EMPEROR NERO

THE SPLENDOUR BEFORE THE DARK

EMPEROR NERO

THE
SPLENDOUR
BEFORE
THE DARK

MARGARET
GEORGE

MACMILLAN

First published 2018 by Berkley, an imprint of Penguin Random House LLC

First published in the UK 2018 by Macmillan
an imprint of Pan Macmillan
20 New Wharf Road, London N1 9RR
Associated companies throughout the world
www.panmacmillan.com

ISBN 978-1-5098-4021-2

Genealogy chart created by JoAnne T. Croft, designed by Laura K. Corless
Maps by Laura Hartman Maestro, based on sketches by Margaret George

Printed and bound by CPI Group (UK) Ltd, Croydon, CR0 4YY

Visit **www.panmacmillan.com** to read more about all our books
and to buy them. You will also find features, author interviews and
news of any author events, and you can sign up for e-newsletters
so that you're always first to hear about our new releases.

To Lydia Margaret
Granddaughter Extraordinaire

MY THANKS

One of the best things about researching a historical novel is the people I have met along the way who have unstintingly and generously helped me and shared my enthusiasm for Nero. My heartfelt thanks to Bob Feibel, a classics lover, who first suggested Nero as a subject; to classics professors Barry B. Powell and William Aylward at the University of Wisconsin–Madison, who translate Greek and Latin for me and keep me informed about new publications and upcoming lectures; to Bela Sandor, professor emeritus of engineering physics at the University of Wisconsin–Madison, a world expert in the mechanics of ancient racing chariots; to Silvia Prosperi, a true "Friend in Rome," who arranged for me to see sites special to Nero's life—Antium, Lake Nemi, Sublaqueum, Portus—that are off the beaten track; to Dr. Ernst R. Tamm and Rosanna Tamm, who translated German texts about Nero for me and helped in the project. Richard Campbell, a Roman enthusiast whose reenactment and Facebook groups, "Roman Army Talk" and "Women in Roman and Ancient Reenacting," has been a font of information on many arcane Roman subjects.

I am also grateful to my enthusiastic, supportive, thoughtful, and discerning editor, Claire Zion; her editorial assistant, Lily Choi; and the whiz publicity and media team at Berkley, especially Lauren Burnstein, Jin Yu, and Jessica Mangicaro, for their excitement and ideas for Nero's story. I appreciate all that Carol Fitzgerald and her team at AuthorsOnTheWeb have done to make mine a world-class website. As always, to my forever agent in the United States, Jacques de Spoelberch, and to my UK agent, Andrew Nurnberg of Andrew Nurnberg Associates International, my deepest thanks. And to all at Pan Macmillan in the UK, who have published all my novels, my appreciation for our happy partnership over the years.

And finally, last but far from least, to my patient family, who have put up with having Nero as a long-term houseguest, my infinite thanks.

THE GENEALOGY OF THE IMPERIAL HOUSE

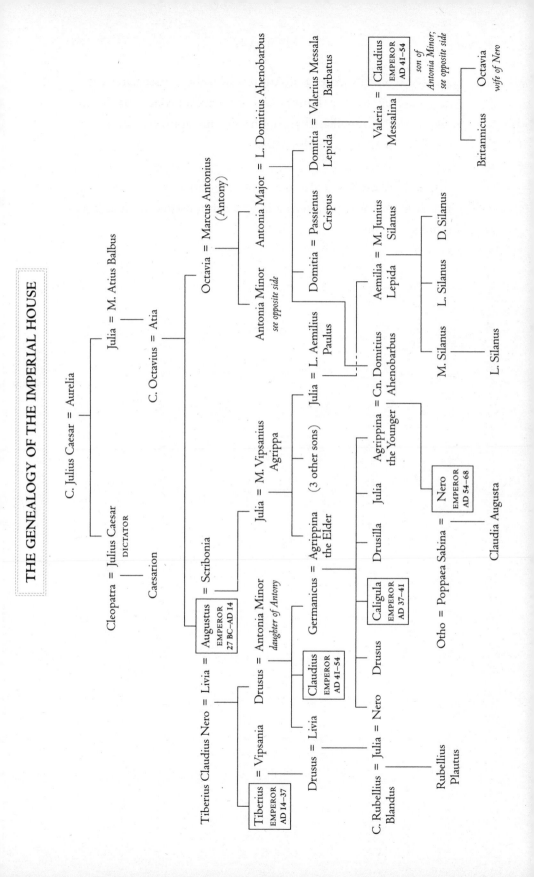

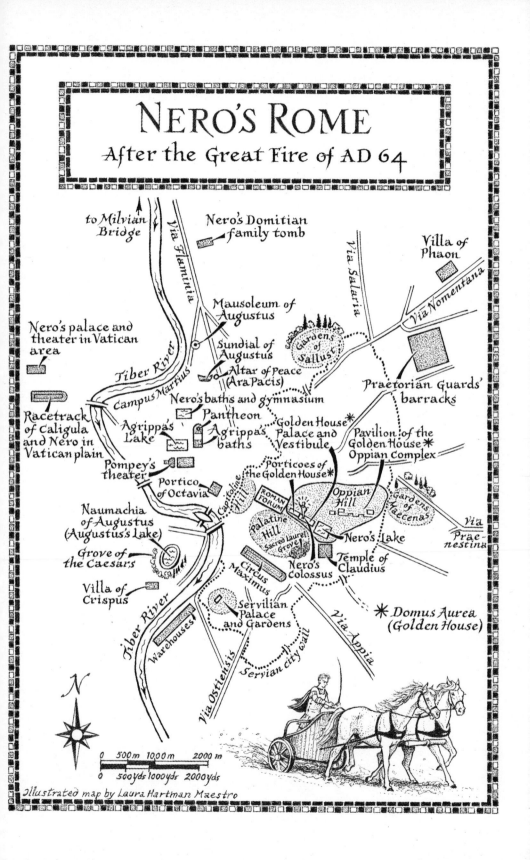

NERO'S ROME
After the Great Fire of AD 64

to Milvian Bridge

Via Flaminia

Nero's Domitian family tomb

Villa of Phaon

Via Salaria

Via Nomentana

Nero's palace and theater in Vatican area

Mausoleum of Augustus

Sundial of Augustus

Altar of Peace (Ara Pacis)

Gardens of Sallust

Tiber River

Campus Martius

Praetorian Guards' barracks

Nero's baths and gymnasium

Pantheon

Agrippa's Lake

Agrippa's baths

Golden House Palace and Vestibule

Pavilion of the Golden House Oppian Complex

Racetrack of Caligula and Nero in Vatican plain

Porticoes of the Golden House

Capitoline Hill

ROMAN FORUM

Oppian Hill

Gardens of Maecenas

Pompey's theater

Portico of Octavia

Palatine Hill

Sacred laurel Grove

Nero's Lake

Via Prae-nestina

Naumachia of Augustus (Augustus's Lake)

Grove of the Caesars

Villa of Crispus

Circus Maximus

Nero's Colossus

Temple of Claudius

Domus Aurea (Golden House)

Tiber River

Warehouses

Servilian Palace and Gardens

Via Ostiensis

Servian city wall

Via Appia

N

0   500m   1000m   2000m
0   500yds 1000yds 2000yds

Illustrated map by Laura Hartman Maestro

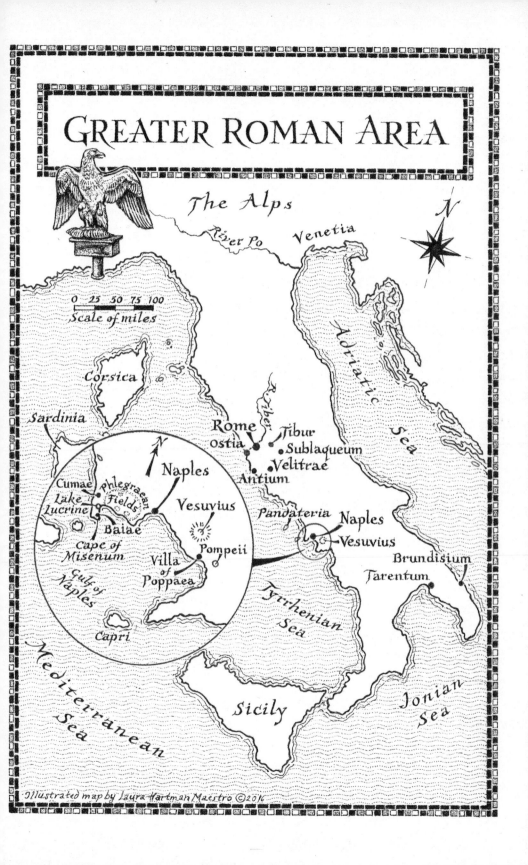

GREATER ROMAN AREA

The Alps

River Po

Venetia

N

Scale of miles
0 25 50 75 100

Corsica

Sardinia

Rome
Ostia
Tibur
Sublaqueum
Velitrae
Antium

Naples

N

Cumae
Lake Lucrine
Phlegraean Fields
Vesuvius

Baiae

Cape of Misenum

Villa of Poppaea

Pompeii

Gulf of Naples

Capri

Pandateria

Naples

Vesuvius

Brundisium

Tarentum

Tyrrhenian Sea

Adriatic Sea

Mediterranean Sea

Sicily

Ionian Sea

I

NERO

I awoke in the milky dawn, that opalescent hour outside time. For an instant I did not know where I was. Thus it must feel to be newborn, unclaimed.

A sweet breeze was stealing across me as I lay quietly. A sea breeze. I was on a shore somewhere. I raised my head, and at once I was back in the world I knew. I was at Antium. I was in my villa bedroom that opened out onto the sea itself.

In the stillness, I arose and left Poppaea sleeping, her lips curved in a smile as she dreamed of something pleasurable. Pleasurable . . . our stay here in Antium had been pleasurable. Far enough from Rome to put thoughts of it aside, to live secluded here by the sea. For a brief time.

Quietly I walked over to the window and pushed back the filmy curtains. The horizon outside was white, making it impossible to see where the sky ended and the sea began. A pale moon was sinking, caught in the clouds. Last night it had been bright, penetrating, high. Now, still full but setting, it faded and became indistinct.

Last night . . . how exultant I had been, performing at last my epic on the Fall of Troy, on the stage here. The hard work of composing it had taken over a year, but with a furious burst the last few days, and now it had shown its face to the world, and I had all the joy of an artist who has birthed a creation after a very long labor.

It was fitting that it had taken place here in Antium, where I myself had been born twenty-six years ago. And after a likewise long and dif-

ficult labor, for I had been born feet first—an evil omen, some said. At
the same time there had been other favorable omens, so which to heed?
Clearly the favorable ones had prevailed, for I had been emperor now
for nine years, having assumed the purple at an absurdly young age.
There had been significant achievements in my reign already, most notably a peace settlement with Parthia, our historic enemy, achieved finally through diplomacy rather than arms. I had gifted the city of
Rome with magnificent baths, a theater, and a covered market, and I
had instituted engineering works that improved harbors and aimed
to protect shipping routes. What I most wanted, though, was to give
Rome the greatest gift of all—a conversion to the Greek sensibilities
and aesthetics. That was much harder than building buildings and
digging canals. But it was coming. I knew it.

The audience last night was proof of that. Many people had traveled from Rome to hear me perform on the cithara. It is a virtuoso
instrument, from Greece. Apollo himself played it. Yes! Their eyes
would be opened, and they would learn to embrace these cultural treasures.

I looked fondly at my cithara, now propped up against the wall,
resting from its labors last night. It was, of course, the finest that could
be made, and I had the finest instructor, Terpnus, who had borne with
me and taught me patiently. I was always reluctant to leave him behind
in Rome, and knowing I was returning to him made it easier to go
back.

Rome. In the growing light, I saw the message cylinders resting on
the table. They had been delivered yesterday, sent by my trusted right-
hand man and Praetorian prefect, Tigellinus. But I could not bring
myself to look at them then. The day was too perfect to spoil with
petty business about import duties or aqueduct repairs or cart traffic in
the city. If you imagine that everything an emperor has to deal with is
lofty and critical, I can assure you that it is not. It is a hundred tax
questions to one diplomatic treaty or one war strategy decision.

I would look at the messages a little later. I had to. But this morning
would be for relaxation and for planning the inevitable return to
Rome.

I had retreated here to escape the hot days in the city, but duty required me to preside over the Feriae Augusti in two weeks, the celebration beginning on August first that culminated on the thirteenth, fourteenth, and fifteenth, commemorating Roman victories over Dalmatia, Actium, and Egypt. As the celebrations featured horse races, the only bright spot was that perhaps then I would be cleared by my trainers to do something I had longed to do: race chariots competitively.

Oh, I had driven chariots, but never in a real public race. It was deemed too dangerous, and it is true, chariot racing has a high accident rate. But it was also the most exciting thing a person could do. My grandfather had been a successful chariot racer, and I liked to believe I had inherited his skill.

"Begging your pardon, Caesar," my trainer had said, "if a celebrated charioteer dies in a race, his family and fans mourn him. But if an emperor dies in one, the entire empire is bereft."

Tigellinus was more blunt. "It's irresponsible of you to think of taking such chances." He paused. "Especially as you have no heir. Do you want to spark a civil war, like we had after Julius Caesar was killed?"

No heir. Oh, the pain of that. I had had a daughter, but she died a baby. And none since.

"No," I admitted. I would not make Rome endure such agony again. But I still wanted to race chariots, calling upon the gods to protect me. Had they not done that so far?

But then there was the nagging thought of a disturbing prophecy I had been given by the sibyl I had visited at Cumae. *Fire will be your undoing,* she had said. When pressed further, she had added, *Flames will consume your dreams, and your dreams are yourself.* But there were no fires at chariot races. So did that assure me that I was safe to embark on that activity?

As for fires, we had a very capable fire brigade in Rome. But perhaps the fire she spoke of was somewhere else? Or it was a metaphorical fire? People spoke of the fire of anger, the fire of lust, the fire of ambition. I was on fire about my art. Did she mean that would destroy me?

I shook my head. Put it out of your thoughts, I told myself. Think only of this fair day before you, a day to walk beside the water, to drink chilled juice of Persian peaches with the wife who is the dearest thing under heaven to you, to wait for the moon to rise upon you once again.

I left her to sleep while I walked outside to see the pearly sky lighten, promising a fair, tranquil day.

It was late morning before Poppaea stirred. I had finished reading the Rome dispatches—they were as dull as I had feared—and reread a portion of my Troy epic with a mind to revisions, when she rose from the bed, trailing silk behind her like clouds of glory. Encircling her neck was the glittering gold collar I had gifted her with last night. She had worn it to bed, and now she ran her hands over it lovingly.

"They say cold metal is a sad thing to lavish love on," I said. "But on you it looks worthy of love." It was studded with gems betokening the planets, moon, and sun, crafted from an Indian design I had commissioned.

"Gold is easy to sleep with," she said. "In fact, it helped me to dream."

"Ah, such dreams as gold gives." I rose and embraced her, the body-warmed gold indistinguishable from her own temperature. "And it is cold no longer."

The sun was midway in the sky, burnishing the waves outside the window.

"Shall we go to the grotto today? We haven't visited it yet." The ancient grotto, down at the far end of the quays, was a large one extending quite far into the hillside. Grottoes held a fascination for me, as so many stories of the gods placed them there. They reeked of the supernatural.

She stretched, raising her arms over her head, shaking her shining amber hair. "I suppose we should. We do not have that much more time here." But she did not sound enthusiastic. "But in the late afternoon," she said. "How do you have the energy, after last night?"

I could never explain to her that performing invigorated me; it was idleness that drained me. "I will meet you on the terrace," I said. I was eager to get outside, to breathe in the fresh air.

Later that day, we sat out on the shaded terrace and watched the horizon. It was soothing and still. And I relished the mindlessness. No thinking. No thinking. Just sit with closed eyes and drift, reliving the night before.

Attendants brought us food, placing the trays down on a stand—platters of cold ham and mullet, sage honey from Crete, bread, eggs, olives, and cherries, with juice or Tarentinum wine to wash it down. Lazily I reached out and took a handful of cherries.

Under her scarf Poppaea still wore the necklace. "For I can't take it off just yet," she admitted.

If only the other people I showered with gifts showed their appreciation so openly, I thought.

I was just passing her the platter of eggs and olives when our idyll was interrupted by a panting, dusty, sweaty messenger who hurried out to us, flanked by two of the villa guards. His face was set in a grimace, matched by the expression on the guards' faces. I stood up, the perfect day suddenly shattered.

"Caesar, Caesar!" he cried, falling to his knees and clasping his hands piteously. "I come from Rome, from Tigellinus." His voice was a croak.

"Well, what is it?"

"Rome is on fire! Rome is on fire!" he shrieked. "It is burning out of control!"

I was unable to take in his words. "On fire?"

"Yes, yes! It started in the Circus Maximus, in one of the shops at the far end."

"When?"

By this time, my wife had risen, too, and out of the corner of my eye I saw her gripping the gold necklace, but no longer languidly. I could sense the alarm and dread that was filling me transferring itself to her as she stared at the messenger.

"Night before last—and the northerly wind fanned the flames so they swept fast, down the length of the Circus. Then it started climbing the hills around it."

Rome was a fire trap, and we had had many fires in our history. To guard against this, Augustus had created his fire brigade of seven thousand men, the Vigiles Urbani, now under the command of Nymphidius Sabinus, a man bearing a striking resemblance to Caligula in looks. Whether true or a coincidence, this allowed him to claim he was Caligula's natural son. But what mattered that now?

"What of the firefighters? Are they out?"

"Yes, but helpless to stop it. The fire is spreading faster than they can contain it. The sparks jump over roofs and fields and flare up in new places. It was starting to climb the Palatine when I left!"

I turned to Poppaea. I felt numb, not even able to truly believe what I was hearing. "I must go," I said. Then I turned to the messenger. "We'll ride together. A fresh horse for you."

It was midday when we set out, trailed by two guards, but darkness had fallen before we approached Rome. All along the ride I felt myself becoming more and more agitated, hoping that the messenger had exaggerated, or that the fire was already contained, or that it had not destroyed much besides the shops in the Circus.

Calm, calm, Nero, you must keep calm, think clearly.

But inside another picture was emerging—of Rome destroyed, people dead or destitute, historical treasures lost forever, all when I was emperor, all happening while I was responsible for the safety of my people.

Rome was ruined under Nero, the city incinerated, nothing left but ashes.

As we neared the top of a hill near Rome, before we could see the city itself, a lurid color stained the night sky, orange and red and yellow, ugly fingers reaching up into the heavens, pulsating. Then we crested the hill and I gazed down on the city aflame. Clouds of smoke roiled upward, and spurts of color, clouds of sparks, and bursts of exploding stone and wood punctuated the darkness. The brisk wind blew ashes in my face, carrying the stench of burning cloth, garbage, and things unnamable.

It was true, all true.

"It's worse!" the messenger cried. "It's still spreading! It's much bigger than when I left. Look, it's engulfed the hills!"

Rome was being devoured. Suddenly I remembered the time when I had visited the Temple of Vesta and been overcome with a strange weakness and trembling, and rendered helpless. I was puzzled by it then, but now I knew it meant I was powerless to protect the sacred flame of Rome. And I understood the meaning of the sibyl and her prophecy that fire would be my doom.

I stood at the turning point of my life. This was my battlefield, the battlefield I had wondered if I would ever face. My ancestor Antony had faced his twice: at the battle of Philippi, when he crushed the assassins of Caesar, and the battle of Actium, when he himself was crushed by Octavian.

Either Rome and I perished together, or we survived together.

But no matter the outcome, there was only one choice: to go forward, to wade into battle.

"Come," I said, urging my horse forward. "Rome awaits."

And we descended the hill, heading into the maelstrom.

II

The hill was not steep, but it was treacherous with winding paths, rocks and tree roots studded everywhere. The moonlight made it possible for us to see, and the increasing glow from the fire added more illumination.

My heart was thudding as if I had just run a *stadion*, and my head was swirling. The air was hot, muggy, and stifling, and the acrid smell of fire made it torture to breathe. We should have been attacked by swarms of insects, but the smoke and soot had banished them. The fire was still too far away for us to feel the heat directly, but I imagined I could anyway. From this distance the city looked as if it were just one mass; I could not discern the individual areas yet.

I stopped. "You say it is bigger now?" I asked the messenger.

"Yes! When I left, it was contained in one area and, from a distance, looked like one campfire. Now it has ignited new sites all around itself."

"It will be light before we get there," I said. And by then, who knew what we would see?

We continued our ride downhill, picking our way slowly. Ahead of us, the demonic glow drew closer.

Fire. What did I know about fire? Very little, to be honest. I had never personally experienced one, not even a house fire; the only fire I knew was the imaginary one at Troy hundreds of years ago. But I had been generous in equipping the Vigiles with whatever they needed, and it was expensive: horse-drawn fire wagons with water pumps, hundreds of buckets, picks, axes, hooks, and even catapults for knocking down houses to create fire breaks. Surely such a trained and equipped force could contain the fire.

But if that was so, why was it spreading? If they could not put it out when it was small, what chance did they have of stopping it as it grew larger?

The wind suddenly shifted, and as it did, I saw a burst of fire in a new place as it ignited there. A column shot up toward the sky, sending embers swirling in a cloud that vanished quickly.

On we went; the moon began dipping toward the west, and a very faint hint of light appeared on the eastern horizon. But it was still very dark, except for the lurid throbbing red ahead of us. We climbed another hill and the city disappeared, but as we reached the summit, we were suddenly close, and the first heat of the fire reached my face. The horses sensed it and began to shy. It was hard to hold them. But I calmed mine, and he obeyed. If only I could calm myself. My hands gripped the reins so tightly the leather was biting into my palms.

"We will have to enter the city from the east," I said. From where we stood, it looked as if the center of the city was not safe, and the fire came up to the Tiber on the west. "Where is Tigellinus? Where is Nymphidius?"

"They were moving to the Esquiline to direct operations from there," the messenger said. "They had to vacate the Palatine and the Forum."

We swung around toward the east, as day finally broke. Now we could see. Clouds of thick black smoke were sending plumes up into the sky, and the fire was roaring, growling like a beast. We got onto the Via Praenestina and immediately were in a sea of fleeing people, tumbling out of the city, carrying their goods on their shoulders, crying and panting.

"Don't go in there!" a family shrieked. "Only a madman would go toward a fire. Run, run!"

"It's the emperor!" another man yelled.

"Save us, save us!" they began to wail.

I stared at them. They truly thought I could save them, somehow command the fire to stop.

"Help, help!" A woman flung herself against the side of my horse.

"I am going to help," I said. "I will direct the firefighters. We will put it out."

Oh, how sure I sounded. What a lie.

More people were pouring out of the city, flooding the road. Donkeys, pushcarts, bags and bundles, screaming children. Slowly we made our way through the crowd, trying to reassure them. We approached the city walls, where the Esquiline gate loomed ahead, jammed with people trying to fit themselves through the narrow opening on the way out. Only when the guards recognized me as emperor did they hold back the crowd to let me in.

I entered the city, and suddenly I was in the arena with the fire. What had been a distant enemy was now facing me. The smoke was much thicker here, and in spite of the sunrise, it cast a dark pall.

"Turn right!" I said, seeking the spot on the Esquiline where Tigellinus would have set up shop. There was a watching post near the Gardens of Maecenas that overlooked the city.

The Gardens of Maecenas! Part of my new palace, the Domus Transitoria, was there! But no, it was safe, it was too far away from the fire.

Too far? It was not so far that it was impossible to link the Domus Transitoria to the old Palatine palace of Tiberius. I had done it, had I not? It was only a mile between them. And the Palatine had had to be evacuated.

I glanced over toward the Domus Transitoria but could not see any damage; it looked intact. This whole area was intact.

At last we reached the top of the Esquiline, and I rushed to the stone house that served as watching post even in tranquil times. Now it was swarming with men, soldiers and firefighters.

I saw Nymphidius, standing beside the door, charts in his hand. His usually placid face was puckered in a grimace. He was conferring with several men, stabbing at a spot on a chart. He glanced up and saw me.

"Caesar! Thank the gods you are here!"

As if I myself were a god. Well, I would have to act like one, hope that somehow for this brief time I could be transformed into something more than myself. "I came as quickly as possible," I said. "Tell me the extent of the fire. Tell me everything."

He pivoted to face the city below us. From this height I saw with horror what looked like a hundred separate fires, each sending up its dark plume, with one massive fire in the middle.

"It started at the end of the Circus where the starting gates are. We think some flammable goods in one of the shops caught fire—they keep oils there to cook snacks for the crowds. It spread immediately to shops next door that store wood, clothes, and such. The shopkeepers, who were sleeping in the quarters above the shops, got out in time but couldn't do anything but run. A strong wind swept the flames down the sides of the Circus, catching the wooden stands, and from there—" He gave an anguished sigh.

"This was at night?"

"Dead night. There was a full moon, though."

The beautiful full moon I had admired at Antium, a benign presence there.

"Who sounded the alarm?"

"The cohort of Vigiles stationed nearest the fire—Cohort Seven." He pointed to its place on the map.

"That's far away, across the Tiber!"

"Yes," he admitted. "Our bad luck."

"Very bad luck."

"By the time the firefighters were roused and equipped, the fire had spread. The flames were roaring through the stands of the Circus, now on both sides. With the wide-open space, there was nothing to stop the spread, and the strong wind fanned it."

A strong wind. More bad luck.

"It leapt up the Palatine hillside on the south side, then fell back down again. Getting the fire wagons in place didn't help; the hoses could not send water that far. So the men fell back, and we called the other cohorts to help. And all this was taking place at night."

A gust of wind flung ashes in our faces, stinging and burning.

"Here." Nymphidius handed me a soaked handkerchief to shield my nose and mouth. I breathed in the cooled air.

"And all the next day?"

"It spread. We were powerless to stop it. The fire seemed to burst out by magic in places far from the source, so we were unable to pull down houses to create an open space. Neighbors helped neighbors fight fire, handing the buckets back and forth, and then would turn and see that their own house was on fire. Some people ran back inside, hiding from the fire, and had to be pulled out, fighting all the way, having lost their senses with fright. We tried dousing the houses with *acetum*, water mixed with vinegar, which fire doesn't like, but there was too little, and we couldn't reach the upper stories."

"By this time, the end of the first day, where was the fire?"

"It was spreading around the Palatine and the Capitoline. Then night fell. We soaked blankets and mattresses so we could lay them out beneath the insulae in the adjoining regions. It was just a matter of time before the fire reached those apartments, and anyone trapped inside would need to jump. We ran through the streets ordering people to evacuate. But some resisted. Denial mixed with fear."

Always. Denial and fear run hand in hand to doom. "The next morning?"

"We had to change shifts, bring in fresh men. We had regrouped here on the Esquiline. The seven cohorts pooled their equipment and men. I ordered the *ballistae*—the catapults—to be brought out and made ready. We had to find a place to create a firebreak. But every place we selected had already been hit by flying embers, and so we had to keep pulling back. At that point we sent the messenger to you. We should have sent him sooner, but even for us it was hard to admit how serious it was."

"Now we are up to this morning. What did you find when daylight returned?"

"The Palatine and Capitoline had been encircled on the east and west sides, with only the north, the Forum, still safe."

"And now?" Never had I regretted my poor eyesight more. I could not pick out the individual areas that were on fire.

"We will have to go into the areas to find out," Nymphidius said. "And to do that we need to be prepared. Wet clothes, masks, hooks and buckets and axes. And the fire engines must be refilled with fresh water."

"We must go immediately!" I said.

He looked at me. "Caesar, you have been up all night. You need rest. Do not join the ranks of the panicked citizens. You need all your strength of mind before confronting the fire."

I did not feel tired. But I did not feel normal, either. "Very well. Where should I go?"

"We have makeshift quarters up here." He motioned to an aide. "Take the emperor to a place where he can rest," he ordered him. "Stay there until the afternoon," he told me. "I will come for you. We will go out together."

The young soldier led me away to a large tent erected on the summit. Inside, on camp beds, exhausted firefighters slept in rows. In the middle a table supplied aid workers with water and food, and physicians were tending to burns.

"In here," the soldier directed me. There was a screened area with private beds. The light was dim, filtered through the canvas walls, and the beds were ready with blankets and pillows. I gladly fell on the nearest one, and the soldier kindly pulled off my sandals and covered me with a blanket. Sleep enveloped me immediately, as my utter fatigue overcame even my horror, and I fell into a dark vortex, as dark as the smoke above the city.

III

I awoke before Nymphidius came in. The last time I had awakened, yesterday at Antium, I had had a moment of disorientation; and so it was here also. I stared up at a dull canvas overhead. I shifted on a narrow cot. I heard odd noises outside, the sound of faraway crowds, and nearby groans. Then I knew. I was in Rome, and Rome was on fire.

I sat bolt upright. I looked down at my dirty hands, streaked with grime and blistered from the long ride. My tunic was filthy, coated with ash and briars. My grit-filled sandals were arranged neatly under the cot. I hastily put them on and ventured out into the tent, where row upon row of beds stretched out in the dim light. Young men, some bandaged and moaning, others unconscious, lay upon them. Casualties of the fire already.

Attendants and nurses were busy and barely glanced at me. That was just as well. I needed to think. Think, Nero, think! But my mind was sluggish, stunned.

The areas of Rome—what was in the path of the fire? Here on the Esquiline we were northeast of the city center, more than a mile from where the fire had started. But fire could run faster than a horse, and it could gallop through the city speedily. How ironic that it had started at a racetrack. Were the gods teasing us?

The Palatine was right next to it. Nymphidius had said the fire had started to climb one side of the hill but then had halted. If it reached the Palatine, all the treasures there would be lost. Historic things, not just luxury goods. Shrines commemorating the foundation of Rome, and—O gods! The sacred laurel grove at Augustus's house. The laurels that foretold the death of an emperor! *My* laurel!

Fire will be your undoing.

Then there were the sacred temples on the Capitoline, and the official buildings in the Forum, and beyond that, closer to us, the Subura where many people lived, many poor, but the wealthy as well in neighboring regions.

Where people lived . . . where did Apollonius, my athletic trainer, live? I knew only it was in the city. What of the genius citharoede, Terpnus? What of Appius, my voice teacher? What of Paris, my actor friend? And the freedmen who served me—Epaphroditus, Phaon? And my childhood nurses, Ecloge and Alexandra, still serving in my household more as friends than servants? And the writers—Lucan, Petronius, and Spiculus? And my friends Piso and Senecio and Vitellius. And . . . and . . . the list went on and on, people dear to me, from all walks of life. For unlike previous emperors, I had sought out people of other classes to mingle with, much to the disapproval of the Senate. There was no part of the city that would not harbor people I was personally connected to. And for the others, I was their emperor and should be their protector, their shield against misfortune.

But the fire . . . the fire . . . it made the beasts faced by Hercules in his Twelve Labors weak and gentle in comparison.

My questions to the firefighters about where my staff and friends had gone were met with shrugs and the admission that no one knew. People had fled when the fire crept close, leaving no word behind.

Just then Tigellinus entered the tent, looking for me. His muscular arms were smeared with soot, his face shiny with sweat. He strode over, grimacing. "You are here," he stated. "Good. Nymphidius says you want to come out with the firefighters. I would advise against that."

"Why?"

"It is too dangerous," he said.

"Like the chariot racing? You would forbid me anything not as safe as a covered carriage trundling out on the Appian Way on a feast day."

"Why do you insist on doing things that are such a risk? It is—"

"Yes, I know. Irresponsible. But the most irresponsible thing an emperor can do is abandon his people in a crisis."

"You don't need to go in person to battle the flames to take care of your people. Someone has to stay safe to direct operations. I am not down there; I am up here, organizing."

"I will go out and see it firsthand. I must do that."

"I—"

He started to say *I forbid it*. But I was emperor, and no one had the authority to forbid me anything. No one.

"I will wait for Nymphidius. He was going to return to the city in the early afternoon. I will accompany him."

I left the tent and stood outside, looking down the hill, seeing the bright rays of sunlight falter and fade as they hit the clouds of smoke hanging over the city. I was on the very summit of the hill. I remembered the day Poppaea and I had come here, walking through the still-unfinished Domus Transitoria linking the old palace of Tiberius on the Palatine to the Gardens of Maecenas here. Its entrance lay farther down the slope. I walked to it; a few nervous slaves were still at their posts guarding the door. I passed them to descend into the tunnel-like passageway that snaked through the lower part of the city to emerge at the base of the Palatine palace.

Together Poppaea and I had selected the ornamentation of the Domus Transitoria; the ceiling was white stucco embedded with gems and sparkling glass. The artist who had done it—where was he? Was he safe?

The passageway was quiet and cool. One would never know conditions were anything but ordinary. But as I walked farther in, I smelled it, faint but distinctive: smoke. Smoke was in the corridor. That meant there was fire at the other end, in the new part where the smell of fresh paint should still linger, but now was replaced by ash and smoke.

I scrambled out and rushed up the hill. My palace was on fire!

When I reached the top, Nymphidius had returned and was standing surrounded by his men. A pile of clothing and equipment was heaped nearby.

"There's smoke in the Domus Transitoria!" I gasped. "That means it's on fire in the Palatine portion!"

"The fire is reaching its arms around the Palatine, then," he said. "Are you still determined to go with us?"

"Yes. I cannot stay here!"

Tigellinus joined us just in time to hear my words. "He is stubborn," he told Nymphidius. "I have tried to persuade him otherwise." He could not say he had tried to *order* me.

"We will be careful. And it starts with putting on protective clothing." Nymphidius pointed to the pile. "I have soaked all this with water, mixed with vinegar. It will stink, but better stink than burn."

I, along with some thirty men, dug out the clothing and put it on: tunic, cloak with arms, high boots, and a close-fitting leather helmet. It was clammy and heavy.

"Now take your equipment," said Nymphidius. "An axe, a grappling hook, a bucket. At the base of the hill the fire engines are waiting, filled and ready, and another wagon with the wet blankets and mattresses to spread out for jumpers. Long before we get to the area of the fire we will encounter crowds. We must stick together and push through them and not get separated. For this I am issuing wide white bracelets. Put them on your left arm. Hold up your arm if you feel you are losing us, so we can spot you."

At his signal, we descended the hill. His instructions had been so spare. He had not told us what to do if we encountered a blaze, if people caught fire, if stones or wood were flying through the air. Perhaps there was nothing we could do but dodge. At the base of the hill the wagons were waiting, as he had told us. I was impressed with his organization and control. The fire engines, filled with water, had hand-turned pumps. The hoses were coiled and waiting, but I doubted they could reach very high. No man had the strength to supply enough power to propel the water higher than about twenty feet.

"Onward!" Nymphidius cried, holding up his left hand with the bracelet. The wagons rumbled forward, and we followed, en masse. As we traversed the streets, everything was still intact, but as Nymphidius had predicted, we were almost swept away by the sea of surging people fleeing the city, out into the fields of the countryside. Ahead of us, the ominous cloud of smoke hung over the city.

But as we came closer to the Forum, passing into the crowded center of the city, the Subura, we suddenly entered an area aflame. We first realized it when swirls of embers began landing on us, sizzling as they were extinguished by our wet clothes. "It's in Region Eight!" yelled Nymphidius, and that was the last thing I heard before the roar of the fires and the screams of the people drowned him out.

Houses were ablaze—but not all of them. One house afire might have houses on either side still safe—but not for long. I saw a stream of water from our hoses directed at one of the houses, but it was puny and had little effect on the fire. The heat was intense, and the heavy clothes I was wearing made it almost unbearable. But I could not discard them—I would roast directly.

Flying pieces of wood glowing with sparks burst out of the houses, landing on people, and crushing some. At my feet a child was felled beneath a wayward beam, and I managed to kick it off, but the child was dead. I looked up at the blazing houses, with yellow writhing tendrils of flame coming from the windows, like a living thing. Then the windows burst outward, exploding in a ball of fire. Screams from within the house stopped as the floors collapsed.

Then I heard Nymphidius again. "This way! The insulae!" And we pushed our way through toward that area. But on the way I was blocked by a group of menacing men. These were not panicked citizens but purposeful agents carrying buckets of tar and sticks and lighted brands. Deliberately they cast them into the houses that were not on fire.

"Stop that!" I cried, grabbing the forearm of one. He flung me off easily.

"Shut up!" he spat. His companions kept dipping their sticks into their tar buckets, igniting them, and tossing them into houses.

"Stop it!" I ordered them, again to no effect. Then I realized they had no idea who I was, disguised as I was by the fire-prevention clothes. Just then I saw them hindering some of Nymphidius's firefighters as they attempted to put out fires.

They held up threatening hands to me. "We do this under authority!" they said.

"Whose authority?" I demanded.

"One whom we obey," they said.

"I am the emperor!" I cried. "I have power over anyone who is ordering you to do this. Stop, if you value your lives!" I commanded them.

The men merely laughed, not believing me. Or perhaps not caring, knowing I could never identify them. But the people around us heard and misunderstood. "It's the emperor! He's telling them to start fires!"

"No!" I cried. "I am not with these men!"

"Yes you are," yelled a woman. "You are with them. Why else are you standing talking to them? And in secret, with none of your royal guards around? Where are the Praetorians? You have slipped away from them on purpose."

Then another house began to sway and fall, and everyone scattered. Everyone but two men who stood, praising their god.

"Oh, great and glorious name of Jesus! It is the beginning. The beginning of the end, the end you promised." One of them bent down and grabbed the end of a glowing stick. "It's the Day of the Lord at last! And we are given the gift of speeding its coming!" He flung the flaming brand into a house. "Thank you, Lord!"

Their thanks was short-lived; as if in answer, the house collapsed and buried them under it.

I had entered a nightmare. I swerved around the collapsed house, hunting for Nymphidius and the other men, but I had lost them. No matter. I knew how to get to the insulae. But I was shaken by the brazen looters I now saw rushing into houses, emerging with armloads of stolen goods, and the religious fanatics who were exploiting the fire for their own ends. I had not anticipated this, but I should have. There is no tragedy that evil men do not repurpose.

Suddenly a river of fire poured out the door of a house; it rippled and shimmered like a real river, but this was pure fire. From inside came a growl, like a monstrous animal, followed by another vomit of fire. I was pummeled and squeezed by the tight-packed crowds fleeing it and carried in a direction I had no control over.

Now I was at the insulae, those tall apartment buildings that were the most dangerous of all. They could be five or six stories, of wood or mud brick, rickety and more flimsy the higher they were. I found Nymphidius by spotting the fire engines and wagons, lined up outside one building. The men were spreading out the blankets and mattresses, and I joined them, hauling the heavy material out of the wagons. The side of the building was a sheet of red-yellow flames already, and people were hanging out the windows, terrified.

Nymphidius gestured to them as soon as the blankets and mattresses were in place. "Jump! Jump!" he yelled. Some obeyed, and the ones in the lower floors landed safely. But the ones in the higher floors hit hard, and not everyone survived.

We stood looking at the dead people, mangled upon the blankets. There were some very small children. They had hit the hardest. I felt sick. One of the firemen beside me said, "It is a kinder death than fire." He was right. But the fire was the true cause of it.

Just then one of the insulae next to us, seemingly untouched, shot out sparks and then suddenly exploded with no warning. Flying debris went everywhere, bodies along with beams and stones and furniture. Charred bodies rained down around us, blackened and unrecognizable as people except for the shoes that were still on the carbonized skeletal feet. Now I did get sick and pulled off my heavy, stifling helmet to kneel on the pavement. But as I straightened up, wiping my mouth, cinders singed my hair and I only saved myself from catching fire by smothering it, clapping my helmet back on my head. Inside the helmet I felt the heat of the embers trying to kill me before they slowly died out, their mission extinguished along with them.

"It is a monster," said Nymphidius. "Have you seen enough? I told you that you should have stayed back at the camp."

"Like a coward?" I said. "I have to see it, have to know what we are facing."

"A fire is a living thing," said Nymphidius. "The apartment building looked safe. But it harbored the enemy inside, an enemy that was feeding, breathing, hiding, waiting, growing strong. Only then did it reveal itself. When it was too late for us to stop it."

"I am not sure we have the power to stop it, only to slow it and to rescue its victims. And even in that we are pitifully weak, outflanked by the enemy." That was the horrible truth of it.

"I need to refill the fire engines," he said. "And my men need to rest, rotate shifts. We must retreat, back to the Esquiline and Region Four."

"I need to see the Palatine," I said. "I have to go on."

Nymphidius did not bother to try to dissuade me. "Not alone. Take one of the Praetorian tribunes with you. Subrius Flavus is by the wagons. I'll call him."

I did not want to return to the wagons and the blankets with their grisly spread. I would wait. Soon Subrius appeared. He was one of those men who looked wide, with a broad face and torso, although he wasn't fat. But under all the protective clothes it was impossible to see what anyone really looked like.

"I will accompany you, Caesar," he said. "Where do you wish to go next?"

I knew without hesitation. "The Forum. And the Palatine."

He frowned. "That is heading into the heart of the fire," he said.

"I have to see where it has spread," I said. I dreaded the sight, but I had to see it. I had to know.

He gave an almost imperceptible sigh and pointed. "This way, then."

We fought our way against the tide of frantic people and past more burning buildings. The noise of the fire grew greater, louder, sucking the air. The smoke became denser, and I had to cover my nose and mouth with a handkerchief. My eyes, uncovered, were stinging and aching. In the artificial darkness created by the smoke, I could not see very far in front of me, but still I could discern the stumbling people, some helping others, carrying invalids and the helpless, others ruthlessly pushing everyone aside and trampling them. Some people were carrying bundles of their own belongings; others were thieves laden with stolen booty.

Then suddenly we were out into the Forum, in the open spaces there. It was intact. It had not caught fire yet. The marble buildings, and the space between them, would retard the fire. But the fire was creeping closer to it, and suddenly I saw a flame shoot up through the open roof of the Temple of Vesta, and I knew it was not the sacred flame.

I stood still and watched. This was the very essence, the heart of Rome, and it was succumbing to ruin. This was the center of the Rome I was responsible for, the Rome I was supposed to protect. I alone knew the sacred secret name of Rome, as Pontifex Maximus, the head priest of the state religion. It was not written down anywhere, only whispered from one Pontifex to his successor. As long as that sacred name was known, Rome could continue, could reconstitute herself. But if something happened to me—if I perished right here—Rome would perish along with me. Tigellinus had been right to try to keep me from danger, but there was danger everywhere. A quiet night alone in the palace could also be dangerous. It was nobler to die on my feet fighting a huge evil than to be ignominiously murdered in a corridor, like Caligula.

I turned from the heartrending sight. "Down here!" I told Subrius, and headed toward the Capitoline end of the Forum. We passed the Temple of the Divine Julius, the arch of Augustus, the Rostra, the Curia, all standing proud and serene as their marble grew darkened by soot and ash.

The Capitoline Hill ahead of us looked safe. To our left was the Palatine, and I pointed to the steep path leading up it. Subrius shook his head.

"Stay here, then," I said. He made as if to stop me but knew he did not have the authority. "Wait for me."

Before he could protest, I turned and hurried up the pavement, although it was very hard to breathe now. But I had to see. I had to. This side was still quiet, but the other side of the Palatine faced the origin of the fire, which was still roaring and spreading. I reached the top and there it was—a hideous, hot, bellowing fire on the other side, its flames so high they bested the top of the Palatine. The waves of heat drove me back, staggering. It was impossible to approach any closer. Crackles and groans rose from the dying buildings. A writhing column of flame undulated on the rim, twisting and turning like a dancer. I stood hypnotized, a captive of its strange beauty. A puff of wind blew the curtain of smoke away, and I saw my Domus Transitoria on fire, hissing and spitting. The place where I had sat with my poet friends and had enjoyed long leisurely meetings, with a fountain splashing gently behind us, was now consumed with fire, the fountain turned to steam, the columns blistered and swaying. Then, mercifully, the veil of smoke fell again and hid the sight from me.

I must retreat. At any moment the fire would spread farther up here, racing from tight-packed building to building. I would be trapped. I rushed down, the heat searing my back, pursued by the demon that laughed behind me.

Subrius was standing impatiently as I joined him. "It's starting to go," I said. "It will ignite completely soon. Let us retreat across the river to my house at the Vatican Fields. I will stay there tonight."

Taking great care to skirt the burning areas, which meant going far afield through the Campus Martius, which looked unharmed, we finally crossed the Tiber across from my Vatican properties. My residence there was safe, and it was unlikely the fire would jump the river and come here.

"Stay here and eat," I told Subrius. "Then return to the Esquiline and give a report to Nymphidius. Tell him I will return in the morning."

The slaves quickly prepared a meal for him, and I was able to tell them what I had seen and assure them they were safe. Subrius said little. Perhaps he was always quiet, or perhaps what we had seen today drained all talk from us. I appreciated his silence as he ate slowly.

It was still light on this side of the river when I sent him on his way. I did not need to tell him to stay far north of the city.

"Thank you," I said.

He nodded and took his leave.

Wearily I sought out my bedchamber, after asking for something to eat. When the food came—just bread and some dried figs, all that was on hand—I found I had no appetite at all.

I took to my bed, having washed off the soot, sweat, and dirt. In spite of the protective clothes, my arms and legs were red and blistered from the heat, and my hair badly singed. But that was immaterial. My city was being destroyed, and I was powerless to stop it, beyond small measures. Only the gods could stop it now. And this day had taught me that between literature and real life lay a chasm. It was one thing to sing of Troy and imagine Priam's anguish, the suffering of the people of Troy, but quite another to behold it actually happening, to have the dead and destitute be people I could touch and smell—my own people.

IV

There was no real dawn, for the fire kept the sky illuminated in lurid red all night. Finally, in the east, the normal color of day appeared. I had not slept, not really. Dreams of fire blended with memories of what I had seen, and it was impossible to tell them apart. I stumbled out of bed, my arms and legs smarting from the burns. As soon as I could dress, I would return to the Esquiline.

Today was the fourth day of the fire. Where had it spread in the night? The red stain in the sky dashed any hopes that by a miracle it had died out. And where were the people who had escaped into the countryside? They must be found, counted, and helped.

I was on my way quickly, telling the slaves to ready the grounds for use as a refugee shelter. I walked by myself, unguarded, so I could pass through the city unnoticed and judge for myself its state. As I passed back through the Campus Martius—which still looked unharmed—I realized the public buildings there could be used as shelter as well. That is, if the area remained safe. Clouds of smoke were hovering overhead and the fire had sent an arm creeping up the city side of the Campus, by the Via Lata. I kept well north of it all, passing through the areas of the Quirinal and Viminal Hills, until I finally reached the Esquiline by noon. In the low-lying areas I could see the fire blazing high and hear the sound of cries and destruction.

Nymphidius and his men were grouped at the top of the hill, ready to put on their protective clothing and venture out again. As soon as he saw me, he came over and relieved me of the gear I had carried all the way.

"Subrius told me what happened," he said. "That you actually climbed up the Palatine. You barely missed being roasted alive. The whole of it is ablaze now. At least, we think all of it is. None is so foolish as to venture close enough to make sure. It has spread to one end of the Forum as well."

"I know," I said. "I saw it attack the Temple of Vesta yesterday."

He grimaced. "Attack. Now you understand. Yes, it's a beast; it thinks and it stalks and attacks and kills. It has a will of its own. Perhaps it even plans."

"We have to outsmart it, then."

"We are trying. But so far it has outsmarted us. Every place we try to set up a firebreak, it jumps over us and mocks us. I swear it laughs."

"It's still safe across the river. We can direct people there."

"If any will listen. They are hysterical. We may have to find them out in the fields. Some have taken refuge in the tombs lining the roads outside the city." He hoisted the leather protective gear over his shoulder. "Are you coming with us again?"

"No," I said. "Not today."

"Tomorrow?" Was he testing my resolve, or was he just cajoling me into thinking he wanted my participation?

"I hope by tomorrow you will not need to go out."

He laughed. "Hoping is not getting." He jiggled the gear. "And you need to take better care of yourself."

"I won't come close to the fire again."

"I don't mean the fire. I mean exposing yourself like this, running around without even a guard. You walked all through the city to get here, didn't you?"

"Yes, but I kept far from the fire."

"I don't mean the fire. I mean assassins! Anyone could have assassinated you this morning. Good gods, Caesar, have you no prudence? You are instantly recognizable, and you were alone."

"I don't think many people would want to assassinate me," I said. Only members of my family wanted to do that, not my people.

"It only takes one!"

"You are right, of course," I admitted. "It would have been easy."

"It is no reflection on you. No matter the person, there is always someone who would prefer they disappear. Such an enemy may even be insane, but his knife is as lethal as anyone else's."

"Yes, yes," I said. I wanted an end to this conversation. The thought of anyone wanting to kill me was unnerving. I should have been hardened to it, but I wasn't.

Turning away, I stood and looked down at the spreading fire. By now seven of the fourteen regions were ablaze—from the south near the Caelian Hill, across the bases of the Viminal and the Esquiline, the entire Circus Maximus, most of the Palatine, half the Forum, one side of the Campus Martius near the theaters. Only the Capitoline Hill stood secure, an island in a sea of flame. Perhaps Jupiter himself was protecting his own. The Subura, the densely packed center where the poor were concentrated, was an inferno. The crooked narrow streets, the overhanging upper stories, the close houses that shared a wall, had made ideal conditions to feed the fire.

If only it would rain! If only one of the thunderstorms for which Rome was notorious would rescue us now. But no, the gods turned their faces away, did not take pity on us. A drenching, pounding rain would put out the fire, or at least beat it back to levels that we could fight. The sky—that part of it not obscured by smoke—remained tauntingly clear.

I busied myself conferring with Tigellinus and other Praetorians about the measures we could take to alleviate the sufferings of the displaced population. It kept me from thinking about the unspeakable things happening below, things I was helpless to do anything about.

"You hiked across the city," said Tigellinus with disapproval. "You could have—"

"Yes, I know," I said, cutting him off. "We must take control of what we can. We need to make provisions for the people who have fled, lost everything."

"There are a million people in Rome," said Faenius Rufus, separating himself from the other Praetorians. "How can we take care of all of them?"

"Faenius," I said, "it is good to see Tigellinus's elusive partner." Although I had appointed him to share the title of Praetorian prefect with Tigellinus, Faenius, a quieter sort, usually disappeared in the broad shadow Tigellinus threw. "All of Rome's population has not fled—yet. So there will not be a million refugees."

"Yes, some of them are dead," said Tigellinus. "So we need do nothing for them. The fire has even cremated them for us, so everything is taken care of."

Faenius scowled. "You're a bastard, Tigellinus."

"So they tell me. That's why I am where I am." He then switched on his charming smile, the one he gave to all the brothel ladies.

The brothels! Most of them were located in the Subura, I remembered with horror. I hoped the women had all fled, they and their customers, in time.

"First, are your men patrolling the streets to limit the looting?" I asked. "That should be one of your tasks. Then, we need to locate and count the displaced people. Only when we have a count can we provide enough relief."

"The numbers keep growing as long as the fire does," said Faenius. "It is not over yet." As if to emphasize the point, a gust of wind laden with soot and foul smells of rot and burned flesh reached us. He held a handkerchief up to his nose and coughed. "And yes, we have units out patrolling. Although it seems hopeless to stop it. And there are even reports that some soldiers themselves are looting."

"I saw both looters and arsonists when I was there yesterday."

"Arsonists?" asked Tigellinus.

"Men deliberately throwing torches into buildings and threatening anyone who tried to stop them. They said they were obeying orders."

"Whose orders?"

"'One with authority' was what I heard," I said. "And then there were different men, calling on Jesus and saying the end times were here and they were to help bring it about."

"Are you sure?" asked Faenius.

"Yes. Absolutely," I said.

"People lose their minds during a crisis like this. They do not know what they are doing or saying," said Tigellinus.

"These people did," I insisted. "But that is not our concern. Our concern is the ones who have survived, but only with their lives. So get a count. Then we will prepare my grounds in Vatican Fields and open the public buildings in the Campus Martius—the Pantheon, the Theater of Pompey, the baths, and the gymnasium."

"They will be hungry," said Faenius.

"The grain warehouses at the docks have caught fire," said Tigellinus. "There is nothing to feed them with."

"Then let us bring grain up from Ostia," I said. "And from neighboring towns. See that it's done."

Darkness came early, twilight masked by the smoke. As we watched from the hill, the glowing red below seemed to fill almost all the empty spaces. Nymphidius and his men returned, exhausted and defeated. Pulling off his helmet, he gasped, "It is still growing. We had to abandon the central part of the city and retreat to safety." He sat down, panting, draping his sweaty arms over his knees.

"Is everyone out safely?" I asked.

"All my men, yes. But for many others, no." He put his head in his hands as if he could squeeze the images out of his mind. "So tomorrow we must destroy everything below the base of this hill. Everything. Every house, every insula, every shop and stable and shrine. We must create a huge firebreak, something so wide it cannot leap it. And we must spend tomorrow doing it, before the fire gets any closer."

There was nothing more to be done in the darkness, so I retired to rest. I lay rigid on the camp bed, pretending to sleep. Perhaps if I pretended, I would be able to actually sleep. But thoughts ran through my mind like scuttling rats. Flames cascading. People engulfed. Destruction of all our history, the tangible remnants of our achievements, shields and spoils and trophies from faraway wars. Fear. What was going to happen? What would remain? Anything?

Poppaea. I should get word to her, let her know what was taking place. But it was frivolous to send a messenger all the way to Antium with a letter, when we needed every hand here. And how could I describe it? And yet, not to describe it would be cruel and disrespectful— to her who would want to know, to those who had perished. I must wait until I was with her to tell her. And when, when would that be? And what would be the world we looked out upon?

The world I looked out upon the next morning was one of utter destruction. The fire beast had gorged overnight and grown again, spreading out like a stain, glowing and pulsating. It was the fifth day of the fire. We gathered on the top of the hill and looked down in anguish. The fire was now visible to our right, encroaching on Region Six, which held the Gardens of Sallust. It was reaching its arms around, seeking to encircle us and obliterate all traces of safe space.

Tigellinus had called out all the Praetorians from their camp on the far east of the city, adding thousands more hands. He had also ordered all the *ballistae* to be brought to the base of the Esquiline, to knock down houses and create a firebreak.

"All sizes," he said. "We have three giants, the kind that can throw stones weighing eighty pounds. But they are huge themselves and hard to maneuver in narrow spaces. So we will use the smaller ones as well. We have about thirty of them."

"We have more but they are too far away in other camps to bring quickly," said Faenius. "Come, let us all get ready and at the signal descend."

Once again I put on the heavy leather gear, which was more uncomfortable now that my skin was blistered. But no matter. I found I was eager to go down, to do *something* rather than stand and watch.

Nymphidius would direct the firefighters and Tigellinus the soldiers. At the base of the hill the *ballistae* were lined up and waiting, along with the Praetorians. I beheld, in amazed admiration, the strength of these machines, put together by Roman expertise. They were instruments of destruction, but destruction could have its own spectacular beauty.

They worked by a wound spring, made of animal sinews, cranked back to high tension. I walked around the largest one, running my hands over it, marveling at its construction of wood and metal. A wagonload of stones waited to be loaded into the machines. Each stone would slide back along a trough, resting against a plate that would be released when the torsion was sprung.

"This can fling a boulder a third of a mile," said Tigellinus, patting it as if it were a pet donkey. "But we won't need to be that far back, if we can get closer to the houses and aim directly at them. Let's go!" he ordered the men. Mules pulled the *ballistae* along on creaking wheels.

I fell in behind them, and soon we had selected our targets: a wide swath of houses and shops that bordered on the Gardens of Maecenas, several blocks deep.

"It's a pity, yes?" said Subrius, standing beside me as the machines were hauled into place. "Rich people's houses, filled with treasures, gardens with rare plants—all to be obliterated."

"Warn everyone!" yelled Tigellinus. "Get everyone out!" Dozens of soldiers ran up and down the streets crying for people to evacuate.

Surely there was no one left inside. But to my amazement, people poured out of the doors. Were they blind and deaf? How could they have stayed here?

They flung themselves on the soldiers and catapults and screamed, "No, not my house! Not my house! My grandfather built it—" or "It's my private property, you have no right to destroy it!"

Now I had to speak. I stepped forward and pulled off my helmet so they could know who addressed them. "We do have the authority," I said. "You will lose your house in any case; this way the sacrifice can have some value. Otherwise it is just wasted. Let us build this firebreak to save other areas."

"The emperor!" one man said. "What would you know about the loss of a house?"

"My own house has just burned, with everything in it, everything I treasured. And for nothing. It is gone, and all it served to do was feed this fire and the horror of it along to what was next."

"You can build another!" he cried. "What of us?"

"You will be recompensed. You can build again, too."

"I won't move!"

"Enough of this!" said Tigellinus. He motioned to his soldiers, who took out their swords. "We are losing precious time. Your house is going to be knocked down. So run inside and take what you can in the next few minutes, then go out the Via Praenestina east and wait in the fields."

"We will be coming to the fields, providing relief, food, and shelter," I said.

The argument was repeated up and down the line of houses, and they were quickly cleared and the demolition began.

The *ballistae* were swiveled into place ready to launch at the houses, and at a signal, one at a time, they released their stones from a safe distance. The impact as they hit was explosive. The bricks and wood crumpled like paper; the stones penetrated inside, and it took only four or five to complete each job. The houses turned into mere heaps of rubble.

We then advanced to the next block and repeated the process. By midafternoon a wide band of debris encircled the base of the Esquiline, a mile long and a quarter mile wide. Then we soaked the debris with vinegared water.

"Good work, men," said Tigellinus, raising his arm in a salute. "Now go back to the camp and get a good rest." The Praetorian camp, outside the city on high ground, was surely in a safe area.

The rest of us climbed back up the Esquiline. And waited.

And got drunk. It began with Nymphidius bringing out amphoras and assuring us not to stint ourselves, there was more, we had earned it. Exhaustion and fear and tension had already debilitated us. Now Bacchus marched in and took command. Soon we were all sitting on the ground, swigging wine, some singing, some weeping, some muttering incoherently.

I kept staring at the fire below us. Even with my poor eyesight, I could see the different intensities of the fire, some places burning with a bright flame, others a deeper red flame, and still others with flames tinged with blue. It was a collection of gems, rubies and carnelian and citrine and topaz, lit from within.

It was hard to think. All I could do was stare at the conflagration, but my mind could not form words. I did not want words to rush in and fill the empty space. No words. Without them, I could keep fear at bay.

I was walking through cool fields, stalks of poppies swaying on either side. Above me a hawk soared, cutting the sky with its wings. "Caesar! Caesar!" someone was calling. I looked but saw no one, only the lone hawk.

"Caesar, Caesar!" The voice was outside the dream; it was by my ears. I opened my eyes and the poppy field melted away and I was staring into the face of Tigellinus. The real world was back, and I was in it.

"Yes?" I said. What now? What dreadful new thing had happened?

"It worked!" he said. "The fire has stopped. Overnight it reached our cleared ground and could advance no farther. And it is dying down in the rest of the city, too. It has run out of fuel!"

I swung my legs out of bed. "Because it has burned everything to a cinder?" I said. Not a victory.

"Not everything is gone," he insisted. "But it would have been without the firebreak."

I pulled on my clothes and ventured out of the tent, eager to see what had happened.

The hilltop was abuzz with activity. Everyone was staring out at the city, which showed only a few spurts of flame and great volumes of smoke. People were cheering and laughing—some hysterically. I saw many faces that belonged to neither the Praetorians nor the Vigiles; these people must have gathered here seeking a safe place.

They were not the rabble but the more refined sort. Possibly aristocrats who had hurried up to the city from their seaside villas when they heard about the fire, eager to know if their property had been spared. Some also looked like local well-to-do merchants.

"Caesar!" A hearty voice called behind me, and I turned to see Epaphroditus, my principal secretary. "The tide has turned!" he said.

"Thank the gods you are safe. Where have you been?" I had been frantic with worry not knowing where my staff had been during the fire.

"I've been staying with Phaon. He has a villa four miles out near the Via Nomentana, far from all this."

What a relief. Phaon, my minister of accounts and revenues, was safe as well. "What of your property?"

"I don't know. It was in Region Two." He shrugged. "I heard about your relief efforts. The emperor, putting on firefighter's gear and going out with the Vigiles," he said. "I don't think Claudius would have done that." He laughed.

"He wasn't able," I said. Claudius had done the best he could, which was all the gods can ask of us. "Caligula was, but he wouldn't have done anything but watch with amusement."

"Well, we have a fighting emperor!" His dark eyes were warm with approval. Epaphroditus was a freedman who had the build of a bull but an affable nature. Nearly all my administrators were freedmen, who were unpretentious and willing to work, unlike the senators. Epaphroditus had just proved the point, having come back into the city to search for me. I had no doubt that once restitution efforts were under way, he would be an invaluable help.

"More of the warrior in me than I thought," I said, smiling. "What did you see on your way in?" I asked.

"I was coming from the northeast," he said. "There were hordes of people in the fields and sheltering in the tombs. They were dazed, some wandering aimlessly. And I heard some calling for death, crying that they had lost everything and begging for someone to put them out of their misery. They called for a dagger, for poison, for a kind soul to strangle them."

"I hope no one answered their calls?"

"Better hope they did," he said. "These people long for death. There is nothing left in life for them."

"But there is always something left in life." Death lasts so long. Why hasten to it? Someone, a poet somewhere, had said, *Someday you will be dead, and then as time passes you will have been dead for a very long time.*

"For an emperor, yes," said Epaphroditus. "For others, not always so."

"Caesar!" I turned to see Calpurnius Piso standing before me, elegantly dressed, looking out of place among the soot-smudged firefighters around us. Epaphroditus diplomatically melted away. "I praise all the gods you are safe! Someone started a foolish rumor that you had rushed out to fight the fire and even climbed the Palatine when it was blazing."

"It was true," I said.

He just stared at me. I knew what he was thinking. His handsome face gave it away. *The emperor, who loves luxury and sings and writes poetry? He would not dare.*

But the grandson of Germanicus would dare. The great-grandson of Marc Antony would dare. "Yes, true," I repeated. I thrust out my burned forearm, a badge of honor I prized. "Here is the proof."

"I would not have such courage," he admitted. "In fact, I have just come up from Baiae. I think my property in the city has been spared. But until it is safe to go there, I cannot know."

I had always liked Piso and spent time at his elaborate seaside villa in Baiae. But that he was a spoiled, soft aristocrat there was no hiding. He dabbled in the arts, acting and writing, but lacked the focus to dedicate himself to them. He was mediocre in every way except his pedigree, but like many mediocre people, he compensated for it by a charming manner.

"What of the others in our literary group? Have you heard anything?"

He tilted his head, thinking. "Petronius is down at his villa near Cumae. Lucan probably is with his father, Mela, and his uncle Seneca at Seneca's country estate outside Rome."

Seneca. The old philosopher who had been my tutor and councilor for so many years, now retired to write. I missed him in many ways, but our parting had been strained. He wanted me to continue following the path of Augustus and behaving in strict Roman fashion, but I determined to follow my own path—the path of Nero, a path that no other emperor had trod. To add to the family disagreements, his young nephew Lucan, a talented poet and eager member of my literary group at court, admired me and wrote paeans in praise of me. And Gallio, his brother, still served me occasionally as an adviser on Judean matters, as he had been a proconsul in Greece some years earlier and had run afoul of local Jewish sectarian quarrels there.

"I predict that Petronius, the voluptuary, will not return to Rome until the banqueting rooms are ready again in the palace," I said. "Did you know my palace burned?"

"Where we used to gather for our literary discussions? The new, lower part?"

"The very same," I said. It hurt to say it, to picture it.

"You will have to build a new one, bigger and better," he said.

"I can't imagine such a dwelling," I said. "And for now I must worry about building simple shelters for all the displaced people."

"Oh, the people!" he said, with a dismissive gesture. "Aren't they used to doing without?"

V

All that evening we celebrated, boisterously, loudly, unbalanced by the strain of the past six days. By the time the waning moon rose—had all this really happened only in the space of the moon going from full to half?—we collapsed, exhausted but dizzy with relief.

But the next morning the dreaded red had flared up again in the city. The fire had not died; it had merely rested.

"Like the beast we knew it was," said Nymphidius. "It slept in its cave, living embers under the ash, and now has roared back."

"It looks farther away," I said, straining to see it.

"It's down near the Capitoline," he said. "Near your estates, Tigellinus," he called to the prefect, who strode over, adjusting his sleeves.

"Gods!" he cried.

"Send men down to rescue the state records from the *Tabularium* archives on the Capitoline," I said. All the history of Rome was in those records. "And get any historic treasures you can reach. They are irreplaceable. Augustus's gold Triumphal chariot, if you can."

Quickly the men left, while there was still clear passage. The rekindled fire rapidly leapt to places spared the first time, roaring through open spaces around the Forum, then sent arms north and south, as if to show us it had only held back by its own decision earlier. Later I was to learn it almost reached my family tomb, outside the city to the north. And to the south, almost to the Servilian Gardens.

It burned another three days, until finally it died away. But no one trusted that it was actually over, and we waited another two days before venturing down from the safety of the hill. Smoking vents in the ash, still hot, made us suspect there were more sleeping fires waiting to roar to life.

"Don't touch it for another two days," Nymphidius warned his men. "Give it four days without a flare-up." In the meantime, Tigellinus assigned soldiers to keep civilians—both honest people and treasure hunters—out. No one was to enter the city until I allowed them to.

"After it cools and is safe, we must remove the bodies. We must not allow them to lie there to greet the returning people," I ordered.

"A ghoulish task," said Faenius.

"A grim but necessary one."

"They won't stink, at least. There will not be much left of them. Just bones," Faenius said.

"There may not be much left of anything," I said.

And so it proved. When it was finally safe to inspect, the damage was overwhelming. Wearing high boots, I waded through heaps of ash in fields, for the buildings had disappeared and the streets no longer existed. An ugly odor permeated the air, compounded of smoke and stone and charcoal and flesh. The desolate landscape spread out all around. What had been the center of the city was a vast empty space, filled with debris and ash. Plumes of curling smoke rose here and there, tendrils trailing off into the air, light fluffy ash dancing in the breeze. Sometimes there was a charred massive beam, too large to have burned completely. There were metal railings, twisted and curled, or merely melted into a hard disc. The surviving stones that poked through the ash were blackened and split from the heat.

I stood in the ruins, knee deep in ashes, ashes that spread all around me like the Phlegraean Fields, that hellish volcanic terrain I had ridden through near Naples. The place I had had to traverse to get to the sibyl at Cumae.

The sibyl who had prophesied *Fire will be your undoing* and *Flames will consume your dreams, and your dreams are yourself.*

Defiant, I surveyed what was left of my city. The flames would not consume my dreams. They would give shape to them. I would rebuild

Rome and dazzle the world. I would whisper the secret name of Rome, and it would be reborn.

I t was time to measure the destruction and its extent and locate the displaced population. My order that no one enter the city until the preliminary cleanup was completed was still in effect. Unlike with earlier fires—and there had been many—we would not build anew on top of the ashes. They would be cleared away, hauled down the Tiber to the Ostian marshes. In addition to giving us a clean platform to rebuild on, it would ensure that there was no hidden smoldering debris left.

A week after the Fire, I set out with Epaphroditus, Tigellinus, and Faenius to see first the inner city, then the outlying areas. It quickly became apparent that it would be easier to count the areas that had survived than to list the ones that had not. Of the Fourteen Regions, only four remained intact. Regio One, below the Circus Maximus where the fire had begun, had escaped because the wind was blowing in the opposite direction. Regio Fourteen lay across the Tiber, near the Gardens of Caesar. It was where Crispus's villa had been, so my old boyhood home still stood. Regio Five, the Esquiline, and Regio Six, farther out, were untouched. But other than that, nearly all the central part of the city was destroyed. The saved areas had lain on the margins.

There was no trace of the Domus Transitoria where it had snaked through the land between the Palatine and the Esquiline. In the Forum, the Temple of Vesta was destroyed, along with the State Household gods, and so was the Regia, the ancient house of the Pontifex Maximus next to it.

The list went on and on. The Temple of Romulus, mansions of the great with their trophies from the wars against Hannibal and of the Gauls—gone.

Strangely, some things survived. Most of the Forum, the western slope of the Palatine, and, as it turned out, several buildings on the Palatine itself remained. The Temple of Palatine Apollo was only par-

tially damaged, and the original palace of Tiberius, Caligula, and Claudius escaped total destruction. Augustus's chariot had been rescued,
under great danger, from its place on the Palatine and was now safe
across the river. Likewise the Capitoline Hill had only been lightly
damaged, and the transfer of the precious archives had been successful.

The wall built by Servius Tullius around Rome five hundred years
ago had saved most of the Campus Martius, keeping the fire at bay, as
it could not leap the thirty-foot height and twelve-foot width—
although it had elsewhere—and I was thankful to see that the public
buildings, where I intended to house displaced people, were in good
condition, if dirty and ash-covered. There was much open ground
there, as well as the large buildings for shelter. The only casualty of the
area was the Amphitheater of Taurus, which lay in a heap of rubble and
tumbled stones.

The ashes were still warm as we waded through them. Teams of
slaves were clearing them, loading them onto wagons to be hauled
down to the docks. It was a race against the weather, for if the rain I
had longed for earlier were to strike now, the whole area would turn
into a sea of sludge, and when the muck dried, Rome would be encased
in a shell of ash. The sky looked clear, but we were in the season of hard
thunderstorms.

"I hope old Jupiter doesn't decide to send his lightning bolts," said
Epaphroditus, reading my mind.

"If he did, people would say he was punishing us," said Tigellinus.
"So he'd better control himself."

"Isn't it clear already that he is punishing us?" said Faenius, no
playfulness in his voice.

"Who can know the mind of the gods?" said Epaphroditus with a
laugh as he kicked ash before him.

I would not let it pass. "What do you mean, Faenius?" I asked.

He stopped and looked at me. "Something like this does not happen for no reason," he said. "It is too monumental for it not to have
been ordered by the gods."

"It was an accident," I said. "Unless an arsonist started it, and to
what end?"

"No matter how it started, the gods were sending a message when they allowed it to continue," said Faenius. "They could have stopped it at any point. But they chose not to."

"We cannot know how they think or how they behave," I said. "All we can do is proceed as if they did not exist. Do the tasks that are set before us. Fight the fire, even if it was sponsored by the gods. Rebuild, whether they bless it or not."

"Are you an atheist, Caesar?" asked Faenius. "For you certainly sound like one."

"In practical terms, yes. By that I mean since we cannot know their thoughts, it is best to admit that and proceed in the dark, unlike ignorant people who think they know and make stupid interpretations."

He glared at me—was he assuming I meant it personally? Then he turned and kept wading through the ashes.

But he was wrong in his accusation. I did believe in the gods; I just did not claim to know their motives. And I believed I pleased them best when I followed my conscience and brought my best efforts to whatever I did. That was what they required of mortals; it was very simple.

I had moved back into my residence in the Vatican Fields, which bore no marks of the fire, other than the dust and soot that had blown in. Workers were readying rows of shelters on the grounds that surrounded the racetrack Caligula had built and gifted with an obelisk straight from Egypt, a great engineering feat. I had driven chariots there, had trained to compete there soon. But now everything had changed, and my efforts must go toward recovery from the catastrophe. These grounds could house thousands of people, and if that was not enough, I would open the other imperial gardens—the Gardens of Caesar, the Gardens of Sallust, the Gardens of Servilius.

At last I could send a message to Poppaea, explaining briefly what had happened and telling her it was safe to join me but stressing that I would be preoccupied with the problems of the fire and that although the palace was intact, she should decide if she would rather stay at Antium for a while longer.

For although I long to see you, it is enough that I know you are safe and will return in due time, when we can be together without care and hardship.

I sealed the letter and sent it off. This was an example of what I believed: that Poppaea herself would decide what to do, and no god would sway her mind, or keep us apart.

I needed to make an inspection trip to the outlying fields. This time only Epaphroditus and Tigellinus came with me. I commented on Faenius's seeming disaffection, but Tigellinus laughed it off. "He's moody," he said. "Haven't you noticed that before?"

"No," I said, thinking that I would not have missed it. Something had changed.

The areas lying north of the city were seas of misery. Clumps of people crouched in the tombs, mausoleums built by wealthy Romans lining the roads leading out of the city. Some had porticoes and shrines that afforded roofs and marble floors to sleep on, protected from scurrying rodents. But they did not have water or food. Hollow-eyed children sat on the lids of sarcophagi, staring out in misery. In the outlying fields, hordes of people dressed in rags wandered the grounds. Some huddled together around cookfires; others lay motionless on the ground. I walked through them, disguised, for I did not dare risk being mobbed by the frantic people. I looked around, trying to take it all in, to grasp the extent of it. First I had to take measure of the problem; then I would solve it. As soon as possible, I would send messengers here to announce a plan to take care of them, to escort them to their temporary location.

All the while there was a lowing, continuous moaning and wailing from the destitute. Some were calling, feebly. A tall figure was walking among them, bending down and listening.

"As I told you, some are calling for deliverance," said Epaphroditus.

"They will soon get their deliverance," I said.

"They want a different sort of deliverance," he said. "They want death."

I looked around, searching for unscrupulous soldiers who might be willing to grant the pleas. But all I saw was the tall figure.

The tall figure . . . the way she moved . . . suddenly I knew her. And I knew why she was there.

"Stay here," I ordered my men. I made my way over to the woman. Her back was to me. She was not a refugee, as she was well dressed.

"Locusta," I said, and she turned.

"Caesar," she said, bowing. Then she straightened and smiled. "It has been a long time."

"An odd place to meet," I said. "I do not need to ask why you are here."

"People need me," she said. "I do not refuse those who ask."

I had once needed her, and she had responded. Without her, I would have been dead. To say I was ungrateful would be hypocritical. To say I hoped I would not need her again was also true. For Locusta was a professional poisoner, much in demand by the royal family in past times, and such was her fame that common people, like these suffering here, knew of her. She was a woman of integrity, which in her chosen field may be a contradiction in terms. But she had chosen to side with me when I had been marked for extermination, and saved me.

"They might not feel the same way tomorrow, or the next day."

"For them, there is no tomorrow. They do not wish to live with what they have lost. It is irreparable."

"I assume you mean people they loved? For no one would kill himself over a house or furniture or even the most precious artwork."

"Yes, that is what I mean. The pain of losing their child is too much."

But it wasn't. I had lost my daughter, and although it felt as if I had died, I had not, and I had gone on. The sting had subsided, although the ache never left.

"If they would only wait—"

"They do not wish to, and is it our right to hinder them in their hurry to cross the Styx and lose their pain?"

I shook my head. I did not know.

"I have missed seeing you, Caesar," she said, adroitly steering away from the subject. "You promised to visit my farm, but you never do."

Ah, yes. After her last completed assignment, I had furloughed her to a farm where she could set up her academy and teach others her skill. She was renowned not only for her poisoning expertise but for her knowledge of medicinal pharmacology, and soon her fame had spread so wide she was overwhelmed with applicants.

"I have meant to, but—" I spread my hands, helplessly.

"I work on antidotes, too, you know," she said. "It isn't all killing. I can reverse the effects as well. Do not assume I am an expert in only one area."

"Oh, Locusta, I would never assume that." It was almost impossible to overestimate her skills. "You know, I have a physician who claims he has an antidote for animal poisons. You should have a duel sometime. On a goat, that is. But then, you don't specialize in animal poisons, do you?"

"Too unstable, they don't keep, and they are hard to collect. But yes, I have them, although plants are my forte."

"Good. Then I promise, I will introduce you. But for now, please— refrain from your work here."

She bowed again. "You are Caesar, and I am bound to obey."

VI

LOCUSTA

But not willingly, I thought. If only he had not seen me. I was peacefully ministering relief to these suffering souls, and now he has interfered. I dare not disobey, for if I am caught the penalty would be dire. Even from this emperor, whom I have known since he was a child. I cannot presume on our friendship. Does an emperor have any friends? Can he afford to have any friends?

Someone was calling to me. I went over to her, bent down to listen. She wanted to die. She had seen her house collapse and trap her entire family inside. The neighbors had pulled her back to save her.

"If only they had let me in," she moaned. "That would have been the kindness." She grabbed my sleeve. "Help me. Help me. I know you can."

"I could. Now I can't," I said. The emperor was nearby, waist deep in the weeds, watching.

"Give me a gentle death," she begged. "Dark and sweet, not the agony of fire."

I stood up. I hated being cruel. "I can't. I'm sorry."

I needed to leave this place, since now there was nothing I could do.

I lived some miles outside Rome, in the countryside where the emperor had granted me land. That was several years ago, following a bargain I had made with him. It seemed fair—in exchange for one of my services, he let me set up a school of pharmacology where I could grow my medicinal plants openly and teach others my arts. I would be officially recognized and licensed—no more jail sentences, to be rescinded only when one emperor or another needed my help. I had worked for Tiberius, for Caligula, for Agrippina, and my professional name, Locusta, was known far and wide. But strictures had meant that my real name be secret. And my trade be practiced in secret. Now I was a free woman.

I had over twenty pupils and more graduates. I was careful not to teach them *everything* I knew; I wanted to retain supremacy in my field. I was the best, and everyone knew it.

But some people are stubborn. The emperor, for example. Instead of calling on me in his hour of need in sending his mother to her reward, he took matters into his own hands. The result was a bungled mess, filled with typical amateurish mistakes. Well. I hope he has learned his lesson.

I was once employed to eliminate him, employed by Agrippina and Britannicus. But then I was persuaded to change sides, and it was Britannicus who perished with the poison meant for Nero. I was especially proud of my skill in that, since Britannicus's tasters were vigilant. But tasters are overrated as a method of protection.

And so young Nero and I had a bond. But as I said, he did not call for me again. It has been eight years since I'd helped him, and I have watched him grow into his command. He was a promising youth when I first knew him; now he is becoming a true emperor.

His behavior during the fire was heroic. But as I have walked up and down the fields, I have heard mutterings from people. Some blame him for being away from Rome when the fire started. Others go further and accuse him of starting the fire himself. And most fantastic, some claim they saw him singing about the Fall of Troy as he watched the flames, treating it as a backdrop for his concert. They said he was on a stage, or in a tower, or on the roof of his palace. Obviously he could not have been in any of those places. His stage was across the river where no one could have seen him; the roof of his city palace was on fire; and there is no tower he could have ascended.

That these rumors are impossible does not make them any less dangerous. I fear for him. Let him act soon to smother them. Or they will grow, like the fire itself, and consume him.

VII

NERO

Quickly the fields were cleared and the people relocated in shelters across the river and in the Campus Martius. Since they were some third of the entire population of the city, I was proud of our efficiency in providing for them. The barges were busy bringing grain up from Ostia, where it was distributed on makeshift docks that replaced the destroyed ones downstream. Other supplies were gathered from neighboring towns. The rubble and dust were still being cleared from the city, but soon it should be finished. My next move was to execute a rebuilding plan for the city, carefully planned and engineered, to prevent any such fires in the future. And at the same time, to change the city's layout. We had a blank slate to start all over; why replicate the mistakes of the past?

I received an odd invitation from Petronius—an old friend who labeled himself my "arbiter of elegance"—but most of his invitations were odd. This one read,

Let us return to the haunts of Pan, to hear the echoes of Nature and lift a cup to the bounty of Life. At the edge of the woods of Aelia, past the turnstile and over the stream. Bring panpipes.

Where was he? Where had he been during the fire—which was now formally called the Great Fire of Rome? How typical of him to issue an invitation with no reference to anything else. I would find out when I got there. I was surprisingly eager to go. It had been a long time since

I had done anything, seen anyone, not directly connected with the Fire. I needed an escape.

W hen the day arrived, I set out for this mysterious place with several attendant slaves. The woods of Aelia were known for inexplicable nocturnal sounds, and local people stayed away from them. They bordered on open fields now planted with wheat and barley, fields that ended abruptly at the stream that flowed at the edge of the woods. As Petronius had said, there was an old turnstile I had to pass through before stepping across the stream.

I stood before the tall forest, a mixture of pines and oaks, dark within. There was a path leading into it, faint but there. Gingerly we walked along it, stirring up clouds of fireflies just beginning to glow. They twinkled ahead of us in the forest. The wind sighed in the tops of the trees, and from somewhere I heard the sound of water tumbling over stones. Then, rounding a bend in the path, voices. A glen opened before me, with an array of couches and a makeshift altar grouped together. Lanterns hung from low branches, like huge moths.

Petronius rose and came over to me. He was wearing a black goatskin and artificial horns. "Welcome, Caesar, in the name of Pan."

I just stared at him, wondering if this was a dream. I had had many odd ones lately.

"Did you bring your panpipes?" he asked, as if it were the most normal question in the world.

"Yes, yes." I held them aloft. They were a simple reed instrument, more difficult to play than one would think.

"Good," he said. "We will call Pan himself to join us." He led me over to the rustic couches, made of boughs and leaves. Lounging on them were several of our old literary group and others less well known to me.

"The place of honor," said Petronius, gesturing to the proper place on the middle couch. "Our last and most exalted guest joins us, to rejoice that we have all escaped unscathed by the Fire. And to celebrate our bond of fellowship, which will endure. We are all Friends of Caesar, are we not?" He alluded to a formal political designation, now endowing it with a deeper personal meaning. He took the position of host at the head of the couch on my right.

I stretched out and looked up and down. On the left-hand couch was young Lucan; next to him was Claudius Senecio; then Aulus Vitellius, just sliding into place. He was obviously the oldest man present and did not seem to mind being in the lowest-ranked place. Besides, there was more room for his dangling limbs that way. He had hip problems, having been run over by Caligula's chariot once. In fact, he had served ignominious appetites of emperors most of his life. As a boy he had been Tiberius's plaything on Capri; he had driven chariots with Caligula and played dice with Claudius. I had had no such use for him, other than as a companion in my early night wanderings and at feasts and drinking parties. He had recently returned from serving an appointment as proconsul of Africa and had executed his responsibility there admirably. His personal proclivities did not taint his professional skills.

Beside me was a louche senator named Flavius Scaevinus, and next to him lay an enormous senator, Plautius Lateranus, whose giant arms and legs hung off the couch. On the right-hand couch with Petronius lay Piso, next a senator named Afranius Quintianus.

I greeted those I knew heartily, delighted to see them unharmed. "Where were you during the Fire?" I asked everyone.

"With Uncle Seneca," said Lucan. "At his estate about four miles from Rome. We saw the smoke and the night sky lit up, but we did not venture closer." He had an open, handsome face and the sort of clear blue eyes that made you believe he was honest. But like all poets, what was truly in his mind was much deeper. "Uncle Gallio sheltered there, too. His town house in Rome may be destroyed. It was on the Caelian Hill."

"Mine, too," said Lateranus. "But I think it survived." His deep bass voice rumbled out of his huge chest. "We can't return to see for ourselves yet." He turned and looked at me for confirmation.

"Not yet," I said. "We are still clearing out the debris, so the rebuilding can begin. Some of the Caelian Hill survived, though. You are lucky."

"We fled my house in Rome," said Scaevinus. "And took refuge in our country villa in the mountains." He had a hawk nose and a large scar above his lip, making his mouth pucker.

"I stayed in Baiae, as you know," said Piso, turning to me. "But returned to Rome while the Fire was still burning." He smiled his charming smile, as if it had been a pleasurable excursion.

"I was also in Baiae," said Senecio, a sly grin on his face. He preferred the attractions of Baiae, that resort area Seneca had called "the inn of all vices," where Senecio felt most at home.

"Ah, the Fire gave you an excuse to spend more time there," said Scaevinus beside me.

"He doesn't need an excuse," said Petronius. "Like all libertines, he openly embraces his true nature."

"We envy you, Senecio," said Vitellius.

"Yours is hardly hidden, Vitellius," said Afranius Quintianus, with a wink.

"We need not advertise it," said Vitellius.

Quintianus laughed. "No, since everyone knows." He smoothed his hair, studded with gems and wildflowers, also advertising his true nature.

"I stayed in Cumae," said Petronius, returning to the subject. "I prayed my property in Rome on the Aventine would survive."

"It may have," I said. "Little pockets in that area were spared. That part was hit in the second flare-up of the Fire." But in truth there was little hope his property still stood.

"The suspicious flare-up," said Petronius.

"Why do you say that?" I asked.

"It started near the property of Tigellinus," he said. "There are rumors he started it."

For a moment I was speechless, remembering the exhaustion and dedication of Tigellinus and his men combating the Fire. Finally I said, "That's absurd. No, worse, a calumny."

Petronius shrugged, as if the serious slander was of no moment.

"Don't pass it off," I said. "Where did this rumor start?"

He leaned forward on his elbows. "Where does any rumor start? We never know. They are untraceable; they just appear."

"It's a vile defamation!" I said.

"There may be worse before long," said Senecio. "People always want to fasten blame, always look for a villain."

"In that case they will have to blame the gods," I said.

"Ah, yes, the gods," said Petronius, taking elegant command. "That is why we are here. Let us put all troublesome thought behind, all anguish or concern over the recent disaster." He got off the makeshift rustic couch and took his place in the middle of our little glen. His eyes, beneath the headdress with the horns, glinted in the lantern light.

He held up his hands for silence. We stayed very still, and as we quieted, the sounds of the forest around us became audible. First the creak of tall trees swaying in the breeze; then the sweet piercing calls of night birds; then, from far away in the glen, a faint croaking of frogs. I also became aware of the dry scent of pine needles, a dusty, spicy smell.

"Pan is the god of wooded glens, of groves, of forests of fir." He brought out his panpipes. "This is his instrument. He plays it exquisitely, not like children who see it as a plaything." He blew into his, coaxing sweet notes from it. "Now you," he said, and one by one we held our pipes and played them, some of us clumsily, others skillfully.

"This is how we call him," said Petronius. "We lure him out of the cave where he is resting."

"Why are we calling him?" asked Quintianus. "Why would we want him here?"

"Because he was declared dead!" said Petronius. "And we must not allow that."

"How can a god die?" asked Vitellius.

"They die when we stop believing in them. And Pan was declared dead back in the reign of Tiberius. Someone on the island of Paxi shouted out "Great god Pan is dead!" to the pilot of a passing boat. But I know better. He is my favorite god, and we will honor him here. I believe he has taken his last refuge in this enchanted forest."

Like most of the entertainments of Petronius, this was exceedingly peculiar. Perhaps he just wanted to dress up in a goatskin and play the panpipes. How very odd for someone who was recently a consul.

He recited the story of Pan, and his companions in the woods, and his affinity for goats, being half goat himself. It was true he tripped about in the woods, dancing and playing the pipes, but he was best known for a voracious sexual appetite, favoring nymphs and nanny goats. That must account for Petronius's fondness for him.

He approached the crude altar and laid the panpipes on it, along with an offering of cut fir branches and a libation of dark wine. Then he stepped back.

"He's here!" he announced. "Can't you see him?"

Playing the game, we all nodded. Then we drank a toast to him, recited flattering poems to him, and bid him good-bye. By that point we could almost see the shrubs part, rustling to let him pass.

We settled back into our places, munching on the tidbits Petronius had provided, washing them down with various wines—all rare vintages, of course. Even in the woods, Petronius remained urbane.

There was no more conversation about the Fire. We all wanted to look elsewhere, see beyond it. Perhaps that had been Petronius's real mission for the gathering. There would come a day when we would assemble again, not in a forest but in shining new halls, in the New Rome I would build.

The woods around me embraced me. Perhaps, in the New Rome, rural and city would meet and marry, no longer separate beings. It was a moment of inspiration in which I envisioned a new kind of city. Pan had brought me this gift.

Flames, far from consuming my dreams, would enable me to dream larger than I could have ever imagined.

VIII

It was growing light before I returned to the Vatican residence after the strange interlude in the woods. Nymphs and moths would be fluttering to their rest, and creatures of the night seeking dark places to creep into. It had been restorative to see a piece of nature unharmed, to know my friends had survived. But the smell of ashes was still in the air as I passed north of the city, and the devastation there was almost beyond comprehension.

From the window of my room I looked over the sea of tents on the grounds, housing the displaced. Those were the lucky ones; others simply lay on the grass, using cloaks as blankets. My gardens were at full capacity for housing people and could take no more. Farther downstream I had set up aid stations where food and clothing could be distributed and boards where announcements or concerns could be posted. I had appointed Epaphroditus to oversee all the refugee work. He was indefatigable and trustworthy; most important, he was a man of common sense, an absolute necessity in making the endless decisions he needed to address.

My city, my people! We stood at a crossroads. Rome would survive, but in what manner? Faenius had hinted darkly that the gods had punished us—but for what? If that was so, then we could not begin anew until the gods were appeased, until sacrifices had been made and accepted. And as Pontifex Maximus, as head of the Roman state, I was the designated one to carry out those rites.

I shook my head and rubbed my bleary eyes. If I did not know our transgression, how could I atone for it? And if I did not atone for it, the gods would continue to punish us.

I lay down on the untouched bed, its smooth silk coverings a caress. What could it have been? How could I know? The gods were mischievous and elusive; often they punished for whimsical reasons. But such a devastating punishment for a small infringement? It would not be possible. Even they were not so cruel. It had to be something enormous, something grand, an unforgivable effrontery. And I was utterly ignorant of what that might have been.

But there had been murmurs of arson. And I myself had seen men throwing lighted brands into houses and heard the strange praise of the Fire from the men just before the house collapsed on them.

But people say and do wild and bizarre things in danger; they lose their heads. I remembered the people who would not leave their houses, and even worse, ran back into them. And then the looters, for evil people always appear like magic at a crisis.

What could it be? What could it be? Desperate, I begged the gods to give me a sign, to reveal the answer to me in a dream.

But my dreams in the predawn were vague and murky, and when I opened my eyes midmorning I was no more enlightened. The day was well on and I needed to shoulder my duties, visiting the refuge stations farther down the river in the Gardens of Caesar and meeting with some of my former advisers from the Consilium—not all had returned to Rome, many having lost their homes, so they were staying in the their villas elsewhere. But enough were here for a quorum as we explored the massive undertaking of rebuilding the city.

Do not think of the scale of it, just attend to each task lying before you; keep your eyes on that. Focus only on what you know, on what you can do, on what you can command.

The day was fair and promised to be searingly hot. I chose my lightest toga—for although I normally hated wearing the uncomfortable garment, I knew the people needed to see me as emperor in one now—and knew it would be soaked with sweat and ruined by the end of the day. Even so, I felt embarrassed at having an intact garment when the people I would be consoling were in rags.

The field with aid stations was past the old naumachia water theater of Augustus, just across from the warehouses of Rome proper. Those had been reduced to smoldering blackened piles, and now ships from Ostia were docking farther downstream to unload their food and take on the cleared debris from the fire. A sea of people swarmed in the field, knots gathered around flags indicating food stations, medical stations, clothing stations, legal stations with property advice, and secretarial stations where information about missing persons and announcements were posted.

Flanked by my guards—for I had taken to heart the assassination warning—I made my way through the crowds. They seemed overwhelmingly joyous to see me; it was hard to believe they would wish me harm. But as Nymphidius had said, it took only one. And there were a lot of people here.

"Caesar, Caesar!" they cried, surging toward me, yelling their petitions.

"My house gone—"

"My son is injured"—holding a child with bandaged legs aloft.

"I have lost my livelihood—my hand crippled, I cannot work copper—"

"See my agents at the appropriate stations," I told them, pointing elsewhere. "They will help, in my name."

But they wanted me to help them directly, as if by magic I could heal their child, their hand. Their houses I could restore, but some things were gone forever. And lives lost were beyond help.

I will restore to you the years that the locust has eaten. Where had that come from? Something Poppaea had quoted once. Probably from those Hebrew writings she fancied. She had liked it, she said, because it promised that not only the grain would be restored but the very years wasted as well.

"Only God can restore time itself," she said.

But which god? And would the Hebrew God want to undo what the Roman ones had visited on us?

Time . . . the Roman gods had robbed us of that as well, for it would take months and years to rebuild what they had destroyed in nine days.

I will restore to you the years . . .

"Caesar, you are here!" Epaphroditus welcomed me to his head-quarter station. He gestured to show me the tables set up, the files, the lists, the busy secretaries overseeing it all.

"We are assessing the damages and filing the losses," he said. "Many claims, of course."

"Can you restore time?" I asked. "Where is the station for that?"

He looked at me quizzically. "Caesar?"

"Names, property, food, all that can be addressed. But time—and life, of course," I said. "Those losses are the ones that sting and wound."

"Caesar, we are not gods," he said. "We cannot restore what only they have ultimate power over and what lives only once. A house has many lives, a man only one."

"True," I said. "And we must admit the limit of our power, although the people here want to grant us more than we have."

"It is their wishes speaking, not their knowledge," he said. "But we are doing what lies in our power to do, and we can rest our consciences with that. No one man can exceed his own limits."

"My, you sound like a philosopher," I said. "And here I thought you were merely my head secretary and administrator."

"To be an able officer, one needs to be a bit of a philosopher as well." He laughed.

"Spoken like both," I said. "Take me to see the other stations, if you will."

The nearest one was one of many distributing food. Several men and women were overseeing the distribution of grain that had been brought in from neighboring towns. The lines were long.

"Many people have come in from the country to help in the aid stations," said Epaphroditus. "They have been invaluable."

The medical station had several physicians attending to patients; tables of ointments, bandages, and instruments were set up, and there were several camp cots for people to lie on, as well as piles of crutches.

The head physician told me, "We are seeing many burns, of course, but also broken limbs and wounds. The wounds are festering; we pour wine and oil into them, but about half do not heal, and the people either die or lose their limb to amputation. Then, some will die from the shock of the amputation." He shook his head. "It is a tragic business. It goes on day after day, and still I see no end to this yet."

I thanked him and moved on from this sorrowful station.

The clothing station was more reassuring. Cheerful workers handed out tunics, cloaks, hats, eagerly snatched by the threadbare suppliants.

"Where did all these come from?" I asked.

"Donations from the countryside," the head worker said. "They have been very generous."

As we turned away, Epaphroditus said, "Speaking of generous, Seneca has offered an enormous donation to help. He seems to have pledged most of his considerable fortune."

"Seneca?" I was astounded, but I should not have been. He had retired, not died. He had busied himself writing in his country villa, but I only heard about him secondhand. My old tutor had cut ties with me, which had hurt, but I lived with it. I had made decisions he disliked, especially marrying Poppaea and daring to perform publicly as a musician, violating his standards of Roman propriety. And, like all teachers, he did not like seeing his pupil grow up and fail to follow his advice obediently. "He will have to come and discuss this with us," I said. Secretly I was delighted that I would now have a chance to see him again.

We approached the saddest station of all—the information center. A large board was filled with flyers and notes and lists, so thick that some were posted on top of one another. A woman stood by a table, helping people compose new notes and filing information.

I walked over to the board and beheld the tablet of pain.

Help find my daughter Paulina Fausta, last seen in Eagle tavern in Circus Maximus night of the Fire, twenty years old, blue eyes, blond hair, wearing green tunic. Report to information station.

Missing husband of Marcia, Albinus Longinus, guard at grain storage warehouse, Regio XIII, forty-one years old, black hair, tall, scar on right shin. Last seen trying to put out the blaze at the warehouse.

Have you seen my mother? She is Metella, thirty-two years old, brown hair, small, wearing white gown when last seen running with me from our house on the Via Lata—we were separated—please find her! Crispina Balba

Our children, Gaius, age seven, and Vipsania, age five, lost in the crowd in the night of the Fire. We pray for your safety and hate ourselves forever that we were not able to keep holding your hands. Nonius Aetinus.

"Show me no more of this," I said. "I cannot bear it." I turned and sought out another station, something to focus on. My eyes were filling with tears, knowing as I did there was nothing I could do to help these people and feeling only one thousandth of the pain they were enduring, and yet it was searing.

"Let us turn then to the legal stand; the dry law dries all tears," said Epaphroditus. Even he was touched, his voice husky with sadness.

The legal station seemed the largest of all. A long table had at least five lawyers seated before it, and behind them were more tables with scribes and filing boxes, as well as legal scrolls. I inquired about their procedures and what they had processed so far, but I was almost deaf to the answers, as the plaintive words on the flyers were still echoing through the chambers of my mind.

Looking over the head of one of the lawyers droning on (admittedly to my own question), I was thunderstruck to see, behind one of the back tables a face I thought never to see again. At the same time she saw me and looked not shocked but disconcerted. Or was my bad eyesight misleading me?

"Acte," I said.

She rose. It was she.

"Caesar." She gave a little bow when she reached me.

"Don't call me that!" I barked. This woman I had loved, whom I had wanted to marry, to make my empress, now would only address me in my formal title?

"What else should I call you? You are Caesar Augustus, that is the truth."

"Yes, but not to you." I indicated that we should step away from these people. She had to obey. I *was* the emperor, she had spoken true. We walked a little way from the eager ears, the guards still trailing me.

Now that we were alone—in the midst of strangers—I could not find words to speak to her. She stood patiently waiting. She had always been calm, a soothing presence for my soul. So was she still.

"Shall I help you?" she said. "You wish to ask me why I am here. I am here to help; all the surrounding countryside is doing what it can, whether in grain or in presence. I still live in Velitrae. That is not so far."

"I know exactly how far it is," I said. *Twenty-two and a half miles in a straight line.* I had traveled it many times in my mind but never allowed myself to do so in reality. "It seems to have treated you well."

She smiled. "Yes, it has." She was lovely as ever, unchanged in the five years since we had parted. But I knew she could not say the same for me. If my looks reflected the changes in my being, I was not the same Nero. Instead, she asked, "And for you? How has the time treated you?"

She would have known all the external things that had happened, and I could not relate the personal things. So I just said, "Well."

We stood awkwardly in the field as busy people flowed around us. There were a thousand things I could say and none of them I would say. I loved my wife, Poppaea, with a passion and a fidelity that was devout, but Acte had known me when I was very young and if not innocent, more innocent than the Nero standing before her now. The remnants of that Nero lived on in my music, my poetry, my art, that side that fought to stay alive and untarnished in spite of the pressing, inexorable grinding of life and of being emperor. To her I would always be that boy, that youth, and in losing her I had lost the one person who saw me that way, and only that way: new and uncompromised. But now the compromised, the mature Nero looked at her and said, "I am pleased to have seen you and know that you have fared so well. And I thank you for helping us in our hour of need." Then I let her go, released her from the bondage of standing there, both of us brimming with the words we would never speak.

IX

ACTE

"No, you don't sign there, you sign here." My supervisor was standing over me, glaring at the paper I was processing. He stabbed his finger down on the spot.

I took up my pen and started to write, then suddenly forgot my full name. *Acte*, I wrote.

"This is a legal document," he said sharply. "We need your full legal name as well."

My name . . . which one? The one I had as a child in Lycia, *Glykera*, before the Romans enslaved me? The one I had as a slave, a single name that denoted slavery, just *Acte*? The one I acquired when I became a freedwoman, through the imperial Claudian house, *Claudia Acte*? The private one Nero called me, *my soul*?

But he had had different names, too, and I had known him first as Lucius—Lucius Domitius Ahenobarbus, before he changed into Nero Claudius Caesar Drusus Germanicus at his adoption by the emperor Claudius. I often called him Lucius in affectionate banter between us.

"Now you've blotched it!" A smear of ink soiled the page and obliterated my signature.

I rose. "I am sorry. I don't feel well." Without waiting for his permission, I left the table and walked away, out into the field.

Did not feel well . . . in fact I was shaking, unsteady. I had not expected to see him, except at a distance. I knew he would visit the relief stations at some point, had heard how he had exhausted himself with emergency measures for the city. But I had not prepared myself to speak directly with him.

Words had deserted me just now, although so many times over the five years since we parted I had spoken to him in my mind. It was I who had left him, but only because he had changed, grown apart from me, kept secrets I could not share. And his dream of ever marrying me, a former slave, would never have come true. I, as the older one by six years, could see things he could not. I knew more of the world than he did, could see that even the power of an emperor had its limits and that he could never have all his wishes.

Someone shoved me. "Look where you are going!" just before I tripped over a basket of grain. I was wandering like a madwoman in the heat, not seeing anything but just him, standing there in the field, saying, "I am pleased to have seen you and know that you have fared so well. And I thank you for helping us in our hour of need."

The formal, stiff phrases he would utter to anyone—a senator from Capua, an army officer, a lawyer from the provinces. Those words from the youth who had held me tightly on our bed of pine boughs in the cool mountains when we slipped away there for him to plan his retreat villa at Sublaqueum. His architects Severus and Celer—strange how I could remember their names today but not my own—had praised him as having the eye of an architect, but I had pleased him more by telling them no, he had the eye of an artist. And that night he had fervently begged me to marry him.

It was always impossible. But oh! what happiness while the possibility still existed.

If my heart had spoken instead of my closed lips, I would have answered him, not let him turn away. I would have said, "I am watching over you, and always will. If you call me, I will come. Always and ever."

Nothing could break or replace the bond formed from having once loved him with as strong a love as mine. I could not say the same for him. He had married *her*, Poppaea Sabina, the most beautiful woman in Rome, and the most vain and clever. And from all reports his madness for her had not faltered in the two years they had been married or through the loss of their baby girl.

No, he was gone. But I never would be free of him.

I had left Rome to make a new life in Velitrae and had prospered there. It was a pleasant place, the home city of the family of Augustus in the Alban Hills. I owned a pottery and tile factory in Sardinia that kept me affluent, as well as other businesses. I did not lack for suitors; now I could believe the myths about marriageable women setting impossible tasks for suitors. In my case the impossible task was that they equal Nero, but failure did not mean they would meet a deadly end, as happened in the stories. Instead their company brought me pleasure and amusement, but no more than that.

I finally reached the end of the field and found a tree to sit under, beyond the milling crowds. I could still see him in his purple toga—how he hated them, I remembered—very visible in the crowd. As I sat quietly and breathed slowly, my heart stopped racing and I could think. I was glad to have seen him, for otherwise I would carry only an outdated memory of him in my mind. He looked different. His hair was singed by the fire, giving him a wild look, like a damaged sun god. He had put on weight—his face was fuller. Once he had seemed younger than his years, but now he looked older than twenty-six. He had borne heavy responsibilities and it was showing. And the task of rebuilding Rome would strain his resources to the limit—all his resources: personal, financial, organizational, and artistic. Now he had a challenge equal to any emperor before him.

Protect him! I prayed to Ceres, my personal god, and then to all the other gods of Rome. Guide him in the decisions he must make, let them be wise and perfect for Rome. Let them make him immortal among emperors.

I did not add, *And let him return to me.* That could never be. And adding it might cause them to reject the entire petition.

X

NERO

I was exhausted and wished I had not summoned what remained of the Consilium to meet with me in the late afternoon. I did not have all the information I needed to lay before them, but more than that, I was so shaken by the suffering I had seen in the fields, and by encountering Acte again after all the years, that I could hardly think. They were mixed up together in my mind, both blisteringly real and dreamlike at the same time.

I limped back into the palace, wilted and dragging. As I had predicted, the toga was ruined—soaked with sweat, covered with briars, and soiled at the hem. Off and out with it. Should I bother to dress in another toga for this meeting? Sighing, I admitted I had to. I needed to show my authority when I addressed them, and the visual always confirms authority.

Acte . . . how was it she seemed unchanged, unaged? Was she truly just a work of art, as I had first seen her, the model for a mosaic in the imperial apartments? Art never ages, and that is what makes it so precious. It outlives us and our desires and griefs, serenely oblivious to the decay of its creator.

But I had seen flickers of emotion in her face—or was that just my fancy? And why had I been unable to speak, except to utter banalities?

Enough of this. Put it aside, put it away. Rome needs you. And the councilors will be arriving shortly. You have only a little while to go over the maps and think of what you are proposing.

. . .

Rome has been virtually destroyed." I stood before some fifteen men who had answered my summons. They were mainly senators, but my own staff were also present—Epaphroditus, my principal secretary; Phaon, my minister of accounts and revenues; and my architects, Severus and Celer; as well as the two Praetorian prefects, Tigellinus and Faenius; and Nymphidius, captain of the Vigiles. "But you do not need me to tell you this."

They looked back at me. Their eyes were wary, and they, like everyone else, had been severely tested in the ordeal, thankful to have survived.

"What you need me to tell you is what we will do now." But I had only a vague idea of what that would be. If they expected details, they would be disappointed.

I took a deep breath. "When Troy burned, Aeneas did not stay in Troy but left the ruins behind and sailed away to found Rome. But we are not Aeneas, and we do not wish to abandon Rome. And it was not an enemy who destroyed it, as Troy was destroyed, but an accident. We have no reason to flee. But we can imagine a new Rome, finer and more shining than the old."

I heard murmuring, so I hastened on. "Yes, much has been lost. I have prepared a report detailing all of it, at least what we know so far. Temples, trophies, artwork, records—the old Rome that was our pride. But we are still here, and we can re-create it, give a glorious city to the future, when the old one has been long forgotten." I nodded toward Severus and Celer. "With my architects, I will plan out a new city and present the design to you soon. For I think we must move quickly. There is no point in waiting; we need a city to live in, and the longer it takes to create it, the more the misery will swell."

"How can we afford it?" asked Publius, a senator from Tusculum.

An astute and painful question. "We will afford it because we have no choice." That was the honest answer.

"Do you plan to do this on credit?"

"No. The imperial treasury will bear most of the cost. We will also bring in contributions from the provinces, and there will be donations from wealthy people." Like Seneca, I thought, but did not name him. "People who can afford it can rebuild at their own expense, and if they meet a deadline in completing it, they will receive a compensation bonus from the treasury." I knew many people still had money; they had investments outside Rome, and not everyone had lost his house. Some had miraculously been spared.

"What about the cause of the Fire?" asked Faenius. "Will the culprits be punished?"

"How can we punish the wind, which whipped up the flames? Or the smoldering candle wick that set fire to rags?" I said.

"Are we sure that is how it happened?" he persisted.

"As sure as we can be," I said. "But still, the gods must be appeased. And I will make the necessary ritual sacrifices to do so."

One senator said, "When will the plans be ready?"

"As quickly as Celer, Severus, and I can do it. In the meantime, think of any changes you want to incorporate. This is your opportunity. We have a blank slate."

After they departed, Epaphroditus and Tigellinus lingered.

"Yes?" I said, sitting glumly at my desk.

"Seeing you gave the people comfort today," Epaphroditus said. "I know that."

"It did the opposite for me."

"I know."

Suddenly I had a request. "Stay while I write a note for the lost-persons bulletin. There are several people whose safety I wish to know."

I pulled a piece of paper toward me and wrote:

Anyone with knowledge about the following people contact the emperor through his representative Epaphroditus at the information station.

> *Terpnus, a citharoede of the highest standing*
> *Apollonius, Greek athletic trainer*
> *Paris, a leading actor*
> *Appius, vocal instructor*
> *Vorax, madam in Subura*

I handed it to Epaphroditus.

"A madam?" he said. "You want a madam to contact you?"

"She is a friend," I said. Tigellinus had introduced her to me on the eve of my first disastrous marriage, and she had imparted invaluable knowledge of a certain sort to a virginal boy, so I was forever grateful.

"Ah, I have friends like that," Tigellinus admitted, grinning.

"Then best ask for them on the lost-persons board," I said.

"Well, if the emperor is bold enough to do so, so will I." He winked, and left.

As I watched Tigellinus's retreating back, I was immensely thankful that he was still here with me. Others distrusted the closeness we shared, fearing that he had too much influence. But they had no way of knowing the bond that had formed between us at our first meeting, when I was still a child and he had entered the palace surreptitiously for the announcement of Mother's marriage with Claudius. He was not welcome there but had dared to go anyway, which impressed me. When he told me he was a breeder of racehorses, I was instantly smitten. Both of us were rebels—he in trespassing where he did not belong, I in wanting to be around horses and charioteers, which Mother forbade. He promised to take me to the stables, and I promised not to betray that he was at the palace. Then and there we formed an alliance that had never been broken.

The day had finally ended, and I thanked all the gods. Off with the toga. Down with a cup of wine. I would not think anymore. I could not bear it. Tomorrow I would face it all anew.

As I readied for sleep, a servant pushed open the door; it turned silently on its hinge, and standing on the threshold was Poppaea, like an apparition. But she moved and came forward, and the servant closed the door behind her.

I rushed to embrace her, the first time I had seen her since leaving that hot noon to rush to Rome. I held her in my arms, beyond joy to see her. All would be well, and now I knew Rome would rise anew and that its golden age was still before it, not behind it in the ashes. Poppaea was here with me, and all would be well.

XI

We stayed up talking, words spilling over one another in our rush to pour out all that we had experienced since our parting. My exhaustion fled, banished into the night skies, as I told her all.

"I waited—I heard nothing—there was no way to know what had happened, or if you were safe—" She reached out and touched my hair. "Then there was a report that you had foolishly rushed into the Fire itself. And here is the proof. Burned hair."

"I didn't rush into the Fire, I just came close enough to observe it and see how much of the Palatine was aflame."

"You were close enough to get burned."

"That was from flying sparks; the air was full of them. My arms were blistered, too, but not badly." I was proud of that; I almost wished the blisters would never heal, a permanent reminder that when the hour came I had not flinched. But they were fading already, my proof of bravery along with them.

"Waiting was torture," she said. "Although I do not mean to suggest that it could compare to what you were facing."

"Not knowing what happened to someone is a torture all its own." I thought of the people I had inquired about on the bulletin board, people I longed to know were safe. "A third of the city is now homeless, people looking for lost loved ones, camped out in all the public venues I could provide."

"I know, I passed by some on my way in. A sea of people! What are we do to with them?"

"That is the question I am wrestling with. I met with the Consilium and will work with architects to design the new city."

"A new city?"

"Yes. It has come to me that this is the opportunity to create a new Rome. A Rome beyond anyone's imagining—a Rome that transcends all the old rules."

She lay back on the bed and stretched her arms. "How grandiose."

"Not grandiose. Visionary."

"Two names for the same thing." She smiled. "Your enemies will call it one thing, your friends another."

"I care only what the future calls it. I am building for people not yet born. Contemporary judgment is often faulty and only corrected by later ages."

"But it works the opposite way, too," she said. "What is acclaimed in one age is pilloried in the next."

Her voice faded in the background as the Rome of my imagination rose in shining towers. A Rome that would stun the world.

We embraced on the bed, safe in one another's arms, my burns soothed against the soft skin of her back. But my happiness was shaded by the dark awareness of the displaced people in the fields surrounding us.

The Vatican residence was smaller than the late lost Domus Transitoria, and smaller even than the sprawling multilevel villa at Antium. I liked to call it my rural palace, lying in the fields across the Tiber from Rome. It had the theater where I had held the Juvenalia, my coming-of-age celebration, and the racetrack where lesser chariot races were run. It was much less formal than any other imperial venue. So it made a suitable place for me to meet with the engineers and architects to plan the reconstruction of Rome, for the homey setting was not intimidating.

I had a large table constructed from flat boards in the middle of the meeting room; here we would build a model of the city. Wooden blocks of all sizes were at the ready, which could be stacked and rearranged, and a map of the old city plan. Severus and Celer, my trusted architects, stood by, waiting. Several engineers were also present, experts in water drainage, brick and stone properties, and vaulting and arches.

They were all looking at me, waiting for me to begin. No one would speak until I did. So I took up my staff and pointed to the empty tabletop. "Two thirds of Rome has been destroyed," I said. Taking chalk, I sketched the outlines of the geography of the area, the river, the hills, the low areas. I filled in the places untouched by the fire, mainly on the margins of the area. The middle was gapingly empty.

"There must be no more fires," I said. "If we are to create a new Rome, it must be invulnerable."

"There are always fires," said one of the engineers. "Along with plagues and wars."

"Yes, because conditions favor them. The middle of the city was a crowded warren of twisted streets, overhanging wooden houses, and flammable goods. It must be rebuilt differently," I said.

"In what way?" Another of the engineers looked skeptical.

"Well, it's obvious," said Severus. "Correct those three conditions and you will go a long way to eliminating fires. No more narrow streets—we will have wide ones. No more overhanging upper stories of houses; there should be open sky between houses. And the houses should not be of wood but built of Gabii or Alba stone, which is fireproof."

"And each house should have its own wall," I added. "No common walls."

Celer spoke up. "The houses should be set back from the road."

"With porticos lining each side," I said, picturing it.

"Where shall these streets be built?" asked another of the engineers. "And where will the shrines and temples go? Those will have to be rebuilt. We can't have a street plan until we have situated the large buildings."

"True," I admitted. "I will draw up a list of the buildings we need to replace." It would be a dreary list, a list of loss. "Then we can proceed from there."

"What about that low-lying area between the Esquiline and the Viminal? The section at the end of the Forum."

"It should stay open," I said.

"But it's swampy and there's no use for it," Severus said.

"Perhaps we could build a large artificial lake there. Like Agrippa's in the Campus Martius. That is probably what it is best suited for."

"Do we need another lake?" the engineer Junius said. "We already have Agrippa's, and Augustus's naumachia across the river."

Suddenly a picture was forming in my mind, indistinct but compelling. "But they are on the outskirts. This would be in the heart of Rome."

I needed to be alone with Severus and Celer. So I told the others we would meet again the next day when I had the list of public buildings for us to plan around. After they left, I eagerly turned to my architects. "I have an idea," I said. I took the chalk and drew a rectangle in the middle. "This can be the lake. And around it"—I took the miniature blocks and began to arrange them—"around the lake, woodlands. Fields."

"What?" Celer shook his head. "This is the middle of Rome. You can't have woodlands there."

"But what if we did—open green fields, trees of all sorts, deer and herons and hawks? People flee to the country, to villas, because the central city is congested and foul, but this would bring the country into the city. And with the wide streets, and the open air, it would be a garden. A garden open to all of Rome."

"It would take up too much space. Real estate in the center of Rome would be sacrificed, and people would be angry. They would say, if we want fields and lakes, we can go to Campania."

"But now they would not have to travel to do so. It would soothe their spirits," I said.

"They care more about their purses and business dealings than their spirits," said Celer.

"I want you to draw up a plan for this," I said stubbornly. "After we decide where the public buildings are going to be re-erected, we can design the rest."

"Your plans always seem to defy nature," said Severus. "The Avernus–Ostia canal, for example. One hundred and twenty miles through difficult country, wide enough for two quinqueremes to pass abreast. We have only got a few miles into it; the engineering is challenging. And the Sublaqueum villa, wanting us to dam up a river and create three lakes."

"Well, you did it, didn't you?"

"Yes, but we have been accused of not respecting the bounds of nature."

"That is the cry of the timid," I said.

"No one can accuse you of that," Celer said.

"I have the greatest confidence that you can carry out these plans, whatever we decide." The meeting was over.

After dismissing them, I knew the next step was to inspect the shrines and public buildings—what was left of them—to decide which ones were the most urgent to replace. The engineers were right; those would have to be planned before we could allocate other space. I set out with Tigellinus and two other guards early the next morning. The bridge was intact, and we were able to cross over easily; inside the city the noise of carts, workers, and demolition made a strangely melodic background. Makeshift roads had been plowed through the areas. We no longer needed boots to wade through. It was eerie to see nothing higher than a bramble bush; everything had been leveled.

"When the areas are cleared, we will survey and then let people return to rebuild," I said. "I don't want them there until it is safe and there are no grisly surprises to greet them." My orders that kept people out still stood; treasure hunters and looters must be prevented.

Piles of debris were being shoveled into carts, to be trundled down to the docks and loaded on barges. Workers had been doing this for some time now, and yet the mounds grew back again like mushrooms after rain. Charred beams, metal grates melted into twisted messes, headless statues, detached wheels, broken roof tiles, and pots with dead plants poked out from the piles of rubbish.

Tigellinus shook his head. "The remnants of lives," he said, with uncharacteristic melancholy. He stopped. "Where do you wish to go first?" he asked.

"The Palatine," I said. I needed to examine it more closely than my earlier quick visit had allowed. "We must assess and confirm the losses there."

Passing by the Temple of Vesta, which was a heap of broken stones, still preserving the round shape of the temple by how they had fallen, we began to climb the Palatine. It was hot, of course, being high summer, but cold in comparison to the furnace blast of heat that had confronted me here last time. At last, cresting the hill, I looked out on a blackened expanse of seared trees, fallen buildings, and clumps of ash, all under a clear and soaring blue sky, the birds wheeling overhead.

On my right, the old palace, the Domus Tiberius, was badly damaged, but portions of it still stood. I tried to remember exactly what was in each room, what irreplaceable treasures had been lost, but I could not. There must be an inventory somewhere—but it was probably lost as well. Luckily many of my personal possessions were in Antium and Sublaqueum, but not all. And the glorious bronze statues from Greece must now be melted lumps inside the palace, the genius of their creator fled from the inert material.

Its annex, the Domus Transitoria, had fared worse, although I knew that, having smelled the smoke in it during the fire. But oh! I had designed it, had watched the painter at work, had selected the marble and planned the sunken fountain . . . this hurt much worse than the damage to the main palace.

"There may be something to salvage here," I said, seeing some of the floor design through the ashes.

"Wishful thinking, Caesar," said Tigellinus.

Now we walked farther across the flat top of the hill, toward the Augustus section, where his modest house had stood, along with the Temple of Palatine Apollo and the sacred laurel grove. This side had suffered less damage, although the flames had been licking up just below from the Circus Maximus. Perhaps the wind had mercifully shifted at a crucial time.

But still the devastation was great. The little temple to *Luna Noctiluca*—Luna Light of the Night, which was kept lit all night and glowed in beauty like a white lantern—had toppled and fallen. Next to it, her brother Apollo's large temple still stood, but the portico with the fifty Danaid daughters in red and black marble had collapsed, and the statues fallen, broken. The library attached to the Temple was heavily damaged, the scrolls probably illegible. The precious Sibylline Books, though, had been rescued along with archival material from the *Tabularium* when the Fire had restarted on the sixth day. And we were fortunate that those things, so vital to Rome, had survived.

I waded out onto the floor of the temple, kicking at the ashes. Here I had laid my wreath, awarded to me as a citharoede in the first games in my name, the Neronia. I had given Apollo the credit for my victory. Now the wreath was cinders. Plaster had fallen from the porticoes, and beneath the ashes I saw a blue tint. As I brushed off the ashes, an image of Apollo playing his cithara appeared against a cerulean background. He was gazing upward, his golden hair flowing, his hands steady on the musical instrument. It was just a fragment, but it was a promise.

Art survives. Art is eternal. I am still with you.

I picked it up and hugged it to myself. It would have a place of honor in my new palace.

"Come," I said to Tigellinus and the guards. "We have one more thing to check." But now I was oddly certain it would still be there. And yes, beside the Augustus house, the sacred laurels of the Caesars still grew. They had not been vanquished, as Apollo had not been.

"Here's mine," I said, locating it. Its trunk was a bit burned, and many leaves were shriveled, but I had no doubt it would survive. Every new emperor planted his own sprig from the original laurel of Livia, and it foretold his fortune. As long as the laurel flourished, so would he. When he died, it died with him. The stumps of the trees of Augustus, Tiberius, Caligula, and Claudius stood in a straight, sad line behind mine with its green leaves. Other descendants of the Livia tree likewise still grew strong, not dedicated to any one emperor but to Rome itself. It and I were still safe, under divine protection.

*   *   *

That night I could not sleep. The room was suffocatingly hot, despite the open windows that had both east and west orientation. There was no breeze, and the sound of the refugees on the grounds was louder tonight than usual.

It was urgent to rebuild the city as quickly as possible, so they could end their exile. What I had seen today gave me a clearer picture of what needed to be done, and in what order.

Beside me Poppaea was sleeping calmly. The heat did not seem to bother her, although she slept with only the sheerest cover, her only surrender to the heavy air. Either she had been stunned by what she saw when she returned to the city, or she did not realize the depth of it, for she had said little about it. I found her groundedness a steadying hand, but I also felt alone and abandoned to my own distressing state of mind.

It was no use. I could not lie there any longer, useless and with wasted hours crawling past. I got up and went to the room with the model of Rome, the guards watching me silently from their posts as I passed.

Inside, I lit the lamps to illuminate the big table. The city-to-be spread out before me, waiting to be created. The lines I had drawn earlier, denoting the vast areas of destruction, now seemed an artist's opportunity, obedient to my touch.

The domed market building—the Macellum Magnum—high on the Caelian Hill had survived with minor damage. I put a large block down on the site. The Curia in the Forum survived; I moved its representational block to the correct place. The Temple of Claudius had its block. Then the others followed, all the public buildings and temples that were still with us. Standing back, I surveyed the way the city now looked. Next must come the buildings we were obligated to restore: the Temple of Vesta, the Regia, the Temple of Fortuna, Romulus's temple to Jupiter, the temple to *Luna Noctiluca*. These must all go back in their original sites. But when I was finished with those and many others, there was still an enormous swath of free space in the middle of the city.

I closed my eyes, remembering what I had heard about the legendary city of Alexandria: white marble, grand boulevards, the lighthouse, the great library, the Mouseion. I regretted never having seen it, but Seneca had lingered there, and my grandfather Germanicus had been entranced by it. It cast a spell, they said, its beauty and its learning making it unique. Why should Rome be second to it? We had conquered it, and should not the city of the conqueror be greater than that of the conquered?

And there was more, a compelling mandate. When I was a child, Cleopatra's son had given me a coin his mother had possessed, telling me, *I surrender her and her dreams into your safekeeping.* So did I have a special mission, to transform Rome into something greater than it had been, an enlightened city of beauty to surpass even Alexandria, as she would have wished? To bring in a golden age?

The center of the city . . . the center . . . what was to go there?

Feverishly, I began to arrange and rearrange the blocks. A strange urgency seized me, as if I had thoughts I could never recapture, thoughts I must pursue now. The center . . . it should be a thing of beauty, of transcendent beauty. Not for commerce or ceremonies but for all the people to enjoy. The idea I had had earlier about an open woodland now rose again. But not just a wood—a re-creation of the entire Roman empire, with the lake in the middle representing the Mediterranean. Animals from different regions, trees and plants from far-flung parts. And a pavilion up on the hill, a huge pavilion overlooking the lake, a palace dedicated to art. Terraces below, hanging gardens, descending to the lake, then a vestibule next to a lower separate palace, leading into the Via Sacra of the Forum. All seamless, all flowing together. Fountains, fountains everywhere. The Temple of Claudius—its platform could be converted into a giant fountain and park.

I saw it all, as real as if it were already built. And the glittering hillside pavilion, facing south to pull in the sunlight, would twinkle and beguile, could deserve only one name: the Golden House, Domus Aurea.

The hours had passed so swiftly I was shocked to leave the room and find the rising sun shining in my face.

"Thank you, Apollo. I will build it all worthy of you," I promised him.

XII

Poppaea was still asleep when I stole back into the room. Even though we had now lived together for two years, I still had difficulty seeing her as a living, breathing person rather than a work of art, her perfection was so absolute. In my mind she was Helen of Troy; she taught me that Helen was real, that such a creature could truly exist, and not just in the imagination of Homer.

Now I stood and looked at her. She was turned on one side, facing the sunlit window, the sheer covering now just over her legs. The rays of the rising sun caught her extraordinary hair, illuminating its amber depths, firing them to a honey luster. She seemed oblivious to the importuning beams of Apollonian light tickling her eyelids. That was appropriate. She had once acted the part of Daphne in a pantomime, playing the role of the nymph who preferred to be turned into a tree rather than submit to Apollo. Later she claimed I was the Apollo she chose to submit to, but she was prone to mythologizing, and in truth it was only my blond hair that she was able to cite as being Apollonian. That, and my cithara playing.

"Stop watching me." Her drowsy voice rose. "I see you. You still gawk at me like a schoolboy." Slowly she sat up, turning to me. Her hair tumbled to her waist.

"You turn us all into schoolboys—or schoolgirls." I laughed, but she had embarrassed me. Fleetingly I wondered if the people who stared at me were likewise embarrassed when I caught them, although an emperor can expect to be stared at.

"You look terrible," she said. "Haven't you slept at all?"

"No. Does it show?"

"Yes. You know that beauty requires a certain amount of sleep. So why don't you get it?"

"I am not trying to be beautiful," I said. "I leave that to you. But let me show you what I exchanged for sleep!" Before she could protest, I grabbed her hand and pulled her from the bed.

"Wait, wait!" she said, tripping over her feet. "I can't go out like this."

"We are only going to another room. Come, now!" I dragged her along, down to the planning room, past the guards who pointedly averted their eyes to show us they weren't looking, proving the opposite. "In here!"

The big table with its model spread out before us, even more impressive now that it was lighted naturally. "I've done it! I've laid out all the city plans." I pointed to each building block, explaining it, and named the new streets, marked out with chalk.

She just stared. Perhaps she was still half asleep. Finally she said, "You did all this last night?"

"Not all of it. I had a preliminary talk with the architects and the engineers first."

"This remakes Rome entirely. As you said. It will shock people."

"My concern is not for the people now but the people yet to come."

"Unfortunately we have to live with the ones here now," she said. She smiled. "But this is marvelous. And what about the palace? I don't see it."

I swept my hand over the area that would be called the Domus Aurea—the hillside pavilion and the lower separate palace by the lake. "Here."

She touched the area of the pavilion. "Very well situated. We will have a fine view of the Forum. And I like the long frontage."

"That's only one part of it." I explained the rest—the lake, the garden terraces, the porticoes, the vestibule. "I will put a colossus up in the open-air vestibule," I said, just thinking of it. "Yes, one bigger than the one at Rhodes, dedicated to Apollo, to the new golden age."

She looked dismayed. "How big?"

"Big enough to be seen from everywhere. The one at Rhodes was a hundred feet high, so mine must be at least a hundred and twenty. I'll have it of gilded bronze." I laughed. "But that will be last, don't worry. Everything else must be completed before we splurge on the colossus."

"Is this wise?"

"The colossus? I told you, it will be last."

"No, turning the center of Rome into your private grounds."

"But it won't be private. It will all be open to the people, except the pavilion. Like the area in Antium that I built, by the shore, with the gardens and the theater. I am giving the city of Rome back to its people."

"The people may like it, but the wealthy you are evicting from their property won't."

She had a keen sense of the practical, but at this moment it annoyed me. "Change inevitably brings loss to someone. There is no help for that. Change is both cruel and rewarding—the good and the evil that Zeus dispenses from his jars at each hand."

"I need to get dressed," she said suddenly, pulling her silk garment closer. "Come with me to my apartments. You seldom visit me there."

I found them a stifling hothouse of femininity, so I usually stayed away. But today, my head still spinning from the exultation of the city planning, feeling immune from any surprises, I decided to come with her.

Her quarters were almost as large as mine, and her attendants more numerous. Perhaps it took more effort to look after an empress than an emperor. Or to look after *this* empress. They were on the west side of the palace, because she did not like morning sunlight.

"I prefer the late-afternoon light," she had said. "The oblique slant-ing rays, the feeling of completion, the excitement of the coming night—that is what I love."

True to her wishes, her quarters were still rather dark, even though the sun was well up now. As she entered, her attendants bowed and pulled back the curtains.

Her bed, unslept in, gleamed with its silks and pillows, a pavilion of pleasure that one would not want to waste in sleeping. I eyed it, but there were too many people about—although Poppaea was not shy at dismissing them whenever she wanted them gone.

She saw me looking at the bed, but this morning she was disinclined to follow me there. Instead she went to her cosmetics table, which was laden with bottles and jars of all sizes and shapes—truly beautiful vessels of silver and thin glass and alabaster. She picked up a hand mirror and examined her face critically. I came up behind her and saw my own face reflected in its uneven surface.

"You could see better if you had better light in this room," I said.

"Perhaps I don't want to see better," she said. "I might see things I wish I had not."

"Never," I said, laying my head on her shoulder, embracing her.

But she continued to stare at her reflection, frowning. "This was not here before."

"What?"

"This crease," she said, touching a barely perceptible line around her mouth.

"Unless you want to stop eating and therefore never open your mouth, there are bound to be lines," I said.

"It wasn't there before," she insisted. She put down the mirror. "I told you, I hope to die before my beauty fades."

"It isn't fading," I said. I did not like the course of this conversation.

"I am thirty-two," she said. "Thirty-two. It will not be much longer now. It's beginning. I see it!"

"Stop that," I said. "You are fixated on this idea. If you do not stop thinking this way, you will bring it about."

"Very well for you to say. You are only twenty-six!"

"If I could change places with you and let you be twenty-six, I would gladly be thirty-two. It has never mattered that you are older than I am. To me you are a goddess, and goddesses are ageless."

"Well, this goddess has lines!"

Now I laughed. "How do you know Aphrodite didn't?"

Reluctantly she laughed, too. "I need the donkeys' milk again. Do you know what has happened to my stable?"

"I must confess, checking on your donkeys has been at the bottom of the list of emergencies. But I will." She kept a stable of two hundred donkeys on the outskirts of Rome to provide milk for her to bathe in.

"If I had the milk again, it would restore my complexion."

"It doesn't need restoring," I insisted. "Truly."

She moved to another part of the huge room and called for her wardrobe servants. Several appeared, eager to fulfill her wishes.

"It will be beastly hot again today," she said. "What are the lightest gowns I have?"

"My lady, which color do you prefer?" a slender woman with sunburned cheeks asked.

"Green today," she said, then called after the woman, "*light* green."

"Do you want the kid sandals or the goatskin?" asked a short woman with penetrating eyes.

"Oh . . . kid." Poppaea waved her on her way.

There were still a number of attendants standing about, awaiting their assignments. One or two stood out because their garments were heavy and concealing despite the heat. I wondered why they were wearing them. But I forgot about them as I saw Poppaea standing near them. Then I looked to my right, and she was still standing by me. I whipped my head back to see the other person: the Poppaea on the other side of the room.

"Call that person," I told her, pointing.

She beckoned to him. "Sporus," she called.

The apparition came toward me, walking just as Poppaea did, moving as she did. Unable to trust my own senses, I looked again at her to ascertain she really was still there beside me.

The person stood before me. Now, close up, I could see it wasn't Poppaea, but so close a likeness as a Roman marble copy of a Greek bronze original. It was a man, not a woman. His hair was not the lit-from-within amber of Poppaea's, but it was nearly the same shade. His features, while almost identical to hers, were not so fine. His body was slender, not muscular, but still it did not have her contours.

"You like my twin?" she said.

Sporus merely stood there, an object.

"The resemblance is uncanny," I said.

"Of course we are not related, that we know of, but there are many unacknowledged cousins in Rome."

"And many unacknowledged sons," I said. "Nymphidius claims he is the son of Caligula rather than the gladiator his mother slept with. Who knows?"

"Sporus is my confidant," she said. "It is like talking to myself. We have many a good conversation, do we not?"

Sporus nodded, with an innate dignity. I wondered what his true background was.

"He knows many secrets of the household," she said. "But he knows how to keep them." She looked tellingly at him.

Just then her attendants came to dress her, and she withdrew into an inner room, leaving me alone with Sporus.

"They say everyone has a double," I said. "But it must be odd to find yours. I have never met mine."

"Yes, it was odd at first. But now I feel as if she is my twin, my sister."

"Yet you are slave and she empress."

"We are who we are regardless of our station," he said. He did indeed have gentility. Perhaps his family had fallen into bad times and been forced to sell themselves into slavery.

"How did you come into this household?" I asked.

"My family is long from Pompeii. And we have known and served the Sabinus family for a long time. My grandfather went with Poppaeus Sabinus to Moesia."

Then how did you end up a slave? I wanted to ask. But Poppaea would tell me. I did not want to pursue it now.

Poppaea returned, her green silk gown fluttering behind her. Sporus was dismissed as she fussed with her brooch.

"Now I know where to find another Poppaea if I need one," I said.

"I hope that never happens," she said. "That you would need another Poppaea."

When we were alone—as much as an emperor can ever be alone—back in my apartments, I asked, "What did you mean, he knows the secrets of the household and how to keep them?"

"I think there are Christians in my household. I told you that, when you were interrogating that prisoner, Paul. When you let him go, I warned you that *they* were everywhere. Sporus helps keep a watch. There is little that goes on that he does not know about."

"At the time I told you there was little to be alarmed about, as long as they served you faithfully. Those two with the heavy clothing—is it them?"

"I think so. They cover themselves up, as if the human body is something shameful. So in hot weather, it gives them away. Stupid people!"

We were in my innermost private quarters, and while all around us the palace was buzzing with activity, we were sheltered from it all. I embraced her, wanting to feel her next to me. She had eluded me all morning, but now I would have my way. It did not matter that the little daybed was small and plain and lacked the sumptuous appointments of the imperial bed; it was meant for daytime napping. But it had the most important elements of all: privacy, secrecy, and two people aching to touch one another, two people who found the human body not shameful but glorious.

XIII

The list is complete," said Epaphroditus, handing me the tablet. I looked it over. Terpnus and Appius were there; so was Paris. "Apollonius?"

Epaphroditus shook his head. "We have no knowledge of him. He has not responded."

A veil of sadness dropped over me. He had been my athletic instructor when I was very young and training under a pseudonym, Marcus. That was before Mother married Claudius and whisked me away to the Palatine and turned me into Caesar, heir presumptive. When I knew Apollonius, I was free to roam and play as I liked. A competitive champion himself in Greece, he had instructed me in racing and wrestling and jumping. The last time I had seen him I was emperor, and he was my guest at the Neronian Games. He had teased me and called me little Marcus and asked how I liked being emperor. He had also told me my days of competition were over, for no contest is fair if the emperor competes. I had argued with him, saying that it need not be so. He said this was one argument I could not win.

"Perhaps he was not in Rome," I said. But I knew better. He had never spoken of any other home or of family or friends living elsewhere. He was gone.

I looked back at the list. Vorax was there. That did not surprise me; she was the very definition of a wily survivor.

Tigellinus entered the room, mopping his forehead. "Another

scorcher," he said. "It is hellish out there in the fields. Very little shade." I handed him the list.

"An encouraging list of returns," he said. "My regrets about Apollonius." He glanced at it again. "Ah, Vorax!"

"She will doubtless be pleased to see her favorite patron," I said. Tigellinus was a connoisseur of brothels, and proud of it.

"I have told them to come to the imperial tent on the relief grounds," said Epaphroditus. "They were gratified to know that the emperor cared for their well-being."

I nodded. "Tigellinus, do you want to come and greet your old confederate in carnality?"

"I wouldn't miss it," he said, grinning.

I was eager to reunite with these people dear to me in different aspects of my life, the non-emperor part of me. To say they had known me when I was quite young did not reveal the full significance, because I was only sixteen when I became emperor, and only eleven when I was adopted by Claudius and effectively removed from normal life, and they had known me before that. I was overjoyed that they had survived the fire and that I would not lose them.

The imperial tent Epaphroditus had erected on the grounds was different only in being larger than the others, not more luxurious. It would have been inadvisable to have anything ostentatious. Inside, although we were shielded from the blazing sun, it was stifling, humid from the crushed grass underfoot. Since it would have been conspicuous for slaves shouldering large feather fans to be seen entering the tent, we sweltered as much as all my subjects outside.

The first dear faces I saw were of Ecloge and Alexandra, my earliest caretakers, wet nurses who were far more motherly to me than Mother. I was so fond of them I kept them on long after I had outgrown their original purpose, letting them serve my household in other capacities.

Ecloge, with her pale eyes and wan face, embraced me, and Alexandra, buxom and stout, cried out, "Oh, how sweet to meet again on the other side of the horror."

"Where have you been?" I asked.

"We fled the palace as soon as the flames started and took refuge with our families in the countryside," said Ecloge.

"The whole sky was red, even miles outside," said Alexandra. "It glowed like a furnace."

"I know," I said. "I saw it from the hilltop when I returned." I looked at them, restored to me. "Thank the gods you are safe."

"Thank the gods we all are."

The next person to greet me was Paris, the actor, whom I had known longer than anyone else. He had been my first teacher when I was a poor relation at my aunt's—my father's estate seized by Caligula, my mother exiled. Upon her return, Mother had dismissed him, disapproving of him. But it was too late. He had already imbued me with a fierce love of the theater and acting. Once I was emperor, I had called him back as friend, and Mother had been helpless to do anything about it.

"Caesar!" he said, his face shining—with both sweat and joy.

"We are here together," I said. "Thanks be to all the gods. Where was your house? Is it lost? Is everyone else safe?"

He was a small man, with the ability to grow taller when he played the part of a tall man; a plain man, who could appear handsome when the role called for it. Now he was just himself, a middle-aged man of medium build and thinning hair. "My house was in the sixth district," he said. "So it was saved. Thanks to the firebreak the Vigiles constructed. And no one was hurt." He laughed. "Since your palace across the river survived, and its theater with it, we can put on plays again before too long."

"Yes, people need that. Especially after such sorrow. It helps them to know that life goes on."

"Oddly enough, tragedies are a remedy for that. They put our own sorrows in context, the context of being human. Suffering is woven into all existence."

"Oh my, perhaps you are in the wrong profession and belong with the philosophers."

"Actors bring philosophy to people in a form they can understand," he said. "I prefer that. It is more useful."

I spotted Appius standing near a table with refreshments, looking lost. I hurried over to him. "I am so thankful to see you here. Your name on the list was a great gift."

"Your asking after me was a gift as well," he said.

"Did you think I would abandon my voice lessons?" I laughed, keeping what was so serious as light as possible. "I needed my teacher!"

He just nodded. He had always been a solemn sort, who seldom smiled and joked less. But he was an expert vocal coach and had coaxed my voice to good performances.

"And here is Terpnus," I said, beckoning to him. "Join us!"

Now the legendary citharoede made his way over to us. As a child I had first heard him practicing in an empty room in Claudius's palace, had stolen in to listen to the supernaturally fluid notes, and made a promise to myself that someday I would have him as instructor. As emperor, I had made that wish come true. Whatever I knew about the cithara—and I had recently been honored for my performances—I had learned from him. In performances I combined the vocal training of Appius with the cithara lessons from Terpnus set to my own compositions. They had both prepared me for my public debut, a nerve-rattling exposure for me, but one that had to happen before I could proceed to the next level.

Terpnus greeted us warmly but then said, "What is this I have heard about your singing during the Fire?"

I was taken aback. "What do you mean?"

"It's being whispered, and more than whispered, all over. That you put on your citharoede robe and sang of the Fall of Troy while watching Rome burn. I don't have to tell you how horrified I was to hear such a thing and how ashamed I was that any pupil of mine could do this, emperor or not."

I kept my temper. "How could you believe such an accusation? Don't you know me better than that?" That was the real sting—that he had believed it.

He looked pained. "In a crisis, people behave oddly. One never knows."

"It isn't true!" I said. "For one thing, my cithara was in Antium!"

That sounded like a childish excuse even to my own ears. "I had performed the Fall of Troy in Antium the night before I learned of the Fire. A number of people from Rome had attended. Perhaps that is why the rumor started."

"However it started, many people believe it."

"Do *you* believe it?"

He looked uncomfortable. Finally he said, "If you say it is untrue, I believe you." A hedged support, indicating that he had believed it easily enough. I felt betrayed.

"I can assure you it is untrue."

"I believe you, Caesar," he repeated.

"I never believed it," said Appius.

"Thank you for your trust," I said.

"But I have to tell you that some others say you yourself set the Fire," Appius said. "So you could rebuild Rome and name it after yourself."

"What? What are they saying?"

"That you want to rename Rome Neronopolis," he said.

"This is how facts get twisted," I said. "As Pontifex Maximus I alone know the secret name of Rome, and I will whisper it when I perform the propitiatory rites at the shrines of the gods, restoring that name intact. It will *not* be Neronopolis." I was stunned by the accusations but angry as well. I had not even been in Rome when the Fire started; my own palace had been destroyed; I had risked my personal safety in helping to fight the blaze and was emptying the treasury to rebuild the city. The ingrates!

"Thank you for telling me," I said. "Now please use your influence to correct these rumors." I supposed I should be thankful that I had access to people whose ears were to the ground outside the palace, but what they had heard was disturbing.

There were others to greet. Fabullus, the painter who had done the frescoes of the Domus Transitoria, now lost, alas. But I promised him I would soon have another, and much larger, job for him.

Now Tigellinus came toward me, Vorax in tow. The tall madam had aged little since I had first made her acquaintance as a nervous

fifteen-year-old virgin on the eve of his marriage, dragged to her establishment by Tigellinus, another instance of using an assumed identity,
that time as Tigellinus's slave. I never knew if the disguise had fooled
her. Did it matter at this point?

Before she could speak, or Tigellinus could make one of his inap-
propriate jokes, I said, "I am pleased to know you are safe."

"Thank you," she said, inclining her head in respect of my office
but offering no other recognition of a relationship beyond the fact that
Tigellinus served me.

"I trust all your . . . employees are likewise safe?"

"Yes. My establishment was in the fourth district, but we fled early,
not wanting to take any chances. Unfortunately, the house was lost."

I nodded. I knew very well what district it was in. At one point my
feet could have gone there on their own. And more than just my feet.

"If you have the means to rebuild quickly, the treasury will repay
you as an incentive. I want Rome to be restored as fast as possible."

"You could even build a larger establishment," said Tigellinus.
"Part of the new and improved Rome the emperor is planning."

"I would welcome you, Caesar," she said.

"Alas, he would not patronize your house," said Tigellinus. "He is
hopelessly devoted to his wife, more's the pity."

"It would be surprising if, given the famous beauty of the empress,
he was wont to look elsewhere," she said. "But I would welcome you as
an honored guest to tour the new establishment." Her eyes twinkled.
"There would be many novelties, but of course we would still offer the
tried-and-true favorites."

My cheeks burned. The tried-and-true favorites . . . Vorax had introduced the custom (now much imitated) of having impersonators of
famous women for clients who wished to make love to Cleopatra,
Queen Hippolyta of the Amazons, Nefertiti—and Agrippina the
Younger, my mother. Perhaps that was the proof that she truly had not
known who I was, or surely she would not have matched me with my
own mother that afternoon. I could never banish the searing and de-
grading details from my mind, burned and imprinted there for all
eternity.

"I wish you all good fortune in your rebuilding," I said. I had to turn away.

Later Tigellinus said, "That was abrupt!"

"I wished her well," I said. "And perhaps I will tour her establishment—in full daylight and with an entourage."

"Ah, do not be so quick to turn your back on her. One never knows . . . it is good to have a friend like her."

"I trust we are still friends, whether I am a customer or not." And I meant it.

Not long after, I left and returned to the palace, where I rested on an ivory bench and tried to tame the fighting emotions surging through me. I was full of the happiness of knowing that my music instructors were well, that my painter was well, that everyone but Apollonius would be part of my life going forward, that even Vorax would set up her business again. But the ugly rumors and blame for the Fire—I had not expected this. And such rumors were dangerous. Unlike the Fire, these flames were invisible. Unlike the Fire, there was no clear remedy for them—no houses to demolish to starve them of fuel. How could I starve these baseless rumors of the fuel they were feeding on? What fuel was it? How to douse it? And like the flames, rumors spread, jumped barriers, and confounded attempts to smother them.

XIV

"Today is the day," I told Poppaea. I sounded resolute, composed, in command. In truth I dreaded addressing the Senate for the first time since the Fire. It was necessary, but my message would be difficult to deliver in a manner that was easily comprehended. And I needed them to understand everything I was proposing.

"It is time," she said. "Nothing can move forward until they have been informed and consulted." She was dressed in a respectful, demure gown with a light palla over her shoulders. But unlike Mother, who had eavesdropped on Senate meetings and openly met envoys, she would not be visible today. "And it is good to see you in your purple toga. If only to remind yourself that you are the emperor."

"As if I need reminding." In fact, there was hardly an instant in my life that I wasn't acutely aware of it, and never more so than after the Fire. But it would remind others, in case they were apt to forget.

The Curia had been spared in the Fire, sustaining only smoke damage and some black scorch marks on its walls. Now the Forum had been cleared of its debris, the Curia scrubbed clean again, and the call sent out for all senators to attend my address. Although there were six hundred senators, obviously not all of them would—or could—come.

On my way through Rome I was pleased with the progress of the cleanup. Almost all of the center had been cleared, and work had already begun on the Temple of Vesta and the Circus Maximus. Next week I would give permission for the property owners to return to their sites and start to rebuild.

As I entered the great doors of the Curia, guarded by the Praetorians Faenius and Subrius in uniform, at first I could see nothing in the dimness after the bright sunlight in the Forum. It seemed a great dark void with murmuring voices. Then gradually things swam into view, lightened, clarified. The benches on either side of the long room were filled, aglow with the white of the senatorial togas. The dais where I would sit on my chair, flanked by the two consuls, awaited.

"Imperator Nero Claudius Caesar Augustus Germanicus!" the official announcer boomed out as I approached the dais. The senators rose in a body.

I mounted the steps and turned to look around the room. "Welcome back to Rome, Rome the imperishable!" I said in greeting. I then motioned for them to sit. But I would remain standing.

"I give thanks that we meet here again, safe and in our old home. Rome has endured many calamities in the more than eight hundred years of its existence, but this ranks as one of the greatest it has faced. But we will prevail, and Rome will be restored more glorious than ever. It will enter a golden age, a sublime period in its history, that men will look back upon and lament they were not here to gaze upon it."

I could not make out the expressions on the senators' faces. Some were still shrouded in shadow and besides that, I was shortsighted. They waited, quietly. I guessed there to be about two hundred of them present.

"As to the immediate task before us, I and my agents have assessed the damage and recorded property loss, listed the missing. All those figures are available for your perusal; I will not recite them now or we would be here for a month." Still silence, no chuckles or even groans. "The relief stations have been dispensing food, clothes, and relocation information. We are compiling lists of missing persons and reuniting those we have been able to locate."

I sat down. This was going to be a delicate and difficult conversation, especially as it was one-sided. "After consulting with engineers, architects, legal advisers, and the senators in my Consilium, I have a plan for the rebuilding of the city." I then told them about the new safety measures, the regulations for fireproof stone, the widening of the streets, the colonnades on street fronts, the banning of overhanging stories and common house walls, the requirements for firefighting equipment in each home. I hastened to tell them that I would be responsible for the expense of this. "Contributions from the provinces and from the near countryside have been generous," I said. "And many wealthy people have also made contributions." I hoped this hint would be heeded by the senators, but they as a group were not as wealthy as the next class down, the *equites*, because of their snobbish shunning of money earned in business and finance. Only income from war and land was respectable in their eyes.

Now for the thunderclap. I stood up again. "I am reserving the center of Rome for imperial grounds, which will include a palace, gardens, a lake, the Temple of Claudius, and a porticoed walk connecting the park to the Forum. It will be an integrated whole."

Now they stirred; now there were whispers.

"These grounds will be open to the people; they will belong to all of Rome." I raised my voice. "Rome will become, at one stroke, the most beautiful city on earth. A golden palace, the Domus Aurea, will crown the golden age of Rome, the new age of Apollo!"

A senator stood to speak. He was fairly close to me, and I saw that it was Plautius Lateranus, that giant of a man. "Where do the people go who are displaced for this . . . this imperial playground?" he asked. His deep voice seemed to come from the bottom of a well.

"They will be compensated and settled elsewhere," I said. "And it is their park as well."

"Wouldn't they rather just have a house to live in than a park to stroll in?" another senator, the flighty Quintianus, stood and asked.

"It is not one or the other," I said. "They will get a new house as well."

"This would bankrupt even Croesus," said Scaevinus, his puckered mouth twisted in disapproval. "It is too . . . ambitious." He all but mouthed the word "outrageous" before he replaced it with "ambitious."

"Croesus is not known for anything now but his gold, but this will give Rome a reputation for the ages," I said.

"Yes, a reputation for waste and folly." Thrasea Paetus now stood. The Stoic senator had dared to say the words the others skirted around.

"It is not folly to wish our city beauty and admiration, but perhaps we should build everything else first to see what the treasury can bear." This was Piso, always the smooth conciliator.

"No, it should be done all of a piece," I said. "So when it is finished, it is truly finished." I waited. No other comments. "There is nothing more tedious than a road that is always being repaired, a building that is never finished, endless construction work with dust and mess and detours. No, we want our city back, and quickly. In time for the second Neronian Games, a little over a year from now. Yes, when that day comes, you will walk on new paved roads, past rebuilt houses, into the wide avenues of the new Rome, and we shall have a grand reception in the open vestibule of the Domus Aurea."

I had wished to describe the particulars, to share my excitement with them. But I hesitated now.

Suddenly another senator rose—it was Lucan, recently elected. "Shouldn't the person—or persons—responsible for the Fire be culpable? Shouldn't they pay?"

"Since it was an accident, how would that be possible?" I asked. "If it was a person who knocked over a lamp, it was not done purposely. Even now the person may not be aware of it, if he even survived."

"People are calling down curses on whoever started it," he said. "They give no names, but they seem to feel that someone did."

"And perhaps it says much that they don't name a name," said Scaevinus. "They know it but dare not say it."

He might as well have pointed a finger at me and said, *You are the man!* as the prophet Nathan did to King David. But Scaevinus was no prophet, and unlike David with Bathsheba, I was not guilty. So I did not answer *I have sinned* because I had not. But suddenly I was furious with the continuing accusations against me.

And what if it was true . . . someone had started the Fire? The people felt it was no accident but could not identify the culprits. So they blamed it on me.

"So, good senators, now I have my task set before me," I said gravely. "Not only to rebuild the city but to track down and punish the guilty, if they truly exist.

"But first the gods of Rome must be propitiated for the violation of their shrines by these evil persons, whoever they may be." I meant it, and I was serving notice to those who disrespected and even suspected me—some of them in this very room.

The room was quiet. I then gave the senators the imperial dismissal and took my leave, walking slowly toward the great doors and out into the blinding light of the Forum. The purple toga seemed to shimmer. *Remember you are emperor,* it seemed to whisper. *You rule, not them.*

Beside me, Faenius and Subrius were silent and I could not read their faces.

T hat was unpleasant," I told Poppaea when we were alone in our quarters. Both Subrius and Faenius had hurried away as soon as we were back at the palace. I called for an attendant to disrobe me from the enveloping toga, which was a heavy weight in this weather. Looking at it folded neatly, I wondered how many shellfish had been crushed to dye it. This was a particularly deep purple, so it had been dyed twice at least.

"You did not expect it to be otherwise, did you?" she asked. "No one is going to applaud your plan for Rome."

"The Senate has been docile a long time; why would they change now?" I sank down on a cushioned bench and motioned for a drink, my *decocta Neronis,* water that had been boiled and cooled in snow. A supply was always on hand, for I found it to be the most refreshing of any liquid. Soon a cup was put in my hand and I downed the drink. It had been so hot in the Curia.

Poppaea also motioned for a cup. After sipping it, she said, "They agreed that the death of your mother was suicide following discovered treason—you can thank Seneca for crafting that defense—and they vote you honors on the slightest pretext, but this is different. First of all, you are rewriting what Rome is. Second, and probably more im-

portant to them, your ideas cost them money. It didn't cost them anything to condemn your mother or decree that your speeches must be
engraved in silver and read throughout the empire, but this hits them
in the most tender of spots—their purses. Some of them will lose
property in the middle of Rome to your grand redesign."

"Of course you are right," I admitted. "But the Fire has cost everyone dear."

I patted the folded toga absentmindedly, feeling adrift.

"Something else is bothering you," she said. How well she knew me.
But we had always been reflections of one another, sharing the same
sensibilities and moods.

"They keep blaming me! They think I started the Fire!" I burst out.

She frowned, put down her cup. "Who is 'they'?"

"Everyone! Senator Scaevinus all but accused me directly. And there
was no dissent from the rest of the room. They just sat there, staring!"

She shrugged. "Scaevinus is a pompous snob," she said. "He is
hardly to be heeded when he speaks."

"He seemed to be quite well heeded," I said. "And Lucan said that
the people were cursing the person who started the Fire, without actually naming him. Implying that to do so would run afoul of someone
powerful: the emperor."

She made a face. "Lucan? That poet nephew of Seneca's? He's jealous of you because you are a better writer than he is."

I shook my head. "There's more to it than that." As for his writing,
he was very talented and gave me close competition. "It wasn't just the
senators, anyway. A few days ago my old cithara teacher Terpnus told
me that the rumor that I had sung of the Fall of Troy while Rome
burned was still rife. Worst of all, he believed it. I know he did; I could
tell. And the other story making the rounds is that I myself set fire to
Rome so I could rebuild it and name it after myself. I suppose there's a
combination story that I set fire to Rome and then grabbed my cithara
and rushed off to sing, while renaming Rome after myself." Anger
enveloped me, but it did not quench the deep sorrow underneath at
these accusations, the sense of betrayal by both the people and the
Senate. "I didn't tell you about it. I should have."

She came over to me and embraced me from the back, putting her head on my shoulders and entwining our fingers together. "You should tell me everything. You know we are one and the same, forged together forever."

"Yes." I held her fingers more tightly. "We are."

She nudged my head with hers, as if she would meld them. "What if someone really did start the Fire?" she said. "It is entirely possible."

"But to what end?"

She thought a long moment. "There are madmen who like to destroy or who are enthralled by watching flames. Those we can never discover. But suppose there was a group that had a purpose in kindling the Fire?"

"I can't imagine such a group. The army? No. The slaves? No; too many of them would perish even if a few gained their freedom. The foreigners who live here? No; they are here for trade and because they prefer living here to their home countries. The Jews? No. They may be violent in Jerusalem, but that is because we are occupying their home. Those are the main distinct groups we have."

"You left one out," she said.

"Which one?"

"The Christians," she said. "You must remember our conversation about them after you let that Paul of Tarsus go. I told you they were dangerous. You laughed and gave me a lecture—you really are insufferable when you give one of your little lectures, dear—about how I was exaggerating and even how having them in my household would cause no trouble."

"Oh, yes. I do remember. You said many converts were here in the palace. But you failed to convince me what was so bad about them. You disliked them because they are an offshoot of Judaism, which you feel kindly toward."

"Everyone hates them! They refuse to participate in the rites of Rome, they meet secretly at night—which is illegal, as you know—they worship a man executed as a traitor to Rome. Shall I go on?"

"No," I said. She was quite irrational on this subject, I now recalled.

I was not in the mood for a diatribe. I took a deep breath, my mind made up. "I will propitiate the gods of Rome whom we may have offended, with the prescribed rituals. Perhaps that will placate the people and these rumors will die out. If not—"

If not, my rule was threatened.

We left the conversation off then, but after dinner I stood looking out the window to the palace grounds below, still full of tents of the displaced, although there were fewer now, as people were returning to the city or moving elsewhere. Torches flickered below, lighting the grounds.

Torches. What of the men throwing torches into burning buildings, praising Jesus during the height of the Fire? And the others who said they were acting under orders? That there had been some deliberate fire setting, I had seen with my own eyes. And what was it that Poppaea had asked Paul directly? Something about the end of the world and how Jesus would return, bringing fire with him. Yes. Poppaea claimed their leader had said he had come to cast fire upon the earth and that he wished it was already kindled. Paul had deflected the question, not denying it but saying he had never heard Jesus say that. The truth was he hadn't heard Jesus say anything because he had never met him! I would find out more about this sect, but through less biased eyes than my wife's.

The sacred days of propitiation were here. I had consulted the Sibylline Books, rescued from the Temple of Apollo on the Palatine, and been directed to lead prayers to Vulcan, Ceres, and Proserpine, with a public banquet to follow. Juno would be honored by rites led by the matrons of Rome.

The timing could not have been more auspicious, for Vulcan's feast day was almost a month since the Fire had burned itself out, and already the city was recovering. Vulcan's altar stood near the *mundus* of Ceres in the Forum, the ritual vaulted pit whose cover was removed once a year to allow the spirits of the dead to mingle with the living. It was also the spot where Romulus, the founder of Rome, had disappeared.

On August twenty-third, the day of Vulcan's annual observance, I stood before his altar near the Curia and intoned the ritual prayers, making a vow to set up altars all over the city on his feast day henceforth, to appease him and protect us from fire. Behind me, spread out all over the Forum were crowds of the common people, watching and wondering. The next day, August twenty-fourth, I invoked Ceres and her daughter as the cover was solemnly removed from the yawning pit to the underworld, offering them gifts and prayers.

The ritual completed, I turned to the people, a blur before me, their clothes making a welcome change from the dull gray of the gutted Forum.

"The rites to honor and thank Juno will be completed by the matrons of Rome. Her temple will be cleansed and fresh sea water sprinkled on her statues, and there will be vigils and banquets tonight. Those the matrons will keep privately, but we will banquet here in the Forum after sunset, and all are invited!" Loud cheers went up.

"For we celebrate the rebirth of Rome!" I cried. "The gods have blessed it—as you know, the Fire started on the exact same day as the deadly fire over four hundred years ago when the Gauls sacked and destroyed much of Rome. But Juno's sacred geese on the Capitoline warned of the attack then, saving many things. And once again Juno's temple has been spared. When Rome was rebuilt the first time, it was done in haste and disarray. But here, before the very sacred site of Romulus, I promise him a new city, planned and executed with care and thought. It is rising grander than ever before and will be done as quickly as the former, but more thoroughly. I, your emperor, vow to you that this time next year you will stand in the new Rome and your eyes will be so dazzled you will blink, and your feet will walk on precious marble." I then bent and dropped an offering into the *mundus*. It was so deep I could not hear it hit bottom. As it fell, I whispered the secret name of Rome into the darkness, bringing the sacred city back to life.

*   *   *

A huge table was set up at that end of the Forum, with couches for some fifty high-ranking persons around it. I had invited certain senators, as well as the priests attached to the select gods, military leaders, and wealthy patricians. The people would help themselves to food and drink from tables throughout the Forum—I had ordered two hundred of them. They were free to walk about and mingle and even approach the imperial banquet table, and many did. I welcomed them all, getting up from my couch to talk to them, to hear their concerns. Mostly they seemed dazed by what had happened and what promised to emerge from the ruins as the new Rome. I heard no criticism. Perhaps the reports that people blamed me were exaggerated or coming from only one segment. Or . . . perhaps they were hiding their true feelings.

Settling back onto my couch, I faced the pulvinar, the ceremonial banquet couch of the gods present at sacred events. There were images of Vulcan, Ceres, Proserpine, Juno, and Claudia Augusta. Claudia, my lost baby daughter. The Senate had voted her a place on the gods' couch after her deification.

I stared at the statue. It was an idealized portrait, a perfect baby with perfect features. The sculptor had never seen her. Perhaps it was kinder this way, that it not look like her. To see her again as she had really looked would have been painful. Now I saw only a representation.

I reached out and took Poppaea's hand. She, too, was looking at the statue.

I promise you a Rome worthy of your memory, I told Claudia silently.

A few days later Phaon, my minister of accounts and revenues, placed a paper before me and stepped back.

I reached out to take it. "You act as if this is a poisonous snake," I said, picking it up.

"It is definitely something poisonous," he said.

I spread it out before me and stared at the figures, covering the entire page, in columns and boxes. Finally I located the summation: twenty-two thousand million sesterces. Was I reading this correctly?

"Is this twenty-two thousand million?"

"That is my finding," he said. "It covers everything." Phaon seldom frowned, and he did not even now. He was relentlessly cheerful and optimistic. "Considering what it includes—a bargain. Just for you, sir, I will give it to you for what it cost me, but I am a poor man—" He wheedled, spreading his palms. We both burst out laughing.

"Can you—can you throw in another temple, sir, if I meet this price—" I countered.

"Only if we use inferior stone, and the emperor has forbidden me to traffic in such goods."

We stopped laughing.

I had known it would be costly. But until I saw the figures . . . still, I could not change course now. The city was gone; it had to be rebuilt. There was no choice.

Of course, it did not need to be rebuilt of marble, or the transparent stone from Cappadocia I had ordered for one of the temples, and perhaps I should not have offered to pay for the porticoes. And the Domus Aurea and its grounds—need they be so extensive?

The answer was Yes! It all had to be done, it had all been promised, promised to the gods, promised to the people of Rome. And it had to be done as promised, not stinted upon.

I put down the paper. "Is there any way we could raise more money?" I asked.

"My thoughts exactly, Caesar. You know there are many wealthy freedmen."

"Yes, you should know, you are one."

"And we long to be full Roman citizens, but only our children are allowed that privilege. What if you decreed that any freedman who had more than two hundred thousand sesterces and committed one hundred thousand of them to building a house in Rome could become a citizen? You would have many volunteers, I daresay."

"You already have a villa here," I said. "So that leaves you out."

"I am only one of many in that class of people, but it is a problem—wealthy people with no position in society."

"Having no position in society would be fair only if half of the work of government weren't run by freedmen," I said. "Your fund-raising plan is an excellent one."

But after he left I spread out the paper again and kept staring at it, as if that would change the figures on it.

XV

Work proceeded apace as I scrambled to increase the treasury income to cover it. But the task seemed less onerous as I basked in the memory of the approval I had felt radiating from the people in the Forum at the propitiation ceremonies. Most dear to me was the bond between me and the Roman people, especially as the one between me and the Senate was stretched thin.

But my peace was shattered the morning Tigellinus came to my work quarters. The burly Praetorian looked both self-satisfied and disturbed, an alarming combination. His square jaw was clenched unusually tight as he leaned close and said, "Caesar, dismiss the others present so we can talk."

I waved the scribes and attendants out, then turned to him. "Well?"

"The rites have not been effective. The people are still muttering about the Fire, and this time they name you directly. My agents have heard this in numerous places—I would never credit anything whispered only once."

A combination of anger, sorrow, and panic took hold of me. "What did they say? Dare to speak it aloud."

"They are quoting what they claim is a Sibylline prophecy relating to the Fire.

"*Last of the sons of Aeneas, a mother-slayer, shall govern.*

"And that after that, *Rome by the strife of her people shall perish.*"

He crossed his muscular arms. "I warned you that the people would not be satisfied by the formal rites, and now I have proof."

Yes, he was ruthlessly efficient at tracking down information.

"I have done all I can," I said. But the mention of Mother was unnerving. Long ago it had been accepted (so I thought) that she had committed suicide after her treason was discovered. The treason part was true, even if the suicide was not. She had methodically plotted to turn me off the throne, even to assassinate me—her own, her only son. As the years went on, it became clear that only one of us could survive, and I had to ensure it was I. That was five years ago, safely buried with her ashes, but now the scandal rose again to confront me.

"Obviously you must do more," said Tigellinus.

"What else can I do?"

"Find the guilty ones and punish them," he said.

"It was an accident . . ." I began as I had a hundred times. "But perhaps not." Once again I remembered the torch-throwers.

"What are you thinking?" he asked.

"There were things I saw . . . suspicious things . . . at the height of the Fire." I reminded him of the mysterious men, their strange words.

"They mentioned the end of the world? Flames?"

"I can't recall their exact words. I was being pelted with falling sparks and timber at the time. But I do remember two of them calling on Jesus."

He nodded grimly, but a slight smile played on his lips. "Christians!"

"What do you know about them?" I asked. "What would be pertinent to the Fire?"

"I'll find some of them and ask," he said. "In the way I do best."

"No, bring them here to me. Let me ask them." I didn't want him to use harsh methods that would just extract false information.

"I'll round some up," he said. "How many do you want?"

Fifteen people were paraded before me in my audience room. They were all ages, and both men and women. As a group they looked to come from the lower classes, newly freed slaves or the very poorest segment, the ones who existed on the free grain dole and what they could earn as vendors or menial laborers. But they stood proudly, not as others in their situation usually did when facing the emperor. They looked me in the eye, directly.

"These all belong to a group they call 'Peter's church,'" Tigellinus said. "It's one of the largest in Rome. It probably has a hundred or so members."

"How many Christians are there in Rome?" I asked one of them, a man who somehow seemed like the leader.

"It is difficult to say, Caesar," he said. "Probably several thousand. But we are small compared to the Jews, who number some forty thousand or so here."

"Aren't you some offshoot of Judaism?"

"Some would call us that, but not the Jews!" He laughed. That disconcerted me; no one else being questioned by me on a serious matter would have laughed.

"What is so amusing?" I asked.

"Our founder, Jesus, was a Jew, and taught the Jewish law, and fulfilled the Jewish scriptures, but he was not accepted by them, and he even warned us that we would not be, either. And it has come true. So we are flattered that some still think we are accepted by the Jews, because that would mean they accept our founder's message. But, sadly, they do not."

I didn't care about their quibbles with other religions. "Explain to me your philosophy about fire." Let us get straight to it. "Or rather what Jesus has to do with fire."

The leader looked perplexed, but a woman beside him with wild streaming hair was quick to answer. "Fire is a cleansing element; it purifies us."

The first man now said, "Peter said that sufferings are a fire to refine us, like gold."

"Who is Peter? I asked you about Jesus."

"Peter was one of his followers, and a leader in the church."

"What about real fire, not metaphorical fire like suffering?"

"The world will end in flames!" a youth cried out. "It will bring the end of the age and usher in a new world, a new order."

"So a fire will hasten this—this new world?" I asked. "And what will be in this new world? Is there a Rome? Is there an emperor?"

The older man silenced him. "Peter wrote about this in a letter. It was his words, not those of Jesus."

"What were those words?"

He closed his eyes to conjure them up. "'But the day of the Lord will come like a thief. The heavens will disappear with a roar; the elements will be destroyed by fire, and the earth and everything in it will be laid bare.'" He stopped and took a breath. "'Since everything will be destroyed in this way, what kind of people ought you to be? You ought to live holy and godly lives as you look forward to the day of God and speed its coming. That day will bring about the destruction of the heavens by fire, and the elements will melt in the heat. But in keeping with his promise we are looking forward to a new heaven and a new earth, the home of righteousness.'"

"Ah!" said Tigellinus. "They admit it. They were ordered to speed its coming, the time of fire!"

The man said, "There were more instructions. 'So then, dear friends, since you are looking forward to this, make every effort to be found spotless, blameless, and at peace with him. Bear in mind that our Lord's patience means salvation, just as our dear brother Paul also wrote you with the wisdom that God gave him.'"

Paul! The man I had interrogated and let go.

"I am the one blameless, not you!" I shouted. "You look forward to a fire and even want to bring it about. I wanted no such thing, yet am being blamed!" I stood up, glaring at them.

"What more do we need?" said Tigellinus. "They have condemned themselves by their own words."

"But they have not admitted doing anything," I said. "Wishing for something is not bringing it about."

"That is why I wanted to read you the rest of the letter," the leader said. "We were instructed not to sin, to trust God to bring about the end of days, to be patient and wait for him to act. Our only obligation was to be ready and keep peace."

"But what about the 'speed its coming'?" I asked.

The woman now spoke again. "It only meant that . . . that . . . we believe in it."

"You don't have an answer, do you?" said Tigellinus. "Nobody would take it to mean just that."

"You say you have letters from your leaders?" I said. "I want to read them. I want to read your instructions. From this Peter. And from Paul."

Paul had been so well spoken, so persuasive, at our interview, and had convinced me he was a thoughtful man, someone I could understand and someone who understood me. We had spoken of competition and which prizes were lasting and which were not. I maintained that the prize of eternal art was the one most worthy to strive for, but he said there was one higher even than that, which was the one he sought. Still, we had parted amicably. I could not imagine him advocating setting Rome on fire.

"There are copies in my house," he said. "I will fetch them."

"No!" said Tigellinus. "You are to be detained here. Let one of these others lead me there and gather them up."

"We will hold you here for further questioning," I said. Once they were let go, they might flee, for all their talk of patience. Where was Paul now, for instance?

True to their word, the Christians surrendered their letters to Tigellinus, and with smug vindication he emptied a sack onto my desk and a heap of scrolls poured out.

"They prize these missives and treat them as holy objects," he said. "But for something sacred, they were housed dismally. The rooms— across the river in a hovel—were a warren of poverty."

I spread out the scrolls, lining them up like legionaries.

"They are written in Greek," he said. "Poor Greek, the common sort, not classical Greek."

"At least they can write," I said. "But I may need a translator for some of it, as I don't usually deal with *koine* Greek. Beryllus can probably do it." In the aftermath of the Fire, my secretary for Greek letters had had little to do. But I would try it myself first. I was curious to see what these people believed, in their own words.

There were a number of letters from Paul to his followers all over— to the Galatians, the Philippians, the Thessalonians, the Corinthians, and the Romans. The latter I would read first and unrolled the scroll.

It began, "Dear friends in Rome" but immediately plunged into a long discourse about Jewish laws and sin and an indictment of the Romans around them.

Therefore God gave them over to a depraved mind, to do what ought not to be done. They have become filled with every kind of wickedness, evil, greed, and depravity. They are full of envy, murder, strife, deceit, and malice. They are gossips, slanderers, God-haters, insolent, arrogant, and boastful; they invent ways of doing evil.

"They don't think much of us," I said drily.

"The feeling is mutual," said Tigellinus.

"You may leave me to this," I said. I would dutifully read on, but it promised to be heavy going.

The letter to the Corinthians was more interesting reading. But it just confirmed what dregs the Christians drew their membership from.

Up to this moment we have become the scum of the earth, the refuse of the world.

Do not be deceived. Neither the sexually immoral nor idolators . . . nor thieves nor the greedy nor drunkards . . . will inherit the kingdom of God. And that is what some of you were.

Well, I wouldn't admit it if I were they! What strange people. But Corinth was known for its freewheeling life and gatherings of foreigners, and the Christians were recruited from that population.

As I read along, I saw Paul's words about competition, the very thing he had said to me in person, when we had communicated so well and he had lulled my suspicions about his sect.

Do you not know that in a race all the runners run, but only one gets the prize? Everyone who competes in the games goes into strict training. They do it to get a crown that will not last; but we do it to get a crown that will last forever.

Yes, I had understood that perfectly. How I wished he were here now so I could speak directly to him, instead of relying on these written messages. Further into the letter he mentioned the end of days.

What I mean, brothers, is that the time is short . . . For this world in its present form is passing away.

But he did not say anything about fire or hastening it on. I kept reading, and then I came upon something else.

The sacrifices of pagans are offered to demons, not to God, and I do not want you to be participants with demons. You cannot drink from the cup of the Lord and the cup of demons too; you cannot have a part in both the Lord's table and the table of demons.

There, in the words of a revered leader, was proof that Christians actually considered the Roman gods to be demons and the Roman religion utterly false. Poppaea had said they were subversive, and now I understood. She had also said they practiced magic, which was a capital crime. And here that transgression was, too.

The things that mark an apostle—signs, wonders, and miracles—were done among you with great perseverance.

Magicians were strictly forbidden in the empire, and that included necromancers, wizards, occultists, diviners, and sorcerers. But it apparently was practiced by their apostles. And Jesus himself was said to have performed miracles—the greatest, of course, being that he rose from the dead, a magic feat if ever there was one.

I set the scrolls aside and called for some wine. When it was brought, I swirled it around in my goblet and looked long at its bubbles beaded around the rim. Wine. Bacchus. What did the Christians mean about sharing the cup with demons? Was Bacchus a demon to them? What sort of Lord's cup did they share in their rituals?

I took a deep sip, savoring the rich red liquid. If this was the cup of demons, why was it so delicious? The Roman gods gave us pleasurable things, bestowing the gifts of the earth on us—Venus gave us love, Bacchus wine, Ceres fruit and harvest—all good, not evil. Yet the Christians would condemn them all, deprive us of their beneficence.

Restored by the wine, I opened another letter, this one to the Thessalonians. He didn't mention sins in this one, and at last I found a reference to the apocalypse.

For the Lord himself will come down from heaven, with a loud command, with the voice of the archangel and the trumpet call of God, and the dead in Christ will rise first . . . Now, brothers, about times and dates we do not need to write to you, for you know very well that the day of the Lord will come like a thief in the night. While people are saying "Peace and safety," destruction will come on them suddenly.

There were a few other scrolls, not written by Paul or the other followers, but collections of sayings for and about Jesus. They were not histories, exactly, but notes about the founder. I waded through them, finding Jesus an enigmatic character who certainly made arresting statements, but his overall mission was incoherent. Perhaps it was the random assortment of his sayings, just jumbled together, that made them so abstruse.

But just as patience in searching the desert for precious gems can finally yield a treasure, I saw this.

As the weeds are pulled up and burned in the fire, so it will be at the end of the age. The Son of Man will send out his angels, and they will weed out of his kingdom everything that causes sin and all who do evil. They will throw them into the fiery furnace, where there will be weeping and gnashing of teeth.

It was us, the Romans, the city, they threw into the fiery furnace, to fulfill this prophecy.

On another part of the scroll I finally found the last proof.

I have come to bring fire on the earth, and how I wish it were already kindled! But I have a baptism to undergo, and how distressed I am until it is completed!

His baptism, whatever it was, had passed. So now, by his own words, it had been time to bring the fire to the earth.

XVI

For a long time I sat motionless in front of the condemning papers. I now had the proof I needed, but that was no consolation.

Many years ago, when I was first emperor, I had to sign an execution order for a notorious criminal and cried, "I wish I had never learned to write," to the amusement of the administrators standing by my desk. Scrawling the words on the document had sent tremors through me. But it had to be. And this, too, had to be.

I stood up and went to Poppaea's quarters. I needed resolution, and something more than that—absolution? She was always firm and decisive and did not look back.

The light was fading in the western windows, the scorching sun having fled the sky, and sweet warm evening was at hand. It would be the quiet time in her apartments; I hoped her barbiton player was on duty tonight. His playing was always soothing; I liked the deep tones of the bass cithara.

I was not disappointed. As I approached the area I could just catch the low, melancholy sound of the instrument. Coming into the room, I saw him on a cushion at the far end, with Poppaea reading on a couch nearby, a half smile on her face, her feet tucked under her. She barely looked up as I walked over, but the player stopped, stood up, and bowed. Only when the music stopped did she notice me.

"Did you find what you were looking for?" she asked.

"Yes," I said.

"Then why so downcast? You look as if you were robbed by brigands."

I sat down beside her. "I have been robbed of something. I am not sure what."

"Uncertainty, perhaps," she said, signaling for the music to start up again. She reached out and stroked my cheek. "You are happiest when things are unsettled, still to come."

"Not now," I said. "This uncertainty has smoldered too long after the real Fire died—the smoke of rumors, speculation, hateful accusations still hanging over us all. But now we can focus on the real culprits, who will be duly punished."

She pulled back and looked at me. "So it was them? The Christians?" She could not keep the delight out of her voice.

"Yes," I said. "They kindly provided the proof we needed, conveniently in writing."

"Whose writings?"

"Oh, various leaders."

"That Paul man?"

"That was one of them, yes." His writings were the bulk of the proof, but I need not tell her that.

"I told you so! I told you he was bad, but you wouldn't listen and let him go. You let him walk out of the room, pronounced him not guilty and free to go."

"He wasn't guilty of anything at that point. We don't condemn a man for something he might do. If that were so, every person on earth would be locked up."

"Maybe they ought to be." She stood up and crossed her arms as she did when she was feeling stubborn.

I stood up with her and put my arms around her. "'Every person' means you as well as them. I don't think you would like your cellmates; your dainty nose would find them offensive."

We walked over to the window on the side where full darkness had fallen. The grounds were now almost empty, as the bulk of the refugees had been resettled. "This grieves me," I said. "But once it is over, the Fire will truly be in the past."

"It will become just part of history," she said. "And history will forget these Christians soon enough." She rubbed my hands. "Do not be downcast, my love. We are facing a new day for Rome."

Before I left, she motioned Sporus to come over. As always, his startling resemblance to Poppaea was unnerving, as if I were seeing double from too much wine.

"Sporus, the emperor is weary tonight. Please ask Hesperos to rise and come over here," she said.

Sporus nodded and fetched the barbiton player.

"Hesperos, I release you for now," Poppaea said. "The emperor is sad tonight; let your music be the remedy. For your melodies can soothe an aching heart as none other."

"I believe that is true," I told him. Interesting that Poppaea understood I needed to be alone, but not completely alone. But then she understood everything about me.

O ver the next few days Hesperos was a great comfort to me. Orpheus could tame wild beasts with his lyre, they say, and other gifted artists were said to do the same. My ears were particularly sensitive to the sounds of the cithara with its many strings, which was why even as a child I had been drawn to the instrument and was now an acknowledged master on it. But the skill of Hesperos was another matter altogether, as his instrument was quite different from the traditional cithara. For one thing, it was longer and bigger. So as he sat playing, absorbed in his own world, the deep resounding notes softened the ugly dispatches from Tigellinus with the latest news about the investigation.

The original captives had named others, and those had named others, so now there was a large contingent of people accused of being Christians. They were being held and questioned by Tigellinus and his agents.

"And here are more of them," Tigellinus said one afternoon, marching into the room and dumping down a burlap sack, its sides bulging with tablets. "We have a nice number now. Enough to provide entertainment for the crowds who will cheer to see the wicked arsonists get what they deserve." He picked up the sack again and shook it. "Aren't you going to look at these? I went to a lot of trouble to compile the lists."

"Later," I said, not wishing to look at them, ever.

"They are eager to embrace martyrdom," he said, shaking his head. "They won't make a bargain, won't denounce their leaders, won't give up loyalty to this dead prophet." He shrugged and helped himself to a plate of fruit without permission. I glared at him, and he put the apple back down.

"In some ways they are to be envied," I said.

"What, being criminals?"

"No, having something so precious that it overrides all else in your life, even your life itself." There were times when I felt that way about my music, but did I really? To that extent? So I would give up everything to pursue it, toss over the emperorship? Sadly, I knew the answer. No, not that much. Almost. But not that much.

"They can be persuasive," said Tigellinus. "Especially that man Paul. One of the captives told me that when Paul was held a prisoner in Judea by prefect Festus and had an opportunity to address King Agrippa, he was so eloquent Agrippa said, 'You come close to persuading me to be a Christian.'" He laughed. "Did he have that effect on you?"

"No, but he was able to convince me we were very similar."

"That's his secret," said Tigellinus. "He can become all things to all men. He even admits it, in one of his tedious writings."

"What are the ones being held doing?" I asked. Paul wasn't among them, I assumed. We would know if he was.

"Praying. Some are singing. Singing!" He laughed again. "They don't sing well. They are painful to hear."

The sweet, beguiling sounds of the barbiton sounded in the background, as if to make a point.

"I will read the dispatches later tonight," I told Tigellinus. "And after that, we must stipulate the punishments and prepare the venues." Get it over with.

He nodded and took his leave.

After he was gone, I stood up and went over to Hesperos. He looked up, waiting for me to speak. When I did not, keeping silent, he said softly, "Would you like me to teach you to play this?"

"Yes," I said. Teach me to play this, let me lose myself in beauty, go into that world that means as much—almost—as the imagined one of the Christians. Let me escape this soiled and fallen one, if only for tonight.

The evidence was in, and before I called the Consilium to meet, I summoned my close advisers and administrators to discuss the action we must take. I wanted to sound them out before presenting conclusions to the larger body.

They filed in, filling the private room, some dozen of them. Most people had returned to Rome now and started either rebuilding or reclaiming their homes, if spared. I welcomed them, inquiring politely about their situations but itching to get to the real business. Finally the formalities were over and I could.

"The mystery is solved," I announced. "We know who started the Fire, and why."

"I thought you said it was an accident," said Faenius Rufus. "Every time you were asked, that is what you claimed." He did not smile, and I took his statement as a challenge. This was not auspicious.

"That is what I believed at the time. Now I know better."

Tigellinus stepped forward, standing at my right hand. "The emperor had questioned why people were throwing burning brands into houses, hindering the firefighters. Didn't you observe that, Nymphidius?"

Nymphidius nodded. "Yes, I did. They moved in groups."

"I heard some calling out the name of their patron, Jesus," I said. "Since then I have learned more about this man and his followers."

"For one thing, he's dead!" said Epaphroditus.

"So how can he issue orders?" asked Subrius Flavus.

"Apparently being dead is no hindrance," said Tigellinus with a laugh. "Not to him! He continues to speak to his followers. He tells them to help bring about the end of the world by fire. That is what they believed they were doing."

"The Christians," said Phaon.

"They even restarted the Fire in my estates," said Tigellinus, "to throw blame on me and the emperor. They are in back of the vile slander that he started the Fire."

"But—" began Subrius.

"They have confessed!" said Tigellinus.

"And I have studied their writings, which confirms it," I said. "They are guilty. Guilty of murder, blasphemous attacks on the Roman gods, and destruction of property."

"The punishment must fit the crimes," said Tigellinus. "What is the traditional Roman penalty for arson? Being burned. What is the penalty for desecration of temples and destruction of property? To be thrown to the beasts, *damnatio ad bestias*. But not just as they are. No, they should reenact the myth closest to the thing they have desecrated."

They all nodded. This was fitting. This was right.

"These executions are public expiation to our gods for this wrongdoing. When it is over, and they have accepted the sacrifice, the Fire will truly be forgiven and Rome can enter a new age," I said. "So the venues will be the circus here in the Vatican Fields and the wooden amphitheater spared in the Campus Martius. Burning and crucifixion here, the beasts in the amphitheater."

The meeting with the Consilium afterward went smoothly. I presented the same information, as did Tigellinus. A few of them—notably Piso, Scaevinus, and Lucan—asked pointed questions, such as demanding to read the transcripts of the confessions and whether the local leaders had been caught and the movement stamped out—but in the end they acquiesced, happy to put it behind them.

Expanding on his earlier announcement about the punishments, Tigellinus said, "Since they destroyed the Palatine temple to *Luna Noctiluca* that shone through our nights, they themselves shall light up the night for us in recompense. The burning will take place at night, along with the crucifixions. Two in one!"

Murmurs spread through the group, but there was no outright dissent.

"And for the beasts—since the fire destroyed our venerable Amphitheater of Taurus in the Campus Martius, the perpetrators will play the part of Queen Dirce, who was impaled on the horns of a bull. Taurus! Understand? Is that not justice? And for those who destroyed the Temple of Diana, they shall become Actaeon, who was attacked by hunting dogs for insulting Diana. They will be dressed in animal skins and set upon by dogs. Besides that, the statues of the fifty Danaids at the Temple of Apollo were destroyed, and so the criminals must reenact the punishment of those brides, carrying leaking jars, but not in Hades. No, they will do it in broad daylight, while being pursued by wild beasts in the arena."

People smiled and nodded. This was standard entertainment combined with the execution of criminals, the sort they were used to.

The findings and the prescribed punishments were published, and soon a howling mob outside the palace demanded speedy action.

"Kill them! Torture them! Rip them limb to limb! The arena is too good for them!"

I closed the shutters in Poppaea's apartments, which overlooked the open fields and the mob. But it did little to muffle the sounds outside.

"It has to be soon," I said. "We cannot endure a lengthy siege of this. And they may grow violent themselves, be as bad as the people they want revenge on."

"Yes, it must be soon," she said. "The guilty should not be tortured in advance, by this waiting."

"They seem to enjoy the waiting." I had not heard Sporus come up behind us. "They are calm, praying, even preaching to convert others to join them. Can you imagine? Why would anyone join them at this point?" he said.

"Even lost causes gain adherents," I said. "Perhaps the hopelessness is appealing. It makes people feel noble and brave. What about Thermopylae? They knew they were doomed."

"But that was for a reason," said Sporus. "There's no point to this at all."

Poppaea shuddered. "Let us stop talking about it."

A burst of sound came through the shutters. "As long as it is not finished, we will not be in peace," I said. "That is why we must proceed apace."

That night, in my inner room, I tried to read poetry, while Hesperos played nearby. He had succeeded in teaching me the fingering on the barbiton, showing me how it differed from the smaller cithara. I broke off and went to sit beside him, studying how he held the base of the instrument.

"You need one of your own," he said, looking up. "You should commission one."

"Recommend a maker for me," I said, running my hand along the base, smooth but slightly curved.

"Damasos of Kos," he said.

"Kos! It would take forever to receive it."

"I imagine it could be speeded to the emperor faster than to someone like me."

"Kos is far away, and it would still have to travel by sea. Don't you know anyone closer to Rome?"

"There's Metan in Luceria. But he's not as good."

"I don't need a perfect instrument to learn. So perhaps I'll order a training one from Metan and by the time I've learned, the one from Kos would arrive."

He smiled. "Perhaps. Tell me, when did you first hear the cithara?"

With pleasure I told him of that magic afternoon in the palace of Claudius and my meeting with Terpnus. "I asked him if I could take lessons from him when I was grown up, and he said yes. Neither of us could have imagined how quickly that would come about." I paused. "Terpnus survived the Fire, thanks be to all the gods."

"We must remember the things that were spared, as well as mourn the things that were lost, and be thankful," he said. "And—"

"Tigellinus requests a meeting with the emperor," a guard said, hurrying over, interrupting him.

"Let him in," I said, standing up.

Tigellinus strode in, clutching documents. He thrust them at me. I took them and put them on the desk.

"I suggest you look at these, Caesar," he said. "It is urgent."

"Tigellinus, I appreciate your zeal, but it is late." I had no desire to read documents now.

"At least read this one!" He snatched one from the pile. "Or perhaps you don't need to. I can tell you what is in it. The net has spread wider and caught more Christians. Just in time for the executions, so we can say we have got most of them. And here's one, hiding under your aegis. Him!" He rushed over to Hesperos and grabbed him by the shoulder, hauling him up.

"What?" I was dumbfounded.

"He's one of them. A confessor named him. And there are several more in Poppaea's household."

Ignoring Tigellinus, I looked directly at Hesperos. "Is this true?"

"Yes, Caesar," he said. I was even more dumbfounded.

"But how can that be?" I asked.

"Do you think an artist cannot be a Christian?" he said. "What would prevent that?"

"They are—they are enemies of the state!"

"Do you truly believe those lies put about? We are not enemies of the state—far from it."

"Then why do people say it?" I pursued the question.

"You should know firsthand that what people say and what is true are not the same. After all, people said you started the Fire. Is that true? No."

"Take him away!" said Tigellinus, motioning to the guards.

I stopped him. "In my palace, I issue the orders." I turned to Hesperos. "I know you did not set a fire. You need not join these others. You are innocent."

"If I do not join them, then I am guilty. Not of starting a fire but of deserting Jesus. And I would rather die than do that. So, call the guards and let me be arrested."

My head was spinning. This was absurd. Why should he rush to his doom?

"If you feel guilty for abandoning Jesus, why did you not speak up earlier? Why did you keep silent all this time?" Now I had him. Obviously he wanted to live.

He smiled. That otherworldly smile I had seen on Paul's face. What possessed these people? "Jesus told us, *When they persecute you in one town, flee to the next.* So we are not to seek persecution. But when it finds us, when it hunts us down, we must stand firm."

"And what does that mean?" I asked. I was bewildered.

"Admitting who we are and who we follow. Jesus told us, *Everyone who confesses me before men, I will also confess him before my father in heaven. But whoever denies me before men, I will also deny him before my father in heaven.* So here I am. I confess before the emperor himself that I follow Jesus. That must count for at least three men."

"Are you joking?" barked Tigellinus. "Insulting his *imperium?*"

"Quiet!" I ordered Tigellinus. This was between Hesperos and me. "If you can do no other, then you can do no other. I grieve for you."

"Don't grieve for me," he said. "Grieve for yourself and for Rome."

Now I truly had no choice. "Take him away," I told the guards.

He turned to look at me. "I give you my barbiton, with my blessing. No need to wait for one from Kos."

XVII

That night I sent everyone—except the ever-vigilant guards—away. The barbiton lay on the floor where Hesperos had left it. It looked like a dangerous animal to me, as if it would leap up and attack me. I picked it up and put it in a corner. Would its notes ever be sweet to me again, or always a poisonous reminder of this dreadful event?

The Christians. What a strange group they were, a mixture of violence and idealism, eager to embrace martyrdom. But other religions had barbarous rites—castration for the priests of Attis, human sacrifice for the Druids. Only the Roman one was supremely civilized, humane, orderly—a state religion that did not require soul searching, sacrifice, and pain, and its formal rituals were done in daylight for all to see. We could be proud of that.

I looked around the chamber. This was my refuge, a space no one could enter unless I specifically allowed it. I looked with distaste on the mound of documents that Tigellinus had left. I did not want to open them. I knew what was in them. Not the particulars but the general.

The mob was still outside, still shouting and milling. Forced to close the shutters to shut out their yells, I likewise shut out the warm, seductive breezes of late summer, and the room was hot and still.

I poured a drink from the ewer into a glass cup. It was the remains of my *decocta Neronis*, tepid from standing now. But I did not care to call for a slave to bring fresh. I gulped it down.

The nightmare that began, appropriately, at night—the Great

Fire—had stretched on and on. It was now two months since the flames had engulfed the Circus Maximus. Flames would now end it, flames that would punish the arsonists and light up the night once again. Then, pray to all the gods, let it be over. Let it be over.

Leaving the room, I sought my bed in a nearby room. Poppaea had graced it many times, turning it into a playground of eroticism. But tonight I would sleep alone, pulling the covers over my head to drown out the sounds of the baying crowd. In the little tent made of my sheets, I fell into a restless slumber and into a vivid dream, if indeed it was a dream and not a true vision. How does one discern the difference?

Apollo appeared to me. He was not in his citharoede form but in his guise as Sol, the sun god. He was driving his chariot and pulled up just in front of me. "Get in," he said, holding out a golden arm.

I did not dare to disobey, even though I knew what happened to Phaeton, Apollo's son, when he got into Apollo's chariot. I mounted it and stood on its flexible floor, looking out over the backs of his four horses. Beneath their hooves was the solar path, stretching out in a gentle climbing arc.

The god was shining and burnished. I could feel a dazzling radiance coming from him, a gentle warmth, not a scorching incandescence.

"Look at me," he commanded.

I had been afraid to do so, for to look directly upon a god is death.

"I said look at me," he repeated.

Reluctantly I did so. His features were my own. He smiled.

"Yes, I am you, and you are me. I chose you when you were born, anointing you with my rays. I gave you my skill on the cithara. Now I give you my chariot. Drive it." He thrust the reins into my hands.

The horses were headstrong. I knew that the moment they began to move. They were nothing like earthly horses, trained in obedience.

"Hold them," he said. "Steer them. Let them know you are stronger."

But I wasn't. They had the power to rip my arms off and run away. I strained to keep the reins steady. They were about to break into a gallop, perhaps even plunge off the solar path, as they had with poor Phaeton.

Apollo touched my arms and infused them with his strength, and I pulled the horses back. "Now let us traverse the sky together, so you are with me from sunrise to sunset," he said.

Far below the solar path I could see the land, could see burned-out Rome and the still-green fields around it, could see the snaking lines of aqueducts carrying water from the hills. So this was what it was to be a god and look down upon the world. No wonder we appeared of no moment and trivial to them.

After what was a day on earth the chariot neared the end of the solar path, wreathed in clouds at its base. Apollo had not spoken during the ride, had allowed me to stare in wonder at what was passing beneath us. Now he did. "Remember I am you and you are me. You are to bring the golden age to Rome. The fire is not the end but the beginning. You see me now. For a little while you will not see me, but you and I will return together, bringing joy to the people of Rome."

The chariot stopped against a bank of earth, hidden in writhing mist. The horses sighed and shook their heads. Apollo stepped from the chariot, took my hand, and pulled me after him. "Now I rest, and rest my horses. My sister is now hurrying toward the start of the path to begin her journey. See her?"

I strained my eyes and caught a glimpse of something silvery. Diana, goddess of the moon and the hunt.

"The moon and the hunt," said Apollo, echoing my thought. "You know what you must do to appease her. She has been mightily offended."

He faded. The mists faded. The horses vanished. I was lying in bed, wrapped in layers of sheets. Had I been transported elsewhere, or had I lain here the entire time? I could not know, not now. In time a sign would reveal the answer.

I extricated myself from the bedclothes and went to the window. It was still night. Slowly I pushed a shutter open. There was still noise below, but not as much as earlier. High in the sky a full moon was at its zenith. Diana was riding in splendor.

Full moon. This was the second full moon since the one that had shone down upon Rome the night the Fire started. It had also shone down at Antium where I had performed that night in the new theater I had just opened for the people. It had been a perfect night. But all the nights since had been cursed. Now the curse would be lifted.

Apollo rose as usual that morning, staining the sky pink and orange. I smiled, reveling in our secret journey together. Now he was back driving alone, but I would forever remember my brief turn at the reins. The clouds scattered as the sun rose higher, shone strongly. *I am you, and you are me.* Apollo and I were one.

I t took two weeks to ready the venues for the expiation ceremonies. The moon rose later and later, finally shrinking away into darkness. The day the last preparations were being made for the ceremonies, the sun left us for a few minutes. A spectacular eclipse occurred, covering the sun at midday.

You see me now. For a little while you will not see me, but you and I will return together, bringing joy to the people of Rome.

He was keeping his promise. This was what he meant. The people in the streets were alarmed as the temperature dropped and the day grew dim. Caged birds ceased singing, bees swarmed, geese tried to roost, owls flew out to hunt, crickets chirped. But the sunlight quickly returned, the dimness passed, and the new day promised by Apollo was here.

T he ceremonies at the Vatican racetrack were not to begin until dusk settled on the city. We were past the equinox now, and sundown came quickly, with little twilight.

As the light faded, Poppaea helped me into my costume—Sol the charioteer. I would mount a chariot and drive slowly around the track, letting the people see that the golden age was being born from the destruction, that Sol was rising on a new world. The symbolism was all-important.

She fastened the belt around my waist and stuck the traditional knife in it.

"Not that you are likely to lose control of the horses and need to cut the reins as they walk slowly around the track."

I patted it. "All things must be in order," I said. I was wearing a short tunic of gold-threaded cloth, and a leather helmet covered in gold leaf, for the sun motif. The chariot was likewise covered in gold foil. Nothing, of course, could equal the celestial chariot of the god himself, but this would remind people of it.

"I will watch from the palace," she said. "I don't care to go out into those crowds." Below us we could see a sea of people waiting. We could also see the poles of the crosses set around the perimeter, shorter than the obelisk standing guard in the middle of the track.

The Praetorians came to fetch me to the waiting chariot. There were only two horses, the better to navigate through crowds, and these were not my prize horses safely stabled outside Rome. These were placid animals who would not be disturbed by crowds and noise.

I drove onto the track as guards parted the crowds to make a path for me. People swarmed forward anyway, and soon the chariot was enveloped, held captive. I spoke as loudly as I could, telling them I welcomed them to the new day that was dawning, but only a few could hear me. Darkness was thickening, and the punishing flames from the crosses threw an eerie flickering light over the scene. I did not look at them; I could not make myself. I had ordered that the victims be offered drugs before the executions. Some had accepted the escape and were unconscious, but others refused and had to endure the agony.

It is only the same agony you meted out to others, to innocent people, I reminded myself. But that did not mitigate the severity of the punishment.

The chariot could not move, so I abandoned it and walked out into the crowd. I remembered the warnings of Nymphidius about the danger of assassins, but I felt invulnerable, protected by Apollo himself, and could a god or his chosen one die? *Remember Pan*. But that was different—wasn't it?

The people embraced me, celebrating wildly, relishing the grisly spectacle of the people being punished. In the yellowish guttering torchlight the faces in the crowd were ruddy and their eyes gleamed yellow like wolves'. *The crowd. They can turn to beasts in an instant.* Now they called me champion and cheered me. *But they are still wild beasts and cannot be trusted.*

But I thrust those thoughts aside. Tonight they loved me. Tonight they were tame, and mine.

The fires had dwindled down, and the crosses only glowed by the time I left the track and returned to the palace. The next morning they were gone, as if they had never been.

XVIII

Morning broke on a quiet Rome. Soft breezes caressed the hollows and hills where workmen were hauling stones into place for the new buildings, and slaves smoothed cement binding fresh-laid bricks. The plan for the new Rome was being translated into real streets, dwellings, and fountains. Severus and Celer were drawing up detailed plans for the Golden House, the orientation and size of the rooms. It was decided that the pavilion would be two stories built into the Oppian Hill, with the front of the building facing due south, welcoming the sunlight. The rooms directly behind the front ones would still receive much light.

The centerpiece of the pavilion was a revolutionary designed vaulted room, with an open oculus in the middle of the ceiling and the weight carried on pillars built into the wall, so the space was open and the dome seemed to float above the floor. When we wished, we could cover the opening and put in a revolving cover that showed the zodiac and showered down petals and perfume.

Below the pavilion, in the valley, would be another part of the palace, this one with conventional rooms, overlooking the artificial lake now being dug and lined with stone. On the other side of the palace a huge open forecourt, with colonnades around the sides, stretched to the beginning of the Via Sacra and the Forum. Gardeners were busy with plantings there, and in the middle, on a square platform, would preside my statue. It was Sol. It was me. It was there to guard Rome. I had summoned a sculptor, Zenodorus, skilled in outsized bronze statuary, to execute this. He would arrive any day now.

Ordinary citizens were now rebuilding, too. The clinking sounds of chisels and the rumbling of carts resounded all day long, but it was a healthy noise, the noise of recovery and growth. The Circus Maximus was restored and ready for races again. On the grounds of the Golden House I rebuilt the ruined Temple of Fortune, with walls of *phengites*, an extraordinary stone from Cappadocia that let in light and seemed to store it, so even on cloudy days it glowed inside. Naturally it was extremely expensive, as Phaon reminded me.

"This month's figures," he said, laying the papers before me, looking pained. "The Cappadocian stone has sent the total soaring."

I looked it over. He was right. The total was a shock. But we had not reached the projected final twenty-two thousand million sesterces. So we were still within the budget, so to speak, except that the budget was outrageous in the first place.

"Perhaps, Caesar, we could trim it a bit," Phaon said. "The statue, for example—it isn't commissioned yet; we could postpone it."

"The sculptor is on his way," I said. "I will have to pay him for his time in any case." As if that were an answer.

"The cost of his time is nothing compared to the bronze, the casting, and—I suppose you will want it gilded?"

"Yes, of course. It has to glitter." Sol was gold; the sun god was gold itself.

Phaon sighed. "Indeed."

"There's no point to it otherwise, Phaon," I said, as if I had to explain to a child. "A statue of the sun god has to be gold. If not gold all the way through, then gilded."

"Polished bronze can gleam," he said.

"Not enough," I answered.

I was eager to resume my racing training, which, like everything else, had been interrupted and suspended by the Great Fire. Before the Fire, I had selected a team of horses from a stable recommended by

Tigellinus, originally a horse breeder himself. They were a carefully mixed team, meant to balance speed, stamina, and power. I had a cream-colored Iberian horse for speed, a black Cappadocian for heart and competitive spirit, a gray Mycenaean for stability, and a chestnut Sicilian, fast but unpredictable. Their colors did not match, but I hoped they would lend each other strength, and that was what mattered.

The ride out to the stables of Menenius Lanatus, where my horses were kept, was a good ten miles outside Rome. It was through a landscape of meadows and farms, with a gray stone aqueduct visible on the horizon. In the late September day the land was dozing, having just been delivered of its bounty by harvesters. Here in the country the effects of the Fire were not visible.

Tigellinus and Epaphroditus had come with me, and it was a pleasure to be able to speak of things besides the Fire, for the first time in months. Tigellinus was filled with stories about his Sicilian stables and his upbringing around horses, and Epaphroditus was eager to hear them. For myself, I was just glad to be outside and back with my horses.

Lanatus greeted us effusively, saying he had kept the horses safe and waiting for us. "They have wondered where you were," he told me. "You will see changes in them. I've had my own trainers keep them exercised, but the Sicilian has become disobedient. There's no point in anyone else gentling him because it's you he has to obey, and he is particular in who he obeys."

"We Sicilians are hard to control," said Tigellinus, who came from there, as did Lanatus. "Aren't we?"

"Only an emperor can control a Sicilian, man or horse. Is that not right, Caesar?" said Lanatus.

I had to strain to control Tigellinus sometimes, and the horse would probably be the same. I nodded.

We spent the afternoon driving chariots around the practice track. Lanatus was right—the Sicilian was skittish and headstrong, unless it was just that I was out of practice in driving horses. By the evening, my arms were aching from the strain of pulling his reins. Weary, I stepped down from the chariot, rubbing them.

Tigellinus nodded approvingly. "Well done. You just need a bit more practice, and then—you will be ready."

That surprised me. I had felt so rusty, fearing I had lost my skill through disuse. I smiled. "Ready at last?"

"Soon," he said. "Very soon. Better order your racing costume now."

Back in Rome, I spent that evening in Poppaea's apartments. Our quarters were so different. Mine were filled with an odd combination of art objects and work paraphernalia—Greek bronzes, painted vases, seals, wax, stamps, cabinets, scrolls, and correspondence. Hers was furnished with luxury items—silks, ivory, fans. I hardly needed to steal away to a secluded retreat when I could walk a mere hundred feet and be in another world.

Both of us pointedly avoided alluding to the missing barbiton player, but his absence loomed large. Several other servants were gone, too, presumably for the same reason.

She had a special vintage wine waiting and poured me out a goblet herself, then stood watching as I tasted it. It was acidic, but I smiled anyway.

"What do you think?" she asked.

"It needs to age a bit," I said. "But it has a rich taste."

"It's from our own vineyard on Mount Vesuvius," she said. "I know it's still young, but I think it has potential."

"My wife the vintner," I said. "I agree." But it would have to age a long time to be really drinkable. Suddenly I remembered something. "Seneca had a reputation as a vintner," I said. "But now that he's become an ascetic, I suppose he's abandoned wine as well as all other frivolities."

"Including the emperor?" she said.

"It's hardly the same," I said. "And he didn't abandon me. He retired."

She snorted. "Is that what you call it? You know he resigned and left court. Now I hear that he is claiming he must guard himself against attempts at poisoning him, without actually naming the person who is trying to poison him."

"Where did you hear this?"

"We have been over this before. You have your informants, I have mine."

I drank some more of the distasteful wine. "Well, I don't believe this one. If Seneca wants to starve himself, it isn't because I am trying to poison him. But I do mind to pay a call on him. He made a huge donation for the rebuilding of Rome, and I want to personally thank him."

"If you go, watch what you eat! He sounds knowledgeable about poisons himself." She laughed. "Let's not discuss that disagreeable old man. Stoicism is a bitter drink, and whoever drinks it becomes bitter himself."

In that, and in that only, she and Mother were alike. Neither had any use for philosophy or philosophers.

She curled up on her silk-draped, padded couch, flinging one arm over the back. "I have been reading more of the Jewish scriptures," she said.

Oh, not that subject! It was all I could do not to wince. I plastered a smile on my face. "In Hebrew?" I asked, hoping that would end the conversation.

"Of course not," she said. "It's been translated into Greek. I'm surprised you haven't read it. You devour everything in Greek."

"Not everything."

"After what . . . what happened, I wondered why the Jews rejected the Christians as being different and thought I might find an answer in their writings." She sat up straighter. "And what things I found! A poem to put Propertius to shame."

"In their sacred books? I doubt that."

"They have a name for you, then—a mocker and a scoffer. But I can prove it. Here, read it for yourself." She got up, selected a scroll, and handed it to me.

"*The Song of Songs,*" I read. "Interesting title." I plunged into the text and was swept away by the passion of the poetry, nothing like a religious tract.

> *Let him kiss me with the kisses of his mouth: for thy love is better*
> *than wine.*
> *While the king sits at his table, my spikenard sends forth its scent.*

She passed her forearm under my nose, and the warm smell of spikenard filled my nostrils.

I found the next verses and read, "'A garden enclosed is my spouse, a spring shut up, a fountain sealed. How fair and how pleasant are you, O love, for delights!'"

She took the scroll back and read, "'I am my beloved's, and his desire is toward me. Set me as a seal upon your heart, as a seal upon your arm, for love is strong as death, jealousy is cruel as the grave.'"

I took the scroll from her and laid it down gently. "We do not need another's words, no matter how beautiful or hallowed. You are already sealed in my heart. You know that full well."

"And you in mine," she said. Then we retreated into our own garden of pleasures, beyond even the words of the poet. Spices, pleasant fruit, water—all that was mundane compared to what we were able to conjure for ourselves but could never describe.

Later that night, tired in the most exquisite way, we lay side by side watching the shadows on the ceiling. Ripples, dapples, wavering splashes of light chased one another across the expanse.

"You will soon have a new Rome," she said drowsily, turning her head on my shoulder. "And a new palace."

"*We* will have them," I corrected her. "They are yours as well as mine."

"They are your gifts to me," she said. "You are able to command vast resources to lay at my feet. But I now can present one to you: we have conceived another child. I was not sure, but now I am."

I sat up. "When?"

She laughed. "When was it conceived, or when will it be born?"

"Either. Both!"

"I think it was in Antium. Just before the Fire. So that means it would be born in April. Around the anniversary date of the founding of Rome. The gods have arranged it!"

"There will already be festivities to celebrate Ludi Ceriales in honor of Ceres. But this will eclipse everything else. Oh, what a joy!" My words were trite, and I wished I could say something more worthy of my feelings. But I was impoverished in my imagination, drowning in happiness.

She put her arms around me, rested her face against my chest. "A new beginning for us all. And that is my offering to the new Rome."

XIX

While Rome was rebuilding I made my promised visit to Seneca in his country retreat in Nomentum, some ten miles outside the city. From the heart of Rome the Via Nomentana led out through the northeastern gate beside the huge Praetorian barracks and into the fields. Along the way other villas and houses grew farther apart as the city dwindled behind. Plane trees lined the side of the road, and the worn paving stones caught the light of the autumn sun.

"Over there," said Faenius, who was my guard on this journey. "That's Phaon's villa." He pointed to a large compound far from the road, surrounded by wild fields. At that point we were about four miles outside Rome.

"It looks neglected," I said. Weeds stood shoulder high in the fields around it.

"He doesn't have much opportunity to spend time there," said Faenius. "He is kept too busy with your account books." His voice was smooth and did not linger over the "your," but was it a re-buke?

"The account books of the empire," I corrected him.

Silently we continued the ride, the early hints of autumn brushing the fields, turning them from green to ochre. It was almost October. Almost ten years since I became emperor. Could it truly be only ten years? The world that had surrounded me then had vanished, the people as well as the city itself. Only Seneca and a few of my companions remained. The rest were swept away. *Soon there will be no one who will remember me as a boy.* A frightening thought.

I should celebrate that anniversary, a momentous one. But it was too early for Rome to host anything. Perhaps I would invite people in to see the Golden House when it was finished enough for visitors. I would keep October thirteenth, my accession day, as a private remembrance.

Suddenly I needed to see Seneca, that remnant of my old life, to clutch it and know it did exist and had existed.

We did not reach his villa until late afternoon. It was, as I expected, tidy and well kept. The fields were not in disarray like those of Phaon, and the courtyard was swept clean. Surrounding the houses were orchards planted in straight rows; the apple trees dangled red fruit ready for the picking. Stretching farther away were the vineyards of his estate, famous for yielding one hundred and eighty gallons of wine to the acre. Seneca had prided himself on his ability to graft various types of vines together.

A servant met us, wearing a clean tunic and sturdy sandals. He tried to appear calm, but clearly he was flustered at our impromptu visit. Turning, he motioned to slaves inside the house to alert the master.

"Caesar, oh, to what do we owe this grand honor?" He fell to one knee.

"You owe it to a whim of the emperor," I said. "I had a sudden longing to come here and see my teacher and mentor."

You should have warned us, he must have been thinking. But he smiled broadly and kept down on one knee.

"Up, up," I said, just as a group emerged from the house.

Leading them was Seneca. But how slowly he moved, like an aged beetle. He was creeping toward us. Behind him was his wife, Paulina; his brother Gallio; and his nephew Lucan.

"Welcome," he said, but there was no warmth in the words.

"Thank you," I said, injecting enough jollity in my voice to count for both of us. "I have long threatened to come here, and now I have carried out that threat." Oh, unfortunate words. Instantly I wished I could recall them, substitute "promise" for "threat." The joke had fallen flat.

"Come," he said, turning and beckoning us toward the house. "Welcome, Faenius," he added warmly.

Faenius looked startled and said, "Thank you, sir."

The house was dim and cool inside. A slave opened the shutters and let in more light. We were ushered to comfortable couches. I looked around. This was hardly luxurious, but neither was it the bare hut of a hermit. Where had he stashed all his money? He had been staggeringly wealthy.

"Rome is rebuilding apace?" Seneca asked politely. He nodded, and a slave scurried off to get refreshments.

"Ahead of schedule," I said. "And you helped bring it about. I am deeply grateful for your contribution to the rebuilding. When you retired from court, you offered to return all the rewards I had given you over the years. I refused. Now you have returned them anyway, when Rome needs them."

He gave a ghost of a smile. "I had no need of those things," he said.

"Stoics aren't supposed to need anything, but no one is free entirely of needs," I said.

"He is experimenting with that," said Gallio. "He is trying to do without just about everything." He coughed, covering his mouth with a handkerchief.

"And succeeding better than I would like," said his wife, a comfortably round woman. "For I do not wish to exist only on bread and running water."

"Is that what you are doing?" I asked Seneca. If so, it didn't show. He was still stocky and had a fleshy face.

"Yes, I am trying." He smiled for the first time. "But we will offer you more than that. I do not require the entire household to follow my example."

Lucan said, "Good. For I am longing for some dainties and indulgences. I need to keep my muse well fed." His fierce blue eyes burned in his face. "I will return to Rome shortly. My new house will be ready soon. I have been pestering my uncle to let me have some of his books for my new library. But he won't part with them."

"It's all I have left," said Seneca. I doubted that. He had several houses and villas in Italy, untouched by fire. Why did he make this pretense? But then he had always pretended things. He had pretended that his relegation—not exile, he had insisted—in Corsica had been a torment, but he had actually lived comfortably. He pretended his wealth meant nothing to him, but he kept amassing more. He pretended to guide me morally but reaped the benefits of my misdeeds, covering them up for political presentation. In fact, he aided and abetted what I called the third Nero, that dark side of me that lived apart from the dutiful emperor and the idealistic artist, that had led me to do unspeakable things. And unspeakable was right, because the morally upright Seneca did not speak of them although he approved them and pocketed the rewards for doing so.

"A pity," I said. I looked around. "How are you spending your hours?"

A satisfied smile spread over his face. "Writing. At long last, I have the time to write. I have written a few plays from Greek mythology and seven volumes of *Natural Questions*. I've also written moral treatises as a series of letters to a friend, Lucilius."

Moral treatises. Do as I say, not as I do. And who was Lucilius? Did he even exist, or was he just a literary persona?

"I envy you," I said. "When the rebuilding is over, I will gather my literary group again. You will join us, Lucan? Or are you too busy now that your work is widely recognized?"

He had been making a name for himself, and his *Civil War* epic had grown into seven books since he started it over four years ago. He had dedicated it to me at the time.

"Of course I will join you. Does anyone say no to an invitation from the emperor?"

No, but how many people would like to? I would never know. "Good. I will see you then."

The meal was an awkward one, with five of us eating from dishes of pork and figs and platters of grapes and nuts, while Seneca munched on a crust of dry bread. The five of us sipped his Nomentum estate wine while Seneca drank water fetched from a stream. The conversation was stilted, and no information was exchanged. There was a lot of coughing from Seneca and Gallio, both of whom had weak lungs. I could hardly wait for it to be over. What a mistake to have come.

But just as we were taking our leave, Seneca hobbled over to me and put his hands on my shoulders. "You carry a great deal, my son," he said. "Perhaps you would like to put those burdens down."

Was he suggesting I abdicate? I just stared at him, at his rheumy eyes and wrinkled cheeks, like an old tortoise's.

"I have rejoiced in being able to put my burdens down," he said. "I recommend it."

"When I am as old as you, I'll consider it." I knew that was rude, but it was the truth. And he had been rude to me, suggesting I should give up the emperorship. "My father." I removed his hands from my shoulders and squeezed them in a farewell handshake. It was farewell. He was as gone as all the other things from my past. I truly had no father now. But I had not for a long time. I had only imagined I had.

O n our way back to Rome, Faenius said, "Seneca is convinced someone is trying to poison him. That's why he is eating as he is. It has nothing to do with Stoicism."

"Who would want to poison him?" Poppaea's spies were right, then.

Faenius waited a long time before saying, "It is reported that his freedman Cleonicus was ordered to poison him."

"Who would order that? Was Cleonicus the man who greeted us?"

"Yes. He is fiercely loyal to his master."

"You didn't answer my question," I said. "Who would benefit by poisoning Seneca?"

He tilted his head. "I don't know. Perhaps you should ask Tigellinus. He has spies everywhere."

Beneath the surface of the court, then, a nest of spies slithered like snakes. Poppaea's, Tigellinus's, Seneca's—and mine.

It was the middle of the night before we got back, so I slept late the next morning. It was not only the ride that had tired me; it was seeing Seneca again. It was not as I expected—but what had I expected? As a result of my oversleeping, I was groggy for the morning ritual of

"Friends of Caesar" paying their respects and giving me a ceremonial kiss in the atrium of the palace. I had enjoyed the hiatus of this tedious custom in the aftermath of the Fire, but now it was fully restored, taking up a good part of each morning. There were two formal groups, the first being of higher standing, the second a lesser status. There was, naturally, a great deal of jockeying to move from group two into group one. I found the whole thing a bore and wanted to abolish it. But it was a good way to keep an eye on senators and magistrates. They had to pass before me, one by one, and look me in the face.

This morning a number of senators had appeared, smiling and praising the rebuilding, its thoroughness and its speed. If they were unhappy with the means of this—the expense—they hid it. The second group—wealthy businessmen, landowners, lawyers—took up the rest of the morning. By the time they left, I was more than ready for the baths. I hurried over there, pleased to see how the Campus Martius was faring. It had not been hard hit and now was bustling. My baths had escaped damage and were thronged with people. The usual crowd of petitioners had followed me but my guards shooed them away, and I sank gratefully into the waters. Afterward I strolled in the yard of the palaestra beside the baths, my pride and joy, one of my first building projects. Now artworks lined the walls of the exercise yard and the reading room was stocked with scrolls, and a person could spend all day here, exercising both the mind and the body.

I needed to go back to a regular exercise regimen; it had been sadly neglected. If I wanted to control horses in the Circus, I needed to be as strong as possible. But the loss of Apollonius, my trainer, had sapped my desire to train. Another part of my past lost, another person who had known me as a boy and not as emperor. I could find another trainer, but not another who would have known me as I once was and, inside, still remained.

Despite these thoughts, the baths relaxed me. But my serenity was shattered when I returned to the palace to find Tigellinus waiting. He was the opposite of tranquility, always suffused with energy and tension. He could smile, but it always looked borrowed. Now he was smiling, but grimly. He gestured to a scroll on my desk.

My skin was still glowing from the hot and cold baths, the rub-down with oil, the feel of a fresh linen tunic afterward. Now this, whatever it was.

"You know how to spoil a man's day," I said, picking up the scroll.

"How was your visit to Mr. Pompous and Pious?" he asked, crossing his muscular arms and leaning against the wall.

In spite of myself, I laughed. "Pompous and pious," I said. "He should go on the stage, he is so good at playacting."

"What was he playing at this time?"

"The humble philosopher," I said. "All that was missing was the whip for self-discipline. He had the other props—crusts of dry bread, cups of water." I unrolled the scroll. It was a play, titled *Octavia*. A list of parts followed:

> Octavia, *wife of Nero*
> Octavia's nurse
> Seneca, *minister to Nero*
> Nero, *emperor of Rome*
> A Prefect
> Poppaea, *mistress and afterward wife of Nero*
> Messenger
> Chorus of Roman citizens

"Where did you get this?" I asked him.

"It was removed from the workroom of Seneca. Not at Nomentum, but at his smaller villa closer to Rome."

I need not ask how it was removed or by whom. *He has spies everywhere.* Had Seneca missed it? When I was there, did he assume I had seen it?

"Do we know he wrote it? Perhaps someone else wrote it and sent it to him."

"The style is identical," said Tigellinus.

"It is easy to copy someone's style," I said. "Or rather, most people's styles. There are scores of imitation Homers and Ovids."

"No matter who wrote it, Seneca had it."

Sighing, I began reading. It was my duty to read it.

It was a drama of how cruel I was, how hated by Octavia, who despised my person and compared me to a lion's wrath, a tiger's rage. Seneca was cast in the role of the wise mediator, attempting to restrain my evil deeds. Poppaea was the incarnation of a scheming hussy. Even Mother's ghost made an appearance, bent on revenge from Hades. There was one line in which Octavia said, "Let him destroy me, too— or I shall kill him!" Well, that had certainly been true. She and Britannicus had tried to kill me. But, oddly enough, our relationship was much more than that, much more complicated than this simplistic play. We had been childhood victims to Mother's ambitions, married to one another for political reasons through no desire of our own, inevitably ending as political opponents. That we had suffered alike in our arranged marriage at the hands of others gave us a strange fellowship.

Seneca stood forth in dignity uttering a series of lines that I answered as we batted clichés back and forth, he always having the last word.

SENECA: *Is that just treatment for those nearest to you?*
NERO: *Let him be just who has no need of fear.*
SENECA: *The more your power, greater your fear should be.*
NERO: *A man's a fool who does not know his strength.*
SENECA: *Justice, not strength, is what a good man knows.*

And so on.

At one point he had me saying, "Am I to tolerate conspiracy against my life and make no retribution?"

Thank you, Seneca, for allowing me this favor! I thought.

He also let me say, about Octavia, "Nor was she ever wife to me in heart and soul." Again, Seneca, thanks for your admission here!

Seneca, having bleated out his tiresome platitudes, vanished from the play, which ended with Octavia being exiled.

Tigellinus was waiting for my response. "I notice you don't fare so well in it, either. But at least you aren't identified by name. Just called 'Prefect.' And look here, he has me saying, 'Here comes the captain of my guard, whose loyalty well proved, and signal virtue, make him fit to hold command over my garrison.' Well, that's true. You are. And somewhere else it says that Poppaea is more lovely than Helen of Troy." I searched for it. "Here it is: 'Let Sparta praise her daughter's beauty, and the young Phrygian shepherd boast of his prize; We have one here, a face more lovely than the Tyndarid—that face that launched a lamentable war, and brought the throne of Phrygia to the ground.' At least he gives Poppaea her due."

"She almost started a war here, too."

"Nasty stuff. It's nasty stuff," I admitted. I rolled it up. It should have made me angry, and it did on the surface, but deeper down I felt sorrow. If he did not actually write it, whoever did had known it would find a welcome home with him.

"Is this really public opinion?" I wondered out loud.

"The divorce was a scandal, as you know. But we managed it; it is over. Octavia's sad end is fading in memory, too. The whole family was cursed—Claudius, Messalina, Britannicus, Octavia, and then your mother for joining them. But all things pass, and the latest scandal or tragedy takes its place. The Fire has wiped out many memories." He raised his eyebrows. "There is nothing like having your own house burn down to take your mind off the misbehavior of others."

XX

ACTE

Autumn was always a busy time for me. The orders for new amphoras, one of my businesses, became brisk, as vintners suddenly realized their harvest was yielding more wine than they had predicted. Then they wanted the extras immediately. I had to take them in order, first the most long-standing customers, without losing the newer customers. It was a difficult juggling act.

As if that were not challenging enough, I suddenly had a spate of suitors. Sometimes I was tempted to take one just to end the siege. But I knew that remedy was worse than the disease. I was thirty-two and past the age for marriage. Not legally but emotionally. It is a misfortune to find a love early in life and then lose him. When that happens, you can spend the rest of your days either memorializing him or searching for him again. In my case, I chose to do neither. I did not need to memorialize Nero; the world did that for me. And there was no point in searching for him. I knew where to find him, but finding him would not change anything. Meeting him again in the fields outside Rome had altered nothing except to prove to me that my bond with him would never fade or break.

People make second marriages all the time. Why not me? It would be easier if the person was no longer on earth but a little heap of ashes in an urn; then it would be like that saying: *a living dog is better than a dead lion.* But if the lion is still alive?

There was one man I had not sent away yet. I hated finalities, and of all the men I had met since coming to Velitrae, he was the most tempting. But I could not bring myself to say yes—yet. So I kept him on, postponing a decision.

My servants had returned from the morning markets and I had finished signing some contracts for the amphoras when a visitor was announced. I was not expecting anyone, but my atrium and reception rooms were tidy as usual. I smoothed my hair, straightened my shoulders, and said, "Admit him."

In walked Claudius Senecio, a man from my past. I was so startled to see him for an instant I was without words. It is always disorienting to see someone from another place suddenly appear where they don't belong.

"I am not a ghost," he said. "Although you look as if you had seen one." He smiled. "Do you not recognize your old paramour?"

"Claudius Senecio," I said, to prove that I did recognize him and had not lost my wits. "Yes, I remember our subterfuge." I motioned him to follow me out of the wide atrium and into the room where I received clients and visitors.

He put his hands over his heart. "Ah, how can you call it a subterfuge? For me it was real."

He had aged little. He still had his thick dark hair and his ready, but insincere, smile on a tanned face.

"It was meant to look real," I said, indicating a chair for him to sit in. "Those were in the days before Nero ceased to care if people knew about him and me. So, as his companion, you provided the excuse for me to be out in his company." Surely he hadn't dwelt on the idea that I might have harbored secret feelings for him?

"It was a pleasure while it lasted," he said, accepting the drink my servant brought over on a mother-of-pearl tray. "And here you are." He looked around appreciatively. "Your liaison with the emperor has stood you in good stead."

He had always had a mean tongue. "Do you mean that he has bought me off? That I profited by my time with him?" I did not take insults from anyone.

"Well, you are a freedwoman and now have this big villa and several businesses, so I hear."

"Some of the wealthiest people in the empire are freedmen," I said.

"Especially mistresses of the emperor," he said.

I set down my goblet. "What do you want, Senecio?"

He shrugged. "I happened to be here and thought I would stop in and see you, as an old friend."

"If you speak like this to other old friends, I doubt you have very many."

"I beg your pardon. Please, do not take offense. Our positions have changed since those early days. Tell me, do you hear from the emperor?"

"Hardly. We are not in contact."

"Oh, that's a pity." He took another sip of his drink. "I have been concerned about him. So have others."

"In what way?"

"Since the Fire . . . It has affected him . . . he seems changed."

"How?"

"It's hard to say. Do you happen to know if he plans to reopen the Macellum Magnum in person? I believe the damage from the Fire has been repaired."

"No, I told you, I don't know what he is doing or plans to do."

"What about the Circus? There are rumors that he plans to race in it himself. Do you know when?"

"What about 'no' don't you understand? I've told you, I'm not in contact with him."

"I am just concerned," he repeated.

"Then why don't you go to him yourself? I am sure you have admittance to the palace."

"Oh, yes, I dined with him not long after the Fire. Petronius hosted us. It was out in the woods. Well, you know Petronius! Always something different. This was a gathering to resurrect Pan."

"Well, then, you have seen him more recently than I have."

"He's gained weight," he said suddenly. "I don't think he looks well."

"As I said, you have seen him more recently than I have."

"Do you truly not see him? They say he is faithful to his wife, but she's a bitch. An opportunist if ever there was one."

And you are not? I thought. "I don't know what he does."

"He couldn't be faithful to her. After all, he's the emperor; he can have as many women as he wants. She is probably driving him away with her demands and tantrums. You've heard about the asses' milk baths?"

I would not take this bait, would not ask about her. "I really can't tell you anything about him nowadays," I said. I stood up. "Senecio, it was good to see you. Now I have another appointment." I rang for the servant to see him out.

I had no other appointment, but I spent the rest of the afternoon in agitated unease. The encounter was disturbing. Why had he come? What did he want to know? Behind the smoke of niceties he had asked pointed questions about where Nero could be expected to be and when.

There may have been nothing to it, but it felt suspect. Should I report it to Nero? No, he would think I was looking for an excuse to write him, to get in touch with him. This sounded flimsy. *One of your old companions stopped by, asking questions about you.* The questions sounded innocent enough when I repeated them.

But what if they weren't, and in concern for what Nero might impute to me, I let them slip by?

I would write him. But how to make sure the letter wasn't intercepted? Suddenly today's impromptu, casual visit took on ominous overtones. He might be surrounded by people watching, spying, making sure he wasn't warned.

Tigellinus. Could he be trusted? The letter would pass through his hands if it was addressed directly to Nero. But if I sent it to Alexandra, his old nurse and my friend who still served him in the palace, no one would bother with it. And she could carry it to him when it was safe.

I pulled out paper and began.

To Nero (alongside the real words I wrote were ghost ones,
To my everlasting love)

Claudius Senecio (that snake) came to my home today, ostensibly for a friendly visit, but he asked several questions about you and your plans. l. He asked if you planned to reopen the Macellum Magnum in person and if so, when? 2. He asked if you were going to race in the Circus Maximus, or open the track, and if so, when? 3. He asked about possible mistresses and who they might be. (He slandered your wife and, incidentally, me, too, saying that I had profited by my time with you.) 4. He professed to be concerned about you and your health and said you did not look well. (Is this true? I pray not.) I am more concerned than he claims to be, for I fear he was spying, to what end I know not. In any case, I told him I knew nothing, which is true. But even were it not, I still would have said it.

With wishes for your health, safety, and happiness,
(Your) Claudia Acte

XXI

NERO

When is he to arrive?" asked Poppaea. We had been waiting all morning for the legendary sculptor Zenodorus to come and discuss the statue I was commissioning.

I didn't know but didn't want to admit it, for Poppaea would lecture me about my being the emperor and how I should command people's appearance at my convenience. She didn't understand that artists can't be commanded, and any attempt to do so just alienates them, even more so if it is the emperor doing it.

"Probably this afternoon," I said to placate her.

"Are you sure he is the right man for this job?" she asked. "You didn't even approach anyone else."

"There is no one else," I said. "No one who could conceivably execute a statue of this magnitude."

Zenodorus had gained fame from his enormous bronze statue of Mercury that stood in the Gallic town of Augustodunum.

"Why must it be so large?" she asked.

"Because it must," I said. I wanted Rome to have its own colossus, bigger even than the one in Rhodes, gone now, tumbled in an earthquake some three hundred years ago, but writ large in memory.

"But it took him ten years to do the Mercury statue!" she said. "You can't wait that long."

"Indeed not. I want everything in place by next spring—the Golden House finished, all the rebuilding, and the dedication of the statue."

"And how will you prod him into completing it in record time?"

"He ran out of money in Gaul. That won't happen here." Money . . . already a problem, dwindling rapidly, and much still left to do. I had to find more sources.

She sighed and leaned back against the arm of the couch. I thought of the reference to her as a latter-day Helen of Troy in the abominable play; even someone prejudiced against her could not deny her other-worldly beauty. Now I looked at her and tried to see her as a stranger would, but it was impossible. She was pressed into my vision, my heart, my dreams. Even Zenodorus could not capture her beauty, no matter his genius.

Zenodorus was announced not long afterward, to our relief, and escorted into the room. He was a short, balding man with bushy over-hanging eyebrows. I had not pictured him to look so negligible, and I was surprised. But I should not have been. There is no connection be-tween a person's looks and his ability to bring forth visions for others.

"Caesar," he said. "I am here as you requested."

"I am pleased to welcome you. How was your journey?"

After more of these pleasantries, I bade him sit while I laid out my ideas for the statue. It had to be taller than any other statue, it should be of bronze overlaid with gold, it should be freestanding, and it should be modeled with my features. He listened without comment.

"You are ambitious," he finally said. "But such a statue would strain the limitations of what is possible."

"Not for you, surely," I said, hoping the flattery would sway him.

"To attempt it and have it fail would do no good to either of our reputations," he said. "If it fell, how would that be interpreted? Would people see it as an omen, that your rule is over, toppled? No, I wouldn't chance it."

"I am not a coward," I said. "Better to dare and fail than not to try. Especially if the reward for succeeding is eternal fame."

"A statue won't assure you of eternal fame," he said. "Although it will outlast you for a while."

"I want the statue! No argument can convince me otherwise. I made a vow to Apollo, to Sol. He will watch over the city, and the golden statue in his likeness and mine will confirm that."

"Very well," he said. "Now, for the particulars—"

He was a gracious loser and immediately put any other path behind him.

He wanted to inspect the area where the statue would be situated, and so we left the palace across the Tiber and went to the site where the complex was rising. A haze of dust from the stone chisels filled the air in the valley where the lake, the main palace, and the courtyard were being built. Sunlight danced in the motes, like daytime fireflies.

Zenodorus looked around, swiveling his head on his wattled neck. "I see now. I see why the statue must be outsized."

I led him into the nearly completed courtyard where bricklayers were setting the pavement and workmen were smoothing the marble finish on the surrounding colonnades. An open space was fenced off, with no plantings yet. "Here," I said. "We will leave the ground bare until the statue is in place, otherwise the plantings would be trampled. The statue will be facing the Forum and the Capitoline Hill, looking west. It will top the colonnades and be visible from anywhere in Rome. So you see why it must be over a hundred feet high."

"Yes, yes," he said. He was stunned.

We strolled through the empty, echoing halls of the attached incomplete palace, awaiting its final touches, and then out to the artificial lake beside it. That at least was done; the stones were sealed and watertight. "We will fill it soon," I said. It was about twenty feet deep, and large enough to carry a pleasure boat. "And over here"—I steered him toward the Temple of the Divine Claudius on the other side, being converted into a giant public fountain on one side. Up on the hill gleamed the veranda of the pavilion, open to the air and the sun; cascading down the hillside were bricked terraces and gardens.

"I truly have never seen the like," he finally said.

"What you are seeing now are the shells. When they are ornamented, then they will be unequaled." Surely then, surely when Rome saw what I had done, their doubts about my plans would fade away and they would glory in their city being the grandest on earth.

Back across the Tiber in the Vatican palace, Zenodorus got down to specifics. He told me to take off my tunic and let him take my measurements. The statue would be nude, and he needed the proportions. Poppaea watched from her couch.

"For a statue this tall, we will need a support. You will have to be leaning on something, holding something," he said, fussing with the measuring string. "A rudder? It has to be long enough to reach the ground. A spear? A shield?"

"Nothing military," I said. "A rudder will do. And in my right hand I'll hold a globe. The head should have a crown of divine rays, since the statue is also Sol."

"But it will have your features," he said. "Won't that confuse people?"

I shrugged. "People understand symbolism," I said.

"This will have to be constructed in sections," he said. "It is not possible to cast anything this large as a single piece. But it can be joined together cleverly so the seams won't show." He noted the measurements in his notebook.

"Make him more heroic than that," said Poppaea suddenly. "Don't use his genuine measurements. After all, this is supposed to be Sol as well."

Embarrassed, Zenodorus looked at me for guidance.

"She is right," I said. "It is the duty of art to elevate the commonplace to the sublime." No, I didn't want my present proportions to be rendered eternal in metal. It was good that Poppaea had spoken up. "Make the measurements Olympian."

He nodded and wrote furiously in his notebook.

After he was gone, I sat down beside her on the couch and laughed. She poked at my stomach. "You don't want this on your statue!" she said.

"I know I have gotten fat," I admitted.

"No, no, not fat, just—burly," she said.

"Fat by any other name . . ." I embraced her and stroked her hair. "But I will lose it all, I swear. When spring comes, you will see me as I used to be."

"So you have six months," she said. "When the baby comes, you will be reborn yourself as a slender man."

The baby. "I want the Nero who holds him to be worthy of him," I said. "Oh, Poppaea, I cannot express how happy I am. The gods have blessed us at last."

"Yes," she said. "Yes." She reached for a honeyed date on a nearby platter and handed me one. I refused. "Ah, I was testing you to see how long your resolve would last. You passed this first test. But there will be others. No more honeyed dates for you."

She went to lie down. She was at the stage of her pregnancy when she was sleepy during the day. I went to my workroom to tackle dispatches and other matters awaiting my attention. It was the usual pile: reports from various provinces, letters from governors, diplomatic questions involving territory or treaty rights. I was hard at work, surprisingly refreshed after the meeting with Zenodorus and the excitement of commissioning the statue, when a servant announced that Alexandra was waiting to see me. I was always pleased to see my old nurse, but this was an inconvenient time. Nonetheless I sighed and said, "Show her in."

The dear lady, still strong with a straight bearing, came in and greeted me. "Dear Lucius," she said, using my childhood name, the one she had known me as. She had license to say and do just about anything with me. I had been mistaken to have forgotten her and her fellow nurse Ecloge in the short list of people who had known me all my life; how could I have left her off?

I rose and embraced her. "And my dear Alexandra," I said. "You are always welcome."

"I have received a letter for you," she said, handing it to me. "I think perhaps it was sent to me to avoid any spying eyes. No one suspects an older woman of receiving important letters."

"Ah, don't speak of yourself that way," I said.

"I can say it; I just don't want anyone else to," she said. She kissed my cheek. "I'll leave you to it. We can chat another time." She had always been practical and astute.

When she left, I opened the letter. It was from Acte. Just seeing her name gave me a jolt, seeing her handwriting. But the contents were chilling. She was right to have let me know.

I folded it up, caressing it a bit too long. Acte. I had seen her after the Fire, that day in the fields: another person who had known me for a long time, but so much more than that. She was the love of my youth, something pure and unstained in an ugly world, the memory of which remained almost holy.

But I mustn't dwell on that. It must remain locked up in its shrine.

What was Senecio asking about? And who wanted to know, besides him? Most important, *why* did they want to know?

I was so absorbed in thinking about it, with the letter reopened, analyzing every word, I hardly heard Poppaea come into the room, did not realize she was there until she came up behind me and put her arms around me.

"You work too hard," she murmured, her voice still drowsy. Then her eyes focused on the paper, the words and the name. She jerked away. "Work! Forgive me, you aren't working; you are mulling over letters from that ex-lover of yours! So you are in secret correspondence with her!" She backed away, glaring at me, red spots rising in her cheeks.

"Don't be foolish," I said. This annoyed me. "She has warned me about suspicious questions from a supposed friend. Here, read it." I handed it to her. At first she refused to take it, as if it were a poisonous serpent, but she finally did.

"This is hardly a love letter, and it is the first I have received from her in years." Poppaea did not, could not possibly, know I had seen her recently, although by sheer accident. "She is not someone to send such news lightly," I said, snatching it back from her. "Now are you satisfied?"

Reluctantly she nodded. "I suppose it was kind of her to send it," she admitted. "But why would Senecio assume she was in contact with you? Why would your friends think you were still seeing her? There must be a reason they would suspect that!"

"It's wishful thinking on their parts," I said. "They could hardly approach you. So they have cast about, fishing for anyone they hope might be close to me. They may have approached others, men as well as women, who didn't see the significance of it." I glared at her. "You should be grateful that Acte, unlike most ex-mistresses, has proved a loyal friend."

"What other ex-mistresses of yours are floating about?" she said.

"It's a figure of speech," I said. "I don't have any other ex-mistresses."

Ex-lovers—partners in sex frolics in Baiae, at Piso's villa, at Petronius's dinners, courtesans from Vorax's establishment, yes, but they hardly counted. In most cases I couldn't even remember their names— and I was good with names.

"That's hard to believe," she said.

"Believe it or not, it's true." I looked at her. "And what about you, divorced twice before you married me? Cheating on your second husband, Otho, with his friend—me?"

And Otho's dreadful warning to us, or was it a curse? *Why do you want this? So you can be empress? Have power? For surely you don't love him. You don't love anyone, not really. I was content knowing that. Will he be?*

"You were my willing partner in that," she said. "I did not commit adultery alone."

"We were willing partners in everything," I said. There had been much more than that. There had been Octavia as well, Poppaea's crime against her and my acceptance of it. I took the letter from her hand and put it back on the desk. "Everything. As we still are." *For surely you don't love him.* "Do you love me?"

"Yes. Of course I do. You should not ask."

"You should not force me to ask. And I love you. I tell you without your asking. But of course you know."

She was not my innocent love of youth but my guilty one of manhood, a different thing altogether, for someone who knows us and loves the dark side as well as the light is a ruby beyond great price.

XXII

I 've changed my mind," I said.

Poppaea looked up from her day couch. "About what?" she asked. She did not seem concerned to know the answer. Her pregnancy had made her languid. Languid and more beautiful than ever, like a vision in slow motion, the sort we chase in dreams.

"About celebrating the tenth anniversary of my accession," I said. "It seems too momentous to ignore. And public ceremonies will be a confirmation that Rome has recovered."

"*Is* recovering, you mean," she corrected me. "It still has a long way to go."

Her criticism, welcome sometimes, annoyed me today. "What has been achieved in three months is almost a miracle. So yes, there is cause for celebration."

"A heavenly miracle brought about by the very earthly treasury."

The treasury. I inwardly winced, thinking of the huge debt draining it. And the accession events would add to the burden.

But no matter. The people of Rome had borne much and deserved a respite and reward.

So later that day, I met with Tigellinus and announced, "I will race in the Circus Maximus." Before he could say anything, I hurried on. "The stands are rebuilt, the track ready. It is fitting that in the place where the fire started, we have our first public entertainment."

He knew better than to scowl outright, so he kept his face in what he assumed was an expressionless gaze. Finally he said, "Races, fine. I agree, nothing will signal to the people that life is returning to normal better than a day of races. But they can take place without you."

Now he, too, irritated me. "You don't think I'm ready?"

"I didn't say that." He shrugged.

"But that's what you mean."

"If you insist, then, yes. But that isn't the main concern. It's that your competing will draw all the attention to you. People will be watching every move, every turn, and—dare I say it?—some may wish that you meet with an accident. When you don't, the idea won't fade away. Do you want to put that idea into their heads?" He looked hard at me, his eyes mercilessly honest.

He was right, of course. People watched the races hungry for gore and spectacular deaths as much as to make money betting. This would allow them to imagine my death anywhere on the seven laps around the course.

But such thoughts were for the timid. The only alternative was to never take the reins on a public racecourse. And for the rebirth of Rome, the beginning of the golden age, my commission from Apollo, Sol himself, to ride out as his incarnation, was absolute. And so I would do.

Soon, the decade celebration of my accession ballooned into a bigger and bigger event. I decided to inaugurate the pavilion of the Domus Aurea as well, inviting not only the senators and magistrates but also freedmen and common people. I would throw open all the rooms, finished or not, and at sunset we would gather on the porch and drink in the vista of the New Rome spreading out before us.

While the dusty work of rebuilding went on in Rome, I practiced my racing out at Lanatus's track. The horses were working smoothly as a team now, and I was able to concentrate on subtle means of communicating with them, using my voice as well as the whip to guide them. The Iberian, the most important horse in the team, pulling on the left side of the chariot, was the most willful but also the fastest and nimblest. I would have to control him on the turns or all would be lost.

"Better and better," said Lanatus, watching me. "I do believe you are ready."

I pulled up before him. "That's not what Tigellinus says."

"Tigellinus may have his reasons for saying what he does that have nothing to do with how well you drive." He walked over to us and ran his hands over the cream-colored Iberian. "I knew you'd be a prize," he said. "Even as a foal you showed your bloodlines."

"I want to be worthy of these racers," I said. "And bring them to the finish without injury."

He nodded. "And yourself as well. How will you race? Will you wear one of the Colors?"

I stepped off the chariot and back onto the firm ground. "No. I'm not a member of any, and if I singled out one, the others would feel slighted. Of course I'd be a Green if I could. But I'll wear my own Color."

"Would that be gold?"

I laughed. "How did you know?"

"What else could it be?"

I reveled in visiting the Domus Aurea and following its progress. The hillside pavilion, which would house art and be the venue for state receptions, was structurally complete, but it was a race to finish the interior.

I strolled through the first row of rooms, the ones opening directly onto the hillside. Sunlight streamed in, beaming on the workmen laying the marble floors. The closer the rooms were to the grand oculus chamber, the more expensive and elaborate the patterns of marble. Gradually they went from black and white to all the colors from the far-flung outposts of the empire—yellow from Numidia, green from Greece, purple from Egypt. The Domus Aurea must reflect the entire empire, advertise its might.

The air was filled with dust where the marble was being laid, but in the completed rooms artists were busy with the frescoes.

The senior artist, Fabullus, who had done the frescoes in the Domus Transitoria, was busy on a scaffold. The ceilings were twenty-five feet high and in the passageways, even higher. They made a person feel overwhelmed, small.

"Fabullus!" I called.

Slowly he turned and looked down. "Good day, Caesar," he said.

"How are you progressing?" I asked.

"I am progressing as I should be," he said. "Art cannot be hurried." He moved a bit to the side, and I could see what he had painted—brilliant blues and reds in a geometric pattern.

"I am not here to hurry you, just to take pride in your work," I assured him.

"I understand you want to open the house for an event shortly," he said warily. "It won't be ready by then, if that is what you are asking."

"I know it won't," I said. "But this will give them a glimpse of the wonders to come. Whet their appetites."

He grunted and flicked one fold of his toga. Yes, he insisted on working in a full toga. I did not know how he could stand it. Who would wear one by choice? "Unfinished art is often unappealing."

"Promised work has a lure all its own," I countered. In any case, unfinished was all that was available.

"The world is full of promised, unfinished work," he said. "For every completed work, there are a thousand uncompleted."

Well, they would not be able to say that about my Rome. It would be finished.

I kept walking through the long row of rooms—some twenty altogether—until I reached the focal point of the building, the vaulted oculus chamber. The marble floor was already laid and polished, the marble cladding on the walls. But the grand finishing touch, the detachable revolving ceiling, was still to come. It had to be done by October thirteenth. This was where I would lead the guests and dazzle them.

I spotted a workman at the waterfall in one of the alcoves. Celer, Severus, and I had designed a cascading river of water flowing down into a pool, murmuring and splashing. He was adjusting one of the blocks so the water entered the pool gently rather than with a roar.

He stood up when he saw me. "Almost ready, Caesar," he said proudly. "Whoever thought of this design, it makes the room sing."

"I am glad it has turned out as pleasantly in reality as it looked on the plans. What of the rotating ceiling insert?"

"I don't know. I am not on that work detail. But the last I heard, umm, they had run into a bit of trouble with it."

"What sort of trouble?"

"It needs to be perfectly balanced or it won't turn properly. And it takes more water power to turn it than expected. They are redesigning it now. It's in a shed up on top of the hill if you wish to see it."

I hurried up there, scrambling over the steep path that would take me to the summit of the Oppian Hill. Inside a makeshift shelter, a great wooden wheel, about thirty feet in diameter, lay on canvas. On its surface were sketches of the zodiac signs to be incorporated in ivory, as well as openings where rose petals or perfume could be sprinkled on those below. Several workmen were bent over it, measuring and murmuring. They snapped to attention when they saw me.

"I understand you need to make adjustments to it," I said.

"Yes, Caesar," a brawny man said. "It was unbalanced. We are trying to find the source of the listing."

"And I see you haven't got the designs on it yet," I said.

"We can't do that until it functions properly. Once the ivory is in it, it won't stand for rough handling."

"Yes, of course." Just looking at the wheel, I could not tell how near they were to solving the engineering problem. "But it needs to be finished soon."

"Yes, Caesar," they chorused.

"I can dispatch Celer or Severus here to help if you need them," I said.

"I think they are busy with the artificial lake," the burly man said. "Putting the finishing touches on it."

"That can wait," I said. We wouldn't be needing that for a while yet. "Let me know your progress. If you haven't solved it in two days, I'll pull Celer and Severus off the lake project."

But when I saw Celer and Severus, it was not about the revolving ceiling, and I had not sought the meeting. They came to me, rolls of blueprints tucked under their arms, the next day. They looked pleased with themselves and, after the proper greetings, said, "Rome is rising like a fast-growing sapling, and soon the branches will give shelter to all."

I bade them sit and offered them refreshments, which they waved away. "Are you pleased, Caesar?"

"Yes," I said. From the flattened blackened ground the white buildings were growing, reaching for the sun. "I was at the Domus Aurea yesterday, and from the terrace the city gleamed."

Before I could mention the ceiling problem, Celer cleared his throat. "In all this, there is something we—I, I should say—have overlooked. This must be remedied. And quickly, before the space fills in."

As if he had been primed to take the next sentence, Severus said, "Something of great importance," in a solemn tone. Being the older one, he always sounded sure of his facts.

"Well, what?" The temples were accounted for, the fountains, the streets—what could be missing?

"The latrines," said Celer. "We forgot to plan for the latrines."

"Latrines?"

"A very important part of civic life," said Severus. "The city depends on them." He scratched his busy gray hair.

"It does?"

"Naturally, Caesar, you would not have . . . have availed yourself of these relief stations, as you have your own in the palace, but most people do use them. In fact, they probably rank next to the games in public awareness."

"And how many of these do we need?"

"I would say . . . at least fifty. Unless you want the new streets to be soiled and stink."

More money! More building costs!

"Yes, of course," I said. "Where should they be situated?"

"At strategic places around the city, as they tend to be gathering places. So they should not be where they would cause a bottleneck of human traffic. And they need to be over existing sewers. Those mostly survived the Fire; we just have to map out their exact route," continued Severus.

"People do pay to use them," said Celer. "So the cost of building and upkeep is somewhat lessened."

"Upkeep?"

"They have to be cleaned, and sponges must be provided for the patrons. And if there is a blockage, well . . ."

I didn't want to think about it. "All right, all right!"

"They can vary in size, but the largest ones have fifteen or twenty seats. Usually of marble," said Severus. "There was a famous one near the Forum of Julius Caesar. It was heated, so naturally it was very popular."

"Perhaps we should build one very posh one, that has heating, marble seats, and even some artwork. Suitable for the New Rome!" said Celer.

"Of course, they don't all have to be like that. Just a few for show," said Severus.

More expenses! But if it had to be, it had to be. And if we could build structures that exalted the necessary into a luxury, would that be brilliant? I began to warm to the idea.

"Unroll the city map and let us see where we might put them. You are right, we must hurry while there is still space. Do you have the sewer plans?" I asked.

Before we were finished, I had elevated the idea and called for Luna marble, sponges from the Red Sea, mosaic floors. Why do things halfway?

When I consulted with Phaon, he was not impressed. In fact, as he totted up the costs for this sudden expenditure, he shook his head. "Regular marble will do as well as Luna. No one's bum can tell the difference. And Red Sea sponges, to be used and thrown down the sewer?" He snorted. "And mosaics! Who will be looking at them?"

"People sitting and staring at them, that's who," I said. "People linger there and would enjoy seeing them."

"What they enjoy more is gossiping with the other people in there. Really, you hear the most scandalous things—" He stopped. "I mean, ordinary people do—you wouldn't know—and besides, the floor will get dirty, and the mosaics will be scratched and muddy."

I sighed. "You have a point. But I think we should have one showcase latrine, in that spot near the Julius Caesar Forum."

"All right, one. But by forgoing the trappings for the rest of the latrines, you have just saved yourself . . . um . . . several million sesterces." He smiled for the first time.

"That makes me feel virtuous," I said. Actually it just made me feel relieved to have lessened the financial burden of the rebuilding.

"Besides, Caesar, it is better to build modestly for such things. You don't want your name forever linked with fancy latrines, do you?"

XXIII

L atrines aside, I watched proudly as the new Rome rose around me, like a flower opening, spreading its petals wide, seeking the sun. October thirteenth loomed ahead. I would be ready for it.

The night before, sitting alone as evening fell and slaves tiptoed in to light the oil lamps, I could not help but go back in time to the same evening ten years ago. Then I was not ready for it; I was a frightened sixteen-year-old trailing in my mother's poisonous wake, seeing the future only as an abyss I must plunge into. A deep dark well that might drown me.

Now, from my safe vantage point, I could know that I had not only survived but achieved victories, political and personal. The empire was flourishing, and after the uprising in Britain and the settlement in Armenia, we were at peace. When the Armenian king arrived in Rome to be awarded his crown by me, I would close the doors of the Temple of Janus, signaling that Rome was at peace everywhere in the world. It had been closed only six times in the entire history of Rome.

I had kept my inaugural promise to the Senate to honor their ancient privileges, to keep personal and state business separate, to bring no civil wars. I was at peace with everyone, except one obstructionist Stoic senator named Thrasea Paetus, who delighted in baiting me. I had a wife I loved, and hope of an heir soon. I had fought the Fire in Rome, propitiated the gods, and punished the criminals.

But of course there had been losses, mistakes. I was estranged from Seneca. The unnatural deaths of my first wife, Octavia, and my mother weighed heavily on me, even as they had brought me freedom. That I was three persons in one—the daylight emperor, the artist, and the dark actor—with only one other person safe to reveal the third Nero to, was painful. And my only child, my daughter, Claudia, had died as an infant.

Life is a mixture, Homer said. Zeus stands with two jars at his side; one contains good and the other ill. As mortals line up, he fills their jugs with either all bad or a mix of good and bad. No one gets only the good. But some get only the bad. So be satisfied if you get the blend.

Rome had burned—that was bad. But it was being re-created in a fuller form, and that was good. I was able to bring good out of the bad. And for that I counted myself blessed by fortune, for that opportunity.

In spite of the glowing lamps, the room was dim. This time ten years ago Claudius was at his dinner, about to be fed the poisonous mushrooms by Mother. I had watched, helpless to do anything about it. Watched while he chewed, contented. First contentment, then a blurring, then oblivion. And Nero the emperor was born.

Gloomy thoughts that did not bear too-close scrutiny. Nero, however you got here, you are emperor now. You have been for a decade. Remember the words of your hero Paris: *The golden gifts of the gods must not be despised, even if they were not what you would have chosen to begin with.* You were given the gift. Do not despise it.

"I want you to wear your most lovely gown," I told Poppaea. "For the inauguration of the new Circus Maximus."

"Of course," she said. "I realize all eyes will be on us."

If only you knew, I thought.

The sun shone brightly on the afternoon of October thirteenth, as it had ten years ago. The Circus was filled to capacity, hundreds of thousands of spectators in the stone and wooden seats. In the rebuilding, I had ordered the Caesar's old water channel to be filled in, increasing the seating area. The floor of the arena was spread with fresh fine sand, clean and raked. The chariots that would race today would be running on a virgin track.

The new imperial box, the pulvinar, was grander and better-appointed than its predecessor; it was perched midway up in the stands on the Palatine side for the best view of both the start and the finish lines. At the finish was the judges' box directly across from us, over the *spina*—the backbone—that divided the track into its two halves. It was laden with ornamental statues, as well as an obelisk, and at each end were crossbars with seven lap markers, for the chariots had to make seven circuits of the track, making a total of fourteen turns at each end of the *spina*, for a total distance of some three miles. It was these hazardous turns that put drivers most at risk, and they called for the utmost skill.

A herald would announce my entrance, but it was I who must host the games. Lesser games could be hosted by magistrates or wealthy patrons, but for this rededication of the Circus, only the emperor could preside. The faint scent of religious rites still clung to the Circus and the games, hence the shrines to Consus, Murcia, and Ceres that were present, and the formal procession of the gods before the races.

I had invited several senators, ones I knew best and often dined with—Piso and his wife, Atria; Scaevinus and his wife, Caedicia; Lateranus; consul Vestinus and his wife, Statilia—to join me in the box. Faenius would stand guard, along with his company soldiers Subrius Flavus and Sulpicius Asper.

Because this bordered on a sacred occasion, I was wearing a purple toga, and my guests were formally dressed. We settled into our padded seats and watched the last of the empty places in the stands fill, until the stadium was a mosaic of colors, the spectators wearing tunics or ribbons in the color of the team they supported—red, green, white, or blue.

The roof of the pulvinar over us provided welcome shade, as slaves offered food and drink.

"I say," said Piso, holding up his goblet and twirling it around, "is this a new vintage?"

Surely Poppaea hadn't insisted they serve the wine from her Vesuvian vines?

She held out her hand to take the goblet and have a sip. She smiled.

"Yes. It's from my own vineyard near my villa, on the slopes of Vesuvius. Do you like it?" She handed it back to him.

"Oh, it is delicious!"

Well said, actor, I thought. Very convincing.

Vestinus likewise took a sip and said, "A dog must have pissed on these particular grapes."

Everyone was silent, but I laughed. Vestinus was a rotund, droll man who did not suffer fools or hypocrisy but nonetheless was quite popular. Until he laughed at *you*.

Once I laughed, the others followed suit. "We have other varieties," I said, indicating that the other goblets should be filled with those. "Dear Poppaea, perhaps you should stick to what you do best."

"Cosmetics?" said Statilia, Vestinus's wife. She meant it as a barb, but Poppaea did not catch it.

"Oh, yes," Poppaea said, "my face cream is renowned. I could make a fortune if I sold it, but as empress it would hardly be seemly. But then, of course, you have no need of such." Perhaps she had caught the barb after all.

Statilia was a mature woman who made no effort to disguise it. But she did not need to. Her slightly jaded features bespoke experience and secret knowledge; her low gravelly voice beckoned you to find out what it was. "No, I do not," she said, looking levelly at Poppaea. It was clear she pitied those who did.

"Is anyone famous driving today?" asked Scaevinus.

"Many," I said.

"Who?"

I named Demetrius, the lead charioteer from the Greens, whose inside horse had won over a hundred races, earning him the title of *centenarius*, and his counterpart, Flamma, from the Blues, who had two such horses on his team. "And others. Check the betting forms. Old Fortunatus is making another comeback."

"They would have to have a special race for great-grandfathers, then," said Lateranus, shifting to get his huge frame comfortable in his chair. That was always a problem for him. "He must be ninety years old."

"No, closer to forty. Charioteers don't live long," said Piso.

"Remember that handsome one, Orestes?" said Atria. She had a little girl's voice, whispery and tentative.

"Yes. Won the Circus ten times with a six-horse team. He was killed when he was only twenty-two, but he had won two hundred and forty-two races by then," said Lateranus. He, like most racing fans, knew all the statistics.

"A short life but a happy one," said Vestinus, finishing his wine and holding his goblet out for more. "Personally I'd rather have a long and only semihappy one."

"*Count no man happy until he is dead,*" said Statilia. "Who said that?"

"Solon of Athens," I said. "He said it, to Croesus."

"Let's not talk of death," said Caedicia. "It is bad luck, especially today." She was a sturdy, matronly-looking woman who wore a severe, middle-parted hairstyle.

"You are right," said Scaevinus. "Let us not talk of death."

All the while Faenius and his cohorts Subrius and Sulpicius stood in the back, not joining in, just standing. Protocol would not allow them to indicate their presence, but I was tired of protocol.

"What do you think, Faenius?" I asked.

He looked startled. "About what, Caesar?"

"About the charioteers. Which faction do you favor? Greens, Blues, Reds, or Whites?"

"I—I—the Reds."

Vestinus booed. "The Reds? How could you?"

I turned to the other two soldiers. "And you?"

A statue could not have looked more startled to be brought to life.

"I am with Faenius in whatever he chooses," said Subrius.

"Likewise," said Sulpicius curtly.

"How boring," said Vestinus. "Are you all duplicates of one another? Do you like the same wines, the same women, and the same music?"

"I don't like music," said Sulpicius.

Vestinus laughed. "I won't ask whether you like women or wine, then. The answer is probably not. Ascetics usually don't."

"Ascetics make the best soldiers," I said, defending them.

"Most soldiers don't have a reputation for ascetic living," said Lateranus. "Haven't you ever seen them in town when they are on leave? Lock up your wives and daughters and hide your amphoras."

Everyone laughed but Sulpicius and Subrius. Even Faenius managed a faint whinny.

But by then, the time had come. The herald, standing at the judges' box, blew his trumpet and announced, "The emperor!"

At that point, I made my way—amid immense cheering—to stand beside him and cry, "We inaugurate our new stadium today. May it resound with victory and last a thousand years."

I waited and watched the ceremonial parade, the *pompa*, of priests with statues of the gods, incense swirling around them. Not only were the Olympian gods honored but the deified emperors rode beside them. The steely gaze of Julius Caesar, the benign one of Augustus, and the vacant one of Claudius beamed out at the crowd. Following them, musicians and dancers pranced across the sands, some dressed as warriors, others as satyrs who wiggled their goatskin-clad rumps in rhythm. When they had finally finished their circuit around the entire track, slaves came out to rake the sand and water it to keep the dust down. At last the races would begin.

When I returned to the imperial box, the couch with the gods had been reverently placed in the back. There, with Jupiter, Juno, Venus, Apollo, and Diana, was little Claudia. I had seen the bust before, but that did not make it less painful. I would remain acutely aware of her behind me. I took my seat.

I was nervous. Very nervous, and I could not show it to anyone. I did not drink the wine, although I pretended to. I had arranged for a substitute. The guests were chattering away, eager for the first race—the most prestigious one, doubly so this important day—to begin.

"Well done, Caesar," said Piso. "We could actually hear you from way up here. Your voice carried well."

"That was only because the crowd was quiet. That won't last long." I took a drink of my pseudo-wine and tried to look relaxed.

"It's impressive, that the Circus was rebuilt so quickly," said Lateranus. "You promised it would be, but I did not see how it could be."

"You get what you pay for," said Vestinus. "And we have paid dearly for it."

"We have gotten our money's worth," said Poppaea. I knew that whenever she had that edge in her voice, she was insulted.

"And what about your other . . . project?" asked Scaevinus. "The one that has taken up four regions out of the city's fourteen—Regions Three and Ten and part of Regions Four and Two." He did not disguise his disapproval.

Poppaea shot a look at me as if to say, *I told you so. People resent it.*

Just as Mother had to pretend she did not know the boat was no accident, I pretended not to grasp his meaning. "It is rising apace, and soon will be finished enough to show. You will be among the select first guests." That usually disarmed people, to be told they were special.

But Scaevinus continued to scowl.

"I will be proud to welcome all of you as my guests for the first glimpses of the finished halls," I said.

"And we will be honored to be there," said Piso, ever the diplomat.

But the others were silent.

Mercifully the impending race put an end to our conversation. We moved close to the edge of the box for the best view. I brought out my emerald eyepiece, in hopes it would improve my sight, especially for the finish line.

The chariots were taking their places in the starting stalls, held back by doors that would be released when a restraining rope across them was dropped. The places were decided by lots, with the most coveted spot the left-hand one, closest to the rails, and the worst one the outside one nearest the stands. Anyone in that position would have to cut across the other three chariots in order to make the first turn ahead of them to take the lead, a dangerous move. Usually teams who drew that unlucky position had to rely on speed to eventually overtake the others, or on accidents that would eliminate some of the competition and clear the field.

The final trumpet blew. The magistrate acting in my name cried, "Let the games begin!" and dropped his white handkerchief, which floated to the ground.

The doors flung open, and the chariots burst out.

The Green had drawn the best place! The Blue the worst! We stood on tiptoe, gripping the edge of the box railing. The horses thundered down the track, maneuvering to the inside. But then they stopped. The judges had not dropped the white rope, the *alba linea*, that was a safeguard against false starts, strung about a third of the way down the track.

The *alba linea*, and how to approach it, was part of the racing strategy. Until that rope was dropped, it was risky to go top speed, for if the horses tangled in it, the chariot would be wrecked, the horses injured, possibly with broken legs. But to hold back, if the rope was then duly dropped, meant you had lost ground to the others, who, more daring, were now ahead.

The chariots wheeled around and returned to the starting gates.

"What happened? What was wrong?" asked Caedicia. She prided herself on being knowledgeable about the races. "I didn't see anything."

"I think the White left the gate before the rope was dropped," said Lateranus.

"How could he? The gate wouldn't open."

"He pushed it and the rope slackened," said Vestinus.

Oh, for such eyesight!

They were shut in again, and the doors closed. The handkerchief dropped again. They took off again.

They drove furiously, hurtling toward the *alba linea*. If it failed to drop, they would all be injured. But it dropped. And they roared across it, making for the end of the *spina* and the first turn around the three huge gold-covered columns, the *metae*, which served as bumpers to keep the chariots off the *spina* but often impaled them and caused as many accidents as they prevented.

As they approached the first turn, the Green, on the inside, had the advantage. Demetrius, renowned for his skill in making turns, did not disappoint. The chariot hugged the turn, his inside horse surefootedly did not break pace, and the outside horse pivoted expertly, guiding the two middle horses to turn smoothly.

Just behind him were the White and the Red. The White tried to maneuver closer to the rail but did not have the speed and fell in just behind the Red. As they entered the straightaway, they crowded to-gether, jostling. Then the Red moved up, almost beside the Green.

"The Red is going to hook the spokes!" cried Lateranus. "Look!"

"He can't! Demetrius is too clever to let him," Caedicia said. As she spoke, Demetrius put more distance between himself and the Red.

"Look out, White, he is coming for you!" Poppaea yelled. Everyone was yelling, and the stands were roaring.

The Red swerved left to try to hook the spokes of his rival White but failed when he fell behind. The Green, Demetrius, was still ahead of them both.

"What's happened to Flamma?" asked Scaevinus. "I had bet on him!"

The Blue was far behind, although he was now on the rail, having it all to himself.

Now the second turn came up, and once again Demetrius navigated it superbly, the dust flying out from the right wheel of his chariot, leaving the others literally in his dust.

"It must be hell on his wheel," said Lateranus. "It may not hold up until the end of the race."

"The turns put an immense strain on that outer wheel," said Vesti-nus. "I heard some were putting an iron band on their rim to strengthen it."

"That would add weight and slow him down," yelled Piso.

After five circuits, the order stayed the same: Demetrius the Green in the lead, the White and the Red running almost neck and neck, and Flamma the Blue behind.

But at the eleventh turn things changed. Demetrius slowed his team as he rounded the *metae* and lost ground.

"It's that wheel, I tell you! It is disintegrating!" cried Lateranus.

The Green fans in the stands shrieked, wept, tore their garments. A wail rose from the stands.

The Red came up behind him once they were on the straightaway. But Demetrius had recovered his speed and maintained his lead, al-though it was shrinking. Again on the turn he had to slow, but the wheel held. Back on the straightaway he sped up. But the others were closer now.

"He's going to lose!" cried Poppaea.

"Go, Red!" yelled Faenius, joining in at last.

The next-to-last turn was coming up, and suddenly the Red steered around Demetrius and made the turn ahead of him on the outside, pulling into the lead. Was it my imagination (and my poor eyesight), or was Demetrius's wheel wobbling? But on the last straightaway it stopped, and he came neck and neck with the Red.

One turn left. Suddenly, Flamma swept past on the outside, rounding the turn and then swinging to the inside, cutting them both off. The Red plowed into a *meta*, wrecking his chariot and going flying, landing on the track, crawling to the side to avoid being run over. Demetrius adroitly steered to the right and avoided the *meta* but lost his speed. The White trailed behind.

Flamma the Blue crossed the finish line to tumultuous applause and cries. Whether you supported him or not, it was a superlative show of charioteering, his victory "snatched at the post," as the saying had it.

"Two of his horses are not *centenarii* for nothing," said Vestinus drily. "I should have known to bet on him." He snorted. "But I got a tip from my uncle's stableboy that one of the horses had sprained his leg. Bah!"

"There are more races, Vestinus," I said. "Plenty of time to recoup your loss."

"Who else is racing today?" asked Poppaea.

We sat back down, exhausted from the strain. "It's all on the betting forms," I said, handing her one, engraved on ivory.

She looked it over and shrugged. "The names don't mean anything to me."

Lateranus took it and pored over it. "Oh, yes, there's the one from Sicily, what's his name . . . Decimus . . . and the driver from Athens, said to be very good, but has never raced here . . . and that Arab, who uses only Libyans." He shook his head. "They are beautiful, they are fast, but that breed is too small. Against a horse with a longer stride, they can't win."

"Oh, look!" said Caedilia. "There's a team from Galatia. Don't they put iron shoes on their horses' hooves?"

"What?" Piso said. "How ridiculous. Think of the weight."

"Those horses have soft feet, living in wet country. Without the shoes, their hooves would shred and peel."

"Like Demetrius's chariot wheel?" said Vestinus with a laugh.

"It held up," said Lateranus. "But one more turn would have done it in."

"We have more good races to look forward to, then. The day is just beginning," said Poppaea.

"Indeed," I assured her.

XXIV

Tigellinus appeared at the doorway to the imperial box. I rose to meet him. He nodded to me but gave one of his dazzling smiles to the company.

"I must leave you for a bit," I said. "Tigellinus has arranged for me to look in at the race stables."

"May I accompany you, Caesar?" asked Lateranus.

Knowing how he loved horses and racing, it hurt to say no.

"We visit only by special permission, and only for the emperor. The horses are easily spooked before a race," said Tigellinus.

Before anyone else could ask, we left the box and made our way out down the aisle of the stands. As I passed, people rose and cheered, showering me with petals, reaching out to touch the hem of my toga. "Caesar, Caesar!" they bayed, like packs of scavenging dogs. Some of them were disheveled from ripping at their clothes at the last race; others were drunk. Still others were nuzzling and embracing, not caring who saw them. The races offered the ultimate in freedom of all sorts.

Once outside, we hurried past the arched sides of the Circus stands and on to the area where the chariots and horses were awaiting their turn to race, in the exercise track by the stables. The gate was firmly secured and only after convincing the guard that I was truly the emperor were we allowed to pass.

We walked out into the grassy paddock, where many teams were assembling themselves.

Tigellinus touched my arm. "Are you sure you want to do this?"

Long ago, when I was still a virginal boy, he had dragged me to a brothel to educate me. Then, it had been he who had insisted I had to go through with it. Now it was the opposite. I felt as strangely excited and nervous now as I was then. But I was more sure of what I wanted to do. "Yes," I said. I had waited for this for years. Now there was no Burrus to say it wasn't seemly, no Seneca to lecture, no Mother to scold. I was indeed free, as free as those patrons in the stands, to do as I pleased.

"Very well." We continued walking. "Lanatus brought the team up two days ago so they could be rested before the race. He has exercised them lightly this morning. The chariot was delivered on time. So was the costume. So, all is in readiness."

I had made decisions about the construction of the chariot, but only with the advice of master chariot designers. It would be as light as possible, with a flexible low floor, wheels of composite wood layers on a wide axle base, and one with the iron rim we had talked about in the box. They—and I as well—felt that as a novice I would put more strain on the right wheel in the turns than a professional.

"And it would never do for Caesar's wheel to fall apart in his first public race in the Circus Maximus," said the designer. "You will have many more races, but this first one must be a success."

By that he didn't mean winning; he meant just finishing with honor.

"Lanatus is over on the other side of the paddock," said Tigellinus, and we made our way there. The grass felt springy under my shoes, and the air was pungent with the smell of horse—horse hair, horse breath, horse droppings. Swarming all around us were the army of professionals who managed the races: the *aurigatores*, charioteer assistants; the *conditores*, chariot wheel greasers; the *sparsores*, chariot cleaners; the *armentarii*, grooms; the *moratores*, who led the horses at the end of the race. There were also veterinarians for the horses and physicians for the charioteers, saddlers, water boys, and trainers. The buzz of voices, the clang of metal, thrummed through the air.

"This is more complex than the government of the empire," I said.

"Oh, there are more workers than these. There are *procurators dromi* to smooth the sand before the races, *erectores* to move the eggs and dolphins as each turn is finished—you didn't think they moved by themselves, did you?—grooms who talk to the horses as they are being led, and—"

Just then we reached Lanatus, who was leaning against a fence, affecting a relaxed pose. But his rapid blinking betrayed his nervousness. "They are waiting for you, Caesar." He gestured toward my four horses.

They had been groomed and their tails tied up, so they could not tangle in the reins. They sensed something in the air, and they pawed the ground nervously.

"I thought the exercise earlier would calm them down," said Lanatus, "but I see they are still on edge. But it wouldn't do to exercise them again. It's too close to the race."

I patted the withers of the Iberian. His coat was sleek and warm, the hairs bristly. "I am counting on you," I told him. He had learned to respond to my voice, and he leaned toward me now, his breath hot and moist. "When I say turn, turn," I said. "When I say slow, go slow. When I say fast, go fast. You know that, don't you?"

In response, he blew out a blast of air from his quivering nostrils and nibbled at my hand.

I likewise patted my other three, their contrasting coats making them easy to tell apart—the gray Mycenaean, the chestnut Sicilian, the black Cappadocian. "They say a team should match and we'll make a motley assembly, but I think you are beautiful. You are from all parts of the empire, and the empire is a rainbow of colors." Suddenly I was seized with a spasm of nerves and turned away. "How much longer?" I asked the men. "What is scheduled before me? Should I get dressed now?"

"There are two more races ahead of you. That will take about an hour, with all the cleanup. And yes, you might as well get dressed now. The clothes are in the private changing room over here." Lanatus led me to the room and left me. On a bench I saw the package of clothes, and I opened it slowly. There was the leather helmet, the leather belt, the leg wrappings, the knife, and the racing tunic, made of golden cloth. My colors. *Sol's colors.* I drew them out and, setting aside my toga and regular tunic, put them on. The emperor was suspended; the celestial charioteer took his place.

All was in readiness. I stood beside the chariot, inspecting it. The smell of new wood and paint clung to it, a dry sweet scent. I ran my hand over the iron rim on the right wheel. It was as thin as it could be and still provide protection.

Lanatus held out a cup. "Drink this, and become a true charioteer."

I sniffed it. It had a sour smell. But I knew full well what it was—the charioteer's drink of dried and burned boar's dung, dissolved in vinegar. It was supposed to confer healing power if I was injured in the race, and also keep horses from trampling me if I fell. I drank it slowly, wincing at the acid taste.

"There, now!" Lanatus took the cup.

"Who am I racing against?" I asked. "And do they know I am in the race?"

"All veteran racers from the clubs, but no celebrities," said Tigellinus. "It was not fixed that way, that was just the way the seventh race of the day was slated."

"All veterans but no famous ones," I said, not believing for a moment that Tigellinus had not arranged it. "That way if I lose, it is no disgrace because they are veterans, and not novices like me, but also an honor to be in competition with them at my level."

"Yes, of course," he said, as if this was the first time he had considered it from this perspective.

"Has it been announced that I am competing?" I asked.

"Not yet. Would you like it to be?"

"No," I said. "If the people recognize me, that is well enough. If they don't, then I have the rare pleasure of not being judged as the emperor. But it is only fair to tell the other charioteers in my race." They would recognize me at close quarters in any case. "Oh, Jupiter, let them not hold back to let me win. Jupiter, Jupiter, hear me and grant this!"

"Charioteers are professionals and respect others likewise as professionals. Not that some don't accept bribes to throw a race, but it would be helpful if we tell them they will be rewarded for running their best race and ignoring you," said Lanatus. "I'll speak to them."

He turned and left us alone. I stood by the chariot, gripping its side. Tigellinus looked at me. "It's here. The hour is here at last. Do your best." He patted my arm. "Just as you did at Vorax's all those years ago."

I got into the chariot, feeling the flexible floor bend under my feet. I put on my helmet and gathered the reins. The two middle horses were yoked to the shaft, but the two outer ones ran on traces and had to be guided separately. I wrapped the lines of the yoked horses around my waist to secure them, and thrust the knife into my belt. The knife was necessary so if the chariot crashed and I needed to get free I could slash the reins to do so. Otherwise I would be dragged to my death, horribly mangled.

But in truth, how quickly could I react? Each rein was a strong piece of leather. How long would it take to cut through them? I gathered the slack lengths of the trace lines up in my right hand, leaving my left to hold the whip. I would not use the whip to make them run faster but lay it on their shoulders to guide them; I had trained them to respond to the touch as well as my voice.

I looked across their curved backs, shining and freshly groomed. Their tails were tied and knotted; their manes were woven with pearls, carnelian, and malachite; they had breastplates of amulets, and I had put Germanicus's ring on the Iberian's for good luck. Finally, around each of their necks was a gold ribbon, my racing color.

The stable handler charged with leading us to the starting stalls took the bridle of the inside horse, and we moved slowly toward the gates. Four other chariots followed. Before we reached the stalls where we would be enclosed, I motioned for us to stop. I wanted to speak to my fellow competitors and charioteers.

The Red chariot had a team of all chestnut horses, and the charioteer was a young man. His heavy helmet obscured his hair so I could not see what color it was, but his eyes were dark. He had a thick mouth that did not smile.

The Green chariot had a tall driver with bushy light hair that spilled out from his decorated helmet. He must be a Gaul, or from somewhere even farther north. Could he be a Briton? His left arm had blue tattoos of triangles, circles, and dots. His team was mixed: two horses were very large with long slender legs, the other two were smaller and looked strong, and these were hitched to the shaft to provide the pulling power.

The Blue driver was ostentatiously dressed, with a leather helmet embossed with Etruscan designs and a tunic bordered with curling fringes. His horses were nondescript, though—one even looked un-groomed, with tufts of hair sticking up all over his rump and back.

The charioteer in the White vehicle was older, his weatherbeaten face betraying him as a veteran of many races. He must be a cautious driver, then, because, as Piso had said, a successful driver usually did not live long; to be successful a driver had to be aggressive. Surely I could beat *him*.

I wheeled my chariot around to face them. They were all staring at me, and not just because I had halted the progress into the stalls.

"Yes, I am the emperor," I began.

Immediately the Blue driver snatched off his helmet. The others started to follow suit, but I said, "Please. That is what I wish to tell you. You must not pay attention to me or race any differently than you would. That is the greatest homage you can pay me—to treat me as your equal, no more, no less."

I feared it would prove impossible, but perhaps not. "Now let us draw the lots, and take whatever we are assigned."

The White driver just grinned; was it a friendly grin or an adver-sarial one? The other three stared blankly, and the Blue driver put his helmet back on.

The judge brought out a device that had hollow arms, each one numbered, suspended over another box containing five color tokens. Then with a swift motion, he turned them upside down. The clunk of the wooden balls dropping from the first box into the second, rolling along the arms, then the low sound as they hit the end of their channel told us fate had spoken and assigned us our places.

The judge carried the box around to show us where we each went.

The coveted number one spot went to the White; the number two to me; number three to the Blue; number four, Green; and number five, the worst spot, to the Red. Now we entered our assigned stalls.

The stalls were wide enough to accommodate the chariots, but the horses did not like being pinned so tightly. On each side of the stall were posts with heads of Mercury, god of speed. I would need his help today.

The trumpet sounded, warning us. Then the doors of the stalls opened, and the track was before us.

It was immense, looking completely different when I was down on it than it had looked from the stands. The brown sand spread out on all sides. But I had no time to think of this, for we all sprang forward and the race was on.

My horses were fast, and I saw that we were keeping abreast of the two chariots on either side. But looming ahead was the deadly *alba linea*. Should I urge the horses on, or be more cautious? They were already at a full gallop; we had trained them to go from a standing start to a full gallop quickly, omitting the paces in between.

Closer and closer we came, but I didn't pull them back. The White was ahead, and if the rope stayed taut, he would be the first to trip on it. That would pull down the rope and let the rest of us cross it safely before we had to stop.

But it did drop, and we ran over it, coming alongside the *spina*, which began at the line of the *alba linea*. Now, until the first turn, we were on the straightaway.

I needed to get over closer to the rails if I had hopes of making a tight turn, and I steered the horses to the left. But the White kept blocking me, wavering and feinting, teasing me but not letting me past. I shot a look at him; his horses were running steadily but not too fast. My first judgment that he was cautious had been borne out, but he was very skillful in his handling.

I would go around him. It took more ground, but I could pass him. So I pulled my team to the right and gave them the command to run all out, and they speeded up and we pulled alongside the White. Now to get around him!

But the old driver turned his head, grinning that grin, and suddenly his horses pulled out a reserve and leapt forward. I urged mine to do the same, but they weren't fast enough, not even trying their utmost.

Not fast enough . . . how could that be? But a team is only as fast as its slowest horse, Tigellinus had cautioned, and the other three were not as fast as the Iberian.

So I fell back on the inner rail behind the White. Just then, coming from behind, the Blue passed me and ran neck and neck with White. Now I had two of them blocking me; I was trapped.

A roar went up from the stands, but although I was aware of it, it didn't register as anything but noise, background noise.

The first turn. I was gripping the reins tightly, but my hands were so sweaty they made the reins slippery. But the Iberian performed magnificently, sure-footedly navigating around the *metae*, while the Cappadocian expertly pivoted and kept the chariot from veering out to the right.

The right! I glanced at my chariot wheel but could not see anything but the dust around it.

For the next circuit all stayed in the same positions, or at least we first three did; I could not see behind me. After the next turn, on the straightaway, the White and the Blue collided when the Blue tried again to pass, and the White went flying, his chariot careening in the air and falling to earth in a shower of splinters. The wheels rolled away on their own. The driver managed to free himself and huddled by the side of the *spina*. His horses littered the track, groaning. I had all I could do to avoid running over them, but I saw their terrified eyes as I passed.

Now, having steered safely past the wreckage, the Blue was behind me but making up his lost time from the crash and closing in. When we passed the spot of the wreck on the next round, workers had cleared the chariot debris, but two dead horses lay on the side. The driver had presumably been carried off in a litter.

A blur on my right side. Green was coming up, trying to pass me. I urged my horses faster, but he passed me anyway, and just after him Blue passed me also. Now I was behind both of them. Red must be behind me, but how far behind? Or had he wrecked himself and was now out of the race?

Ahead of me for two long laps the Blue and the Green battled for first place, jostling, attempting to hook one another's wheel and jerk it off, even hitting each other with whips. But both clung to the lead, running even. Both negotiated the turns and did not lose their place. But then, subtly, the Green's horses began to slow. They must have been a fast breed that lacked endurance and it was telling now. The chariot began to slip behind, little by little, and the Blue saw it and urged his horses faster, demoralizing the Green, who could not call up one more token of speed from his team. He fell back behind the Blue but was still ahead of me.

Another turn. This time, my chariot skidded out to the side, but mercifully on the side of the stands and not the unforgiving *metae* side. The Cappadocian did not steady the team enough and went wide. Was he tiring? The Red was now right behind me.

All the while, with my every sense alert and straining, time seemed suspended, unreal. I saw what was happening on the track around me, but it unfolded slowly, as if I floated. In reality it was happening so fast I could barely comprehend it. I had never experienced such a feeling, of elation, vigilance, fear, and desire simultaneously. Such are the chariot races, and the emotion is conveyed and magnified in the audience of tens of thousands who share it with the charioteer.

Suddenly my team found new strength and speed and hurtled toward the next turn. I was able to guide the Iberian through it with only my voice, not needing to even touch him with the whip, and we gained ground with that perfect turn and now I was just behind the Green.

"Go, go!" I cried to my team, and they obeyed, running faster still, calling on reserves of power they had saved. With a sudden burst of speed, we passed the Green on the outside. On the outside! Covering more ground, but still going faster!

The last turn. Oh, make it perfect! I called to the Iberian again, but this time we did not execute the turn as sharply and lost ground. It was impossible to overtake the Blue, who was well in the lead. So much for my thinking his horses were nondescript. They may have been ungroomed, but they were blazingly fast.

The finishing line was just ahead, and the roar of the crowd was loud as thunder. Out of the corner of my eye I could see wild movement in the stands, but I had to keep focused ahead on the horses. We crossed the line at full speed, and it took until the end of the straightaway for the horses to slow to a walk. Then we waited until the others finished, the Green just behind me and the Red after that.

At the judges' station, we lined up in order of finish. Two judges came down on the field, awarding the Blue the winner's wreath. They stopped by my chariot and said, "Well done, Caesar," awarding me the ribbon for second place and the Green, one for third.

I stepped out of the chariot. The solid ground felt odd beneath my feet, and my legs buckled. I touched the iron rim of the wheel, and it was hot from the friction and speed it had endured. Turning to my team, I petted each of the horses in turn, telling them how proud I was of their performance. The ring of Germanicus was still on the Iberian's breastplate; it had indeed brought us luck.

Second place. I had competed in the Circus Maximus and won second place! I was suddenly overcome with the enormity of the achievement.

My fellow racers came over and congratulated me.

"A brilliant debut," said Green.

"As you can see, we did not let you win," said Blue.

White, who had been released from the medical station, hobbled over on crutches, his head bandaged. "No, really, it was all staged—couldn't you tell?" He laughed, a painful wheeze. "I went to the trouble of being wrecked just to prove I wasn't favoring you."

"Your loyalty is impressive," said Red.

"I am grateful to all of you," I said. "You have given me a gift beyond the precious."

Before anyone could reply, we were swept away by the crowd pouring down out of the stands, engulfing us. I was surrounded by people crying out, "Nero, Nero, Nero!" waving palm branches, scarves, and ribbons. None were gold because no one had known I was competing, but all the other colors were there, and they covered me with them. Wreaths and flowers followed, spinning through the air.

"Our emperor!"

"Our god! Sol! The sun himself!"

"Shining upon us!"

They tried to lay hands on me and hoist me up, but a group of Praetorians who had hurried down to the track prevented them. "No, don't touch him!" they barked, pulling out their swords.

Gently I pushed the Praetorians back. "Let them," I said. "It is their day—it is *our* day."

At the sound of "our" the people let out a roar, and an enormous man, with his fellows, hoisted me up on his shoulders, shouting, "Behold our emperor, who dares what none other has dared!" The stands, which were still far from empty, erupted in screams and cheers.

I was borne around the entire circuit, to the cry of the crowds in the stands, and as I looked at them, and felt the strong shoulders beneath me bearing me up, I was wedded to them all in a mutual passionate love.

XXV

It was dusk when I returned to my palace quarters, exhilarated beyond all telling, my tunic sweaty and stained, wilted wreaths of flowers drooping around my neck. Fatigue had not set in yet; instead I felt as powerful as a god.

Poppaea was waiting, sitting on one of the ivory-footed couches. Instead of rising, rushing toward me, and embracing me—as the crowd had done—she just lifted her chin. There was no smile.

I had been walking toward her, but I stopped.

"That was a pretty show!" she said, her voice cold. "It was hideously embarrassing. What a kind surprise to present me with. You could at least have warned me."

"No one but Tigellinus knew. It had to be that way."

Did the others in the box feel the same way? I wondered.

"Not only was I frightened that you would be injured—or worse—but I was shamed that the emperor would perform before a hundred thousand people. As a *charioteer*! Slaves are charioteers, not the upper classes, let alone the *emperor*! You have dishonored yourself, can't you see that?"

I looked at her, at her perfect face, now set in judgment over me. "You are wrong. It was the opposite. The people were proud of me. They in effect crowned me, directly, today. In that way *this* is my true accession day."

"The Praetorians and the Senate crowned you ten years ago, and they are the ones who matter, not the rabble." She fingered her gold-

and-emerald necklace, sliding it around her throat. "The love of the rabble avails you nothing and even costs you in the esteem of those in power."

"In power? If they are in power, it is because I allow them to be. One word from me and they cease to be in power."

I went over and sat on the couch with her. I longed for her to put her arms around me, belatedly congratulate me. I *had* done something praiseworthy today.

Instead, she held her nose. "You smell like a horse. And the stinking crowd."

"A sweet smell to me," I countered.

"Why did you have to do it? Why race chariots?"

"It was something I have wanted to do since I was a child."

"But you are no longer a child. Or are you? You behave like one."

"If I behave like one, it is because deep inside the child is still there." I shuffled my feet, stuck them out, and flexed them in the sandals. Sand fell out onto the green marble floor.

"Childhood is a phase of life, to be put aside as one grows up."

"No, it should be cherished, because it is the truest part of ourselves, the part that came into being first." I had always had a fear that I would lose that, that somehow when I was an adult all the essence of the real Nero would be lost, drowned in a sea of dreamless days. But I had preserved him, he was still there, and today he had shown himself in all his fullness. "It is when we are our childhood selves that we are closest to the gods." It was true. Sol had come to me in dreams; he had come to me today. He did not attend Consilium meetings.

She softened and put her head on my shoulder, even letting the crushed roses around my neck grind into her hair. "I loved you for the boy in you, the radiant youth—but it does get a bit tiresome," she said, stroking my cheek. She kissed me. "I do want a man as well."

Outside in the fading light, dark shapes, flocks of birds, filled the sky, going to their rest.

"And you shall have him," I promised. "Now." The perfect end to my perfect day.

＊   ＊   ＊

E lated from the triumph at the Circus Maximus, I sent out invitations to the Senate, my friends and administrators, and the general public to the inauguration of the Domus Aurea at noon a week later to continue the celebration of the first decade of my reign.

"But you must come with me and tour it first," I told Poppaea. "I want to see it through your eyes."

"Is it finished?" she asked.

"Not completely, no. But well enough that we can entertain in it." We were taking a leisurely breakfast in our small dining room.

The sun shone through the murrhine goblets holding our fresh pear juice, making them glow. Poppaea held one up, playing with the light effects. She sighed. "I don't feel so well. Perhaps another day."

"We can take a litter. You need not strain yourself," I said. "This is the perfect day to see it."

She nibbled on a dried fig. "Very well. But is there any place where I can lie down if I need to?"

"I'll have a bed brought," I promised her.

T he litter deposited us on the top of the Oppian Hill, where delicate porticoes and gardens were being laid out. We stepped out and stood looking upon the city, with the rising residential palace and its lake below us. The waters on it sparkled; it had just been filled from the Claudian aqueduct.

"The residential palace should be ready for us to move in by winter. As you can see, the lake is finished. The gardens and grounds are being landscaped, and we'll have the animals last of all."

"Will we have peacocks?" she said. "I do fancy peacocks."

"I have already ordered a dozen from a supplier in Sicily."

"And overseeing all this will be the colossal statue." She giggled. "How is Zenodorus coming along with it?"

He was slow, that I knew, and even in the best of cases, it would take a long time. "Well enough," I said.

A dry, playful wind blew across us, carrying leaves along with it. They danced and tumbled, and the ones that landed on the ground chased one another around our feet. We crunched some of them, loving the crackling sound.

I pointed to an open area beside the hilltop gardens. "I plan to construct baths here, with both sea and sulfur water," I said. "But that is for later."

"Thank Zeus *something* is!" she said. "Is this your attempt at economy?"

I laughed. "Perhaps. Perhaps. Come, let us go into the pavilion itself." I took her hand, and we descended from the brow of the hill down to the wide stone terrace onto which the rooms opened. As far as we looked, the facade of the building stretched away.

She gasped. "Where does it end?"

"You looked at the plans. You know it is twelve hundred feet long. It has over two hundred rooms."

"But a plan doesn't show you what it really will look like. O gods, this is—this is—"

"Extravagant?"

"That isn't the word I was searching for. *Dangerous.* It is dangerous, politically, to have built such a thing."

"It will fulfill a need. Rome needs a central place for art, for gatherings, for celebrations, apart from the living quarters of the emperor, which should be private. You will see. It will be used constantly, and Romans will not know how they ever got along without it." *And it will fulfill another purpose, a grander one. It will reflect the glory of Sol and his chosen dwelling place.*

She did not reply.

"Come, come!" I motioned for her to follow me into the building. Every room opened directly onto the terrace, and with no inner doors to close, the sunlight was able to penetrate far within, into the second row of rooms and beyond. Gold leaf gilded the stucco, magnifying the light, making the room glow. Glass and gems also caught the light, sparkling as we turned beneath them.

"Now do you see why I called it the Domus Aurea, the Golden

House?" I asked her. "The light and the gold together make it the royal house of the sun." *The sun god. Sol. Inaugurating his house will usher in the golden age of Rome.*

She walked around the perimeter of the first room, marveling at the vivid frescoes and the marble inlays.

"This is one of the smaller ones," I said, leading her back toward the peristyle court in the interior. Even here, the light followed us.

Now she gasped. The rush of water filled our ears; a waterfall at the back of the peristyle court emptied into an enormous footed porphyry basin, easily ten feet across. We stood at its rim, glimpsing the bottom through the very clear water. Over the lip of the basin, water flowed gently into a channel and out of the room.

"Oh, there's more," I said, turning to another room, with the theme of Ulysses. High on the ceiling was a mosaic of Ulysses offering the cup of wine to Polyphemus—the first of many, which would lead to his drunken downfall. "A ceiling mosaic—something never done before."

"My head is spinning," she said. "I need see no more."

"Oh, but you must. You need to see one more thing before the guests do, so when they are amazed, you can be blasé." We walked farther east, to the large garden courtyard where I would first welcome the guests, and stopped.

"Close your eyes," I said. "Don't worry, I'll guide you." I took her hand, and we stepped outdoors into the courtyard.

"We are outside," she said. "I can feel the sun and the air."

"Don't look yet," I said, turning left on the terrace and walking until we came to a large open entrance. We entered it and I led her almost to the center.

"Now," I said. "Open your eyes."

We were standing in the octagon room. The sun was a brilliant circle of light shining through the oculus, beaming down on the dazzling white marble beneath. It was so bright it hurt the eyes.

She was silent, looking up in wonder. Then she turned to me. "Forgive me," she said. "I questioned you, as if this were an ordinary palace. I did not know it would rival the gods."

I pulled her toward me, hugging her to my side.

"The huge open space—how does the ceiling stay up without pillars? It soars into the air as if it were air itself," she said.

"It has eight supports, but they are incorporated into the walls." I pointed to one.

"It is magic," she said.

"With help from Celer and Severus," I said.

Only after our eyes adjusted to the bright light did she see the artworks arranged around the edges of the space—bronzes of Galatians slain in war, taken from Pergamum; an Amazon from Athens; and the statue of the priest of Troy and his two sons attacked by a sea serpent, from my own villa in Antium.

"I will use this space as an art gallery, with works that can be changed. The five rooms opening off the octagon are part of the complex and share walls with it, so they can be used as well. The largest one has a waterfall and a fountain."

I would not reveal the last surprise about the octagon room—the revolving ceiling. Yes, the workmen had fixed it and now it waited, covered, to be put in position as night fell on the night of the celebration. Something had to be reserved for her amazement, along with everyone else.

She walked to the room where the water flowed into the fountain. Mosaics framed it with sea scenes—blue waves, fish, starfish, and shells. She sat on the rim of the basin and dipped her hand into the water. "It is so tranquil here," she said. Even the waterfall murmured, rather than splashing.

I sat down beside her. The water rippled in the basin, soothing, orderly.

"I still do not feel well. Has the bed come yet where I can lie down?"

I stood up. "I'll see." I had ordered it brought to the Hector room, which was nearby. The room was only a few feet from the octagon chamber, so I quickly checked and saw that the bed had arrived.

"Yes, come," I said, returning to her side.

She sought the bed, not looking at the room itself, and lay on her back, her eyes closing. "I don't know what it is. It comes and goes during the day." She took several deep breaths.

"Rest, then."

Is it not a fine thing to be emperor and have a bed brought wherever you wish?

After a few minutes she began to take interest in her surroundings and looked at the frescoes done by Fabullus.

"What is this one?" she asked, pointing to a large one on the upper reaches of the wall, within a painted frame of brown, blue, and ocher. A helmeted figure with a very long spear and a shield was facing a cloaked woman with a child, standing before a city wall, and another cloaked figure in the doorway.

"It's Hector and Andromache," I said. "Hector bidding farewell to her before he faces Achilles."

"So it is their final farewell," she said. "Why did you choose that scene?"

"Because I am interested in the human side of the characters in the Iliad, not their heroics. That farewell, not fighting Achilles, was the bravest and hardest thing Hector did."

There was an empty matching frame facing it yet to be filled in. "What will go in there?" she asked.

"I haven't decided yet," I admitted.

"Then let me," she said. "Please have Fabullus depict Protesilaus and Laodamia. It was the first tragedy of the Trojan War." She sat up. "When Laodamia got word that her husband had died, she begged for just three hours more to be with him, and the gods granted her wish. If anything should ever happen to you—as I was afraid it would in the chariot race—I would beg the gods for the same."

A chill ran through me. "As would I, for you. Three hours more . . . just three hours. But now we have infinite hours, or what feels like it. Oh, to cherish them while we have them!" I buried my face in her hair, unable to permit myself to imagine her not with me. "Yes, I'll commission it from Fabullus. I promise."

XXVI

I could expect thousands to respond to my citywide invitation, but I had asked my literary group to come first for a private tour. The group had lapsed, and I wished to revive it and provide the utmost incentive to do so—an ambiance that would encourage the creative experience.

Petronius was the first to arrive. I had not seen him since the Pan gathering.

"I've been back at Cumae. Really, all the dust and noise of Rome's rebuilding was just too much. Wake me when it's over," he said. We were standing on the stone terrace, looking down at the lake, waiting for the others. "You must be descended from an ancient Babylonian. How else to explain these hanging gardens?" He gestured toward the descending terraces, hung with vines. "But then, this . . . house . . . seems inspired by Persepolis."

"Are you hinting that I am Nebuchadnezzar and Darius combined?" I asked.

Instead of laughing and denying it, he said, "Well, you do have a bit of the eastern love of luxury in you. Quite un-Roman." He looked at me, amusement on his saturnine face. "What is this you are wearing?" He flicked his hand toward me.

I had forgone a toga and chosen a long tunic in shimmering gold thread. I knew what it betokened, but that was my secret. It would have been insulting to Sol to inaugurate his palace in anything else. "I call this the Golden House, and my attire reflects it."

He shielded his eyes. "Reflect is right. It's glaring."

Like the sun. As it should be.

"Have you been writing in Cumae?" I asked, changing the subject.

"Yes, I've got more chapters of my *Satyricon* done."

I was about to tell him I was eager to read it, when Spiculus and Lucan arrived simultaneously. I turned to welcome them.

Spiculus, a poet who also fought as a gladiator, had a wide grin. "Greetings, Caesar," he said, inclining his head slightly.

Lucan, beside him, said, "To what do we owe this honor?"

His question surprised me. "As my friends and fellow writers, you are the first I wish to welcome."

"As you say," he replied evenly.

"It *is* an honor," said Spiculus. "One I do not take for granted. Of course, I am only a gladiator, not a senator like you."

"In the house of the Muses, all are equal," I said.

Just then Piso arrived, formally attired in his finest senatorial toga. "Am I late?" he asked apologetically.

"Not at all. Let us all stand here a moment and look out. If you have any questions about the grounds, please ask me."

I turned to face the valley. It was late morning, and the October sun was swinging around to the south, where it would soon shine full force into the pavilion. A slight breeze, spicy from fallen leaves, blew up from the valley to us.

But they stood silent, until finally I said, "Let us go inside." I led them to the first open door and then back through the labyrinth of rooms, all sunlit, to the fountain room with the Ulysses mosaic, and now with something else—a marble statue that sat in majesty across from the fountain, and the fresco of Apollo the lyre player I had rescued from the ruins around Augustus's house near it on the wall. Pillowed couches were arranged on the black-and-white marble floor, their colors matching it. Architectural engineering ensured that the chamber received natural light, but there were several bronze lamp stands at hand.

"This will be our retreat, a space dedicated to art." I swept my arm around the room.

"Do I recognize—is it Terpsichore?" asked Petronius.

"Yes. The Muse of lyric poetry," I said. "Who more fitting for us?"

"But this isn't the original," said Lucan, cocking his head. He circled it critically.

"Of course not," said Petronius. "Praxiteles worked in bronze. Everyone knows that. This is marble, a copy."

"Gladiators aren't so expert," said Spiculus.

"You are expert where it is crucial," I assured him. "When words are futile and feeble, a sword offers vital protection."

"Ah, but I am here to improve my words, not my sword arm," he said.

Piso stood in front of the fresco. "This speaks to me," he said.

"And to me," I said. In the indoor light, the colors were softer and warmer, enhancing the portrait.

I waved them to couches and took my place on one as well. "Petronius has been busy with his *Satyricon*," I told them. "I confess I have done little of late, for obvious reasons. What of the rest of you? Only outside Rome could you have enough peace to produce creative work."

Spiculus shifted on his couch, trying to find a way to lounge comfortably with his muscular body. "The arenas have been closed, so outside of training, I have had an unusual amount of time to compose. I've been working on a series of pastoral poems."

"Ah, a peaceful gladiator!" said Lucan. "A contradiction in terms."

"We are all contradictions, Lucan," said Piso. "You more than others, I think."

Lucan just laughed. "True." He paused. "What about you, Piso?"

"As a contradiction or as a writer?"

"We can let the first go. What have you written since last we met?"

"I've written two plays. They won't put Sophocles out of business, but—"

"Or Seneca, either, I hear," I said. "Has anyone here read his plays?"

"No," they chorused quickly—too quickly. So they had. They had read the *Octavia*. That answered my question, as to whom Seneca had written it for; he had written it for all educated Romans to read.

"I have," I said pointedly. "I've read them carefully. He has a very active imagination. But then writers need that. We create beings and places out of our airy fantasies. But, being unreal, they melt away when we try to prove them true."

They stared back at me innocently. A long stretch of silence ensued.

"We should invite Quintianus to join us," said Piso, steering the conversation away from the shoals of Seneca. "He writes poetry."

"He does?" That was a surprise. "Well, then, I'll ask him."

It was time for refreshments. I motioned to the slave on duty, and he appeared a few minutes later with wine, quinces from Kos, and almonds from Naxos. He poured out a sample of the wine into the murrhine cups I kept for the occasion, and I tasted it, then nodded for him to fill the other cups.

"To go with our Greek Muse, we have the legendary wine from Lesbos."

They murmured in delighted surprise. Lucan said, "I thought it no longer existed."

I smiled. "There are a few stores yet."

Is it not a fine thing to be emperor and call up whatever rare wine you wish?

The slave handed the cups around. Petronius sipped, then held out the cup and looked at it. "I have two like this," he said. "Well, actually, with more rainbow color."

"I'll gladly buy them," I said.

Petronius shook his head. "No, I am too fond of them." He sniffed the rim. "The stone has a delicate scent of its own. Extraordinary!"

Everyone sipped, and quickly the cups were empty. The slave refilled them.

The wine of Lesbos was renowned for its bouquet; it had a faint tang of sweet grasses. I inhaled and felt myself in a meadow far away, on the island, with the waves washing the shore and the wind blowing through the reeds.

On our third cup, the mood mellowed. I asked each of them what written line of someone here they liked best—if they could remember from the last time we met.

Spiculus thought for a moment, then said, "I liked your lines, Petronius, that went: *Unhappy Tantalus, with plenty curst / 'Mid fruits for hunger faints /*

'mid streams for thirst: / the Miser's emblem! who of all possessed / Yet fears to taste, in blessings most unblessed."

Petronius was touched, I could tell. "Thank you, Spiculus. What a memory! And those lines are something I am adamant about—we should avail ourselves of the plenty around us. Do not hold back. The worst miser is he who turns his back on what he should grasp." To make his point, he grabbed a quince and bit into it noisily.

Then why was he critical of the Golden House? In constructing it, hadn't I done exactly what he was extolling?

"My favorite lines are from Lucan's Third Book of the *Civil War*," I said. *"Either no feeling is left to the mind by death / or death itself is nothing."*

"Thank you," said Lucan. "I would have thought your favorite line would have been one in the opening praising you. Don't you like, *Whether you choose to wield / the scepter or to mount the flaming chariot of Phoebus / and to circle with moving fire the earth entirely unperturbed / by the transference of the sun, every deity / will yield to you, to your decision nature will leave / which god you wish to be?"*

Was he accusing me of the Fire? What a sly dig. But what he could not know was that I *had* mounted the chariot of Phoebus, Sol himself. His mockery only confirmed the truth, little did he know.

I did not react. Instead I said, "What is your favorite line of mine?"

"Oh, I could never forget *You might think it thundered 'neath the earth.* I can hear the very rumbling, the growling, in the bowels of the earth. Yes, the bowels."

Outside I could hear the noise of the arriving guests. I dismissed the group, telling them to come and join the others outside. I helped myself to a handful of the almonds; they were sweet and crunchy. Then I readied myself for the main event.

The courtyard was filling with people, gathering outside and milling about. A sea of white togas swam before my eyes, stark beneath the noon sun. The overall effect was softened by the women's gowns of various colors, azure and yellow and rose. As I joined them, everyone swung around to look at me, making a whorl with me in the center.

"I welcome you to the Golden House," I said. "It is your house as well as mine; it is a house for all of Rome."

I could have sworn I heard a mutter off to one side. *Fair enough. It takes up all of Rome.* But all I saw were smiles and nods.

"Please enjoy the views from here, feel the sunshine, and shortly I will lead you into the house as my guests."

Whenever there were crowds, even of ostensible friends, it was prudent to have the Praetorians on hand, discreetly stationed. Tigellinus and Faenius were on guard, wearing their dress uniforms, and their colleagues Subrius Flavus and Sulpicius Asper were nearby but keeping to the shadows of the portico.

I stopped to talk to Tigellinus and Faenius and ask if they had noticed anything out of order.

"No," Tigellinus said. "The people seem more curious than anything else."

"I heard some mention of the Circus Maximus race," said Faenius. "They chose their words carefully, for they knew I might overhear."

"Well?" I asked.

"They were . . . They looked askance at it."

"That's because you do, Faenius," said Tigellinus quickly. "Admit it. You hear what you want to."

"We all do," he answered. "That does not mean it wasn't said."

"I did not hear such words," said Tigellinus.

"As you just said, you hear what you want to."

I looked at Faenius. Of late he had changed, there was no doubt of it. His boyish face still looked honest, but what was really going on behind it? An honest face could be the best mask of all.

"Keep your ears open today, as well as your minds," I directed them, turning to seek out Sulpicius and Subrius in the shadows. I greeted them, thanking them for their service.

Sulpicius would have shrugged, but his rigid posture, as well as his rigid demeanor, made that impossible. If wood could come to life, it would look like Sulpicius. "It is my duty," he said.

Subrius smiled, fingering his sword. "We will be vigilant," he said.

He looked around, turning his stocky body, surveying the crowd. "They look harmless enough."

"As for the common people who will come to the lower terraces, we've stationed twenty other Praetorians. Those are the people likely to cause trouble," said Sulpicius, disapproval written all over him.

"Or not," I said. "It is not always obvious who will cause trouble. Carry on."

I was grateful to have such professional soldiers to guard me, but why did they make me uneasy? I remembered Caligula and his guards. I must speak to Tigellinus, who I trusted. But should I trust even him?

Shaking off these thoughts, I turned back to the sunlight and the people.

Standing together were my erstwhile guests in the imperial box, whom I had not seen after the race. Poppaea was with them. For a moment before joining them, I stood and watched her, her yellow gown complementing the rich depths of her tawny hair. The breeze stirred the delicate material, letting it hug her body, but she was still slender and her pregnancy was not betrayed.

I joined them. Vestinus was nearest Poppaea, and he greeted me effusively. "I lost money on that race," he said. "Why didn't you give me the insider's tip?"

"I couldn't have," I said. "I didn't know the odds."

"Funny, if the emperor is racing, the odds are no secret," Lateranus boomed.

"They would have been wrong," I said. The race wasn't thrown. How could anyone but me appreciate the preciousness of that?

"Why didn't you tell us?" Scaevinus was accusatory. "Why did you keep us in ignorance?"

"Maybe he was afraid he wouldn't go through with it," said Lateranus.

"You are being rude," said Poppaea. "The emperor is no coward. But neither is he obligated to announce everything he does, any more than you are."

Lateranus made a clucking sound. "Excuse *me*."

As the conversation turned elsewhere and people drifted away,

Statilia sought me out. "Pay them no mind," she said. "They are envious. Not one of them would have dared to do it, and they know it. And *you* know it. And they know that you know." She laughed, a deep, throaty laugh. "The truth is, you were impressive. At least, I was impressed." Her tone hinted that she rarely was.

She was standing very close to me, but not close enough to be improper. I could smell her perfume, a mossy smell that echoed her voice—deep and heady.

"Perhaps you are right," I said. "I will not let their remarks spoil my pride in it. I had wanted to do it for years and been forbidden to."

She gave a skeptical sound. "Forbidden? The emperor?"

"I assure you, there are many constraints on the emperor."

"Tell that to my husband, the republican."

I was startled—first at the idea, then at her boldness in proclaiming it. "There are still republicans?" It had been almost a hundred years since the end of the Republic and the ascent of Emperor Augustus, transformed from plain Octavian. There were no living people left who had experienced the Republic personally. But the idea of it, the ghost of it—did it linger?

"There are still republicans," she confirmed. "They long for it, as only someone who has never actually lived under it can. It's a fantasy, of course."

"A harmless one, I hope," I said. "Come. It is time to go inside." I motioned to Poppaea, and she joined us. The rest of the crowd fell in behind us.

I led them into the room opening directly from the courtyard, an enormous reception room with an elaborately decorated and gilded ceiling, glowing in the sunlight, its rich, multicolored marble walls from far-flung places in the empire shining. Even as large as the crowd was, the room swallowed them up.

Everyone fell silent, stunned, craning their necks to take it all in. Then an appreciative murmur swept through them. One man called out, "This is the house of a god!" but I answered, "No, it is the house of a human being. It is not Olympus. It is only our feeble imitation."

The tour continued into the west wing, with its indoor courtyard

garden and waterfall ending in the porphyry basin, then to the room
with the Ulysses mosaic and the statue of the Muse, which I called the
Literary Room in my own mind. People lingered en route, looking into
the rooms on each side, marveling at the patterns of different marbles—
intense Taenarus red, Numidian yellow, serpentine green from Egypt.
Then, turning back toward the east wing, I took them into a large reception room with frescoes of the Trojan War, a magnificent Achilles
as a centerpiece high in the ceiling. But it was Achilles only just assuming the guise of warrior—the moment when he embraced his destiny
and first took up the sword and shield at Scyros. That is the true great
moment in a person's life—to recognize one's calling and heed it. That
is what separates heroes from the mass of men.

Now we were near the octagon room. Intense light was spilling out,
drawing us to its source like a beacon. I led them in, then stepped back
into one of the alcove rooms, letting them behold the room suddenly
and personally. The great open circle to the sky let in the sun like the
eye of Zeus, beaming down hot and white. It seemed to blind them as
they stood stunned beneath it.

For long moments they were speechless, and the thrill of seeing
their wonder made me tremble. Yes, this was what art could do, what
art should do. Render us mute in awe. Beside me Poppaea took my
hand.

Finally they moved into the adjoining rooms, making space for
those following, who duplicated their astonishment and awe.

Only when the amazement had begun to wear off did the people
notice the artworks arranged around the alcove—masterpieces that at
any other time would command exclusive attention but were dimmed
by the architectural marvel above them.

By the time everyone had seen the room, it was late afternoon, and
the banquet was ready in the Hall of the Gilded Vault. The huge
room swallowed up the couches and tables and could accommodate all
the diners easily. In the middle of the room a gigantic table, with several
levels, displayed the food. Guests could walk by, make their selections,

and have the slaves bring it to their table. Likewise with the wine—amphoras of many varieties were lined up, with slaves to designate the vintages. Before people drifted to their couches—they were free to choose their own dining companions—I welcomed them.

"It is with great pleasure and pride that I invite you to dine with me here," I said. I had to raise my voice so it could carry to the far corners of the room.

While I spoke, the slaves were lighting the elaborate candelabra, for we would soon lose the daylight. The sinking sun was painting the upper walls and the vault a honey gold, but it was fading.

"Rome is a mighty empire," I said. "It stretches from the far north, Britain, to the first cataract of the Nile. From wild misty woods to hot sand. And each place provides its own delicacies. I have offerings from them here." I walked up and down in front of the table. "Here we have ham from Gaul. Salt fish from Spain. Pomegranates from Cyprus. Olives from Portugal. Dates from Jericho. Mackerel from the Hellespont. Pears from Syria. And a favorite—snails from Majorca."

A contented sigh arose from the crowd.

"And of course the usual array of local seafood—sardines, anchovies, lamprey eels, octopus, mullet. Game—hare, wild boars, deer, partridges. Fresh from gardens and fields—beets, leeks with peppermint, cucumbers, mushrooms, truffles, hearts of palm, wild flower bulbs in vinegar. Cheeses, smoked and flavored. All the nuts you could name—walnuts, beechnuts, pistachios, chestnuts, hazelnuts, almonds, pine nuts."

All this was arrayed on gold platters, artfully.

"But even the mighty Roman empire cannot command the seasons, so cherries are not here today." A faint ripple of laughter. "But we still have apples, pears, figs, grapes, and blackberries." I gestured toward the heaps of fruit. People stared, an unmistakably hungry look in their eyes.

"And last, if you crave a sweet, there is honeycomb in old wine, pudding, and pine nuts."

I stepped aside then to allow them to come up and make their choices. I retired to the set of couches at the back of the room, set off a bit from the others, where I would dine, although later I would make the round of the other couches to speak personally to the guests.

Poppaea, of course, was with me, and Vitellius took his place on one of the couches. Quintianus wandered by, looking lost, so they waved him over. Piso and Atria followed, and then a man named Antonius Natalis, a friend of Scaevinus's. Finally Vestinus and Statilia joined us, making the nine.

I stretched out on the couch, glad to get off my feet. They were still a bit sore from bracing myself in the race chariot, holding my footing on the flimsy floor.

Poppaea leaned over, whispering, "I am glad to lie down."

"As am I," I answered. That worried me—was she still not feeling well?

Antonius Natalis settled himself down across from me and leaned forward. He had a cap of dark brown shining hair that reminded me of a sable pelt. "Fine driving at the Circus," he said. "It was the ultimate surprise to look down and see you in the arena that day. But I have to confess, not knowing you were competing, I had bet on the White."

"You bet against the emperor?" asked Vestinus, false shock in his voice. "Don't you know that's illegal?"

"Is that your republican sentiment, Vestinus?" I asked lightly, as if I were joking.

"Hardly. Just good common sense!" he said, holding out his goblet to a passing slave. "A good republican is thrifty and wouldn't bet at all."

We flagged the line of slaves over to choose from their amphoras. They dutifully recited the available ones: from Tarentinum? Calenum? Albanum? Spolentinum? Falernum? Chios? Knossos?

"Take what you like, not what you ought to like. Petronius isn't here to judge you!" I said, gesturing for the Tarentinum, a light wine that did not easily make one drunk. I wanted a clear head tonight.

Atria looked to Piso to make all her choices, holding out her goblet to take the same wine and having identical food on her plate. The others made individual choices. Natalis wanted the Albanum, the dry variety. Quintianus chose Calenum, a light wine much prized by connoisseurs. He sipped it daintily.

With arched eyebrows, he smacked his lips. "I say, superlative vintage for this one!"

Everyone groaned.

"Quintianus, how precious is your taste!" said Vestinus. "As for me, give me Nomentanum, if you have anything so lowly."

"The emperor would not, my dear," said Statilia. She looked directly at me with her smoky gray eyes. "He is much too refined. You will have to resort to the slaves' store after we return home and help yourself."

Vitellius shifted his bulk, rolling almost onto his stomach, trying to find a comfortable position for his injured hip. His wide shoulders hunched as he stared at his plate. "There are worse places to go," he said. "I should know; I've availed myself of their offerings—of all sorts—many a time."

"I say, let us drink to the man who is at home wherever he finds himself," said Piso, raising his cup.

Several groups of musicians, with lyre and flute, were playing in the corners of the room, but they were barely heard over the chattering voices. Later entertainers would arrive—acrobats, dancers, actors reciting famous lines. The food tables would be removed, and the middle of the floor would belong to the entertainers.

When they arrived, it was obvious I had hired the best, and they gave spellbinding performances, enthralling the onlookers, who even stopped gossiping and drinking to watch.

At length the banquet was over. At the end of the entertainments, I walked around the various couches, speaking to people. I spotted Senecio at one of the farther corners. I went over to him, remembering what Acte had told me about his visit and his questions.

He sat up, startled, pushing his hair off his forehead.

"You should have joined us," I said, pointing to the place where I had been. "It has been a long time since I have seen you. Not since Petronius's party, I think."

"Yes. I have been away from Rome," he said.

So I hear. "And where have you been? Traveling?"

"Yes, visiting my villa near Naples. You know, waiting until the rebuilding is over here. So much noise, and then so many roads still being paved." He gave a bleating laugh.

"That's amusing?" I asked. I had no desire to put him at ease—quite the opposite.

"No, no, not really," he said. "Forgive me."

"For what?" I let the question hang. "Not for laughing, surely. For one must find humor in what goes on around us if at all possible. It is what makes life bearable."

"Indeed," he said.

I left him and made my way to the center of the room. Night had fallen, and the only light, from hundreds of oil lamps, glowed yellow. The time had come to address the entire company and present the grand finale.

"Follow me now, for the final presentation of the day," I said, then turned toward the octagon room. It was in almost complete darkness when I arrived, a black cave, aside from small lamps on the floor. Not until the crowd had gathered did the slaves light the big lampstands, flooding it with light.

Above us the ivory ceiling was in place, turning slowly. The slaves thrust flaming torches aloft to illuminate it as it rotated.

"The sun by day," I cried, "and the stars by night!"

The twelve signs of the zodiac were etched on the ivory, and from the center of the disc rose petals rained down, a shower of red and white.

The entire company was gripped with silence, standing open-mouthed in wonderment.

XXVII

They had left. The great company had departed out into the night, murmuring and clutching keepsakes—flower petals, napkins stained with rare wine, pilfered oil lamps stamped with images of the Golden House. Even senators were not above helping themselves to the lamps and even small gold platters tucked into the folds of their togas.

"They want some tangible reminder of the event," I said to Poppaea, not without satisfaction.

Around us slaves were clearing up, sweeping the crushed flower petals, carrying away the goblets and cushions.

"Come. Let us go outside," I said. I had not had a chance to observe what was happening on the lower levels yet. We stepped out onto the stone courtyard, the brisk autumn wind carrying the sound of revelry toward us. As we walked closer to the edge of the terrace, I could see torches below, could hear singing, could see lively dancing. They were celebrating, and it pleased me.

"The common people stay up later than rich people," said Poppaea. "Just listen to them! What a raucous bunch. Worse than a barnful of roosters."

I laughed. "Or peacocks. Considering that the peacock is Juno's special bird, I am surprised it has such an ugly voice."

"Everything beautiful has an ugly side."

I put my arms around her. "Not you." I drew her close.

"You don't see it in me because you don't wish to," she said. "But there are strands of things running through me that taint the rest."

"For all the gods' sake, don't tell me about them, or I will look for them and looking, find them."

"Sometimes I wish you would see them, so we would be equal—human beings with faults. For I know full well you aren't perfect."

"As you often remind me," I said. But I had always found it a comfort that she could see the things I hid from others. The three Neros—she knew them all. The daylight Nero was visible to all, as he performed his imperial duties clad in a toga. The artist Nero strove now to show himself publicly. But the third Nero, the dark one who enabled the other two to exist, who stopped at nothing to protect them—ah, that Nero must never be revealed, except to the one person who could understand him and forgive all his faults, including that one. "Come, it's too cold to stand out here. I have one more thing to show you."

"Oh, no more! I am tired." She pulled on my arm. "I want to go to bed. I want to take off these sandals. Jeweled sandals hurt!"

"Take them off, then, but come with me." She bent down and untied them, and I led her back indoors. Only a few slaves were still padding about but most lamps had been extinguished, and the ones that remained were on the floor and threw flickering light only halfway up the walls. The ceilings were lost in shadow and could have been a hundred feet high.

I led her through the largest alcove room with its splashing fountain and then from one adjoining room to the next, passing deeper into the building, away from the open south side. Voices echoed from distant rooms as the slaves finished their work, dying away as we got farther from them.

"Where are we going?" she asked, tugging at my hand. "I can't see anything. I told you, I want to go to bed. No more displays!"

We rounded a corner, and there it was—our room. A black room, high-vaulted, with delicate cream, red, and blue painted threads weaving a pattern on the dark walls. A lampstand in a corner was only partially lit, making the room feel like a cave.

"You didn't!" she said.

"I did," I answered.

"But it doesn't match the rest of the building, the frescoes," she said. "What did Fabullus say?"

"I didn't ask him to paint this room. I wanted it to be entirely different from anything else here, so we could go away to Pompeii without having to travel." The room was set up with a bed, a couch, small tables, lampstands, and braziers. "You said you wanted to go to bed," I said. "It awaits."

She walked slowly toward it, as if she did not believe what she was seeing. Finally, patting it gingerly, she sat on it.

"You see? It is real," I said.

Her face softened. "You did this to duplicate the room in my villa?"

"I know we can never duplicate what happened there, because that can happen only once. But the memory is as precious to me as a shrine." I sat down beside her.

"We were a thousand years younger then, it seems. But oh!" She reached up and touched my cheek. "I would not take back a single day we have had since then, even to restore that first rapture."

"I want the baby to be born here," I said. "Not at Antium." I need not explain why. "A new place for a new beginning. Just as Rome is starting over, so will we be."

"Hold me," she said. "Hold me, here, in our black room." She crushed herself against me, and we toppled sideways onto the soft bed. "Our black room . . ."

It was long since we had been together in total privacy or without looming worries and pressing decisions, those deadly enemies of passion. The black room would serve as our island from all that, from now on.

"*My beloved is mine and I am his*," I said into her soft ear. "You taught me those words."

She ran her hands over my back, slowly and gently. "*How fair and pleasant art thou, O love, for delights.*" Her voice was drowsy, thick.

But no words, no, not even the finest poetry, could capture the depth of my love for her. "No words," I whispered. "No words." We must have utter silence, no sound but the faint sigh of the fountain in the far room and our own breathing. Thus we create our own sacred space.

Later, Poppaea lay languid beside me, limp from our lovemaking. I cradled her, feeling her sweet warmth, her smooth flesh. But I was invigorated, quivering with energy. I wanted to get up and walk around but could not bear to leave her, to forgo even the briefest instant of lying close to her. So, while my body lay still, my mind was racing, running down forgotten—or repressed—roads.

The baby. *I want the baby to be born here. Not at Antium. A new place for a new beginning.* Lying in the dark, the smell of the fresh-painted room enveloping me—stronger than Poppaea's myrrh perfume—I felt that everything was beginning anew. The Fire had cleansed Rome and given it a rebirth.

But the old Rome? Did it linger on in survivors' minds, unscorched by the purifying flames? The old patrician families, the ones going back hundreds of years—they were still the pillars and foundations of Rome, not buildings. I could update building codes but not citizens' moral codes and prejudices.

The baby, coming now in a few months. The last of the dynasty founded by Julius Caesar—my five-times-great-uncle—would take his place on the stage of history. All the rest were gone. Some by natural causes and others by political ones. I myself had removed several of my cousins from the family tree, bearing in mind Augustus's warning, *It is not good to have too many Caesars.* So now there remained only one living male direct descendant of Augustus—me. The weight of the entire dynasty hung around my neck like a spiked collar.

Did I regret having pruned those branches? I never regretted an act of survival, for the cousins would have done the same to me—indeed, they wanted to. But having survived my mother's attempts on me, no one else came close to her as a threat. I had learned from the best and could protect myself against all others.

The baby. Would his life be in jeopardy from the moment he arrived? I was a little child when Caligula tried to drown me and not much older when Messalina sent assassins to kill me in the cradle. Not only is it not good to have too many Caesars, just being a Caesar is dangerous.

I must be here to guard him. I had been all alone—my father dead, my mother exiled, leaving me to the mercy of others. My mother . . . I wonder why she had no other children. She was young enough—she was only thirteen when she married. And the list of her lovers, reputed or real, was enough to sire a stable of children.

Against my will I started to laugh, and Poppaea stirred. I stifled the laugh as best I could. But one of Mother's lovers was supposedly Seneca, and the thought of that pompous, sanctimonious philosopher in the role of lover was so comical I guffawed. Oh, the things Mother did to advance her schemes! But surely, bedding down with Seneca must have tested even her resolve.

But was that worse than Claudius? And what about Rubellius Plautus, a cousin eyeing the throne? He was younger, at least. And then there was her own brother, Caligula. Yes, my mad uncle and my mother.

How was it she had only me? Were there others, done away with in the dark of the moon? Spirited away to be exposed on a hillside or drowned by an obliging midwife? Anything could be true.

But that was over now. All that was over, the perpetrators of such unnatural vice dead and gone. The Fire swept over their tombs and blew away their spirits, and Rome was clean again.

XXVIII

The welcoming reception at the Golden House caught the last of the warm weather, convincing me that Sol himself had assured its success. Now he retired behind his bank of clouds and a chill descended on Rome, foretelling winter. But much of the rebuilding had progressed to the point that people would not be unsheltered in the cold—it had happened at miraculous speed. And the miracle in back of it was money.

Money. We were only halfway through all that needed to be done, but already the bottom of the treasury could be glimpsed, shiny and bald. I would have to raise more, somehow.

But the building continued apace, and soon we were able to move into the lower quarters of the Golden House, finished enough to let us live there. The private rooms overlooked the lake, so its water reflected light into the interior, dappled rays that played on the ceilings and walls. The new furniture arrived daily, fresh from the workshops, gleaming with ivory, ebony, and silver fittings. I had dispatched agents to Greece to procure artworks, particularly bronzes. I did not want to move the ones already at Sublaqueum and Antium, because I wanted them still there to greet me.

Poppaea continued to be often exhausted, with little appetite. There were some days when she was content just to sit, wrapped in a soft wool robe, and look out at the lake. Other days when she seemed like her old self, she rose and attended to business. Sporus, her lookalike, teased her about it, offering to be active when she rested and to rest when she was active.

"So there will always be a Poppaea on duty," he said. "Would you like me to accompany the emperor on his official appearances? Perhaps no one would be the wiser."

"Until you spoke and your voice gave you away," she said, laughing. "So you would have to be silent."

"Sporus, silent?" I said. "That would be a rare occurrence." Sporus was one who chattered a great deal, but unlike many who did, he was amusing rather than annoying.

Privately I asked him about Poppaea. He had known her since childhood and was more familiar with her longtime habits than I was. "Has this ever happened before?" I said.

"No," he said. "Yet she does not seem ill, just tired and lacking in strength."

"Not all the time," I said.

"It comes and goes," he admitted. "It must be the pregnancy."

"This did not happen at her last pregnancy."

He blushed. "You need to ask a midwife, not me."

Perhaps I would. In the meantime I watched her closely and tried not to show alarm. I also stayed nearby, conducting most of the imperial business in an inner workroom.

The literary gatherings would resume in the new year, and each of us was assigned the task of writing a satirical poem about one of the members, after drawing the names from a pot. I had drawn Afranius Quintianus. That would be easy. The man was a walking butt of jokes as it was; I could hardly improve on the original.

I was working late one night—Poppaea had retired early—sitting in the snuggest of the rooms, small enough to be easily warmed by one brazier. I closed my eyes and pictured Quintianus, hoping for inspiration. There he loomed in my inner eye—a large, bulky man with unruly curls that fell like nettles around his face and down his neck. In them he liked to twist flowers and fake pearls, making him look like Medusa rather than the Apollo he was aiming for. He had feet the size of triremes, which he made even larger by the thick-soled sandals he favored. His verse was, surprisingly, light and nimble. So I would write a poem contrasting his earthly form with his intellectual one.

> *Phoebus cannot arise; he lies caught in the thicket of your hair;*
> *He is imprisoned there, fighting to extricate himself;*
> *But close to your ear, he whispers his poetry . . .*

I went on to the feet, to the oversized tunics he fancied, each one having a god entrapped within, a god that served to inspire Quintianus's writing.

I reread it. It would do. It was meant to be funny, nothing more. There would doubtless be more clever ones composed for the evening, but I need not labor on it any longer. I set it aside.

I wanted to write a poem to Poppaea. A gift for her, as she was awash in jewels and luxuries, but a personal poem was a unique gift. I pulled a fresh piece of paper in front of me. Then I sat staring at it.

Poppaea . . . fairer than the air of summer . . . clear white star of evening . . . intoxicating beauty . . .

It was no use. No phrase came to mind. I leaned my head on my elbows and stared out the window. Even this small room had a view of the lake, and it was a sheet of shimmering light from the moon overhead.

The moon. Something about the moon. I found my Sappho scroll—didn't she write something about the moon? A fragment . . . an evocative line? I unrolled it and looked.

> *The stars around the beautiful moon*
> *Hiding their glittering forms*
> *Whenever she shines full on earth . . .*
> *Silver . . .*

I went to the window and looked up at the inky sky. It was true; the moon made the stars near her invisible. As Poppaea did when she stood next to any other woman.

But I couldn't copy Sappho, and my own words were clumsy beside hers. I began to read other poems; it was hard not to.

I came to one on Aphrodite. It jolted me.

Come to me now, then, free me
From aching care, and win me
All my heart longs to win.

Acte and I had recited those lines when we first spoke, and instantly we knew one another for close spirits. So long ago . . . Britannicus was still alive, Octavia still my wife, I barely emperor.

Acte. I had never replied to her note warning me about Senecio's visit. I owed her a response. But Poppaea had reacted so jealously that I had set it aside to answer later. The truth was, I would prefer to thank her in person, but that was unlikely to be. Seeing her in the field station, speaking to her, had been so awkward and difficult for me that I was loath to do it again. Yet if we spoke again, after a bit it might be more natural, and there was so much left hanging, so much unsaid that I longed to say.

I would write the note another time. I would write the poem another time. Clearly the Muse was not with me tonight.

The light in the brazier was throbbing, its coals glowing. I welcomed the warmth. I understood why Augustus wrapped his legs with wool strips in the winter. But he was so mocked for it that I did not want to follow his practice. So I shivered.

The coals threw a reddish glow on the painted walls, but the rest of the chamber was dim. I put my head down and rested. It was late. But I was not ready for bed. I thought of the Golden House and its frescoes . . . Fabullus was now finishing in the Hector room . . . of the name we would choose for the baby . . . of the new coinage I had approved showing the rebuilt Temple of Vesta, attesting to Rome's recovery. I jerked my head. I had fallen asleep. But I saw, briefly, a dark shape in the corner of the room. It moved furtively. I turned to look, and for an instant I saw myself, a shadowed figure that stared back at me. Then it was gone.

Obviously it was a dream. Time to go to bed, Nero, I told myself.
You are sleeping at the desk.

A round us the palace and its environs rose, the finishing touches
now dusting it with splendor that the shell had only promised.
The buildings surrounding the lake had been faced in red-veined marble, and the triple colonnades linking it to the Via Sacra and the Forum
were spreading their arches. The rest of Rome was keeping pace. By
next summer the last damages of the Fire would be gone, just a memory. We would be ready to host the second Neronian Games in the
autumn. And the summer following, to ceremonially receive King Tiridates, the Armenian king whose obeisance would mark the end of all
war in the empire.

That didn't, of course, mean there was no trouble, nor enemies. I
had promised in my inaugural speech to the Senate that there would
be no more secret treason trials as there had been under Claudius, and
I had kept my word. But over the years several spy networks had grown
up. Tigellinus ran the largest one and reported everything to me, so in
a way it was my network. Poppaea had her own, and many of the senators likewise. Unfortunately, the spies were necessary to investigate
malcontents and rumors. Rumors had almost done me in with blame
for the Fire, and failure to keep abreast of them was foolhardy.

So I was not surprised when Tigellinus requested a meeting with
me one chilly morning. He strode into the larger workroom, the one
meant for meetings of the Consilium. He looked around approvingly.
"Ah," he said, "this is an opulent place to do business." He ran his hand
over a bronze bust of Alexander, looking the man in the eye. "If you
want to rule the world, that is."

"I do rule the world." Why not say it?

"Yes, you do." He eyed a chair, and I motioned for him to sit. He
sank down, flexing his strong arms as he grabbed the carved lions'
heads adorning the chair. "And this setting is entirely worthy of your
position."

I waited.

"So, I have a report . . ." He fished in his leather satchel and brought out a sheaf of papers. He started to riffle through them.

"Why don't you just summarize what's in them?" I asked. Get on with it.

Instead of complying with a smile, he looked away. "Very well. If you want the details, then—" He motioned to the papers.

"I can consult them if need be."

"Ah. Well, my first report is a happy one. The people are still talking about your race in the Circus. They are delighted about it. The senators less so."

"Oh. Them. Of course. I know that."

"There is . . . err . . . grumbling about the space the Golden House is taking up."

"Grumbling by whom?" The senators again, obviously.

"Uh . . . by many people. The poor as well as the rich."

"But it isn't finished yet. The parks have yet to open. When they can use them, they will be content."

"I hope you are right," he said. He brightened. "The latrines are very popular."

Ah. The latrines.

"The fancy one near Caesar's Forum is much frequented."

It ought to be. I had made it especially attractive—as much as a latrine could be.

"It is a prime site to place spies. People are unguarded in there; they'll speak more freely than at a tavern. They seem to feel that anything they say while baring their privates is . . . private. Not so."

"So, what have you heard?"

"It's Lucan."

"Lucan?"

"Yes. He was in there a few days ago and, after letting loose a tremendous fart, quoted the line from your poem." Now he glanced at his notes. "He said, *You would have thought it thundered 'neath the earth.* Since your poem has been published and widely read, the other patrons recognized it, gathered their tunics and togas around them, and rushed out."

"He mocked my poem?"

"Yes. And took pleasure in doing so. He laughed and laughed as the people fled."

He had quoted the line to me as his favorite. The bastard!

"And I have a copy of his latest work on the *Civil War*. Books eight and nine. He doesn't bother to hide his republican leanings."

"Oh, why do you find these things?" I cried out. "First Seneca's plays, now this!" It was painful, painful.

"Would you rather not know? Be ignorant of what your erstwhile friends are writing and thinking about you?"

"No." But oh! To have them thinking it!

"I have even heard that he's writing something else, something worse, about you. But I haven't been able to get my hands on it yet."

"Maybe it's not true."

"For your sake I hope not. But if it is true, I'll find it."

XXIX

Lucan. The young man with a prodigious talent, and Seneca's nephew. Alone of the people in the writing circle, he would take his place in Roman literature; I was sure of it. I had encouraged him and taken his suggestions and criticisms of my own work to heart, as someone whose opinions mattered.

And he had always respected me. More than respected me, had praised me in his own poetry, dedicating the first book of the *Civil War* to me, even saying I would ascend to the realm of the gods.

But . . . he had changed. He had been gruff and abrupt at the Golden House. And was that where he had cited *You would think it thundered 'neath the earth* as his favorite of my lines? Mocking me, I now knew.

I looked out the window to the pavilion of the Golden House up on its hill. The workmen had finished with the last foundations for the terraced gardens; next spring they would be planted and the architectural vision come to life.

I command all this. I spoke true to Tigellinus—I do rule the world. I command fleets and legions. So why fret over what someone has said about my poetry?

I turned away from the view and paced in the room. The marble floor was chilly; it seemed to store the cold in its whiteness. Because my poetry is me. *Even the emperorship is not uniquely me like my poetry, because other men can wear the title "emperor."*

But this is foolish, juvenile. And besides, no one artist is universally admired. Some say Homer is boring, others that Euripides is too emotional.

As I was attempting to talk myself out of my consternation, Poppaea came into the room and caught me midpace.

"What is troubling you?" she asked, coming over and laying her hand on my shoulder, stilling my movement.

"Nothing," I said. It was too petty to tell; too embarrassing to admit how it bothered me. I turned and looked at her. She was pale but seemed better. "You look like your old self." Not quite true.

"I feel stronger," she said. She looked around. "This room is finished," she said. "When did that happen?"

"You have been missing quite a few things," I said. "But is it not good to have a few surprises?"

She laughed, then made her way over to one of the couches, stretched out on it, and said, "How lovely to lie on a new couch." She waved her arms. "Have some figs and cheese brought. I am actually hungry."

Soon a slave appeared with a tray heaped with not only figs and cheese but also bread and sausage. A second slave brought cups and a jug of juice.

I took a piece of cheese. It had a tangy flavor. A rich, piquant zing.

Tangy . . . piquant . . . strong flavors that could cover other flavors.

Seneca is convinced someone is trying to poison him. Perhaps it was not Seneca who was being poisoned but Seneca who was himself a poisoner. Or Lucan, whose dislike of me was now exposed. I almost dropped the cheese. Not that this cheese was poisoned, but any strong flavor could serve to disguise a telltale taste.

Was Poppaea being poisoned? The strange weakness and lethargy that came and went, could it be the subtle workings of poison?

"What are you staring at?" Poppaea asked. "You look as if you had seen a spirit. Really, what's wrong with you? You are acting very strange this morning."

I did not want to alarm her, but I said, "This weakness and feeling of illness . . . when is it strongest?"

She shook her head. "I don't know."

"Think!" I ordered her, so curtly that she winced.

"Perhaps . . . a few hours after I eat. And it lasts until the next morning."

"Does it wear off gradually or all at once?"

"Sometimes one way, sometimes another."

"Which is more usual?"

"I don't know. Why are you asking me these questions? I came to join you to have a pleasant morning, and instead you act angry and interrogate me." She stood up. "I am leaving."

"I am angry, but not at you. And you are not leaving. You will stay here while I send for Andromachus."

"I've had enough physicians. They didn't help. They didn't know how to treat my illness."

"That was because they didn't know what to look for. Now this one will." I grabbed her arm and made her sit back on the couch.

Would my sudden suspicions be confirmed? I dreaded the answer.

Andromachus took his time about coming. The tall Cretan had moved into the palace with us and had several suites of rooms, but they were a far distance from ours that faced the lake. Finally he was announced and came forward in his usual dignified manner.

"And what does Caesar require?" he asked, bowing. He was looking at me with his keen eyes. Although he was my personal physician, I saw him seldom, as I was rarely sick.

"It's not me," I said. "It is my wife."

Now he turned and observed her. Then he moved closer, as if he were inspecting a painting. "Wan color. Puffy eyelids." He took her wrist and rotated it. "Limp muscles. May I ask you to stand up?"

Poppaea obeyed. He turned her around and made her balance on one leg.

"Hmm. Of course, she is pregnant, and that changes the body."

"You can speak directly to me, Andromachus," she said. "My hearing hasn't failed—yet."

"Of course, Augusta. I see that you are suffering from some upset of the natural courses of the body. How much to blame on the pregnancy I cannot say."

"I felt well throughout my last pregnancy."

"We know all pregnancies are different, just as all children are different. They manifest their differences even in the womb. And your last was a girl. Perhaps this means this one is a boy."

"Boys!" I laughed. "Troublemakers from the start." But my words covered my anxiety. I was not convinced pregnancy was the answer. "Shall we retire to more private quarters?" I said, eyeing the guards standing around the perimeters of the room. *Tigellinus has spies everywhere.* And not just Tigellinus.

In our inmost room, with only one entrance and sealed off by a series of doors, we could speak freely. And I did.

"Is she being poisoned?" I asked.

Poppaea gasped. Andromachus did not.

"Possibly," he said.

"You are the expert on poisons," I said.

"I am an expert on the treatment, not the poisons themselves," he countered. "You know my special antidote, which covers all poisons."

"Yes, yes. Sixty-one ingredients. It's in your poem. But for all the gods' sake, why did you write the recipe in the form of an elegiac poem?"

He smiled and swayed slightly on his feet, like a supple reed. "Poetry will last longer than prose," he said. "And it's harder to alter. Changing it would mess up the meter of the verse."

Perhaps I should have included him in my writers' group, then—this scientist who wrote his formulas in verse.

Naturally he produced a copy of it. He was a true writer, then. Our eagerness to display our art is ever present. Now he unrolled it and began reading the dedication to me. "'Hear of the force of the antidote with many ingredients, Caesar, giver of freedom that knows no fear, hear, Nero!'"

Flattery. Didn't Lucan write, *every deity / will yield to you, to your decision nature will leave / which god you wish to be?* Now the words taunted me, stung, trumpeting his hypocrisy.

"You needn't read it all. Just remind me of the ingredients. I remember that squill bulbs, opium, and pepper were main ones."

"Ah, but you have left out the secret one, the one that crowns the whole. Chopped vipers!" He beamed.

Poppaea almost retched. "Now I *do* feel as if I will vomit. I won't take such a concoction."

"You may not need to," Andromachus said. "Unless it is used as an antidote, it can cause harm in itself. So we would need to prove you have been ingesting poison. Or exposed to it—it can be in ointments or even in the air. It can be in clothes, or on surfaces—"

"Enough, enough!" I said. "There is someone who will know. And we will go there, together."

Locusta. The queen of poisoners. I had long owed her a visit.

The fields were quiet and autumnal after we left Rome behind, heading north on the Via Flaminia toward Locusta's establishment, her academy of pharmacology, as she called it. I called it the college of poison. I could call it whatever I liked, since I was its patron. Yes, I had set her up in business in gratitude and acknowledgment that I owed my life to her skills and my throne as well. I had outbid my opponents in vying for her expertise. Now I was emperor and they were ashes. Afterward I had freed her from the dreary round of imprisonments and releases that she had endured at the hands of the capricious imperial family. She had earned her safe haven. I had hoped never to need her actual services again but to keep her as a consultant in case lesser Locustas targeted me.

The harvest was in, the countryside resting, clothed in shades of soothing brown, dull green, and gray. The land lay hushed and satiated. It had been a plentiful harvest this year, especially for grapes, causing a run on amphoras when the vintage was ready.

We trundled along the paved road in the carriage that was best for Poppaea's condition. Locusta's academy was some distance outside Rome. Through the windows came the tangy scent of fallen apples, and, more pungently, rotting pears under trees. As we came to the hills, where fields gave way to orchards, and began to climb, I could see wild meadows rippling under the autumn wind, and crows flapping overhead, black shadows against the cloudless sky.

At the top of a gentle hill Locusta's establishment spread out, covering the entire area. There were several buildings, long low ones, and three with glass sides. Not entirely glass, of course, no one sheet of glass could ever be that large, but many panes soldered together. There were also long rectangular plots with neat planted rows, some plants still green. A number of people were working in the rows, pruning, raking, and watering. We came to a stop, and the people looked up, curious. I saw a number of other carriages and horses there; business was apparently brisk. Was Lucan one of the customers?

A barrel-shaped woman came hustling over to us, frowning. She was going to tell us to park elsewhere or that the business was closed for today. Her mouth was open to say it when I stepped out. She shrieked. Then she fell onto her knees.

"Oh, oh! Caesar, Caesar, I never thought to see you—like this—an arm's length away—"

Once such reactions were flattering. Then amusing. Now they were merely tiresome. I would have to soothe her.

"Please rise," I said. "What is your name?" That usually pleased them, to be asked their names.

"Portia," she said. "Oh, oh—"

Before she could go on, I said, "I have come to see your mistress. Please direct us to her."

Confused and giddy, Portia pointed to one of the smaller buildings and led us there. She kept stumbling over her own feet. Bowing and bending, she left us at the door and went to warn Locusta. But she need not have worried; Locusta would not have been flustered. Nothing flustered Locusta.

Soon Locusta, tall and magisterial, appeared at the door. She smiled.

"You are come at last!" she said. "Welcome, welcome!"

"I promised," I said. "And I keep my promises." I indicated Poppaea and Andromachus. "I have brought guests. My wife, the Augusta, and my personal physician, Andromachus of Crete."

"All the more welcome," she said. "Come."

She led us through several rooms with shelves of glass vials, vases, jugs, and bottles until we came to a large chamber that looked like an office. There was a long trestle table, with scrolls, tablets, pens, and inks at the ready. Comfortable chairs were scattered about. Two bronze braziers glowed with welcome warmth.

"As you can see, I have used your bounty well," she said, indicating the room. "If you care to see my books——"

I laughed. "I have not come as a landlord but as a friend. And as someone seeking a consultation."

Her expression did not change. She showed neither alarm nor curiosity. She merely smiled reassuringly. "Speak what is on your mind. I shall try to answer."

"My wife is not well. Whether it is by natural means or unnatural, that is what we want to know."

"Tell me all," she said, and we did. She listened intently.

"You were wise to come to me," she said. "And you, Andromachus, to warn that an antidote, where one is not needed, can become a poison itself." She sighed and addressed Poppaea directly. "Your symptoms are vague. They do not fit the known pattern of familiar poisons. And you have suffered from this for several months. It is much more difficult to make a slow-acting poison than a fast one. Of course, if it is fed in continual small doses . . . but that requires that the poisoner act over and over and over, without being detected. Someone would have to live with you in order to have that opportunity and proximity."

"Then perhaps we should give the antidote as a general precaution," said Andromachus. "As I say in the preface to my recipe, it gives freedom from fear."

"I am not convinced about the efficacy of the antidote," she said, "begging your pardon. I would have to see it demonstrated to believe it. And I understood that your antidote was specific only against animal poisons."

"Not so, not only animals. I will bring some samples and we can test them against your poisons composed of either plants or animals," he said. "We can use pigs and goats."

She shot him a look. "Yes, that is what I use as testers. Did you think otherwise? People, perhaps?"

He spread his hands. "Well, one hears things . . . with someone as famous as you, naturally things get exaggerated."

"You are famous yourself," she said kindly. "But I believe the emperor has another physician with a rival antidote remedy. What of him?"

Andromachus laughed dismissively. "Oh, Xenocrates of Aphrodisias? His remedy is disgusting—eating human livers and the secretions of hippopotami and elephants."

"Obviously a quack," said Locusta.

"I'm not so sure," I said. "Maybe he should come and join in with the testing."

"All this talk is not helping me!" cried Poppaea. "I want your diagnosis. That is all I care about."

Locusta thought a moment. "I cannot confirm that you are being poisoned. There is no convincing proof of it for now."

Poppaea almost burst into tears, then controlled herself. "So all I can do is wait? See if I get worse?"

"For now, yes," Locusta said. "That, hard as it may be, is the safest route to take." She sent for a slave and ordered some food and drink. "You may rest assured it harbors nothing harmful," she told Poppaea. "While you and Andromachus stay here, I would like to show the emperor my academy. After all, it may be a long time before he returns. And I think what I have done will impress him."

She proudly led me inside the sheltered brick buildings, where rows and rows of plants were growing in pots—hemlock, henbane, tansy, monkshood, oleander, azaleas, small yews. "We bring them outdoors most of the year, but this way the winter does not end our business," she said. Another building was kept dim and dank. This housed beds of lethal mushrooms—the death cap with its ghostly white crown, the death angel, and several others. "There's no antidote to these," she said cheerfully. *Yes, just ask Claudius.*

Another kept bees, but not ordinary ones: these were fed on oleanders and azaleas to produce poisonous honey. A barn had rows of cages with snakes, spiders, toads, and scorpions. Tanks held stinging jellyfish, sea snakes, sea anemones, the lovely striped zebrafish of the Red Sea, with poison in its fins.

"You can see why I need such a large staff," she said. "Feeding the spiders is particularly demanding. They eat constantly!"

"Yes, I can see that. Tell me, how is business?"

"Doing well. I am forever grateful to you for making it possible for me to practice openly."

"It was the least I could do," I said. "Since you are the foremost in this . . . profession, has anyone come to see you asking about—me?"

She frowned. "No. You know I would come immediately to Rome to tell you."

"A would-be poisoner might realize that and go to someone else. Someone not so skilled but not so loyal to me."

"This is not an idle question, then. Do you have suspicions? Is there any reason to think you are in danger?"

"No . . . it's just a feeling I have, an apprehension." *An overblown one. Mocking my poem with a fart is not the same as poisoning me. Writing a play about Octavia does not mean the author is out to kill me.* But still . . . "It is probably just my imagination."

"An emperor needs an overalert imagination if he is to survive," she said. "Keep a close watch. I promise to let you know if anyone comes to me or if I hear anything."

XXX

LOCUSTA

In the falling dusk I watched the imperial carriage pull away and head down the hill. The wheels chewed at the gravel path, and the carriage would lurch until it reached the paved road farther on.

The carriage. Its swaying and jolting was a far cry from the chariot Nero had driven at the Circus Maximus. Then he had flown like the wind, so I heard. Like everyone else, I have my spies. I could hardly operate without them. But I did not need spies to report his race to me. All of Rome was buzzing about it. Knowing him as I did, I imagined that for those brief moments he had transcended time and earthly cares. But it had ended abruptly when he crossed the finish line. Now he was awash in cares again—the burden of being emperor. He stays awake so that we might sleep in peace.

If, all those years ago when the prospect of being emperor was a poison mushroom away, did he have any comprehension of what was waiting on the other side? No, how could he? He was just sixteen and saw only the escape that being emperor offered—escape from bondage to his mother, from strictures and denied dreams. Now he had entered fully into another kind of bondage, with no deliverance as long as he lived. Emperors did not retire into private life, like philosophers. There was only one retirement for an emperor— the grave. And if he is lucky, a natural descent into it at an advanced age.

But the past record for that was not encouraging. There were rumors, never proved, that Augustus was helped into his divinity by Livia, that Tiberius was put onto Charon's boat by Caligula. Caligula himself was assassinated in broad daylight.

Claudius at night at a banquet. And we all know what happened to Julius Caesar.

If I believed that the gods were kindly and cared for our welfare, I would sacrifice and pray, *Protect him, protect him, do not let him come to harm!* But they are oblivious to us and our needs and concerns. There is no help in heaven. We must help ourselves, and that is all there is for us.

It was almost dark, and lamps had been lit inside the main building. A mist was rising from the valley, obliterating the features below. The carriage would have to plunge into the mist; the trip back to Rome would be a slow one. I shivered and hurried into the building.

Several workers were waiting to talk to me. I took them in turn. A gardener was concerned about the tansy.

"I brought it inside two weeks ago, but it is drooping anyway," he said. "I have been careful not to overwater."

"Do we still have stocks outside?" I asked.

"A few. There is always a reserve that survives the winter."

"Keep a watch. Cover those at night to blunt the cold. Then if the potted ones die, we will still have the outdoor ones." Tansy was the tried-and-true remedy for ending pregnancies. It was much in demand.

Another person was concerned about the henbane. "There are too many flowers," she said. "It is using all its strength in flowering and the leaves will be cheated."

"Then pinch them off, but wear gloves." I laughed. "The pretty white flowers will make a nice bouquet, but remember that the water they are in will be poisonous. Dispose of it where it won't do harm." Henbane caused the heart to beat so hard it killed itself.

A man complained about the jellyfish. "I got a vicious sting from one of them."

"You must have forgotten your gloves."

"No. He stung right through them." He held up his hand, covered with red welts.

Problems, problems. They were constant in this business. But I wouldn't want to do anything else.

I retired to my workroom and went over the books for orders and payments. Business was constant—poisonings knew no seasons, which was why I had to have indoor facilities. Illnesses knew no seasons, either, and the curative potions I could concoct were at least half my business and a growing one. Perhaps in a little while it would be my main business, bringing health and freedom to those trapped in a cage of sickness.

In the yellow lamplight I noticed an order for powdered cobra venom. That was unusual. I looked more closely. I did not recognize the customer's name, but the address was Rome. I called my secretary.

"Do you recognize this name?" I asked, pointing to it.

He shook his head.

"Did we fill the order?"

"No," he said. "We don't stock it."

"That's because it is hardly the drug of choice, unless you have fangs. If you just drink it, it is harmless. So someone would have to dissolve it, then smear it into an open wound. Hardly very subtle."

"Perhaps he wanted to commit suicide."

"There are easier and cheaper ways. Powdered venom is horribly expensive—it has to be imported from India. The snake charmers there milk the cobras." I shuddered. "Not for the faint of heart." I rattled the order book. "Even if we had it, he probably couldn't have afforded it." I had another thought. "Have you received any inquiries other than written ones?"

"Someone appeared a week or so ago, asking vague questions. I took him for a potential business rival, so I told him nothing and sent him on his way."

"I see. Next time let me know." I must be vigilant. I sensed a halo of danger around the emperor.

XXXI

ACTE

When the official summons came from the palace, for an instant I believed he had sent it. The soldier who delivered it in its shining cylinder served the personal dispatches of the imperial household, not the political ones.

Once inside the privacy of my workroom, opening it with unsteady hands, I saw the seal and thought, Yes! He has called for me. But when I broke it and unrolled the letter, it was not from him. It was from *her*.

How did she even know who I was or where I was? But there was probably nothing mysterious about it. She must have intercepted the letter I had sent Nero warning him about Senecio. Perhaps he had never even had the chance to see it. But I did not regret sending it, trying to warn him. And unappealing as the prospect of meeting Poppaea was, it would give me the chance to deliver the message about Senecio again. I would tell her, and whatever her faults, Nero's well-being would be her paramount concern.

Now I looked more closely at the details. The Augusta requested my presence in three days at the lake location of the Golden House, at the eighth hour.

That was all. No explanation of what or why. But I knew it wasn't to order amphoras or tiles.

* * *

I stood in the outer atrium of the famous—or infamous—Golden House. Even in Velitrae, there was constant talk about it. Amazement at its glittering magical beauty. But there were other less laudatory murmurs. *It's an extravagance and an insult to the people who were made homeless by the fire. Homeless first by the fire, now by the Golden House that takes up the whole center of the city.* And *it shows what he considers important—experiments in architecture. A disgrace!*

It seemed many had quickly forgotten all his efforts to help after the Fire. They hadn't seen it; I had. But those efforts weren't advertised like the Golden House. They were seen once, fleetingly, while the bulk of the palace remained, tauntingly, every day.

I took advantage of the visit to see the inside for myself. I looked around, my eyes taking in the many colored marbles on the walls and the floor, the open view straight through the columns and out into the sunlight. It was dazzling, if overwhelming. Its scale was so large it made me feel small. Perhaps that was the intention of it.

"You are to come with me," a voice behind me announced. I turned and stood up. Poppaea herself! But no . . . the voice was a man's.

He smiled. The face was Poppaea's? Of course not. But it disoriented me. Perhaps that, like the huge atrium, was the purpose of having such an attendant—to unsettle visitors.

I followed him through what seemed miles of corridors and connected rooms, until we reached large gilded doors, the apartments of the Augusta. He flung them open, only to reveal another long corridor. He led me down that one until we finally reached a room that glinted with reflected light from the choppy waves on the artificial lake outside, stirred by a stiff breeze. Seated at the far end, like an eastern idol, was a woman who looked like the attendant. But her color was pale and her arm appeared thin when she waved me forward. *So this is the legendary Poppaea, the most beautiful woman in Rome, the second Helen.* I was prepared to disagree. But as I came closer and her features came into focus, I had to admit it—she was indeed glorious, even in a diminished state, as she was also clearly unwell.

"Thank you, Sporus," she said to the attendant. Then she turned to me. "Do I address Claudia Acte?" she asked. Her voice was rich, beguiling, melodic.

"Yes, Augusta." I bowed.

"Come closer," she said. "I want to look at you."

I took a few steps nearer, coming to within ten feet of her. Her chair, set on a dais, enabled her to look down at me. For long moments she said nothing. I had a desire to turn and leave.

"What does the Augusta require of me?" I finally asked.

"It is not for you to ask me questions," she said. She made me wait longer. Then slowly, carefully, she descended from the regal chair. Suddenly her manner changed, like switching masks. "I wanted to thank you for your warning about Senecio," she said. "The emperor is grateful to you. As am I."

"It was my duty," I said before thinking. That was true, but only a small part of it. I had been so alarmed at the thought of a plot against him that I had not slept that night. And I still shivered thinking of Senecio's sly grin.

She turned and walked toward a group of couches in another part of the enormous room, which was big enough to host a dinner, a lecture, and acrobatic acts simultaneously. She sank down on an especially cushioned couch and beckoned me to take the one nearest her. Her small feet barely touched the ground, and she lay back on the couch, arranging her gown to cover them.

Without openly staring, I tried to steal looks at her clothes, her jewelry, her face. As she found a comfortable position, I suddenly saw that she was pregnant. The sight sent a jolt through me. I did not want to see it. Nor did I want to see her. But she was the empress and could command me.

She leaned toward me as if we were friends. "Yes, we are grateful. One cannot be too careful. We would appreciate it if you would continue to keep us apprised of any such information."

We are grateful . . . *we* would appreciate . . . So did she mean I must now report to him through her? No more private correspondence to the emperor?

"I will, though I hope there is no further need to. And if there is, the official courier is not the best way to send it. You should provide me with a trusted channel to send it through."

"I will. And next time I will not send the soldier."

Next time. Did there have to be a next time?

"But I had only the information of your work address to summon you. From now on . . ." She clapped for a slave and ordered sweet wine, figs, and cheese without asking me what, if anything, I wanted. She swung around on the couch, and her eyes bored into me. "Are you wondering where the emperor is?"

I had been but would hardly say so. "I came to see you," I said. "Not the emperor."

"He's at Ostia for the day," she said. "I thought it would be better if we had our privacy."

But so far she had said absolutely nothing that he could not hear.

"As you wish, Augusta."

"It is as I wish," she said. "And I wished to see you for myself. Now that I have, I can forget all about you. As a rival for the emperor's affection, I mean. I see that you are harmless."

I wanted to say, *It is only the emperor who can truly know how harmless I am. Only Lucius. You never knew him as Lucius, but I did. I do. My Lucius.*

I was suddenly seized with the desire to laugh and sweep my hand around the opulent room and say, *This could have all been mine. Me in the chair on the dais. My head on gold coins. Me draped in jewelry. Me as Augusta. But I walked away.* Oh, what would her face have looked like then?

"Indeed I am, Augusta. Indeed I am." I smiled.

The only thing I envied her, with a sharp sorrow, was that she carried his child. The rest she could have.

XXXII

NERO

The visit to Locusta had allayed my fears but only somewhat. That she was unable to pronounce definitively that yes, poison was at work was reassuring. But she did not rule it out, either.

Were we to imitate Seneca and eat only bread made in our presence and drink only water from running streams? Perhaps we should try it and see if Poppaea improved.

The journey back to Rome, in the swirling fog, had taken a very long time, but it had been bracing to leave the city for a bit. I could think better away from it. As the carriage bumped and rumbled, I began plans for next spring, when the baby would be born and the rebuilding of Rome finished, with ceremonies to commemorate that. There would be much to celebrate—that less than a year after the catastrophe, Rome had recovered, with improvements and new amenities. And beyond that, there were innovative architectural experiments to add another dimension to the city, not the least of which was the Golden House.

And in the autumn, we would have the second Neronian Games. I would build, perhaps, a new stadium where they could be held. And this time I would race chariots myself. By the time we rolled into the palace gates long past midnight, I had it all planned.

The next day, at my orders, we went on what I laughingly called the Seneca Diet.

"We will eat only fruit we have peeled ourselves, bread that can be made from grain in special guarded fields, ground in front of us, and baked in a little oven we'll install in our quarters, drink only water from a running stream," I told Poppaea.

She rolled her eyes. "Shall we just move into the kitchen, then?"

"This is for you. You do want to recover, don't you? Or prove that it isn't poison?"

"Yes," she said. "More than anything."

"Then we will have to follow this plan for a while." I sighed and patted my stomach. "This will ensure I finally lose weight," I said. "I have not made much headway so far."

I needed to shed a lot more before I was svelte again. The honeyed cakes, the wine, the roasted piglets . . . all had done their worst. In an effort to shame myself into action I had allowed unflattering profiles of myself to be portrayed on coins, exaggerating my double chin. It had not worked; all it did was broadcast to people who had never seen me that the emperor was portly.

I had neglected my exercise, too. Too busy in rebuilding Rome to attend to that. Well, the upcoming Neronian Games would provide the incentive I needed.

We followed this dreary diet for five weeks. I found that after a spell I lost my appetite and had trouble eating the dry bread. Perhaps I could make a good ascetic after all. There was less willpower involved than I had assumed. I did get thinner; I could see it in my face and in how my belts tied. But I was the only one who benefited from the regimen. Poppaea did not feel better. So we abandoned it as Saturnalia approached, although I vowed to curb my eating from now on, tempting cakes or not. I did not want to lose ground again.

"Yes, you are almost back to the lithe man I married," Poppaea said. "It is nice to see him again."

But I could not say likewise; I could not say, *You are the blooming woman I married*. I held her close to me. She was not being poisoned. It was something else.

We plunged into the darkest time of year. The sun did not rise until we had long been up, and even then its light was so wan we kept the oil lamps lit. It set in a blaze of yellow in the south so early there were hours left until bedtime. Its rays lit the pavilion longer as it was on the hilltop, but the high ceilings there made it difficult to heat so we seldom went there. Fabullus had finished working there for the season, as his paints did not behave well below a certain temperature.

"It would make a fine setting for a Saturnalia party," I said wistfully. But not this year.

"Or for your birthday," said Poppaea.

"But not this year," I said out loud.

"Perhaps we could have a small gathering here," she said. "Should not the emperor's birthday be celebrated?"

"We celebrated the accession in October, and the legions and the magistrates will pledge loyalty at the New Year. We need not add another celebration." Poppaea was not up to it in any case.

W ork did not cease, even in this time of year. I sent out a number of dispatches concerning various shipping projects—the harbor at Ostia, the canal between Naples and Ostia, the docks at Antium. The smiling courier took the cylinders and said, "Nothing for Velitrae today, Caesar?"

I looked at him. "No. Why should there be?"

He shrugged. "I had to deliver a message there not long ago. I wasn't sure of the exact address of the party I was looking for. But I know it now should there be more messages."

I knew instantly the address he was looking for and who had sent the message. I rose in anger—not at him. He I sent on his way with a cheerful wave. Then I marched into Poppaea's apartments.

She was lying down, surrounded by her attendants, who were pampering her with sweetened wine and tidbits; a lyre played softly in one corner. I ordered everyone out. Sporus stood by respectfully.

"You, too," I told him, and he melted away with the others. When he was gone and we were alone, I looked down at Poppaea. "Why did you send a message to Acte?" I demanded.

She raised herself up on her elbows in complete equanimity. "I wanted to thank her for her warning."

"Without me there? Was it not my place to do that? Did you wait until I was away to issue this . . . invitation?"

"You were busy at Ostia." She turned her head and fingered the fringes of the blanket covering her, finding them very interesting.

"You planned it that way. Don't lie to me. What did you really want with her?" I was embarrassed, furious that she had done this. "You are talking to me, remember? Me, who understands how you think."

Now she took herself off the bed, slowly. She stood before me, looking plaintive. "I meant nothing devious," she said, in her most beguiling voice.

"I said don't lie!" I barked. "Don't you dare insult me that way!"

She stepped back as if the force of my words had hit her like a blow. She stood, thinking. I knew exactly what she was thinking. Shall I confess or prevaricate? Finally she said, "I sent for her because I wanted to see her."

"Obviously," I said. "This tells me nothing. *Why* did you want to see her? And don't lie about thanking her. What a pitiful cover story. Surely you are more creative than that. But don't try to outdo yourself and come up with something else. Just tell the truth. It is so much easier."

"How would you know?" she spat. "You who betrayed your friend Otho and took me from him."

I laughed. "With considerable help from his loving wife. Enough of this. It is past, and I don't make a habit of lying. And I'm not the one in question here."

But it was my lie about Mother's death, and my tryst with Poppaea, that had driven Acte from me. She had said, *I do not want a liar for a husband, even if he is the emperor.* I had had to lie then. But I hated thinking of myself as a liar. I ascribed that to what I called the third Nero, the one who did bad but necessary things. I had not had to summon him in some time, like Locusta, and I hoped never to again.

"Very well, then," she said. "I was curious to see her. Because I love you, I am jealous of anyone you have ever loved or who ever loved you. If you can't understand that, you have never loved."

But I thought it was more spite than love that made Poppaea jealous of Acte, more competition than curiosity.

There was no point in arguing. "It is true, I have seen both your husbands. There is peace of mind in that. For those of us who have a jealous nature." Her first, Rufrius Crispinus, was much older and had been the Praetorian prefect under Claudius. Her second, Otho, an amusing and wealthy dandy, was now governor of Portugal. Neither one would excite much jealousy, at least in looks. "So, having seen her, what do you think?"

She sighed. "That I can see why you were taken with her." She tilted her head. "What a pity she was so far beneath you. A slave."

"A captive from a noble family in Lycia. A former slave. Now a businesswoman of great success."

"Thanks to your generosity."

"I just helped her get started. She is on her own now," I said.

"As she should be," retorted Poppaea.

I let it go and returned to my own quarters. What was I most angry about? That Poppaea had gone behind my back to see Acte? Or that I was not there to see her myself?

Petronius was to host a Saturnalia party in his new house in Rome, hastily constructed on the Aventine, near his old damaged one. "All the world is flocking to the New Rome," he said, "and so one needs a place, be it ever so small." Knowing him, I knew it was not likely to be small.

I pondered who to disguise myself as. Someone from mythology? From history? A living person? In my new thinner state, I thought of a wandering philosopher, one of those who lived on shriveled apples and scummy water. But I would have to walk around spouting pompous platitudes and that would be tedious.

Thinking of philosophers brought me back to Seneca. I decided to look through *Octavia* again, to read it more carefully, more thoroughly. The first time I had been aghast and read it hurriedly. Now time had passed and I could analyze it.

The attacks on me seemed even more vicious than they had the first time I read it. But now something else struck me. Mother's ghost spoke directly, cursing me and Poppaea.

> *The avenging Fury has a death prepared*
> *Meet for his crimes*
> *A scourge will fall upon him*
> *Let his proud majesty build marble halls*
> *And roof his courts with gold*
> *The time will come, the day will surely come*
> *When he will pay with his own poisoned life*
> *The forfeit of his crimes; the day when he,*
> *Ruined, abandoned, naked to the world,*
> *Will bow his neck beneath his enemy's sword.*

Build marble halls and roof his courts with gold . . . the Golden House! And an avenging Fury loosed on me?

Then she spoke of the most dreadful crime that *she* had committed, the incest that I had told no one. Had Seneca guessed at it, or was this just his most foul imagination?

> *Would that wild beasts had torn my womb to pieces*
> *Ere I had brought into the light that child*
> *Or held him to my breast.*
> *You would have died all mine, flesh of my flesh*

Yes, that was what you wanted, Mother, me all yours, and flesh of your flesh. I had thought death had sundered us. Now I was not so sure. I shuddered. I had put those thoughts far away, and now they were back like a screaming throng.

And she did not spare Poppaea.

> *My bleeding hands infernal torches bring*
> *To greet this impious marriage; by their light*
> *My son shall wed Poppaea: these bright flames*

The avenging hands of his infuriate mother
Shall turn to funeral fires.

But this was a play, a play written by a man, not a ghost. Obviously a man who hated me. Still, it was a work of imagination, not fact.

And there was something else. Octavia described Poppaea thus:

His haughty concubine goes proudly decked
In stolen riches of the royal house

This could have been Mother protesting. Once I had gifted her with a jeweled dress from the royal wardrobe. Instead of thanking me, she complained that I had cheated her, as once she had had all of the wardrobe at her disposal and now I returned her only one small part of it. What bounty was it, she asked, to be given back what was already hers?

Poppaea had taken a fancy to the dress and worn it once. I had ordered her to take it off. I could not bear to see it again, nor to see Poppaea wearing it. Too much of Mother lingered in it.

XXXIII

I awoke on the morning of my birthday aware of an unnatural light in the room. Poppaea was in her own quarters; I was alone. The shutters were closed, but somehow the strange illumination seeped in around them.

I got up and made my way barefoot across the chilled floor, sliding on the smooth marble. I pushed open the shutters, and they creaked as they swung on their hinges to reveal a blindingly white world. Rome was covered in snow! The sunlight dazzled as it struck the drifts and mounds, and the sky was ringingly blue.

It was hushed and still outside. No one had ventured out yet, and the world looked new-made, unsullied. Sharp corners and smudges were blanketed and erased. I stood breathless before it, overcome by its crystalline beauty.

"Rome has given you a birthday gift." I had been so transfixed by the scene outside that I had not heard Poppaea steal into the room and come up behind me.

"The best one I have ever had," I said, turning to her as she embraced me. "It so seldom snows in Rome, and almost never this deep."

"Now you need to bask in the first rays of sunlight, like you did on the day you were born," she said.

I was standing in the sunlight but did not consider it a reenactment. Some things happen only once, giving rise to personal myths. Such was the story of my birth. "I am just happy to see the sun again," I said. "It has been so gloomy and muffled for days."

"If the snow stays, how will that affect Saturnalia?" she asked.

"Nothing will stop Saturnalia," I said, laughing. "Nothing in the world, not even a volcano. Romans must have their holiday."

"Look, the snow is floating in clumps on the lake," she said in childish glee. "Like foam on ocean waves."

To me it looked like clouds on a blue sky, upside down. So the world was already upside down, ready for Saturnalia.

Two days later I stood in the Temple of Saturn in the Forum to offer prayers and formally proclaim the festival in his name. Whether Saturn really had any concern with it was irrelevant at this point. What did the gods really think of us and the things we claimed for them?

The snow had not melted, and it was bitter cold. Paths had been cleared through the Forum and the steps of the Temple were shoveled, but our thick mantles dragged in the snow anyway. However, the sparkling city had everyone in a jolly mood, cold and wet mantles be damned.

Back in the palace, the first thing I had to do was attend the daily "Friends of Caesar" reception. Normally the people lined up to pay their respects to me; now I must pay respects to them, as Saturnalia demanded.

They were gathered in the atrium, clustered around the blue-tiled impluvium. This first reception was limited to an elite group, deemed to be especially important or close to me. Another, larger group came to a later reception. To be banished from the "Friends of Caesar" membership was a sign of their being out of my favor.

Now the figures turned toward me as I approached. Instead of smiling, they scowled. Everything must be reversed.

I went down the row, making humble obeisance to them, fawning and uttering outlandish compliments to them. To a bald senator I praised his shining pate. To a rotund man I praised his athletic prowess. To a plain praetor I praised his Apollonian looks. I hoped in this they would recognize how comical their effusive compliments sounded to me every day.

Back in my quarters, Faenius and Subrius were on duty but not in uniform. Instead they wore loose long-sleeved tunics and civilian shoes. I almost did not recognize them.

They lifted up a cuirass and helmet and ordered me to put them on. "You need to protect us," said Faenius. "As we do you, day in and day out."

"Yes, your safety is paramount with us," said Subrius. "We think of nothing else, no matter where our duty calls us."

There was an undertone to his words that betrayed something beyond a lighthearted game.

"I know you do," I said. "And I trust you with my life." I put on the cold metal helmet and strapped on the weighty leather cuirass. Suddenly I felt invincible, military, stalwart. I laughed. "I feel quite transformed," I said. "Now you must trust me with *your* lives."

They looked at one another. "Of course," they said in unison. "Absolutely."

In my military glory, I went to Poppaea's apartments. People blinked when they saw me, taken aback. I loved it.

I went through the nest of rooms to reach Poppaea's. She was seated on a chair high on her dais, with her slaves and servers looking on. But no! It was Sporus in the chair, and Poppaea attending him, wearing the gown of a slave. But even this became her. For a fleeting instant I remembered Acte serving Octavia in her household, with grace and dignity. But I had never truly thought of her as a slave, although others did.

Sporus looked up haughtily. "Do we welcome the great Germanicus?"

I bowed slightly. "At your service."

"Ah, I see the family resemblance to the emperor. But it can't be Nero, because he doesn't know a *gladius* from a *pilum*."

Saturnalian license to speak words forbidden any other time . . . I felt my face growing red while the company laughed uproariously. And I wasn't that ignorant of arms!

"My grandson fights in other fields," I said, defending myself.

"Yes, the effete parlors of poetry!" a slave yelled.

"He is rather skilled with chariots," I said.

"Yes, once," the taunter continued. "But could he do it again? Not like you, mighty warrior, who had the barbaric hairy Germans on the run."

"We shall see," I said, leaving the field of retorts. I took my place at the back of the room while Poppaea ostentatiously waited on her double. I was stung by the insult, but I determined not to let it show. It is better to know secret thoughts than to be ignorant of them, keep ears open rather than shut them.

Should I apologize for Sporus?" asked Poppaea when we were getting ready for Petronius's party. "I know it hurt your feelings."

"No, no, it didn't," I insisted. "But I won't wear these again. It was Faenius and Subrius who put them on me." The helmet and cuirass were sitting neatly on a table. "I will go as something so far from what I am that there can be no comparisons. I will go as"—I thought fast—"a muleteer."

She burst out laughing. "With a mule in tow?"

"Let's get one of the slaves to dress as one," I said. "But since everything is unreal, he will be a talking mule."

"I shall go as myself, but veiled. What would that make me? What anyone wants to imagine. And it saves me the trouble of thinking of a costume."

"If you don't feel up to it, you needn't go."

"I feel better today. If I need to, I can leave early."

Suited up in my muleteer's outfit—thick boots, leather leg wrappings, a long-sleeved unbleached tunic, a greasy mantle—we set out in a litter toward Petronius's dwelling on the Aventine after sunset, the pretend mule sitting behind us in his furry costume with big ears. Although it was barely dark, the streets were thronged with costumed revelers, shouting and pushing, most of them drunk. They jostled and tilted the litter; in spite of my disguise, I was recognized, and leering faces peered in at me. One woman, in rags—was she really a beggar or disguised as one?—thrust a doll at me, saying it would protect me against assassins. Before I could respond, she was swept away in the crowd.

I turned it over. It was a simple cloth doll, the sort children have. Its features were crudely drawn and its hair yarn. I set it down in the litter. But Poppaea clutched my arm. "Didn't someone hand Caesar a doll when he was on his way to the Senate on the ides of March?"

"It was a note, and he didn't read it."

"What did it say?"

"It had the details of the plot. But he just stuck it with the bundle of petitions to read later."

"Don't go to Petronius's!" she cried. She leaned forward to the bearers. "Turn around!" she said.

I pulled her hand off my arm. "Don't be foolish," I said. "I am sure Petronius has guards, and we are among friends. Where is the bold Poppaea of old, the Poppaea I married?" I turned the doll in my hand. "This is just a child's toy." I started to throw it out the litter, but she grabbed it.

"No!" She held it to her chest. "That would be as foolhardy as Caesar."

Our litter climbed the hill overlooking the Circus Maximus, a not very steep grade. Even here the crowds were thick, careening and bumping. The snow crunched underfoot and the damp air stung; it had an astringent smell not unlike weak vinegar. Bobbing torches were a swirl of yellow moons.

A variety of buildings covered the Aventine, from luxurious mansions to more humble dwellings. Our bearers set the litter down before an elegant jewel of a house and announced, "The residence of Gaius Petronius Arbiter."

Its size was modest, but its design was innovative, daring, and extravagant, a child of the reborn Rome. We made our way to the door, I leading my mule, who had hooves of polished ebony and ears that waved over his head, stiffened with wire. A slave opened the door, but no, it was Atria, Piso's wife. I started to greet her as such, but she put her finger to her lips.

"Lesbia, to serve you and welcome you to the home of Catullus." So that was who Petronius claimed to be tonight. She bowed and ushered us in. The atrium was crowded, almost as crowded as the streets. Peo-

ple were wading in the impluvium, baring their legs and shrieking.
Mounds of food listed from overladen tables, making the floor slippery
with crushed grapes.

"The private party is this way," she said, steering us through the
atrium and a doorway into a surprisingly large room off an indoor
garden. Opulently dressed slaves welcomed us to "the garden of delights," and indeed, flowers—lilies, roses, iris—were fastened around
the walls, imported from warm countries, and heady clouds of sandal-
wood incense spewed from censers hanging from the ceiling.

"Oh, my, a mule driver!" Petronius was beside us. "And his mule.
With what is he laden?"

"Some tokens that can be redeemed with the puzzles."

"Oh, good! We are about to begin the games."

He looked at Poppaea. "The goddess of Fortune?" he asked.

"The goddess of *my* fortune," I said. "You can ask her a question."

Petronius cocked his head. "Will my venture succeed?"

Muffled behind her veil, Poppaea said, "You must describe the venture in more detail. You must have several ventures upon which you
await the outcome."

"Ah, if you were a true prophetess, you would know *which* venture."
He winked. "But it is better if you don't. Come, partake of some refreshments."

In the middle of the room stood a silver-legged table bedecked with
at least thirty pots and dishes. Petronius was eager to show them off,
but in truth they were merely one type of food disguised as another—
pastry that mimicked meat, meat that looked like fruit, and so on.
After our visit to Locusta we were loath to eat anything here; too many
people had access to it. I even demurred about the wine, confounding
Petronius.

In an adjoining room a master of ceremonies was announcing the
beginning of the questions and forfeits. It was impossible for someone
of Lateranus's size to disguise himself, so I recognized him despite the
mask, the wild wig, and the barbarian trousers that ballooned out
around his treelike legs.

"I, the master of revels, will put a question to you all. Answer it as best you can. But be careful. A wrong answer gets a punishment." He turned his backside out and slapped his butt. Turning back, he asked, "What is the best time of day to have sex?"

Someone dressed as a pirate said, "Midnight."

"I said *day!*" roared Lateranus. "Paddle him!" he ordered one of the slaves.

"Right as the sun comes up," said a gladiator—who turned out to be Vestinus.

"That's because you are old!" said Lateranus. "The only time you have enough energy! Paddle him!"

"I'm not that old," protested Vestinus. But he submitted good-naturedly.

"I say right after the baths," said Quintianus—I recognized his voice, coming from a Circe costume.

"Wrong! That's backward. You should take a bath afterward, not before. But then, you probably want to smell like perfumed oil. The paddle for you!"

After many wrong answers, my mule said, "Any time of day!"

Lateranus swung around. "Leave it to a dumb animal to know the best time for sex! All the time! Yes! Here's our winner!"

"And he gets a reward from his very own pack," I said, opening his saddlebag and pulling out a token, labeled "a parrot with an obscene vocabulary." There was a squawky one at the palace I wanted to rid myself of.

There were many other questions and riddles. How many cups of wine make a man drunk? What's the rarest hair color? Is there a foolproof test for virginity? Has anyone ever brought a dead person back to life?

But other people ignored the puzzles and continued talking with one another, downing cup after cup of wine, answering the question for themselves of how many cups were needed.

Suddenly Lucan, wearing an ivy wreath, took the floor, shoving Lateranus aside. He swayed slightly on his feet, swishing his wine cup aimlessly.

"The Greeks knew their w-wine! Yes, the great poet Euboulos said, 'I prepare only th-three cups for m' guests—the first f'r health, the second f'r love and pleasure, the third f'r s-sleep.'" Lucan drained his. "This is my suh-sixth! So what does he say about th-that? 'The f-fourth is not the host's any longer but buh-longs to bad buh-havior, the fifth is for shouting, and the suh-sixth is for rudeness and insults.' So here is wh-where I am!"

"You stammer like Claudius," said Piso, coming out of the shadows.

"You don't need six cups of wine to be rude and insulting," I said, glaring at him. Let him know I knew about the latrine joke. "You can do it dead sober."

He turned slowly, trying to focus his eyes. He shrugged. Perhaps nothing could penetrate his mind at this moment. "More!" he cried, holding out his cup, and General Vespasian, dressed as a slave, filled it. "Now," said Lucan, licking his lips. "Number seven—hmm—'seven is f'r fights.'"

He deserved a fight, but it was not fair to fight with a man so drunk he could barely stand. I turned away. When I confronted him, it would be at a time he couldn't hide behind Bacchus.

"Riddle, riddle!" called Lateranus, seeking to regain control. "Does anyone know the rest of the rhyme? Our friend here is too drunk to proceed." He motioned for someone to pull Lucan away from the center. True to the poem, he tried to fight, but he was so uncoordinated he fell in a heap and was dragged away into the shadows.

"Yes," said a throaty deep voice I thought I recognized. A woman dressed as Boudicca, tossing her head with its long red wig, tapping her spear, said, "The eighth is for lawless behavior, the ninth for vomiting, and the tenth for insanity." As if on cue, the sound of vomiting came in the direction where Lucan was last seen. "He must have skipped the eighth," said Boudicca. Everyone howled.

Lateranus continued smoothly. "So, here is another riddle! What is it that is both mortal and immortal but lives as neither god nor man, is born anew and dies each day? Is seen by no one but known to all?"

While everyone was thinking, I looked around. I knew most of the people, but some were strangers. The disguises did not help. The smoke from the censers blurred the faces, and the corners of the room were murky. Petronius looked on, arms crossed. What was going through his mind? I had never understood him; he seemed to stand outside the general breed of men yet desired to be part of that company, hosting entertainments and presiding over clubs, but always at a remove. So was he here—looking on from the shadows.

"The answer is *sleep!*" proclaimed Lateranus.

General Vespasian, standing next to me, snorted. "Don't hold with riddles," he said. "Foolishness." The old general was back in Rome from his time as governor of North Africa. "I see you are disguised as me," he said.

"A general?" For a moment I was confused. Then I remembered. Incurring so many debts in Africa, he had had to go into business as a muleteer, earning the nickname Mule Driver. "Oh, I meant no disrespect. In fact, that cruel label was so far from my mind I didn't even remember it."

"Do you like mules?" he asked. "I don't. Annoying beasts. But there's money in them. Saved my skin."

"Had you not been so honest, you would have come back rich from Africa, not poor." Almost alone of governors, honest Vespasian had not used his office as a way to make illegal money.

"Ah, honesty. Where has it got me but the name Mule Driver?"

"Your career is not over yet," I said. But he was not young—he was one of the soldiers who invaded Britain for Claudius twenty years before.

Boudicca was making her way over to us. "You! You!" She pointed at Vespasian. "You brought the vile Romans to my country!"

"Not me, lady," said Vespasian. "Blame Julius Caesar. He started it."

She laughed, throwing her head back. Now I knew her: Statilia Messalina, Vestinus's wife. "It is something you will all regret!" she said. "My country has little to offer worth the trouble of garrisoning it."

"It has your bravery and nobility. A country that can produce such a leader must be a special one," I said.

"Nonetheless you defeated me," she said.

"Not easily," I admitted.

She sighed and pulled off the heavy wig. "It is late. I have had my three cups of wine. Time to go home." She looked around for Vestinus. "Time to be Statilia again."

I put the wig back on her head. "Be Boudicca for a little while longer. For I always wanted to talk to you and never had the opportunity."

And so we playacted, she speaking for the lost queen and I saying all the things I had wanted to ask her, had I ever had the privilege of seeing her in person. But the only way I would ever have seen her in person was if she had been brought to Rome in chains, humiliated and paraded before jeering mobs. I was thankful she had been spared that. No one knew what happened to her—some said she took poison, others that she just disappeared and would come again someday to lead her people. I preferred the latter story.

The room was slowly clearing; people were drifting away. It must be long past midnight. Poppaea was talking to Scaevinus and his wife, Caedicia, as they lingered near the door. Taking advantage of the ugly scar on his mouth that gave him a sinister look, Scaevinus was dressed as a highway brigand, while Caedicia was a mermaid, covered in shiny scales tinted green.

Poppaea had taken off her face veil. In the wavering light she suddenly, horribly, looked like Mother. I rubbed my eyes to banish the sight, but when I opened them again, Mother stared back at me, her eyes seeming to pop from her head. Her teeth were bared like a wolf's. Horrible, horrible. I turned away and saw, even more horribly, myself in a far corner—a dark figure who looked like me, slinking away through the shadows and out the door.

Without thinking, I ran after him. It wasn't an apparition; I had to prove it wasn't, I had to lay hold of him and see who this was. I heard his footsteps on the tile floor; the feet of spirits make no noise. I saw his robe flying out behind him as he turned the corner and fled out the main door.

Why was he running? He must be a real person; ghosts don't flee, why should they?

I reached the front door and looked out at the paved walkway. Nothing. He had vanished into the night.

Our journey back to the palace was quiet and subdued. The raucous crowds had gone, although there were still a few merrymakers out on the streets. The half moon was low in the sky, near to setting. It threw forlorn light on the snow, trampled and dirty now. The doll was still in the litter.

XXXIV

Although the dawn was not far away, I took to my bed, casting off the muleteer's clothing with relief. At Poppaea's insistence I had carried the doll inside, and now it rested on a nearby table, its arms flopping over the edge. The strange spell of the last few minutes of the party lingered; if only I could cast them off as easily as the muleteer costume.

I fell into a deep, surreal sleep. I was floating over the city, watching each of the seven hills, swooping down lower to see more closely. First I hovered over Petronius's house, and in the light (for it was full daylight in the dream) I searched for the dark man who had scurried away but saw nothing, only chattering guests departing. I drifted away, wafted on a supernatural wind, and looked down at the Golden House, its sparkling lake, its green-bronze roof, its veined *Gallia antica* marble columns. Up on the hill the pavilion gleamed, its long facade welcoming the rays of the sun. How lovely it was.

Then before my eyes it shimmered and dissolved, leaving bare ground, overcoming me with a profound sense of dread and sorrow, and a voice whispered in my ear, "Not one stone shall remain standing upon another, nor anything that you hold dear."

I cried out but my throat was frozen, and then suddenly it opened and the sound I made rang out in the room, and I was back there, solidly in my bed. The room was intact, the marble walls shining and whole. Gingerly I got out of bed and looked out at the lake. It was still there. It was all still there. In wonder I touched the wall, rejoicing that it was real.

But I had seen it in ruins. I had *seen* it, and it was too real to have been a dream. It was a vision, not a dream. My beloved Golden House would not survive.

And the second part: anything that I held dear.

Shaken, I sat down on a couch. I did not want to return to bed, lest I dream again, lest the dream continue. It was not over; I had just prematurely ended it by my scream. It was waiting to come back, to finish its dreadful portent.

Was this a manifestation of the Furies? Was this how they visited, not as maidens with snake hair, dog's heads, and bloodshot eyes? Did they invade sleep and torment in this way?

Mother. I had felt her presence recently, speaking from the play, altering Poppaea's features, even being reminded about Germanicus, her father and still beloved of soldiers.

The Furies—those avengers of wrongs of the young against the old. They haunted and punished, and their victims died in torment. Orestes had suffered from them because he killed his mother, Clytemnestra, avenging her murder of her husband and Orestes's father, Agamemnon. Honor had compelled him to avenge his father's death; honor equally demanded that he protect his mother. He could not do both.

Mother had killed both my adoptive fathers. Was I not justified in seeking revenge?

You told Poppaea you did not lie, so do not lie to yourself. You killed your mother, Agrippina, not because of Crispus and Claudius but because she would not let you live without her, and you could not breathe. She strangled you and put you in manacles to serve her purpose. It could not go on. She would not let you be emperor except as a toy—a doll like the one on the table—that she could control. And she even tried to take control of your body itself, drugging you and pulling you into her bed. Incest worse than Oedipus, who sinned in ignorance, not deliberately. But nothing was taboo to her. No, it could not go on. You could not both exist in the same world.

But as Orestes discovered, the Furies did not reason. There were no extenuating circumstances with them. In that way they were like puppets themselves, unthinking agents.

Perhaps they were tormenting Poppaea. If it was not poison attacking her, what was it besides the Furies?

How did one overcome the Furies? Orestes had appealed to Apollo, who in turn asked Athena to intervene. But I needed something quicker than that. The gods could take years to answer, if they answered at all—didn't Orestes wander for ages?—and Poppaea and I must be freed immediately.

I knew of . . . I had heard of . . . Chaldean magi who had the power to exorcise ghosts of the dead. They could even speak to them. I shuddered. These things were forbidden in Rome, but not to the emperor. That is, no one could prevent the emperor from pursuing what he liked. *Is it not a fine thing to be emperor and call anyone you please?*

Tiridates of Armenia was coming to Rome to be crowned by me. He was even a magus himself. But that was a long time off. He would take forever to get here, refusing to travel by sea as it was against his religion. I must find Chaldean magi now. Luckily Rome harbored many nationalities and religions. There must be some somewhere.

In feverish haste, I called for my slaves to help me dress and sent for Tigellinus.

Within the hour, he was there.

"Good morning, Caesar. How was the Saturnalia party? I hope you did not mind that I sent Subrius in my place yesterday. I had . . . er . . . other things to attend to."

I could imagine but didn't want to hear about them. His excursions to the brothels kept them in business, and they were especially inventive at Saturnalia. "It was well done, as the parties of Petronius are known for." I related the episode about Lucan.

"He is probably recovering as we speak. He's young and can drink to oblivion but be fine the next night. In the meantime, I've found another of his writings, and it isn't about the wars of the last century." He thrust out a scroll at me.

I didn't want to read it right then. "What is it?" I asked.

"Read the title. It will tell you all."

I unrolled the scroll just enough to see *De Incendio Urbis—On the Burning of the City.* I stared at it. "Does he blame me?"

"He doesn't blame an accident, put it that way. Or the Christians."

What had turned him against me? Was that the work of the Furies as well? To poison others' minds against me? They worked in evil, insidious ways. Lucan especially grieved me.

"It is unfortunate," I said. But I had more pressing concerns. "Do you know of any Chaldean magi?" I asked.

He laughed. "Priests and religions are not my specialty." But when he saw I was serious, he said, "I am sure I can locate some. One can find anything in Rome."

"Then do so," I said. "As quickly as possible."

There was a reason why Tigellinus had risen to such prominence and why I relied on him so much. By noon he had located two Chaldean magi who lived—ironically near to Petronius—on the Aventine, where many foreign cults and temples flourished, as it was outside the old city boundary.

"They prefer to come at night," he said, describing them. "The position of the stars is very important to their—their conjuring, or whatever it is that they do." He grinned, waiting for me to explain what they did and why I wanted them. I let him wait. The grin faded from his square-jawed face. "Is there anything else you require?"

"Did they specify anything?" I asked.

"They asked for meat from a black dog," he said, wrinkling his nose. "They said no salt must be present. They prefer stormy weather, but of course we can't control that." He looked out the window, where the sky was overcast, gray like the aging snow beneath it.

All was in readiness. Poppaea and I waited in my innermost room. She was bewildered but acquiescent to whatever I required of her. I had made sure we were alone; the ever-present guards were relegated to the outer doors. A covered platter of cooked dog meat stood on a table. This room, although small, had excellent views of the heavens from two windows. And outside, although it was not stormy, fog from the melting snow hugged the ground. I had done all I could. Now we awaited the knock on the door—the knock that I hoped would deliver us from whatever had tormented us.

It was almost midnight when a gentle tap came. I myself opened the door to find two men standing there, their glittering dark robes adorned with zodiac signs. I ushered them in.

"Welcome," I said. Then I suddenly wondered what language they spoke. Should I have had a translator at hand? Tigellinus had spoken to them, but he had not said how he managed that.

"Thank you," the taller of the two replied, in Greek. What a relief.

They walked into the room. I waited to see what they wanted to do—stand or sit, and where? It was all up to them. "I have the proper dog meat here, and there is no salt, as you requested."

"That is acceptable," the smaller man said in a soft voice. "We require very little." He motioned toward the window. "The stars supply our power. All we need now is your birth date so we know what the stars said when you were born, and we need to know the entity who is troubling you. Is it a regular demon or a deceased person?"

He had a bushy beard that overpowered his small, foxlike face. But his voice, though gentle, was authoritative.

I related both our birth dates and then said quietly, as if to admit it was dangerous, "It is a person."

"How long has the person been deceased?" the taller man asked. His beard was tamer, but his dark penetrating eyes made him seem wilder than his companion.

"Five years," I said.

"A pity. If it were recent, we could perhaps reanimate the corpse."

"She was cremated," I said. How ghoulish, to think of meddling with Mother's body. Suddenly the question at Petronius's party slid across my mind. *Has anyone ever brought a dead person back to life?*

"Then we shall summon the spirit."

"No! She is already present. I want you to banish her, send her away. Don't strengthen her presence here with us!" I cried.

"We have to summon her, call her to heel, to answer to us, before we can send her away," said the smaller man. "We shall prepare the ritual."

He went over to the table and lifted the cover off the meat. "We eat dog to honor Hecate, the goddess of death. Her companion is a black dog. And we cannot have salt present, for salt is a preservative, the opposite of decay."

He opened the bag he carried and extracted two plates with an unknown writing on them. He handed one to his companion, and together they put the dog meat on the plates, mumbling something before they ate it. Then they swayed on their feet a long time, before saying, "Now extinguish all but one lamp. We must have darkness."

All the lamps gone but one, the flickering faint light threw long, jumping shadows on the walls. The taller man asked us to stand with our backs to the lamp.

"Now." He spoke in a low voice. "Do you have any possession of the deceased?"

"Yes," said Poppaea. She held up the jeweled dress from the imperial wardrobe.

"Good. Now, you will tell me the name of the person."

I whispered in the right ear of first one magi, then the other. "Julia Augusta Agrippina." I paused. "And the *Erinyes*, the Furies, whom she has sent."

If they were taken aback, they did not show it. "Now we shall call her. It is good that it is misty outside. The spirits show up better against fog."

"I don't want to see her!" I said.

"Then don't look," one of them said. "Perhaps we alone will see her. It often happens that way."

I shut my eyes. Poppaea did likewise. And the men began to chant in a high singsong voice, in an unknown tongue. How could Mother understand them? Or did the shades know everything?

What was happening? Was she there?

Then they spoke so that we could understand.

"In the name of Hecate, in the name of Proserpine, in the name of Pluto, we command you to retreat to the depths of Hades and never come no more. Cease your torment of these people who stand in the sacred place here. You are banished, you are dispelled, you are vanquished."

Utter stillness prevailed. How long should we stand there? When was it safe to open my eyes? The magi began chanting again, a discordant sound. Then they stopped.

Finally one of the men touched my shoulder. "It is over, Caesar. The spirits have come and gone." Slowly I opened my eyes. The lamplight still wavered. The room was empty of anyone but us. Poppaea was weeping softly in the corner, sunk down on a couch.

"Did you prevail?" I asked.

"We used our strongest magic."

"But did you *prevail?*" I had to know.

"Only time will tell."

XXXV

I stood on the cliff edge, looking down over the steep drop to the dark woods below, where the rushing river sang its melodious notes. Although it was cold here, with snow on the ground, the river was not frozen. Nor were the three artificial lakes higher on the mountain, a gift of the river as well. I was in Sublaqueum, appropriately named "under the lakes," for I had created those lakes and built my cliffside villa beneath them. It was one of my earliest architectural experiments, and it had been successful. Now this villa served as my special retreat, a place where I could withdraw and think.

I had desperate need of it after the encounter with the magi, which had left me more apprehensive than ever and even more protective of Poppaea. It was out of the question for her to travel with me here, but she had urged me to go.

"You must regain your peace of mind, your equilibrium," she said. "I depend on you for that." She herself would rest in her apartments.

Once I was away from Rome, my mind cleared. Every mile I traveled lifted the confusion and disquiet that plagued me, and by the time I arrived at Sublaqueum I felt tranquil.

The villa lay in the Apenninus Mountains, the chain that ran down the center of the country, whence came the snow I used for my *decocta Neronis*, the drink I loved more than wine. It was secluded, but not remote and inaccessible. Before I entered the building, I stretched my legs outside, walking along the precipitous path, being careful of my footing. The lower valley was already dark; light lingered only at the top of the mountain, kissing the roof of the villa before retreating. The air was bracing, pine-scented. I drank in deep lungfuls of it, feeling it better medicine than anything Andromachus could prescribe.

"Caesar, the footing is dangerous in the dark; you should come inside," my accompanying slave said. He was right. I turned away and followed him into the villa, which he and the others had prepared while I was outside.

Although I had not been here in a long time—and Poppaea had never come here—it felt like home as soon as I walked in the door. It was small enough to feel private and snug, large enough to house some of my favorite artworks, a series of white marble statues of Niobe and her fourteen children. In the low light they seemed to glow white; they were scattered throughout the various rooms, so that each could be appreciated separately. In contrast, a long table of black marble graced the main room, so reflective that candles placed on it doubled their light. A line of them flickered now.

I kept a library here with my favorite books—histories and poetry. I selected one or two I had wanted to reread—but never had time in Rome—and settled down on my couch with a glowing brazier beside me. The evening was mine. The time was mine. No one could intrude.

"Please make me a *decocta Neronis*," I asked one of the slaves. That was what I needed as a final soother, and the snow to make it was just outside. He would gather a bowl from the cleanest drift, to cool a cup of fresh-boiled water. I might add some dried mint to it.

I felt safe here. Mother had never set foot in Sublaqueum and could not muddy my memories. Instead, Acte's presence was very real here, as she had come with me when I first plotted out the design for the villa. We had fled Rome, away from censuring eyes, and slept outdoors in a makeshift tent. I had asked her to marry me. She said it was impossible. I said I was emperor and could make it possible. I was very naïve.

That was a lifetime ago, it seemed. But here it was just yesterday, alive and fresh. I wondered what Acte thought when Poppaea summoned her to the palace and whether she believed I was avoiding her by not being there. If I ever saw Acte again I would have to conquer the tongue-tied awkwardness that gripped me when I saw her after the Fire.

Tiredness crept over me like the long shadows at sundown. One moment I was reading Livy, the next my slave was touching my shoulder, clutching the fallen scroll. It was time for sleep. My bedchamber beckoned.

Whether it was the invigorating mountain air or the cumulative exhaustion of the past few weeks, I slept more soundly than I had in months. No dreams, no Furies, nothing but blessed darkness, as dark as the long table. If death is like this, why do we fear it so?

The darkness rolled slowly and kindly away, and my wakening was gentle. I looked around the chamber, seeing so much more now than I had at night. One of the statues, a fallen daughter of Niobe, was near the window. I lingered beside her, studying her face. Her head was turned sideways, as if she slept on a pillow. Her lips were parted, but whether in a dream or in death it was impossible to know. How near they were, death and sleep. And how utterly beautiful she was, suspended between the two.

I have long prayed that I would die before I lost my beauty, Poppaea once said. Only a statue could keep beauty from fading, free from death.

Turning away from the statue and its melancholy, I dressed and decided to walk up to the lakes in the morning. There were three of them, strung out like beads on a necklace, created by damming the river Anio. The flat expanse of water twinkled in the sunlight. I dipped my hand in and it was stinging cold. I had swum in the lakes, finding them chilly even in summer. When I was training my voice, my vocal coach advised me that swimming in cold water would strengthen my lungs.

My music . . . when would I return to it? When could I return to it? So much had been set aside since the Fire. I missed it. But the Fire tainted even the thought of music, because I now associated it with the barbiton player and his instrument. I couldn't bear to touch the thing, as much as I had wanted to learn to play it.

The lakes, pristine and pure. When I swam in them, they rinsed me clean and unstained. But it was too cold today.

Returning to the villa, I sat at one end of the long dining table, where daylight made the small inclusions in the black marble top gleam. This slab of stone was a replacement; the original had been shattered by a bolt of lightning a while ago. Since the old adage held that lightning never struck twice in the same place, presumably this table would not be put to the same test.

The table made a perfect racetrack facsimile, and as I had a collection of toy chariots here, I enacted a few races on it. I was proud of my collection; the star was a bronze one Claudius had given me. It was a perfect replica of a real chariot. I treasured it not only because of its accuracy but because, in giving it to me, Claudius had shown that he understood the passions of a little boy.

I would give it to my son. I would hand it to him when he was old enough, say six or seven, and tell him, *The emperor Claudius gave it to me when I was a boy. Take good care of it.*

My son. I so longed for his arrival. I realized I did not have a name for him yet, perhaps out of superstition. When I saw him, when I held him in my arms, would be time enough to choose his name.

T he days passed in quiet solitude, healing days, each evening leaving me more restored. I planned to return to Rome shortly; I did not want to leave Poppaea for very long.

But a messenger arrived on the sixth morning, telling me it was urgent that I hurry back. He carried no written instructions, just verbal ones, which said I was needed in Rome for personal matters.

"What sort of personal matters?" I asked. "I need to know more than that." He was a trusted servant, and I knew his business was official, but I did not want to rush back for a trivial matter.

"It—it is the Augusta," he said. "She has sent for you. And Andromachus also asks that you return."

"Is something wrong?"

"Caesar, I do not know. Whatever it was, they wanted it kept secret. But I assure you, I was dispatched by the Augusta." He held up her seal.

Indeed it was hers. And the request of Andromachus meant it was a medical emergency, not a state one.

"Let us go at once!" I cried. We hurried out of the villa and took to the road.

The entire way back I was plagued with worry, shattering my hard-won tranquility. By the time I reached Rome it was as if I had never left, never had a respite from this oppression. I rushed into the palace, straight to Poppaea's apartments. I tried to read the guards' faces, but they averted their eyes. I brushed past them and walked the long passageway toward the room that was Poppaea's main chamber. Slaves were standing about but did not look at me. At the chamber door two more guards bowed and opened the door, silently. Neither said *Greetings, Caesar.*

I took a deep breath, standing on the threshold. Several people stood, backs to me, shielding the bed. I approached, then parted them to look. Poppaea lay inert, her head turned, her eyes closed, her lips slightly open. *Like the statue.* O gods! Was she dead?

My heart stopped, frozen. "Poppaea!" I cried, bending toward her, clasping her. She was warm. "Poppaea!" Her head lolled forward, limp. I hugged her as if I could force her to breathe. Then I felt a slight tremor as her muscles quivered.

I laid her back down, saw her chest rise and fall. Only then did I ask, "What has happened?"

A middle-aged woman, a midwife I assumed, said, "She had the baby. It was born too early to live."

"Where is it?"

"Taken away. It was early this morning. She sent the messenger last night, when the labor began. She sleeps now, because the physician gave her a draft. It was a difficult labor, with no reward."

"Does she know?" I asked.

"Yes, she knows." The midwife laid her hand on Poppaea's forehead, called for cold clothes. "She will sleep for another few hours. When she awakens, I warn you, she will be devastated."

As was I. Crushed and stunned. But Poppaea lived; the tragedy was not entire. "I will stay with her," I said. "You may go, and rest."

I sank down in a chair beside her as the attendants drifted away, leaving us alone. I put my head in my hands, as if that would ease the pain, drive it out. Hours passed while she quietly slept, eventually becoming more restless, finally opening her eyes. She gave a ragged smile.

"Your face is the first thing I see," she murmured. "You came."

I leaned forward and kissed her forehead. "I never should have left."

"It would have made no difference." Her voice was weak. She struggled to sit upright but lacked the strength. She reached her hand out to mine. "The baby was too small to live. He—"

"It was a boy?"

"Yes, a son. But he never breathed. He was so small. He should not have come for another four months." Her voice held steady, but tears slid down her cheeks. She took a deep breath. "You must divorce me," she said. "It is clear that I cannot give you a living child, and you must have an heir. You are young and strong and must not be tied to me."

Her words appalled me. Surely this was the shock affecting her mind. "No, never," I said. "You will recover, you will feel better, and such thoughts will go back where they belong—nowhere."

"You are not practical, my love. You refuse to see the stark truth. I am thirty-three and have had two pregnancies and no living child. You cannot go on like this—you need a younger wife."

"I can't live without you!" I cried. I had thought she had died and then rejoiced to see her breathe. Now she wanted to leave me anyway.

"Yes, you can, and you have to. I love you enough to insist that you look to your own safety, even if you must cast me aside."

"I won't! I won't do it!" I grabbed her hand, squeezing it so tightly she winced. "You made a vow. *Whenever and wherever you are Gaius, then I am Gaia.* That means that no matter where we are, no matter what is happening around us, we are one. If you did not mean the vow, you should never have spoken the words."

"Oh, my love, you forget that these words apply to everyone but the emperor. What is happening around him alters everything, and he must then think of his own survival."

"I can't survive without you."

She sighed, as if I were an obstinate child. "You will not let me go, then?"

"No."

She lay back down, closing her eyes. "I am glad, then," she murmured. And slept again.

XXXVI

Poppaea slowly recovered. The color returned to her cheeks and the strength to her limbs. We held the sorrow of our lost son close inside, so secreted that we dared not talk about it, lest it loosen the grief again, a flight of woe, like the evil creatures Pandora had released. And I was afraid she would again offer me a divorce. No! Life without her was for me unthinkable.

We went about our daily lives, the never-ending round of ceremonies, rituals, official correspondence, diplomatic meetings. The sheer monotony of it acted as an anesthetic, numbing us while underneath the grief lessened, diluted, losing its first fierce strength. And there came a day, as winter ebbed away and the subtle signs of spring were at hand, a rare day when there were no official duties to distract, a forgotten feeling of almost-happiness came to me, for a moment. A moment that seemed bright and hopeful and, if not joyous, held the promise of joy.

The Festival of Ceres was at hand. It was the ominous date when the baby would have been born, but the festival must go on regardless. I had looked forward to the festival, thinking then to have my own celebration to double the significance of it, but now there would be only a single meaning. Nonetheless it came at a lovely time of year—April twelfth to nineteenth, and two days later was the official birthday of Rome. On the last day of the festival there would be chariot races at the Circus Maximus, and I planned to preside over them. The racing season would begin, and that would lift my heart.

On that last day, the games would not start until noon, but I was up early to sign papers and put business behind me. Outside the window I could hear birdsong, loud chirping in a chorus that died away as the sun rose. It was hard to be downcast with such exuberant bursts of rapture outside. It was warm enough to open the window, and I went over to do so.

Before I reached the window, there was an urgent knocking at the door, and Epaphroditus hurried in.

"Caesar, I do not mean to disturb you so early, but I must!" His usually calm face was flushed and his eyes bulging.

"What is it?"

"There's a plot to assassinate you! Today!" He waved a dagger.

I shrank back. For a moment he looked as if he would thrust it into me. Was *he* the assassin?

But then he said, "A slave, along with his wife, has come to us, betraying the plot of his master."

"Who is his master?" I dreaded the answer.

"Flavius Scaevinus," he said.

My friend! Now I felt as if I *was* stabbed. "What did this slave say?"

"His name is Milichus. I will bring him in, and he can tell you the story directly."

"Very well." I braced myself against the desk, leaning on my knuckles. Oh, Zeus, give me strength for this. How can I hear this? The dagger lay before me, glinting in the early-morning sunlight—the thing meant to be plunged into me up to its hilt.

In a moment Epaphroditus returned, a burly, bald man in tow, with his stocky wife. They bowed low.

Epaphroditus said, "Now repeat to the emperor what you told me."

Milichus nervously wrung his hands. "Caesar, my master has acted strangely. Yesterday he rewrote his will with extravagant bequests. Then he called me in and gave me this dagger, which he said he had taken from the shrine of Fortune at Ferentum, said it was too dull, had lost its edge, and I must sharpen it. He also told me to lay in a supply of bandages."

Odd, but not damning. "What else?"

"Then he gave a banquet for his friends from the Senate, and it was obviously a farewell banquet, from the toasts and the speeches."

"Has he made travel preparations?"

"No. The only preparations he made were the knife and the bandages."

"So . . . a journey that involved bloodletting and bloodshed?"

"I assume so."

"Perhaps he was preparing for suicide." But why would he? However, we cannot know what is eating at the peace of mind of someone.

"No. He was—the mood was wrong for that. He was nervous, jumpy."

"Wouldn't you be, if you planned to kill yourself?"

"From what I understand, suicides are calm, and their only worry is that something will prevent them from carrying through their plan."

I nodded to Faenius, the Praetorian on guard today. "Send soldiers to bring Scaevinus here," I ordered.

Within an hour, Scaevinus was brought in, a soldier holding each of his arms.

"Hello, Scaevinus," I said.

He looked around and saw Milichus. Immediately he drew himself up indignantly. "Caesar, what has this slave been telling you?" he demanded.

I recounted the accusations, and Scaevinus was dismissive. "He's a lying scoundrel." He pointed toward the dagger. "This is a family heirloom, kept in my bedroom, and Milichus has stolen it. As for the bandages, he made that up, so he has a charge that can rest solely on his own evidence."

"What about the banquet and the bequests? Why the change in your will?" I asked.

He looked at me. "Is it a crime to be generous? You, who are generous to a fault, would not call it so. I have given slaves their freedom and made bequests before, but this time I made them larger because with my dwindling estate I wanted to distribute it before my debt collectors swooped down." He laughed. "With these lies from Milichus,

I am glad I did not give him a bequest. Perhaps that is why he wants revenge."

It made sense. I felt an immense relief. There was no plot after all. I started to set Scaevinus free when Milichus's wife spoke up to her husband. "Aren't you forgetting something, my dear? Our master spent all afternoon closeted with Antonius Natalis." She turned to me. "Why don't you send for Natalis and question him as to what this conversation was about?"

"Yes, ask them!" said Milichus eagerly.

Again I nodded to Faenius. "Bring him in."

While we waited, Scaevinus attempted to make pleasantries but then fell silent. Milichus and his wife stood quietly. Soon Natalis was escorted in, and his face fell when he saw Scaevinus.

"Wh-what is this all about?" he asked.

"I have a few questions for you," I said. "It has to do with a conversation that you and Scaevinus had recently."

"Oh, we will gladly answer, Caesar."

"Separately," I said. "Take them to different rooms and interrogate them," I ordered the soldiers, along with scribes to record their words.

Now I must wait. I was seized with a chill dread. Scaevinus and Natalis. And the dagger was to be used today . . . where? When? It would soon be time for the Ceres festival and my opening of the games. But should I go?

Hours passed. I did not go. In midafternoon the soldiers and scribes came back with their report.

"Their stories did not match. We put them in shackles and told them they were under arrest. We laid out torture implements, and the mere sight of them was enough. They confessed."

I braced myself. I did not want to hear. I had to hear.

"Natalis broke first. He detailed a plot to assassinate you and replace you with Piso. They had suggested killing you when you visited Piso at his villa, but Piso said it would taint his good name. Natalis named many more people, including Lateranus and Seneca, who were in on the plot."

Lateranus! Seneca!

"Then Scaevinus confessed and named Quintianus, Lucan, and Senecio, as well as others."

Lucan and Senecio were no surprise, but Quintianus was.

"Tell me the details."

"It was to be today at the games. Just as you were to open them, Lateranus would kneel before you with a petition, but really to tackle you and hold you down. Then they would take turns stabbing you, with Scaevinus striking the first blow. It was to be modeled on the assassination of Julius Caesar. Hence the sacred dagger."

O gods!

"Piso was to be waiting at the Temple of Ceres nearby, and when you were dead, to be escorted to the Praetorian barracks and proclaimed emperor."

"Is he still waiting?"

"Presumably."

"Arrest him!"

How many of them were in this plot? The soldiers had spoken of "many more'" and "others." The named ones were Scaevinus, Natalis, Seneca, Piso, Lateranus, Lucan, Senecio, Quintianus—eight people. But oh, what people! They had been my friends, had been in my writers' group, had sat with me in the imperial box at the races.

I could not grapple with this horrible betrayal, this perfidy. They had eaten at my table, drunk with me, kept me company, known me well for years. And I trusted them. One of those Hebrew poems Poppaea was so taken with flitted through my mind.

For it is not an enemy who taunts me—then I could bear it; it is not an adversary who deals insolently with me—then I could hide from him. But it is you, a man, my companion, my familiar friend. We would share personal thoughts with one another . . . Even my close friend in whom I trusted, who ate my bread, has lifted his heel against me.

As it sank in, my legs turned to jelly and my mind fell into darkness.

The day had started normally, with minutes and hours passing at the usual pace. Now they were suspended, stretched out, elastic. As in a dream when there is no real chronology, so time felt now. But unlike a dream, where I need do nothing, I was called upon to act, to think, and quickly.

They wanted to kill me. I thought that danger was past, once my own family was gone. (What a damning admission!) Britannicus and his sister, my wife Octavia, had had my funeral pyre built; I was saved by Locusta when Britannicus died by the poison meant for me. Mother, too, had her schemes and threatened to kill me. And then there was Uncle Caligula, who tried to drown me. And cousin Messalina, who sent assassins to my cradle. All dead now, no longer a threat to me.

But my friends and companions! Lateranus wanted to truss me up for Scaevinus's dagger. It was already midafternoon. Was I supposed to be lying dead on the steps of the Circus Maximus by now, and Piso en route to the Praetorian barracks? What would the people in the stands have done—fled in panic? Who would have escorted Piso? My Praetorians were loyal. And . . . what would they have done with my body? Left it lying, sprawled out, wrapped in a blood-soaked toga? Or would they have done the dreadful deed of cutting off my head and dragging my body to the Tiber? Would the people have stood for that? Only soldiers could have cut through them to make it possible. And the soldiers would not have done it.

Would the assassins have fled, gone into hiding? Or would they have been on hand to welcome Piso into the Senate as their emperor?

The Senate. These traitors were all senators, excepting only Senecio and Natalis, who trafficked with them. I had always felt the contempt and hostility of that body of patricians but never thought it would come to this. This was different from the assassination of Caligula. Although senators were involved, that was a desperate, makeshift venture, done out of sight, whereas they meant to elevate my death into a public spectacle. And without the help of the disaffected Praetorians, Caligula never would have fallen. Mine were loyal, as were the *equites* class and the freedmen.

Tigellinus arrived, snapping me out of my panicked thoughts. "Caesar, Faenius told me of the plot. Heinous! Send me where you will, and I shall carry out your orders without delay."

My orders . . . my orders . . . "Arrest . . . arrest Lucan, Quintianus, and Senecio. And send someone to Seneca to interrogate him. He's been accused as well."

"I'll send Gavius Silvanus to Seneca. Where is he now?"

"I assume at Nomentum."

"We will check. I'll send Subrius to Lucan, Sulpicius to Senecio, and reserve the pleasure of Quintianus, that pederast, for myself."

"I don't think he is that," I said.

"He's a pervert. Everyone knows that," he said with a snort.

"Being a murderer is worse," I said. "And he is certainly that."

"Disgusting," said Tigellinus. "Not a redeeming quality in him."

"Call out all the guards to secure the entire city. I want the river blocked, the gates closed, and the streets patrolled. The Circus will be letting out soon—the races must have gone on unimpeded—and the crowds need to be managed."

Think only of the measures that must be taken, safety measures. Do not think of the monstrous implications behind them. Only think of what must be done, step by step. Just as your chariot horses must look only at the track ahead in a race.

"Take any suspicious persons into custody," I said. "We cannot take chances. At this point we do not know how wide the conspiracy is."

"Yes, Caesar."

"And send Silvanus to me before he goes to Seneca."

"Yes, Caesar." Tigellinus turned smartly on his heels, eager to begin his hunt.

Gavius Silvanus appeared only a few moments later. The tribune was a handsome man with a perpetually boyish look, freckle-faced and open-eyed. "Caesar?" he said, saluting.

"Has Tigellinus told you of your mission?"

He frowned. "Only that I am to find Seneca and question him. But I do not know what questions to frame."

"An assassination plot has been exposed."

The color drained from his face, making his freckles stand out. "A plot? Who was involved?"

"Some senators and their friends. Under interrogation, Antonius Natalis has named Seneca as a co-conspirator with Piso, the figurehead. Apparently Piso sent this person, Natalis, to Seneca with an urgent message to meet with him, but Seneca refused, saying it would not be in his or Piso's best interest to meet or have further communication. He then added, 'My own well-being depends on Piso's safety.' What did he mean by that? How were they involved? I need to know."

"What shall I do with him when I am there?"

"That depends on his answers. I want him to be innocent. But if he condemns himself, or confesses, you must arrest him."

"Yes, Caesar."

I sent for Poppaea. Time for her to know. By now, probably, the news had leaked out and the streets were full of gossip. That was why the Praetorians and even the new soldier recruits would be needed to secure the entire city. The rats could not be allowed to escape.

"Oh, my dear!" She rushed into the room, embracing me, smoothing my hair, running her hands over my face.

"My head is still attached," I assured her, taking her hands in mine.

"Don't joke!" she said. She clutched at her own throat as if she would choke.

"We have caught it in time," I said. "Due to the observant eye of a slave and his loyalty in reporting it."

"Thanks be to all the gods! To Jupiter the Savior. Only by the help of the gods have you escaped, within hours."

I held her in my arms, needing to feel her next to me.

For months now I have had this feeling of danger, of something lurking, just out of sight. What this it? Was this what I sensed?

"The doll," she said. "The doll the woman gave us. You didn't want to keep it. Thank all the gods you did. She told us it would save you from assassination. Maybe she sensed some threat."

"Maybe she knew about this one." A chill thought. "Maybe a lot of people knew about it." And I the only ignorant one. The unknowing victim to be.

I had eaten nothing. I should call for something, keep hunger at bay, keep strong, in order to think. "Come," I said. "Let us go into the dining room." A change of scene, a room that was the opposite of a workroom.

I leaned back onto a couch and looked at the garden frescoes on the wall of the triclinium while waiting for the food. It was a restful scene, crowded with flowers, shrubs, flowering vines, and songbirds, immersed in a blue-green not actually seen in nature. The flowers were so realistic, though, I expected to smell them, and to hear the birds.

Birds twittering. How many years ago did I hear them? Could it truly be only a few hours?

A silent slave set a tray of grapes, figs, and bread and a pitcher of wine down for us, passed by a taster. I did not want any of it, but I must make myself eat. I took a cluster of grapes and a bun. "There should be a tortoise in there," I said, pointing to the mural. "A garden without a tortoise is not complete."

"You can transfer that one from Antium," said Poppaea.

"Oh, no, he's lived there so long a change of scene might kill him," I said. "We'll find another one. A Roman one."

"Let him be loyal, then. Not a turncoat tortoise." In spite of herself, she laughed. "He would turn slowly even if he turned."

"Perhaps these traitors turned slowly, too." How long ago had they turned against me? When we sat together at the races? When we were at Petronius's Pan party? Or did it go back even before that? Had it ripened slowly, or had the decision come like a thunderclap?

And what had I done to any of them to deserve their enmity? Or to the Senate as a whole, for that matter? Had I not kept my inaugural promises to them? Was not the empire quiet and prosperous? Was Rome not rebuilt in astounding time, and much more beautiful than before?

Suddenly anger, white hot and glowing, seized me. The ingrates, the slinking, grasping, duplicitous deceivers. Piso was not the only actor among them. In fact, he was not even the best one.

I threw down my napkin and stalked out of the room.

I was restless the remainder of the day. By the time the sun was going down and I joined Poppaea in the main room, my heart was still racing. Then Tigellinus returned, sweat pouring off his face. I jumped up.

He took his helmet off and ran his hands through his soaking hair. "The net is cast," he said. "Large numbers have been arrested. There isn't room enough in the palace, so they must stay out in the grounds where the statue will go." He helped himself to a large cup of juice. "Quintianus is locked up, awaiting trial. The same for Senecio and Lucan. We got Lateranus, too. He put up a good fight, but he was no match for four soldiers."

"Where is Piso?" I had given specific orders to arrest him.

Tigellinus laughed. "He's gone to his ancestors." He took a big swallow of juice. "Before we could get him at the Temple of Ceres, he had been told the plot was betrayed. His fellows urged him to take to the streets and plead his case, that the people would follow him—what were they thinking, why would the people follow him? So he did, wandering aimlessly for a little while before going home and committing suicide. Oh, and leaving this for you."

He fumbled in his belt and pulled out a scroll. "His will. He was madly in love with you, to hear him tell it here."

I didn't want to read it. "It was only to save his family's estate," I said. "So transparent. Really, disappointing of him."

"He never had much imagination. That's why his poetry stank."

Even that made me mad. I had been so polite about his pitiful verse! For what? I threw the scroll on the table.

"So who will try these people?" Tigellinus asked.

"It can't be the Senate. The traitors are from their midst. I will try them myself. In a court here in the palace. The proceedings will all be published, so no one can claim they were unjust. And all the details will be public."

More hours passed, and then Silvanus returned, dusty and tired. Tigellinus and I leapt up; Poppaea stayed seated.

He dragged himself into the room, then asked leave to sit. "I found Seneca," he said. "But he wasn't at Nomentum. So that was a wasted few hours. He was at his other estate closer to Rome."

Suddenly it made sense. "And when did he move there?" I asked.

"Last night," said Silvanus.

"What a coincidence," said Tigellinus. "He just happens to move close to Rome the night before the plot is to take place. He wanted to be near at hand. What I heard was that Seneca was a second choice for some people. He didn't want to be too far away in case the call to duty came." He spat on the floor. Poppaea frowned at the disrespect to the mosaic.

I was too stunned to care. Seneca saw himself as a possible emperor?

"What did he say when you found him?"

"He maintained that he was innocent and that you wanted to kill him. He said, 'Well, having killed his mother and his brother, what is left to him but to murder his old teacher?' Begging your pardon, Caesar, those were his words."

To think he would fall to this. He, who had helped himself to the booty from Britannicus's estates, and had composed a speech to the Senate exonerating me for Mother's death, would now mewl and play innocent. I wouldn't dignify his charge with an answer. "What did he say to the specific charges?"

"He was haughty and said that he had rejected the overtures from Piso for a meeting. And as for the phrase 'my well-being depends on your safety,' it was only a polite ending. He had no reason to especially value the health of any man, except—except an emperor's. And this emperor knew that he, Seneca, was not one for idle flattery, so had no reason to flatter Piso. Nero himself could attest that he was no flatterer."

Except when it suited him, which was often. "What was his mood?"

"He seemed oblivious to any danger. Or perhaps that is how Stoics behave in such situations."

Stoics . . . suddenly I remembered a passage in one of his essays, to the effect that if a ruler proved insane or cruel, there was no remedy for him but death. Was that what he thought of me? That I was a tyrannical madman? Why would he think that? But the only thing that mattered was that he did think it. Had he not said as much in the *Octavia*? He had called me *Master of every evil art . . . foul emperor . . . monstrous tyrant . . . whose infamous yoke oppresses all the world . . .* Those were his own words, not the persons whose mouths he put them in. I fit his description of the ruler who should be put to death. *Perhaps you would like to put those burdens down,* he had said not long ago.

"Was there any hint that he might be contemplating suicide?" He had spoken of it often enough, and it would be the better way now. That, too, was part of his Stoicism. And since he had made a show of pretending I was poisoning him, he must have his deathbed scenario, complete with speeches, prepared.

"No. Not that I detected."

I sighed. "Then he will have to be ordered to it. Return in the morning to deliver the verdict."

Silvanus bowed his head. "As you wish, Caesar."

"I don't wish it, but it must be."

He left. Then I asked everyone else to leave as well, even Poppaea.

Outside, where the birds had sung, it was silent. The bushes rustled slightly. I had pronounced a death sentence on the person I had known and esteemed for so long, who had steered me through boyhood and on into manhood until the light had faded and we parted ways. I had never thought I would have to make such a choice. Or that I could make it and sleep thereafter.

Sleep. I was beyond exhausted, almost too tired to rise and go to bed. I sat staring in the dim light. I was not surprised to see the dark figure, the one who looked like me, in the shadows. My decision had called him out; he ran parallel to me, keeping pace with me, coming closer all the while.

XXXVII

The second day of the foiled conspiracy dawned, and now there stretched the wretched task of capturing the rest of the traitors and administering justice. The Senate, the Senate should have that responsibility, but no. They could not police their own; they could hardly be honest. How many of them were corrupted, part of the plot?

And during the night my anger at the betrayers had grown, not ebbed. These, my erstwhile friends, had received nothing but bounties from me. I had done them no wrong. What were their claimed grievances against me?

I had no doubt that others could have real grievances. No ruler is perfect; we all make mistakes, omissions, insult by accident, forget obligations. But those injured by such mistakes were not the plotters—no, the streets were quiet, there was no outcry against me, no marching mobs.

But my false friends, what were they hoping to gain by deposing me? They had plenty already, thanks to my open hand!

I told Epaphroditus to prepare the largest palace chamber for the hearings. It was one of the most beautiful and now would be forever tainted from these proceedings. But it was the safest place to hold them. It couldn't be in the Curia—the Senate House—nor in the Forum in one of the basilicas, because those were public places.

I dressed formally and would sit on a high bench at the end of the room. The accused would stand before me, guarded on both sides by

Praetorians. I would not be the only one to question them. The two prefects, Tigellinus and Faenius, could, as well as court officials and lawyers who wished to. At the end of the hearings I would pronounce the sentence. Two scribes would record all the proceedings as well as the verdict.

I had always enjoyed hearing cases and had a keen interest in the law, but this was a heavy duty. If I were truly mad, or a tyrant, I would not be competent to preside. Now let them listen to me and let the world judge whether I fit their false accusations or deserved their wish to kill me.

The proceedings would begin that morning when I would see Lateranus—fitting, since he was the designated first to lay hands on me and set the plot in motion.

He was led in by two soldiers, his leg chains clanking as he walked. He was so strong that the heavy chains did not hinder his gait. He stood in front of me, staring at me as if I were the one on trial.

"Plautius Lateranus, you have been accused of planning the assassination of the emperor," I said.

He just continued staring. Then he jerked his head in a dismissive gesture.

"Speak. You are ready enough to speak on other occasions." At Petronius's party, for example.

"I have nothing to say."

"Read the charges against him," I ordered the court lawyer.

The lawyer held the paper out at arm's length and said, "That you were privy and part of a plot to assassinate the emperor on the last day of the Festival of Ceres in public view at the races. Your assignment was to kneel before him to ask a favor and then overpower him. To use your friendship with him to approach him to harm him."

Lateranus just continued to stare, a slight smile on his face.

"Is this true?" asked the lawyer.

Lateranus shrugged.

"You are in contempt of court to refuse to answer," said the lawyer.

"We'll make him answer!" said Faenius roughly. He grabbed Lateranus's shoulder.

Lateranus laughed, and Faenius cuffed him, spinning him around. He drew back his hand to strike again.

"Enough," I said.

Lateranus cocked his head. "Do you truly want me to speak, Caesar?"

Enough of these games! "Of course I want you to speak in your own defense."

"What difference does it make? I am going to die."

"I want to know what you are willing to die for."

"Do you, then? Well, I'll tell you. For the Republic!"

There was a collective gasp in the room.

"The Republic?" asked the lawyer. Lateranus might as well have said, *the ancient kingdom of Babylonia*, the Republic was so obsolete, except in poetry.

"Yes, there are those of us who still believe in it and will do anything to bring it back, to restore to the Roman people their freedom from the iron rule of these emperors, so alien to our true way of government." Now that he had decided to speak, the words rushed out.

"And to do this you were willing to kill me?"

"Of course. That's obvious."

I felt chilled to the bone. Even my fingers grew numb. "Then the sentence is equally obvious. Lateranus, you are condemned to death for crimes against the emperor and the state." I motioned to the soldiers. "Take him out. Now."

"I want to go home and say good-bye to my family first, and write my will."

"You should have thought of that before you joined the plot. No. You will go the way you had planned for me to go. Were you going to allow me to say good-bye to my family or my people? I think not." I nodded, and the soldiers dragged him out.

I should have felt sad at the pronouncement, but instead I felt a fiery vindication.

The court was dismissed until afternoon, when Quintianus and Senecio would be tried.

In the meantime I conferred with Faenius and Tigellinus as to the ongoing investigation. Soldiers had fanned out everywhere, searching.

Many of the people who had first been rounded up were let go, and the remaining ones were under closer questioning.

"They are vermin!" said Faenius. His face was red and his usual handsome features contorted.

"My, you are incensed about this. I've seldom seen you so worked up," said Tigellinus.

"I can't help it!" he said. He took a deep breath. "I wanted to kill him right there in the courtroom. Insolent bastard!"

"He will be dead before the court reconvenes," I assured him. "Just not by your hand."

Fortified by the short respite from these grim proceedings, I returned to the room to preside over the next trial.

Quintianus was led in, his head held high. He, too, wore chains, but they were lighter ones and he could move easily. He did not look so much the dandy now. His night of incarceration had dirtied him, flattened his curls, and given him a different perfume than the scent he usually wore.

"Afranius Quintianus," I said, repeating the formula, "you have been accused of planning the assassination of the emperor. You are here to answer these charges."

"Who accused me of it?" he said. "I don't know why I am brought in here."

The lawyer read out the accusation, ending with, "Flavius Scaevinus accused you of being part of the assassination plot," he said.

"Scaevinus! I am innocent. That man is a liar!" Quintianus said.

"So you claim to be innocent?" I asked.

"Yes. I swear it!"

I looked at him. He was a weak man, hardly the stern stuff of assassins. But in a pack of hyenas, individual strength is not as important as numbers.

Tigellinus and Faenius were sputtering with disgust at the man, ready to drag him away.

I leaned forward. "Quintianus, I have known you as a friend. If you will confess what you know, you will have immunity." By that I meant that I would be as lenient with him as the law allowed.

He jumped at it eagerly. "Immunity?"

I expected him to continue to protest his innocence and say he had nothing to confess. Instead he poured out a list of names of his friends— the senators Novius Priscus, Annius Pollio, Glitius Gallus, Musonius Rufus, and six more. Then he added four *equites* for good measure.

I sat back, trying to keep the shock from showing on my face. That made seventeen senators and six *equites*—so far. Seventeen senators!

Then, feeling safe, he said, "And I confess that I myself was a plotter. I hated you because you wrote that insulting poem about me. About my hair!"

I motioned to Faenius. I did not trust Tigellinus to keep from strangling Quintianus. "Take him back to wherever he is being held," I said.

"You promised me freedom!" he protested.

"I promised you immunity. They are not the same thing. And we need to hold you a bit longer in case you remember other things. You may know more than you just told us."

Shaken by his revelation, I asked the court to break for an hour. I hurried back to my private quarters.

Seventeen senators. Six *equites*. Twenty-three traitors, right in the bosom of the government. I told Tigellinus to order the newly named to be arrested.

What were their motives? Were they as high-minded as Lateranus about the Republic, or as petty and personal as Quintianus and his wounded vanity?

A great foreboding came over me. What really was happening beneath the placid surface of the inner circle of Rome? I was suddenly privy to a clear view of the depths of it; until now I had only perceived the shallows.

Thank all the gods that the people, and the soldiers, were still loyal.

When again I was seated on the judgment bench, Senecio was brought in. Led by two guards, he was sauntering as best he could with shackles on his legs.

"Claudius Senecio, you have been accused of planning the assassination of the emperor. You are here to answer these charges." How many more times must I say these words?

He merely bowed his head and gave his sly smile, the one I knew so well.

The lawyer read out the charges. "You are accused of being part of the so-called Piso Plot to assassinate the emperor and replace him with Gaius Calpurnius Piso. How do you plead?"

"I am not guilty. Why am I here?"

"You were named by one of the key conspirators."

"Who?"

"Scaevinus," I said.

"Surely you don't believe that man?" he said.

"And why should I not believe him?"

"He wants to drag others into his scummy pond."

"Why would he want to do that?"

"How do I know?"

"Scaevinus will have his own trial. This is yours," I said.

"I am innocent. This is a mistake."

"Then perhaps you can tell me why you made inquiries about my whereabouts—the hour and day I would be somewhere. Why would you want to know that? You need not go to the Macellum Magnum to see me, or to the Circus. Why, you were my *friend*—you did not have to search for me in crowds."

"Who told you that?"

"Someone I trust utterly, to whom a lie would be unthinkable." To my misfortune. "You should admit what you know. If you do, I will give you immunity."

Now he gave a full smile, the sort a man makes after he has concluded a sale with a merchant to his own advantage. "Very well. I am pleased, now that it is safe and I cannot be touched, to name my co-conspirators—for yes, I am one!" And he spilled another list of names. More senators and *equites*.

"Take him away," I said.

He squawked a protest. "No, I am to be set free!"

"I never said that," I said. "Immunity is not freedom. Take him away," I repeated.

Faenius leapt to it, pushing him so roughly he almost fell. He stumbled and righted himself. The smile was gone from his face, replaced by fear. He was led out, back to prison, where he would be held.

T hat was enough for the day. I needed to stop and hear what was happening elsewhere. I dismissed the court and took two Praetorians and Epaphroditus back to my private workroom.

It was late afternoon, a balmy spring day. Somewhere outside the palace ordinary people were strolling in gardens, enjoying the sweet air and the butterflies. Would their lives have been markedly different if Piso instead of me sat on the throne? Did it matter who was emperor?

This was sophomoric. Of course it did. Augustus was different from Caligula.

Ah, but to the people in the gardens, was he?

I sank down and poured out a cup of wine. There were more inquiries to be made.

"What has happened to Seneca?" I asked. "Send for Silvanus."

Faenius hurried off to do so, while Epaphroditus, Tigellinus, and I waited. Soon the two returned.

"You delivered the verdict to Seneca?" I asked Silvanus, who looked distressed.

"Not I," he admitted. "I sent one of my staff officers."

"And how was the command received?" I asked.

"Calmly, so it was reported. There was a meal, farewell words. He took the knife. But it did not work. He was too emaciated; his veins had shriveled. He then took hemlock."

"Ah, in imitation of Socrates," I said. Posturing to the end.

"But it did not have an effect, either," he said. "He had so fortified himself against poison that he was immune to it." He shook his head. "Seneca and his wife, Paulina, then cut their wrists together. He then sent her into another room so she would not see him suffer."

"She was not under sentence!" I said.

"We knew that, Caesar, so the staff officer sent soldiers and slaves into the room to bandage her arms and stop the bleeding. She survived. Apparently she was glad to be saved, in spite of telling her husband she was privileged to die with him."

A relief. She lived. "What of Seneca?"

"When all else failed, he was carried into a hot bath where he expired. He sprinkled a few drops of the water on his slaves and said it was a libation to Jupiter. Then he was gone."

"Gone."

"Yes, cremated under his own instructions. Paulina is recovering."

It was over. Seneca was gone. I felt a great weariness fall like a mantle on me, and a deep loneliness in its wake.

The night passed slowly—but probably not as slowly as it did for Quintianus and Senecio. Lateranus was dead. He had been executed in the afternoon, at a spot reserved for the punishment of slaves. Apparently the first blow did not end him, but he bravely braced for the second. There were no speeches, no words, no accusations. He died silently.

I fell silent, too. I did not want to talk to anyone, not even Poppaea. The accusations of Lateranus, Quintianus, and Senecio echoed through my mind. Senecio I had suspected, but not Lateranus and Quintianus. They had questioned the expenditure of the Golden House, but nothing hostile beyond that. How little we can penetrate a disguise if it is well maintained.

In the morning the trials began again. The next to be tried was to be Lucan, and I dreaded it. Of all of them, Lucan had been the closest to me, as the only true poet in the group, a man of immense talent. He had admired—no, idolized—me. But that had changed—why? Perhaps it was only the natural evolution of an artist. We start out with giants that we admire, but as we grow in our own art we see them only as people, and finally as equals or even inferiors. Although we outgrow them and cast them aside as models, that should not mean we want to kill them.

It was a rainy, blustery day. Black-bottomed clouds hung low in the sky, and thunder rumbled. Today my wool toga was not unwelcome, for the warmth it provided.

Tigellinus came up to me and said, "I am posting two more soldiers behind you on the bench," he said, indicating the large crowd. "Faenius and I are handling the prisoners, so we need Sulpicius and Subrius to focus their entire attention on the room in case of trouble."

I just nodded. One never knew what might happen; I had quickly learned that lesson in the last three days.

Lucan was brought into the room, wearing shackles like his predecessors.

"Marcus Annaeus Lucanus, you have been accused of planning the assassination of the emperor," I said. A world of disillusion for me in those few words.

He smiled, that winning smile—it had won me from the beginning, but no more. "Really?" he said.

Faenius spoke up. "Address the emperor with respect!" he barked, smacking Lucan's shoulder.

"Yes, *really*," I said sardonically. "Will the court lawyer please read the charges?"

The lawyer once again held out a paper and read, "That you were privy and part of a plot to assassinate the emperor during the Festival of Ceres in the so-called Piso conspiracy."

Lucan shifted on his feet, weighing his words, as if he were at a party deciding which witty phrase to use. Oh, if only he were not so fair in looks, if only his blue eyes did not seem so honest, it would not be so difficult to see him clearly and fairly.

"I deny this charge," he finally said. "And may I ask who accused me?"

"Of course you may. All is out in the open. It was Scaevinus."

Lucan gave a twisted smile. "Oh, *him*. Never trust the words of a man with a scar, I always say!"

I was appalled. This was not a joke. "Answer the charge," I ordered him.

While Lucan was thinking—most likely of another bon mot—

Tigellinus suddenly spoke up. Extracting a scroll from his satchel, he said, "While the accused is delaying, here is hard evidence of his treasonous thoughts toward his emperor." He handed it to me.

De Incendio Urbis—*On the Burning of the City.* I held it up for Lucan to see.

"Where did you get that?" he cried.

"Why, are you ashamed of it? Do you want to polish its phrases a bit more?" I asked. "I think even clumsy words do the work well enough. You paint me as an arsonist, as having caused the Fire." Oh, would this bogus charge never die away?

From the back of the room, Scaevinus, who was waiting to be tried in the afternoon, and doubtless was stung at the jibe about his scar, yelled, "He promised me he would give me your head as a gift, Nero!"

Behind me, Sulpicius and Subrius stiffened and put their hands on their swords, moving closer to me.

"Remove Scaevinus from the court," I said. I did not want the two prisoners exchanging information, playing off one another. I turned to my guards. "No need for worry," I assured them. I turned back to Lucan. At that moment there was a tremendous clap of thunder, echoing several times.

"Clearly there is much here that needs exposing. I am surprised that you should harbor these grievances against me, considering our past. I prefer to believe that the last accusation was a fabrication of a desperate man, Scaevinus. He wants to drag others down with him. But if you will cooperate and tell us what you know of this plot, you will be granted immunity."

Now his demeanor changed. "Immunity, you say? I may speak freely?"

"Yes," I said. "It would be helpful."

He took a deep breath, like a man preparing to dive into cold water—ready for the shock, but still holding back, still hesitating. Then he leapt. "Very well. Here it is: I hate you. You have hindered my career, forbidding me to recite my verses in public. It is because you are envious of me. You know I am the better poet, and your verse cannot stand up to mine."

I hate you. He had said it. It was I who had the shock of the cold water after all, not him.

"You may well be a better poet," I said. "That is not the question. But your verses of the *Civil War* are treasonous, advocating the Republic. That is why I don't want them read in public."

"You were willing enough to have my verses read in public when they eulogized *you*! Oh, those phrases I had to write, sickening, sycophantic praise, it was a parody, I didn't mean a word of it. But you were too blind to recognize it. You believed it."

"I believed it because I believed you were an honest man and an honest poet."

"No one can be honest to the emperor. Don't you know that even now? How can someone who is a master of Greek, of music composition, of architectural designs be so stupid?"

Faenius stepped in. "He's said enough. Stop these treasonous words!"

"No, let him speak. I want to hear it—all of it."

Suddenly Lucan realized he had gone too far out onto the ice to come back, and it was cracking under him. So be it. Down he would go. "Tyrant! Oppressor! Yes, I'd offer up your head if I could get it. And here's something for you, here's my gift to you; you want the names of other conspirators. Add my mother, Acilia, to the list! My mother! Now you know I am modeling myself on you—that's what you wanted, wasn't it?—everyone to admire you and applaud you? I am ready to kill my mother—like you did yours!"

The courtroom was silent, and suddenly another loud boom of thunder rang out.

"Take him away," I said. I was too stunned to say anything else, even to respond. Again the guards had moved closer behind me.

Faenius took Lucan out of the room and to prison.

"Court will reconvene this afternoon," I said, my voice so low Tigellinus had to lean close to hear it.

XXXVIII

Tigellinus and Faenius escorted me back to the private room. Perhaps they were afraid I could not stand on my own, or might collapse, and they must be there to catch me. But my walking was not what was affected.

Poppaea was waiting, with food and drink. But I wanted none of it. The only drink I craved was the waters of nepenthe, that would erase sorrow, make me forget. The drug of forgetfulness that Homer extolled. Where was it? Where could a man go to find it?

"Rest, Caesar," said Faenius. "That last was difficult to hear." He patted a couch, well pillowed. I sank down on it. The judgment bench's wood was hard. But that was the least of it.

"What has happened?" asked Poppaea.

"I can't talk about it," I said. "Not now." There had been too much, too fast—the widening plot, the death of Seneca, and now the revelations of Lucan. His accusations rang in my mind. He had called me stupid, blind. Perhaps he was right. How could I not have known?

But . . . I had sensed something amiss. Yes. I recalled now the cutting remarks of these conspirators about the Golden House, about the rebuilding of Rome, about people cursing *whoever* had started the Fire, about the Circus Maximus race being "fixed." But a ruler who took umbrage at every little remark would soon become so suspicious and touchy that he would degenerate into what they had called me—a tyrant. I had thought to be no such thing. But, perhaps a ruler who did *not* take umbrage readily was soon a dead one, oblivious to danger around him even as the knives flashed.

No more. This morning saw the death of my tolerance. It would be buried with Seneca's ashes. The gods had saved me from my own folly of trust, but they would not do it again. Inside, something hardened that had grown soft over the years, the years since the dangerous passages I had navigated as little more than a child in order to survive to manhood. I had not forgotten my skills, just let them sleep, thinking I was past needing them. I was wrong.

There was still this afternoon to get through, the trial of Scaevinus. Later there would be trials of all the others named, but those were not my personal friends, and the level of betrayal was not so monstrous.

The afternoon trial opened as the others had. The skies were still stormy, and rain was pelting down, rattling on the roof. Subrius and Sulpicius took their places behind me. Seated on the bench, I watched Scaevinus make his way back into the room. His chains dragged; he made no attempt to pick up his feet, just shuffled along. He stood looking at me.

"Flavius Scaevinus, you have confessed to planning the assassination of the emperor." The phrase repeated itself now like a litany.

He just stared back. Finally he said, "Yes, I confessed."

The lawyer read the formal charge. "That you were privy and part of a plot to assassinate the emperor, and claimed the right to strike the first blow."

"That is what my slave claimed."

Before I could correct him, that he had confessed it himself, Faenius yelled, "Do you deny it? You yourself admitted it!"

Scaevinus swung around and gave him a withering look. "Oh, yes, that is correct."

"That is not all you confessed," I said. "You named Lucan, Lateranus, and Senecio as accomplices."

Scaevinus nodded.

"Do you stand by these accusations?"

Oddly, Faenius shook his head, slowly, looking at me. Behind me I heard Sulpicius and Subrius relax the grip on their swords. They were very close to me.

I turned back to the men in front of me. Faenius was frowning. Then he hissed at Scaevinus, "Who else? There must be others! Stop hiding them!"

Scaevinus shrugged. "I am doomed. I may as well speak freely. And here are the names I know for certain: Petronius and Vestinus."

Petronius!

"You coward! There are more than that!" said Faenius. "Tell the truth, or you will be whipped! Who are the rest?"

Scaevinus smiled. "No one knows more than you do, Faenius. Why not share your knowledge with your emperor?"

Faenius went pale and could not reply, beyond an incoherent stammer.

"Yes, he is well informed about the plot, since he is part of it!" Scaevinus pointed at him. He shook his head. "Such ferocity to mask your own involvement. Such overacting!" he said. "Pity."

I gave orders for Cassius, a soldier as big and strong as Hercules, to bind Faenius. Then Scaevinus called out, "Sulpicius! Subrius! Come and join your commander!" Behind me they tried to bolt, but more soldiers grabbed them.

I was aghast. My Praetorian prefect and two of his closest subordinates! Scaevinus went on, naming more and more Praetorians, until he ran out of breath. Oh, so fortunate—the gods were protecting me once again—that the room was filled with loyal soldiers. I had stationed them there to keep order from the observers, and now they had to capture and restrain their own fellow soldiers.

I ordered the room cleared of everyone but the plotters and the military necessary to arrest them. Then I came down from the judge's bench and stood before Faenius. His hands were tied behind him, and Cassius had a muscular arm around his neck. He remained silent. I waved my hand to have him taken away, and Cassius steered him out.

Now I confronted Subrius. His broad face betrayed no fear. He burst out, "I am not one of them. Do you think I would lower myself to be involved in a plot masterminded by these effete civilians?"

Scaevinus laughed. "It seems that the answer is yes."

Suddenly Subrius sneered, "Yes, it is true! You were only saved by Faenius just now. I had my sword ready to plunge into you, but he shook his head. Why did he stop me? It was ludicrous, four of us who wanted you dead, you unarmed, and us pretending to fight one another! Thanks to his faintheartedness, we lost our chance."

The sound of the hands on the swords behind me . . . I shuddered. "Why have you forgotten your oath of loyalty? As a soldier, that is part of your honor," I said.

He glared at me. "Because I detest you!" he spat. "I was as loyal as any soldier in the realm as long as you deserved my respect. I began hating you when you murdered your mother and wife and became a charioteer, actor, and incendiary!"

His strange, garbled accusations rang out—that driving chariots and acting were on a criminal par with murder. Or arson.

"But I didn't want Piso," he continued. "I told them, why replace a lyre player with an actor? No, some of us, including me, wanted Seneca."

So that was where Seneca came in. Now it made sense.

"I had a mind to slay you when you were unguarded during the Fire. Or better yet, in sight of thousands while you were onstage!" he crowed.

I stared at him, stunned. Then I turned to Sulpicius. Even bound, he kept his rigid posture, back straight as a lead pipe, head aloft. "And you?" I asked.

"It was the only way to put an end to your evil ways. The only remedy at hand."

Four more Praetorians were bound and waiting in line, among them Silvanus.

I faced him. "And you?"

"That is why I could not deliver the death command to Seneca. Faenius told me I had to go through with it or arouse suspicion, but I couldn't."

At least he had a tattered remnant of honor in his behavior.

"Take them all away!" I ordered the loyal soldiers holding the prisoners. I could bear no more.

I withdrew into my inmost chamber in my apartments. Outside the rain kept pounding, blowing sideways and splattering through the windows, while the bushes whipped their branches back and forth.

The stunning revelation that many Praetorians had turned against me was so devastating that I almost could not even repeat their names to myself, as if that would conjure up more evil, open more abysses. I felt as if I had fallen into one, a long bottomless black one. It would take me a long time to come to terms with this deep betrayal by those pledged to protect me and whom I trusted utterly. And in the meantime I had decisions to execute—oh, that word!—that could not be delayed.

The doll lay on a table in the corner. Could that truly have been the talisman that saved me just hours from death? I could never know. Fate is inexplicable.

Eventually I sent for Tigellinus. He was loyal—wasn't he?

"*Is anyone?*" I cried to the blank walls. "*Is anyone?*"

Tigellinus entered gingerly, bringing a wine pitcher and a plate of fruit. He set them down carefully, then said softly, "Caesar, here is some refreshment."

"Refreshment?" My head was buried in my arms on the table. Now I looked up. "There is nothing that can ever refresh me again."

"I hate to be so down to earth, but you will feel better if you eat."

"Ever the soldier," I said. But I made no move to pick up any food.

"Shall I send for Poppaea?"

"Not yet," I said. No, not yet.

"They are dead," said Tigellinus. "Faenius, Sulpicius, and Subrius." But their hatred would live on. "Oh," I said listlessly.

"Don't you want to hear?"

"You obviously want to tell me," I said.

"Faenius wrote a whining will lamenting his sad fate," he said.

"So I will be kind to his family," I said. How tedious. How predictable. Where were his noble principles now—begging to the charioteer he hated?

"Subrius complained about the grave that was dug for him. He said it wasn't up to military standards, proof of how discipline had fallen off under your command."

Any other time that would have made me laugh. But now, no.

"Let him rest in it in peace," I said. "Even though it isn't up to standards. He will get used to it."

That night I lay motionless on my bed, floating as if in a warm and still sea, my mind emptied of everything but desolation and despair. Perhaps this was what the Furies really were—not wrinkled horrors with dogs' heads, but—*this*.

L ucan was allowed to return to his home, under guard, and permit-ted to commit suicide in his own time. His mother was not ar-rested. He had accused her, likening her to Mother, only to wound me. He had succeeded.

His demise was witnessed and described by his guards; three days afterward I read the report. As he weakened from loss of blood, he had recited lines from his poem about a wounded soldier who had also died of blood loss. He had made sure his last words were literary, and thus he would be remembered—as a poet, not a traitor.

Vestinus followed likewise, committing suicide in an upper cham-ber while his dinner guests sat downstairs, surrounded by guards. He made no speeches or statements. Neither did Scaevinus, Senecio, or Quintianus. Those three had gallant deaths out of keeping with their lives. Their exit from the stage of life proved their bravest moment.

T he trials went on. And on. In the end there were forty-one con-firmed conspirators—nineteen senators, seven *equites*, eleven sol-diers, and four women. Fourteen senators were sent into exile, as well as Scaevinus's wife, Caedicia. Three people were pardoned, including Antonius Natalis. One was acquitted—the conscionable Gaius Silvanus. Lucan's mother, Acilia, was never charged. These people had not been actively involved, or, like Lucan's mother, were named out of spite or revenge by someone with no proof. There were enough actual traitors without drumming up false ones.

Petronius was the last to perish. In characteristic fashion, he hosted a dinner at his house on the Aventine. The guests arrived after he had already cut his wrists. But he bound them up, entertained, then loosened the bandages again, and so on all night, dying little by little, but making it seem a game. His entertainment was not lofty words nor philosophical discourses on the immortality of the soul à la Seneca but light verses and frivolous poems. When he finally expired, it looked natural, as if he had dozed off after too much wine—something the guests had witnessed many times before. Thus he laughed at death, treating it as inconsequential.

Will my venture succeed? Thanks be to all the gods, the answer was "no."

It was finished. From mid-April until late May, Rome had been in the grip of the upheaval of the conspiracy and its aftermath. I published an edict of the proceedings of the trials, appending statements of the informers and confessions of the convicted, and their sentences.

For Rome, it was over. For me, it never could be.

XXXIX

I had hardly noticed the spring, and now it was summer. An entire season had passed, slipping by, while I grappled with the trials and the dismaying consequences. It was June—a luscious, rose-scented June—when I had to address the Senate, or what was left of it.

That was a turn of phrase. In truth, the loss of the nineteen senators did not strip the Senate of its numbers. But they did strip it of my trust. Looking out at the remaining senators, I could never know how many were traitors in their hearts, who had just not been detected, or who might become traitors in the future. They had murdered my sense of safety if they had failed to murder my person.

Nonetheless I must play my part and play it better than Scaevinus and Faenius had played theirs. I wore my finest lightweight imperial toga to address this august—in their own minds—body. I was flanked by the two consuls of the year, one of them being a substitute for a substitute, as consul-elect Lateranus had been first replaced by Vestinus, who had likewise proved a traitor, and a replacement had been found for him as well.

A hundred faces looked back me, hard to see with the light against them. It being warm, the great doors of the Curia had been left open, and the bright summer sun streamed in, caressing and heating the marble floor.

Before I could speak, two senators came forward, bowing and prostrating themselves. "Oh, blessed emperor!" they said. "We thank the Sun himself for miraculously preserving our most glorious emperor."

Sol. Yes, Sol had protected me. In doing this he had shown me that I was his true son, as he had revealed in the dream.

"Rise," I said. The two men stood up.

"I thank you," I said. "I am truly blessed, as you call me, but blessed in having such loyal subjects as you all before me. We will not speak of those who have forfeited their places here; you can read all the proceedings in the edict I have issued and posted all over Rome. What is important is what remains—the foundation of Rome and your emperor, chosen by the gods to protect it and you." I sat back down. Was that flowery enough?

Then poured out the honors and flatteries. There were to be formal thank-offerings to Sol in his ancient temple in the Circus Maximus, the site of the planned assassination. A Temple of Welfare would be constructed. The month of April, the month I was saved, was to be renamed Neroneus. There would be a memorial in the temple from which Scaevinus had taken the dagger.

"That is not enough!" a senator from Tarracina suddenly said, rising and addressing the entire body. "We must erect a temple to his divinity, to the god Nero, who is more than a mortal and should be worshipped as such."

Everyone leapt to his feet and cried, "Yes! Yes!" They bowed toward me, as toward Sol himself.

Now I rose. "No, no," I said, holding up my hands. "That is not fitting. I refuse to allow it."

They then extolled my godly humility.

But it was not my humility. Since traditionally an emperor is only deified after death, there would come men who would take it as a mandate to help me enter that state where I would indeed be eligible for the title. Let me not tempt fate.

"I myself will dedicate the dagger on the Capitoline to Jupiter the Guardian," I said, to mollify them. "That is enough for me."

I held the dagger in my hands. Milichus had not sharpened it, disobeying the order to do so, and it was dull and rusty, but could have carried out its task well enough. It would have been even more painful than a sharp, clean blade. Now I ran my thumb along it, feeling its rough edge. A dagger fit for an emperor? If assassination is the goal, any dagger is fit for it.

I had finished dressing for the ceremony at Jupiter's temple on the Capitoline. A new imperial purple toga, with a fold of it draped over my head. If I would face Jupiter, I must face him in the trappings of my high office—not only emperor but Pontifex Maximus.

The outer grounds of the main palace were now connected to the Via Sacra, the Triumphal route that ran through the Forum and then up the steep path to the Temple of Jupiter. I set out, with all the ceremony needed to endow this action with its necessary gravitas, accompanied by my Praetorians and the many orders of priests of the Roman state religion. We passed the Temple of the Divine Julius, the two basilicas, the Rostra, the Temple of Saturn.

I was walking the Triumphal route of Claudius that I had watched from a crowd when I was only seven, dazzled by the glory of the procession, standing on tiptoe to see over taller heads. Now others strained to see me. The day was sweetly warm, and the scent of roses from the quarters of the Vestal Virgins spread out over the Forum, strongest as we passed by.

I came to the place where Claudius had descended from the Triumphal chariot and made his slow, painful way on foot up to the Temple of Jupiter. I would not have trouble with the path, but I wondered if there would be another Triumph during my reign. They celebrated military victories. But could there not be a Triumph celebrating achievements in other endeavors? Why only military?

I approached the great, towering Temple that crowned the Capitoline Hill. Its vast dimensions made it a fitting dwelling for the ruler of all the gods. A huge seated statue of Jupiter awaited me, one of his feet peeking out from under his robe, his stern visage inspecting me. At the base of the statue lay withered wreaths of honor, plaques of vows and gratitude, and cut branches of evergreen oak and olive, sacred to him. I bowed and then knelt.

"Jupiter, greatest and best, avenger of wrongs, and great guardian of my fate, who has saved me from the danger of this dagger by divine intervention, I dedicate this spoil to you." I leaned forward and laid the dagger at his feet. "In thanksgiving, I vow a gold coin to Jupiter the Guardian, Jupiter *Custos*."

I stood, trembling. It was not hyperbole. To have come so close, to be delivered only hours before the assassination was to take place, and by the hands of those close to me who I trusted, could only have come from a god. The mightiest of them, the ruler of heaven, protecting their ruler on earth.

The warm weather called me back to the pavilion of the Golden House, empty during the winter months while we lived in the main, better heated, palace below. Poppaea and I returned to it eagerly. The artists had been hard at work for several weeks, and the stonemasons had almost finished their installations. Now the polishers would buff and shine the marble. Painters were carefully applying gold leaf on the highest plaster of the ceilings.

The midsummer sun streamed in, warming the rooms. In spite of their beauty, the rooms had melancholy echoes for me. I ordered the statue of Terpsichore to be moved out of the Odysseus room to an outside covered portico. There was no more writer's room; I would never write a line there.

Our black room was still beguiling, and Fabullus had finished the fresco in the Hector room, the one of Protesilaus that Poppaea had requested. We stood before it, appraising it.

"It is dark," she said.

"It is a dark subject," I replied. "The first death in the Trojan War, and a wife only allowed to see her husband again for three hours before he must return to the underworld."

"The colors are muted and murky," she said.

"As they should be." I held her close to me. "But if we should ever lose one another, would not a cloudy glimpse be better than darkness?" I held her closer. She was almost entirely recovered now; none of the weakness that she had suffered earlier. Perhaps it had been the pregnancy after all.

"Come, let us go outside." We walked through an open door and out into the courtyard, where we could look down into the valley of the city. The gardens were taking shape; another growing season and they would look as we had envisioned them in the plans. The vines were growing lustily and the saplings had survived the winter and were covered with fresh new leaves and green-stemmed branches.

"It is near the solstice," said Poppaea. "The longest day of the year will soon be upon us."

The time when Sol would be riding highest. Sol, who had anointed me his chosen one, his son. I should have a celebration for him, but I did not want to plan one now. It was too soon after the conspiracy to celebrate anything. But in the autumn the second Neronian Games were scheduled, five years after the first ones. It would serve as a return to normalcy.

We sat on a marble bench and felt the gentle wind, watched the white and yellow butterflies darting in and out of the bushes. The characteristic acrid smell of sun-warmed boxwood rode the breeze.

Gardeners were working on the far side of the plot, their shoes crunching on the gravel, their low laughter a happy sound. But as we sat luxuriating in the majesty of early summer, a quicker crunching of footsteps hurried our way. Tigellinus came bearing a box.

I rose. "What is this?" I asked.

The sun struck his face, illuminating the high cheekbones, the strong jaw. His jaw was clenched. "It seems Petronius left you something in his will." He handed me the box. "Shall I stay while you open it?"

"If you wish." It might have a cobra in it for all I knew. Or a poisoned pin. But most likely it contained a will in which he had left me, and Tigellinus, most of his estate, along with fulsome phrases of flattery. Almost all the other condemned men had composed such wills.

The box was a richly ornamented one, citrus wood with inlaid ivory and shining brass hinges. I opened it slowly.

Something glinted inside. As I raised the lid, the sunshine hit shards of precious stone, turning them into glowing rainbows. Pieces of his murrhine cups, the ones I had admired and offered to buy from him. I picked up one of the pieces, feeling a deep sense of loss. Such beauty destroyed. And for what?

Underneath the shattered cups was a note.

You wanted these. Now you have them!

"The vindictive bastard," said Tigellinus.

"Never mind," I said. "Here's the will." I unrolled a scroll and started to read it aloud, but soon stopped.

The last will of Gaius Petronius Arbiter:

I leave the items below to the emperor Nero Claudius Caesar Augustus Germanicus:

Herein a list of the emperor's sex romps and partners:

> *With the lady Aelia, and the lady Junia at same time, at Piso's villa, positions x, y, and z (see below for positions chart and key)*

> *With the courtesan Lucilia 3 times at Petronius's villa in Cumae, positions f and g, with salt water and honey*

> *With the noted madam Maxima, in costume, at palace, with gold dust and olive oil, positions t, r, and q*

> *With Poppaea Sabina, then Otho's wife, on Tigellinus's pleasure boat on Lake of Augustus, under the sail covers, position t*

The list continued, a very long one.

Poppaea had been reading it over my shoulder and burst out laughing.

"How does he know all this?" she asked.

"He liked to watch," I admitted. "Not just me, everyone. He said he was taking notes for scenes in his *Satyricon*. Maybe he was."

"But how did he know about us on the boat?"

"Someone must have told him. Maybe Otho himself. He seemed proud of it at the time."

She took the scroll away and read it down to the end, some twenty-five or thirty more names.

"All that was before I knew you," I said. It sounded a lame disclaimer, even to me.

But she just laughed. "I like this one," she said, pointing to the key for "position r." "Shall we try it?"

"I may have forgotten how," I said. "It was a long time ago."

"I am sure it will come back to you. It's like swimming. Once you have done it, you never forget."

"Shall I leave you alone so you can pursue this?" asked Tigellinus. "I find it strange that *you* find it so amusing."

"He meant to hurt us, to crush us like he did the cups. Instead he has inspired us," said Poppaea. "Yes! He miscalculated. It seems, my dear husband, he did not know you as well as he thought he did. Just one of his many misjudgments." She rose, took my hand. "Come. And yes, Tigellinus, you may leave us now."

I handed him the box with the broken cups but kept the will. "We will need this," I said. "A timely instruction manual."

Laughing, we ran through the gardens and back into the pavilion, hurrying to the black room, where the bed awaited. We fell on it, still laughing, and rolled over and over, tumbling like children, until we stopped, and the laughter ceased. My face was only a few inches from hers, and I looked at it in wonder, that such a creature was mine and could love me. She lay still, looking back at me. Then she kissed me, at first softly, then with eagerness and hunger. I slid my arms under her, pressing her to me, as if I would bind her to me forever, meld us into one.

"Never mind about position r," she whispered. "I cannot wait. Save it for later."

But I didn't have to wait, as I hadn't forgotten after all.

XL

LOCUSTA

My suspicions were, alas, too real. But in my profession, an acutely sensitive sense of suspicion is a basic requirement. So there was a plot, a widespread one, against him. Forty-one people, including—most ominously—the military.

From what I have heard, except for the two or three who wanted the Republic back, the rest were a sorry lot of mixed motives, mainly petty. Some had personal grievances against him—those were of his inner circle—and the soldiers disapproved of what they considered his embarrassing public performances. But Faenius, despite his high-sounding denunciations of the emperor's behavior, actually was motivated more by personal jealousy of Tigellinus, who had the emperor's ear, to the exclusion of Faenius.

The conspiracy had no clear goal, except to remove Nero. Some wanted to replace him with Piso, but the soldiers preferred Seneca, and planned to kill Piso and exchange Seneca for him. It all came to nothing—because it was betrayed by a suspicious slave on the very morning it was to take place.

Nero, however, believes that only Jupiter saved him at the last moment, that he was divinely protected. But he now takes measures to avert any repetition of this close call and has increased his oppressive spy network's vigilance.

In the first ten years of his rule, he was lenient and merciful. There were no executions and only two banishments, one for treason and one for libel on the emperor. Even in the aftermath of the conspiracy, more senators were banished than executed, and one of the conspirators was even acquitted. But his peace of mind is gone now.

At present, in an attempt to start anew, as if the conspiracy was merely a detour from an otherwise straight track, Nero is preparing to put on the second Neronian Games in Rome. Whether the population will warm to this is anyone's guess.

I keep myself informed. I can only watch and wait and warn him if anything comes to my ears.

XLI

ACTE

Oh, my heart aches for him—for them, yes, for her, too. The broad outlines of the plot were heard here in Velitrae, growing more and more detailed as the specific facts came out. The dagger and the slave. The coterie of his friends, not only the despicable Senecio (who has paid the price) but other friends of his idle hours like Petronius and Lucan. The Praetorians, pledged to defend his person against all enemies, becoming those enemies. Whatever world he believed he inhabited, it is shattered now.

Even their child is lost, and I chide myself for my jealousy of her. She has sorrows enough without my wishing any on her.

So we go on, walking ahead through a changed world, unbowed. We have no other choice. In this, and this only, we live.

XLII

NERO

The glorious summer filled Rome, Sol himself reassuring me. That, and Tigellinus's trained informers bringing him—and me—reports of what was happening around me. Never again would I slumber, trustingly, in my palace bed. Now the watchword was: on guard.

Before the Fire, I had hosted all the city with games, lakeside entertainments, and banquets. Now the second quinquennial Neronia, the Greek-style competitions in the arts and athletics, would revive the tradition, reassure my people that the city, and their emperor, were restored. That all was well.

I announced this to the Rump Senate (as I called it privately), adding that I planned to compete myself. Almost before I could finish, three senators rose and cried, "No need for that! We hereby offer you the crown for both eloquence and song. You need not lower yourself to compete with those—others."

"What about the chariot race? For I plan to compete there, too."

"Naturally you are entitled to the prize there as well."

How transparent they were, attempting to keep me off the stage. "No," I said. "Why should I be exempt from competition? Let the judges decide. I am not afraid to be compared to the performances of others." Without comparison, we can never know our true standing. Why should the emperor alone be denied this knowledge?

* * *

Back in the imperial apartments, Poppaea and I laughed about it. All the windows were open so the summer air could circulate freely, and outside the bees were busy in the oleander bushes. The curtains rose and fell in warm puffs.

"They were so serious," I said. "It was comical."

"One of the complaints of the traitors concerned your lack of gravitas," she said. "Perhaps you should be careful."

"I'm through with that," I said. "Now I shall do as I please and just double the guards and informers. Whom do I hurt by performing? No one."

"Their sense of the old Roman ways, that is all."

"It's a new Rome now, and it's time they accepted it." I sighed. "I am eager to go back to my music, so neglected. And to race again in the Circus."

"Just don't neglect Rome itself," she said. "If only to guarantee that you have a stage to perform upon."

"A stage . . . they accused me of performing while that stage, the city, burned. How dare they!"

She rose and came over to me, standing behind me and draping her arms over my shoulders in the way I loved. She kissed my ear. "That is over. Do not dwell on it. It will eat at you, and there is nothing more futile than being devoured by the past, a past you cannot change. The only thing you can do to change it is to overwrite it, make the people forget it. Like the scribes overwrite old manuscripts."

I heeded her words and embraced my arts again with the eagerness of a reunion with a lost lover. I had hesitated to call Terpnus back, after his insinuations about the Fire, but I decided to forget about that, as Poppaea advised. As I knew only too well, my skills had declined with lack of practice, and he could revive them.

Indeed, once he arrived, he did not allude to the Fire, and neither did I. Soon we were back in the old teacher-pupil relationship we had, where nothing mattered but the cithara and my expertise in it.

Reluctantly he said, "You are better than I dared to hope after all this time away. It may not take too long for you to be back where you were."

"I want to be better than that," I said. "But for now I will settle for reclaiming what I once had."

I spent evenings revising my *Troia* epic poem. I wondered at the advisability of reciting it, since I had been accused of performing it during the Fire, but it was the best poem I had written, and in a contest, why should I not offer my best? Second-rate poems would guarantee a second-place finish.

And it was with immense joy that I returned to the stables and the racetrack. Tigellinus kept me company, and I could leave the Praetorians at the palace under Faenius's trusted replacement, Nymphidius Sabinus, promoted from head of the fire brigade. Being outside in the summer sun, straining to control the horses, practicing the turns, was as close as a mortal could get to flying—and leaving earthly cares behind.

The Theater of Pompey was selected for the setting of the poetry and music competitions. It was a huge stone theater in the Campus Martius, undamaged by the Fire, that held some eleven thousand people, a fitting place for performances. Statues of the fourteen nations conquered by Pompey graced niches around the arena, and the building was well lighted.

The Neronia started with a week of lesser contests and recitals. But today only the most acclaimed poets would read. Secretly I had packed all the accouterments of a citharoede: the flowing chiton, the light shoulder mantle, the special thick-soled boots for the feet, a gold wreath for the hair, nestled with the instrument itself and hidden offstage, for a different performance. But for now I concentrated on reciting my lines.

Several others went before me, but Apollo help me, I did not really hear them, I was so keen on the moment I would follow them. It was all coming back—the anxiety, the racing heart. I strode out and took my place, seeing the audience as only a blur before me in their seats. My poor eyesight served me well now, sparing me from seeing individual faces.

I acknowledged the judges and the audience, then began. There was a murmur as it became clear I was reciting a part of my *Troia*, daring the public audience from all walks of life to think badly of me, daring them to think of the Fire. But the murmurs faded away, as they were caught up in the story itself. After I finished, there was tremendous applause.

I bowed and left the stage, while they cried, "No, don't leave! You must show us all your accomplishments! We demand it!"

I kept walking away, and the voices rose. "Display all your accomplishments! More, more!" Vitellius, who had been helping on stage, came after me.

"Come back," he said. "As we arranged."

"Let me change my clothes," I said. Quickly I went behind the stage and put on the citharoede costume, then clutched my instrument and returned to the stage. People screamed with delight.

"I will sing the 'Niobe,' a song of my own composition." One that I had feverishly composed in the last few days.

I held the heavy cithara, its strap across my right shoulder, its weight resting on my left wrist. I had to use the fingers of both hands to play the strings—plucking from one side with a plectrum, pressing from the other with my fingertips to temper the sound. And in addition, to sing. Let no one accuse anyone who plays this instrument, even badly, of not being a virtuoso, for even at the lowest level it demands much of the musician.

As tense as one of the strings, I concentrated so hard that sweat dripped down my face and my fingers grew slippery. When I got to the end, I was exhausted, drained—yet aflame.

The audience responded, my trained cadre of Alexandrian clappers leading the different rhythms, until the sound was deafening. I stood, running in sweat, melting. Finally I bowed and left the stage, too sapped even to speak.

•   •   •

Poppaea had been in the audience. Five years ago it had been Acte there, nervously watching me as I convinced myself that the oracle who had told me *There is no respect for hidden music* had meant that I must perform publicly. And after the performance, in a dazed state, I had wandered onto the pleasure boat and hence into Poppaea's arms. I was still married to Octavia then. Five years ago. Was it only five years ago? Now, once again in a dazed state, I wandered in the aftermath of the performance, half flying, half lost.

After we returned to the palace, Poppaea said, "That was a victory. Over your own doubts and those of others. I applaud you, now that you can hear me. For it would have been lost in the cacophony of the crowd." She clapped daintily. "And now I add to the prizes, one only I can award. I am with child again."

It was too much—too much happiness, too much excitement. Beyond happiness, beyond excitement, into the realm of ecstasy. I grabbed her and swung her around, until her feet hit a pedestal stand and knocked off a vase, shattering it.

We sank down on the floor, laughing, holding one another, with the pieces all around us. I did not care. I cared for nothing but the glory of the gifts I had been given that day.

The Neronia continued for another two weeks, the entire city thronging to the events and clamoring for more. This time Greek dress was not required, but some people wore it anyway, so that I got a glimpse of what one might see in Athens. People were in a holiday mood. Clearly they wanted to put the past behind them, to walk on the freshly paved streets, no longer complaining about the direct sunlight since shading overhanging stories had been banned as fire hazards, and to sit by the new fountains, dipping their hands in the splashing water. The conspiracy had not touched them; it was confined to a circle that the common people had no involvement with—the aristocracy and the soldiers.

My staff, made up almost exclusively of freedmen, were all loyal and still with me. Oh, how I had been criticized for employing freedmen, criticized by the aristocrats, because it kept them at a remove from power. But the aristocrats did not want to do this work, did not want to demean themselves, as they saw it. And how fortunate they did not, because had I been stupid enough to employ them, I would now be lacking a principal secretary, a secretary for Latin and Greek letters, a minister of accounts and revenues, a minister of correspondence, and so on all down the line.

The expenses of rebuilding were still rolling in. But thanks to the conspiracy (if one can be thankful for it), the estates of the traitors were now going directly into the imperial treasury. There was still a deficit, but not a catastrophic one.

Most of the thousands of Praetorians had remained loyal, and I rewarded them with a donation of two thousand sesterces per man, as well as free grain for life. Naturally this was very expensive, and it was fine justice that the estates of the traitors were paying for it.

The public gardens were crowded with strollers, and the much-maligned—by the people who had been in the Piso plot—grounds of the Golden House were enjoyed by the common people. Zenodorus had not completed the statue yet, but its base was already in place in the outer garden. For now, people sat on the flat platform and pic-nicked.

But in all this calm, this recovery, I was wary, like a forest animal alert for any misstep. They had not murdered me, but they had mur-dered my serenity. Would I ever sleep restfully again?

The grand finale of the Neronia was the races in the Circus Maxi-mus. Once again I would compete, and this time it was known well in advance. There were no surprises as there were last time, when all my company in the imperial box had been ignorant of my secret intentions. Now they had perished in the conspiracy, those nonchalant souls who had bantered with me beforehand about wine and which charioteer to bet on. Gone, gone—Piso, Lateranus, Vestinus, Scaevinus, and the two Praetorians guarding us, Subrius and Sulpicius. Now let their ashes disapprove of my race.

I said as much to Poppaea. "You sound pettily vindictive," she said.

"Petty? What they tried to do to me was hardly petty."

"If you turn into a bitter, suspicious person, they will have killed the man you used to be after all."

"He's gone," I said. Or, rather, the softer parts of me had had to shrink back and give space to the third Nero, the hard one who gives no quarter. The dark figure I had seen slinking in shadows who looked like me—was I now him in corporeal form?

She smoothed my hair. "No, no, he isn't."

"He is here only for you. Like a person who is fey, you are the only person now who can see him."

"He will come back," she said. "When the burn heals."

I did well in the two races I was in. I had altered the rein length for the two horses on traces, and it made for a more sensitive handling of them. The chariot axle had been broadened, making it more stable in turns. I came in third in one race and second in the other. If I never won a first it would not matter; what mattered was the skill in driving and the bond between me and my horses. And the supreme feeling of moving supernaturally fast.

The Neronia concluded successfully, and I was content. The anger and bitterness coated the surface of my mind but did not penetrate deeper, where my happiness with Poppaea, my pride in the rebuilt Rome and in my Domus Aurea, resided, untouched and untouchable. Often at night we would sit quietly in the lamplight, she resting with her feet covered with a light wool blanket, me reading and writing poetry. Sometimes when she was not looking, I would steal a glance at her, a wellspring of joy flooding me, too much to be contained. Too much to be borne. Too much to last.

XLIII

After the games ended, I suggested that we leave Rome for a while. The last few months had been all-consuming and soul-devouring.

"We could go back to Pompeii," Poppaea said. "I have not been back since we married."

"Back to your old home, where you seduced me?" I said it lightly, but in truth I wondered if I could bear to return to the Bay of Naples and gaze across the peninsula at Baiae. Baiae, where Mother . . .

"Or the other way around," she said. "Oh, let's go back. I want to see it all again, to see how well they've repaired the earthquake damage. And besides, I need to inspect the vineyards."

"Where the vines grow that produce that abominable wine you foisted on us at the Circus?" The Circus, and the people in the box drinking it, all dead now, all traitors . . . Would everything I see, everything I hear, remind me forever? If only there were an instrument to remove it from the head, cut it out as neatly as we pit a peach.

She smiled. "The same. I tell you, in years to come it will prove its worth. You'll see."

"I'll be an old man. I can hardly wait to taste this wine then. Age will have dulled my sense of taste!"

We left less than a week later. We passed by Naples, with the bay sparkling before us. Hundreds of boats were bobbing on the water, dipping up and down between white-capped waves. The wind was strong off the waters, bringing the tang of salt with it. Naples was my favorite city for its Greek ways. Besides, as the site of my first public performance, it held a special place in my heart—even though the theater had collapsed in an earthquake just afterward.

In the distance Vesuvius spread its purple shadow. We headed toward it; Poppaea's villa was not actually in Pompeii but closer to Vesuvius and the water. We passed under the umbrella of the mountain's shade and then down the long road to the villa itself. As we approached the heart of its extensive grounds, the landscape came back to me as a friend. The wide paved path to the colonnaded entrance . . . the grove of plane trees and olive orchards, stretching into the distance . . . it had the familiarity of home, but not quite home, because this was Poppaea's own estate, and I had come there as a hesitant visitor three years ago. I had arrived at night, greeted only by flaming torches and guards at the door, and passed into rooms that seemed mysterious and magical, where *she* waited for me.

"We are here!" she cried. "Oh, it is so good to be home!" Like a child, she rushed toward the doors. I followed at a more leisurely pace.

Inside was the hushed and odd suspension of time in a place where one has been absent. Slaves and attendants had overseen it and, upon notice that the mistress was returning, had opened rooms long closed. But the lack of a presence here meant that it had slumbered.

She turned around several times in the wide atrium, seeing the dancing motes in the shafts of sunlight that poured through the roof opening into the impluvium—empty now.

"They didn't fill it," she said, disappointed.

"Wait for the rain," I said. We strolled through the rooms, all immaculately clean but with the odor of disuse. We came at last to the western room that overlooked the bay, being on a cliff high above it. She flung open the doors to the portico and let the wind in, singing from the sea. The curtains danced and twirled. We went outside and stood looking down at the water, its piercing blue almost hurting our eyes.

Back inside, as we passed back through the room, the fresco of Apollo at Delphi, and the oracle's tripod, caught my eye. Suddenly, as if the oracle had actually spoken, the words whispered in my mind. *Delphi. Home of Apollo. You must go there.*

I stood, rooted to the spot, while she walked on.

Delphi. Delphi.

She turned, frowning. "Why have you stopped?"

"I was . . . I was remembering this fresco and what you said about it. That you were fond of Apollo."

"And I said you were my Apollo."

"Sheer flattery, but I loved it."

"I knew you would." She smiled slyly, holding out her hand for me to join her.

In the late afternoon we went to the small enclosed garden, its frescoes of flowers and shrubs blending with the real ones growing around its border. It was here we had exchanged our marriage vows. *Whenever and wherever you are Gaius, then I am Gaia.* Silent, she took my hand, and we stood for long minutes there.

Then we entered the adjoining triclinium for our dinner, a simple one for this first night. Her longtime attendant had prepared her favorite dishes—sweet melon with mint, cumin-flavored chickpeas, and grilled mullet—and tactfully offered other wine than the estate wine. She thanked him for remembering her favorites and asked him if there were any problems at the villa that he wished to report.

He shook his head. "All is in order, Augusta. The earthquake damage has been repaired, and there have been no tremors since. It was a onetime event."

"Thanks be to all the gods," she said.

After dinner we lingered in the library, taking out various scrolls, unrolling them, only to put them back. We were too tired to want to read by lamplight.

She took my hand again, as she had three years ago, leading me through her domain. "Now we go there," she said.

I knew where she was heading. Soon we stood before the door of the black room, the place where we had thrown prudence aside, had embraced our transgression, joyfully and defiantly. Now I did not want to look at it; a place once sacred can become ordinary if revisited. But before I could stay her hand, she flung open the door, and the darkness yawned before us, a beckoning cavern of desire.

A slave hastily scurried in and lit the lamps, then hurried out. We entered the room. It was still sacred after all.

"I built you a replica in Rome," I said. "But there can be only one room where everything truly started."

A wide bed was made up with linens and blankets, fresh and smelling of open fields; clearly she had sent orders ahead. She fell on it, holding out her arms to me.

"Is it different here now, being married?" she murmured.

"Yes," I said. "Nothing is ever the same twice." I kissed her. "Nor should it be."

"No," she said. "We would not want it to be."

She was my wife now, the companion of my soul, soon to be the mother of my child, no longer the wild stranger who beckoned me down forbidden paths. I would have it no other way.

Since that first night in the black room, we had made love many times, so many times I would not have thought there was any novelty left to us. But returning to the origin of our passion anointed us with a special gift from Aphrodite, a singular experience worthy of the gods themselves. For that little space and that little time, we ourselves were allowed to be gods.

Strangely shy the next morning, we ate a silent breakfast of eggs and cheese in the inner garden and then went outside to walk the grounds, which were extensive. It felt good to walk, to feel the brisk morning air on my face. When we reached the formal gardens, the wallflowers and larkspurs were blooming lustily, but the roses were not in season.

"You have not seen my rose garden," she said. "I told you I have three varieties, all in different shades of red. We must come again at the time they bloom."

"Roses are sacred to Aphrodite, are they not?" I asked. "I think they were in bloom last night. That's why they are withered here."

She smiled. "Yes, that explains it."

Not until we stood on the wide stone terrace overlooking the sea did the words come to me, all at once. I had to raise my voice to be heard over the crash of the waves below. "The Neronia—they aren't enough. I want to go to Greece itself, compete there."

She turned to me, puzzled. "What do you mean? Greece?"

"I have tried to bring the ways of Greece to Rome, and the Neronia have been a success as far as it goes. But the true competition is in Greece. At Delphi. And at Olympia. And Nemea and Isthmia. To go there—that is my deepest desire."

Just then a gust of wind blew her palla off, and her hair tangled in the breeze. She grabbed it, smoothing it down, and her gold earrings swung back and forth. "But . . . how long would this require? Surely you cannot be away from Rome that long. After all, the games don't all take place in the same year. The whole cycle of them takes four years."

"I know that. But, as you and others never tire of reminding me, I am the emperor. Greece is a Roman province, no matter its art and music—they were no match for Roman armies. I can ask them to re-arrange the order of the competitions."

"Order them, you mean."

"Yes, that's what I mean."

"What about your duties in Rome? Tiberius lost control when he retired to Capri."

"He was gone eleven years. I will be gone only a year."

She turned and hugged me to her. Her voice trembled with tears. "They attacked you for your art. Boudicca insulted you as a lyre player, and so did the Praetorians in the conspiracy, and rivalry in artistry turned Lucan and Petronius into enemies."

"They are dead, gone. I do not think others will want to follow in their footsteps."

"It is over. Do not tempt anyone again. Do not become a full-fledged artist, desert your calling in Rome, giving weapons to enemies. And don't say 'what enemies?' There are always new ones; the supply is inexhaustible."

She didn't understand. "I must do this," I said. "Apollo himself—

when I saw him again in the room here, I knew what he was calling me to do."

"The gods often lure us to destruction. They enjoy doing it. Don't listen to him!"

I wanted to say, *He is more than just a god; he is Sol, and Sol is me. We are one and the same. He would not want to harm me. He is me.* But I could never explain it, could not convey the transcendent experience I had had in his chariot. So I just said, "It would not be for another year at least. I need time to train, to compose verse and song worthy of the fiercest competition. For that is where the best people compete—Greece."

Still she clung to me and said in a trembling voice, "You need to be here when the baby comes. Do not desert me, not even for Apollo."

"Do you think I would ever be anywhere else? I am as joyful and hopeful for this child as you are." I held her close. "I will be with you."

XLIV

We stayed in the Pompeii area until the nights grew too chilly to sit outside after sunset. Pleasure boats still plied the waters, but there were fewer of them; soon they would be taken in for the winter. Poppaea visited some of her relatives in Pompeii proper, and they welcomed her with all the pomp due an Augusta, a rank far beyond what anyone else in the family had dreamed of.

We also ventured to some of the other villas lining the coast, some of them as sumptuous as any palace. The wealthy aristocrats—the snobs who scorned my music—wanted showplaces where they could entertain and impress their clients, and the coast of the bay was the prime spot to do it. The sprawling complexes were adorned with statues, the walls were frescoed in bright and costly colors, the floors covered in precious stone mosaics, and most of the places offered baths and gymnasiums and exercise yards as well.

Suspicious as I was of them—for I could never trust that class again—I felt it wise to make gestures of friendship, for I would have to work with them in Rome. An emperor does not have to wait for an invitation; the mere hint that he might like to come was enough to elicit one. I enjoyed the days with them, in spite of myself, although I viewed them as an investment, learning to know new people, with the ranks of the old destroyed. I would have to start all over again building up relations within the Senate. And where would it be less of a chore than here?

They tiptoed around the Subject, which was fine with me. I did not want to discuss it, to have it brought up. I was still wounded by it, but the wound would heal in its own time; nothing could hurry it, certainly not discussing it with these men.

Yet they, in their lightweight way, were good medicine. They seemed to have little in their heads but furnishing their villas, overseeing their fishponds and gardens, and attending the races at the Circus. Cautiously they congratulated me and asked questions about my horses. They inquired about the coming state visit from the Armenian king Tiridates, asking when he would arrive. I laughed and said the gods only knew. He would travel the long land route, bringing his queen with him. I promised them there would be a grand welcoming reception and a splendid ceremony in which I bestowed his crown. And after that, I said, I would close the doors of the Temple of Janus.

It was a great feat. But what credit did the conspirators give me for it? Did Seneca appreciate it? No. Did Faenius? No. Or any of them, the vile— I stopped myself. I had to stop letting it consume me like this. I had to. I turned and smiled at my hosts.

Back in Rome, the eleventh anniversary of my accession loomed. Memories of the ceremonies, overlaid with images of the traitors who attended it last year, blighted the idea of a repeat event, and I decided to let it pass without recognition.

But Poppaea objected. "If you forgo it because of *them*, they will laugh from the underworld. You have much to be proud of. Last year the Golden House was barely finished. Now it is nearly complete. The gardens have taken hold and are a pleasing vista from the terrace. The Neronia was a success. The rebuilding of Rome is almost finished. Eleven years of reign. Is that not something to mark?"

She seemed oddly insistent on it, as if it somehow reflected badly on us if we did not have one. So once again invitations were issued to celebrate the accession. They went out to the entire Senate, public servants, and this time, freedmen of standing. Yes, let Phaon, Epaphroditus, and even important slaves like Sporus come. And I invited the common people to stroll the lower gardens and help themselves to food from the long trestle tables I would set out. Free wine for all.

The day was a fair one, a mellow golden blaze. Warmth from the sun-soaked valley wafted upward, enveloping us as we stood waiting to welcome the throng. I warned Poppaea that she need not stand the whole time and to lie down whenever she felt the need. She claimed, however, that she felt well and that the weakness that had plagued her last time had not returned.

She was wondrous fair in a sky blue gown that, with its airy folds, disguised her growing size. Her rich hair, licked by the reddish sun rays, glowed a fiery bronze. She reached out her hands to me, and I carry forever the image of her face as she did, lit by the sun, touched with color.

The guests arrived in a rush. A flurry of white togas, gowns the color of summer gardens, and embroidered cloaks crowded the terrace. Eager heads bobbed in the sea of people, all heading toward us to greet us extravagantly.

"Caesar, I am humbled, let me kiss your hand—"

"Augusta, your beauty blinds me—"

"The honor is too much—"

"I cannot breathe in the exalted air around you—"

And so on. These were the faces of the senators who had kept out of the conspiracy—who knew what was in their hearts?—and who had proposed the excessive honors to me, such as building a temple to my divinity. They were my new reality, and I would have to know them, but my capacity for trust was exhausted.

Phaon and Epaphroditus stayed back, and when I was through greeting the unctuous politicians, I was able to speak to them.

"Caesar, forgive us if we do not bend our knees," said Epaphroditus, a smile on his broad face, glancing over at the crowd. Phaon nodded.

"You know too much," I said. "How can you bend your knee to the same person you have discussed latrines with?"

Tigellinus joined us, Nymphidius at his side.

"A goodly crowd," he said. "Purged of its rot." He looked around smugly.

Nymphidius stepped closer to me, saying, "It is an honor to work with Tigellinus in this position."

I looked at him. Did he resemble Caligula, his purported father? Like Caligula, he had a grim triangular face with small eyes. "I welcome you as Praetorian prefect," I said. "You proved your abilities in directing the firefighting efforts."

He smiled grimly, like Caligula, whose smiles were dangerous. Perhaps the rumors were correct. In any case, he would work well with Tigellinus. There would be no rivalry there; they were cut from the same cloth. Cloth that I could use to fashion what I wanted.

I had to give a formal welcome, so I made my way to the center of the terrace; Tigellinus and Nymphidius clapped for silence.

In the past I had written out my thoughts, or at least practiced them. Now I would just say what came to me. "I welcome you here to share with me the anniversary of my becoming emperor. Eleven years ago I set out from the palace on the Palatine a prince and returned an emperor. In those years much has been accomplished. But in those years much has befallen us to challenge us. Not only a rebellion in the province of Britain, turmoil in Armenia and Parthia, but destruction of our beloved city by a conflagration, the likes of which has never been seen."

And a dastardly conspiracy, aimed to kill me like a sacrificial ox in your sight.

They were quiet, looking at me with benign faces.

"But we have overcome all these misfortunes. Britain is secure, pacified. The Armenian question has been settled definitively, with the king agreeing to acknowledge Rome as his source of power. Even as we speak, Tiridates has just set out on his way here to receive his crown from my hands. When that happens, I will be able to close the doors of the Temple of Janus, something rarely done, in fact not done for almost seventy years since the Divine Augustus, and only six times through our history."

They were nodding and smiling.

"And Rome has been rebuilt. Yes, what you see around you is our gift to you. A shining city, modeled on new architectural visions, a people's park in the midst of the city, and this pavilion and its gardens to serve as a center for art and beauty."

Again they nodded, as if the Golden House and its expense had not been a matter of fierce opposition. And as if much of the cost of rebuilding Rome had not come from confiscated estates of traitors.

"And now I invite you to dine with me in the Golden House!" Slaves threw open the doors into the reception room, ready and waiting with mounds of food on long tables, rows and rows of amphoras with enough wine to supply Agamemnon's army, rose petals covering the floor, musicians, and tall bronze lampstands blazing with dozens of lamps.

I led the way, and they streamed in behind me, filling every corner of the room. They fell on the food like starving wolves, eager to taste what they presumed was expensive imported fare usually out of their reach. They were correct—I had ordered boar from Lucania, aged cheese from Bithynia, and heaps of sea urchins from Portugal, in addition to the usual milk-fed snails from Sardinia and anchovies from Spanish waters. There were even flagons of that exotic barbarian drink, beer, for the truly adventurous. Let them eat well and drink deep. We celebrated the rebirth of Rome and the end of troubles.

It was past midnight when the last of the celebrants departed, leaving us standing on a floor of crushed rose petals, dropped food, and spilled wine. Slaves cleared away the tables and the debris and started to sweep and clean the floor, but I said, "Later." So they left us alone.

"I told you it was the right thing to do," said Poppaea. She leaned her head on my shoulder.

"Entirely the right thing," I agreed. "You were correct, as you usually are." I kissed the top of her head.

It had been a success. I was elated that it had gone so well. In my feverish exuberance, the floor beneath me seemed to pulsate, pieces of the mosaic peeking out between the rose petals, puddles of wine glinting.

I turned Poppaea to face me, took her hands. "I am the happiest of all mortals," I said. Seized with a desire to move, to express my exaltation, I swung her out in a circle, as we had done once before, the time we knocked off the vase. As I spun around, her legs flew higher, and I spun faster, she squealing in delight at the weightlessness of it. Faster and faster, and then my feet slipped on the sleek floor, I lost my footing, she flew out of my grasp, hitting one of the lampstands, knocking it to the ground, and I followed, landing on top of her, crushing her between the lampstand and my body.

She moaned, and I tumbled off her. In the dim light I could see her head tilted back at an unnatural angle, her legs twisted away from her body. On my hands and knees I crawled closer, trying to see better.

I called out her name. I screamed out her name. But no answer. I sat up and took her head on my lap, frantically smoothing her hair. Her lips parted, and she groaned, tried to form words. "I . . . fell . . ." she whispered.

"No . . . you are safe . . . you are well . . ."

"I . . . weak . . . can't stand . . ."

"You are safe, all will be well," I kept repeating. Her eyes were open. She was speaking. All would be well.

But when I looked down I saw an ominous dark shadow spreading out around her beneath her hips. A jolt of horror went through me. Not taking my eyes off hers, I put my hand down to the shadow and it came away red with blood.

I wouldn't scream. No, I wouldn't. It would frighten her, so with all my self-control I said, "Let me move you from this floor." I picked her up, acutely aware that I must be wary of my footing, more difficult now that I carried a heavy weight.

We were nearest the Hector room, and I knew a cot was there that the painters had used. So, moving slowly, I took her in and laid her on it; she winced and cried out when I put her down.

There was one lampstand burning in the room, enough that we could see. I watched helplessly as the stain appeared again around her and was soon dripping beneath the cot on the floor. I needed to call someone, but I dared not leave her. I took her hands. They were cool.

"Poppaea, we need help. I have to call someone. I have to find a slave; they are somewhere here but not nearby." I squeezed her hands, willing them to return the gesture, willing strength into them.

"No . . . do not leave me . . ." Her voice was soft.

"I have to, to get help!"

"Stay with me, don't leave me," she repeated. "Please!"

So I knelt beside her, murmuring assurances, all the while seeing the blood seep around us, until it reached my knees where I knelt.

Even as that was happening, she seemed to regain strength, which dulled me to the danger. "I told you . . . I said I could not give you a child, you should have divorced me . . . now this . . ."

"Don't think of it!" I said. "You will be well again, child or no child."

"No . . ." She smiled. "Do you remember, I said . . . I did not wish to live longer than my beauty would last. I wanted . . . to die beautiful."

I did remember that, but I said, "No, I don't. It's a foolish wish. You will always be beautiful to me."

"I am granted my wish," she said. "I . . . feel it."

"No, no!" I cried. "You are wrong."

Her eyes held mine. "Dear Nero. You always have trouble . . . seeing reality. You live in the then and the maybe . . . not the here and now."

"I see you, here now."

"Not . . . much longer. Hold me."

I leaned over and took her in my arms without making her sit up. "Whenever and wherever you . . . are Gaius, then . . . I am Gaia," she said. "Remember that . . . when I am gone. I will always be . . . your Gaia." Now her voice was fading again. I gently moved her, to restore it.

"And I your Gaius," I whispered.

She turned to look at the opposite wall. "If I can, I will come . . . back like Protesilaus . . . did to Laodamia . . . good . . . I requested that . . . story . . ."

"I won't let you go!"

"Three hours . . . we will have three hours . . ."

Three hours. What were three hours out of all the ones we should have had?

Her eyes closed as if she slept. Her hand went limp in mine. Now I pulled away, leaving her, running through the connected chambers of the palace, shouting out for someone.

I found a group of slaves in the peristyle garden, far from the Hector room. "Midwife! Midwife!" I cried, frantic, hardly knowing what I was saying, only that I had to explain, so they could help. But words failed me; I was incoherent. I took a deep breath, struggling. "I need a midwife. A physician. Anyone with medical knowledge. Hurry, find him or her or all of them! Bring them to the Hector room. The Augusta is there."

They looked puzzled, then leapt into action, scattering.

I rushed back to the Hector room, finding Poppaea unchanged. Standing back from the bed, from this distance I could see the extent of the blood on the floor. Could anyone survive the loss of so much blood?

Once again I knelt by her, my knees in the sticky blood. Her face was pale, and her hands still cool. Her lips had a bluish cast.

"Speak to me," I said, willing her to, commanding her.

She smiled, faintly. Then she whispered, "Farewell . . . my love . . . let . . . the earth lie lightly . . . upon me . . . Now I rest . . . among the dead . . . while still youthful . . ."

It was no use. I had to let her go, not vex her spirit by restraining it. "The gods granted you your wish," I said.

There was no answer, and she slipped away from me even as I held her.

"You are now a goddess," I said, touching her face. She would join Claudia. But what comfort to us left behind?

As I waited for the now-useless midwife or physician to arrive, I trembled. I had done it. I had taken her hands and swung her out, and slipped and caused this. Foolhardy and clumsy. I had smashed the dearest vessel in the world, not deliberately as Petronius had crushed the murrhine cups, but blindly, stupidly. Persia had rocks aplenty that could yield more cups, but nowhere in the universe was there the means to create another Poppaea.

XLV

I sat by her side, seeing her sink into stillness, that stillness that no living creature can claim. Her features grew paler, and the hand I held grew cooler. I cradled it, as if I could transfer the warmth from my own into hers, could infuse it with life again. But it continued to grow colder.

The blood congealed on the floor, turning dark. I could not think, could hardly even feel, as if a lightning bolt had wiped my mind clean, leaving only pain and confusion. The lamps flickered on the wall, coating the frescoes in yellow light. Hector and Andromache. Protesilaus and Laodamia. Bereavement from long ago, sealed over in time, prettily preserved in celebrated verse, rendered stale and impotent. Not searing, fresh, and bleeding.

And I had caused this. Had I not been so filled with joy I would not have swung her around. But no, I had swung her around another time, with no mishap. Yes, but then I didn't lose my footing. But this floor was slippery, and if I had only let the slaves clean it up . . .

But . . . but . . . but . . . a thousand buts, a thousand ifs, a thousand other ways it could have turned out, and I would not be gazing on a lifeless Poppaea. But it turned out only one way. This way. This horrible, fatal, final way. With no restoration from the gods, in spite of the tales we love to hear.

A slight hint of daylight illuminated the chamber, dulling the lamplight, when two midwives and Andromachus appeared, along with several slaves. They peered into the chamber, apprehensive and hesitant, carrying cloths and basins. Then the older midwife approached, followed by the others.

"May I see closer?" she asked.

"Yes," I said. But I left the chamber. I could not bear to look, to see them examine her. I waited in the next room, hearing them murmur, hearing the scrape of the cot on the floor as they moved it.

Andromachus came for me. "Caesar, we have finished," he said. "Come." We returned to the chamber. Poppaea had been moved away from the bloody floor and covered with a clean linen sheet. Her hands were crossed on her chest.

"She died from loss of blood," said Andromachus.

As if anyone but a blind person could not have seen that.

"The injury to her abdomen caused the child to dislodge, suddenly, and rip away from the womb. When that happens, the loss of blood is so catastrophic that the mother dies, and usually the child as well," said the midwife, more practiced in this area than Andromachus.

I had done it, I had done it.

"I must tell you that this sometimes happens for no apparent reason. No injury, no warning. Just a sudden onset. And the Augusta has had problems in childbearing. So she may have been predisposed to this."

Yes, but I set it in motion.

"The child is lost, too," said Andromachus, pointing to a bundle, wrapped in another linen. "It was still too small to survive."

I did not want to break down in front of them, but I could not help it. I waved them away, out of the room, and wept.

They were gone. Everyone was gone except Poppaea, who lay serenely on the cot, her slender, pale hands clasped. In death she was beautiful in a way she had not been before—in absolute stillness and perfection. A beauty that could not change. A beauty that was immortal.

When it was full day, Epaphroditus appeared at the door. Wordlessly, he came in and stood looking down at the figure on the cot. He turned to me, protocol forgotten, and touched my shoulder. His silent gesture caused me to weep again.

"Caesar, we must . . . make preparations," he said. "For the Augusta . . ."

"Preparations?" I did not understand.

"The funeral."

The funeral. Yes, there had to be a funeral.

"Shall I arrange to have the cremation site readied?"

"No!"

"We will carry her with the utmost respect and care."

Onto a funeral pyre. Laid on a pyre, set aflame. Crackling and melting and turning black.

"No! No cremation! I won't have her destroyed!"

"But, Caesar, it is a necessary rite. The customary Roman rite."

"Not for my daughter and not for the Augusta. She will be embalmed."

I had not yet allowed myself to step beyond the *now*, the overwhelming *now*, and enter the world of *next*, the world of practicalities and what shall we do with the body of the Augusta? But instantly I knew she must be embalmed, preserved, not obliterated.

"Embalmed?" He sighed. "But the spices necessary for an adult, the quantity, so different than for an infant."

"Am I not the emperor?" I cried. "Is not procuring a mountain of spices within my power? Get them, get them, send for all the merchants who deal with Arabia, but get them!"

Shocked, he retreated, bowing and hurrying away, leaving me alone with Poppaea again.

I knelt by her side. "I won't let them harm you. You wished that your beauty would never fade, and I promise you it will not."

Eventually I was persuaded to leave the room, to return to the lower palace, and attendants took Poppaea away in a closed litter to the place where she would be prepared for eternity.

Once in the palace, I felt marooned and lost. How could all this be unchanged? How could the couches still be as they were, the round tables be oblivious to the loss? They were inanimate, and I hated them for it—hated their immunity to our mortality. *Things* rusted, they rotted, they disintegrated and eventually fell into dust, but they weren't aware of it and were not mourned by their fellow pieces of furniture. I kicked the little table that usually held a pitcher of juice, smashing it. Then I turned to the neighboring table and said, "You don't care, do you? You won't miss it!" I wanted revenge on the furniture for their protection against all loss and care. I wanted revenge on everything that was not wounded by the loss of Poppaea.

Then the rage was replaced by a dullness, a softness that the armor of anger had kept at bay. Pain and sorrow crept in, little fingers that clasped and then grasped, squeezing the breath out of me. I flung myself down on my bed and lay motionless all day, feeling dead myself. Perhaps I was.

Finally my closest attendants tiptoed in. "Caesar," one said. "We have food for you. You must eat."

The light was fading. It was almost dark. The first full night without Poppaea was about to begin. The first full day without her had passed.

I can't live without you. I can't survive without you. I had said that. But now I would have to. And I did not know how I could.

When the embalmers had finished their task and laid Poppaea in her coffin, I was called in. I gazed down at her. She looked as if she still lived, which was painful. *Why is this possible? It is more of a torture than if the embalmers had failed. Then I would see that you are no longer here. Instead I think you should stir, arise. I wait for you to do so, and you do not.*

I nodded. "Thank you," I said. "Thank you for your skill."

Once again I was alone with her, and all that remained was to close the lid and say farewell upon this earth. I took one last lingering look, then did it. And resisted the temptation to raise it again for just one more glance.

She was to have a state funeral, with the bier resting on the Rostra, where I would address the people in the Forum. It was a cloudy day, blowing misty rain. I was flanked by members of the four orders of state priests, as well as a cordon of magistrates, Praetorians and leading members of the Senate. They blocked my view of Poppaea, now resting where everyone could see her—everyone but me. I had said my farewell.

I looked out at the crowd, dressed in muted mourning colors, their heads covered. Waiting. Waiting to see what the emperor would say. How many times had I experienced that? But today, I hardly knew what to say. The emperor was at a loss for words. But there had to be words.

I motioned to the priests' acolytes to light the incense, heaped in high stands on both sides of the Rostra. Clouds of smoke rose, sending the voluptuous scent of myrrh and cassia to surround us and waft out into the Forum.

"Today there are no official mourners but one. Your emperor. My loss and my mourning are so vast that an army of official mourners could not equal it. I have lost the Augusta, my beloved wife. She was a woman of incomparable beauty, of goodness, of intelligence. Of wit and compassion. And she was the mother of the Diva Claudia Augusta, who is on the couch of the immortals. She now takes her place on that couch beside her as a goddess in her own right, Diva Poppaea Augusta."

People began to wail and keen, as customary in funerals. The sound grew and grew, resounding off the buildings in the Forum.

"She will be entombed, intact, in the tumulus of the Julian family, where our daughter now lies. She, too, will have a shrine dedicated to her divinity, as does Diva Claudia. I will lead the procession."

Through the dreary drizzle I walked, with Poppaea's closed coffin on a royal litter borne before me, with swaying priests and chanting mourners behind me, a long line of mourners snaking through the Forum and out to the Campus Martius. The tumulus, an imposing, high mound where the ashes of Julius Caesar himself rested, had two bronze doors, now open and waiting. I stood as Poppaea was taken inside, to the place where I could not follow.

XLVI

Life must go on, they say. But in what way? For days afterward I kept to my chamber, but she was still there. All the things she had gazed upon, touched, remained, mocking me. I felt her presence, but when I turned to see her, she was gone. Silent servants came and went, bringing food, taking it away untouched.

Stoic philosophers would argue that my folly was in forming an attachment to an earthly thing. One had gone so far as to say that when he held his wife he was always aware of her skeleton and that she was just a piece of flesh that would decay. If we can stay aloof from all that perishes, then we do not ache when they leave us.

But that is not to live at all. I could find no consolation in philosophy or in clever ways of restating facts to try to alter them. The poets knew more than all the philosophers put together and offered me the only solace I could find, and even that was meager. Homer said,

The life of man is like a summer's leaf.

And Archilochos said,

Now, I have no desire for poetry or joy,
yet I will make nothing worse by crying,
Nor worse by seeking good foods and pleasure

And he was right. But Sappho was the only one who truly understood:

The moon and Pleiades
are set. Midnight,
And time spins away.
I lie in bed, alone.

And so the days and the nights passed.

Since, as the poet said, I felt no better or no worse regardless of what I did, eventually I returned to my duties, signing papers, meeting with the Consilium, consulting with my true advisers—Tigellinus, Nymphidius, Epaphroditus, Phaon. To them and them alone could I speak freely, not guarding my every word.

In addition to these official duties, there was the melancholy one of dispersing Poppaea's household, her servants, her slaves, her possessions. There was even the question of what to do with her stable of donkeys that she kept for their milk to bathe in. I visited her apartments and surveyed the objects—the luxurious bed, the ivory-adorned couches and tables, the array of costly perfumes and ointments in their slender-necked alabaster vials and delicate glass. And the jewelry. I took the necklace I had commissioned for her, the gold collar with the nine celestial stones, that she had worn on the last day before the night that everything changed, when Rome caught on fire. I would keep it, remembering her joy at wearing it. For the rest, it should be sold and the money deposited in the imperial treasury.

We had no child to save these things for, and keeping them would be a continual stinging reminder of that.

The slaves and servants would be absorbed into other households, but I wanted to keep her musicians and Sporus. His uncanny resemblance to Poppaea meant that sending him away would, in some way, be losing her again. The first time I saw him again, it was both a pain and a comfort. Long ago I had said, *Now I know where to find another Poppaea if I need one,* and she had answered, *I hope that never happens, that you would need another Poppaea.*

Easy to laugh and joke about it then. I freed him as a gift to Poppaea's memory, but he chose to remain in the palace, as near to her as he could be in this life.

It was a long time before I was able to return to the Golden House, once my joy and treasure, its majestic beauty now tarnished with the sorrow of that night. I stood in the Hector room, seeing that the mosaic floor had been retiled, presumably because the stains of her blood had permanently damaged the original. The painting of Protesilaus and Laodamia, reenacting their tragedy for eternity, leered at me. I ordered it painted over but changed my mind, realizing it was the last thing she had seen, and she had specially commissioned it, and to destroy it was to deny her wishes. But I never wanted to see it again. Let later generations admire it. I would never stand in that chamber again and ordered it closed.

But would there be later generations to see it? What of the dreadful prophecy in my dream? *Not one stone shall remain standing upon another, nor anything that you hold dear.*

Was there any use, then, in striving against the Fates, against oblivion?

Tigellinus came to me one day with a further taunt to my loss.

"Another malicious rumor," he said, laying a paper before me. I looked at it, listlessly.

"Just tell me," I said. What now?

He was truly reluctant to speak. But he was charged with finding out all the dangers and secrets harbored in Rome. "Some say that you caused the death of the empress."

I above anyone accused myself of that. But only I and the physician and the midwives knew what really happened; even Tigellinus didn't. "What do they say?"

"That she scolded you for coming home late from the races, and in a fit of anger you kicked her even though she was pregnant."

I sighed. What evil imagination. "There were no races, I didn't return late from any, and I don't hit or kick people." I had never struck anyone in my life. But it wasn't Tigellinus I needed to convince.

"I know that, Caesar," he said. "But how to refute it?"

I had learned my lesson after the Fire. It was almost impossible to snuff out a rumor that was determined to burn. "We can't," I said. "Only Poppaea could refute it." I didn't care anymore. I was weary of the unfair rumors and accusations. Let them flame, let them smolder. But the unfairness of them made me sick at heart.

XLVII

ACTE

Like everyone else, I heard about the death of Poppaea and Nero's responsibility for it. Yes, even in Velitrae—or perhaps especially in Velitrae, for the farther a place is from the origin of a story, the more it changes—the tale circulated. She had nagged him for coming home late, and he had kicked her, the story went.

I could well believe that she could scold him. She was imperious and demanding, as I knew firsthand from her summoning of me and her cutting words. But I could not believe he would harm her or anyone else by striking them. He was capable of striking people, but only from a distance with arrest warrants, and only for his enemies who tried to strike him first. And that he loved her, I had no doubt, loved her to madness.

I grieved for him—what would he do now, without her? She and Tigellinus had been his closest companions and advisers. Now there was just Tigellinus. All the political personas who had crowded the stage when he and I were first together were gone, swept away—Agrippina, Seneca, Burrus, Octavia, Britannicus, now Poppaea.

Only he and I survived. Odd thought. May we endure and live.

I attended the state funeral, standing in the crowd before the Rostra. Why did I go? It is hard to answer that, even to myself. I can only ask myself questions. Is it because I still want to share, even at the margins, his life? Is it because I feel protective of him, more so now than ever? Or did I simply want to see him again, even at a distance? How strange not to know oneself better.

The day was cold, drizzly, windy. Poets would say the skies wept. Common people would say they should have remembered to bring a hat. An enormous crowd had gathered in the Forum, a testament to his popularity among the people.

The Rostra was filled with officials, standing behind the bier with Poppaea's form stretched out upon it. She lay pale and slender, surrounded by myrtle boughs, her amber hair waving around her shoulders. Two enormous incense burners flanked the bier, and when they were lit, heady smoke poured out, almost enveloping the Rostra.

Then he appeared, wearing a mourning toga of dark color, and started speaking. At first his voice was so low I could barely hear him, but it gained strength as he went on. He spoke of her in the highest terms, but even as he enumerated all her qualities and his vow to build a shrine to her, and declared that she was divine, I knew—I could sense—that he wished just to cry out and scream to the heavens rather than deliver this measured, calm speech.

He looked ravaged, far older than his twenty-seven years. Where was the boy I had known?

The speeches over, it was time to transfer the bier to the cremation spot. Reverently they closed the coffin and descended from the Rostra. Nero followed, and then all the officials and last the rest of the people fell in behind him.

He passed by me but did not see me; his eyes were focused on the swaying coffin ahead of him. I waited and then followed at a distance. We snaked through the Forum and then toward the Campus Martius. But we did not stop in the open field, the traditional spot for cremations. We kept walking, and around me people were murmuring, wondering, and then someone said, "He won't cremate her. He had her embalmed. She's going directly into the tumulus of the Julians."

"No cremation? That's un-Roman!" a man next to me cried.

"Foreign—like the Egyptians!" muttered a woman.

"He likes foreign things. What about those Greek games?" the man said.

"But embalming!" a boy said in alarm, as if it were perverse.

"It must have cost a fortune. All those imported spices. And the incense at the Rostra—a year's worth!" said an old man, hobbling along with his walking stick.

But I remembered, if they did not, that he had done likewise with his daughter, Claudia. Perhaps he simply could not bear to think of them burned. Or perhaps he merely wanted to believe they slumbered rather than ceased to exist.

The tumulus rose before us, a great mound that had been heaped over Caesar's only daughter in her sarcophagus, then over Caesar himself, and held the embalmed body of Drusus, the first Germanicus. Nero was not the first in Rome to have someone embalmed.

There were brief prayers before the yawning doors of the dark interior, and Nero touched her coffin, then nodded for it to be conveyed inside.

He turned away, unseeing, although I was close by. But then, even without grief, he had bad eyesight. Once he had given me an emerald he used to improve his eyesight at the races. I still had it; it rested on a table in my workroom, a poignant reminder of how vulnerable even an emperor can be.

XLVIII

NERO

I had to select a site for Poppaea's shrine. The Senate had voted formally on her deification, but it was up to me to find the proper place for her temple. A task that would, for a little while, keep her with me.

Would it be in Rome? She was empress here, and here she rested. But her cry *Oh, it is so good to be home!* when we returned to the area of Naples meant that her heart was there, and there she would want her shrine. And Naples was a spiritual home to me, too, in that its temperament was Greek, not Roman.

I chose a site on a hill overlooking the bright bay, where her villa was just visible. I would design the shrine, and when it was done, would call to her, "Come home again."

Now the melancholy tasks of laying her to rest were over, a sadness in itself. For in mourning rituals, in the clearing away of the beloved dead, we put away something precious in ourselves that we know we will never see again.

I returned to Rome. The palace was still, deserted—or so it felt without her. In truth it still bustled with slaves and petitioners and messengers. But at night, when they had left, emptiness descended, along with haunting thoughts. *Mother.* In returning to Naples and the bay, I had also evoked her memory, inextricably tied to the area, along with Poppaea's. And now her mocking curse in the *Octavia* rang through my mind as I sat, nursing a cup of wine, in the shadow-filled chamber.

My bleeding hands infernal torches bring
To greet this impious marriage; by their light
My son shall wed Poppaea; these bright flames
The avenging hands of his infuriate mother
Shall turn to funeral flames.

I took a big swallow of the wine, feeling its tart sting slide down my throat. *You were wrong in that at least. There were no funeral flames.* I set the cup back down; it was empty. I refilled it, up to the brim.

I did not need to consult the actual manuscript. The words were burned into my memory. Mother crying,

In the face of all this evil
Your stricken mother's anger should be silent,
Whom in your wickedness you killed?

She had succeeded. She had punished me with an ultimate, ironic, cruel revenge—by watching me, cursing me, so that I now had killed the person dearest to me in the world by accident, just as I had killed her by intent.

She was Hera to my Hercules. Hera, who had driven Hercules mad so he killed his wife and children by accident. And when he regained his senses, did endless penance, felt endless remorse.

I drained the rest of the cup of wine. Endless remorse. And for me, no Twelve Labors—no killing the Nemean lion, no destroying the Lernian hydra, no cleaning the Augean stables. Just being emperor, guarding and guiding the Roman empire as wisely and bravely as I could, amid criticism and opposition as well as cloying sycophantism and opportunism to wade through. And at the end, ambrosia and a welcome on Mount Olympus, like Hercules? No, the best I could hope for was an honorable place in history—mortal history.

The emperor must go on, go on the stage of political affairs that were so much less interesting than the real stage in the theater. Why is it that the reality is dull, whereas the stage, impersonating reality, seems so much more real?

The state visit of Tiridates would take place in late spring; he had been traveling from Armenia for four months already but still had a long way to go. I must plan it, must arrange a spectacle suitable for the occasion. At the same time, the idea of going to Greece to compete in the contests refused to evaporate; instead it grew stronger. If I were to do it, I would need to practice my arts and compose new material— difficult to do even in times of exuberance; almost impossible when the spirits are low. Yet I knew that Greece might be the only thing to cure me of my despondency. Not only would I compete in the arts, but I wanted to drive a chariot, perhaps with more than just four horses. Set myself a high challenge. If my mind and body were preoccupied with these tests, it would banish everything else from my head.

In the meantime I faced a test of another nature. The immediate mourning period over, a number of senators were ambitious for their daughters to become the next empress. They hinted, at first coyly, that I might like to invite Drusilla or Flavia or Quintina to the palace for an intimate dinner. When I did not respond, they became more strident, swarming like bees on a warm day. I fled.

But alone in my quarters, I had to ask myself honestly: did I intend to remain single for the rest of my life? I was twenty-eight. I still needed an heir. I was solitary and it felt right that I be, but—forever? If I did take up with one of these daughters, would I feel less alone—or more?

At length I relented, capitulating to the siege. I invited Aelia Paulina, the daughter of Senator Aelis, to dine with me at the palace. Dine—and what else? Not stipulated, not even to myself.

She was fifteen, a willow of a girl with light hair and an oval face. She was escorted to the palace by her father and two slaves. The father, after bleating out the customary greetings, melted away. The slaves stayed, as chaperones, but did not follow us into my dining chamber.

I motioned for her to sit on one of the couches. I had a slave bring us wine and olives, to put her at ease. She sat primly on the edge of the couch, with folded hands, and looked at me with rounded innocent eyes.

"You are frightened of me, aren't you?" I asked, gently I hoped.

She nodded, now casting her eyes down.

"You needn't be," I said. I won't bite.

"But you rule the whole world!" she said.

Oh, that. "One gets used to it." But she never would, I could see that. She was too young. She was a child compared to Poppaea.

Further awkward conversation revealed that she had been tutored at home, could weave and play the flute and had a pet parrot. Other than that, there was little to say, those being the sum of her interests.

She was very sweet, very modest, and way too virginal in all ways for me. I returned her to her father in the same condition she had arrived.

The next invitation went out to Horatia, the daughter of Senator Horatius. This one held more promise; I knew she had studied Greek. I was beginning to feel I was back at Lanatus's stable, choosing a horse for certain qualities.

Like her predecessor, she was brought by her father and had two slaves in tow. Unlike with the first candidate, though, her father wanted to be treated to the meal as well, and he had to be dissuaded and told he would have an invitation at another time.

Horatia was a strapping girl, tall and broad-shouldered, and almost seventeen—late to be unmarried. Was there something wrong with her, or was she just picky? Instead of sitting rigidly on the edge of the couch she had chosen, she draped herself on it and crossed her legs, exposing muscular calves.

She was not afraid of me, oh, no. She asked me questions, some of them personal. Did I like to bathe in cold water? For how long? What sort of ointments did I fancy?

She ate voraciously, rather than daintily. Her fingers were soon greasy. She quoted a line about eating from Pindar—yes, it was true she knew Greek—and then asked me to match it. We embarked on a Greek quote contest.

The meal being over, musicians came in to play and we continued the conversation—or rather, she continued it. At length I motioned to the players to quit. When they were gone, she came over to me and put her hands on my shoulders and tried to kiss me.

"Now for the last course of the dinner," she said.

I backed away. "That wasn't on the menu," I said, trying to make light of it.

"It is on mine," she said. "I will carry the memory and the honor of being in the emperor's bed with me the rest of my life."

Now I felt like the horse being chosen, rather than being the chooser.

"I fear I cannot say likewise," I replied.

She, too, was returned to her father in whatever state she had entered the palace.

It was some time before I ventured down that road again, and this time almost by accident. Senator Gaius Tullius, whom I liked, happened to mention that his daughter had become obsessed with the Greek games and wanted to go to Olympia and run in Hera's race, the only one in all the games for girls.

"Is she fast?" I asked.

"Yes, very. But there are so few contests where she can test herself."

"What's her name—Atalanta?" I asked, joking.

"Tullia," he said.

"I should like to meet her," I said, and meant it. It had been years since I raced, but I was still keenly interested in the sport. And a girl who did it seriously was unusual.

Tullia was brought to the palace, and this time I was pleased to have her father join us in the beginning. The conversation was pleasant, and Gaius explained that his wife, Tullia's mother, had died and it was just the two of them in the household. Tullia was a comely girl, sixteen, with a ready laugh and an ease beyond her years.

"How long have you been running?" I asked her. "And where do you run?"

She smiled. "I've run since I was a child. Children's races. I was always the best. I beat the boys." She spread her hands. "But that stopped when I got older. The boys had the trainers and the training grounds and the races. The girls had nothing. So I do not know if I am still fast, or if it is just a memory."

Yes, I knew about that. It had been so long since I had run an actual race. But I had switched to another venue, chariot racing, whereas she could not.

"I found out that in Olympia they do have a girls' race. It is dedicated to Hera. It is my dream to go there."

On impulse I said, "You shall. I shall take you there when I go."

She and her father stared at me. "What do you mean?" he finally said.

"I hope to go to Greece and compete in all the games," I said. "Soon. You may join my retinue." I looked at her father, assuring him, "There will be many people with me; she will have much company."

Although until that moment it had only been a hope, suddenly, for the first time since the conspiracy, since Poppaea's death, I felt a surge of true excitement for a concrete and immediate goal. I *would* go to Greece.

"Truly?" she said. "That seems—beyond anything I could have expected."

"Start training," I said. "You will need all the time to get ready. Only the best compete there."

Her father discreetly left after the meal, telling her cheerfully that he would be waiting for her at home.

Now we were alone. But awkwardness did not descend. I was glad she was there; I welcomed her company. I trusted her and she, me. It seemed entirely natural to end up in the bedroom by the end of the evening. I took her in my arms, and she fit. She was neither shy nor bold, but at ease, relaxed. I kissed her, and that felt natural, too. But I would go no further without asking her, if not in so many words, then in my actions. And she said yes, wordlessly but definitely.

To hold another woman in my arms instead of Poppaea, someone who felt different, who was made differently, smaller and stronger and with a different scent, was strange to me but not unnatural. She responded as if this held no fear or hesitation for her, as if it was the race she had yearned to run. And I responded likewise, losing myself in her, losing the heaviness that had pursued me like a dark gloom, weighing me down. I was set free, free to feel joy and pleasure again.

Afterward we lay and talked. It was astounding, a miracle, for me to lie thus again. She said, "I hope you do not think I only wanted to be taken to Greece." But I knew she knew better. In our desire to compete in Greece, we were kindred spirits, and that had opened the door for us to know one another.

I played with a strand of her hair, drawing it across her forehead to make a headband. "And I hope you do not think I only offered to take you there to end up here tonight instead."

She smiled. "No, I don't." She put her head down on my chest with a sigh. "I enjoyed this journey on its own merits." Then she said mischievously, "But when do we leave?"

"Mid-July," I said. There. I had decided. Made a commitment.

I would be pleased to have her in Greece, to make her dream of racing come true. But she was a girl still. For empress I needed a woman, a mature woman of experience. Tullia would be a friend, a fellow competitor and companion, but she could never be my wife.

XLIX

With the spring, I renewed, fresh sap pushing the sludge of winter out of my being. For the first time since the early days of last spring, when I was still ignorant of the conspiracy, I could look out on the world and see it as benign and even pleasant. As the Feast of Ceres approached again, I noted it but did not plan to attend the ceremonies. I would give thanks in my private chambers for having survived, but I would spend the day at Lanatus's stables, choosing new horses and ordering a new chariot. The open countryside sang of life and warmth, and riding through it was a balm.

I confided to Lanatus my growing desire to drive more than four horses and my plans to go to Greece.

"Horses don't travel well," he said. "Even in the special ships built for horse transport. You would be affecting their stamina. Why do that?"

"Because I want my own team there. I can't use just any local horses."

He stroked his chin. "It's true, Greek horses are not the best."

"And they wouldn't have been trained by me. We would have no way of speaking to one another."

He relented. "I can see you won't change your mind, so let's get down to business and look at some." He stood back and said, "I can only tell you I am glad to see you here again."

I knew what he meant. No need to dwell on it. "Thank you," I said.

We strolled over to the paddock, and he pointed out several horses he could recommend. He was particularly enthusiastic about the long-legged bay at the far end. "He'll be five this summer. Perfect. He learns quickly and will adapt to you." He waved his hand toward some others grazing together. "What size team did you have in mind?"

"Ten," I said.

He whipped his head around, staring. "Ten? Are you insane?"

I laughed. "There are those who think so."

"Now I am with them. You can't drive ten horses. Almost no one can. Name me anyone who has."

"Mithridates?"

"I mean, that you have seen with your own eyes."

"I haven't," I admitted.

"And with good reason. They can't be controlled. There is only one shaft, with two horses yoked to it. The other eight would be on individual traces, controlled separately. Eight separate reins! No, forget it."

"But I've heard it can be done."

"Leander swam the Hellespont, too. Could you?"

"No, but if I practiced . . ."

"You are childishly stubborn," he said. "But this is dangerous."

"A refrain I have heard all my life. Anything worth doing seems to be dangerous: racing chariots, competing—being emperor! Especially the latter."

"Yes . . . well . . . another drawback is that the chariot team is so wide it takes an enormous flat track to accommodate it. You know the tracks in Greece aren't like ours. They are much more primitive, just open fields, really."

"Good. A field ought to be wide enough."

He sighed, then put his arm on my shoulder. "Let us start selecting."

On my other ventures, poetry and music, I spent most evenings composing. Like the Neronia that they inspired, the Greek festivals had three categories of competition for me: poetry, music, and chariot racing. But they were huge ventures compared to ours, many more contestants, and many more contests. They were held all over Greece, at

Olympia, at Delphi, at Isthmia, at Nemea, at Actium, at Argos, and there were numerous other local festivals as well. Some ran on a four-year cycle, others on a two-year cycle. But they would adjust their schedules so I could attend each of them in their own cities. It would be an exhausting tour; it would be an exhilarating tour; it would be my rebirth.

In writing to the game officials to request the changes in schedule, I was committing myself. It was with great determination that I sent the letters off. The Senate did not object. They wouldn't dare, not these days.

The evenings were oases of quiet and contentment as I worked on my poetry and Tullia read nearby. She was a soothing presence, a friendly companion as excited about the Greek expedition as I was. I had assured her a place and time to train at the palaestra beside the gymnasium and baths, along with several other girls who wanted to cross over to Greece with us. As a bedfellow she was pleasurable and undemanding, if not torrid and experienced, which I missed. She told me that a bed could only hold one such person, and it had it in me; there should not be two of us. But I knew better—that is the true meaning of the word *experienced*.

So by day I drove my horses and trained my neglected singing voice under the tutelage of Appius, and by night I composed, and day and night I had to plan for the imminent arrival of Tiridates. It had taken him nine months to make the journey, but he was now entering Roman territory from the north, having come all the way on land with an enormous company—not only his wife but three thousand Parthian horsemen and a huge baggage train. This was a unique occasion, similar to a Triumph but not truly one. We had not conquered a foreign enemy but made an ally and vassal of him, and he would parade in the streets of Rome but as an honored guest. There were many questions of protocol to be settled.

I relied on my trusted freedmen and the Praetorian prefects to discuss things with first; next would come the Consilium and last the Senate. The Praetorians had common sense; the freedmen were all trusted ministers. In addition to Epaphroditus, Phaon, Tigellinus, and Nymphidius, I had rediscovered an old freedman of Claudius's, Helios. He had served Claudius well behind the scenes, never rising to the prominence of Pallas or Narcissus; all the better. So I assembled my little private group of advisers, and we tackled the particulars of the Tiridates visit.

The first concern was where and how I would receive him. It was decided that I would meet him in Naples and then lead him into Rome myself.

The next concern was in what capacity he would be received. As a guest? As a client king?

We met in one of the smaller workrooms in the palace, gathered around a long wooden table that held a map of Rome and the surrounding country.

"Since this is unprecedented, I propose to receive him as an honored ally, but one whose kingship is dependent on Rome. He surrenders his eastern crown and I place his diadem on his head. This will be in public ceremony in the Forum," I said, looking around at the men.

Tigellinus just nodded curtly. So did Nymphidius.

Helios said, "What sort of ceremony will this be?" He was a stocky man, solid but not weak, balding, with dark penetrating eyes.

"We will have to create it ourselves," I said. "The obeisance and exchange of diadem for crown should be on the Rostra where the most people can see it."

"The Praetorians will be needed to keep order in the Forum, manage the crowds," said Nymphidius.

"From the Forum we will proceed to the Theater of Pompey for more ceremony. I will order the interior to be gilded, and over the open sky, a giant silk purple awning with the stars and me driving a celestial chariot in gold."

Phaon began to fidget. "The expense . . . I will have to compute it. The gold leaf . . . the silk awning . . ."

"And I will order white robes for the people in the Forum, so they are all in white when the sun rises," I said, suddenly seeing it. Yes, a multitude in white.

"Robes? For everyone?" he asked, his voice squeaky.

"We will process from the Theater to the Temple of Janus, where I will formally close the doors. Then there will be a celebratory banquet."

Phaon now grimaced. "Caesar, I fear the treasury cannot support this. You have already given Tiridates an exorbitant travel allowance, thousands of sesterces a day. And he has been traveling for nine months! What does this add up to?" He reached for the pitcher of juice on the table and poured himself a big cup.

Epaphroditus asked, "What of the problem of his dagger? It is his official emblem of rank, but weapons are not allowed in the emperor's presence."

Helios massaged his cheek and said, "Let it be nailed to its scabbard so it cannot be taken out. A diplomatic solution to a diplomatic problem."

Oh, he *was* good. How fortuitous that I had found him.

"The banquet will conclude the festivities?" asked Phaon.

"No, we have games the next day." And I would race, but I didn't tell them that.

"*Then* is it over?" begged Phaon.

As the time grew closer, one idea gave birth to another, as if the event had a mind of its own. It swelled and swelled, billowing out in my imagination.

A Triumph. Up until now, Triumphs were celebrations of military victories, rejoicing over the conquest of a foreign enemy. During the Republic, the Senate granted generals the right to celebrate a Triumph, and famous ones like Scipio, Sulla, and Pompey paraded through the streets on the predetermined route from the Campus Martius through the Forum and then on to the Temple of the Capitoline Jupiter. There were strict requirements: the general had to have won a major land or sea battle and ended a war, and killed at least five thousand of the enemy. But since then, the privilege of celebrating a Triumph was reserved to the imperial family, and the rules became less defined. Augustus had had a triple Triumph, celebrating his victories over Dalmatia, Actium, and Egypt. In the last, the three children of Cleopatra and Marc Antony marched as captives. Germanicus had had a Triumph for his wars in Germany. And I had watched Claudius's in recognition of his conquest of Britain. All of these celebrated military victories. But why should a diplomatic victory, a bloodless one, not be equally worthy of honor?

A diplomatic victory was more than equal to a military one; it was superior to it. Lives were spared. Cities were not destroyed. Treasuries were not emptied. Hatred between conquering and conquered was avoided. Trade was not disrupted.

And I had achieved this. I had brought about peace with Parthia, peace with our perpetual enemy, peace that had eluded us up until now. True, I had had to direct the military strategy and the stalemate had not been achieved without generals, but they had only laid the groundwork for the negotiations.

Parthia. The country that had defeated Crassus, beheading him and then pouring molten gold down his throat in mockery of his wealth. Parthia, the country that had annihilated the army of Marc Antony, starting his long fall from power.

Parthia, the country Julius Caesar was on the eve of setting out to conquer, considering that a victory there would be his greatest achievement.

But I, Nero Claudius Caesar Augustus Germanicus, had done what none of these national heroes had managed to do.

L

There were a thousand details to manage, and I relished tackling them all. To absorb myself in choosing the exact degree of whiteness of the robes, the length of the palm branches to be carried in the Forum, the thickness of the gold foil to be applied to the wood in the Theater of Pompey—all these purged my mind, channeling it away from the places to which it wanted to return, the loss of Poppaea, the perfidy of the conspirators. Nothing could ever restore that fullness of content, of trust, shattered and lost forever. But to dwell on it only increased its power; better to lose myself in what I realized was trivia, but diverting trivia.

Oh, how I imagined what Poppaea would say. How she would comment on all these details, teasing me and suggesting changes. As I looked around the room, seeing the empty couch where she liked to sit, the unpressed cushions mocked me.

What I would give to speak to you on the most trivial subject. But no amount of gold, nothing I possessed, would make such a swap possible.

And the conspirators, some rotting in their graves, others a tidy pile of ashes in urns—for how long would I continue to see their features stamped on living senators and soldiers, invading and tainting the present?

Agitated, my morning disturbed, I turned back to the charts drawn up for the ceremony in the Forum, and all that would follow.

There were people moving about the chamber, fussing with curtains and trays, gliding soundlessly about. More distractions. I turned around and saw them, looking like a lot of mice, scurrying here and there. And then, among them, in the shadow of a corner—Poppaea.

I strained to see. Could a ghost move among the living? But no. It was Sporus. I motioned for him to come over to me. The dim light did nothing to dispel the impression that it was she, she herself.

"Take a look at this chart," I said, pointing to the one with sketches of the tunics. I waved the other attendants away.

Come closer. Let me see you. Come back to me.

He smiled, happy to look, to give an opinion. He bent his head over the drawings.

"These are for the morning at the Forum?" he asked.

"Yes. We will give out the tunics the night before, so the people can spend the night there, already waiting and attired at the first light of dawn."

"As the night gradually flees and the sky turns purple and then opalescent, the robes will glow," he said.

"Yes," I said. "But we must have a clear sky."

"The gods will grant it," he said. "I am sure of it."

The voice. The words. As she would say them. As she *was* saying them.

He stood and we looked at one another, our faces on the same level. I bent toward him—toward *her*—and kissed her full on the mouth. It felt the same.

Instantly I recoiled. Was I mad? This was another person entirely. But was it? The resemblance—more than a resemblance, an exact reproduction. But no. Not exact. No.

"Forgive me," I said. "It was—it seemed—"

He touched my shoulder. "I miss her, too. We mourn together. If I can ease your grief, I am honored. And if I can make her live again, my own grief is lessened."

I waved him away, shaking my head. What had I done?

But for that moment, my pain had vanished.

And now that I knew it could vanish, how could I keep from seeking that solace again?

When word came that Tiridates was within a hundred miles of us, I had a two-horse carriage meet him to convey him and his queen south to Naples, where I would receive him. I went early, always eager to be in Naples. I visited the site where Poppaea's shrine was being built; work was proceeding apace, and the foundations of the building were already laid. Soon the columns would rise.

The shrine would commemorate her life and divinity. The memory of the living Poppaea would be subsumed into this inert structure, while the warm breathing one . . . the warm breathing one lingering on in another guise, in another being . . . was she still with me after all?

A t last I gazed upon the face of Tiridates, so long almost a make-believe figure to me. He was a dark-eyed, short, wiry man, a few years older than me but still young, somewhat bandy-legged but quivering with energy. His queen, wearing a golden helmet to comply with Roman custom rather than the veil traditional to her culture, kept mostly silent, so unlike our chattering Roman women.

I was relieved that he spoke Latin, for I certainly did not speak Parthian, and it is always better to forgo a translator. We were able to converse quite freely, and he told me of his country and its neighbors, Colchis and Pontus. He invited me to visit Armenia, and on impulse I accepted, which led him to propose that we launch a joint exploratory military campaign through the Caucasian Gates, which lay just north of Armenia and from which we could smash the troublesome Alani tribe.

"You can name your legion the Phalanx of Alexander the Great," he said. "Have only very tall soldiers." He leaned over and whispered, "People in my region are short, and this would strike fear into them."

I laughed. "Alexander, alas, was short himself. So the name would hardly be descriptive."

"What matter? Who will know?" He smiled. "He has grown tall in legend."

I liked the man. I liked him even better when, at the exhibition games put on in his honor at Naples, he displayed his archery skills in killing two bulls with a single arrow.

"The Parthians are known for their prowess in archery, but I have never witnessed anything like this," I told him. "The person I admire most in the Trojan War was Paris, and he was an archer."

Tiridates laughed, showing little white teeth. "He did what the heroic Hector could not, slaying Achilles. Arrows are mightier than swords."

"The modern usually destroys the antiquated," I corrected him. "Or, it is always safer to kill from a distance."

All was in readiness in Rome; I waited in satisfaction that the next day was the day. I had a new imperial purple toga at the ready, and for once I did not mind wearing it. The wreath made from fresh-gathered branches from my sacred imperial laurel at Livia's house was plaited and rested on a golden tray.

Helios tiptoed in at the dividing line between day and night, when the sky dims and the first stars appear.

"Caesar," he said, bowing, "all the signs of rain are with us—there is a ring around the moon. The hawks are flying low, and seagulls are flying inland."

I leapt up and went to the window. Sure enough, there was a halo around the moon. And the breeze hitting my face felt damp. Curses! We would have to postpone the ceremonies.

"Notify the Praetorians, and halt handing out the tunics," I said. "There must be clear skies for this!"

"Caesar, I have already warned them about it. They only await your official orders."

I nodded. He seemed to anticipate everything. "Good," I said. "You are resourceful. I appreciate that."

But oh! What a disappointment. Things postponed lose their luster.

In the morning the skies were leaden but no rain fell, and by late afternoon the sun was out. The ceremonies would proceed the next day. That night the city was lit with torches and garlands hung from buildings, and the streets were thronged with people. Celebrants, clad in their white robes, poured into the Forum where they would wait all night, and stood on the rooftops of all the surrounding buildings, so thick the roof tiles could no longer be seen.

I awoke very early, before the sun even tinted the eastern sky. I needed to be attired and waiting with the guards and senators long before the procession actually got under way through the Forum. There had been no rehearsal, for that would spoil the element of surprise. So the first time had to be perfect.

The new toga, rich purple from the dye of a thousand snails, draped lightly around me. The smooth laurel leaves circled my head and felt cool against my hair. Their subtle scent spoke of solemnity.

Now I would go forth to complete the Neronian triumph of diplomacy.

By the time I stood with my companions at the eastern entrance to the Forum, the sun was just about to rise. We made our slow way toward the Rostra at the western end, walking in pairs. The cohorts of soldiers in parade dress fanned out through the Forum to direct the crowds, and I ascended the Rostra and took my seat on the magisterial chair, surrounded by military standards.

The sun suddenly burst out from the clouds, hitting the white garments of the people in the Forum, flashing off the armor, weapons, and standards of the soldiers, hitting me full in the face. Tiridates appeared at the far end, walking through a lane of soldiers, then stopping at the foot of the Rostra where he and his entourage did obeisance to me.

"Master, I am the descendant of Arsaces, brother of the kings Vologases and Pacorus, and your slave. I have come to you, my god, worshipping you as I do Mithras. The destiny you spin shall be mine, for you are my Fate and my Fortune."

The crowd gave a mighty roar, and when it subsided, I stood, looked down upon him, and said, "You have done well to come here in person, so that you might enjoy my grace. For what neither your father left you nor your brothers gave you and guarded for you, this I give you freely and I make you King of Armenia, so that you and they may understand that I have the power to take away kingdoms and to bestow them." I then motioned for him to ascend to the Rostra by the special ramp that had been built and to sit at my feet.

He did so, moving supplely, and took his place at my feet. I bent over, took his hand, and raised him up, while I stood with him. I removed his tiara and replaced it with a diadem, and shouts of celebration rung out, resounding in the Forum and the open air.

"Rome crowns you," I said. "And with this diadem, all nations know you are recognized as the legitimate king of Armenia."

Now I would lead on to the gilded theater, I who had been equated with Mithras, the eye of the sun. The Golden Day would continue, blessed by Sol.

He—Sol—shone down upon us as the people processed to the theater, in orderly files, to take their appointed places within. There was room only for eleven thousand people, and thus, unfortunately, attendance was limited.

After enough time had passed for the audience to be seated, Tiridates and I descended from the Rostra and made our way through the cheering crowds, a dazzling sea of white with splashes of green from the waving palm branches.

"This was worth the nine months' journey," he said. "We hear of the splendor of Rome but few of us have seen it, and the only crowds of Romans we know are the legions of soldiers come to fight us."

"From now on, our legions fight *with* you," I assured him. I dodged as a shower of roses was flung over us, with cries of excitement.

"Rome is so wealthy she can even trample roses underfoot," he said in wonder, as he stepped on them, crushing the petals beneath his boots. The drowsy warm scent surrounded us. Then we passed on.

The great facade of the theater was hung with garlands; we stood before it for a moment, then entered. The sun was almost directly overhead, shining through the purple silk awning stretched across the open air, bathing the interior with violet light, giving the white robes of the audience an otherworldly glow.

We stepped into the theater, and the audience rose, cheering. Once inside, my eyes were bedazzled by the luminous glow of the gold walls that seemed to pulsate. And above, pictured on the purple awning, myself in a chariot surrounded by stars, all in gold. I turned once around, basking in the beauty and symbolism.

"Mighty Imperator!" the people cried, rising to their feet. "Imperator!"

Imperator. I now could assume the title, meaning supreme victorious field commander, permanently by popular acclamation. So be it. I held up my hands for silence. "I humbly accept the title, by your bestowal. And we are here to celebrate this great moment in Roman history, a conciliation between us and our ancient enemy, and the gift of peace. Peace all throughout the empire. As such, I will close the doors of the Temple of Janus."

"This is truly the Golden Day!" they cried. "We are surrounded by gold, immersed in it! And peace, a golden moment, crowns it!"

Tiridates and I ascended the stage, and ceremonies of speeches and gift exchanges followed. As I looked out over the rows of white-clad spectators, the sunlight moving slowly across them as Sol made his journey in the sky above, I felt transported. The warmth of the sun on my head seemed to anoint me. *All will be well. The troubles are over and gone, and sun returns after the storms.*

Tiridates presented me with a prized possession, a Parthian sword, encased in an enameled scabbard. Handing it to me, he said, "It is a match to mine. We can carry our swords when we march through the Gates of the Caucasus as brothers."

I had to admit, the idea beguiled me. Perhaps if one lives long enough, one finds delight in discarded ideas after all.

I presented him with a Roman counterpart, a finely wrought *gladius* in a jeweled scabbard.

Speeches followed, dull ones by ambassadors and senators. The sun shifted from overhead to west. People began to fidget; I could see the movement in the audience. There was one thing left to do.

A herald stepped forward and said, "In closing, the emperor will perform a poem he has written for the occasion."

I had worked on the poem, and its accompanying music, for some time, along with several others I was practicing to perform in Greece. It had been difficult to enter into that frame of mind, but if I could not harness my energy to create material, I could not think of going to Greece.

The cithara was placed in my hands, and I took it reverently, passing the strap over my shoulder and positioning the instrument so my left arm supported its weight. I looked out at the audience.

Apollo, Sol, guide the hands and voice of your son if you want him—and you—to be honored.

I began. For the first moment the old terror, the old awkwardness, seized me, and then Apollo enveloped me and they vanished, and there was only the music and the poetry and the joy of expressing them. I was freed from where I stood, an earthly creature, and soared into the realms of imagination and eternity.

LI

I never left them. In all the hours that followed, I was still transported, not really of this time and this place, although I trod the stones of the streets and stood on the mosaics of the banquet hall. But a glow suffused them, so they seemed unreal, and my actions likewise. Was this a protective shield given me by Apollo?

Still in my Triumphator's robe, with crowds behind me, I climbed the steep hill to the Temple of the Capitoline Jupiter, standing before his statue. I removed the laurel wreath from my head, feeling its smooth leaves slide away, and laid it before the marble feet of Jupiter.

Here is my Triumph crown of the sacred laurel, my offering to you. Accept the symbol of this personal Triumph, a departure from tradition.

Did its leaves quiver, or was that just the breeze? I was used to gods now, to their silences and their whims, their favors and their desertions, and would not stay to fret about it. I could only offer what I had, and what I was, and there was no arguing with a god's decision.

Now I must perform a duty not as emperor but as Pontifex Maximus, and a place was provided for me to change into the appropriate robes, then set out for the Temple of Janus near the Forum. Back down the hill, and the shadows were long now, stretching out, as the glorious day of Sol was coming to its end. I must perform this rite while it was still daylight. But in May the light lingers long.

I reached the temple just as the last warm rays of sunshine were caressing it. I turned to the people, still in their white robes, still filling the streets and Forum, now bathed in the rosy light of sunset.

"Good people of Rome!" I said. "I am come here today to celebrate a profound accomplishment—the entire empire is at peace. There is no war anywhere. From the wilds of Britain to the cataracts of the Nile, from the sands of Persia to the Pillars of Hercules in the west, strife has ceased. Therefore we can shut the doors of the temple of the god Janus."

Cheers went up, and the now-bedraggled palm branches waved.

"Why do we open and shut the doors, and what have they to do with peace or war?" I asked them.

"Janus has helped us in times past!" a man called.

"True. He is the god who guards the inside and the outside, the east, west, north, and south, what is past and yet to come. Endings and beginnings. But long ago he caused a torrent of boiling water to surge forth from his temple and overwhelm our Sabine enemies. So we leave his doors open when we are at war, so he can help us again. When we are at peace, and do not need his aid, we can close them. I do so now, for the first time since the days of Augustus."

I turned and faced the ornate bronze double doors, now gaping open on their hinges, with a statue of the two-headed god inside—the two faces of Janus, looking forward and backward. A ray of sun slanted into the interior.

I could not stretch my arms wide enough to pull both doors, so I closed them one at time. They creaked and groaned, their hinges rusty. They were extremely heavy and it took all my strength to move them, but only the Pontifex Maximus could do it. The first door clanged into place, making a hollow ringing noise. The second followed, fitting it-self beside the first, sealing the interior shut. Now that they were closed, I could marvel at the fine bronze work, the six panels on the door with a large arch at the top. One of the acolytes then hung a garland across it in celebration.

"It is done!" I said. "May the peace last forever!"

Oh, what a dream.

* * *

The formal banquet would be held at the Golden House pavilion—where else? I had spent little time in it since the horror of Poppaea's death there, but I could hardly abandon it, for political reasons. People had murmured against the expense and the expanse of it, and not to use it now would be foolhardy.

Consulting not only with Helios and Epaphroditus but also with the head cook of the imperial kitchen, I had settled on a menu that included Parthian dishes, incorporating even the costly and rare silphium plant. I had also engaged Parthian minstrels to provide music, as I understood that their culture set great store by it.

For the invited guests, I had, albeit reluctantly, invited the senators, as well as the ranking Praetorians, and scholars who studied eastern literature and history to mingle with the Parthian entourage. I had also made sure to include translators.

As this was a diplomatic and formal occasion, I kept on the Triumphal purple toga and wore a wreath of gold laurel leaves. The dusk was thickening as I stood in the courtyard waiting to welcome the guests. Torches flared all up and down the long facade, and the sweet winds of May swept up from the blooming gardens below, warm kisses of perfume.

I fairly ached from loneliness. But here came my guests—a thousand people, but no one who could make this feeling abate. Still, it was better to be surrounded by noise, light, and music than to be alone, if only a little better.

A tinkle of chimes signaled the approach of Tiridates and his company. He had changed into formal regal Parthian wear: multicolored layers of tunics, vests, and overcoats, loose billowing pantaloons, and red leather shoes. He proudly wore the just-bestowed diadem on his elaborate headdress. In the interval between the Temple of Janus ceremony and the banquet, he had had his beard dressed with jewels and curled; likewise his hair, which protruded from the headdress and hung to his shoulders.

"My brother," he murmured, leaning forward to bestow a ceremonial kiss on my cheek. I did likewise with him. "My queen," he said proudly. Beside him, a woman with dark eyes bowed her head. She now wore a veil that made it hard to see the rest of her features.

Behind him were lined up his senior officials, his envoys, and Zeus knew who else—we emperors and kings have many in our trains.

Soon the Romans arrived, their jaded eyes open wide with curiosity. Quickly the noise of many voices was reverberating off the walls and the Parthian minstrels could scarcely be heard over the chatter. But that the guests were engaging with one another was the important thing.

"You are another Alexander," said Tiridates, suddenly by my side. "Look! Togas and pantaloons, side by side! Bare heads and conical hats. Shall we have a mass wedding, like Alexander did in Susa? Having his Greek officers marry the daughters of Persian nobles?"

"How many nobles here brought their daughters?" I asked. I looked around; there were many Parthian women.

"Quite a few," he said. "They were curious to see Rome."

"Curious enough to remain here with a Roman husband?" I asked. I did not mention that such a marriage would be illegal in Roman law, which did not recognize the union of a Roman citizen with a foreigner. Marc Antony found that out, as had even the Divine Julius.

Tiridates laughed. "Who can say, until we ask them?"

We strolled over to one of the tables displaying some of the dishes to be served. Mounds of Parthian beans, Parthian lamb, and Parthian bread were the centerpiece, arranged on gold platters.

Tiridates helped himself to a tidbit.

"How authentic is it?" I asked. "My cook could only work from guesswork."

He nodded. "It comes close," he said diplomatically. "I can taste the silphium. However did you come by it? We have to substitute asafoetida."

"We have our ways," I said. The truth was, it was almost impossible to obtain, had cost a fortune, and had strained the business connections of our source in Cyrene.

"Mmm," he said, savoring the taste. "Like Alexander, you can do the impossible."

What was he leading up to? Or was this just routine eastern flattery?

"Not always," I said, waiting for the request.

"About the new legion," he said.

So that was it. "What about it?"

"I was serious when I proposed the joint venture. As you know, we have been threatened by the Alani tribes just north of us, over the Caucasian Mountain pass. I know Rome wants to settle the Black Sea piracy problem once and for all, and you can only do that by encircling the sea and putting an end to the independent countries there. So your interests coincide with ours. If you contribute a legion, and we contribute our archers and horsemen, we could cross the pass and destroy the Alani, expanding our territory and ending the threats to both of us." He grinned, his lips spreading his bushy beard wide.

It was an inviting proposal. "It has many things to recommend it," I admitted. As it stood now, Rome controlled the lands encircling the western part of the Black Sea, but if we could control the eastern portions as well we could close the gap and turn the sea into another "Roman lake" like the Mediterranean. The Alani tribes lurking near the Black Sea could not stand up to Roman legions, and so we had little to lose. That part of the world had beckoned and beguiled Alexander himself. The campaign would be at best an adventure and at worst a waste of time. But it would confer Alexander-like glory on me and give me military laurels at last.

"Before I depart, we should make an agreement. While we are standing face-to-face, not thousands of miles apart, where messages take weeks to go back and forth, if they arrive at all."

I nodded. "I believe in swift decisions," I said. "But for tonight, we must concern ourselves only with the entertainment and protocol. It is time to announce the banquet and the order of seating. We will revisit this question in privacy." I signaled for the master of ceremonies to address the company and for the servers to bring out all the dishes.

The royals would dine from a long table, in keeping with eastern custom, on a dais built at one end of the hall; others had a choice of Roman couches or smaller tables, whichever they preferred. Tiridates and I would sit side by side in the center of the table, looking out at the rest of the diners. I had provided drinking rhytons for the Parthians, although the Romans were welcome to drink from them as well. Most were decorated with animal heads—bulls, lions, boars, and griffins.

The presenter held up the platters of special Parthian dishes and described them, but in truth they were not unfamiliar to us in Rome; they were already a popular novelty.

I was eager to speak to Tiridates about horses, as the Parthians were renowned horsemen.

"Well, as the saying goes," he said, "we learn to ride almost before we can walk." He held up the rhyton, inspecting it. "Because we can't put a rhyton down, since it has no flat bottom, we have to drink it fast. I suppose that is why we end up so drunk."

"Don't do that here, or you will be thought truly barbarian!" I warned him.

"What, the Romans don't get drunk? You can't expect me to believe that. I have heard much about your drunken parties."

"All true, but we like to imagine we are more refined." I took a sip from my own, footed goblet. "You see. No need to gulp." I smiled. "But about the horses. It is curious that you ride them, one man on one horse, whereas we harness them to pull chariots."

"Do Romans not ride, then?" He seemed puzzled.

"Yes, in the cavalry, but most of those are auxiliaries, not Romans, although they serve in the Roman army. And of course some ride for travel, or as couriers, or as acrobats in circus stunts. But we don't often race on horseback."

"It is strange how different customs arise," he said. "I understand you race chariots. Did other emperors do that?"

The servers put down platters of Parthian chicken, Parthian beans, cucumbers, and melons before us and refilled our drinking vessels.

I laughed. "Now I know you are a foreigner! No! And it is considered scandalous that I do. But having endured the scandal, I have no plans now to stop racing. In fact, I am going to race here at the games celebrating the treaty. The Greens have invited me to race in their colors, a great honor."

"So I will be able to watch?" he asked, his eyes twinkling. "What horses do you have in your team?"

I told him about the selection I had made, and he nodded approvingly.

"And here's a secret." I leaned toward him. "I am training to race a ten-horse chariot."

Now he looked surprised and impressed. "Where?"

"At Olympia. I am going to Greece soon to compete in the games there."

"Now *that* is something I would love to see."

"Come with me, then. Delay your return to Armenia."

"I am tempted. But a new crown needs to be guarded for a while. I need to return to make sure my title is secure."

"I understand." He spoke true. Nothing is more wobbly than a newly minted crown.

The banquet proper being over, the gathering devolved into a drinking party. Tables were cleared away, the Parthian minstrels stopped chanting and lamenting, and acrobats and dancers took their place. Amphoras were wheeled out, and stacks of cups were set by. Both red and white wines, plain and flavored, were offered. So, too, was the barbarian favorite, beer. It was all there for the taking—and more taking. The Parthians contributed their own magicians and fire-eaters to entertain us, and under the flickering yellow light of hundreds of oil lamps they wavered before us.

The crowd was close around me, but Tigellinus and Nymphidius were keeping a keen watch. The days when I could carelessly assume no one wished me harm were as dead as the conspirators. But even so I felt a slight pull on my clothing, subtle but there. I stood very still, pretending to watch the fire-eater standing on his hands in the circle before me, but holding my breath. There. It came again—the tug on the back of my toga. Even through the layers of cloth, I could feel it. Such is the sharpened power of discernment that comes after barely escaping assassination. I waited for it to come again. When it did, I whirled around, grabbing the back of someone bent over the hem of the toga, cutting it with a small knife.

I should have yelled "Assassin!" but I was too stunned. Instead, by instinct, I yanked the person up and shook her. Yes, it was a woman. She glared at me.

It was Statilia Messalina, Vestinus's widow. I twisted the knife out of her hand, forcing her to expose her palm, which clutched a small cut square of the gold border of the toga.

No one around us had noticed. It had happened so swiftly and silently that it had not even interrupted the entertainment.

"What are you doing?" I asked. I had not seen her since the trial of the conspirators, and I had not invited her to the banquet. I'd assumed she was in mourning and would not want to come to such a celebration, especially one hosted by me.

She continued staring defiantly at me, saying nothing.

"Answer me, or I will turn you over to the guards, who will make you talk."

"Like you made the innocent people talk in their trials?"

"They weren't innocent," I said.

"My husband was," she answered.

I looked around. We needed to leave this room so we could talk privately. I kept a hold on her arm and steered her out a door at the far end. I nodded to the guards. "It is all right," I said. "She feels faint, and we will go outside for fresh air."

Once outside—although there were other guards posted nearby— I let her go. "Now tell me."

She rubbed her arm. "How trusting you are, still. I may have another knife, a bigger one than the one meant for cutting cloth."

"I doubt it." I waited. She stayed silent. "If you did, you would have cut me rather than the cloth."

"I needed the cloth, and it can do the job of a knife well enough."

"What do you mean?"

"A little patch of the imperial toga, worn on a day of self-congratulation and smugness, carries with it all the traits of its owner."

She was going to curse me. She wanted the piece of toga as something that not only had been on my person but had symbolized my office.

"This makes you a traitor, too," I said. "For you know the law—anything that endangers my person is lèse-majesté and is treason."

"The law. What do I care for the law?"

"Be careful what you say," I warned her. "Do not doom yourself with hasty words."

"I have already doomed myself. I have been caught. Come, do what you will with me. Call the guards!" She started to gesture to them. Once again I grabbed her arm.

"That is too easy," I said. "You will tell me exactly why you tried to kill me. I deserve that much. And this is no court; only I will hear you."

She took a deep breath, thinking. I remembered how I had enjoyed her company at the races and her words at the opening reception for the Domus Aurea, telling me I had done well to race the chariot. She had seemed to be a sympathetic and wise friend, able to see beyond the obvious and the mundane. Someone, even, to confide in. So this stung more than if she had been someone else.

Her husband, Vestinus, was another matter. I had not been surprised that he was one of the conspirators, for he had always been rather dismissive of my ideas and sarcastic in his evaluations of my policies. And he had never made a show of sham friendship as had Petronius and Lucan.

"You condemned my husband without hearing his defense and only on the evidence of others."

"The evidence seemed convincing to me," I said. "And he chose not to say anything. He had the opportunity. Instead he held a dinner party and then killed himself upstairs while his guests waited downstairs." I gave a bitter laugh. "At least he didn't make a parody of it, like Petronius."

"For those of us waiting at the dinner table, it was horrible and interminable. And then you had the effrontery to send a message that the guests were free to leave!"

"I didn't mean it to be insulting. Quite the opposite."

"I couldn't leave! I had to wait at the table for hours, not daring to go upstairs. When finally a slave came to tell me it was over, I had to go and see what awaited me up there. They had cleaned him up, but the bloody towels were still in a pile. He had left me a letter."

"I am sorry for your loss, but it was a loss for me as well."

She gave a short, choking laugh. "What loss for you?"

"A loss of trust, a loss of friendship. Although I suppose you'll tell me I never had those things, only the pretense of them."

"So you see why I wanted to curse you? I want you to end your life miserably, perhaps forced to kill yourself like my husband did, and the gods only know who will be waiting downstairs? Perhaps no one. Perhaps that is the worst curse of all. To have no one there. No one waiting. No one who cares."

Her voice, rich and vibrant, had always been her most compelling feature. In the past she had spoken words that smoothed and amused. Now they pronounced a curse. No need for the cloth or spells. It was simpler than that; words did the conjuring.

"Now you have doomed yourself," I said. "You condemn yourself by your own testimony."

"Call the guards. Get it over with. Do not toy with me, as my husband toyed with our dinner guests."

"Only I know of this."

"Soon everyone will. There is no saving me past that point."

As if in answer to her, a warm, beguiling puff of air from the gardens, laden with the heady scent of roses, washed over us. And then, walking across the terrace, just visible in the torchlight, Poppaea. But of course it was Sporus. It was no true ghost, just the reverberation of one. My longing for her clutched at me, momentarily searing my soul. But it was a chimera.

"Marry me," I said suddenly, shocking myself. "Become my wife. That is the only thing that can save you, make you immune from any charges."

She stared at me. "That is your remedy? Marry you? The person who widowed me, the person I have admitted I want to curse?"

"Yes. The conspiracy has bereaved us both. We are both alone, victims of either the conspiracy itself or its aftermath. Statilia—I cannot call you Messalina; that name chokes me—I have always felt an affinity for you and from you. Tell me I am wrong, that it is only in my own imagination, and I will still release you. I will let you go without charges. As I said, no one knows of this but us. No one heard your words but me."

She stood, speechless for a moment. Then, quietly, she spoke. "I am free, regardless? Then I will voice my true thoughts. It is not your imagination. I have felt a kinship of the mind with you, a sympathy of thought. But the conspiracy—"

"It is over. We are both the poorer for it. But we survive. We are still here. And we must clothe ourselves in what comfort we can, in what remains. Will you be my wife?" I paused. "There will never be another Poppaea for me, and perhaps never another Vestinus for you. But they are gone. Do you not think they would want us to go forward, remembering them but also remembering that life is short and soon we will join them, in the interim snatching whatever the gods will grant us, lessened though it may be?"

She waited long moments, moments that drew themselves out while I asked myself, *Do you really want this?* but feeling that somehow it was right.

Finally she said, "Yes. I will marry you. But I will not marry someone I have not tried first in bed. So until you can prove yourself that way, it is a conditional acceptance."

I let her go. "Very well. In the meantime, would you like to come to the imperial box at the Circus Maximus? Like old times? I am racing tomorrow, wearing the colors of the Greens."

"Yes, I will come," she said. "I will wish you victory."

She turned and walked away, a free woman, and dropped the square she had cut from the toga. I held it up and fitted it into the empty space it had left at the hem. Perhaps someone could mend it.

What had I done?

LII

I prepared for bed. I was exhausted. The day had been indescribable, one the people called "golden" and one I would never forget. It had begun with the kiss of the light at sunrise in the Forum and ended with a marriage proposal to a woman I barely knew.

The lamps were guttering, about to run out of oil. It was long past midnight. I needed to rest if I had any hopes of doing well in the races tomorrow. I climbed into bed, drained.

The races . . . I could not concentrate on them. I knew what I needed to do, I had trained, and I had no control over what the other racers would do, or even over the weather and whether the track would be muddy or hard.

But my marriage proposal . . . I had just asked someone to become my empress. And she had accepted—on condition. On condition of how well we fitted together in bed. Well, that would remain to be seen, and there was nothing I could do about it in advance, either. Although the thought of it was titillating, I had to admit.

That she came from an old patrician family, that of the consul Statilius Taurus, I already knew. Her family name gave that away. But I would ask Epaphroditus to look further into her background.

What had made me do it?

When I had been with her on other occasions, I had sensed some connection, some mutual understanding. Perhaps I was wrong and she had lied to me to save her own life. Or to try again to take mine, although I did not believe that. And that I needed an empress was clear. And she seemed ideally suited for it. She was older—I must find out how old, but I believed she was somewhat older than I—but not beyond childbearing years. She seemed to come from the right family background, proper enough to satisfy the sternest critics in the Senate. And I felt, rightly or wrongly, that I could speak openly to her.

The all-consuming, wild love I had had for Poppaea could not be repeated. I would be foolish to look for it. That was what I told myself.

The day was fair. The race would be on dry sand, making for a faster time and more skidding. My race was the first scheduled, and I was just as glad, because the wait to compete could induce such apprehension it might worsen my performance. Once I had prepared and could do no more, it was best to plunge in and have it over with, the quicker to return to normal breathing.

I was proud to be wearing the colors of the Greens, honored that they had offered me that place. Donning the green racing tunic and fastening the ribbons on the harnesses, I tried to think only of the race and its strategy and put all else out of my mind. But it was almost impossible. Waiting for me in the imperial box was Tiridates and his entourage and Statilia.

My team was skittish and eager to run, though, and sprang out of the starting box like demons released from a cage, jerking the chariot forward so quickly it strained the fittings and stretched my arms painfully. All the teams were fast at the start, but we did not tangle, hurtling toward the *alba linea*. Had it not dropped, the chariots would have been wrecked, but it did fall just in time and we flew past. I was in the second lane and dared not turn my head to look back, but I could hear hoofbeats behind me on both sides, and soon, on the left, the Blue came alongside me. I urged my team to speed up, and they obeyed, so we left him behind, but the first turn was ahead of us, with him on the inside, and he got around it faster than I did.

From then on it was a lost cause. My horses seemed to lose their spirit, or their stamina, and responded sluggishly. Or is it true that animals can sense the master's mood and reflect it? Certainly I was distracted and only half there, and on the last turn, with both the Blue and the White ahead of me, I steered too close to the *metae*, glancing off them without (thank Zeus!) destroying the chariot or the horses, but careening off to the right and across the path of the Red, just barely missing him. Although I regained control of the horses and guided them around the turn way on the outside, my finish was a victory only in the sense that I managed to cross the line intact.

My competitors were gracious and congratulated me anyway.

"Thank you for not crashing into me!" said the Red, grinning. Well, that took at least *some* skill, so I deserved a little credit there. No one had been hurt.

"Don't thank him," said the Blue. "He robbed the crowd of seeing a grisly accident." He turned to me. "How could you be so thoughtless?" But he was grinning, too.

"The emperor ran a good race," said the White. "But, of course, he was competing against *us*, the best in the land."

"You are not far off the truth," I said. "You are the best Rome can offer."

After the track was cleared and swept, the next race commenced, and I made my way to the imperial box, shielding myself from the showers of flowers thrown at me and waving in response to the deafening cheers. I think the people liked me best for coming in last and laughing about it. People are strange; that is why pleasing them is fraught with mystery.

The box was draped with garlands and racing colors, and as I entered, the company stood and greeted me. I had not changed clothes and still wore the charioteer costume, drenched in sweat and covered with a light coating of fine sand.

Tigellinus grasped my forearm and made a face. "Covered in grit! You could sand down a piece of wood."

"A souvenir of the race," I said. "Proof that I did it."

Tiridates inclined his head in a slight bow. "So now I have seen the Roman method of horse racing. When you come to Parthia, we will show you ours."

"Going to Parthia?" asked Nymphidius. "When?"

"Tiridates and I are planning a joint military venture," I said.

Tigellinus barely suppressed a guffaw. "Military?" *You?* he might as well have said.

I had not decided yet, but the scorn and disbelief that I could be interested in a military campaign irked me. "Yes, a campaign against the Alani tribes north of Armenia," I said. "After I return from Greece. You remember, I am leaving for Greece in July. But after that, when the new legion is raised, I will lead it."

"What new legion?" asked Tigellinus. "What are you talking about?"

"I am recruiting a new legion with men from Italy, the first one raised from here in over a century." There, did he think I knew nothing of the history of Roman legions? "They must be at least six feet tall, and we will call them 'the Phalanx of Alexander the Great,' although their formal name will be the *legio I Italica.*"

"Why have I not been told of this?" Tigellinus asked.

"It has only just now been decided." *This very moment, thanks to your skepticism.*

"Perhaps you should recruit from the barbarians instead," said Nymphidius. "They tend to be enormous."

Tiridates quickly said, "We have come to an understanding, then? You promised to decide quickly, and you have fulfilled that promise." He turned to the company. "Endless debate and procrastination are a plague, a sickness your emperor is wise enough to avoid."

Or foolish enough to ignore.

Wine was poured to celebrate the informal agreement, and we drank. It was a luxury to permit myself the ease of wine erasing my jitters now that the race was safely over. For the sparring that now lay ahead, wine would help rather than hinder.

"So the emperor will go a-soldiering?" said the husky voice of Statilia, who had stood quietly in the back. As if to make a point, she was wearing dark clothing that betokened her mourning status.

"Yes, it's time, don't you think?"

"The emperor excels in all he does," said Tiridates eagerly. "So he should make a valiant warrior."

Now Tigellinus had to visibly stifle a laugh, his shoulders shaking.

Damn them all! I was the grandson of Germanicus, and if I wanted to be a soldier, I had no doubt I could be one. A good one, too. "With you by my side, brother, we will vie for valiancy," I said. I could spout eastern flattery, too.

"Yes, it is time," said Statilia, ignoring the interchange between Tiridates and me. "I believe the strength of Rome lies in its legions, and the strength of the legions depends on the strength of the individual soldiers in them."

"Well said, descendant of the great Titus Statilius Taurus, consul and Triumphator," said Tigellinus.

"I do have many of his decorations and honors," she said, "which I inherited. I would be pleased to show my emperor the collection any time he pleases, in my house in what is left of the Taurian Gardens."

And thus was the place of assignation decided. It would be on her grounds, not on mine. And not in the house where her husband had died but in the house she retained from the little Mother had let her keep when she seized her family's garden on a trumped-up charge of sorcery and made them imperial property.

"I would be most pleased to view them," I said.

She nodded, and her eyes met mine.

I set out from the palace at twilight. Birds were winging their way through the glowing sky, black outlines against the tender blue. The Taurian Gardens were not far from the pavilion of the Domus Aurea. When I stood on the terrace and looked northeast, I could see the house where Statilia had bid me come, a rich yellow set in the greenery of the gardens around it.

I would go by litter. That meant observers could know where I was going and how long I stayed, but there was no help for it. Privacy was not something an emperor could have, a privilege beyond his grasp.

The evening breeze was sweet as only May wind can be. I told myself not to think of what the next few hours would hold for me. That did not stop me from thinking about them.

I am accustomed to performing. I have stood on stage and sought the approval of hundreds of people. I have driven chariots and sought the approval of thousands. But the approval of one person, in private, and an audition for which there is no practice?

The bearers set down the litter on the graveled path before the entrance to the house. It was large but not imposing, built in a simpler time. Her ancestor Titus Statilius Taurus had fought in the dying gasps of the Republic a hundred years ago, commanding the land forces of Octavian in the battle of Actium. His reputation as a general was such that Antony's forces surrendered to him without a fight, rather than face Octavian's greatest general after Agrippa. He returned to Rome a hero, building what was then a showcase of a house. Its shrunken grounds—all the rest had been appropriated by Mother—were well tended, with rows of plane trees, boxwood hedges, and pebbled paths framing the dwelling well.

A slave with a lighted torch appeared at the door, coming to me where I stood beside the litter.

"Caesar," he said, bowing. He motioned me to follow him into the house, and I dismissed the litter. Before I got back into it, much would have passed.

The atrium was shadowy; it was that time of day when the outside light has waned but lamps do not help much. A faint glow still outlined the opening above the impluvium, reflected dully in the water beneath.

Statilia came out of the shadows and greeted me. "Welcome, Caesar," she said. "You have come to view the honors of my illustrious great-great-grandfather?"

"Indeed. Is that not why I was invited?" What an odd game we were playing. But let it commence.

"Yes," she said. "A glimpse at the old Republic, her honors, and what mattered then."

Oh, gods. She was going to make this political. That should not have been a surprise to me, as Vestinus was a committed republican.

"Show me," I said.

She led me to the back of the atrium, where her ancestor's Triumphator toga in purple and gold was displayed on a stand, its folds falling to the floor and so artfully arranged I expected to see feet protruding. I reached out to touch it and nearly made a hole in it. The material had deteriorated and was as fragile as a spider's web. I stopped just in time.

"It is exactly a hundred years old," she said. "We never touch it, except to brush it with feathers to keep the dust off."

"A hundred years ago," I said. "When Antony and Cleopatra were still alive."

"He won it for his campaign in Africa, when Octavian and Pompey Sextus were at war." She gestured toward a marble bust on a pedestal, protected by a little barrier of urns. On the white brow of the bust a withered wreath drooped above the eyebrows. It was a duplicate of the laurel wreath he had worn the day of his Triumph.

"Don't touch it!" she warned. "It will fall to dust!"

Suddenly it seemed pathetic to me, this futile attempt to preserve what was perishable. The years had turned the once-green leaves black and twisted, making it a mockery, not a tribute.

She led me on into the adjoining room of the house, where the funeral mask of her ancestor was displayed, the one used in the mourning rites. He stared out at us, a mild-looking man in spite of his martial prowess. He looked trapped, as if he wanted to flee from this dusty museum.

Flimsy old robes, long-dead leaves, wax masks—was I in a mausoleum?

"Thank you for showing me," I said.

"There's more," she said. "Much more. He had many other honors and distinctions."

I took her hands in mine. "Doubtless they are very meaningful to his family, but I need see no more once I have seen the tokens of his highest distinction."

She pulled her hands away. "Oh, you have had so many, these must seem boring and paltry to you. From the days before there was an emperor, before one man hogged all the honors."

"I didn't come here to fight with you or to discuss politics," I said. "I understood that we had another mission."

She smiled. "Oh, yes. That."

Perhaps she was as leery of it as I was.

"But first, let us have some wine," she said.

Yes. Let's.

A slave appeared with a pitcher of wine, a jug of water, and two stemmed goblets on a tray. He set it down and carefully poured out the wine, then added water. We each took our goblets.

Ah, wine. Gift of Bacchus. Bosom friend of Aphrodite. I drank deep of mine—after letting her drink hers first. Just in case.

"Let us sit out in the garden," she said, leading me to the peristyle and taking her place on a marble bench. In the falling light slaves lit lanterns, and we watched the last colors of day leach and fade from the flowers, so that only the white ones were visible. Soon they drew pale moths, their fluttering wings hovering over the petals. After the gaudiness of day, peace reigned.

Now she took my hand, holding it between hers. "This is my favorite place," she said. "I like to come here at close of day. That is why I asked you to come at this time."

"Why do you like it best?"

"The day is done, for well or ill, and I can contemplate it calmly, knowing there is nothing I need do for the next few hours and nothing I can do to change the last few hours. There is profound peace in that."

"Is peace what you seek?"

"An underlying peace, not a static life," she said. "There is a difference."

"So philosophers would say."

"Yes, they would. They do."

"Have you come to peace with what happened between me and Vestinus, or is that too much to expect?"

"Now I have. But first I had to do what I did at the banquet. I had to, for his sake. I owed it to him."

"To take revenge, or try to," I said. "It is a basic desire. But perhaps, trying to take revenge and failing fulfills the obligation well enough?"

"Yes, it does. In the eyes of the gods, it is the same. Now I am spared from cursing you. To curse you would be to curse my own life, if it is tied to yours."

"Is that the only reason?" If she still wished me ill, then I had no desire to yoke my life to hers. "If we are not together, then you would just as soon I go down to doom? Not a very complimentary opinion."

"No," she said. "I would not want any harm to befall you." She took my head in her hands and turned it to look at her. "But we still have one thing to settle."

She took me up the stairs to an upper room, where her bedchamber was situated. It was open to a roof terrace, and from it I could see almost the whole of Rome, punctuated by the light of thousands of torches.

"This is mine alone," she said. "My ancestral home." She paused. "Vestinus has never been here. We lived in his house."

No shadow of the past here, then. No site of either happiness or sorrow with Vestinus. Just her own life, her own memories, from before she knew him.

She took my hand, and together we went inside, toward the bed. The room was dark, and when she made to light a lamp, I stopped her.

"Leave it," I said. The dark was tender and embracing. From the two small windows came only a faint light from the dying day. Framed by the windows, the first stars twinkled feebly in the sky. Faraway music, perhaps a flute, floated in the evening air. So did the sounds of the streets, people calling to one another, the cries of playing children.

I took her in my arms. She fit there well. I was no longer apprehensive or self-conscious. She bent down and pulled away the blankets, exposing the smooth, untouched sheets beneath, running her hands over them, inviting me there.

She was an experienced woman, knowing what pleased her and how to give pleasure to someone else, unblushingly. There is no substitute for that, and if there cannot be wild adoration, there can still be passion, sensuality, and satiety.

Neither of us spoke the word "love."

We were married in that house a week later. By the time I had climbed back into the litter in the morning light, it was all settled. I had passed her test in bed—"surprisingly well," she had said, a thought I did not care to pursue. What had she expected? Did I want to hear? No.

"So I see no need for delay," she said.

Nor did I. This way Tiridates could be a guest, making it somewhat of a state occasion. And so we stood in the atrium and spoke the words that bound us together, all but one phrase—*Whenever and wherever you are Gaia, I am Gaius.* I had made that vow to Poppaea and even in death I would not break it. Besides, in the underworld, when we are pale shades looking for one another, I wanted no confusion.

Statilia did not object. Even the marriage itself seemed a practical arrangement to her, and thus the ceremonial details were not fraught with meaning. She did not even seem curious about what would now be at her fingertips as empress. Perhaps she was so self-possessed she had no need even to ask.

Tiridates presented us with a magnificent gold sculpture of a horse, with the promise that he would send a selection of his best steeds for breeding purposes. His entourage put on an archery exhibition for our entertainment, and we had the usual banquet to celebrate. At length, as the sun sank, we had the traditional wedding procession to the home of the groom, in this case my small residence in the Servilian Gardens, one I seldom visited as it was inconveniently located in the southwestern part of the city, near the road leading to Ostia. But for this bride, I wanted a place with no ghosts, at least for the first few days.

Alone at last in the privacy of the bedchamber, she gave a great sigh.

"So it begins," she said. She turned to me. "A late marriage is as different from a first one as a violet from an aster. But we have glorious examples of those late unions—Julius Caesar himself had been married three times before he met Cleopatra."

But he loved her more than the others, I thought. It was not the order in which love came but that it came, late or early. "Both the violet and the aster are beautiful in their own season," I said diplomatically.

LIII

We stayed at the Servilian Gardens residence for a week, shutting ourselves off from the rest of Rome. I tried to sort out my jumbled feelings about this marriage and about Statilia herself. That I needed an empress was obvious; I was not yet thirty and could not go through life alone. There was also the practical matter that I needed children, or there would be no one to succeed me, and Rome would be thrown back into the strife that followed Caesar's death. But should I have married *this* woman?

Too late for that, Nero, too late. It is done and settled. There is some satisfaction in that, some peace of mind.

We were alone except for the slaves, and the daily visit and briefings from Tigellinus and Helios, who had become increasingly important to me. Tiridates had departed for Parthia, and the recruiting for *legio I Italica* was progressing nicely. It seemed that many men were eager to join.

Seated on one of the stools in the workroom, Tigellinus winked. "And how are . . . things . . . Caesar?"

"Well," I said curtly.

"I am sure Vorax would welcome a visit," he said, "if things are not so well."

"I am well aware of my choices, Tigellinus," I said.

"I am just reminding you, Caesar."

"My memory is not failing."

Would that it were. If my memory of Poppaea were not so vivid, perhaps I would be less troubled. When Statilia was in my bed I was able to vanquish it, because Statilia was a seasoned voluptuary and drove all other thoughts from my mind at the time, but they crept back afterward.

But in the enclosed world we were occupying, secluded and protected, we were able, gingerly, to get to know one another, what and who we were before the conspiracy.

She was three years older than I, being thirty-one. She had married Vestinus when she was seventeen but had taken many lovers.

"Well, that explains it," I said.

"Explains what? As if I do not know."

"Why you had to settle that before all else with me. Comparisons?"

She sighed and reached over to take a fresh-cut fig resting on the nearby table. "They are inevitable," she said. "That becomes the curse of marriage. They say that the best matches are made between two virgins because they know no better and are satisfied with whatever they get." She bit into the fig, and juice ran down her chin. She wiped it off quickly.

I laughed. "That does not describe you."

"Nor you," she shot back. "Did you know, there were rumors that I was your lover and that Vestinus was named in the conspiracy so you could marry me?"

How had Tigellinus failed to pick up that rumor? "Absurd," I said.

She laughed. "Are you sure we have never been lovers before?"

"Wouldn't I remember it?"

"Well, you were quite drunk that time at Piso's . . ."

O gods! Was she one of the ones on Petronius's list? Or was she teasing me?

"I surely would never have forgotten," I said gallantly.

"You have improved since then," she said. "If you hadn't, well—" She spread her hands, laughing.

"If I was that drunk, it is no wonder I am better now." But was she serious? I doubted we had ever been together. But I would not pursue it.

As the days passed, the old easy feeling I had had with her in the past returned. We spoke of many things, and her low, throaty voice, which I had always found attractive, was beguiling. She exuded a sophistication that shunned conventional judgments and allowed her to speak her mind.

"If I trust someone, mind you," she said. "And for some reason I have always trusted you."

"Why?"

"Because you had the courage to be openly yourself in the face of disapproval. To be an artist in spite of ridicule and opposition."

"Ridicule?" I bristled.

She draped herself over the edge of a couch, carelessly, like a thrown scarf. "Surely you must know that there were people who laughed at you."

I knew there were people who condemned me, but laugh? "I didn't hear them," I said.

"Good. But I did. Never mind. Because you were true to yourself, you are honest through and through. And I could trust you. To listen, and to keep it to yourself." She smiled. "You are not a gossip."

"How do you know that?"

"I just do," she said serenely. "I can tell. My mother told me that she had the ability to read people, to know them after they had spoken just a few words. I inherited that gift."

"Is it a gift, or a curse?"

"It's a painful gift," she admitted.

It was one I wished I had, painful or not. Then I would not have been shocked at Piso, at Seneca, at Lucan or Faenius or any of them. Perhaps I could now rely on Statilia to be my eyes and ears. She might be better than Tigellinus.

Emerging from our cocoon into the turmoil of Rome, we relocated to the Golden House and Statilia moved into Poppaea's quarters, a bittersweet event.

The rooms were furnished with pieces more to Statilia's taste. She brought her own slaves, wanting those to wait on her as always. Thus, little by little, whether we want it or not, the present consumes the past.

Statilia was introduced to the Senate and the people of Rome as my empress. We were duly congratulated and feted. No one dared do otherwise.

"You, who excel at mind reading, tell me what they really think," I asked her after the long ceremony had come to an end.

"I am sorry to disappoint you, but I don't think they really care," she said.

"Oh," I said. I *was* disappointed.

"They are more concerned about your upcoming trip to Greece," she said. "They don't like to be left alone for such a long time. That was part of the concern about Caesar—he was going to Parthia for at least three years. It is dangerous to leave Rome for too long."

"I've served Rome like a slave for twelve years, never leaving it! I deserve a respite, a chance to do something else," I burst out.

"What you deserve and what is wise are two different things," she said, shrugging.

"Other emperors have left Rome, going off to conquer territory."

"Then perhaps you ought to go on the campaign with Tiridates first, then go to Greece. People will be satisfied that you have first done something for Rome rather than yourself."

"My competitions in Greece will win glory for Rome. I am doing it in the name of the people of Rome."

"People don't identify with artistic pursuits in Greece or anywhere else. I don't notice your Neronia making any converts."

"What do you mean? They were well attended!"

"I don't see the games or races being replaced by them. As soon as they were over, people went right back to their old familiar Roman favorites, racing and fighting."

"I can't campaign with Tiridates first," I said. "He needs more time to prepare. And the schedule of contests in Greece are all arranged."

"As you wish," she said. "You are the emperor." Clearly she thought I was making a mistake.

By early July the preparations were all in order. An astounding number of people wanted to accompany me on the tour, belying the naysayers who predicted the trip would be unpopular. A number of senators, including Cluvius Rufus acting as imperial herald, high-ranking military leaders like General Vespasian and the head Praetorians, and, not surprisingly, hordes of artists and athletes, joined the group.

Before taking leave, I addressed the Senate. They turned out in full measure, knowing this was the last meeting for some time.

I stood and adjusted my toga. At least I wouldn't have to wear the wretched formal thing for a long time. "Noble senators of Rome," I said. "I am embarking on a journey no emperor has undertaken before. Not a journey of conquest, except in the realm of the arts and athletics. I go to Greece, the cradle of our customs and inspiration, where the sacred games are still held—the games of Zeus at Olympia, the games of Apollo at Delphi, the games of Zeus again at Nemea, the games of Poseidon at Isthmia. And also important, the games of Actia, which the divine Augustus founded to commemorate his decisive victory at Actium that ended the civil war." I looked around, scanning the faces from left to right. "Some of you have asked to come with me, and of course, I welcome you. Should anyone else wish to join us, it is not too late. We leave in two weeks."

A rotund senator stood and asked, "But how long will you be away, Caesar?"

"I will attend the full cycle of games, and that will take a year."

"A year!" a cry went up.

"Perhaps some of you might wish to come for one or the other of the games, rather than the entire time. The games are staggered throughout the year. I think the Olympian one in summer will be the grandest."

Another senator rose. "We aren't concerned about whether we go but that you will leave us for so long."

"I have appointed loyal and qualified representatives," I said. "Helios will be my principal deputy, able to transact business in my name."

A stunned Senate stared back at me. Finally one man rose and said, "A freedman! You appoint a freedman to sit in the judgment seat of the government?"

"No, I am still in the judgment seat. Helios is merely acting in my name."

A thin, nervous man stood. "Forgive me, Caesar, but this is—this is—"

"Outrageous!" cried another man. "To leave us in the hands of a servant, a freedman—" Someone jerked on his toga, and he quickly sat down.

His companion now stood. "Of course, Caesar is never outrageous, he has our best interests at heart always, but what my friend was trying to say is that—can we really go on without you?"

"It is only for a little while. And I will return with honors earned in your name that will glorify Rome and the Senate."

If that answer did not satisfy them, they kept it to themselves and smiled back. In a body they rose and wished me well.

Tigellinus, Nymphidius, and I went to review the newly raised troops of *legio I Italica*. They were stationed in a camp outside Rome and were lined up in formation for my inspection. From horseback, we looked out at the orderly rows of men, their special helmets with added height gleaming in the sun.

"A goodly sight, Caesar," said Tigellinus. "But can they fight?"

"What do you mean?"

"They are pretty, I admit," said Nymphidius, "but they were selected for their height more than anything else. And a tall, thin tree is not necessarily the strongest."

"Neither is a shrub," I shot back.

We dismounted, and the commander of the new legion led us down the ranks of soldiers. The standards, with their newly selected emblem of a boar, stood proudly over them. Although I am tall myself, I had to look up at the men. I nodded as I passed through their ranks.

Returning to a platform to address them, I said, "Greetings to you all. I, your emperor, am proud to welcome you to the company of the twenty-seven legions who guard Rome, knowing you will be equally valiant. You know your name: *legio I Italica*, having been levied exclusively from Italy, the first in a century. And your other, special name: the Phalanx of Alexander the Great—*phalanx Alexandri magni*—because

you will follow in his footsteps, to a region he visited but passed by—
your mission being to the gates of the Caucasian Mountains and
beyond."

So disciplined were they, there was no movement, no swaying, no
shuffling.

"And I myself will lead you!" I cried. "I myself will fight with you!"

A great cheer rose in the summer air. I believed it myself. At long
last I would embrace the side of me so long suppressed, the blood of
Germanicus and Antony calling out to me.

But first, the games in Greece.

And a letter I must write.

LIV

ACTE

So he married again. And so quickly. He was not made to be alone—he always needed a companion, a mirror, a confidante, that I have known always. But I was still oddly disturbed when I heard it.

His new wife is Statilia Messalina, an aristocrat of the first order, coming from an old Roman family, with an ancestor, Statilius Taurus, who served twice as consul and celebrated a Triumph. His name lived on in popular memory in the amphitheater he built, the Theater of Taurus, the first one in Rome built of stone. It was destroyed in the Fire, a great loss.

Her husband perished in the conspiracy, so it is odd that she would marry the man who made her a widow. But if that man is emperor, how easy to overlook a little thing like that!

Oh, I am being unkind. But is it not suspicious? It is hard to think her motives untarnished. And she was known to be a libertine, like her cousin the empress Messalina, Claudius's wife, only not as extreme—as if anyone could be.

Yesterday I received a message from the palace, as unexpected as the first one from Poppaea. I have let it rest on the table overnight. Not that I will accept the invitation, but I want a little interval to elapse before I say no, a little space where in my own mind I can still say yes.

To the Lady Claudia Acte, in Velitrae:

Imperator Nero Claudius Caesar Augustus Germanicus sends greetings.

The emperor invites the said Claudia Acte to accompany him to Greece to celebrate the Panhellenic Games there, which will take place in Corinth, Delphi, Nemea, and Olympia.

Particulars: the company will depart Rome on July fifteenth, journeying to Brundisium along the Appian Way. You may join at any point of the trip. From the port of Brundisium boats will ferry the company—which includes government officials, soldiers, artists, and athletes—to Greece. Housing and food are at the expense of the imperial treasury.

The emperor would be pleased if you accept the invitation.

Then, in his own handwriting, a postscript:

My dear Acte,

I am late in thanking you for your timely warning about Senecio, which was all too accurate, and for which I am grateful.

You, who watched my first public appearance, know only too well what my performing in Greece will mean to me. And you can judge best if I have improved since then. There are many people coming to watch, but none as meaningful to me as you.

> *Your friend and grateful emperor,*
> *Nero, or Lucius*

The answer was—had to be—no. I did not wish to be part of his adoring entourage, and besides, I could not take that long an absence from my business. The thought of traveling with a troupe of actors, athletes, and soldiers was unappealing.

But I was telling myself that while knowing that obviously he would single me out of the crowd and bring me into his inner circle. I would not be bumping along with the spectators but part of his own group.

How would Statilia feel about that? After my treatment by Poppaea, I had no wish to put myself in the sights of another empress.

Still, still . . . perhaps I could go over separately, see one of the games myself, just to watch, to see him perform. Be invisible. Be there just for myself, as I had seen him previously at funerals.

I had to answer. I had to respond. But I hated to write the words.

LV

NERO

All was in readiness, except my own expertise in the arts, always unknown to me until I actually stood on the stage. I had practiced the cithara until my fingers were raw and my supporting arm ached; I had memorized the words of *Oedipus in Colonus* so obsessively that one night Sporus came running to my bedside when I shouted "Dread brood of Earth and Darkness!" in my sleep. There were five other plays I had had to master as well.

As I had reminded Acte, I had first performed in public seven years ago, but it was to a small and selected audience, and I had been shaking when I stepped out on the stage. Partly because I knew how shocked everyone would be to see me in a citharoede's robe but also because I could not trust myself to acquit myself well. Now, at the legendary Greek games, the level of skill required was much higher, and I was left with the same nervous worry as when I was a novice. But always there was before me the stern prophecy I had been given as a child, by the oracle of the goddess of Fortune at Antium: *There is no respect for hidden music.*

Most of the people who had witnessed that first performance were gone now, but Acte was a link to that early stage in my dramatic career. It would have been meaningful on many levels if she could have accompanied me to Greece. Unlike Poppaea, Statilia would have been unconcerned. But she had declined the invitation. I wondered, truly, if we would ever meet again. Life is long, but meetings can be rare when they are left to chance.

. . .

We gathered in the south of Rome, at the start of the Appian Way, the famous road called "the queen of long roads" that stretched three hundred and fifty miles from the Forum to Brundisium on the southeast coast of Italy, from whence we would sail for Greece.

There were five thousand Augustiani, three hundred Praetorians, senators, military officers, and men. There were two hundred athletes, including Tullia and the girls who would race at Olympia, and five hundred actors and singers. That made a total of some six thousand, and Phaon, Tigellinus, and Nymphidius would oversee the logistics of this company. For we had, of course, slaves and craftsmen to provide for all these people, swelling the total number to around ten thousand.

Traveling slowly by hundreds of rumbling carts, we would reach Brundisium in around seventeen days. Until we actually sailed away, I was easily reachable by a fast courier.

I stood on a makeshift podium and looked out at the sea of carts and people, primed to start the journey. I had done it. I had brought this about. A dream had been realized, and we would embark for the greatest artistic challenge, not in imagination but in reality.

"We are the select, the blessed, who sail for Greece. You are my companions, all, my brothers in art. Let us begin!" I gave the signal, and my cart lurched forward, down the beckoning smooth-paved road, lined with marble monuments to the dead, sheltered overhead by umbrella pines, whispering above us, *Come, come, Greece awaits.*

We proceeded at a languid pace—how could it be otherwise, with so many baggage carts? But the journey was pleasant enough. The moment we rolled out of Rome I felt a great peace descend on me. I was on my way, keeping a promise I had made long ago to a little boy—myself.

The Appian Way leads first through the causeway over the Pontine Marshes, partially drained but still with foul pools of insect-ridden water, then emerges into green country of Campania, a tranquil sight of peaceful fields and trees.

I was letting its quiet beauty soothe me when Sporus, sitting beside me, whispered, "This stretch has ghosts."

"I don't feel them," I said.

"You should. Six thousand ghosts are crying out—the six thousand who were crucified for the Spartacus rebellion. The crosses lined the road from Rome to Capua. A hundred and twenty miles of crosses."

Yet their shadows had vanished in the sun. I shuddered. "Let us not seek out ill omens," I told him.

But too late. Now I could see the shadows of the crosses falling across the road, lengthening as the day came to a close. He had called them forth, and they sprang to life after almost a hundred and fifty years.

Once we passed beyond that stretch, the mood lightened and I could hear singing from the carts behind us, felt the air begin to cool as we climbed higher and breasted the Apennines, the mountain spine that ran down the middle of Italy. In the July heat the stretch through the plains, and especially through the Pontine area, had been humid and oppressive, but the mountains offered a respite.

All too soon we were on the other side and halfway there. I had traveled so little, seen so little of my own country, never having gone more than about a hundred miles from Rome. Now I was already well beyond that, and the wide world was opening its arms to me, after I had been held captive in Rome my whole life. I would escape its claws, would go on to taste what was beyond it. Greece. Troy. Egypt. The eastern campaign. I felt my blood sing; I felt like Hercules bursting his bonds.

At last we approached Brundisium, and the Adriatic Sea came into view, a sea I had never seen, that washed our eastern shores and bound us to Greece and the east. It sparkled from the distance, with a white haze on the horizon where sea met sky. Actually glimpsing it meant the journey was real, and I would soon leave the shores of Italy behind.

As we approached the city, I recited to myself all I knew of it. It was founded by one of the Homeric heroes, Diomedes. It had been attacked by Julius Caesar in his war against Pompey. Octavian and Antony had reconciled here, with Antony agreeing to marry Octavian's sister. And the poet Virgil had died here, returning from—where else would a poet travel to?—Greece.

This was a Greek city in spirit, founded by a Greek, facing Greece. "I am in Greece already!" I cried, throwing up my hands in joy. If the carriage had not been moving, I would have danced.

I remembered the part Brundisium had played in my own begetting, too. Antony and Octavian had made a pact there, sealing it with Antony's marriage to Octavia. The marriage, a legendary disaster, resulted in two daughters, both of them my ancestors. Two years later Octavian asked Antony to meet him in Brundisium; Antony traveled there, only to find that Octavian did not appear. At that point, Antony sailed away back to the east and Cleopatra and never set foot in Italy again. I wondered how he felt as he shrugged it all off and, like Caesar crossing the Rubicon, knew the dice were thrown.

The harbor was a forked one, with the town lying between the two forks. The deep water made it an important port, as it could shelter a sizable number of boats. The road sloped down, heading directly to the water, where two fifty-foot granite pillars marked the end of the Appian Way, waves lapping against their base.

I leapt out of the carriage and stood at the water's edge. The land road ended here. Beyond was the sea road, the route to Greece. The salty air ruffled my hair. Seagulls screeched overhead, wheeling and cawing. Soon our sails would imitate them, try to harness the wind, and let us fly to our destination.

LVI

When I finally stood upon the sacred ground of Greece I felt that the very earth beneath my feet was imbued with energy. I smelled a subtle, distinctive difference in the breeze-borne scent, new to me but somehow seeming familiar from poetry. Pine trees of a different shape than Roman ones framed the sky, their dark boughs calling forth legends. It was all true. Greece existed, and not just in the imagination. I stood surrounded by it, a homecoming to a place I had never been but belonged.

Greece, I embrace you. Welcome me as a son.

The crossing had been smooth and uneventful, one glorious day following another, no squalls, no becalming. Poseidon had been kindly, guiding us. It took us only three days to reach Corcyra on the island of Corfu, and then just another day and a half to sail to the mainland at the Gulf of Actium.

We had landed near the site of the pivotal and world-changing sea battle of Actium, where eight years after the rift, Octavian had soundly defeated Antony and Cleopatra, making the whole Roman empire his own. He had founded Nikopolis there, adorned it with the trophies of rams from the defeated fleet, and decreed that every four years, on the anniversary of the victory, celebratory games would be held on the spot. I had arrived in time to participate. I had mixed feelings about celebrating the fall of Antony, but it would be a less demanding event than the four older traditional ones and a good introduction for my first competition.

I stood on the hilltop overlooking the Bay of Actium below, a wide bay with a narrow opening. Once the army of Octavian had been camped here, looking across at Antony's camp, cruelly located on a site rife with malaria on the other side of the bay. Now on this hillside a theater had been built, as well as a monument with the rams, and temples and a stadium for the games. A clean, tidy commemoration for a bloody and messy event.

The officials of the games swarmed around to welcome us, telling me that special quarters had been built for our lodging. The games themselves would commence in a week, "or whenever Caesar feels rested," the chief official said in Greek. I spoke Greek as well as my own Latin and had no trouble communicating with him.

They were eager to please and arranged a welcome banquet for the evening. But I postponed it. Everyone was tired and salt-stained, and a quiet bath, supper, and rest would be best for now. They nodded obsequiously.

But late at night, my company being settled in the temporary housing erected for us on the crest of the hill, I rose and stole out of the quarters, allowing only two guards to trail me at a distance. A full moon's piercing light shone down, turning the water of the bay below into an oblong mirror, outlining the monuments in edged shadows. Supreme silence had fallen over the site like a mantle, cloaking it in hushed reverence, with only a chorus of singing cicadas thrumming in the background.

I walked slowly downhill until I reached the large platform of the open-air sanctuary Octavian had dedicated to Apollo. The flat pavement bespoke the calm that descends after a battle is in the past, its cries and crises now relegated to history, history that is its own mausoleum.

Yes, that was what this was. A mausoleum to a battle fought a hundred years ago, all its participants dead, even those who died a natural death. Over my head a quick darting dark shape, a bat winging past, briefly threw a shadow on the pavement, flitting by and then gone.

Just below the wide pavement was a wall bristling with the naval rams of captured battleships from Antony and Cleopatra's fleet. I walked over to the edge and looked down. They gleamed in the moonlight, throwing sharp shadows. There were thirty-six of them, of all different sizes, wrenched from ships, now fitted into sockets in the wall. Gingerly, watching my step as I went, I descended to a lower walkway and moved along it, passing the rows of rams. They were affixed at shoulder height, and I could inspect them closely. I ran my hand along one; the bronze was cold and smooth. If I closed my eyes, I could almost hear the ring of the rams striking wooden ships, the anguished cries of the sailors, feel the moment that all was lost.

But all was not lost. I patted the ram. Octavian won the battle, but the war was not over. There was now an emperor who saw the east as equal to the west, who prized the glory of Greece, and who had a mandate from Cleopatra herself: *I surrender her dreams and ambitions into your keeping.* The dream of an empire that encompassed both east and west did not die with Alexander or with Antony and Cleopatra. It was alive in me. And I would bring it about. This journey to Greece was the first step.

We stayed in Actia well over a month, accustoming ourselves to the area. In early September the Actian Games were held, in accordance with the September second anniversary of the battle of Actium. They had never had the cachet that the traditional Panhellenic Games did and did not draw the large crowds or the big-name competitors.

I competed in only one event—the musical composition. I did not sing, only played the cithara, a tune of my own invention. The audience, though small, was enthusiastic, and I felt at that moment that I had been entirely right to strive so hard to come to Greece to compete. Not to win—although I did this time—but just for the joy of it.

These Actian Games were a gentle introduction to the prestigious ancient games that I would participate in later, with one of the most important coming up soon—Delphi.

Delphi. The very word trailed clouds of glory. The center of the world, on the slopes of Mount Parnassus, home of the Muses, source of the Castalian Spring. The shrine of the oracle of Apollo. The first contests to include drama and music, as befitting Apollo, in addition to athletic meets. The place where Dionysus spent the winter months in revelry. Site of pilgrimage from all over the Greek world, rich from donations and filled with priceless artworks.

We sailed there on the Gulf of Corinth, that long, thin finger cutting Greece in half, leaving the Peloponnese dangling by a four-mile isthmus from the mainland. The day was fair and the winds high, but not dangerous, and inside the Gulf we were sheltered and slid along the shore. We disembarked close to Delphi and could see Mount Parnassus rearing up before us, blue as twilight, wreathed in mystery.

It was beautiful beyond words. No wonder Apollo had sought it out for his home, no wonder the Muses lived on the mountain. This was the lodestone that had drawn me all my life, and now I stood at its threshold.

People were gathering around me, but for a few moments all I was aware of was the jagged shape of the sacred mountain and the slender cypresses standing like nymphs on the slopes. I could see the outline of the monuments scattered on the heights.

No one could move until I did. Finally the spell was broken and I said, "Come," and we set out toward the site. The ground rose slowly, rugged rocks guarding the pathway, while pines, cedars, and laurel rustled in the sweet wind. The only colors were stone gray and dark green, restrained and calm.

Halfway up, the path became steeper. The air was clearer and delicately scented with wild thyme and fennel, as well as the warm fragrance of the bay laurel, Apollo's own plant. Ahead of us, at a bend of the path, the rock-cut basin for the Castalian Spring greeted us, dappled light playing across its surface.

"Are you going to bathe in it?" asked Statilia, who had huffed up the path behind me.

I looked at the rippling water, being fed from its source higher up. Should I bathe in it, or drink from it merely?

"Some people wash only their hands or hair, but murderers have to wash completely," she said.

Murderers. If I bathed in it, would everyone assume I was trying to cleanse myself of guilt?

"Are you planning to visit the oracle?" she persisted. "If so, you have to purify yourself."

"Not today. Today I drink from it, imbibe the source of literary inspiration." I motioned to my body slave, who proffered a golden cup. I went to the edge of the water and dipped it in. The water was pure as rock crystal. I sipped. It was cold and had an indefinable taste, something that, if it had been a color, would have been pale blue.

"Now, Apollo," I whispered, "nourish the artist inside me."

Statilia held out her hand. "Let me taste it."

I held on to the cup. "No. Each person must have his own." I indicated that the slave should hand her a cup.

She plunged it into the water, bringing it out dripping. She took a long swallow. "Cold. Rather tasteless," she said. "I don't feel moved to create."

Tasteless? Perhaps only some people could taste it; perhaps it kept its secret flavor for those sensitive enough to discern it.

Walking ever upward, now on the Sacred Way, we soon came upon the splendor of the vast Apollonian site, the buildings strung out like beads of a necklace on the slope, cascading in seven terraces.

Building after building crowded the terraces, some small, some large, but the long colonnaded Temple of Apollo dominated the scene. Within was the famous oracle, where people came from all the world to seek advice. I, too, would, but not today. I had to ready myself for it. I stood in the outer courtyard and looked into the shaded interior. On the entrance portal was carved KNOW THYSELF, NOTHING IN EXCESS, and MAKE A PLEDGE AND MISCHIEF IS NIGH. I could embrace the first but not the second, and as for the third, I believed in pledges and always tried to keep them, even if mischief followed, for a vow should be honored.

Above the temple, hovering on a terrace, was the theater where the music and drama contests would be held, honoring Apollo. Soon I would stand on its stage and make my offering to the god.

* * *

We were housed in luxurious quarters to one side of the theater, built for us. They overlooked the entire valley, and when shadows crept down the mountainside at sunset, the valley glowed with blue mist for a short time. Then the glory faded.

That evening I studied my lines from *Niobe*, which I would perform in a few days. The story had gripped me always, and the villa at Sublaqueum had a group of statues depicting the stricken and dying sons and daughters of the proud queen. In my sleeping chamber there was one statue in particular of a woman who was either asleep or dead, her head resting sideways, showing how one state could shade into another. Whenever I gazed on it upon awakening, it made me grateful that my sleep was not of the eternal kind.

There was another statue in the atrium of a son wounded in his back, thrown off balance and trying not to fall, an expression of surprise and dismay on his face.

Another showed a woman, half kneeling, reaching behind herself, trying in vain to pull an arrow from her back. Niobe had had seven sons and seven daughters, and incurred the wrath of Leto, the mother of Artemis and Apollo, by saying she had the better of her, with more children.

But Leto was a goddess and no one has the better of a god or goddess. So she ordered her children to slay Niobe's. They shot them down without pity, until fourteen bodies lay before their tragic mother. She wept so incessantly that the gods took pity on her and changed her into a rock, from which streams of water flowed.

Both Sophocles and Aeschylus had written plays about Niobe, and I chose the one by Sophocles. In the one by Aeschylus, Niobe sits mourning in silence, and that is no way to win a drama contest! Silence may be eloquent, but it does not allow us to display our emotions.

I needed to be alone to summon up the proper mood, so I dismissed everyone and sat by myself, willing myself to become Niobe, to experience her profound grief at the irreversible loss of her children, in spite of her pleas to the hardhearted Apollo and Artemis. I knew the pain of losing my daughter, and sons too young to survive, also stricken by the gods. Yes, there was no other explanation for it. The gods, envious of the happiness Poppaea and I shared, decided to punish us, to inflict crushing pain on us. A mother's grief is different from a father's, and I could only become Niobe by becoming Poppaea first.

I had had a mask made in her likeness, and I would wear it when performing, share the experience with Poppaea, bring her back to life in front of the audience. Yes, the play was about irreversible loss, but I would show that it was possible to reverse it, if only for a brief hour on the stage.

I put the mask down on a table, propped up so I could study it. The eyes were empty, waiting to be filled by a living presence, but the rest of the face reproduced her features in perfect detail. I could see the small dimple that had been on one side of her mouth only, could see the line of her high cheekbones that gave such definition to her face.

"Why aren't you real?" I cried. "How can you be so real, and not speak?"

I would speak for her. I would give her words and life again. And her cries for our lost children would embody and echo those of Niobe.

It was late. The hours I had spent sharing Niobe's grief had somehow flown. Sporus glided in, so quietly I did not know he was there until he stood behind me, gazing on the mask.

"The likeness is uncanny," he said. "That makes it more painful."

I looked up at him. "I could say the same for you," I said. "Unlike a mask, you can move and talk and toss your head." His likeness to her, especially in the dim lamplight, was as good as the mask's.

He bent down and took the mask in his hands, examining it. The two identical profiles seemed two halves of a whole. He put on the mask and turned to me.

"Is she here now?" he asked.

"What do you think?" I knew she wasn't . . . was she?

"I think I can do better than this," he said.

"What do you mean?" I sensed danger, although of what kind, I could not articulate.

"There is one thing lacking," he said. "Or rather, there should be something lacking that is not."

"What is lacking is the breath of life," I said. "Poppaea lies in the tomb, and we cannot restore her."

"Are you sure of that?" he asked.

"I am not sure of anything anymore," I admitted. Not of friendship, nor of promises, nor of endings.

"You will see," he said.

LVII

I spent the next few days exploring Delphi and practicing *Niobe*. The sacred site bristled with donated artworks, exquisite marble and bronze statues that in any other place would reign supreme and solitary, here so crowded together that masterpieces looked commonplace. A bronze of a winning charioteer, along with his horses, had been given to commemorate the victory of Polyzalos of Syracuse. It showed him in his slow triumphal lap, after the race was won, all calmness and control, rather than in the heat and strain of the race itself. That was the Greek ideal: calm and order. But after winning a race a Roman charioteer was anything but that—he was exultant and covered with sweat and dust. In that I was more Roman than Greek.

I passed the Temple of Apollo at least once a day, seeing the pilgrims entering, seeing the smoke rising from the sacrifices. At some point I would enter myself, put a question to the oracle. If I did not, I was a coward, since other rulers had dared to ask their fates. But the oracle was known to be tricky and misleading. Inhaling the fumes from the deep fissure underneath the temple, she entered another state of mind, where she heard Apollo speak, but sometimes in a garbled manner.

Sometimes her translation of it was puzzling and tantalizing. To one man, asking advice about whether he should go to war, the oracle replied, *Go, return not die in war.* Was the correct interpretation *Go, return not, die in war* or *Go, return, not die in war?*

King Croesus of Lydia was told that if he made war on the Persians, he would destroy a mighty empire. It turned out to be his own.

Alexander, angry that the oracle had not confirmed his own belief that he would soon conquer the known world, telling him to come back later, grabbed her by the hair and dragged her outside until she screamed, "You are invincible, my son!" As soon as she said it, he let her go, saying, "Now I have my answer!"

Alexander put much stock in prophecies. In Egypt, at the oasis of Siwa, the oracle there recognized him as the son of Ammon, and from that moment on he behaved as if he were truly invincible, chosen.

Would I believe what she said? How much would I allow myself to?

I continued to delay my visit, and the days passed pleasantly, or would have, had I not grown more and more nervous as the contests drew near. First was the drama competition, and two days later was the music contest. The athletic events would be last. Preparing for them all was harrowing—I hardly knew which one to concentrate on. But obviously the drama, coming first, ought to receive the most attention.

The night before the contest, the closest members of my company gathered in the atrium of our quarters. Tigellinus said offhandedly, "Another day, another competition. Caesar, you must be used to it by now." He popped a handful of walnuts into his mouth, crunching them.

If only he could know, could understand. It did not matter how many times a performer stood in front of an audience; each time was terrifying in its own way. And here, where the best in the world would stand on the same stage, it was overwhelming. Last night I had hardly slept.

"A true artist never gets accustomed to it," said Epaphroditus, trying to reassure me. "Only a pedestrian performer is not concerned. After all, he has nothing to live up to."

"But he enjoys himself more," said Tigellinus.

"What will you be wearing?" asked Phaon.

I showed them the traditional thick-soled boots worn for tragedy, the purple robe for majesty and goddesses with its gold border, and finally the mask. The mask stunned everyone into silence.

"Yes, it is the late empress. For the performance, she and Niobe are one," I said. "United in sorrow for their lost children." I put it down and changed the conversation. "I believe there are twenty other competitors. One has come from Rhodes, another from Cyprus."

"A long way to travel just to lose," said Tigellinus, with a hearty laugh.

Everyone politely joined in. I did not.

Statilia, from her chair farther back, said, "You realize that the competition can never answer the question of who is best?"

"It's subjective," said Epaphroditus. "That's the trouble with art, unlike numerical figures."

"No, I mean that the judges cannot rule against you. Even if Apollo himself were competing against you."

How dare she? What if Apollo heard? And especially as I was performing *Niobe*, in which he avenged an insult.

"I disagree," I said. "They are to forget I am emperor."

She laughed. "As if anyone could, even behind the mask."

"When I perform, I am no longer the emperor," I said. "I am someone else." That was the wonder of it, the mystery and the escape.

"To yourself, perhaps, but not to anyone else," she stubbornly persisted.

"Where is Sporus?" asked Tigellinus suddenly, looking around, to draw attention elsewhere.

I shook my head. "I have not seen him since yesterday," I said. I only just now noticed.

After everyone had gone their ways to bed, I took Statilia to task. "Why did you say that about the competition in front of everyone?"

She twitched her mouth. "I was not thinking," she said. "I should not have said it publicly. But it is what everyone knows."

"My athletic coach said the same thing once. He said I could never have a fair competition." *Your competing days are over . . . No one will risk beating the emperor. So you are doomed to never truly know your worth on the field of competition.* "But I thought—I hoped—I dreamed—that at this very highest level, beyond the local boys' races and the festivals, it would be different."

She sighed and touched my arm. "The emperor is always the emperor, even at the far-flung corners of the empire. More so there, perhaps."

The afternoon was fair and calm, a halcyon day sent by Apollo himself, a day touched with only the faintest hint of autumn, and a soothing golden sun. I had asked to be in the middle of the contestants. I had no wish to be first or to be last. It was not modesty. People are overly critical of the first performers and bored by the time the last finally appear.

I watched, my heart hammering, as the first declaimed their parts on the stage. In these contests, the entire play is not performed, only an excerpt, chosen for its poetry and its action. Thus, Agamemnon being stabbed in the bathtub, Oedipus blinding himself, and Medea killing her children were favorites. But the judges' familiarity with them might rob them of some of their impact. *Niobe* was not so often performed.

Then the moment came. I walked out onto the stage, seeing the world through Poppaea's eyes, *becoming* her and Niobe. The words flowed as if I had spontaneously thought them, as if Sophocles had nothing to do with it, coming from the queen herself. Out in the audience, I could see heads but it was a blur; they were hardly real to me. Some were bowed, as if deep in thought. Others were staring straight ahead, riveted. I felt the bond between them and me, or rather, between them and Niobe.

At last it was over. It seemed to have lasted forever, as long as it had taken Apollo and Artemis in real life to slay all the children. It seemed to have passed in an instant.

Then I had to step down, and the next ten followed me.

The judges huddled after the stage was cleared and all the performers had returned to their seats. Then they rose as a body and held up the laurel wreath, cut from the sacred tree of Apollo.

"We award the emperor Nero Caesar the crown for his performance of the tragedy of *Niobe*," they said. The theater burst into cheers.

I felt that I would die with relief and exaltation. I rose and went over to them, lowering my head for them to place the crown—oh, sweetest crown of leaves, fairer than any of gold!—on my head. Then I turned to the people. "I accept this crown in the name of the Roman people and the empire." Yes, the victory was ours together. I did this for the glory of Rome as well as my own. Only later did someone notice that I had omitted the customary "and the Senate."

Afterward I hosted a great celebration. Wine, food, dancers, and music—not by me but by the other musicians in the company, professionals. A sea of heads bobbed in the open-air terrace where the festivity was held. I saw Tullia, who rushed over to congratulate me.

"Wonderful!" she said, her face flushed with excitement.

"Thank you," I replied. "I know it will be a while yet before you yourself compete, but may the day be as fair for you as this one was for me."

"I am drinking in all of it," she said. "I thank you for making it possible for me to come. All of us girls from Rome scarcely believe we are here."

"Believe it," I said. But I knew how she felt.

Tigellinus sidled up a few minutes later. "Very impressive, Caesar," he said. "You make a convincing woman." He laughed his horsey laugh, close to a whinny.

Right behind him, General Vespasian was eyeing me. Tigellinus stepped back, then said, "General, I saw that you were so lost in the performance it looked as if you slept."

Vespasian glared at him. "I wasn't sleeping, although one of the ushers thought so and prodded me!"

"I am honored if you tried to close your eyes and concentrate on the words," I assured him.

"I watched as well," he said. "Truly a magnificent performance. And to see the empress again, with us in person . . . beyond pleasure."

Tigellinus rolled his eyes. Vespasian did not see.

Our guest quarters were large enough to permit Statilia and me to have separate apartments, and tonight I wished to be alone. My foray into the forbidden realm of bringing Poppaea back, letting her participate in my life again, had left me strangely agitated, and I needed solitude. Her mask rested on a table, and beside it, the laurel wreath. Both together. In the dim light of the oil lamps, the mask seemed to glow like ivory, but then her complexion had been her pride, often compared to ivory. I stood up, walked over, and ran my hand over its smooth surface. But of course it was not warm, thereby betraying its true nature: inanimate.

I should go to bed, call the slave to prepare me. But instead I stood staring at the mask and the crown. I should be happier. I *was* happy, but . . . I reached out and took the crown, turning it over and over in my hands. The leaves were still firm and green, the victory fresh.

A slight noise behind me made my hair stir on the back of my head. There was supposed to be no one here; I thought myself alone. I whirled around in the direction of the noise. A ghostly white figure stood in the shadowy corner.

Oh, all the gods! An apparition! I dropped the precious crown, and it fell to the floor.

The figure came closer, and I backed up. It was walking stiffly and painfully toward me.

It was Poppaea. Poppaea herself. I stood, paralyzed, held helpless between joy and terror.

She did not speak, but approached, slowly and deliberately, until she was an arm's length away. Unable to stop myself, I reached out and embraced her.

This was no bloodless spirit or cold mask but a warm being. Her hair, the luxuriant amber curls that were her personal glory, tumbled under my fingers. I grabbed her head, plunging my hands through the hair, and, pulling her face to mine, kissed her, the long kiss of yearning and reunion.

I could not question it. She was here again. She had promised, she had said that if at all possible, she would return, like Protesilaus had done, if only for a brief time. Perhaps only for a few moments. No matter, I would seize those few moments, if that was all we had.

But the shock of it made me unable at first to feel true joy or wonder; it stunned me, and in the fear that she would disappear momentarily, I could not pause to think clearly again. I embraced her feverishly, clutching at her, covering her with kisses.

She felt the same—but not quite the same. Or had I forgotten already, forgotten some small personal characteristic? Then at last emotion returned, and the ecstasy of having her again overcame any hesitation, and I felt like a starving man confronted with a heap of food, not knowing what to taste first.

Formally, as if we were in a ritual, I took her hands and led her to the bed. Still neither of us spoke, as if that would break the spell. Perhaps it would. Time enough for that later; I did not dare shatter the illusion, the apparition, or whatever it was. It was here, it was with me, it was warm to the touch, solid and breathing.

To hold her once again . . . it was impossible, but it was happening. Or was it? Was it just one of those vivid dreams, dreams that seem entirely and frighteningly true while we sleep but vanish in the dawn, leaving a strange aftertaste for the rest of the day? I was plunged into the hallucination, embracing the phantom Poppaea, so like her in some ways and so alien in others. In the hours that followed, I cannot even recall them exactly, because like a dream, they made no sense, they were illogical and jumbled and perceived through a haze of wonder and fear. After hours of it, I finally fell into a fitful sleep.

The voice that awoke me shattered my illusions.

"I have done what I promised." The voice in the dawn was not Poppaea's but Sporus's. "I told you I could do better than the mask. Now I have kept my word."

I sat bolt upright. "What have you done?" But, suddenly, I knew.

"There is no going back," he said. "Now you have your Poppaea again, as near as flesh can make her."

The stiff and painful walking . . . "No!" I said. "Why?"

"I have told you. I could not bear seeing you suffer so, missing her. Now you need not."

"But it was in vain! Nothing can bring her back. You are not she."

"Ah, but will you know that? After a while, we will merge . . . and the real Poppaea will be swallowed up in me. You will accept me as her."

"You've made a eunuch of yourself for nothing! I will always know it is you."

"You didn't last night."

"I was stunned, hardly able to comprehend what was happening." But didn't I, at some level? Even in the dream, it wasn't right. It was not a true woman I held in my arms.

"But your heart was lightened for those hours." He reached out and smoothed my hair. "Admit it."

"Even so, last night can never be duplicated." The shock that had disabled my reasoning would not come again.

I was, illogically, angry at Poppaea herself. She had betrayed me; she had not come back as she had promised. There was no Protesilaus and Laodamia or us. The painting she had ordered in the Golden House was a cruel mockery.

"Do not be so sure. What the heart wants, it creates."

"Leave me!" I ordered him. "Leave me!"

As the first rays of the sun lightened the chamber, he stole away, taking her with him. The auburn wig that had felt so real last night lay abandoned in the bedsheets.

The victory wreath was still on the floor where I had dropped it. I got out of bed and picked it up. I had trampled the leaves, stepping on them on the way to bed. I smoothed them out, aghast at the desecration. How could I have damaged this crown, so precious to me?

But I had lost my mind, been overcome with a loss of reason like no other. All else had fallen by the wayside. I suspended my awareness because I needed to. *When the gods grant you an impossible wish you do not question them, and if anything seems amiss you do not question that, either.*

He was right—I had been truly happy for those brief hours. But they had been based on a willing delusion on my part and on a ghastly and appalling sacrifice on his.

LVIII

Tigellinus was the first to know, followed by Statilia. Neither seemed troubled by it. Tigellinus joked, saying, "I can perform a marriage ceremony if you like. We are, after all, here in Greece where such things are not amiss." He looked over at Statilia. "Or would that make him a bigamist? He is, after all, legally married to you."

"Marriage ends at death, so lawyers assure us," she said. "As did his to Poppaea, and mine to Vestinus. However, marriage to a ghost—well, there is nothing illegal about that!"

I was rather shocked. Was nothing sacred to her? Did she not regard our marriage as something to be defended? I had hoped that she would be pregnant by now, but so far, nothing.

"I am glad you two think this is amusing," I said. "Perhaps you can cheer Sporus up in his recovery. He would probably appreciate a nice bouquet of flowers."

They just laughed.

Suddenly I wanted to go to bed with Statilia, to wash the episode of the night before from my mind, to expunge it. But did I really want to forget it?

I left them both chuckling and spent the day watching the other competitions, trying to lose myself in them and regain my equilibrium.

The sweet air wafting across the mountainside whispered of vanished history, lost deities, stories from the beginning of time. Here was supposedly the center of the world, the place Zeus's eagles had identified, marked now with a large stone, the Omphalos, resting in the inner sanctum of the Temple of Apollo.

Here, far away from the rest of the world on the slopes of this sacred mountain, it was easy to believe that life was meant to be calm, kind, devoted to the arts and to higher things. But below us on the plain, easily visible, lay old battlefields, and on the other side of Mount Parnassus lay Thermopylae. Greece had been the site of many battles, and their warriors were as extolled as their poets. In spite of the warm cedar-scented breezes, the quiet beauty of the trees standing like green sentinels on the rocky slopes, my mind could not be serene.

Sporus. The encounter in the night was deeply troubling, in a way that no walk around Delphi could soothe. For a few hours Poppaea had been brought to life, brought back by my extreme longing and Sporus's devotion. The door to Hades yawned open; the barrier that no one could cross had suddenly been breached. I had held her in my arms, suspending disbelief for a few hours in my shock and joy. But once I knew, I had fallen back to earth with a jolt, further from her than ever. Like Orpheus, I stood once more on familiar ground, alone. And she remained below, taken from me a second time. My true battle had been against death, a contest I could never win.

From a distance I could hear the sounds of the lyre competition in the theater. The notes were faint, but they reached me where I sat overlooking the steep drop to the valley below. Shadows were creeping across the landscape, lengthening toward the close of day. I closed my eyes and let the music speak directly to me. In just this way had Orpheus played his lyre, the liquid beauty of the melody reaching directly into the heart of his listeners.

Liquid . . . liquid took many forms, assumed the shape of its container. Could identity be the same? Was it truly fixed, one person a man forever, another person a woman forever? The eunuch, who is an altered man, does not become a woman, but he is no longer a man, either. What was Sporus? He had been a man, and now he was not. He could simulate Poppaea but could not duplicate her in the most intimate fashion.

But did that matter? If I could have her partially back, would that be better than nothing? Or is a faulty imitation only a mockery?

If the demarcation line between man and woman is indistinct, one perhaps fading into another, then why could not I assume whatever identity I pleased on any given day? Or anyone else do the same, for that matter? The whole world might be a dancing sphere of beings who constantly took other identities.

Was that not what the gods did? In our stories of them, were we merely recognizing what we instinctively knew? Zeus took many forms—a swan, a bull, even an ant. Apollo sometimes assumed the guise of a mortal shepherd. Sporus could sometimes be Poppaea.

And I could sometimes be emperor, other times an artist and charioteer.

Why did others have so much trouble with this?

How dreary to be the same day after day, one person only, imprisoned in one identity!

I would have to consult the oracle. I could not shirk it. Delphi was renowned for the oracle, not the games. And although I trembled to know my future, better to know it and prepare for it.

The first step was to bathe in the Castalian Spring, to purify myself. I could not approach her otherwise. I gave orders that the basin where the spring emptied be cleared of sightseers and gawkers, so I could have privacy. They obeyed—I was the emperor, after all. Early the next morning I stood before the hollowed rock basin and looked at the placid clear water, a few ripples traveling across its surface. It would be cold, that I knew. It was known to be frigid, bracing. I threw off my loincloth and plunged in.

My feet could not touch the bottom, and I paddled furiously. My arms were numb already, and my legs were paralyzed and heavy. The water came from a source not far removed from winter snow. I swam back toward the lip of the basin. Surely I was purified now.

The day was overcast, with lowering gray-bottomed clouds hanging over the valley. Wearing the white robe of the petitioner, I approached the temple, where I had to offer a goat in sacrifice, Apollo's preferred animal for this site. When the priests doused it with sacred water, it trembled from the hooves up as it was supposed to, meaning the god had accepted me. They then slayed it and put it on the altar in the forecourt.

Three priests came forward to escort me into the temple. The oracle was in her sunken grotto at the back of the building.

What would I ask her? There were so many things I longed to know. *Will I ever be happy again? When I return from Greece, what shall I do? What should be my vision as emperor? What will be my legacy? How can I shape it?*

All of these questions burned for an answer. I had been happy with Poppaea. I was happy now in Greece, because I was suspended between two worlds. But beyond that? Did I want to take my place among the imperial immortals—Julius Caesar, Augustus—or among great artists? Truly, where did I belong? And would the ages remember me, or would I disappear into obscurity?

I settled on one question. *What does the future hold for me?*

The three priests walked with me into the dim interior of the temple, past the sacred hearth, then left me standing at the top of the short flight of steps that led down into the grotto, the *adyton*. After a few moments, a young acolyte dressed in white robes came to me and whispered, "Do you seek the revered oracle?"

"I do," I answered.

"Follow me, then." She turned and led me down the steps. The room opening up before me had a low ceiling and was divided into several small sections. From the corner of one eye I could see the tripod the oracle sat upon, but I was guided to another side of the room, where a curtained partition held benches for petitioners to sit. Today, though, there were no other petitioners, by my order.

The acolyte said, "You may tell me your question and I will relate it to the revered oracle." She edged up close so I could speak.

"I will present my question myself," I told her. Now was the moment to speak. "I am the emperor."

"Oh, most gracious leader, forgive me. I did not recognize you." She knelt.

"All the better," I said. "Here I am an ordinary suppliant."

"Never ordinary," she said.

"Here I am ordinary," I said "But I prefer to speak for myself."

"Very well. Follow me." She led me out of the curtained area and into the grotto; I followed the slight form into the darkness. "Here I leave you," she said.

The chamber was cold, and I could hear dripping noises and the sound of an underground stream.

I stood in the dim light and awaited the arrival of the oracle. I could see the sacred Omphalos, guarded by statues of two golden eagles, and a large statue of Apollo holding his laurel sprig. A strange odor filled the little room, unlike any I had smelled before.

At last a figure appeared. She was tall and graceful, wearing a long white robe. She was not young, but a mature woman.

"What do you seek of the oracle?" she asked. Her voice was odd, otherworldly.

"To know my fate," I answered.

"And whence do you come?" she asked.

"From the seat of the Roman empire," I said.

"Indeed?" she asked. Her voice was reedy and wavering.

"I am the emperor!" I proclaimed. "The very person of the empire. The embodiment of it. Ask the god, What does the future hold for me?"

"I shall consult Apollo," she said. "Return to the place where you shall wait." She pointed toward the curtained area.

"Apollo is my patron," I cried. But did she hear me?

I made my way back to the bench, but instead of sitting quietly, I stood and pulled the curtain back enough that I could watch what she did. She made her way over to the tall-legged tripod and took her place on its seat, her legs dangling. An acolyte handed her a cup, filled, I presumed, with water from a sacred stream. Next she handed her a sprig of laurel, cut from a little bush to one side of the tripod. Then the acolyte began fanning at the foot of the tripod. There seemed to be an opening there, a crevice of some sort, deep below. She worked vigorously, directing the air upward toward the oracle, who kept her eyes closed and inhaled deeply.

I did the opposite; I tried to breathe as little as possible. But even so, I could smell the peculiar vapors, and they spread coolly in my lungs. Little by little I could feel them in my head, too.

The oracle was taking great gulps of air, panting. I heard her speaking, but the words made no sense; they were not any language I could recognize. She raised her voice and twisted on her seat, then cried out with an eerie croak.

I waited for what seemed eons. The Trojan War could have passed. The war against Hannibal passed. The fumes from the sacred fissure below must be affecting my brain. Time was at a standstill. Finally the acolyte pulled the curtain aside, bade me emerge, and led me to the oracle, who was standing stiffly, her limbs jerking. She glared at me and recited, "Your presence here outrages the gods you seek! Go back, matricide!"

I leaned forward, clutched her white robe. "There is more to it than that; surely the gods know all!"

She backed away, saying, "Nero, Orestes, Alcmeon, all murderers of their mothers!"

"But for a reason!" I cried. "All of us, for a reason!"

"Go back, matricide! Leave this place!" she recited.

"I did not ask you about the past," I said. "I have purified myself of the past in the Castalian Spring."

"Nothing can purify you!" she replied.

"You did not ask Apollo the question I put to you. *What does the future hold for me?*"

"Yes, I asked him. He said, 'Beware the seventy-third year.'"

The seventy-third year! That was ages away. I was only twenty-nine.

I rushed toward her, to embrace her, so relieved was I. But she pushed me away. "Do not touch me!" she said. "Now go."

I stumbled out into the sunlight. The seventy-third year! Forty-four years from now. I had a very long time ahead of me. Years and years. Forever.

LIX

I fairly skipped up the Sacred Way back to my quarters. Forty-four more years. What things I could accomplish, knowing the gods had given me the gift of longevity. I could complete my engineering projects, could compose music that would surpass all I had done so far, could father sons and watch them grow to maturity, teaching them all I knew, sharing with them all the beauty of the world. I could administer and reform Rome with the care it deserved. I could campaign at the Caucasian Gates. I could visit Egypt and sail down the Nile. The years stretched out before me, a flowery carpet, unfolding benignly into the distance.

But for now, there were only a few days left in Delphi. The athletic contests were next, and the games would conclude with the equestrian events. Despite the words of the oracle, I would not leave Delphi until I was ready. But her words haunted me—the gods expelling me from their presence.

Perversely, I decided I would enact *Orestes* in the next dramatic contest. Let me embrace my fellow matricide, then. Let me take my place in that brotherhood—all of us having done away with our mothers, but as I had cried in vain, for a reason, for a reason! The mothers were not innocent, and their sons were avenging wrongs. Still, the stain remained, and no waters of Castalia or anywhere else could wash it away, she said. So that meant I could never go to Eleusis or be initiated into the Mysteries there. And if I went near Athens, would the Furies pursue me as they had Orestes?

But the world was a wide place, and if those were the only two places barred to me, I would not challenge it.

Sporus returned from wherever he had gone to be by himself and heal and took his place in my company again. I welcomed him, not asking where he had been. It was enough that he was back.

He looked more like Poppaea than ever, probably because he was rested and at peace with himself.

"You are no longer Sporus," I said. "From now on you are Sabina. You had long served that family, and now you shall have their name." I could not call him Poppaea, but her full name had been Poppaea Sabina, and so he would share part of it.

Whatever people thought, they kept it to themselves. I was past caring, as having the pseudo-Poppaea nearby made me happier than I had been. To outsiders it would appear scandalous, but so be it.

Our last night in Delphi, we sat watching the dark terraces below, illuminated here and there by torches, which made the gold statues glint. The white stone buildings seemed to glow, as if they had stored up light during the day. Truly this was a sacred place.

Tigellinus said, "Before we leave, let us have that wedding I offered to celebrate. The emperor and his bride!" He stood and took Sabina's hand and joined it to mine. "We are here in the center of the world, are we not? At the very navel of it. Then, what better place, where every-thing whirls together?"

I looked at Sabina. Yes, let us make this gesture, theatrical as a mask, artificial as anything on the stage. Were we not at the very birth-place of theater? And was this not the ultimate act of theater?

We were "married" by Tigellinus in the early-morning sunlight, Sabina wearing the traditional bridal veil, I acting as groom. Not only our own inner circle of friends and attendants, but whatever passersby happened along, were witnesses. It was, as I said, a piece of theater. But at a deeper level, I had accepted his sacrifice and bestowed my blessing upon it. Since there was no undoing it, it would have been the cruelest act to reject the gift.

* * *

As we prepared to leave Delphi, couriers arrived, fresh from Brundisium, with chilling news. There had been another conspiracy, this one centered in the town of Beneventum, a place we had passed through on our way to the port. I received the messengers in the cool of the early evening on the terrace overlooking the valley below, as the deepening twilight grew more purple.

The taller of the two couriers, a soldier, looked grim as he handed me the message in its wrappings. His companion kept his expression blank and his posture rigid.

I quickly skimmed the contents. The plot had centered on our passage through the town, but the conspirators had been unable to organize in time, and thus we had come and gone unharmed. The head of it was Annius Vinicianus, a Roman consul who had escorted Tiridates to Rome.

"He is also the son of a conspirator against the life of Claudius," Tigellinus reminded me when I handed him the report.

I remembered Vinicianus—a young man, not yet thirty, but with a face leathery from his time out in the field. He had served in General Corbulo's forces in Armenia and had married Corbulo's daughter.

"Gnaeus Domitius Corbulo!" said Epaphroditus ominously. "If the Piso plot failed for lack of a suitable leader, a conspiracy with Corbulo as its figurehead would have no such weakness. He is the foremost general of our age. And rumor has it that he feels unappreciated by you. A dangerous combination."

I took the report back. "It is your duty to report all such rumors to me," I upbraided him.

"Very well, then," said Epaphroditus, "there are rumors as well about the Scribonius brothers, Rufus and Proculus, the governors of Upper and Lower Germany."

"What sort of rumors? Spit it out!"

"They are disaffected and in questionable communication with Corbulo."

"If the generals of the western and eastern armies joined forces against an emperor they perceive as unmilitary . . ." said Tigellinus.

The words of a Praetorian conspirator, accusing me of unmanly conduct, echoed: *I was as loyal as any soldier in the realm as long as you deserved my respect.* Were these men feeling the same way?

The tall soldier broke in. "The conspiracy at Beneventum has been crushed. Helios had the traitors executed. But the generals, that is a bigger question. They are still in command. Rufus has the armies of Upper Germany, Proculus of Lower Germany. Together they command seven legions. And Corbulo is without command at the moment but revered by the troops in the east."

Was this never going to stop? Would I never be safe? And how dare they disrupt my peace of mind at a time like this, when I was in the very cradle of art and beauty?

"Tell Helios to gather more information," I said. "And as for the rest of you, never keep rumors from me again."

After they left, I stood looking down the steep slopes to the valley, completely dark now. I felt as if the darkness were creeping upward to engulf me, too.

We left Delphi and its sacred mountain behind and set out slowly for the plains of Argos, where we would winter, waiting for spring and the resumption of the games. We wound our way down through the Isthmus at Corinth, bypassing Athens. I would not give the Furies a chance to attack me by coming anywhere near it. What need I of Furies to torment me when I had ever-new conspiracies at my back?

The city of Corinth was an impressive one, really two cities in one—a lower one that had the port, and a high one on the slopes looking down. It had been utterly destroyed by the Romans and then rebuilt by Julius Caesar, so it was a little outpost of Rome here in the midst of sublime Greece. It hosted the Isthmian Games, in which I would compete later.

As we crossed the narrow isthmus, where I could see the sea on either side, it was so close, I suddenly envisioned a canal cutting through it, allowing ships to avoid the dangerous sailing around the Peloponnese. I mentioned this to Phaon. He groaned.

"Not another engineering project!" he said.

"This seems more feasible than the one from Lake Avernus to Ostia," I said. "This one would be only about four miles long."

"You are overly fond of canals," he said.

"No one could accuse me of doing it to glorify myself," I said. The accusations about the Domus Aurea still stung. "This would benefit commerce."

"Yes, but at what cost?" he said. His round face seemed to deflate.

"That, my dear minister of accounts and revenues, is for you to investigate," I said. "I would like to bestow a gift on Greece, as a token of my esteem. And to help them, as they are struggling against poverty."

"Beware of a Roman bearing gifts to the Greeks," he said.

"Very funny," I said. "Just find out what it would cost—if it is even feasible."

More news filtered in about Corbulo and the Scribonius brothers, and it was dark. Corbulo, at large in the east with no command, was in communication with them, and making no secret of the fact that he would like a command. A big one.

"A command beyond the army," said Tigellinus. "A command of the empire."

We were sitting in the main room of our winter quarters near Mycenae. I had insisted on lodging there to be near the legendary home of Agamemnon, although few traces of it remained. We were staying on a windy plain, flat and well-watered, close to many sites that loomed large in epics.

Several braziers were burning; Greece in winter had a stinging damp cold. We huddled around the largest one, warming our hands. "That's absurd," I said. "He has no connection to the imperial line."

"Does he need to?" asked Statilia. She often joined in consultations, and I welcomed her incisive intelligence. Her amused tolerance of Sabina sealed my appreciation of her; truly she was an unusual woman.

"Of course he does," I said. If that were not so, all my cousins had perished in vain.

"Piso did not, and neither did Seneca," she said. "Perhaps a day is coming when emperors will come from another source."

"A more likely source is the military," said Epaphroditus. "That is where Caesar came from. A general is always an attractive figure, able to draw followers. And their followers are armed soldiers, not the crowd at a market."

Or at a concert. Or at a chariot race. Or at a drama. He did not need to name them: my followers.

They all looked at me, waiting for direction. It was an order I had thought to leave behind, to be done with. But safety is never permanent. The Nero who knew how to respond to danger had not flown away; he had but merely rested.

"Send a command to Corbulo, Proculus Scribonius, and Rufus Scribonius to report to Corinth immediately. Tell Corbulo there will be important orders awaiting him."

Then I settled in for the winter. It would take the men weeks to arrive. In the meantime I tried to put it out of my mind. I was, after all, in the very heart of Greece, of the places that I had long known by name, the places where Hercules had performed his labors: Lerna, where he slew the Hydra; Nemea, where he killed the lion; Olympia, where he cleaned the stables; Stymphalos, where he overcame the evil birds. Hercules—he who, in a fit of madness brought on by his enemy the goddess Hera, killed his wife and children and was tormented by guilt. Apollo had provided the only remedy: redemption through heroic works.

I visited Lerna, seeking out the swamp where the many-headed Hydra had lived, now a famed spot. The swamp was filled with reeds, but there had been an underwater den where the Hydra had lurked. I stood looking at the bubbles forming in the murky water, rising and bursting with evil smells, and thought how like Hercules' my own journey was, as I was tormented by the death of Poppaea, trying to bring her back. These Greek games and competitions were my labors, and the benefits I wanted to bestow on Greece were my good deeds.

"I can't slay a lion," I said to whatever gods still listened at this place, "or visit Hades and bypass Cerberus—although I have tried to—but forgive me my lapses."

As I stood there in silence, an idea came to me. There were still other feats I could undertake. Was not the bottomless Lake of Alcyon near Lerna? Was it truly bottomless? Could I find out? Could I verify the story, or disprove it, add to our knowledge of the world, a science esteemed by the Greeks?

The Lake of Alcyon was small and it was black, as if it truly was bottomless. I stood on its reedy shore with two Praetorians and a local man who supplied a small boat for us, as well as rope with lead weights and length measurements. But it wasn't long enough. It was only about three hundred feet. I ordered it to be doubled, and by noon the man had returned with another rope, which he fastened to it. But that still made it only six hundred feet long. I wanted another four hundred.

"If after a thousand feet it has not touched bottom, we can say it is a good day's work," I said. "Obviously if it is truly bottomless, no rope would be long enough."

By the time we had the coils of rope in the boat, there was room for only two of us. I left one Praetorian on the shore with the boat owner and we set out to row to the middle of the lake, getting clear of the reeds that bristled along the rim but did not extend far, a clue that the lake was, if not bottomless, quickly very deep. I peered down into it, unable to see anything but black. Perhaps it was like a well, not large in diameter but a funnel deep in the earth. When we reached the middle—it did not take long—I ordered the Praetorian to begin lowering the rope.

He stood up carefully and, taking the end of the rope with the lead weight, bent over the side of the boat and dropped it. Quickly, like a serpent, the rope began to uncoil, making the boat lurch. The Praetorian grabbed it to gain control, and then lowered it little by little by his own hand.

The coil grew smaller.

"I don't feel anything yet," he said, when he reached the end of the first rope, at three hundred feet.

"Keep going," I said, peering over the side of the boat. The water, although dark from its depth, was clear and showed the rope as a pale snake disappearing into the darkness.

We came to the end of the second rope. "Six hundred feet," the Praetorian said.

"Keep going," I said. Now I wished I had asked for more rope, although it would have required a larger boat.

Hand over hand he played out the rope until it came to the end. "A thousand feet," he said. "And I still feel no bottom. The rope is swinging free."

I was disappointed. All I had proved was that it was at least a thousand feet deep, not that it was bottomless. But to show it was bottomless, there was not enough rope in Greece, or in the whole world. Perhaps, as with all true mysteries, we must content ourselves with half answers.

Corbulo and the Scribonius brothers arrived in Corinth two months later, where they were handed, instead of promotions and recognition, orders to commit suicide.

Corbulo obeyed immediately, drawing his sword and stabbing himself in public, saying only *Axios*—Greek for "you deserved it" before he fell to the ground.

The word was customarily said in acclaiming an athlete's victory. So what did he mean? Was he admitting that he deserved the punishment? Was he angry at himself for being caught? Whatever he meant, like the true depth of Lake Alcyon, it would remain a mystery.

The Scribonius brothers, handed their orders, obeyed and committed suicide privately in a meek and quiet manner, uttering no complaints or comments for people to puzzle over.

I appointed Verginius Rufus as governor of Upper Germany and Fonteius Capito as governor of Lower Germany, both men who had no imperial descent and no personal ambition. It turned out that the Scribonius brothers had had some imperial blood connections after all, as well as descent from Pompey the Great. I would not make that mistake again, appointing such men to positions of power.

LX

True winter closed in with fierce winds and icy rain. Even then, Greece had a sublime beauty. The very starkness revealed the intricate patterns of bare-branched trees against the white sky. Mornings spread a carpet of glistening frost across the fields.

This was not the time for practicing for the chariot race; the frozen and uneven ground was dangerous for the horses. But it was perfect for practicing indoor events, music and drama. I particularly pursued the drama, now that I had decided to perform *Orestes*. I would also perform *Hercules Gone Mad*, as well as *Cadace in Labor*, a scene from the *Aeolus*. I embraced my past, as that was the only way to acknowledge it and rid myself of the curse of it.

Greek playwrights did not shrink from the subject, and neither should I. As I fastened the heavy tragic mask and willed myself to become Orestes or Hercules, I felt every drop of their suffering and every curse hurled at them. Such is the power of art.

When I put on the Poppaea mask to play Niobe or Cadace, I transformed myself into a woman. I became entirely female and discovered—there is not that much difference. Where does being a man leave off and being a woman begin? There were of course stories about that, such as the one about Tiresias, who went back and forth between being a woman and being a man, being thus part man and part female. But are not we all?

Now I could unleash to my attraction to men as well as women. Beauty was my criterion and always had been, but now it need not be confined to one type of person only. Oh, the freedom of Greece! What vistas had it opened to me!

Rome seemed very far away—and it was.

But its troubles were not. Ominous messages came, concerning the province of Judea. More couriers, more dispatches.

Judea had long been a troubled spot in the empire. It was a small country but a fiercely xenophobic one. They did not submit readily or easily to being under the control of Rome, and trouble flared up periodically. But it was nothing we could not manage. The Jews, who resolutely refused to acknowledge or worship any god but their own, had wangled the concession from us that they would sacrifice *for* the emperor but not *to* him at their temple in Jerusalem. All very well. A compromise that saved honor on both sides.

Two soldiers and a courier scrambled over the bumpy ground to my quarters one dreary day, their heavy wool cloaks stained and studded with burs. They begged to see me immediately, and Epaphroditus complied. Usually he detained such visitors and questioned them, but he looked dismayed and frightened as he presented them straightaway.

"Gaius Erucius, centurion, and Publius Hosidius, tribune," he said. "They are from Caesarea, the prefect's headquarters. Marcus Liganus, official courier."

I stood, eyeing them. "Yes?"

"Caesar, the situation in Judea is almost out of control," said Publius.

"It is not *almost* out of control, it *is* out of control," said Gaius.

I nodded for Epaphroditus to summon Tigellinus and several of the Praetorians. "Explain yourselves," I said.

"Earlier in the spring, the Jews launched protests against the taxes and began attacking individual Romans, people who were just going about their everyday lives. There were riots in Caesarea. We put that down. But then the zealots, who are gaining control of the country, stopped the sacrifices in the temple for you. Then prefect Florus went into the temple and took silver from the treasury," said Marcus, the courier.

The fool! The Jews had rioted when Caligula tried to have his statues put there. The temple was sacrosanct to them, and any non-Jew entering it was to be put to death. I groaned.

Tigellinus and the other soldiers arrived. I repeated the news about the sacrifices and then said, "Continue," to Marcus.

"Things quickly got out of control. A band of armed zealots attacked the Roman garrison at Masada and the Antonia Fortress in Jerusalem."

"And?" I asked. Surely they were repelled.

"Horrible! Horrible!" said Publius. "The same day, Greeks, in retaliation, attacked Jews in Caesarea and killed twenty thousand. Both sides declared war. Prefect Florus asked General Cestius Gallus in Syria for help, as the forces stationed in Judea were not enough. He set out with the Twelfth Legion, the Fulminata, as well as cohorts from other legions and auxiliaries. He had thirty thousand men."

Ah. Now surely the rebels were quelled. "Good. Is order restored?" I asked. Why had no one told me about this earlier? But no matter. It was over now.

"No!" Gaius wiped the sweat off his forehead, which was running in rivulets down his cheeks in spite of the cold. "He arrived in Jerusalem but found the resistance fierce, and he—first he—the Antonia Fortress had fallen—"

"What was the outcome?" Never mind about the intervening details.

"He was destroyed. He lost everything but his own life in the retreat from Jerusalem."

"Retreat?" barked Tigellinus. "Retreat?"

"He had to retreat. He was beaten. The dishonorable lying rebels promised him safe conduct if he withdrew, but they massacred his rearguard, over five thousand men, and he was forced to abandon his transport train and his artillery, which the rebels have now seized."

Oh, all the gods! Beaten! Driven from Jerusalem like a whipped cur, the mighty soldiers of the Roman army. The shame!

The province—we were in danger of losing it, then. For the second time in my reign, a province might slip away. First Britain, a few years ago, now Judea. And in both cases by armed but untrained rebels.

"Who is their leader?" I asked. Was it another woman, another Boudicca?

"There does not seem to be any clear-cut command," said Publius. "They fight even among themselves. There is no unity. But they have sixty thousand out in the field now."

This was a fire out of control, like the one that had raged through Rome two years ago. But we had better means of combatting it than the Vigiles Urbani and their wagons and buckets. We had the finest army in existence, and if we could not crush this uprising, then we did not deserve the name of master of the world.

I listened to the details of their report, then asked that they be fed and given quarters to rest from their long journey. They were ushered out and the door closed behind them.

Tigellinus sprang. "What, I wonder, has happened since these men left? Every day counts, and they have been gone a fortnight. A fortnight, while the rebels there roam the countryside and strengthen their position." He leaned on his knuckles on the work table, bending forward, his keen eyes fastened on me.

"I must think," I said. "This is crucial. We cannot make hasty decisions, as we will not have a chance to undo them."

"Think quickly," he said. "Think quickly, or all will be lost."

Many of the entourage were wintering in Corinth, so I sent for senators and officers who were knowledgeable about that part of the world. A day later they gathered in the meeting room and offered what they knew, but opinions differed. Some thought it was not an emergency and could be controlled quickly by larger forces; others that the rebels' means of fighting were difficult to counter with traditionally trained troops. What everyone agreed on was that we must move fast.

I needed a general, a capable one. Corbulo would have been the obvious one. Who else was there? Who could be dispatched quickly? Who was already at hand?

Vespasian. Vespasian had come to Greece, at least initially. Was he still here? Or had he left for the winter?

Luckily he was in Athens, and thus Titus Flavius Vespasian was able to stand before me three days later.

"Caesar?" he asked. His broad face, with its wrinkled forehead, seemed stolid and reassuring to me.

I explained the military situation and gave him the dispatches to read for the details. "You served Claudius in his invasion of Britain over twenty years ago," I said. "But it was not your war. Now you have the opportunity to make a war your own, to wed your name to a conquest forever. I want you to take command of the Roman response to the uprising in Judea. I have utmost confidence in you."

"I am to leave my mule trade?" he said, smiling.

"You can leave the mules behind," I assured him. "Your future lies elsewhere."

After he had carefully read the dispatches and questioned the messengers, we met again. He would take command of two legions in Syria—the Fifth, the Macedonia, and the Tenth, the Fretensis. His son Titus would bring up the Fifteenth, the Apollinarius, from Egypt. That would make a force of fifty to sixty thousand.

"Gallus thought it would be easy. I will not make that mistake," he said. "I will leave Jerusalem for last. I will reduce the rest of the country, destroy the rebels in the field, so there is no one left behind us as I take on Jerusalem. It will be slow but methodical and inexorable. We will advance foot by foot if necessary, but whatever we conquer stays conquered."

"I wanted a wise and thoughtful general, and I have found him," I said.

These military disturbances upended my protected oasis of tranquility and escape. I sat brooding for hours at night, thinking how difficult it was to manage the empire, to contend with ambition and treachery on our own side and rebellion on the other. Now I began to question my planned campaign with Tiridates to fight at the Gates of the Caucasus. This was not the time to launch an expansion of the empire but to stand firm in its defense. Reluctantly I admitted I would have to call it off.

As always, when something went deep with me, I tried to convert it into art, to wrestle it into another form, one I could confront. For the upcoming cithara competitions in Nemea, I would abandon the Trojan War and write a composition about war itself and its meaning.

It is always easier to write about an action than an idea, I soon found out. Hector and Achilles, and their swords, yes. The concept of war, very difficult, partly because I did not know myself what I truly thought about war. I came from a family of warriors, the most notable being Germanicus. The entire empire was built on war. Through war Rome had expanded from a small inland town in central Italy to rule the world. We had done it through increments, the way Vespasian was going to fight the Judean War. The slow, inexorable expansion had been more solid and lasting than Alexander's lightning conquests that did not outlive him.

More than a half century earlier, Horace had written *Dulce et decoram est pro patria mori*—It is sweet and honorable to die for your country. It was the Roman theme, as well as the Greek. But so many lives were lost in unnecessary wars, wars started by the greed or vanity of one king. Thousands would die because of the stupidity of a leader. Was that sweet or honorable?

I said as much to Statilia one evening as I struggled to compose the words for the poem.

"Another subversive idea from you," she said. "That to die for Rome might be a waste." She leaned back in her chair and eyed me, teasing as she often did. "An emperor who sings, dances, and races chariots and now questions the sacred idea of war?"

"I don't question war itself," I said, picking up the cithara. "There are only two classes of people: the conquerors and the conquered. In order to avoid being in the latter, you have to protect yourself by fighting. I am only questioning the idea that all wars are equal. Some are foolish. The soldiers who die for them die in vain, yes. It is the legionary who pays the price, not the king who sent him."

"A fine distinction," she said. "People may not see the difference."

"What people? The audience at the competitions who will hear me? I am lucky if they stay awake!"

I began to touch the strings of the cithara. The liquid sound, as always, transported me. The notes were sweet . . . sweet . . . yes, I could adapt Horace's words, then refute them . . . contrasting the sweet sound of the cithara and the very word "sweet" itself with the carnage of war, marrying the two art forms, music and language, into one. Yes!

I wrote it in a white-hot heat. It was, I felt, my masterpiece. How odd that an incident I did not welcome had given birth to the finest work I had ever done. Even the melody sprang naturally from the words, and I felt joy in performing it. I would be ready when we moved to the first games of the new year, those at Nemea.

Spring came to Greece in all its legendary glory. An undercarpet of wildflowers surrounded the orchards, the trees drooping under frothy white blossoms. With each wind, clouds of loose petals flew aloft, scattering and swirling. The sky was a piercing blue, the air soft and rich with the scent of honeysuckle and cyclamen. Dancing poppies around the creamy white Temple of Zeus at Nemea rejoiced that winter was over.

Nemea was situated below a ring of low hills studded with pines and wild olive trees. Like Olympia, the games here were dedicated to Zeus, and his temple loomed over the site, framed by a sacred grove of cypress. When the games began, the valley would fill with tents, but for now it was peaceful and empty. We had arrived early.

I stood at the starting gates for runners at the fine stadium, looking down the long track. My running days were past, but now I regretted that. The thirteen lanes stretched like ribbons before me, beckoning. I put my toes in the marble grooves that served as the start line and inspected the intricate wood and rope mechanism that released all the runners at once. Very clever. Across the way was the tunnel leading from the athletes' changing room out onto the track. I entered it, reading the notations athletes had scratched on the stones. *I win. My strength to the gods.* In my mind I swore the competitors' oath that was administered there before each race: *Do you swear to abide by the rules of the Nemean Games and to do nothing that would bring shame to you, your family, or the spirit of the games? Yes. Then go forward into the stadium, and be worthy of victory.*

I walked slowly through the tunnel, imagining that I had so sworn, emerging out onto the track. The desire for the coming contests surged through me. I was eager for the games to begin.

As contestants began arriving, tents sprang up in the valley and turned Nemea into a city. We were housed in fine temporary wooden quarters built for us, but I often went out strolling in the cool of the evening to visit the tents and to watch the athletes training. In the changing room they shed their clothes, oiled themselves, and practiced in the stadium. I had not noticed before, but a fresh water channel circled the track, so that competitors could drink or cool themselves off. Again, very clever.

The music and drama contests would take place elsewhere, in a temporary theater constructed some distance from the stadium. Walking toward it with me one twilight, Statilia asked, "Do you know yet who your competitors will be?"

"No," I said. "I can guess at some of them, but they can come from all over the Greek world."

The setting sun had turned the Temple of Zeus rosy and softened the new stone of the theater. As I stood in a field before it, plants tickled my ankles and I bent down to pull one up. Wild celery. What an auspicious omen. I said so, taking the stem and twisting it into a circle to make a wreath.

"How so?" asked Statilia.

"The winners here receive a crown of wild celery." I held it but would not put it on my head. It would be bad luck.

"So perishable," she said. "So fragile."

As was everything, I knew to my sorrow. But that does not diminish the shining moment.

The competition for the champion of musical composition and performance will now commence," a black-robed judge intoned. He stood on the floor of the theater and further explained the rules. Each contestant would perform only one piece. There could be no wiping of the face, no dropping of the instrument, no clearing of the throat. To do so would mean immediate disqualification.

He then introduced the competitors. There was a man from Crete, another from Patrae, two from Sicily, one from Rhodes. And then came the thunderbolt. "Terpnus from Rome," and Terpnus stepped out and bowed.

Terpnus! My teacher from my youth, the man who had first shown me the magic and beauty that the cithara alone could command. I nodded to him. To compete against my teacher! I was suddenly unnerved. There was no way I could ever be better than he was.

But I steeled myself. A performer is only as good as he is on that particular occasion, I told myself. A great citharoede could have a lesser presentation one time. And a poorer one could give the performance of his life.

Then an unexpected emotion surged through me. I wanted to beat Terpnus. He had all but accused me of starting the Fire, obviously harboring bad thoughts about me. For someone to believe the worst of you, they had to have thought badly about you to begin with. I had not deserved that; he should surely have known me better than that. The cordial years we had spent together were suddenly swept away, and I wanted revenge, the only revenge that would count: vanquishing him in his chosen field of virtuosity.

"Diodorus of Rome," the judge announced. Another citharoede I had known and practiced with!

So, both Terpnus and Diodorus had made the journey here but disdained to be part of my company and did not even have the courtesy to inform me they were coming, as any true friends would have done.

More were announced, from various places: Philippi, Naples, Naxos.

Then another shock. "Pammenes of Athens." A wizened man tottered out, clutching his cithara. He was legendary but must be ninety years old.

We would perform in the order in which we were announced. That meant I was in the middle, the position I favored. I listened as my predecessors stepped out and presented themselves, then sang their chosen pieces. They were all astoundingly good, but then, no one but the best journeyed to the games here.

Think only of your own composition, your own words. Hold them in your mind, do not be distracted.

Then it was I on the stage. I faced the audience and said the customary words to the judges.

"I will do what I can to the best of my ability, but the outcome is in the hands of Fortune. You are all men of judgment and experience and will know how to evaluate fairly and eliminate the role of Chance."

They looked back at me, as expressionless as stones.

Now it was here. The moment I had longed for and dreaded. One chance. One chance. I took the cithara, holding it on my left arm, and made myself ready. I breathed deeply. No throat clearing. Then I began, and once past the first few notes, I thought only of the message of my song and its reinterpretation of the glory of war. People needed to hear this; they needed to ponder it. It was not a song about nymphs or centaurs or Zeus. It was a song about today, about choices we had to make today—or tomorrow. Choices that ordinary people, who fought in the ranks of soldiers, would encounter, not deciding which of three goddesses is the most beautiful. Choices that their commanders must make. Thus art can be urgent, can raise burning questions and leave it to us to answer them.

Sweat was gathering on my forehead, running into my eyes, but I could not wipe it away. It blurred my vision, making the audience swim before me. It made the cithara slippery in my hands. Then, miraculously, the song was over.

Suddenly my legs almost buckled under me as I stood trembling on the stage for recognition that I had completed my presentation satisfactorily. Then the weakness passed, and I left the stage to make way for the next.

After several of them, Terpnus took his place on the stage. He played one of his signature pieces. He played it perfectly. But there was nothing exciting about it; it was as conventional as it was possible to be.

Next was Diodorus, whose selection was melodic but whose voice was not at its best, and the rule against clearing the throat doomed him.

More contestants, and then old Pammenes appeared, shuffling out.

In a wavering voice he addressed the judges, then straightened himself and began to play. Miraculously, his voice transformed itself into a strong one for the duration of the song.

A few more, and then it ended. Now we waited, pretending to be calm but in reality so apprehensive it was difficult to sit still with straight backs. At length the judges rose, and the chief judge announced, "We award the crown to Nero Caesar for his composition and the execution of it."

The sweetest words in the world! I rose and went to the judges, bowing my head while they placed the crown of wild celery on it. The leaves were cool on my damp forehead; this crown was real, not one I had made myself.

"Nero Caesar accepts this crown in the name of the Roman people," I said. Oh, the joy of saying it, and feeling the crown on my head.

Afterward there was a celebration, put on by the officials; the contestants, their guests, and enthusiastic audience members milled around. Statilia, Sabina, Tigellinus, Epaphroditus, Phaon, and others from my household congratulated me, but I could tell they were surprised. At that moment, in spite of everyone here surrounding me, I wished Acte could have been here, could have shared this. Had things been different, I would have wished my teacher could have seen it, instead of competing against me.

"So the pupil surpasses the teacher." Terpnus was at my shoulder, and I whirled around.

Should I say, *Oh, no, it should have been you?* Should I apologize? But that would be to deny what was.

"On this particular day," I said. "That is all. And what you taught me is the foundation for all else."

"Yes, you were always a studious pupil," he said, holding up his wine goblet.

Studious pupil. Synonyms for *ordinary, mediocre, mundane, workmanlike.* I smiled. I wore the celery crown, not him.

"I did my best," I said.

He took a long swallow of his wine. "We can quench our thirst at last, can mop our brows."

"Yes, it is over," I said. "At long last."

It had been two years since he had uttered his insulting words about the Fire, saying he was ashamed to have a student who had sung of Troy when Rome was burning, and refused to say that he did not believe the rumors. Now I could forget about him and what he thought. It was truly over—between him and me.

LXI

The sweetness of spring turned quickly to summer, and the delicate scent of early flowers was replaced by the dusty dry smell of heated leaves. Spring is brief in Greece, as fleeting as the nymphs associated with it.

Olympia loomed ahead on the calendar, scheduled for the hottest stretch of summer, August. *The Olympics.* The largest and most venerable of the Panhellenic Games, honoring Zeus and celebrating the physical prowess of athletes from the world over, its prestige unmatched. I decided to move there straightaway, to make at least the surroundings familiar to me, so that by the time the games started I would feel at home there—as if that were really possible. Could any contender truly feel at ease as he approached the crucible of competition there?

The distance between Nemea and Olympia was a long one, crossing the entire breadth of the Peloponnese and separated by mountain ranges. To follow the valleys increased the distance but with our large contingent it was the prudent path to take. We set out, our wagons groaning, our company in high spirits, and none more than me, my wreath, ribbon, and palm branch from the cithara contest carefully packed away between layers of paper to preserve them, but radiating my victory beyond their storage box.

At Olympia another test awaited me. There I would race the ten-horse chariot as I both longed and dreaded to do. At this point I could not turn back. Not only could I not bear the ridicule, I could not bear my later regret if I failed to go through with it.

Tigellinus rode up beside the imperial wagon as we trundled along, leaning in, grinning. "Take a last look at Nemea," he said, gesturing behind him.

I turned and watched it receding into the distance. Already it was being swallowed up by the low hills around it. But the image of it would be indelible in my mind.

"On to Olympia," said Statilia, sitting beside me.

On to Olympia. To her it was a simple thing, just on to the next, as a spectator who had no trepidation and faced no demands. How easy to be a spectator, an observer, rather than a participant, a consumer rather than a producer. But that was alien to me. If I cared about something, if I had an interest in it, I could not keep from participating. How much more advisable it would be for me as emperor to be like Statilia. That way I would garner no criticism, no censure, raise no eyebrows. That way I would not be Nero.

"Yes, on to Olympia," I said lightly.

"Your Augustiani claque is in full practice," said Phaon, sitting behind me. "Just listen. You can hear them all the way up here."

From far back in the train I could hear the rhythmic clapping of the group, my faithful supporters and cheerleaders. They had several special types of claps, depending on how they smacked their palms together in unison.

"They sound like a tree full of rooks," said Statilia. "Noisy but enthusiastic."

"Just as long as they don't leave a lot of droppings!" said Phaon, laughing uproariously. I was not amused. His laughter died away.

"Ahem . . . I have sent messengers ahead so that our quarters will be prepared," said Epaphroditus, in his official's voice. "They were not expecting us so early. But all will be ready."

"Good," said Statilia. "I want to be comfortable." She stretched in her seat. "By the time we get there, I will be pounded into a porridge."

"I will be stiff as a dried ox hide," said Epaphroditus. "Perhaps I should get out of the wagon and travel on horseback like Tigellinus."

"You sound like a couple of old women," I said. That ought to snap them out of it.

Suddenly I longed to be with youth, with people who did not complain about their joints, who saw the move to Olympia as an adventure rather than a chore. Perhaps that was really what differentiated youth from age: to see your surroundings as exciting and filled with opportunities. It had nothing to do with being bald or having a full head of hair. It was what was inside the head that determined age, not what was on the scalp.

Was I still young? Or had I joined the ranks of the old? Here in Greece I felt young; in Rome I had felt old, which is one reason I had fled it. But what would happen when it was time to return? Could I dutifully leave youth behind and put on the mantle of age, of caution and ennui, again? Those days of feeling hollowed out, listless—could I bear them again?

Olympia came into view in its serene, green splendor. A flat plain lying between two rivers—one quiet and the other lively—cupped by gentle hills, and filled with temples and groves, its very air seemed sacred.

Olympia was a huge site. Like Delphi, there were monumental buildings, treasuries and offerings from various states, sublime artwork on display. Unlike Delphi, it was not stepped on a steep hillside but spread out in glory like a peacock tail on flat ground. At the far end was a conical hill, Kronos, rustling with pines, that oversaw the oldest of the buildings, the temple to Hera. I stood, blinking, before this august place. It was still a good two months before the games would commence, a month before the crowds would be arriving. We had it to ourselves.

All around me people were climbing out of the wagons, and more wagons were rolling up. An official hurried over, flanked by assistants, to welcome us.

"Caesar," the man said, bowing. "We rejoice to behold you here. Your quarters are ready; we prepared them before starting anything else. They are over there"—he pointed—"just beside the chariot racetrack."

What a favorable omen. I smiled. "We all thank you and look forward to the games. As you know, I am entering the chariot race."

He kept his smile the same. "Yes, Caesar, we have been informed of that. The stables are prepared as well. Many contestants arrive early so their horses can be acclimated to their surroundings. Will you be driving the *tethrippon*? I understand you have driven that in Rome."

"No, not the four-horse chariot," I said. "You could call mine a *dekarippon*."

"What?" He was puzzled.

"In Latin, *decemiugis*. Ten horses."

"Ten?" Now his smile melted.

"Ten," I repeated.

"Then . . . we will have to limit the number of entries for that race, as the width of your team will be greater and we have only so much space. The track is about two hundred feet wide. I will inquire as to what other entries we are expecting in the . . . over-four category. It would be best if you all ran together."

"As you say," I said. "I trust your judgment."

"It will be peaceful here for a while," he said. "But once the month of truce before the games opens, the crowds start coming, and the valley will be filled with tents. We expect many thousands. Enjoy your solitude now."

"I have ten thousand in my own entourage," I warned him. "So already there is no solitude."

"An emperor brings his own city with him," he said.

"Not a city but certainly my court and my athletes," I answered.

"We have not had an emperor here since Tiberius," he said. "But at that time he was not yet emperor, as Augustus was still alive."

So I was the first. Let it be so. Another favorable omen. "I would be pleased to see my quarters," I told him. "Please show us."

I was unprepared for the elaborate building they had erected for our stay. It abutted onto the large structure used to house high-ranking guests to the games, with its spacious dining room, its walkways and courtyards. Ours was a square structure with many rooms, cool and airy even in the midday heat.

"You will, of course, be able to use the adjoining building whenever you wish as your own. This evening, we invite you to partake of a welcoming treat in the dining room, for your immediate company and anyone else you care to have."

Statilia must have made a face, for he hurriedly said, "This I can guarantee you is something you have never had before."

That was unlikely, but I smiled and said, "Thank you. We are pleased to accept." Let the adventure begin.

I wandered outside, going first to the chariot racetrack, as yet ungroomed. Weeds and grass grew over it, with even a flock of goats grazing on it. But beneath the vegetation the outline of the track was clear. A magnificent pillared portico was at one end of it. There the chariots would line up in front of it in an ingenious starting order, forming a wedge, pairing the two on the outside lanes farthest back, then the two in the next lanes, until finally the last pair, in lanes right next to one another, would start. Thus the ones farthest back started first, then the next, and so on, with the last two to start the ones who had the shortest distance to go. When all the chariots were abreast, the judge then officially called the race started.

The starting mechanisms had not been set up yet. I walked around the near end and then climbed up the embankment serving as a viewing area for people. Cresting it, I found myself looking down on the stadium that served for the foot races, wrestling, boxing, the pankration, and the hoplite race. It, too, was still ungroomed. Soon it would look entirely different, with white earth marking the running lanes and the starting mechanisms set in place. The pits for the jumps would be dug and lined with sand.

The sun was halfway down the sky; the air was still and heavy, pressing down with the fiercest heat of the day. Entering the main area of the site, I walked slowly, the bristly grass brushing my legs. Ahead of me, unmistakable, was the great Temple of Zeus. A crowd stood in front of it. People came here at all times of the year, for the statue within was acclaimed as one of the seven wonders of the world. It was said that anyone who gazed upon it could not meet an unhappy death. So I would make sure to see it.

As I crossed the grassy yard, I saw a slight movement. I approached it and looked down; nestled in the green I saw the distinctive yellow and black markings of a large tortoise. Bending down to pick him up, I raised him to eye level. He sleepily blinked at me, his eyes all-knowing.

"On Mount Olympus, the tortoises there are sacred to Zeus," I said. "Have you made a pilgrimage here? Or are tortoises in this area equally sacred? I don't see why not." I carried him over to put him in the shade; his shell had been rather hot. "This should be better for you," I said. Let it not be said I failed to help one of Zeus's creatures.

Entering the temple, I saw that even in the dim light the enormous seated statue of Zeus commanded the space. He was made of gold and ivory and was so large that even seated, his head touched the ceiling. His eyes—what were they made of? I could not tell, but they seemed alive, boring into me. I moved to one side, and they followed me.

There were other worshippers, tourists, and pilgrims here, but his eyes seemed only for me. There were low murmurs around me, but they seemed unimportant. I saw a wavering reflection of myself in the shallow pool of olive oil at the base of the statue; it was there to make sure the ivory did not dry out. The yellowish shadow of my figure in the oil was eerie.

Suddenly the name of the month swam into my consciousness: June. It was June. What of it? Then a group of people walked solemnly past, and I counted them. One, two, three. Four, five, six. Seven, eight. Then one last one. Nine.

The ninth day of June. That was today. Zeus, why are you calling it to my attention?

An attendant knelt at the side of the pool of olive oil and poured more oil into it from a tray of small vials. It took five of the jugs before the level of the olive oil in the pool reached the lip.

June ninth. Five. What could it mean? Five. Five what? Five years? In five years I would be thirty-four. Was there something I should know about that year? Tell me, Zeus!

But his visage did not change. The eyes still focused on me, inscrutable.

Five years ago? I was twenty-five. I had just married Poppaea. I had . . . divorced Octavia. Exiled . . . she was exiled. June ninth. She had died on June ninth. By Poppaea's orders, pretending to be me. A crime. A lie.

This day was an evil one. But this sanctuary would protect me. Would it not?

As I turned to go, the attendant bent down again and selected another jug from her tray. Holding it high, she poured out the oil in a golden stream.

One. One year. One year either backward or forward. Last year at this time—nothing truly noteworthy. Tiridates' visit and my marriage had been in May. So it must be next year. Next year on June ninth. Something. Something ominous.

But seeing the statue of the mighty seated Zeus was supposed to protect against an unhappy death, so it could not be that. And anything other than death could be overcome.

At twilight we gathered in the assembly room of the Leonidaion, the adjacent building for notable guests. I had asked that the Roman girls competing in Hera's races be included, as that event preceded the opening games proper. And now they joined us, glowing in their clean gowns, their eyes eager, cauldrons of energy among their elders. I saw Tullia immediately and motioned her over.

"You see I kept my promise," I told her. "You are here, and you will race."

"When we arrived this morning, I could hardly believe I was actually at Olympia," she said. "I have been training, but I do not know how I will fare against people I do not know."

I put my hand on her shoulder. "No one knows that. That is what makes each race unique. Always unforeseen factors."

"There are to be three races, of different ages. I will be in the last, oldest group." She leaned closer and whispered, "I fear I may be disqualified."

"Why?"

"The race is only for virgins," she said.

"Oh." I had not known that, but it made sense. The races were dedicated to Hera, hardly a virgin herself, but holding them in high esteem. "Then let us keep our secret," I said. *Is it not a fine thing to be emperor and decree who is a virgin and who is not?* "But after the race is over, let us . . . spend time together." I had missed her, missed her good-natured physicality and easygoing nature. A sunny disposition free of guile and foreboding.

I asked the entire group of girls to come over to me. I guessed the youngest group to start at around seven; they must have traveled here with fathers who were competing. The next group began around twelve, already tall. And the last, with Tullia, were in their teens and would likely be married shortly after this. All told there were about fifteen of them.

"You are no less athletes than the men competing here," I said. "The winners will receive crowns of wild olive and the right to dedicate statues of yourselves in the customary place. I myself will pay for them, for I will be proud of our winners from Rome. So, go and may the gods give you victory!"

Statilia glided up to me. "I see that you care for them," she said.

Did she suspect about Tullia? "I urged them to come. I think it is important that girls and women should compete. After all, the Amazons are warriors, and Atalanta ran faster than any man."

"Both from mythology," she said. "Name me a real woman who has done these feats."

"There are gladiators," I said.

She thought a moment. "Yes, true. And that is no easy profession." She cast a knowing glance at Tullia and smiled. "I wish her luck."

The Hellanodikes, head official of the games, announced that the surprise of the evening was now being unveiled. "We are honored beyond words that our emperor has come to Olympia, not only to compete but to be a patron," he said. "What can we offer him that is unique to us? Rome has many things we do not have, but Greece is supreme in one thing: our honey."

There was a collective chuckle and sighs of relief that it was not a droning recitation of philosophy, that other item Greece was supreme in.

"Yes, honey! The honey from Mount Hymettos is famous, and exported everywhere, but our local honeys, ah! You can only get them here, and when you taste them you will swear they are the very nectar of the gods!" With a flourish, he motioned for the servers to come forward, each with a large jar, and place it reverently upon a stone table set up at the end of the room.

Heaps of fresh bread and bowls of cheese curds were also on the table, along with plates and spoons.

The official walked to the first jar, indicating it with a flip of his hand. "Our honeys are of two types: the forest honey, from the fir and pine trees, and the mountain honeys, from the wildflowers growing on the slopes. The taste is particular to that one plant." He lifted the lid on the jar and dipped a stick into it. A golden liquid, tinged with dark flakes, dripped seductively from it. "This is thyme honey. Taste it and know ecstasy." He held up the stick. "But!" Oh, he was a master of the dramatic moment. "Not so fast! There is more to judging honey than just gobbling it down. There are four steps to it. First, examine the color. The flower honeys are light, the tree honeys darker. See if the shade is pleasing."

He dipped the stick in again and let the bright stream drip.

"Now the actual tasting. You must note your first impression of the honey as it touches your tongue. Next, the full taste. And finally, just as important, the aftertaste. What lingers in the mouth. Now, for each person it will be different, but there are some general observations. The flower honeys have a strong taste and perfume, and a strong aftertaste, and are runny. The tree honeys are softer in taste and aftertaste, and stickier."

He walked down the long table. "Since no one eats honey by itself, spread it on bread or pour it on the cheese. Then allow a few moments to pass before trying a different one. Here are the types, labeled: fir, pine, chestnut, thyme, sage, clover." To demonstrate, he dipped a stick into the fir honey jar and held it up, gazing at the color, a dark brown. Then he spread it on a piece of bread to taste. After a moment, he pronounced it sublime. "You must do your own testing now." He stepped back.

I was expected to go first, so I selected the jar with the pine honey. It took a long time to drip from its stick, as it was thick. Its color was a pleasing dark bronze, and it seemed a promising choice. But it was oddly bland once I tasted it. I said so.

"The pine honey is the least sweet of honeys," the official said, as if anyone who did not know this was deficient. "That is why it stays liquid longer than the sweeter honeys."

The table was open for the rest of the company. I stepped back and let them crowd around.

"That was rather cheeky of him," said Phaon, spooning honey off his plate, joining me. "Who wants honey that is not sweet?"

"There are wine snobs and art snobs, but I never suspected there were honey snobs," said Tigellinus. He smacked his lips as he munched on a piece of honey-smeared bread. "This is delicious, though."

"What kind are you trying?" I asked.

"The sage," he said. "It comes from Crete. Or so the expert says."

"There are snobs in every field," I said. "They consider themselves our guides. And perhaps they are. Mountain honey and forest honey—who knew?"

"Who needs to know?" asked Nymphidius. "I plead ignorance. I never felt a lack in my life not knowing the difference between clover honey and sage honey." He cocked his head, looking down at the honey-covered cheese curds. "This one is very good. That's all I know."

"Which one is it?" asked Epaphroditus.

"I don't remember!" He laughed.

"I understand you have visited the Temple of Zeus," Epaphroditus said to me, attempting to steer the ship of conversation onto a more stately course.

"Yes, I did," I answered, confirming it.

"So now you won't have an unhappy death!" Nymphidius was not to be dissuaded from his antics. "We should all go!" He spun around.

"You have it wrong," said Phaon. "The maxim is *Count no man happy until his death.*"

Tigellinus joined in. "And what did the face of Zeus look like?" he asked. "Any resemblance to Caligula?"

"No, he didn't succeed in having his head swapped for Zeus's," I said. "The face didn't look a thing like Caligula."

"Or me?" said Nymphidius, posing. He must have been drinking before he got here. "You know, he's my father."

"I know you claim so," said Epaphroditus.

"So did my mother," Nymphidias said.

"Ah, yes, I see the likeness. Little ears. Triangular face. Shifty eyes . . ." said Phaon. "I am sorry your sire was killed, but the Zeus statue was spared, and that probably pleased Zeus. And it is better to be on the right side of the king of Mount Olympus than the emperor of Rome."

Caligula had wanted to move the statue to Rome, but experts said it could not withstand the journey, so he ordered the head to be remodeled in his own likeness. Luckily for Rome and for the statue, he was assassinated soon after giving the order.

"He must have been struck by a thunderbolt first," said Nymphidius, still laughing. "Zeus is like that."

LXII

The air crackled with anticipation and excitement. In only two weeks the games would begin, and athletes from all over the Greek world were pouring in, setting up their tents, then rushing to practice in the gymnasium, the open-air palaestra, the stadium, and the chariot racetrack. Not only did they want to familiarize themselves with the venues, but for the first time they had a chance to size up their opponents.

High-ranking personages from many countries converged on Olympia, eager to see if their athletes would bring home honors for their towns. If they did so, rich patrons would gladly pay to erect the customary statues in their recognition, so that their victory should never be forgotten. Some of the monuments dated back five hundred years. Already the poets, artists, and sculptors had arrived, advertising their wares, promising odes and paintings of the winners for a bargain price.

The day was a fair one, and I was tingling with anticipation as I dressed. Here in Olympia I had flung off my Roman persona almost in entirety and embraced my true self. I had let my hair grow long, so it fell to my shoulders, an unruly cascade, like the locks of Apollo. It had stayed the blond of my youth, not darkening as happens to most people. It was also wavy, and I no longer made any attempt to tame it.

The toga was gone, replaced by loose and flowered tunics. I often added a neck scarf of a bright color, useful for wiping away sweat in the baking heat. Until I ventured outdoors, I remained barefoot.

Statilia came in just as I was tying the neck scarf.

"Oh my," she said. "Saffron today! Are you sure it goes with the pattern on the tunic?"

I whirled around; she was teasing.

"And if it doesn't?" I asked.

"No matter," she said. "You are the emperor."

We both burst out laughing.

"It's a good thing your contest is the chariot race and not the nude stadium races," she said. "Tunics can cover many faults."

I knew precisely what she meant, but I pretended otherwise. Let her come out and say it, if she dared. "I won't be wearing a tunic, but the customary long chiton," I said.

"Even better," she said.

"So, the more covered, the better?" I asked.

"Well, you are not exactly Apollo—except in the face and hair, of course. And in your music."

"In other words, I am fat."

"You said it, not me."

"You didn't need to say it, after everything else you said."

She laughed. "What was the motto at Delphi? *Know thyself?*"

"It's true I am heavier than I was," I admitted. "But I am not *fat*."

She encircled me with her arms. "I can still get them around you, so I suppose you are right."

"I prefer the word 'husky,'" I said, and again we laughed. She kissed me and we laughed again.

Just then Epaphroditus was announced, and I sighed. "An emperor can have flowered tunics but not privacy." I let her go and said, "Enter."

He came in, a great bear of a man, always seeming larger than he really was. His dark eyebrows drawn, he said, "Caesar, a contingent of senators are here. They have just arrived and beg leave to see you."

Senators! All the way from Rome? I was surprised but pleased. "I will receive them in the atrium." I smoothed my hair and adjusted the scarf, then strode out.

A group of some fifteen men were standing in the atrium. They all wore togas. As I entered the room, a slave announced, "The emperor!" and they turned to greet me. They looked thunderstruck. I realized they had not seen me since my hair had grown, and I had embraced a different wardrobe. And—I had forgotten to put on sandals in my haste to greet them, and was still barefoot.

"Welcome to Olympia!" I said, spreading my arms wide. "Welcome to the games!"

"Caesar," they murmured in unison, staring. Finally one said, "You are—looking well."

"I am well. I am in the home of the gods," I said. "And you honor me by coming. It is a long journey, and I am touched. I compete on the third day, in the chariot race. The entire games last only five days. Five days, but it takes years to prepare."

One senator said softly, "The games are legendary, but I have never had a chance to attend them. We are grateful to you for providing us the opportunity."

I walked around them, looking for one I recognized. There were many new men in the Senate now, and I knew few of them. "Your arrival is timely. We can arrange for a tour of the historic site before the events begin," I said.

"Caesar, we—Aulus Largus, Sextus Scaurus, and I, Titus Vetus— would speak to you privately first," a tall man with ginger hair said.

"Of course," said Epaphroditus, standing by. "I shall arrange it. As for the rest of you, please wait here and take refreshments. The emperor and a games official will then take you to see Olympia shortly." Smoothly, he gestured for stools to be brought and for a slave to bring refreshments. Then we followed him into a private room.

He drew the curtains—already the hot sun was heating the air in the small room—and said, "I will have refreshments brought here as well, and then you can speak freely." There were comfortable padded benches for us, and I motioned the three men to sit.

"Speak, please," I told them. But they only stared silently. "Do not be shy," I said. "You asked for a private audience, and you have it. You did not come all this way to be mute."

The ginger-haired man, Titus, who had initiated the parlay, finally said, "We of course have come to see our Caesar compete, but matters in Rome also drove us here."

"What matters?" I asked. Before he could answer, the slave appeared with his tray of olives, melon, and cheese, and set it down. Silence reigned until he left.

Aulus, a young man with a severe haircut, said, "We in the Senate are anxious for you to return," he said. "There is . . . there is a feeling of unrest."

"A feeling? Please be more specific," I said.

"I can't," he said. "It is just something in the air."

"I think what Aulus means is that the emperor's absence gives an opportunity for certain elements to grow," said Sextus, a stocky older man with a fringe of gray hair around his otherwise bald head. "I have heard grumbling about Rome being neglected and murmurs about the length of the Greece trip."

"How long *do* you intend to stay away, Caesar?" asked Titus.

"Until I have completed the historic circuit of games," I said. "After Olympia, I will go to Corinth for the Isthmian Games."

"And they are when?" asked Sextus.

"In November," I said.

They looked dismayed. "Another few months?" Titus finally said. "You have already been away a year!"

"Is not Helios managing affairs? He sends me regular reports." Helios had been more than diligent; he had been resourceful and efficient.

"There is no substitute for the emperor," said Aulus. "The very presence of the emperor is in itself a stay against mischief."

So how did my presence prevent the Piso conspiracy? It was not a convincing argument. "I will return, and not so long from now. You may rest in that assurance."

"Caesar, we are here in Olympia, where the shadow of Zeus presides," said Aulus. "We feel his presence here even if we do not see him, because his great temple and statue are a visual reminder of him. People need to see things to believe in them. Only the Jews seem to believe in a god they cannot see; no one else has been able to manage it. A Caesar far from Rome, invisible to the people, does not rule it. Not for long." When I did not immediately answer, he said, "Forgive me for the blunt words, Caesar, but we did not travel hundreds of miles to tell anything less than the truth."

I looked at him, at his open face, now showing consternation. "I admire you," I said. "I, too, believe in speaking truth." The gods knew how I had hated all the lies surrounding me as I grew up and my vow to speak truth as soon as I could escape them. "But for the moment I cannot abandon what I am doing here. What I do will bring honor to the Roman people and allow me to do something I have waited years to do. Surely the gods will protect me and Rome until I accomplish this."

What could they do but bow to my words? But the truth of it— truth, my favorite word?—was that one could not rely on the gods to do what you wished of them or even what was right.

As promised in the early hours, the day was hot. Very hot. We hurried from one pool of shade to another as the official led us on a reverential tour of the site. Sweltering in their togas, the senators trudged along. Soon enough the majesty of the place seeped in even for them and their faces registered awe.

The first thing to behold was, of course, the Temple of Zeus, now thronged with sightseers. A long line waited for entrance, and I urged our group to return later, when they could enter more easily.

"Zeus cannot be appreciated if you are crushed together in a crowd. Wait," I said.

The official gave a quick recitation of the size of the temple, the making of the statue, the sovereignty of Zeus over the games, as he had judged the winner of the founding Olympic chariot race between Pelops and Oinomaos for the hand of Hippodameia, daughter of Oinomaos. He went on to explain how Pelops had cheated. The senators mopped their brows.

We followed him behind the temple, where he halted in front of a huge olive tree. Luckily it threw a big shadow that we could crowd under. "This is the sacred olive tree, from which we get branches for the victory crowns, which the winners are awarded on the last day of the games. They must be cut with a sickle of gold, by a boy who has two living parents. We fashion them and display them in the temple to Hera until the ceremony, where you can see them."

"Is that all they get?" one senator muttered under his breath. "A crown of leaves, like the sort we wear at banquets and trample underfoot afterward?"

"I think they also get a ribbon," his companion answered him. "Maybe a palm as well."

"Oh, how exciting!" the first senator sneered.

Then I heard my name, spoken low. "Nero has tried to bring such games to Rome, but they haven't taken root."

"Thank Zeus," said another man, then laughed. "Or perhaps I should not invoke him. At least, not here." He nodded toward the temple.

The official heard the snickers and snorts and glared at the senators. He then led us around the temple and past statue after statue commemorating victorious athletes.

Xenokles of Mainalon, winner of the wrestling competition. A group statue of two brothers and their father—*Akousilaos and Damagetos and Diagoras of Rhodes, boxing and pankraton.* A large stela with the list of winners of the chariot race.

Philip II of Macedonia. Yes, I knew that Alexander's father had won the chariot race. My eye went down the long list until a name jumped out at me: *Germanicus Julius Caesar.* My grandfather!

I stopped dead as the group went on. My grandfather had raced in the Olympics. Why had no one ever told me? Mother! Mother must surely have known; she was his daughter and worshipped everything about him. Yet she derided me for my interest in horses and chariot racing, making my life miserable and doing everything to keep me away from the stables. Indeed, that was why I had first formed my secret bond with Tigellinus, as he was a horse breeder.

I looked carefully at the date. It was only two years before Germanicus died; he had been thirty-two then. Near my age. I stared at it. *May my name join yours, Grandfather.* For the first time I did not resent him, but felt a great kinship with him.

And just a few paces away there was a statue of him, standing tall and victorious in bronze. How had I missed it? The limestone block beneath said that M. Antonius Peisanus attested that Germanicus Caesar had won the *tethrippon* at the one hundred and ninety-ninth Olympics. I was stunned and proud.

I had to hurry to catch up with the group, now standing in front of the temple to Hera, the oldest sanctuary at Olympia. It had thick golden columns, standing serenely in front of the wooded Kronos hill.

"Hippodaemia ordered this temple to pay homage to Hera," the official intoned. "And here, in her honor, every year sixteen women weave a robe for the goddess, and host three races for unmarried women. These are run before the Olympics begin. As you know, women cannot compete in the Olympics, or even watch them. But they have their own competition here."

"Imagine if women weren't allowed to watch the gladiators in Rome," one of the senators said.

"Yes, the stands would be half empty!"

"And the gladiators would have empty beds," said another.

It was well known that highborn women found gladiators attractive and indulged their appetites with them.

"Perhaps it's the naked men here that make it forbidden," said the first senator. "Imagine if the gladiators fought naked."

"Ouch!" groaned his companion.

Again the official glared. I felt I should apologize or rein in the conversation, but the Romans were hot, tired, and uninterested. It was time to end the tour.

"We are grateful for your explanations," I said. "And now, I invite the company to retire to the baths, on the far western side of the site, by the river Kladeos."

They did not have to be asked twice and immediately headed there. I watched as they disappeared behind the shrine to Pelops. I then thanked our guide and went inside Hera's temple.

It was blessedly cool, and dark enough that for a few moments I could not make out any structures. Then a statue of the goddess swam into view, its white marble making it the first thing visible. I walked toward it; gradually the surroundings came into focus and I could see the gold and ivory table in front of the altar, with rows of victory wreaths laid reverently on it. I came closer and bent over them. I wanted to touch one but felt that it might disqualify me in the eyes of the gods, as if I were claiming something I had not yet earned. The shiny gray-green leaves of the wreaths were expertly woven so they chased one another around the circlet, overlapping in the most pleasing manner. Oh, most beautiful of sights, this emblem of excellence at the highest level.

The girls would receive one, too. Three wreaths, one for each of the winners of the three age groups. The race would take place tomorrow.

Someone was behind me, breathing softly. I turned and saw that it was Tullia. Shyly she said, "I wanted to see the crowns. I thought if I saw one, it would be real to me, and I could imagine wearing it."

She was so young, so winsome. I could almost love her, and never more than at this moment, when we both had been drawn to the victor's table, pulled there by the same love of sports and competition.

"I am afraid," she confided. "I don't want to run tomorrow."

"Everyone is afraid," I assured her. "In fact, anyone who is not afraid is not a true athlete. It means he or she doesn't care."

She looked straight at me. "Are you afraid?"

"Yes," I admitted. "Not only of winning or not winning, but driving a chariot is dangerous, and none more dangerous than a ten-horse one."

"You don't have to. You could change to a regular four-horse one."

"You are wrong. I must do this."

"So must I." But she looked miserable as she said it.

"I will be there tomorrow when you run," I promised her. "Don't disappoint me."

"By losing?"

"No, by not starting."

LXIII

The day dawned clear; there was even a light sheen of dew on the grass, a cooling balm. The girls' race would take place in the stadium, but the course was a hundred feet shorter than the men's *stadion*, making a total length of about five hundred and twenty feet. Tullia and I had discussed the mechanics of the race. It was a long time since I had run, but I remembered the tactics well.

"There are really only two methods of winning," I said. "Either you have to take the lead from the first and run the others off their feet, or you have to hang back—but not too far back—and come from behind at the end in a burst of reserved speed. But to lead from the beginning, you have to know you are faster and stronger than the others."

She tossed her hair. "That's the way I always race," she said.

"Ah, but that is against local girls. Here the competition is much more selective."

"I won't know how fast they are," she said. "I will have to race as I always do."

After we parted I made my way down to the stadium, passing the row of Zeus statues paid for by fines of disgraced athletes who had cheated, a warning to all the competitors who had to pass them. *Victory at Olympia is to be won not by money but by swiftness of foot and strength of body,* they were admonished.

The crowd was surprisingly large; to them it was a novelty event, one they didn't want to miss. The girls now entered the stadium, walking single file. Unlike the men, they did not race naked. They wore the prescribed costume of a short tunic, fastened only on the left shoulder, leaving the right bare to below the breast. Their hair was unbound, to signify their maiden status. They each in her way looked like Artemis, and perhaps that was the intention.

The youngest girls raced first, their slight forms making them seem like flying wisps of mist. The race was so short it could be run almost on one breath, and it seemed over too quickly. Too quickly for those of us who were nervous about the last race.

The winner, a thin girl with very dark hair, got her ribbon and palm and then retired to the side.

Next came the older girls. The differences in height were more pronounced. Some had grown quickly and were almost adult height; others had yet to have a growth spurt. That would make for an unequal race even if they were the same age, for long legs cover distance faster than short ones.

Sure enough, the tallest girl won, although a shorter one, who pounded the course fiercely, almost beat her.

Now came the last group. As they sorted themselves out and lined up at the incised marble slab that marked the start, I saw that Tullia was flanked by a large, muscular girl with wheat-colored hair. On the other side was a willowy girl with very long legs. This was not good.

Tullia stared straight ahead and stood tensely. She was clearly so nervous she was stiff. This was not good, either.

Time felt interminable while the girls stood at the ready for the race, which seemingly would never begin. Then, suddenly, they were off.

Tullia burst from the starting line; she clearly had practiced her starts. But after the first few steps the larger girl passed her, with the long-legged girl just behind. Tullia's tried-and-true tactic of running ahead of everyone did not work here. I could almost feel her surprise and panic when they both passed her.

After that she did not lose ground; the gap between them did not widen. She was about one length behind both of them, who were each fighting for the lead. The rest were farther back, but I paid them no mind. They were irrelevant to the race at this point.

Now the two leaders were halfway to the finish, their hair flying out behind them. Now three-quarters to the finish. Then the long-legged girl pulled slightly ahead. The blonde was flagging, having overdone the first part of the race and tired herself too early.

Only about a hundred feet left. Then, like a bird taking wing, Tullia closed the gap, running smoothly and strongly. Twenty feet left. The front runner heard the feet behind her and made the fatal mistake of looking back, slowing herself just enough that Tullia shot past her and finished first.

I let out a whoop of glee; I was more excited than if I myself had won. A throng rushed to the finish line to congratulate the final winner. Tullia was surrounded by well-wishers as the judge handed her the palm and the ribbon. I hung back, not joining them. This was her moment, not mine.

While everyone was exulting and praising her, I watched the losers slink off the track. They had all done well and were probably the best runners of their age group in the world. But in Greek contests, there are no runners-up; there is only the one winner.

I sent a congratulatory note to Tullia where she was staying. *Come to my quarters so I may tell you in person how proud I am,* I wrote. *Bring the ribbon and palm!*

She came as the evening was settling in and the first stars were appearing. Her face was shining and her cheeks glowing.

"You have been to the baths," I said, touching her hair, which was still wet. "How could you bear to wash away that sacred dust from the race?"

She laughed. "Because I was hot and dirty."

"You had to take off your ribbon," I said.

"I couldn't wear it forever," she said.

She was practical, clear-sighted. She would do well in life. People of that temperament usually did. "No, I suppose not. But for one day?" Especially as it was the only one she would ever get.

"All things must end," she said.

"Not this day. Not yet."

She held out the ribbon and the palm and I took them, examining them closely, feeling the stiff bristles of the palm and the smooth weave of the ribbon. "You have done it," I said. "You won your city the race. Now you will get free meals the rest of your life." I laughed. "Although they don't do that in Rome, only here in Greece."

We walked to the open terrace, where the sky of day, still laced with pink streaks from the setting sun, was tender. I put my arm around her shoulder. "I am so proud of you," I said. "And all the more proud because I was surprised. I thought you had lost when I saw your competition, and I knew your strategy of leading from the start had failed."

"For the first time," she said. "But you were right, the competition was of a different caliber here. That is why I was so surprised when the leader made that amateur mistake of turning her head."

"It's one she won't make again," I said. "Now, we must commission your statue," I said.

"No," she said. "It isn't necessary."

"Yes, it is. If you cannot stay here, your likeness can, so that forever after your victory will live on. I have enjoyed seeing the dedications and statues of past winners." *Like the one of my grandfather.* "This way no one can forget you." I turned her to embrace her. "I know I never will."

She turned her face up to kiss me, then said, "When I said all things must end, I meant more than just wearing the ribbon." She pulled away a small space and then said, "I am to be married. My father was waiting until after the Olympics, but now I must prepare for another life. A different one. One I am not sure I want but which I will submit to. And so, since you have declared me a virgin"—we both laughed—"I shall remain so until my marriage day."

So be it, then. I stepped away from her and handed her back the ribbon and the palm. "Cherish these," I said. Of course she should not enshrine them as Statilia had done her ancestor's awards, but just keep them in a private place.

"I cherish them, but more than that I cherish the encouragement you have given me, the opportunity to come here. Without you, I never would have known this moment."

A slight, warm breeze had sprung up, caressing the evening. We turned once again to look at the sky. An almost-full moon had already risen, pale at first, but growing brighter as the last of the day fled.

When it was full, in two days' time, the great sacrifice to Zeus, a hundred oxen on his altar, would take place.

"You will receive your victory wreath along with all the winners on the last day," I told her. "There will be a big banquet. If I do not win, I will not be there. So tonight may be our farewell, although I hope not."

"Do you mean you hope it won't be our farewell, just because, or because you might not be at the winners' banquet?"

"Both," I said. "I will be sad for both."

The night passed slowly. I had thought to spend it with Tullia, but now I had no desire for company. There would be enough of that in the coming days. I did not sleep well; I kept awakening, seeing the moonlight moving across the floor. It faded in the pearly dawn, and I arose.

Today was the start of the Olympics, the two hundred and eleventh, the twelfth since Germanicus had competed. I sent up a silent plea to him to watch over me. Now it was time to go forth.

Athletes, judges, and trainers would gather in the Bouleutarion, the headquarters of the Olympian council and keeper of the archives, to take our oaths and be registered. As we crowded in, I looked around at my fellow competitors. They were of all types—dark and light, burly and slender. But they were all young. Past a certain age, competition was pointless—unless you enjoyed losing or were fulfilling a lifetime wish to come to this king of all contests and never mind the results.

Zeus Horkios, Zeus of the Oath, glared at us in the form of a bronze statue in majesty and danger, wielding thunderbolts in both hands, ready to smite anyone who cheated. The base of the statue repeated the threat, in case the depiction failed to stir us. In front of it was a table with slices of wild boar's meat.

The presiding official stood before the statue and led us in the oath.

"Upon my honor as a man and an athlete, I swear to do nothing evil against the Olympic Games. I touch the meat to confirm this." A rumbling of voices filled the room as all swore. We then filed up to touch the meat.

Now the judges had to verify the athletes as to age, which did not concern me; it was mainly to make sure the boys' races were run by boys and not men. But the horses had to be examined, and that meant all ten of mine must be cleared.

They had arrived in Greece in time to become acclimated to the weather and the food. I had, as was my preference, a mixed team— some for speed, some for strength, some for steadiness. They were of all colors; the artist in me wished they could have been all white, to make a striking image, but the competitor in me would rather have a smooth-running team.

They passed the qualification test, as I expected. The judges, however, were skeptical that I could run a ten-horse team. Then they said, "There is no one for you to compete against. No one else has entered such a team."

I was immensely disappointed—surely someone else in the Greek world could drive a ten-horse chariot. "I can't run on an empty track," I said. "The horses need to run against something, not by themselves."

"We will have two *tethrippon* chariots run with you, but only to pace you," they said.

What a letdown! But I could hardly refuse to go ahead now, after all the effort of preparing for this, my dream race. I tried to console myself by knowing that just driving the ten horses was challenge enough, but the disappointment was sharp.

The chariot races would take place on the next day. So soon! I had planned for this so long, but it had always danced in the future, tantalizingly, and only in the imagination.

One of the other charioteers had overheard the judges and followed me as I led the horses to the side of the field where I could talk to them and reassure myself that they, and I, were ready.

"Caesar!" he called, catching up to me. "Do you know what this means?"

"It means that a ten-horse team is not a popular choice," I said. But I had known that.

He cocked his head. "It means that you will win a crown. For sure."

He paused. "There is a rule that if there are no competitors, the lone entry is awarded the victory prize."

"But—" Was that a victory or just a consolation prize?

"It happens rarely, but it happens," he said. "Sometimes in the month before the Olympics, the athletes are intimidated by their competitors, or get injured, or just drop out, leaving only one man for the event."

"That's hardly a victory," I said.

"It will be inscribed as one. And what does a victory proclaim, but you are the best in that event on that day and at that time? So if you are the only one, that is still what it means." He grinned. "Congratulations, Caesar!" Bowing smartly, he hurried back to his horses, leaving me with mine.

I stroked their backs, one at a time, loving the smooth, shiny coats that bespoke their healthy diet, and the unique smell of their hides. "We will still run," I assured them. "We will run as if we were competing against Pelops himself." Even if the crown was inevitable, the outcome, the actual race itself, how the horses would run and how I would control them on a real track, was still a question mark.

That night, I tried on the Greek charioteer costume, so different from the Roman one. It consisted of a long chiton with a wide belt. That was all. No helmet, no leather leg or arm guards, no protective corselet.

"You wanted to go all Greek," said Statilia, circling me. "Now you have your wish." She fingered the chiton material. "Very thin. This won't help if you crash."

"No need to remind me of that," I said. And the obvious retort would have been, *I don't plan on crashing*. But no one plans on crashing.

"I heard something that will hearten you," she said. "I overheard two men talking about the chariot races tomorrow. One said that although the owners get the victory wreaths, very few were brave enough to drive their own teams, letting the charioteers take the risks while they took the prizes. Then another one said, 'The emperor Nero is one of the very few who dares to do it. Cheers to him.'"

"Did you really hear that?" How encouraging, after nonstop criticism from all quarters, calling me crazy, vain, stupid, foolhardy, and arrogant—anything but brave.

"Yes, I did," she assured me. "There are probably many people who share his opinion. I am one of them."

"You are?" She had never voiced it.

"Oh, yes. But until today, it was never certain you would go through with it. Too many things could have interfered. I will be there, watching. As I was at the Circus Maximus for your first race."

"But women aren't permitted."

She laughed. "It's a big open field. Who will be able to enforce that rule?"

The next day, the second of the contest, I was oddly calm, as if all the waiting had drained away the tension, siphoning it off into space. I put on the flimsy costume and, accompanied by my supporters, headed for the race field.

The first events were the *tethrippon* races, and there were at least a hundred chariots entered. The track could accommodate as many as twenty chariots at a time, but in the interests of safety, only twelve would run at once, giving them more space. The odd staggered starting gates were ready, and the teams entered them.

It was very different from a Roman race. The flat open field for spectators, rather than stepped viewing stands, meant it was difficult to see the progress clearly. There was no dividing wall in the middle of the track, so the two sides blurred together, and a chariot might easily veer out into the oncoming lanes. There were no stands or *metae* to crash into, but the chariots could run into one another or lock wheels. There were only lone turning posts to mark the end of each lap.

It took most of the morning to run the four-horse chariots, and that was followed by the *synoris*, the two-horse chariots. There were fewer of them; it was not as popular. Soon, too soon, it was over. Next would be my race, announced by the herald as "the ten-horse chariot, driven by Imperator Nero Claudius Caesar Augustus, the son of the

Divine Emperor Claudius, from Rome." It sounded comical, but it was protocol, allowing for a challenge to my credentials, like all the other Olympic competitors. Because the *tethrippon* chariots were not actually competing, they were not announced.

We dispensed with the starting gates. My team would not fit into one, and with only the two other chariots we could start at the same line.

I had decided to extend the yoke of the chariot so I had six horses tethered there, three on each side. That still made four to run on traces, with four separate reins for me to hold, as well as the gathered ones of the yoked horses. Unlike in Rome, I would not tuck them into the belt, and I had no need of a knife to cut me free. If I was thrown, I would not be dragged by horses as in Rome; I could just drop the reins.

The two trace horses that would be closest to the turns were the most nimble and obedient, as the success of the race depended on their executing the turns. The two trace horses on the outside had to be the strongest, to steady the chariot as it turned, which created a tremendous strain on the wheels and pulled the other horses outward. At home, at Lanatus's track, they had performed well. But here?

Before I had finished gathering the reins properly, the trumpeter blew, and the race started. I was jerked forward, almost pulled over the rim of the chariot, as the horses leapt ahead.

Quickly the four-horse chariots were ahead of me, but that was to be expected. Four can always outrun ten. But no matter. Now I must concentrate on my own race. The yells and calls of the crowd faded; all I saw were the backs of my horses and the track unfolding in front of me. The pounding of their hooves threw up a cloud of dust into my eyes, and I kept ducking to shield them. My eyesight was bad for distances, and this hindered me further. But the horses were running effortlessly, and before long we had rounded the first turn.

Things went smoothly, if somewhat boringly, with no one beside me and no way to measure our speed. But after several turns, the four-horse chariots were now on the opposite side of the track, with no protective barrier, and when my horses saw them galloping right toward them, head on, the inner two suddenly bolted to the right. They crashed into the other horses, pushing them to the side and making the chariot careen to the right. I dropped the reins, but before I could grab the bar, the chariot veered again, throwing me out and forward, under the feet of the outer horse. I rolled away just as the hooves passed over me.

Wonderingly, I stood up, bruised and dusty. The chariot was not overturned. The horses remained hitched, and the yoke was unbroken. The chariot was far to the side of the track, facing the wrong direction. The four-horse chariots had made the turn and were now heading toward us at breakneck speed. I limped over to the chariot, got in, gathered the reins, and took off before we were run down. Even in my dazed state, I heard an explosion of cheers from the viewers.

I crossed the finish almost in line with the four-horse chariots. Never had a finish been more welcome. Trembling, I climbed out of the chariot. The other two charioteers embraced me, and the judge hurried over.

"Are you injured?" the judge asked.

"I don't think so." I felt my arms and legs. They were bloody with scrapes and stinging, but they weren't broken and the cuts weren't deep. I felt my head. Miraculously, it had not been hit.

"You should immediately sacrifice to Zeus," he said. "For surely he protected you."

"Yes, yes." Doubtless he had. Or perhaps it was Germanicus.

The herald announced me as winner of the ten-horse chariot race at the two hundred and eleventh Olympiad. The judge tied the ribbon around my dusty head and handed me the palm. I do not think there was anyone present, on that great wide field, who begrudged me the decision.

The crowd rushed over to surround me, yelling and cheering. Never had I felt more valued and respected. Their admiration was genuine, not because I was emperor but because of my fearlessness and pluck.

Whatever the cost, it had been worth it.

I looked out at all the faces; I would try to remember them always: strangers whose giddy exuberance lifted me aloft. Then I saw a face that once was the best known, the dearest, in all the world to me, but now was that of a stranger: Acte.

*   *   *

F ind her!" I ordered Tigellinus late that night.

"But, Caesar," he said, "there are tens of thousands of people here!"

"She was at the race, in the field with the spectators." Statilia had been right; no one enforced the rule against women, perhaps because the track was out of the main area and had no entrance gate.

"So were thousands. Honestly, I do not see how it can be done."

I looked at him. "Tigellinus, I have every confidence in your ability to do the impossible."

He groaned and took his leave.

He had to find her. I had to see her.

LXIV

The third day: the morning of the great sacrifice at the Altar of Zeus, the central ceremony of the games. A procession of priests, judges, athletes, and ambassadors from Greek city-states made their way solemnly through the site and to the huge conical altar of ashes from previous sacrifices, driving a hundred perfect oxen to be slaughtered. The crowd gaped at the rich robes and lowing beasts, but I was scanning the faces for that one face. There were many women there, as this was not a restricted activity, and that made it harder to find any particular one.

How could she have come and not told me, after my personal plea in the letter? In fact, she had told me she wouldn't come.

Another group of people pressed forward to watch the procession. I eyed them, but no Acte was among them.

After the sacrifice—in which the thighs would be offered to Zeus and the rest divided for the people—there would be a huge feast for everyone. The ambassadors would host tables for their own country-men, using only the best gold vessels; the common people would sit on the ground, just as hungry and just as gleeful.

Perhaps she would come to the table for Romans. I went to it, but she was not there, and I had no appetite for the smoking ox meat nor for the Olympian wine—known locally as "headache wine"—so I did not stay.

I wandered about aimlessly, then felt a slow anger spreading through me.

I drove my ten-horse chariot, something I have always longed to do. I acquitted myself well. And she has robbed me of my joy in it!

But that was foolish. I had robbed myself of it, by obsessively seeking a woman who clearly did not want to see me. How shameful!

The feasting over, people rose and headed to the stadium for the afternoon events: the boys' races and contests of strength. I had to go; I would hate myself afterward if I missed anything here, but I didn't really care. I cared about only one thing, like a madman.

Get hold of yourself, Nero. You are disgracing yourself in your own eyes.

I willed myself to stop thinking of the search for her. I concentrated on the events before me. The boys would run the same distances as the adults—first the long race, about five miles, then the double *stadion*, about twelve hundred and fifty feet, and last the stellar event, the original *stadion*, about six hundred and twenty feet. The boxing and wrestling would finish the program.

In the heat of the afternoon the crowd was somewhat stuporous after their big meal. The keenest observers were the families of the boys. No boys would compete if they had not reached a good height and strength, so none were so young as some of the girls in Hera's race. In fact, one of the worries of a youth being examined that first day was that he would be deemed too well developed to race with boys and be shunted off into the adults, despite his age.

The speed and precision of the competitors was impressive; they would grow up to be adult champions, I thought. Later in the afternoon, the boxers and wrestlers were well trained, using skill rather than strength. They had great promise, and if they could hold their skill level and combine it with the strength they would grow into, they would be formidable.

Buoyed by the glow and potential of the youths I had witnessed, I left the stadium in a better frame of mind than I had entered it.

That night I dined with Statilia, and she recounted exactly how the chariot race had looked from the perspective of the crowd.

We were seated in the enclosed terrace off my bedroom, at a low table. It was still too early for lanterns, but the moon, full now, rose like a ghost in the east.

In deference to the heat, the table was set only with light, cooling foods: melons, cherries, currants, cheeses, and pitchers of Thasian wine, with its scent of apples.

"After the ox at noon, I have little appetite tonight," she said, smiling. I did not tell her I had forgone the ox meat and all the rest of it. She seemed mellow tonight. She reached out and took my hand. "I was afraid you would be killed," she said, the smile fading. "It looked as if you were doomed when you were thrown out and under the horse."

"It happened so fast I knew only to dodge the hooves and roll away. I did it without thinking." I shook my head. "I am so fortunate I wasn't belted in by the reins."

"More than lucky, it was a miracle." Her chin trembled a bit. "I did not know until I saw you fall how devastated I would be without you." She stood up, came over to me, and embraced me from the back, putting her head on my shoulder. "I care deeply for you. I do not want to lose you."

Still not the words "I love you." It was as if we had a pledge never to say it, a pledge forged at the beginning.

"You won't," I said. But how could anyone guarantee that? Lovers believe it fiercely, but they are not all-powerful against fate and circumstance. We left the table and in the thickening twilight seized what we had at that moment, at this time, and made celebratory love—rejoicing in my survival, her loyalty, and promises we wanted to keep.

O n the fourth day the culminating competition of the Olympics was held: the men's stadium events. The winner of the *stadion* was honored by having his name bestowed on the entire Olympics of that year.

The excitement was so strong it could almost make the leaves of the trees quiver. But when Tigellinus stood before me early in the morning, his usual proud posture was drooping.

"Well?" I asked, knowing the answer.

"I have had no luck," he said.

"If you rely on luck, you never will find her," I snapped. "There are only two days left. And many people will leave tonight after the stadium events. They won't stay for the awards on the last day."

"I know, I know, but I am doing my best."

"You know what she looks like," I said. "You knew her when she was in the palace. I can't dispatch anyone else who has seen her." Besides, employing more searchers would be embarrassing.

"You know her better than I. Where would she be likely to go? Whom would she be likely to be with?"

I thought hard. She probably had not come alone. That would have been dangerous. But whom would she have traveled with? People from Velitrae, where she lived? "Try a group from the Velitrae area," I ventured. "Or from the surrounding area of Campania. They must be camping together."

After he left, I readied myself to go to the stadium. I would see the best in the world doing what they did best, performing as mortals emulating the gods, pushing themselves to their furthest human level, almost touching the divine.

The stadium was packed. As emperor, I had my own reserved spot, along with officials and other persons of rank, just across from the judges' station. The other forty thousand spectators were squeezed together and looked like they could barely breathe.

The first event, the long race, won by a man from Pylos, served to prepare people for the coming program. Since it took a while to complete, people could also let their attention wander and talk to their companions.

Next came the double *stadion*. Now attention quickened. Some athletes would run this as well as the *stadion*, but most would choose one or the other, conserving their energy. Each competitor was announced by the herald—his name, his hometown. They came from everywhere. As they took their places at the marble ground marker, digging their toes into the grooves, leaning forward, they were like a Greek vase sprung to life, as artists painted this scene over and over.

They were off, streaking down the track. For the first quarter, they were close together, then the faster ones pulled ahead, and by the time they reached the turning post, there were three in the lead. It was a close finish between the three, and I hoped the judges had better eyesight than I, for I could not choose the winner.

But they had one, and he was awarded the ribbon and the palm, with screaming cheers from his compatriots.

There was a pause before the crowning event, the one going back to the first Olympics more than seven hundred years ago. The tension built, the audience was gripped with silence, waiting. Finally twenty-two young men came through the tunnel, passing the statues of Nemesis placed there to remind them of the dangers of pride. They shone with youth and strength and took their places at the starting line before their lanes. The herald called out their names—one would go down to immortality.

They were quickly off. Not one was slow, and all moved with the ease and power of animals, not men. They had been transformed into another species, at least for this magic instant. Then it ended, and one man was proclaimed the winner. The rest fell back to earth, ordinary mortals once again.

"The winner is Tryphon of Philadelphia in the old kingdom of Pergamum now the Roman province of Asia," the herald cried in his thick, penetrating voice. "From henceforth this Olympics will be named the one in which Tryphon of Philadelphia won the *stadion*."

Screams and cheers erupted from the spectators. By the time they died away, the atmosphere in the stadium changed, as people relaxed.

The following contests of strength and skill—boxing, wrestling, jumping, throwing the javelin and the discus—were impressive but lacked the urgency of the *stadion* runs. These were all abilities valued in a soldier, necessary for warfare training.

Thus ended the two hundred and eleventh Olympiad. The grass would grow again in the running lanes, until it was pulled out in another four years for the next Olympiad. And so it had been for hundreds of years.

The winners would feast and celebrate tonight, and the tents would glow with lights and music. The losers and their supporters, as well as spectators who were mere sightseers, began to depart. Soon the valley was jammed with wagons, carriages, and horses, heading out.

So quickly the mood deflated. I should have felt elated, as I had just witnessed such performances as I would never see again, but I felt bereft. Deserted. The higher the high, the lower the fall when it was over.

You still have Isthmia, I told myself. But nothing could equal Olympia and its games. Nothing could equal what I had seen today. Or what I had done yesterday.

Weary, I returned to my quarters. I heard the others of my household laughing and singing in other rooms. They would drink and go over and over all the details of what they had seen. Good for them. But I did not wish to join them.

In fact, I thought, I shall drink, but alone. I walked over to the table where several jugs of wine were waiting, many types to choose from. I poured out some red Corcyraean wine. I might as well stay Greek all day.

After the first cup, the jagged edges of melancholy slid away and I felt much better. Enough better that I even laughed out loud as I remembered the saying about certain kinds of men: *He is three drinks below normal.* Perhaps I was one of those. Or at least one drink below normal. Make that two. I poured another cup and sipped it slowly.

The day had truly ended. It was dark outside. I could hear the carousing from the tents on the grounds. I savored the wine. The Corcyraean type was growing on me.

The door opened, slowly. How annoying. Could they not even knock? Ask permission? The answer would be no if they did ask.

I turned to see the door almost fully open and Acte standing on the threshold.

I stared. The room was dark, as night had fallen while I sat with my wine, and I had not bothered to light a lamp. But my eyes were used to it as it had come gradually. "Tigellinus found you," I said flatly. I was too stunned to speak otherwise.

She stepped into the room and closed the door behind her. "Tigellinus? No, I have not seen him."

"How did you get in here?"

"People of your household still recognize me. It was not difficult."

"Why did you tell me you were not coming?" I jumped up, all my hurt pride and frustration bursting from me. "I invited you to come to

Greece! You answered that you would not. Now you have been here the entire time, without telling me. I saw you by accident after the chariot race. Where else have you been? At Delphi, at Nemea as well?"

She drew back. "No greeting? Is this the welcome I get?"

"You don't deserve a welcome!" I could hardly believe the words I heard coming from my mouth. I had tormented myself for two days wishing to see her, and now I would drive her away. But when I saw her, standing there so self-possessed, I was enraged. "After hiding away, why have you come now?"

"Now I ask myself the same question. I wish I had not. I will go."

"No!" I grabbed her arm. "You will not!" She tried to pull free, but I spun her around. "Look at me!"

She raised her eyes to mine. Within them was not deviousness but honest puzzlement. My anger seeped away.

"I am sorry," I said, letting go of her arm. "I just don't understand. Tell me why you came to Greece at all and why you are here now."

Like a wary animal, she stood ready for flight. I motioned for her to sit on one of the couches. I sank down on one across from her. "I am glad you are here," I said. "Really."

She laughed in that warm way I remembered. "Really?"

"Yes, really. Now tell me."

She drew a deep breath. "I was honored by your invitation. But I could not take off so much time from my work. Your tour is lasting longer than a year. And I did not wish to be in your household. I didn't belong there, and it would give rise to ugly gossip." She smiled. "Once again you have a wife. I have been the mistress before; I have no desire to repeat that."

No desire . . . no desire . . .

"No desire?" There, I repeated her words, to my own horror. I could not seem to control what I said. It must be the wine.

"No desire to be in that position," she clarified, a smile playing about her lips. She seemed pleased that I had objected to her words. "It is not an enviable one. But I wanted to see you compete; as you said in your invitation, I was at the first competition, and it would be fitting if I saw you now."

"I gather you saw the ten-horse race," I said.

"Yes. But it was less than happy for me. For a moment I thought I had traveled all this way just to see you get killed. I cannot . . . There are no words for my joy when you crawled out and back into the chariot."

She got up from the couch, came over, and knelt in front of me, taking my hands. "You are safe. I came here tonight to take your hands and hold them again, giving thanks that I can, that you are uninjured. I needed to assure myself that you were still as you always were."

The touch of her hands was too much. I stood and pulled her up with me, embracing her. "I am here. As I always have been." I kissed her deeply and fiercely; the years apart fell away, and we were both as we always had been, all the intervening events and people faded, dissipated into the night air.

She returned my kiss hungrily, no hesitation, no holding back. We were together again; in some ways we had never really been apart.

As had happened the first unexpected time we had been together, we were swiftly in bed and ravenously making love. Time enough later for talk.

And talk we did, in the languid hours that followed. All the questions that had once seemed so important now did not. I did not want to demand answers, only let her speak so I could understand her. I lay staring up at the ceiling, just dimly visible, listening to her.

"I have seen you many times but you have not seen me, since—since we parted," she said. She turned toward me, putting her head on my shoulder, where I could hear her soft voice.

"I saw you at the relief station after the Fire," I said. "I remember saying something stiff and stupid. But it was so awkward."

"And this isn't?" She pressed her naked body up to mine.

I laughed. "No, it isn't."

"I felt awkward, too," she admitted. "I couldn't fill out forms properly at the aid station, I was so confused at suddenly seeing you."

"That was the last time I saw you," I said. "But we have come close. There was that time Poppaea summoned you, knowing I was away.

And I did want to thank you for your warning about Senecio." I leaned over and kissed her again. "There. I have thanked you."

"I have seen you other times, though," she said. "I came to the two funerals. You passed right by me and didn't see me."

"So you have made a habit of watching me from a crowd?" I asked. "That is what you have done here, too."

"It was a safe way to see you."

"Why was it important to see me?"

She fell silent. I thought she would not answer. Then she whispered, "Because I love you."

The unexpected words sang through me. But she took my silence for disbelief.

"When we parted, I said I would always love you. I meant it. I keep my promises. Don't you remember my words?"

"Yes," I said. "But at the same time you said you would not marry me."

"I said I wouldn't marry a man who lied, as you did."

"I don't lie anymore. I don't need to. I lied only because I had no choice at the time. So that is over. Is that my only fault in your eyes? If so, then you need to find another one to keep us apart."

"Are you forgetting you are married?"

"This wife is not like Poppaea. She would not resent you."

She laughed. "Oh, Lucius. You are still Lucius, very naïve about women!"

"Ah. How good it is to hear you call me Lucius again." I pulled her close to me. "Whatever we want to call ourselves, and whatever we are to each other, please do not leave me again."

"But—my work is in Velitrae."

"I did not mean we had to be together all the time. Only that we should never be apart in our souls again."

"At our first parting, I promised to never leave you. And in my own way I never have," she said.

LXV

ACTE

The night seemed short; the night seemed very long, as when Zeus had stretched one night into three as he lay with Alcmene and conceived his heroic son Hercules. It could not have been too long for me; would that it had been longer.

It was hot, but a cooling breeze blew across us from the terrace, fanning us solicitously. I could hardly believe that I was here, with him, like this.

But isn't that what you wanted? I asked myself. Why did you come all the way here? To hide in a crowd and look at him secretly, as you have done back in Rome?

Yes, partly, I answered in my mind. That was safest. But finally that was unsatisfactory. Let him dismiss me, so I can be free of him, I thought. And the only way for that to happen was to reveal myself to him.

He was asleep. I could tell from his breathing. He lay absolutely still. He must be exhausted, with an exhaustion an ordinary citizen could never know. As I had from the beginning, when he was only eleven and I seventeen, I wanted to protect him.

In my mind I could still see the boy he was, called Lucius then, lost in that crowd at the palace, wandering about. I, a servant in the royal household, had offered him a goblet of drink. He remarked that I did not look Roman. Astute of him, as I was from Lycia. The evening was to celebrate his mother's marriage to the emperor Claudius. He and Claudius's children were hauled up on stage to acknowledge the union. All three looked miserable, as they were.

Later, when he had been renamed Nero and forced to marry Claudius's daughter Octavia, I had revealed a palace plot to murder him—not the first and not the last. By then he was seventeen and I twenty-three, and we became lovers.

Anyone but Lucius—Nero—would have accepted our status as the traditional emperor-mistress one, but he wanted to marry me and tried to bring it about. At the time he was still too young and inexperienced to know how to get his own way against the advisers and gatekeepers. But it was a romantic and valiant try. By the time he could have brought it about, it was I who backed away. But had I ever, really?

And back to the question: why am I here? What does it achieve?

The answer: do I have to justify happiness, even fleeting happiness?

He sighed and rolled over, his arms seeking me. Drowsy, he smoothed my hair and traced his fingers down my cheek. Burying his face against my neck, he kissed my throat, sending shivers down my arms. Languidly, we came together again, a slow contrast to our first heated coupling.

The dawn was coming; I could hear it in the faint morning noises of birds outside, could feel a change in the breeze wafting over us. In the light of day, what would we do?

As the room lightened, I could study his profile as he lay on his back, eyes closed. I knew he was not asleep, just stretching out our secret time as long as possible. But it could not last much longer.

I raised myself on an elbow and peered down at him. "We have to get up," I whispered.

He groaned. Then opened his eyes and smiled. "Do we have to?"

"I do," I said. "I must be dressed if I want to avoid a scandal."

He laughed. "It's been a long time since you have been in the royal quarters, and your concern is out of date," he said. "There is no scandal, no matter what I do. It has taken me years to find that out. The dispensation comes with the word 'emperor.'"

"It's been seven years since I was here," I said. "Perhaps you are right. Finding a woman in your room pales in comparison to the other things you have been accused of in those seven years. In fact, people might be relieved that you have embraced such a mundane transgression."

He laughed, a true laugh, and got up, grabbing his discarded tunic and pulling it over his head.

"Your wardrobe has changed," I said, pointing to the vivid flowers on the knee-length garment.

"Do you like it?" he asked with a grin.

"It's different," I said.

"I feel at home in it," he said, smoothing its wrinkles.

"And what about your hair?" His hair was a mass of tumbled waves past his shoulders.

He tossed his head. "It gave the visiting senators something to gossip about," he said, seemingly unbothered by this.

Oh, Lucius! Do you not see? "What did they come for?" I asked.

"To see the games, of course. At least that was their excuse, although when I questioned them they did not seem to know much about them. Their real reason was to see me and tell me to come back."

"Perhaps you should consider it."

He frowned. "Let us not talk about Rome now," he said. "It is far away and I do not wish to think about it."

Oh, Lucius! Do you not see? "Very well," I said. I put my arms around him. Oh, how I wanted to protect him—from himself.

We had a leisurely breakfast on the terrace, speaking of other things.

"Whom did you travel with?" he asked me.

"A company from Velitrae," I told him. "People curious to see the games and visit Greece."

"When?" he asked, sipping his juice, looking at me.

"We arrived in time for the games at Olympia, a week ago."

"How long will you stay?"

"We are leaving in a few days," I said. "Such a long way to travel for such a short time, I know."

He leaned over to me, reaching for my hand but not taking his eyes from mine. "Will you stay and come to Isthmia with me?"

It hurt to say, "Alas, I cannot. My business . . ."

He sighed. "I have two important projects to unveil at Isthmia. I wish you could be there to see them . . ."

"It cannot be. But tell me of them," I said gently.

He rose. "I will later, then. Now I must get ready for the final ceremony, receiving my victory wreath. You *will* come to that!"

We walked to the Temple of Zeus, out in bold daylight together. But once there, we separated as he took his place with the victors in front of the temple and I joined the spectators, a noisy and jubilant crowd, waiting to shower the winners with flower petals. I stood on tiptoe to see him bow his head for the wreath of wild olive branches to be placed on it, with the announcement that Nero Claudius Caesar Augustus Germanicus had won the crown for the ten-horse chariot race. His voice ringing through the crowd, he cried out that he accepted it in the name of Rome and the Roman people.

There were a great many awards still to be handed out; it took all morning. After that there would be an official banquet for the victors, and the two hundred and eleventh Olympiad would be formally declared at an end.

Buoyant and with shining eyes, surrounded by his household and the senators, Nero sought me out afterward. The gray-green wreath sat proudly on his brow. Loose petals covered his hair and shoulders, flung by the cheering crowd.

"It belongs there," I said, reaching out to touch it. He was so supremely happy, believing that he had earned his honors, not letting himself doubt that the judges were fair. He needed this above all things, and in my eyes it made him achingly innocent.

He glanced around at his company, quickly introducing me to some of them—Epaphroditus, Phaon, Nymphidius. I might have known them in passing long ago, but my memories of them were fuzzy. Then I almost fainted as Poppaea appeared—I went cold.

"Sabina," said Nero. "Or, as previously known, Sporus."

The person—it could not possibly have been Poppaea herself—nodded in acknowledgment. Gulping, I knew I must ask later about Sporus.

"You are all coming to the victors' dinner," he said. "All!"

✦ ✦ ✦

It was a rowdy affair, with boisterous abandon as the athletes could eat and drink all they wished, their victories now secure, and their friends could indulge to the maximum along with them. I watched Nero bounce around gleefully, greeting everyone familiarly, whether he knew them or not. The women stayed on the sides, looking on keenly. Statilia stood in dignified silence, by herself.

Should I approach her? What was the protocol? Was there any? What should I say? *Hello, Empress. I enjoyed last night with your husband.*

As if she had read my mind, she walked over to me—no hurry, just a deliberate pace.

Had I seen her before? No, I did not think so. She had come into his life after I had gone. She was a mature woman, probably a bit older than he was, like me—why was he drawn to older women? Was he even aware of this? Poppaea had been older, too. Poppaea . . .

"I believe you are Claudia Acte?" she asked. She had a deep, soothing voice.

"Yes, Empress," I said, lowering my head.

"I have been waiting for you," she said. "It was just a matter of time."

I bristled at this. As if I were a dog who had come to a whistle. "I am not sure what you mean," I replied, trying to keep my voice neutral.

"Only that when there is a longing, it finds its way home."

I let the silence stretch out.

"I have heard about you," she said. "Oh, not from him, but from others. You left a deep impression on many." She laughed. "You turned him down. Not many emperors have that experience."

Why was she so sanguine about it? Did she not feel bad—either about taking a man who had been turned down or that his feelings had been hurt? The first would mean she had no envy, the second that she didn't care about him.

Again, as if she read my thoughts, she said, "It was good for him. There should always be someone or something one can't have. Or else we are sated; better to always be a little hungry."

"You are wise," I said. Best leave it at that. I watched her shrewd but nonjudgmental eyes, with their slight lines at the edges.

"Yes, I am," she replied, answering my thought. "And so you know, I can read people, and that's a gift and a curse. So I knew what you were—probably—thinking, and I answered it."

"You are frightening," I blurted out.

"There, I didn't need to read that," she said. "Don't be frightened. Without this gift, I would not have survived. You do not need it; you will survive. You are a wise person, too. He is in good hands."

"He is not in my hands," I said.

"He is in both our hands," she said. "But yours are stronger than mine."

In keeping with her wisdom, she did not visit his quarters that night, leaving us to ourselves.

"What an understanding wife you have," I said. "You are right; she is different from Poppaea."

Having carefully removed his victory wreath and set it reverently on a stand, he lay down on a couch and propped up his legs. "You have heard the tired old joke, *My wife doesn't understand me?* This one does," he said, laughing.

"It was considerate of her," I said. "She will have you back shortly. My party is leaving in a few days."

"If only you could come to Isthmia," he said. He waited for me to say something. "But since you cannot, let us enjoy these last days. The last days here, at any rate. Olympia will remain the place where I have been happiest in all the world, with you here to crown it with a joy above the victory crown for me."

LXVI

NERO

Olympia was quickly drained of people and excitement. The temporary buildings, erected for visitors and ceremonies, were dismantled. Only the workers and officials stayed on, and they would soon depart, too, and Olympia would revert back into a sleepy green site, slumbering through the next four years before awakening.

Most of my party departed for Isthmia and nearby Corinth, but Acte and I lingered behind. I still could hardly believe that she was here with me, after being a phantom in my mind for so long. But soon, like Olympia, she would disappear, like a dream.

As the grounds emptied out, we explored them, walking beside the two rivers and seeing how different they were—the Alpheios was slow and sluggish, the Kladeos unruly and rushing. From the top of the Kronos hill we could see the sea and liked to sit on a rock at the very top, staring out. There was always a cool breeze that soothed our faces, blew our hair, and rustled through the pines all around us.

"Across that water lies Rome," she said.

"I know," I said. "A different world."

"This one isn't real, you know," she said. "The real one is across the water."

"They are both real," I said. "I prefer this one."

"You can't live in it. It is a world that has passed, that rises like a ghost every four years and then fades away."

We climbed down off the rock and hunted for a level place to have our picnic. We found one under a large, twisted pine that had made a soft cushion of dropped needles all around us. I spread out a blanket, and we opened the packages of food and set out the jugs of wine.

Feeling closer to her than I had to anyone, able to speak with no censor in my mind, as if we were one person, I said, "I am thinking of not returning."

She looked stricken. "That cannot be. That is irresponsible. That is unthinkable."

"I am thinking it."

"Stop thinking it. You cannot desert your command. It would be—treason."

I laughed. "How can an emperor commit treason?"

"You could, if you desert your post."

"I want to be happy. I am happier here than I have ever been."

"You sound like a five-year-old. Grow up, Lucius! You are no longer Lucius, but Nero. You cannot go back to that child."

I leaned over and poured us each a cup of wine.

"You are always the voice of reason," I said, downing my cup and refilling it.

I set out pears, cheese, and small loaves. There was even the famous thyme honey, which I had told her about. I spread some on the bread and offered her a slice. She took it and munched.

"You should know," she said, "the senators were right. There is unrest in Rome; your absence is becoming a problem. Only you can restore order there."

"Is there an actual breakdown of order?"

"No," she admitted.

"Then I shall come when I am ready," I said, sounding more firm about it than I really was.

"What of Ecloge and Alexandra?" she asked, pointedly changing the subject. "I was able to send you that message about Senecio through Alexandra. Is she still there, and well?"

"Yes, both of them. As steady as the north star. Never changing." At least something was.

We nibbled on the first grapes of the season—still not quite ripe—

and some local goat cheese with herbs. Lying there on the blanket in the green shadows, it was easy to feel that peace itself was palpable. I could reach out and grasp it. I took a handful of needles and squeezed them, loosing the sharp smell of resin, mixed with a dusty dryness. "The crowns at Isthmia are of pine," I said.

"Stop trying to tempt me!" she said, smiling. "I have to return to my business. You know that. But I would like to be there to see— whatever it is you are announcing."

"One is an engineering project, the other a political decree. But"— I reached out and touched her cheek—"you will just have to wait and see, like the rest of the world, since you won't come. You might be surprised—I do think of revolutionary projects that are beneficial as well."

She shifted on the blanket. "Tell me, who—or what—is this Spo-rus person?"

"He was a slave in Poppaea's household who resembles her," I said.

"Is that all?" She looked pointedly at me.

"His grief for Poppaea became extreme. He . . . wanted to be-come her."

"For himself, or for you?" She was relentless.

"For both of us," I admitted. "I think . . . it was a form of mourning."

"Has it helped?"

"A little. But in some ways it has made it worse. I wish it had never happened," I burst out. "But it cannot be undone."

"I see."

But how could she, really?

"Let me explain . . . as best I can. There are stories of statues that are exact replicas of a dead person. And there are ghosts that can look like them but cannot be touched. And if there could be such a thing as an apparition that was *almost* the person, would that do? No. Ultimately it is a tease and a torment. So, no, it has not helped—either of us."

"I see," she repeated.

"But he has suffered enough, so I pretend it has helped. Now do you understand?"

"I think I do. My heart is heavy for you and for him."

"Thank you." I drank another cup of wine. I could not change the subject fast enough.

Soon a warmth spread inside me, courtesy of the wine. I saw her leaning back against the trunk of the old pine, her dark hair shining, her beauty undimmed from the first time I had seen her. She seemed immune to aging.

"Are you a goddess?" I burst out.

"What?"

"They don't age, and neither do you. You must be part goddess."

She laughed. "Not that I know of," she said. "On the other hand, we know you are part god. Wasn't Caesar descended from Aphrodite, and are you not also from that branch of the family?"

I laughed. "So many generations back, there cannot be much god left in me."

Here in our secluded mountain retreat, I was overcome with my desire for her, especially as the day of our parting came closer, and we were more alone here than any other place. I rolled onto the blanket, looking up through the branches of pine, feeling the needles crunching under my back. I pulled her over to me.

"Remember Sublaqueum?" I said. "When we slept out in the woods?"

"Oh, yes," she said. "Oh, yes."

"Years have passed since then, but I feel the same," I said. "And want you just as much."

"I will always love you," she said, her words giving me supreme happiness. "And I will never leave you."

"Here." I reached into a small package I had brought all the way up there and took out a bracelet of ivory and ebony. I fitted it on her wrist. "Whenever you want to see me, send this to me and it will serve without words. And we will be together."

LXVII

Corinth is the premier commercial city of Greece, a cosmopolitan port that is home to both the most refined citizens of the land and the human dregs of society who crawl in from the surrounding area. That gave it a pulsing, vibrant life, but after the quiet beauty of Olympia, I found it jarring. The city, destroyed and then rebuilt by Rome, served as Roman headquarters in Greece.

It had the usual temples, agora, theater, stoas, and council house. The sanctuary for the Isthmian Games was nearby, almost abutting on the city, making these games urban competitions, unlike Delphi, Nemea, and Olympia.

"The prostitutes will be setting up booths of convenience near the agora," said Tigellinus. "If the customers can't find the ladies, the ladies will come to them!" He was chewing noisily on a pear. "Successful businesses know how to cater to their customers. Convenience, convenience, is the key!" He tossed the core into a basket. "Well, Caesar, what is it today? We have settled everyone at last. Most are on the plain a mile or so from town."

"We should go out to look at the isthmus," I said. "The place where the canal will be dug." I had sent Roman engineers ahead for preliminary measurements to see if my grand project was feasible. "Are the prisoners of war here yet?" General Vespasian, from his campaign against the rebels in the Galilee, had promised six thousand Jewish prisoners of war to dig the canal.

"They are just arriving on three ships. We will settle them near the place where they will be working."

"Then it will begin!" My long-dreamed project was going to be realized. "I want to inspect the site before ground is broken. Let's go there this morning."

We rode out through the city, its markets and stalls doing crowded business. The theater seats were empty of patrons, but merchants had claimed them, spreading out blankets with their wares. The air was tinged with the smell of the nearby sea.

My mind was still filled with images of Olympia and my parting from Acte. But I felt a leap of excitement when we reached the edge of the isthmus, where the sea touched the shore and where workers would soon be digging. We dismounted and walked up the hill before us to its crest and looked down at the tiny four-mile strip of land separating the two bodies of water. The ridge where we stood was some hundred feet high, and higher yet in the middle. I kicked the soil; it was shallow and underneath was hard rock. But was it this way all the way down?

"We will have to drill shafts to see exactly what sort of rock we are dealing with and how deep it goes," I said. If it was this hard all the way down, the task would be very challenging. No wonder no one had been able to do it.

"If you can do it, you will be lauded as a genius. If you fail, you will be castigated as a fool," said Tigellinus, scraping at the soil with his hands, baring the rock.

"I'm used to that," I said. I pointed to the site below. "We will start the digging from both sides and the workers will meet in the middle."

"I heard a so-called expert from Egypt say that the water levels on each side are different and if you join them you will flood Greece," said Tigellinus.

"I have brought in real engineers, the Roman kind, who are true experts in water levels, to check on this. After all, our aqueducts are engineering marvels and demand great knowledge of water behavior."

I turned slowly to see the entire panorama. Before me stretched the Peloponnese; to my left was the Aegean Sea; to my right the Bay of

Corinth, with the city of Corinth nestled beside it. I turned in the opposite direction, where the mainland of Greece lay, with Athens and Mount Olympus. A goodly land. A land soon to be free. I saw it all and felt my heart swelling with what was to come.

The games opened with great solemnity, and I was hailed as Sol, the new sun risen to illuminate Greece. The competition had been held elsewhere for many years and was only now returned to its original site, the sanctuary of Poseidon, because I was coming. It was under the auspices and in honor of Poseidon, god of the sea, fitting because of the location. His sacred pine grew nearby and provided the branches for the victors' crowns.

My quarters were in the city, a large palace complex located near the theater. Statilia had quietly moved back in with me, discreetly never mentioning the reason for her voluntary absence in Olympia.

"The last lap," she said, settling herself on an elaborately carved couch provided for our comfort. She tucked her legs under her gown and waved a goblet of wine in her right hand. "And then home."

Home. Where was home, to me? The question had assumed increasing urgency and needed to be answered. Soon.

"Yes." I poured myself a goblet and joined her on the couch. "I have a few events here, but mainly I am content just to watch." I was honestly exhausted from all the other competitions, one after another, month after month. It had seemed reasonable when I planned it; now I saw how unrealistically grueling it was. Normally the succession of contests were staggered out over a four-year period, and with good reason. By now the number of people in my company had dwindled and only a stalwart few Romans remained. The field of competitors had also thinned, and most here would be local.

But the main event had nothing to do with athletics. Only I knew what that was, and I would hold it close until the day itself.

"That's unlike you," she said. "But you have the canal project to initiate, and perhaps that's enough for one place."

I twirled the goblet in my hand. Its bubbles swirled, making a little vortex inside: my own miniature Charybdis. "I am getting used to local Greek wine," I said, savoring its sharp resin taste. "And it took some getting used to."

"I'll be glad to get our own back again," she said, draining her goblet. "Won't you?"

"I don't know," I said. "The taste of Greek wine will always be inextricably mixed with memories of the games."

"Surely you have better ways of remembering them." She laughed her deep, throaty laugh.

Oh, yes. I smiled. "You are right," I said.

She poured herself another goblet. "I am a glutton for punishment," she said. "Or perhaps I just like wine. Even this." She sipped it.

"In the two-day pause in the middle of the games," I said, "I am planning the ceremony for the canal. The engineers have completed their plans and measurements and pronounced it ready to proceed. There is no difference in the water levels on each side after all. And I myself will dig the first shovelfuls."

She set the goblet down and looked at me. "Your eyes are shining. You are never happier than when you have a new project. I hope it succeeds. I shall watch you dig the dirt with pride."

"The shovel will be of gold," I said.

"Of course!" She laughed and squeezed my hand.

Sol himself beamed down upon me in symbolic approval of his chosen one as the company of officials gathered for the inauguration of the Isthmus Canal. Dressed in a purple toga for the occasion, to underscore its solemnity (quite a concession from me), I looked at the sparkling water around us and addressed the company.

"Noble officials of Greece, honored Romans, citizens of Corinth, I, Nero Claudius Caesar Augustus Germanicus, Imperator of Rome, here bequeath a gift to you: a canal to allow ships to pass directly from the Bay of Corinth to the Aegean Sea. No longer will ships have to endure the stormy danger of sailing around Cape Malea of the Peloponnese. This canal has been dreamed of, and needed, for centuries.

Your own king Demetrius, Julius Caesar, the emperor Caligula, all wanted to build it, but none succeeded. What they could not do, I will, with the help of the gods."

I then led a series of carefully worded propitiatory odes to the gods of the area: Amphitrite, Poseidon, Melicertes, and Leucothea.

"And now, the first earth is broken." I picked up the golden shovel and held it aloft, then turned to a ready plot of earth and dug enough to fill an entire basket. I hoisted it onto my shoulder and carried it to a place where I could empty it. Ten other men, selected for reasons of protocol, followed me, and the mound of fresh-turned soil grew.

There was a stirring, a murmur, cheers. Then came a faint voice from the crowd. "Apollonius of Tyana says you will never sail through it."

A gasp, then silence. I looked around, searching for the speaker. "Who is Apollonius of Tyana?" I said with a laugh. "I say this: Apollonius of Tyana will never sail through it."

People then laughed, and the work began in earnest. But later Epaphroditus said, "That was a bad omen. I didn't like it. You recovered yourself well, though."

We were gathered at what was supposed to be a celebration of the successful event. "Omens, omens." I shrugged. "Anyone can quote something and pretend it's an omen. I thought it was just outright rude."

"It certainly was that," he agreed.

Statilia glided over. "It went well," she said. "I would not trouble myself to remember that man's disruption. It was nothing. *He* is nothing." She stroked my shoulder. "The gold shovel glittered in the sun! It hurt my eyes."

The games continued, with a heightened mood after the announcement of the canal. As the final day approached, I sent out word that there would be a special ceremony in the stadium before the customary victors' banquet.

I had closeted myself until late at night agonizing over the exact wording of my speech. It seemed impossible to convey precisely the weight, the significance and momentousness of what I was doing. I consulted secretly with legal and constitutional experts but told no one else. My mind was at ease that all was in order for my command, and that it would stand, but I could not predict the reaction to it.

Once again, for the second time in as many days, I put on my most formal imperial toga. I adjusted a gold wreath on my head—although I had won pine wreaths, I spoke to the people now as emperor, not a fellow competitor—and, clutching a copy of the speech, entered the stadium, where the last races had just been run. The crowd filled the banks and the track, thousands and thousands deep.

It was late in the day, and the sun sent slanting shadows across the field. A fresh breeze from the sea sprang up, a relief after the heat of midday.

The moment was here. I looked out and unrolled my speech. But I did not need to look at it. The short speech was burned into my memory.

"Men of Greece! I present you an unexpected gift, although since I am known for my magnanimity, perhaps nothing can be thought unexpected coming from me. But this is a gift so vast you could not hope to ask for it."

The silence was profound as they waited to hear what it was. But I would draw it out a bit longer. "If only I could have bestowed this when Greece was at its zenith, so that more people could have benefited from it. But I make this benefaction not through pity but through goodwill. I thank your gods, whose watchful providence I have always experienced both on sea and land, that they have afforded me the opportunity of so great a benefaction."

I stepped back and raised my arms high, up toward Sol. "Other emperors have freed cities. Nero alone frees a whole province!"

If silence could deepen, it did now. Time seemed suspended.

"From henceforth you are liberated and freed from Rome and Roman taxation. This is freedom you have never experienced, as you have been under the yoke of foreigners or one another for most of your history."

I then stepped down and through a path of people that opened as silently as a door in a dream. How long they remained speechless I would not know, but it was important to leave before a cacophony of voices and questions would break out. Let them talk and react among themselves. Like a god, I could make my pronouncement and then withdraw, leaving humans to interpret it. I smiled. The victory banquet would be very different now. But I would not attend.

Have you lost your mind?" cried Tigellinus in the privacy of my rooms, where I spent the hours others were at the banquet. "What have you done?"

Close beside him was Epaphroditus, his face a map of worry. "This is a disaster! What will Rome say? How can you do this without consulting the Senate?"

I had foreseen all the objections and put them to my legal advisers. "I didn't need their advice. And the Senate is an advisory body only, not a legislative one. Only I have the power to enact laws. I *am* Rome."

"But oh! Oh! The loss of revenue. That is unthinkable, it's . . ." "Treasonous" trembled on his tongue and was replaced by "*irresponsible.*"

"Greece has been a senatorial province," I said. "I will replace it with the imperial province of Sardinia. The Senate should be pleased with the substitution. The truth is, Greece is a poor country and didn't contribute much to the imperial treasury."

"But it sets a horrible example! What do you think the Judean revolt has been about? They want to be free of Rome as well. And have you forgotten the Boudicca revolt? Britain wanted to be free, too. This is madness! Take it back!" said Tigellinus.

"I cannot. Then I truly would appear mad, someone who is unstable and doesn't know his own mind. And I do not want to take it back. It was a gift. If those other countries want a similar gift, let them earn it! Let them be creative geniuses. I don't see any poetry from Britain or great artworks from Judea."

"They have other strengths," said Phaon, who had just joined us. "Territory, goods we can trade, warriors."

"But the Greeks are unique," I said. "Their gifts are of a different species."

Suddenly Statilia, who had been sitting quietly in the corner, sprang up. "You have blown your admiration for Greek art to ludicrous proportions. Yes, they paint lovely vases—or did. Yes, they carved beautiful statues of marble. But have you noticed? That was long ago. Now they are just like everyone else and only living on past glories. Everyone but you can see that! You have become blinded to the reality of today."

I turned around and looked at her. "Only a wife can speak to her husband in that way." I laughed and addressed the men. "I imagine your wives have taken you to task a time or two as well."

"If you mean that I should be ignored, then say it!" she said. "But think of what I have said. You gave yourself away when you lamented that Greece was no longer at its zenith. It isn't, and hasn't been for a long time. You are in love with a ghost!" She then withdrew and left me with the advisers.

"What does this mean, legally?" asked Epaphroditus. "And when does it take effect?"

"It means that Greece is free of tribute to Rome and can govern itself, within limits. We do not surrender our right to include it in the empire, and Corinth will continue as a Roman city."

"A small consolation," said Phaon. "That we are not expelled, at least."

Winter was closing in. We would stay in Greece until the seas opened for safe sailing in the spring. I allowed myself to imagine staying there forever, of sending everyone else back. But it was pure fantasy, I knew.

As the winds grew in ferocity I often went to the site where the canal was being dug. Watching the waves whipped up into a fury, I thought how useful the canal would be, sparing sailors from the open hostile sea. The workmen had carved an image of Hercules in the rock, as if to say, *This is the thirteenth labor of Hercules.* Certainly it ranked with the other twelve in difficulty.

I was utterly unprepared when Helios, the freedman I had appointed my deputy in Rome, appeared at my quarters, pale as an apparition.

"Are you real?" I cried, leaping to my feet.

"Yes, Caesar," he said. "All too real, and battered from my journey."

"I don't wonder. This is not the season for safe travel."

"I didn't have the luxury of waiting," he said. "You must return to Rome with me. Now."

"Calm down," I said. "Sit." I called for someone to bring him food and drink. "Catch your breath." I sat down, trying to model serenity. But my heart was racing. What was this?

I let him breathe for a few minutes. Then I said, as gently as possible, "Now, what is this about?"

"There is a plot. Another conspiracy. I can't control it. You must return and put it down, or there will be nothing to return to."

He had been sending importuning letters for my return for some time, but they had not been specific.

"Who is it?"

"A group of senators. Malcontents. And the news of the Liberation of Greece has incensed them."

"It takes a long time to get here," I said. "Your news is old by now."

"I left seven days ago."

That was well nigh impossible. "Unless you flew with Hermes' sandals, I cannot believe it."

"Believe it. I risked my life to come here to fetch you, Caesar. Rough seas, a near shipwreck—but I am here. If I could have flown, I would have."

I was touched. I was also alarmed. "It will be equally difficult to return now. Perhaps that is why they have stirred up the conspiracy, assuming that word won't reach me, and even if it does, I cannot get back in time to do anything."

"Undoubtedly that is what they think."

Immediately I made up my mind. "Then they will get a surprise." I never shied from a challenge.

LXVIII

We set out the next morning in high seas that battered the dock and turned the boat into a bucking horse. Spray flung itself inland, and the foam left behind was thick as a snowfall. I had spoken of the protection the gods of Greece had given me on land and sea. Now I hoped they would continue to do so, as I was flirting with death to board that ship.

We left from the somewhat sheltered inland channel, but the moment we hit the open Adriatic Sea, the waves rose up like monsters and at one point almost dashed us on a rocky shore. It loomed closer and closer, with black jagged teeth waiting to bite, but another gust of wind blew us past it at the last instant. I clung to the rail, limp with relief. The whole trip was beset with storms, and when we finally landed at Brundisium I was too drained to have any thought other than the feeling I had escaped a dire fate. Now I had to go forward and confront another dire fate in the making.

The land journey back over the Appian Way retraced the earlier, jolly trip when we were carefree and had the games before us. It had been summer then, and summer in our minds as well; now it was ugly, icy, muddy, and inhospitable. And all the way I wondered what I would find when we got to Rome. The wagon rumbled and slid over the slippery stones while we shivered inside.

What did I expect as we approached the environs? Three and a half years ago I had crested a hill to behold the Fire. I half expected today's danger to manifest itself palpably, to paint the sky black. But Rome slumbered benignly under a leaden winter sky, looking harmless when we arrived sixteen days after leaving Corinth.

I entered the palace, which had also slumbered, waiting for its master to return. How odd it felt to be back here, as if the Nero who had lived here was another person entirely. It was familiar but not familiar; the furniture was the same but somehow the setting felt different. The servants were effusive in welcoming me back, and, dazed, I walked around the apartments, touching this and that to convince myself it was still there, to anchor myself to it, but my mind was still in Greece.

The next morning, having slept off the exhaustion of the journey, I woke up truly back in Rome.

I quickly called a meeting with all my freedmen administrators. In addition to Helios, there were five others, but he was the one with the highest authority. Outside the palace, the December winds were howling, driving sleet against the windows. Even in the morning, it was gloomy enough to require lamps to be lit.

I sat rigid in a chair, watching them. They were unimpressive in appearance but had quick minds. Nonetheless they were widely disliked by the senatorial class and considered upstarts.

"Let us begin with the conspiracy discovered that brought me back here. I want the details," I said.

"We dealt with it," said Halotus, the next in importance behind Helios. Helios gave a start.

"You did?" he asked.

"You have been gone more than three weeks. It was urgent that we move at once. The suspects have been executed." When Helios did not respond, Halotus added, "Caesar, you gave us power to act in your name. And we have done so when we deemed it necessary, while you were away."

"Just how many of these executions have there been?" I asked.

"Some . . . oh, perhaps twenty," Halotus said. "We could not tolerate the merest suggestion of a plot. Rome had to be kept safe for you."

"To be honest, Caesar," said another man, Polyclitus, "most of these malcontents were from the old aristocracy, a faction always hostile to you. However, our . . . severity . . . in dealing with their members has hardened them further against you."

"We have had to rely on informers, which made us disliked, of course. But if it were not for informers, how would we know about the traitors? They, and their sympathizers, will hardly turn themselves in," added Halotus.

I groaned inwardly. What had I come back to? This was ominous.

"What else?" There must be more, and I must hear it.

"The grain ships have been erratic in arriving, and people are short of bread. The ongoing war in Judea has disrupted shipping." Although Vespasian was making steady progress, the war was far from over, and the region was in turmoil.

So now the common people had reason to be angry with me as well.

"I shall order extra ships to take the place of the ones tied up in supplying Judea," I said. At least that should alleviate the acute problem of the grain here in Rome.

"And there have been anonymous placards and graffiti appearing on statues and walls," said a short, keen-eyed man named Coenus.

"What do these say?" I asked.

He was reluctant to answer, pretending he didn't remember the exact wording, just that they were critical of me.

"Bring me a report quoting them, please," I said. "But take them down once you have read them, and scrub off the writing on walls. What else?"

"That is all, Caesar."

"It is enough to keep us busy making amends," I said. "But I have plans to share my Greek trip with the entire populace, and that should please them. We begin anew. It is almost New Year's Day, when a fresh, empty calendar awaits whatever we choose to write upon it."

It was customary for the legionaries to pledge fealty to me on New Year's Day, and for me to appear before them in white robes shot through with gold thread to accept their allegiance. And so I stood on the Rostra on that chilly morning, dazzled by the winter sun striking the frost on the white monuments, making them twinkle like stars. Before me stretched rows of soldiers filling the entire Forum.

I was flanked by Eagle standards on each side and by censers emitting clouds of incense to mark this as a binding and sacred rite. In unison thousands of voices united to recite the pledge, the *sacramentum.*

"In the name of Jupiter Optimus Maximus, I swear allegiance to Imperator Nero Claudius Caesar Augustus Germanicus as supreme commander. I will obey the emperor willingly and implicitly in all his commands. I will not depart my commander in order to take flight or through fear, nor to retreat from the line except to recover or obtain a weapon, strike a foe, or rescue a friend. I will always be ready to sacrifice my life for the Roman empire."

I in turn said, "I accept your pledge of loyalty and vow to lead you in good faith and with courage."

Greece was magnificent in its faded glory, but Rome, in its muscular grandeur, inspired awe, even in me, this morning.

Coenus delivered his compilation of the insulting graffiti and placards, as well as the names of the people who had put them up, thinking they were anonymous. But informers could ferret out everything. I turned the list over to the Senate but told them not to pursue punishment for the culprits. I had incurred enough animosity to want to avoid stirring up more. And publicizing the taunts might inspire more of them.

Clearly there was much going on beneath the surface in Rome; these visible signs of discontent were just a warning. There is never just one mouse in a house, although you may see only one.

My long absence had given the mice a chance to flourish. The senators had been right to worry about it. But I had brushed their misgivings aside, so eager was I to depart for Greece.

So things were now taken in hand, with Rome settled, or seemingly settled, and I could embark on the final leg of the Greek tour, the customary *eiselasis,* the triumphal return home of the winning competitors. In Greece, their hometowns would tear an opening in the city walls and parade their victors through the streets, showering them with flowers and accolades, for the honor belonged not only to them but to their cities as well. In my case, I had accepted every victory in the name of the Roman people and the empire, and they deserved to share my prizes with me. I hoped, also, that in my return in this new year, the eight hundred and twenty-first year of Rome, I could renew my frayed bond with my subjects.

Antium being my actual birthplace, I had an *eiselasis* there and was wildly greeted by the townspeople; I had come home to them. Antium was always a refuge to me, a retreat that, with its sea vistas, promised horizons that were large beyond comprehension, and I treasured it.

Next I went to the place where I had been "born" as an artist when I had first performed on a public stage, Naples, and had a larger *eiselasis*, the entire city filled with ecstatic people. The citizens of Naples, always emotional and immoderate, showered me with so many flowers that the streets were knee deep in them, being trodden into treacherous footing before long. No matter to them; they would cheerfully clean it up as the proof of their extravagance.

But it was Rome that would have the greatest *eiselasis*, an adaptation of the Triumph, remade into a parade of artistic, not military, prizes.

This took careful planning; no aspect could be overlooked. The date of the Triumphal entry was announced, along with its Greek name, but I withheld any further details. To describe an event in advance is to dilute the impact of it on its day.

Sol was kind to me, his chosen son, on the day in February I selected for the event. He shone warmly; even though the leaves were not yet open, it felt like spring, not late winter. As a token of the traditional *eiselasis*, a small ceremonial breach was made in the city wall. Through it marched men carrying the wreaths, palms, and ribbons I had won, with placards citing where and when. Then, behind them, I entered the city, driving the gold Triumphal chariot of Augustus—that I had rescued from the Fire—wearing the Olympic crown of wild olive, and holding the Delphic one of laurel. I was greeted with such cheers and shouts that my ears rang, and flowers, ribbons, and sweetmeats rained down on me. Beside me in the chariot was not the slave muttering, "Remember you are mortal," as in a traditional Triumph, but a lyre player holding his instrument. Four white horses pulled the chariot, and I wore the purple and gold-starred robe of the Triumphator. Along the route the streets were sprinkled with saffron perfume. As we moved slowly through the Circus Maximus and then toward the Forum, the sun struck the half-finished statue of me that stood in the grounds of the Golden House.

Sol, thank you. I promise to give it your features.

Now in the Forum the monuments were hung with garlands, there were blazing torches, and rows of senators and legionaries stood at attention on their steps. They, and the common people surrounding them, shouted in unison, "Hail, Olympian Victor! Hail, Delphic Victor! Augustus! Augustus! Hail to Nero, our Hercules! Hail to Nero, our Apollo! The only Victor of the *Periodonikes*, the only Roman from the beginning of time! Augustus! Augustus! O, Divine Voice! Blessed are they that hear you."

It was head-spinning, but more than that, it vindicated my belief that Greece had been as much for them as for me. The stormy past between me and Rome had been healed, smoothed over, and now we could go forward together. Or so I wanted to believe.

The chariot of Augustus rolled slowly through the Forum, and I passed the spot where I had stood as a boy watching the Triumph of Claudius. Now I had converted his military model to an artistic one, completing my attempts to show Rome a different emphasis.

I came to the spot where the Triumphator customarily stopped the chariot and ascended on foot up the Capitoline Hill to the Temple of Jupiter to dedicate his crown. But I turned the other way; I stepped out and made my way up the Palatine to the Temple of Apollo. As I climbed the height, and looked back to see the sea of people thronging the Forum, exultation filled my being, higher and stronger than even the actual moments of victory in Greece. Nothing would ever eclipse this supreme moment for me.

I made my way to the restored Temple of Apollo that honored him in his guise as citharoede. The fresco fragment depicting him that I had found in the ashes after the Fire still hung in my palace and still spoke to me of art and its survival.

Now I fell on my knees and spoke to him. "Great Apollo, you have blessed me beyond all worthiness. I am your servant. Allow me to keep this mortal token of my victory in your sacred games, this laurel wreath, and accept this gold one in its stead." Respectfully I held them both up. "If I can keep this laurel near me, cut from your own tree, I know it will kindle the flame of inspiration in me, directly from your divine fire."

I looked up at his face, impassive and calm. I sensed that he would allow me this.

Rising, I walked to the nearby house of Augustus, standing proudly on its crest. Much of it had been spared in the Fire, and today all was restored. I had made my peace with my ancestor, and at last I believed he would have been proud of me after all.

Turning the corner around the house, I went to inspect the sacred laurel grove. But . . . where was it? Had it not always been just behind, and to the side of Augustus's house? Yes, it had stood there. And now—

In the knee-high grass I saw them: a row of stumps, long dead. I rushed over to them. Where was mine, where was mine? Had someone cut it? It had survived the Fire and was green and flourishing the last time I had visited it. I pawed through the grass, my purple robe catching on weeds, my heart pounding. Finally I found it. It had not been cut; it had withered. It still had branches at its lower stump, but they had blackened and it had no leaf buds, even though it was almost time for them to open.

It was dying, almost dead. The others behind it—Claudius's, Caligula's, Tiberius's, Augustus's—were further along in the process, barely looking like tree trunks at all, but mine was joining them. This was not the work of human hands but a sign from the gods.

The gods! The omen was lethal. The trees signified the very life of the family of the Claudians and the Julians. I was joining my deceased ancestors, or soon to. I gasped and blinked, hoping to dispel the sight of the shriveled dark leaves, but they refused to vanish.

I was suddenly very frightened, standing alone in the grove, the wind rustling in the grass around me.

LXIX

The *eiselasis* over, there remained but one other intensely personal task, one I longed to fulfill. Poppaea's shrine near Naples was now completed and must be dedicated; it would be the last earthly homage I could offer her. Yes, I had declared her a goddess; yes, I had promised the shrine. Now I would crown it by the rites there.

I took Sporus with me; he would want to be a part of the ceremonies. If people gaped, so be it. The important question was, what would Poppaea think of his being there? I believed she would be touched, as she was very fond of Sporus.

I left Rome behind, still exhilarated by the reception there but uneasy over whatever lingering resentment there was over the excesses of the freedmen while I had been away. And the sacred laurels . . . I had given orders that mine be tended, fertilized, and watered, in hopes of staving off its demise. Of course, I reassured myself, it truly did not mean doom. There could be another interpretation. I had planted it with Mother; perhaps the withering was reflective of the end of her influence on me, a sign that I was finally free of her and my own man.

Reaching Naples, we beheld its bay sparkling before us, with its singular singing blue, most sublime of colors, but impossible to capture in paint or tile. As always, the beauty of the site swept over me like a cloud, but one with a dark underside. Poppaea and I had been divinely happy here; now she was divine and I was alone in our favorite site.

The temple to the Divine Augusta Poppaea Sabina was beautifully simple; it had solid side walls and two columns in front, modeled after the earliest temples in Greece. A large statue of Poppaea filled most of the interior. Around the base ran the dedication, also simple: it stated her titles, adding that she was anointed by the goddess Venus and was the mother of the divine Claudia Augusta and the wife of Nero Claudius Caesar Augustus Germanicus. It omitted the most significant of all: beloved and mourned by her husband.

I had appointed ten priests to serve in perpetuity in rituals at the shrine, and they stood behind me, intoning prayers and putting the seal of officialdom on the ceremony. But I left them behind me and motioned for Sporus alone to follow me into the dim shrine to see the statue privately. We stepped over the high base and entered the hush of eternity.

She stood before us, transfigured into Venus herself. But then, she had always been Venus to me, a warm, breathing incarnation of her. Now she was frozen in cold marble. But there was no other form she could continue to exist in.

"It's a fine likeness," said Sporus.

"Likeness, yes," I answered. "As you are a likeness. This stirs up less controversy. But your likeness is more of an offering."

He blushed. "Mine will perish with me. This will endure."

Mother of the divine Claudia Augusta. My only child, my only daughter, ours together. Was that what the withering sacred laurel meant? The end of the dynasty if I did not have children to succeed me?

Bowing to the statue, we bid her farewell.

Once we were outside, after bringing the ceremony to an end, only then could I let my thoughts continue along the lines that had sprung up inside the shrine. It was disrespectful to Poppaea to think them near her statue, but the lack of living children was now a problem. I was not so young anymore—I had turned thirty just as I announced the Liberation of Greece. There was unrest in Rome, although so far no rival claimants to my throne. I had taken Statilia to wife partly because of the nagging recognition that I needed an heir. But nothing had come of it thus far. Soon we would be married two years. Did the problem lie with her or with me? Or had some vengeful god decided that I would not have children?

*   *   *

I decided to stay in Naples for a while. I wanted to finally catch my breath after the continuous events of the past few years, one after another. The Fire. The conspiracy. The death of Poppaea. The arrival of Tiridates. The Greek trip. One after another, tumbling almost altogether upon me. The truth was, I was tired. I needed to rest. And Naples was the ideal place for it. Except for her ghosts.

As chance would have it, it was the time of the Festival of Minerva that took place from March nineteenth to the twenty-third. I had thought never to be here at that time again, for that was the time that Mother had met her doom. At my hand. There were still graffiti and placards about it, and there was of course the pronouncement of the oracle at Delphi. It would never fade from public consciousness, as it had never faded from mine. This time nine years ago, the bay looked just as it did today, and looking out over it the deed seemed as close as today.

Feeling sullen and disaffected, I went to the gymnasium, which was hosting a series of wrestling matches. I was keenly interested in wrestling, and in Greece I had closely observed the best in the world. Watching now would be a distraction and welcome relief from the tenure of my thoughts.

I was so focused on the match that at first I did not hear the whisper in my ear. The shouts and cheering around me drowned it out. But it was repeated, more insistently. I turned and saw the official courier from Rome.

He carried dispatches from both Tigellinus and the Senate. I rose and left the meet, thinking, oh, what now? Could I not be left in peace to enjoy a wrestling match?

His face did not betray the message. He would let the documents do that for him. The first, from Tigellinus, was terse.

Caesar, there is trouble in Gaul. You should return to Rome as soon as possible.

The one from the Senate was more detailed, and more alarming.

The governor of Gaul, Gaius Julius Vindex, has declared an uprising against you.

He is calling on surrounding generals in Germany, Spain, and Portugal to join him. His motto is "liberation from the tyrant."

"Is there any return message, Caesar?" the courier asked.

"Not now," I said. "Later."

I was so stunned I could not make a reply then, so I turned away quickly.

An uprising! In Gaul, that supposedly pacified region. There had not been a rebellion there in years. They enjoyed all the privileges of Roman civilization. Why would this upstart claim he was under the thumb of a tyrant?

I was not afraid—not yet. There was no chance we could lose that province, the heart of Europe, and surrounded by legions in Germany. But it unnerved me nonetheless. Any rebellion is a threat to the stability of the empire, and we were already engaged in Judea. Vespasian's campaign had its successes, but the war was far from over there.

I left them and walked down to the quays, where the waves were high and the water was splashing. Cold spray misted my face. The bay was filled with decorated boats and merrymakers. Oh, yes, I remembered that. So happy were they nine years ago in the fateful week of the Festival of Minerva.

Vindex. Who was Vindex? I knew he was the son of one of the Gallic chieftains admitted to the Senate by Claudius. The family had seemed thoroughly Romanized. But perhaps you can take a barbarian out of the wilds but you cannot take the wilds out of a barbarian.

There was something else familiar about that name. Was it—could it have been—that he had come on the Greek tour? There were many Romans along, and he was a Roman citizen. Had I met him, talked with him? I conjured up an image of a huge, hulking, hairy man I had seen in the rear of the audience. But that was just the caricature of a barbarian. He was probably more sophisticated than that. After all, his father had been a senator . . . and yes, he himself had even served in the Senate at one point! I remembered that now. No wonder there was something familiar about him. The serpent!

In any case, it was of no matter. Vindex was no Boudicca, was no

Jewish zealot. Those provinces had genuine grievances against Rome, fretting under our yoke, but what gripe did Vindex have?

I soon found out. The grievance was not against Roman rule but against me as ruler.

Two days later another dispatch arrived, forwarded from Rome. An attached note informed me that these dispatches had been made public.

It is impossible to keep people from knowing about them, so we deemed it better to post them than let popular imagination exaggerate them, wrote Epaphroditus.

They could hardly have been exaggerated by imagination, as they were an all-out attack on my person.

Join me in an attack on Nero, because he has destroyed the flower of the Senate and does not preserve even the semblance of sovereignty, Vindex had cried to his followers.

What did he mean by that? The so-called flower of the Senate (did that include him?) had set out to destroy me, not the other way around.

I have seen him, my friends and allies—believe me—I have seen that man (if man he is) in the circle of the theater, that is, in the orchestra, sometimes holding the lyre and dressed in loose tunic and buskins, and again wearing high-soled shoes and mask. I have often heard him sing, play the herald, and act in tragedies. Will anyone, then, style such a person Caesar and emperor and Augustus? Never! Let no one abuse those sacred titles. Therefore rise now at length against him; succor yourselves and succor the Romans; liberate the entire world! the rebel had addressed a gathering of his countrymen.

So I was right. He *had* been on the Greek tour. He must have been lurking in the audience, thinking his hostile thoughts.

His language and insults were eerily like those of Boudicca, calling me a woman and unworthy of being a Caesar. Maybe barbarians kept a common sourcebook of phrases for character assassination?

Who was he surrounded by? Gaul, considered safe, had no legions. Seven legions were guarding the border in Germany, four under the command of Fonteius Capito in Lower Germany, and three—the Fourth, the Twenty-First, and the Twenty-Second—under Verginius Rufus in Upper Germany. There was the one under Galba in Near

Spain. Otho in Portugal had only a few men. But it was Verginius in Upper Germany who had the strongest army in the west and was close to Vindex. It would fall to him to put Vindex down. Nothing to worry about.

In the days following, Vindex roared on, spewing out insults in his speeches to his followers, now reported back to me.

This Domitius Ahenobarbus, a truly pitiful lyre player, has no right to be your ruler! was one of his diatribes, dutifully forwarded from Rome.

I was not ashamed of my birth name, but he meant it to delegitimize and question my adoption as a Claudian. And as for the taunt of being a bad musician, he obviously stole that from Boudicca as well. She had also called me "Mistress Domitia." No originality of thought on his part; he had to filch even his insults from her!

I was boiling mad now. I must take some action. I retired to my quarters and dictated a formal letter to the Senate, ordering them to put a bounty of ten million sesterces on Vindex's head. "Avenge the insults to Rome and your emperor!" I commanded them. I threw down the stylus and called for a messenger to deliver it immediately to Rome, riding through the night to do so.

Then I sat back to wait. I did not have to do so for long.

A week later the Senate forwarded me Vindex's response.

Whoever brings me the head of Nero is welcome to mine in exchange.

It was time to return to Rome. I had waited too long already, reluctant to leave my favorite city, Naples, and thinking I could manage this crisis from here. I could delay no longer. I must take control.

I entered the city on a mild spring day, as sweet as a purring cat. But the news of the Vindex rebellion, public knowledge now, had changed the mood in Rome. I could feel it in the air without even being told; the curious, guarded stares I got as I passed through the streets spoke volumes. I hurried into the palace and called for Tigellinus to meet me immediately in my private office.

Tigellinus strode in, rasping and coughing. Nonetheless he had enough energy to rant about Vindex.

"The cur!" he said. "You can't trust these people, not even after they pretend to be assimilated. They are only waiting to strike, like a wolf brought into a household."

I gave a weak laugh. "Perhaps that is why Augustus felt he had the worst of the spoils, when he was awarded the west, with its empty forests and hostile tribes, while Antony got the soft, rich east."

"Sometimes I don't know why we bother with most of the provinces," he said. "Take Britain, for example. It still doesn't produce anything to justify the expense of garrisoning it." He gave a new great hacking cough.

"Here," I said, calling for a slave. "Greek honey will soothe you."

"I hope it's not that dreadful pine honey," he said. "Oh, what an evening that was."

Our smiles faded. "Do you think anyone will answer Vindex's recruitment speeches?" I asked.

"They already have," said Tigellinus. "A lot of tribes—possibly as many as a hundred thousand men. But Boudicca had two hundred and fifty thousand. A horde of barbarians can't overcome a trained army."

"I mean—the Romans. If a legion defected, that would be a different story."

He thought carefully. "Otho in Portugal has no reason to love you," he said. "Britain is loyal now. Capito? I don't know about him. Verginius is the key player. He can easily squash Vindex, but if he joins with him . . ." He coughed again. "Order him to march against Vindex, and see what he does."

I did as he advised, immediately drafting orders to Verginius and dispatching them. The soldiers' recent oath of allegiance to me— would it hold? Tigellinus gave me messages from governors of the other provinces—Aquitania, Lugdunensis in Gaul, Farther Spain, and Belgica. All reported Vindex's attempts to recruit them to his cause. But there was one gaping omission in these loyal reports. General Galba, governor of Near Spain, was silent.

I also took measures to mobilize other legions reasonably nearby that could be dispatched to Gaul quickly, from Britain and the newly formed legion originally meant for the Caucasus campaign but never sent.

Next I convened the Senate, gathering them in haste, summoning as many as were in Rome. The afternoon was drawing to an end before I stood before them. It had been twenty long months since I had last formally addressed them, on the eve of my departure for Greece. To many I was a stranger. Others had visited me in Greece; a very few were old-timers from way back. On either side of me sat the consuls—Galerius Trachalus and Silius Italicus. I was glad to see Italicus. Not only had he proved himself loyal during my absence, informing Helios of suspicious people, he also wrote poetry, which surprised and pleased me. He nodded to me and smiled.

I rose and looked out over the faces. Some of them frowned, staring at me. I was wearing the requisite toga, but then—oh, yes, I forgot—my hair was still long. That was it. I tucked it behind my ears and proceeded.

"Senators, you are well aware of the rebellion of the governor of Lugdunensis Gaul, Gaius Julius Vindex. A man who has sat among you, has called himself your colleague. Now he has betrayed his loyalty to the empire and is attempting to subvert other governors and generals. Rest assured, I have given orders to Rufus Verginius and his legions in Upper Germany to put this rebel down." The rebellion was old news to them, as the dispatches and edicts of Vindex were public. What they did not know was that I had already taken steps to control it.

"The criminals will soon be delivered their punishment and die the death that they so thoroughly deserve!" I ended.

The senators rose and yelled, "Augustus, you will do it!" A pause. "Augustus, *you* will do it!"

The wording, and the tense, gave me pause as I realized it could also mean, "Augustus, you will have it happen to you."

All their faces turned toward me were benign. I was imagining things. "I have also begun recruiting a new legion from the fleet at Misenum, to be named First Adiutrix, and have sent the Fourteenth Gemina from Britain, under the command of Petronius Turpilianus, to Gaul. The three legions detained for the eastern campaign and the new *legio I Italica* have been reassigned to the command of Rubrius Gallus and sent north. So fear not, the situation is well in hand."

"Augustus, *you* will do it!" they chorused. *You, you, you* . . . I didn't like the twist they gave the word.

"And so, my friends, let us stand firm in defense of Rome. I will inform you of every new development, and may you do likewise with me. Good night."

I motioned to a few of them, men I wished to speak with privately, and held them back. I invited them to come to the palace with me, so we could speak further on these things.

In the room I used for business, I bade them be seated and called for refreshments. They sank gratefully onto the stools and couches and took the drinks from the silver trays.

It had been a long day for them, and their faces showed it. "I know we are all tired," I said, "so I will not keep you long. But we have been parted for a long time, much has happened, and now we have a crisis in one of the provinces. I know we will meet it; as it stands now, it is minor, compared to the one in Britain seven years ago and the one now being crushed in Judea by General Vespasian. But unhappy subjects anywhere make for an unhappy emperor." I expected them to laugh at this, but they merely smiled wanly. Obviously they were tired. I would say only a little more.

"This is different, though, in that Britain and Judea wanted freedom from Rome. Vindex wants liberation from *me*. He wants another emperor in my place."

A rotund senator said, "Perhaps your releasing Greece from its tax bonds to Rome has caused resentment with the other provinces. It is dangerous for the Pater Patriae of the empire to favor one province over another, Caesar. It can give rise to movements like Vindex's."

I nodded. He had a point. I had been too sanguine about it.

Silius Italicus said, "Perhaps you should visit other provinces as well as Greece. Let them see you in person. As it is, they have only seen your likeness on coins."

"Ah, but have there not been complaints that I have been away from

Rome so long? If I made like visits to all the provinces, I would never be here." But suddenly I realized I had taken the loyalty of the faraway provinces too much for granted.

One of the oldest senators, who had been present thirteen years ago when I gave my first speech to the Senate as emperor, said, "You are needed here, at least for a good while. Much is in need of repair." I knew he did not mean the aqueducts and roads. And I would be wise to heed his warning.

"Thank you, Gaius," I said. I looked around. No need to continue the discussion with this exhausted group. It was full dark outside, and a brisk wind was rising.

"For your amusement, since you are here, I will show you a novelty—a water organ. Its tones vary by the pressure of the water . . ." I demonstrated it for a few minutes before bidding them good night.

The next day it was all over Rome that the emperor, after calling a trusted group of advisers to come to the palace, refused to discuss the crisis in Gaul, entertaining them by playing a water organ instead.

"It's a lie!" I cried.

"Well, *did* you play the water organ? I know you were tinkering with it recently," said Statilia.

"Yes, but—only after I had talked with them about Vindex and the state of the empire. They were tired; I thought to give them some little amusement before sending them home."

"Obviously this rumor was spread by one of the men who was there," she said. "No one else would have known about it."

"Yes, but who? And why? You are such an expert in reading people's minds, perhaps I should reconvene them and let you test them."

"You are joking, right?"

"Only partially," I admitted.

"These days it is hard to tell when you are serious." She came over to me and massaged my shoulders. "I can feel how tense you are. I fear sometimes you are not thinking straight. You get so excited and flustered . . ."

I leaned back against her. "Wouldn't you? Oh, I am so tired of all this! I wish—"

"Oh, don't say you wish you had stayed in Greece. That's so childish."

"I wish—I wish—I could lay down the burden of being emperor."

"Stop that!" she hissed close to my ear. "Someone might hear you and be all too glad to help you do it."

"Not that way. Just to . . . resign, and go elsewhere. Not to Greece. To Egypt."

"Egypt?"

"It has a mystique," I said. I was curious about it.

"You need to stay here," she said flatly. "The very existence of rumors like the one about the water organ, meant to discredit you and make you sound deranged, show that the danger is not over, no matter how many plots have been discovered and disrupted."

Plots—here and far away. No safety anywhere. As it was when I was a child—danger all around me.

"I want to put this burden down," I insisted. "I am tired of carrying it."

"Augustus said the same thing, but he couldn't. He was mature enough to know he couldn't, or he would be damaging Rome."

"Even Atlas wanted to put his burden down!"

"That's a myth. You must stop confusing myth and reality. There never was an Atlas, and he never held up the earth. Do you understand that?"

"Yes," I said reluctantly. "But it is a pretty story."

LXX

The days of April crept by. I saw spring come in all its glory to Rome, but I did not really see it. It was all happening outside my windows, while I kept inside, reading dispatches, pacing. Puffs of grass-scented breezes tantalized those of us held captive indoors and awaiting word of events hundreds of miles away.

Tigellinus did not improve, and I ordered him to go to his country house and recover. He protested, but I said I needed him at his best, and only rest could bring him back to that.

"Nymphidius can take over, at least for a little while," I said.

He coughed. "Watch him," he said. "I am not completely sure of him."

"In what way?"

"Never forget who his father is," said Tigellinus. "And if Caligula isn't really his father, all the more reason to be wary, for it means he lies."

I looked at him. He was pale and had grown noticeably thinner. "I thought you liked him."

"Did I say I didn't? But liking and trusting are not the same thing. Great Zeus, Caesar, you of all people should know that."

His illness was making him tetchy.

Not long after he left, Statilia announced that she wanted to visit relatives in Campania. I let her go; there was no point her being held prisoner here, too.

But as a result I was soon more alone than I had been in some time.

Alexandra and Ecloge, in my household since my childhood, steadfastly stayed in Rome, and it was them I saw first thing in the morning and last thing at night as they brought me morning drink and food and filled the oil lamps at dusk. It was a comfort, seeing the faces of those so loyal to me. Those had known me through my entire life. Such people were a rare thing.

The palace quieted at night, and I had solitude and privacy. I often played the flute or the cithara just for myself, or sometimes just listened to the night noises outside, the humming of the cicadas, the echoing voices of revelers out in the Roman streets, stumbling home.

I thought of sending for Acte, but I hesitated. Statilia was right—I was too tense to be good company now. Acte and I had shared glorious, happy moments in Greece, and I did not want to erase that memory in her mind so quickly. But oh! I wished I could see her. My first love, early found, early lost, now found once more, never to be lost again.

Alone, I brooded on the thought I had blurted out to Statilia. It had been half formed then, but just saying it had given it a shape and existence. I did wish I could lay down the burden. It was pressing me, draining me, like a stone pressing down on olives, crushing the oil out of them. The weight of the empire oppressed me.

An astrologer had told me once that I would fall into poverty. At the time I had answered that I could always support myself by my music. It had been half wishful thinking, half a question. If I lost the throne, would I be simply a penniless musician?

The idea of poverty did not bother me—or so I told myself. But as I looked around the room with its marble floor and ceiling, its precious art objects, I realized that wealth enveloped me like a blanket—or a shroud. Could I really live without it? And could I really be content to be Lucius Domitius Ahenobarbus again, after years of being Nero Claudius Caesar Augustus Germanicus? The first time I could not claim, to myself, that no one had the authority to forbid me anything, I would feel even more helpless than I did now. I would have no recourse but to endure the slights and insults heaped on the common man every day. To say I was not used to it was a vast understatement.

It had been so long since I had experienced it, I honestly could not remember what it felt like.

Oh, but you will remember it soon enough when it happens.

The truth was, at this point I would make a poor private citizen; like an exotic plant, I had been in the hothouse too long to be transplanted.

T he spring nights made for good sleeping. The sweetness of the cool air was lulling. I barely needed a light sheet. One night in bed I lay staring out the window, through the leaves of a tree that rustled and threw odd shadows, slithering and dancing, before I drifted into sleep.

I dropped through space, into an abyss that was gray and bare. I fell freely, turning over and over, and landed on a soft gray mound. Then, before me, I saw the Mausoleum of Augustus. Its round shape filled my whole vision, and then, slowly, the two great entrance doors began moving, opening, exposing the dark within. An echoing voice said, "Enter, Nero!"

I stood up, trembling.

"Enter, Nero!" the commanding voice repeated.

Inside were rows of urns containing the remains of Augustus and his family and descendants, their lives finished. I backed away, but a strong invisible power tried to envelop me and pull me in. I thrashed and cried, "No! No!"

I awoke, tangled in the sheet. That was what had enveloped and captured me. I untwisted it and flung it off.

A dream. It was only a dream. But so real . . . I could have sworn I was standing in the Campus Martius before the great hulk of a building.

As I looked beyond the foot of my bed, I saw that my own two bedroom doors were standing wide open. They had been firmly shut when I went to bed. I was sure of it. The force that had tried to suck me into the mausoleum had invaded my room.

I lay quiet until light stole into the room, freeing it from the grip of night. The yawning doors of the room stood as silent witnesses that it had not been entirely a dream. I got up, shakily, and closed them before attendants could arrive and wonder. Just walking in the light of day steadied me, and the shades of night and its terrors faded, blurring into invisibility.

The day itself seemed benign. The April sunshine was warm and beguiling. Suddenly I realized what day this was . . . April nineteenth, the anniversary of the day for my intended assassination three years ago. The evil had been averted, but did it linger still, attached to this date? Was that why the mausoleum was still hungry for me?

I had barely had time to think this when Nymphidius and Epaphroditus arrived, bearing dispatches. Their faces were grim, and they were sweating even on this cool morning.

They knelt and handed the messages to me, as if they could not look me in the eyes. I took them and unrolled them one at a time.

General Galba had given an address at a tribunal in New Carthage, announcing that he had joined Vindex in his rebellion and henceforth renounced his allegiance to me. He denounced me and my regime as tyrannical and unfit, and displayed statues and pictures of my victims. Then he announced that he was seizing all the imperial property in the province.

That was in the first dispatch. In the second one, the story continued. The audience hailed him as imperator, and Galba accepted the title, saying that he was now the representative of the Roman Senate and people but—with false modesty—said he could only assume the title after the Senate had formally granted it. He issued a proclamation calling upon the whole province to join the cause. Otho in Portugal came forward and joined, bringing gold and silver to be melted into coin, as he had no legion to contribute. So . . . it had taken six years, but Otho had his revenge on me.

I dropped the rolls on the table and let them rest there. I could hardly speak.

"Galba has only one legion, the Sixth, Victrix," said Nymphidius. "One legion does not a revolution make."

"And he's old. He's seventy-two, reportedly not in good health," added Epaphroditus.

Seventy-two. *Beware the seventy-third year.*

Everything went black. Vaguely I felt myself falling, heard a clatter as I hit a chair, then nothing.

I awoke to find Ecloge and Alexandra bending over me, wiping my forehead. Nymphidius and Epaphroditus were nowhere to be seen. For a moment I thought I had been transported back in time, looking up into the faces of my childhood nurses. But the faces were lined now, and I was not a child. I tried to sit up.

"You have had a shock," said Ecloge. "Do not move until you feel ready." She wiped my face again, gently. Someone had put a pillow under my head, but I still lay sprawled on the floor where I had fallen, one leg twisted under me.

They must have told her the dreadful news. Or perhaps she had read the dispatches, lying open on the table. A civil war was beginning. The unthinkable, which the founding of the empire was supposed to prevent forever. This was much worse than Vindex's declaration of rebellion. Galba was a trusted governor and a noted general, a stalwart member of the governing elite, and had now provisionally accepted the title of emperor. Emperor!

I still felt stunned, but then I sat up, despondency flooding me, grief taking possession of me. I reached for the neck of my tunic and ripped it, as mourners do, relishing the rasping sound of the tearing fabric, echoing the tearing within me. I beat my head against the legs of the table, hitting it again and again. "It is all over!" I cried. "The oracle foretold it. This is my assassination day after all."

"You must bear up," said Alexandra. "Rome will look to you now for guidance."

Ecloge spoke calmly. "You have not been driven off the throne. You are secure here in Rome; Spain is far away. Your commander Verginius is moving toward Vindex and will likely fight him before Galba can reach him. Then Galba will be alone, stranded, and branded a traitor."

She had always been sensible, tough-minded. Steadying. With her help, I stood up, shakily. Only with Ecloge and Alexandra could I openly show such weakness. It was comforting that I could, and I gave thanks for them.

* * *

Calm. I must pretend to a calmness I did not possess, if only to inspire it in others. I pulled myself together and called a meeting of the Senate the next day. Once again flanked by the consuls, I rose to address the senators.

"At our last meeting, we vowed to bring Vindex to justice," I said. The faces looking back at me had worry writ large on them. "And we will," I said.

Show no weakness or hesitation. What Ecloge and Alexandra saw—the emperor in despair—must never be seen by others.

"But a new danger has arisen. General Servius Sulpicius Galba, governor of Near Spain, has declared himself for Vindex and put his one legion at the rebel's disposal. He has confiscated all the imperial property in the province, robbing us. But more dastardly, he has accepted the title of emperor, which the people there bestowed on him. He calls himself in the meantime the legate of the Senate and the people of Rome until you grant the actual imperial title to him. He shall get another title from you instead: enemy of the public! Declare him *hostis*, that damning judgment."

I was yelling then, all my anger pouring out. Despondency had passed into rage.

They rose and did as I asked, pronouncing the sentence on him of public enemy of Rome. He was now officially a traitor.

The empire was in crisis. There was one more thing I must do now. I turned to the two consuls and said, "You must step down. I will take your places as the sole consul, as is traditional in emergencies. It is said, *Only a consul can subdue Gaul.* That consul should be the emperor."

There was a controlled gasp from the floor. The faces showed different reactions: some frowned, some looked stunned, some were pleased.

"I will take sole command and deliver us from this danger," I assured them.

I sounded so certain, even to myself.

* * *

In the days that followed my moods continued to fluctuate wildly—from abject despondency to intense and detailed planning. We heard nothing of Verginius and his legions and where they were. The five legions under Gallus and Turpilianus were on their way north. I did not give orders to prepare defenses in Rome, as there was no danger of being invaded. But I did have the breach in the wall filled in.

I went out to inspect the city to see if there were any other glaring weaknesses that needed to be repaired. As I made the rounds of the streets, I felt a surge of satisfaction in the rebuilding that had been completed in only four years. If Augustus could claim he found Rome a city of brick and left it a city of marble, Nero could claim to have found Rome a city of ashes and left it a city of rational planning. My wide streets, my mandated fireproof stone, my open spaces and greenery were a vast improvement over Augustus's narrow-streeted and congested Rome.

Returning to the palace, I saw with satisfaction that the statue, my colossus, was finally finished and stood tall over the city. It gleamed in the sunlight, dazzling from any vantage point, the final capstone of the rebuilding and remodeling of Rome. We were the greatest city in the world, and we should have the highest monument to proclaim it.

But no sooner was I back in my rooms than I was plunged into panic, the gloom that alternated with lucidity. It gripped me with its evil whispers, infecting my mind and enervating me. When I passed through the doors to the room, I remembered them swinging open to usher me to the mausoleum. Images of the withering laurel tree floated by. *Beware the seventy-third year* echoed in my head. I had other dreams, too, so that I dreaded to sleep at night. I was in the Theater of Pompey, where I had celebrated the Golden Day with Tiridates. This time the statues came to life and hemmed me in on the stage, giving me no escape, converging on me to crush me between them.

I was indeed hemmed in, a prisoner in Rome, held immobile in the robes of the emperor, I thought when I awakened. Was there no escape?

Egypt. I could go far away, far from Rome, take a different identity. They could never find me there. They might look for me in Greece but would not think of Egypt. What a world was awaiting me there—the allure of the ancient wisdom and monuments that were old before Rome was born. The ghosts of Antony, of Cleopatra, of Alexander would welcome me.

Cleopatra. I hunted for the coin, found it, and started carrying it on my person. *I surrender her and her dreams into your safekeeping.* I had tried, I had tried my best to transform Rome, to bring an eastern sensibility to its stony coldness, but I had failed. Now I needed to take refuge in a more compatible place while I was still young enough to make a new life. I would take Acte with me. She could no longer object to being an emperor's wife. She would be a simple musician's wife.

But no. Quickly a lassitude overcame me. Nothing mattered; it was all one, whatever happened. This must be how the gods felt, who would go on for eternity but nothing could touch them. And they could not truly care for anything.

I made plans, strange plans for what I could do with Vindex. I would go to Gaul and address his troops, appeal to them so touchingly that they would all throw down their arms. I was a good orator, and the sight of the emperor would be so arresting I would win them over.

Thus alternated these delirious moods, played out against backgrounds of a thudding heart by day and terrifying dreams by night.

There could be one infallible means of escape to set my mind at ease. I sent for Locusta.

It has been a long time, Caesar," she said, standing before me as tall and stately as ever. She seemed unchanged, one of the few things that were. "How may I help you?"

I had been slumped on a couch but straightened my back when she came in. "Much as I enjoy your company, there is only one reason I would send for you," I said.

"For whom is this intended, and in what setting?" Ever the professional.

"For me," I said.

Now her expression changed. "Why?"

I noted that she did not launch into a lecture about how wrong it would be. "It may be necessary. There is rebellion in the empire, and a rival emperor has declared himself. If I lose . . ."

She did not argue or say that was unlikely. "You would rather not be here to greet him," she said. "I understand."

"I want this only for peace of mind," I said. "Only as a last resort. I am not ready to depart the stage." *The stage, with its statues come to life.* "But when the audience does not applaud any longer, it is time."

"Very well," she said. "I am saddened to hear it. I had thought danger came from Rome and that it had passed after the conspiracy. It has been many years since there has been an insurrection from the army."

"Yes, it has," I said. "But when a soldier's loyalty to his commander is stronger than to the emperor, the seeds are sown." *In the name of Jupiter Optimus Maximus, I swear allegiance to Imperator Nero Claudius Caesar Augustus Germanicus as supreme commander. I will obey the emperor willingly and implicitly in all his commands.* Would that vow hold? Or was it already trampled underfoot?

"So . . . where and under what circumstances do you see the use of this?" she asked.

"In privacy. While I still have time. In a quiet hour of night."

"I assume you want it to be quick?"

"Oh, yes. But not painful. If I have to compromise speed for comfort, that is acceptable."

She thought for a moment. "I know how to compound it. I will include a pain easer to mask the effects so you will not . . ." She did not need to go into details. "It will be quick as well. You will have exactly what you want."

"I knew I could rely on you," I said.

The business concluded, we then talked of the things old friends would—my days in Greece, her academy, challenges and successes in her business, my marriage to Statilia, the shrine to Poppaea. Just the concerns of our everyday lives.

* * *

A few hours later, I held the vial in my hands. It was a slender glass cylinder of the sort that usually held perfume. But this was a perfume to infuse a shroud. I tilted the bottle, and the dark liquid within winked as it shifted.

It was startling to see death in a bottle and to know that it had the power to remove me from life and whisk me to the underworld, to the grim gray shore lined with asphodels. It was very close, that shore.

I looked around the room, where the victory wreaths from Greece were hung. In the competitions in Greece, I had tasted the very essence of being alive. Now if I unstoppered this bottle I would taste death. It was incomprehensible.

I could throw it out. But death would come in some form, sooner or later. I could not banish death. But this way I could harness it.

I put the bottle in a gold box. Out of sight. After I had hidden it, I suddenly wondered what had possessed me. Was I mad? I would never be able to bring myself to use it. I was too intensely alive.

LXXI

LOCUSTA

I had heard of the turmoil in Gaul, and of Galba's move. But I had let Nero tell me of them. My part was to listen and be of service. At last the poison I had prepared for him at the first, that later found its home in another, was being called back to its first target. Thus we fight hard to evade our own fate but cannot always succeed. I hoped that he would keep his intention of not using it unless the situation was hopeless. But I knew also that his weakness was what has been described as too easily elated by small victories, too easily cast down by small defeats. In just such a frame of mind he might drink the potion.

I could have given him a harmless one, but that would have been unprofessional and would rob him of the death he needed, if he needed it. As well as I knew him, I knew he would have been humiliated by such patronizing treatment. He had an ancestor, Gnaeus Domitius, known for his cowardice whose physician had done just that. The man had downed the potion and then in a panic summoned the physician, who assured him he had watered down the poison, knowing Gnaeus would back out. So the indecisive man was relieved. But he was not an emperor facing the loss of his throne. Would Cleopatra have been relieved if the snake's venom had lost its potency? It depends on what one is facing if the poison fails.

Much had happened since he and Poppaea had paid their visit to me at my academy, consulting with me about Poppaea's health. As I looked at him now, he seemed to have survived the subsequent upheavals intact, perhaps aided by his long tour in Greece, which may have bolstered his bodily health while injuring his political health.

I had watched him grow from a boy to a man and then to an emperor. In first protecting him from my own poison, I had felt entrusted with his survival ever since, and I had never betrayed that trust. In answering his call now, did I now betray it—or would not answering it have been the true betrayal?

LXXII

NERO

"Caesar!" Nymphidius stood beaming before me, holding an armful of dispatches, spread out like a peacock's tail across his forearms.

I eyed them. Where to begin? From the grin on his face, I knew I could choose any of them and be pleased with the contents. "Just tell me," I said. Cut through the Gordian knot of the dispatches.

"Vindex is defeated!" he crowed. "Beaten. Dead."

I sank down on a couch, first astounded and then elated, and motioned him to do likewise. "Let us send for others, so we do not have to repeat the story." I could wait for the details. In fact, the longer I waited, the hungrier I would be for them, and the better they would taste.

I called for Epaphroditus, Phaon, Helios, and the leading Praetorians on duty at the palace. I also called for the best Falernum, both the amber kind and the aged black kind. Let the celebration begin!

Once everyone was gathered, Nymphidius gestured toward the pile of dispatches. "Are you sure you don't want to read them out yourself, Caesar?"

"Later," I said, nodding to him. "You summarize it for us." I could feel the eagerness in the room.

"Verginius, after taking his time, finally faced Vindex near Vesontio and utterly destroyed his forces. Twenty thousand Gauls fell. The Roman legions were especially brutal as they had built up a hatred of Gauls and wanted the plunder."

"How did Vindex die?" I asked.

"He killed himself, after lamenting that he had failed in his mission."

"And no one else helped Vindex? Where was Galba?" I pressed.

"Where he was then, I can't say. He didn't join the fight. But I can tell you where he is now: cowering in Clunia, a small town in the mountains of Spain. The word is that he was making ready to kill himself when a faithful retainer stopped him. He is a beaten man, though. Broken. Done for."

It was all I could do not to jump up and yell in victory. But I restrained myself and said, "Thanks be to the gods for our deliverance. And the legions under Gallus and Turpilianus were not needed?"

"No. I am not sure how far they got."

No matter. No matter.

My blood singing, limp with relief at my deliverance, I stood up. "Oh happy, oh fortunate day!" I cried, embracing the men one by one. "Rejoice with me!"

I looked around at them. "We will have a huge victory banquet. And all of Rome is invited!"

Twilights are lingering in early June, and I watched the pink-tinted sky above Rome change slowly to violet as the guests converged on the Domus Aurea. I had not used the entertaining pavilion since I returned to Rome, living exclusively in the lower part of the palace, but now it would be reinaugurated in all its glory. It was not completely finished in all details; that would take years. But the gardens were exuberant in their blooms and fragrance, the frescoes on the outer wall were complete, and there was no view so magnificent as the one sweeping across the valley below and on to the nearby Caelian Hill. The colossus glowed in the sunset, the last beams of sunlight winking off the tips of the crown.

So many people who had thronged the courtyard in times past were gone—both from natural causes and from treachery and violence. Tonight Tigellinus was also absent, still recovering in his country home.

But the senators were here, friendly and smiling. My enemies had been purged from the Senate, and now I could be at ease with them once again. Statilia stood with me greeting them, and if I ached to have Poppaea there beside me, I told myself sternly that it could not be. I kept Sporus away; I did not want to cause a scandal or expose him to ridicule. In Greece it was accepted well enough, but Rome was a different matter.

As before, I opened the lower gardens to the general public, providing wine, food, and entertainment for them, and the sound of their voices carried up to the courtyard terrace where we all stood. Later we would go inside for our banquet, but for now it was so pleasurable to stand in the warm evening air and watch the flocks of birds winging away in the sunset, in great numbers, wheeling and diving. Such freedom, the sort men would never know.

Darkness was falling; torches were lit. The servers ushered us inside, where the ivory inlaid couches, the food-laden marble tables, the lotus perfume droplets falling gently from the oculus, awaited us. Yes, much was taken, much was missing from the past, but tonight promised hope and fulfilling days to come.

Before the banquet proper began, I addressed the group. "Dear friends of Rome—for so are we all; no, more than that, sons and daughters of Rome—we gather here to celebrate the deliverance of the empire from the rebellion in Gaul. This is the third rebellion since I have been your emperor, and in all three, our loyal Roman legions have put paid to the enemy." Everyone was listening intently, their faces earnest. "This one was the most unnerving because it was closest to home, and from a province thought to be entirely friendly," I continued. "So friendly, in fact, that we did not think it necessary to station troops there. So friendly that its citizens were welcomed into the Senate."

The guests stood utterly still. "So the shock was all the greater. After all, if a viper turns and bites, who could be surprised? It is in his nature. But if a beloved dog charged with protecting the household suddenly turns into a wolf, yes, we would be more than surprised. That is what happened with Gaul. But rest assured, the wolf is no more and the land is safe."

Murmurs of approval swept through the company. "So I invite all of you to join with me in this celebration of victory and safety," I concluded. I called for a goblet, had it filled, and took a long swallow. "Drink with me, keep me company!"

The evening unfolded without incident; all was polite and in order, if a bit subdued. Perhaps that was the new guardedness, born of the recent upheavals. So be it.

After dinner I had provided lyre, flute, and harp musicians, who played at one end of the room. Suddenly one of the senators said, "You have been a generous host, but still you withhold something from us. Your music. We have known of your prize-winning compositions in Greece but have not heard them. Please play one for us."

I was touched. No, let me be honest: I was flattered. I demurred at first but then sent a slave to bring my cithara from the lower palace. Upon his return, I sang the song of Troy I had composed that questioned the necessity of war.

Whether flattery or not, I was supremely contented to be here in the Domus Aurea, one of my creations, while playing another. I needed to create in order to fully live. And I needed an audience to share it with me.

Afterward, in the lower palace, Statilia wearily removed her gold earrings and replaced them in her mother-of-pearl jewel box. "I would pronounce that a success," she said. "At least you weren't pelted with rotten fruit." She flopped down on one of the couches, kicked off her sandals, and put her feet up. Tilting her head back, she unfastened her hair bindings and let her hair tumble free.

"I wasn't expecting to be," I said. "Why would you say that?"

"I hear murmurs in Campania," she said. "The Liberation of Greece was not popular. Neither was your long stay there. The people were quite outspoken about it."

"Well, that's over," I said. "I am back now." More's the pity. "I have gotten over my fit about it. Now I am just a placid donkey, plodding along obediently."

She laughed. "Ha. Never. Though sometimes you do act like an ass."

Usually I enjoyed her sharp tongue, but not tonight. "I don't appreciate that," I said. "I have had very difficult days since you have been away. The crisis in Gaul—Galba—"

Nightmares. Omens. An imperial rival.

"Yes, yes," she said. "And we are all thankful it has turned out as it has. Come, don't pout." She got up and came over to me, leaning over and kissing the top of my head. "I do say, perhaps you should cut off the Apollo locks now." She ruffled them.

When would people stop telling me what to do? "I will when I want to."

She picked up her jewel box. "I need a bigger one," she said. Suddenly she made for a chest under the window and opened it, running her hand along the bottom. "The last time I looked, I saw a carved box in here," she said. "I think it was ebony."

I jumped up. "No, there's nothing like that in there," I said.

Her hand had found the gold box with the poison vial. She brought it out. "This is pretty," she said. It was locked.

"I will order one just for you," I said. "This particular one has a special meaning for me."

Disappointed, she shrugged and put it back. "If you do, put some emeralds on the lid to dress it up."

The next few days passed, somnolent summer days of thick honey-sunshine, drowsy shadows, rustling hedges. Statilia departed for Campania again. Such a hush lay on the land that even the butterflies slowed as they fluttered from flower to flower. Time seemed suspended, a rope bridge swaying over nothingness.

Then, on the eighth of June, in the late afternoon, Nymphidius and Epaphroditus hurried into my quarters. I had just seated myself before a table and was preparing to have supper. My favorite cups of delicate murrhine were waiting to be filled with Massic wine, and I was turning one of them over in my hand, admiring the play of light in the stone, and the carved scene from Homer, showing Achilles and Ajax.

This time there was no proud confidence, no strutting. Silently, cringingly, they handed me several dispatches.

"Which one first?" I asked.

Timidly Epaphroditus pointed to a red canister. "This one, Caesar."

I unrolled it gingerly, as if an asp lurked inside. It did.

Rubrius Gallus had turned his legions over to Galba and declared his loyalty. Petronius Turpilianus, with his one legion, had been deserted by his troops. The legions of Verginius in Germany had hailed him as emperor and he had not declined it. The other four legions in Germany under Fonteius Capito had kept silent, not confirming their loyalty.

I set down the message as if it were hot and would burn the table. "Next," I said, and was handed a brass canister.

Clodius Macer, with the Third Legion near Egypt, had declared for Galba and was raising auxiliaries.

"The last?" I asked. A third was handed to me.

Galba had emerged from his hideout in Spain and was moving, with Otho and the governor of Farther Spain, to meet up with the legions supporting him. Along the way, he was picking up followers, and the surviving Vindex partisans were flocking to him.

The armies were no longer mine. I was undone—legions and generals all over the empire were deserting me.

I was seized with emotions strong as a thunderbolt—currents of fiery anger, icy fear, quivering waves of shock. I stood up and overturned the table, which fell on the hard floor and sent its mosaic pieces flying. The cups flew through the air, their iridescent beauty shattering against the wall. Then I let out a howl that must have reverberated through the entire palace, the howl of a cornered animal.

Nymphidius and Epaphroditus did nothing. They merely stood like statues, waiting for my fit to subside. Finally I sank back down onto the couch and muttered, "What shall I do? What shall I do? All is lost!"

They had no ideas, offered no advice. My mind started churning, roaring, and I was no longer cognizant of them even standing there. A thousand ideas ran scampering like drowning rats through my brain, all to the throbbing refrain *you are doomed, you are doomed, Rome is lost, the empire is lost.*

But no . . . perhaps not. Calm! Calm! But even the word "calm" was racing and staccato in my panic.

Ideas, ideas . . . what to do? What to do? What could I possibly do at this late hour? Late hour . . . too late . . .

I could go to Galba, submit to him, ask him to spare me and let me go to Egypt as a private citizen . . . I could go to the Rostra in the Forum, dressed in black, and address the people of Rome, beg pardon for any offenses . . . I could go to Armenia, be taken under the protection of Tiridates . . . But in the end, I think Egypt is the best choice for me. Yes, Egypt. I will go to Egypt.

"I must flee Rome," I finally announced in a normal voice. "It is my only hope!"

They did not contradict me, but they did move their heads and look at one another. Finally Nymphidius said, "Shall I alert Ostia and have a fleet prepared? When?"

"Now!" I said. "Immediately!" And in those words, I felt a gush of relief. I had freed myself from Rome. Not as I had intended; it had been forced on me, but perhaps otherwise I never would have had the courage—or the madness—to cut myself free. "Go!"

After he left, Epaphroditus said, "It would be best if we moved so you will not have to traverse the city to get to the Ostia Road. We cannot know how safe the streets will be later on as the word gets out to the people. The Servilian Gardens are well situated."

"Yes, yes!" And so I would leave the Golden House, just like that, turn my back on all I loved there and had labored over, the place that held Poppaea's spirit firmer than any other. I would fly free, not away from something but to it.

I grabbed only a few things, stupid, inconsequential things—oddly enough, I did not plan for the journey itself, as if I truly would fly there and had no need of clothing or shoes or money. I was not thinking, of course. I was in a dream, a panic, and such details never figure in a dream.

The streets of Rome were already in a stew, with crowds milling and a current of excitement and fear mixed together permeating the air. They knew. They had heard. The news had leaked out; the dispatches were now public knowledge, in that mysterious way that information travels.

I know, I know, I feel the same, my people. Excitement and fear as I exit this life.

People peered into the litter, trying to see who was in it. I held a cloth up to my face so they could not.

Farewell to all this. It was oddly like the day I had been declared emperor, when I was borne through the streets, past the crowds, past the fountains, to the Praetorian Guards' headquarters. Now I went in the opposite direction, in all senses of the word.

LXXIII

The Servilian Palace was closed and smelled musty. I had rarely visited it since my honeymoon with Statilia. But now my eyes did not see or appreciate what was around me there; they barely recognized anything. Epaphroditus had rounded up my administrators to accompany us, and Nymphidius had transferred a contingent of Praetorians there before he left for Ostia.

Could it really have come to this? *There is none so blind as he who will not see.* I had looked left and right, always on the alert for danger, but watching in the wrong direction, thinking the threat would come from within my own family, or from Rome, never suspecting it could come from the provinces.

Why had I not visited the legions all along to ensure their loyalty and show my respect? Why had I not listened to Statilia's advice to mount the eastern campaign first, before going to Greece? I had belatedly raised legions, preparing at last to lead a campaign as a true descendant of Germanicus, but in vain now. Time, always my friend, now turned against me.

The sun would be setting soon, bringing on the night—my last night in Rome. Was I sure of that? Was I absolutely committed to that course of action?

I went into the bedroom, where slaves had transferred some of my personal belongings, including the chest. If I had not thought of clothes, of mantles, of shoes, they had. And thank all the gods, at the bottom of the chest remained the one thing I must not be parted from and which I had forgotten to save in my panic: the gold box.

I sat down at my desk, reserved for personal correspondence. It was always stocked with paper, seals, and ink. Perhaps I should compose a speech that I could deliver on the Rostra, defending myself. It might be necessary if my getaway plans failed. I spread out a paper and tried to do it.

My beloved subjects. I stand before you here your suppliant, entirely at your mercy.

No. Wrong approach.

My most dear subjects, you may have heard rumors of . . .

No. Do not reiterate information they already have.

People of Rome! I have led you, protected you, cherished you, lavished gifts on you for many years, and led the country into many triumphs, diplomatic and military. Shall I continue as your chosen emperor?

Better. But still not right. I put them all aside. I had best discuss the transfer to Ostia with the Praetorians on guard; it would have to be early in the morning. I had heard nothing yet from Nymphidius about the readiness of the fleet, which he was arranging. But if only one ship was ready, that would suffice.

I went out into the courtyard where the guards were congregating. There were about fifteen of them on duty. I spoke to Publius, the rank-ing guard.

"Tomorrow I transfer to Ostia, early in the morning. Make all preparations and be ready to depart before sunrise," I said. "I invite you to make the entire journey with me, boarding at Ostia."

"Journey to where?" asked a burly young guard.

Should I tell them? Caution advised against it. "I will tell you once we are there," I said.

He shrugged and glanced at the man standing next to him, who said, "I do not wish to march to Ostia tomorrow."

Did I hear correctly? He refused my order? "It is your duty," I said. "What of your oath?"

He laughed. "What of it?"

Publius stood quietly, not reprimanding his soldier. "Publius!" I said. "What sort of officer are you, to allow such insubordination?" I waited for him to apologize and force the other man to as well.

Instead he looked straight at me and quoted Virgil. "*Usque adeone mori miserum est?* Is it so hard then to die?"

"What?" was all I could manage to say.

"We have no wish to die alongside you," said Publius. "Do we, men?"

This must be a dream, a continuation of the nightmares. It felt real, but it could not be. Speechless, I backed out of the courtyard and took refuge in my rooms. I bolted the outer doors, protecting myself from the guards who were meant to protect me. I still had my personal bodyguards, and I stationed them around all the rooms of my apartments.

The sun had fled the sky, and soon darkness would close in. The darkness within and without enveloped me. I undressed and lay down to think, trying to comprehend what had just happened. It was not in the script I had written for myself, when I thought I could order the scenes, the dialogue, and the actors. Suddenly I was seized by sleep, as if Morpheus himself had abducted me. Perhaps in his mercy he had.

I awoke with a start, far from rested but my mind crystal clear, as if all the muddy sediment had been vacuumed out while I slept. I rose and looked out the window. From the position of the stars, I could tell it was around midnight. Accidentally falling asleep so early, I had not had lamps lit, and I called for a servant to bring light.

Silence. I called again. Silence. Carefully, I felt my way around the room, groping for the door. I pulled it open and stared out into darkness. There was no one here. The bodyguards had deserted. Far down the corridor a lampstand flickered, making jumping shadows. I took an oil lamp and lighted it from there, then went through the rest of the palace knocking on doors to rouse the people who were supposed to be with me, but got no response.

So this, then, was the end. Not a journey to Egypt. Not a speech on the Rostra. Thank all the gods I had the means of self-deliverance in the gold box. I returned to my bedroom, only to find that there must still have been people hiding nearby, because my sheets and bedclothes had been stripped and the bed lay bare before me. An old cloak and a tattered hat lay strewn on the floor—cast off by the thieves?

The chest! I rushed to it and threw open the lid. Empty. The clothes, which I would need for my earthly journey, and the poison, which I would need for my otherworldly one, were gone. Stolen. I was utterly abandoned.

"Have I neither friend nor foe?" I cried, so loudly it rang out through the house.

Shoeless, I rushed out of the palace, into the garden, and then a little way onto the street. I would throw myself into the Tiber and drown, having no other quick way to end myself and disappear. I could see its faraway glint from where I stood. But being thrown in the Tiber was a mark of disgrace, a mean and sordid death. No. I wouldn't do it. I couldn't.

Slowly I returned to the palace, feeling every pebble under my bare feet. The Praetorians had fled, so I encountered no one until I was almost at my rooms. Then I heard voices. Epaphroditus, Phaon, and Sporus were huddled near my door.

"Thank the gods, Caesar, we did not know—we feared—"

"That the Praetorians had done to me what they did to Caligula?" I asked. "These had not the courage for that. The best they could do was quote Virgil."

"Your room was empty, your belongings gone," said Epaphroditus. "What else could we think?"

"The streets are starting to fill with people, expecting trouble," said Phaon. "It may not be safe to stay here. They will seek out all the imperial residences, looking for you. And with no guards, they will have easy access. Remember how they tried to storm the palace in support of Octavia?"

All too well. "Have you any word from Nymphidius? Perhaps we should transfer to Ostia now."

They looked at one another. "No," said Epaphroditus. "We have heard nothing."

"I need a place to think, to plan," I said. "A safe haven."

"Come to my villa," said Phaon. "It is between the Via Nomentana and the Via Salaria, four miles out of Rome. It is in the opposite direction from Ostia. They will not be looking in that vicinity."

What choice did I have? "Very well." I was in my night tunic, barefooted. The plunderers had left me the faded cloak and old hat and I grabbed them. I also grabbed two daggers, which they had missed.

We took four horses from the stable and mounted them. "Follow me," said Phaon. Our route would take us through the heart of Rome to the northeast corner, past the Praetorian camp, but there was no help for it.

On we went, passing sites of my former glory: the Circus Maximus, the Forum, the Domus Aurea and its colossus, mocking me now. The streets were indeed filling up, but no one noticed us. The hat and the handkerchief I held up to my face disguised me, and the bare feet helped. No one expected to see the emperor thus.

We emerged near the Praetorian camp and had to skirt so close that I could hear conversations from the soldiers outside.

"Galba will defeat him utterly," one said, and I had no doubt who the *him* was.

"Yes, crush him!" said his companion.

Just then they saw us passing by. "They must be a party hunting for the emperor," one said.

"Is there any news of Nero in the city?" cried one. We did not reply but hurried by.

Suddenly my horse shied; there was a stench from a dead body in a nearby ditch. I wasn't thrown, but I had to use both hands to keep the reins, exposing my face. An old veteran standing close to the road recognized me and saluted. So not everyone had turned against me. Even the words of the Praetorians in the camp had been noncommittal.

Soon we were past the camp and safely out on the Via Nomentana. A long time ago we had ridden out to see Seneca this way. Seneca . . .

one of the earlier betrayals. Long before Seneca's house Phaon said, "It's here!" and pointed to a path leading off the road. "Leave the horses."

We dismounted and started pushing our way through a path hedged in with briars and weeds that caught on my cloak. The path was stony and also overgrown with nettles and thistles, so Epaphroditus and Sporus laid down their cloaks for my bare feet. How far was this villa? It took a long time to reach it at this pace. Overhead the sky was still dark, with thousands of stars, but the villa was not visible.

Finally Phaon said, "Just up ahead here," and pointed. I saw nothing. "We should not go in the front," he said. "There are slaves in there; we don't want them to see. We will have to make another entrance." We crept forward, and at last I could see the outlines of the house.

We finally reached clear ground around the house and a gravel path. "We will dig a secret entrance so we can get into the basement unseen," said Phaon. He handed Epaphroditus and Sporus tools that had been resting up against the back of the house, and they set about digging. He pointed toward a gravel pit and told me to hide in it until the secret tunnel was ready.

"No! I refuse to go underground while I am still alive," I said, and sat down by a small pool of muddy water beside it.

Around me the cicadas were humming and there were crunching and snapping noises as animals stalked through the undergrowth. From another villa dogs were barking, and a night bird shrieked from a marsh. I shivered, pulling my cloak around me. It was studded with briars from the passage through the meadow, and I tried to pull them out, but there were too many; they had torn the mantle in many places.

I was terribly thirsty. I had had nothing to drink since . . . since before I had spoken to the Praetorians. I leaned over and, cupping my hands, took some water from the little rain pool. It tasted of mud and slime. But it was wet. I scooped up another handful and drank it, too.

"So this is what my *decocta Neronis* has fallen to," I whispered. I could almost taste the pristine boiled and cooled water that had sustained me in good times and bad. But there was no time as bad as this, and now foul pond water must take its place.

"It's ready," whispered Phaon, tugging at my sleeve. I went over to the makeshift tunnel that was dug under the foundation and crawled through the little hole. Once I was through, I found myself in a low room with a filthy mattress covered by a stinking mantle. I flung myself down on it, almost gagging with the smell.

The others followed me through the hole, and Sporus handed me a piece of stale bread and a cup of lukewarm water. I smelled the bread and turned it aside, but I was still thirsty and had to drink the water.

They left me, and I could hear them speaking together in low murmurs in a corner of the room. There was nothing to do but lie quietly and wait for the light to come. Lie and think.

Stale bread in place of a banquet table. Warm water in place of snow-cooled water. Three freedmen as my entourage, when I had paraded through the Forum leading hundreds only a little while ago. A ragged cloak, a tunic, and no shoes, when I had been clothed in silk, gold, and softest leather. A hunted man, formerly the ruler of the world. The fall was complete.

How had this happened? How much of it could be laid at my own—now bare—feet? In my life, I had had to survive, and then I had turned my back on what I had survived for, and attempted to escape into art. Now I would have the ultimate escape, forced upon me, no way back. I had performed lines from plays written by someone else, had assumed other personas on stage. I had played the part of a beggar, and now I was one. This day, in these last dwindling hours, I was the only actor in my own play, and I had to play myself. I had to write the lines myself and perform them myself. But what role should Nero assume? What should I write for myself?

"I have taken too little thought of this," I cried. "Too little thought, and now it is too late!"

My projects all unfinished: the Domus Aurea, the Corinthian Canal, the Avernus Canal, my epic poems, the music I had yet to write. Nothing complete. Oh, what a world this artist was losing—so much yet to explore, to understand, to create.

I was born an artist, but two other Neros arose alongside that person as I grew up. There was Nero the emperor, who carried the weight of the state on his shoulders, and the third Nero, who protected and guarded the first and second by whatever means were necessary, even the darkest.

Now in my last hours I could cast away the other versions of myself, needing them no longer, and return unencumbered to my true and only self: the artist.

Once I had told Tigellinus that Christians were to be envied, for having something so precious that it overrides all else in your life, even your life itself.

So I had said. But silently I had admitted, *There were times when I felt that way about my music, but did I really? To that extent? So I would give up everything to pursue it, toss over the emperorship? Sadly, I knew the answer. No, not that much. Almost. But not that much.*

But now the answer had changed. In the final test, I had given all to art: going to Greece to pursue art and staying had cost me my throne and possibly my life. The end of a dynasty—the sacrifices of Augustus, the thwarted dreams of Tiberius, the madness of Caligula, the struggles of Claudius, and Mother's ambition, all collapsing with me. I was taking them all down with me. And I mourned them, even as I had struggled against their legacy all my life.

Forgive me. You did not think to perish thus. All the murders and schemes, to end in nothing at a freedman's villa. The last laurel has withered and will not grow again.

Light slowly crept into the dank cellar, and Phaon came over and said, "We should go outside now."

He would get no argument from me, and we crawled out the same way we had come in. The fresh June air was exhilarating after the dank cellar.

"There is no word from Nymphidius," said Epaphroditus. "And we—we three—have been conferring, and realizing what you are facing—as they will find you sooner or later—we think—we believe—that you should spare yourself this fate."

Phaon and Sporus nodded solemnly.

"You say there is no word from Nymphidius?" Again they nodded. Suddenly I knew. I knew Nymphidius had never gone to Ostia. And that he had told the Praetorians they were no longer to protect me, so they deserted me. The son of Caligula had destroyed me, where his father had failed. And Phaon had led me here, far on the other side of Rome, to make sure I could never get to Ostia. Were Epaphroditus and Sporus also part of this plan?

"Nothing," they said in unison.

What a surprise. They might have heard something, but not anything they could tell me.

"So you advise me to kill myself?" I asked.

"That would be best, I am grieved to say," said Phaon.

"I am not skilled. Could one of you, out of loyalty, kill yourself to show me how?" Now what would they say?

"I—we could not. We must be here to see to your body, your burial. We must protect your remains," said Epaphroditus.

"I see. How could I overlook that? Well, then, get busy and dig my grave. You can measure it for me now, since I am right here. And gather up any pieces of marble that we can use to line it and to mark it. And we will need wood for the pyre and water to put it out. Plus an urn. Can you get an urn?"

Was I really having this conversation?

"Yes, Caesar," was all they said, stealing glances at one another. *The emperor has lost his senses. He is hysterical.*

Perhaps I was hysterical. Nothing seemed real; everything seemed too real, too brutal, too sharp. While they busied themselves digging, I looked at the glory of early summer all around me and burst out, "What an artist the world is losing!" Earlier I had said the artist was losing a world, but the world was losing her most passionate artist with his best works still undone. We were a couple, entwined and dancing together, and now the dance was ending.

The three turned and stared at me, then continued digging.

The grave was almost complete when a runner found us at the back of the house. He handed Phaon a note, but before he could read it I snatched it away. It was my fate, let me read it for myself.

The Senate—the Senate I thought was now my friend—had met at an emergency session during the night. They had declared me a public enemy, just as they had Galba only a little while ago. They had ordered my arrest and execution under the ancient style.

"What is the 'ancient style'?" I asked.

Phaon looked evasive. Finally Epaphroditus said, "The person is stripped naked, then his head is put into a forked yoke, and he is beaten to death with rods."

O gods! No, I must rob them of the chance to do this to me. I looked around, at the waiting grave, the shovels, the wood. Where were my daggers? The daggers. I needed them.

"Here they are, Caesar," said Sporus kindly, handing them to me. I had left them in the cellar.

I took them, tested the blades. I held one up to my throat. But the day was sweet and there was no commotion. I threw them down. "It is not yet the hour!" I said.

They recommenced their digging, and I walked around in a fog, muttering to myself in both Greek and Latin.

How can my life have come to such an end?

This behavior does not become Nero, does not become him! It is not seemly!

One should be resolute at such times. Be resolute—come, pull yourself together. Rouse yourself!

All the while the shovels were scraping, scraping.

The early-morning birdsong had died out, replaced by the stillness of midmorning in the fields. But there was a distant sound—a rhythmic sound, a pounding.

Hoofbeats! They grew louder and unmistakable. This was not one rider but a whole company of them. Come to take me. They had found me, but not by themselves. Someone had told them where I was.

I looked at the three people with me. Which one was it? Or was it all three? I had survived many betrayals, but what was it Seneca had once said? No matter how many people you kill, you cannot kill your successor. He could just as well have said, no matter how many betrayals you survive, you cannot survive the last one.

The horses were getting closer. Suddenly a line from Homer burst from me:

"'Hark to the sound I hear! It is hooves of galloping horses!'"

Now with all my strength, I took up the dagger. No more hesitation.

Nero—Lucius!—be worthy of yourself!

LXXIV

ACTE

The June day was glorious in Velitrae. Our hilltop location guaranteed us cooling breezes, but this day did not need them, as it was perfect. I stood on the terrace of my home, looking out across the valley, toward Rome. Brown and yellow butterflies flitted in and out of the potted flowers nearby, joined by buzzing bees.

Like everyone else, I had heard of the unrest in Rome, which Nero had returned to, and the upheavals in the provinces, and the treason of Galba. I had planned to see Nero when it died down, knowing he did not need any distractions when he was so beleaguered. I constantly wore the ivory-and-ebony bracelet he had given me, never wanting to take it off, as if it were an invisible cord binding us together.

That there was danger to him I knew. I had warned him of that when he was so carefree in Greece. But even so I was unprepared for the sweating messenger who arrived, panting, at my doorstep and thrust a cylinder into my hands before sliding down the wall and nearly collapsing.

"I've come from Rome," he managed to get out. "Emergency."

I had the servants take care of him and went out onto the open terrace to read the message.

It was from Alexandra.

Nero is dead. It falls to us to bury him. Hurry. Time is not on our side.

The friendly warmth of the sun, the sweet scent of the flowers in their containers, faded all around me into a white nothingness.

Nero is dead.

Impossible words. Impossible thought. How could the world be here and he not in it? At that moment there was no world around me, either, and the white web of blankness enveloped me. The loss of such a presence as his should have sent shivers and quakes through the land. But the ground under me did not move.

I arrived at the palace with near otherworldly speed, to find Alexandra and Ecloge awaiting me in Nero's imperial apartments. I had never been in his; it was Poppaea's I had been summoned to. The palace was oddly deserted, although there were guards at the entrance. But the atrium was empty, and rather than servants, soldiers strolled the halls.

As soon as I entered, Ecloge embraced me, weeping. I had yet to cry; shock had stopped all tears, paralyzed all thoughts except the one that I must get to the palace as quickly as humanly possible. But now a deluge of tears poured from me, all the hours of crying released at once, choking me so that I could hardly breathe. She guided me to a couch and lowered me gently. It was a long time before I could look up at her, and even so my vision was blurred, making her features indistinct.

"Tell me," was all I said, and she understood.

"He was betrayed," she said.

O gods! Was this the cause of his death? Not a noble reason but a lie?

"Who? How?"

"Nymphidius told the bodyguards and the Praetorians that Nero had fled to Egypt, deserting Rome like a coward. He then promised them each a bounty of thirty thousand sesterces—many years' wages— if they would declare loyalty to Galba as emperor. He also announced to the Senate that Nero had fled, and they joined with the Praetorians in saluting Galba as emperor. Then they pronounced Nero a public enemy, as they had pronounced Galba one only a short time before. That is how honest the Senate is! For sale to the highest bidder!"

"But where *was* Nero?"

"At Phaon's villa," said Alexandra, sitting down beside me.

"Why in the world was he there?" I lifted the hem of my tunic to dry my eyes.

"We don't know," said Ecloge. "He was persuaded to leave the palace and go there. But once again, betrayal came into it. Someone alerted the Praetorians searching for him just where to find him."

"It must have been one of the ones with him at the villa," I said.

"All fingers would point in that direction," said Ecloge. "Who else would have known?"

"Who was with him?"

"Phaon, Epaphroditus, Sporus."

One of them, then. Or all of them.

"They are waiting for us now. They have his . . . him . . . ready for burial."

Now I understood the hurry. "But where will he lie?"

"Galba's henchman, Icelus Marcianus, has given permission for a formal funeral. He can be interred in the mausoleum of his father's line, the Domitians. I took the liberty of ordering a sarcophagus of red porphyry and an altar of white Luna marble."

"They cost two thousand gold pieces," said Alexandra.

"I hope that is not why you have called me," I said. "But of course I will pay." I would have paid a thousand times that to keep him from the ignominy usually accorded an overthrown ruler—a shabby grave if at all, or worse, desecration of the body.

"We called you because you were his first love, and we knew he never stopped caring for you. We hoped you still felt the same. His last rites should be carried out by those who care for him."

Of course they would have had no way of knowing anything that had passed between us in Greece. How fortunate they remembered me at all at this time.

"Oh, yes. I do care. More than that." I stood and wiped my eyes again to clear my vision. "We must hurry, as you said. What shall we take with us for him?"

"I thought the white robes with the gold thread he wore at the New Year ceremony, when the legions swore loyalty to him, would be most appropriate," said Alexandra, pointing to a folded bundle on the table.

"What loyalty?" I said. "Is this what he would want connected to his burial?"

"The Praetorians were loyal, until they were deceived. When they know the truth, they will repent."

"It won't bring him back," I said.

"It is true his last words were about the troops' loyalty," admitted Ecloge.

His last words. "What did he say?"

"This is what Epaphroditus told us. He said the emperor knew his hour had come but refused to take the final strike until he heard the sound of the approaching soldiers. Only then could he bring himself to do it. Barely a few moments later the centurion arrived, to find him almost dead. Leaping off his horse, he rushed to Nero's side, and held his cloak up to Nero's neck, to stop the bleeding—so he could be saved, only to be executed later. Nero, still conscious, looked at him and said, 'Too late. So this is your loyalty!' He died right after that, thwarting their plans."

So he knew. At the end he knew the bitterness of betrayal, as well as the small consolation of having eluded his captors and a shameful execution. Oh, my dear Nero, what a horrible death, to die with such knowledge.

Now my eyes filled with tears again, blinding me. Finally I dried them, rose, and went over to the folded robes. Privately I thought he would have preferred one of his outrageous flowered tunics, as a last gesture to his Roman critics, but this was certainly more dignified. I stroked the fine white wool, felt the roughness of the gold threads running through it. "This will do," I said.

Only now that my eyes had cleared did I look around the chamber. Hanging on the wall, in a place of honor, was the crown of wild olive from Olympia, the winner's wreath that he had cherished. "We need to take this," I said.

"And his cithara," said Alexandra. "I know he would want it with him."

I took the wreath off the wall. Some of its fragile leaves, almost a year old, crumbled. But the rest were well preserved.

* * *

It was a long, dusty ride out of the city to Phaon's villa. Along the way, once we were out in the country, birds swooped and dove over the fields, and hedges were in bloom. It seemed peculiarly and personally insulting to him that the world persisted in bright colors and singing birds when he lay dead.

The villa loomed ahead, surrounded by untended fields of tall reeds and bramble bushes. Phaon had done well for himself; the villa was large and sprawling. We entered through a grand front door, and Phaon's slave greeted us. He quickly led us to where Phaon, Epaphroditus, and Sporus awaited us in the light-filled atrium. Which was the traitor? Or were all three guilty?

"Thank you for coming," said Phaon. "We are grateful you can . . . help us."

"And grateful to the powers now in control that he is permitted an honest funeral," said Epaphroditus, a man with dark features and heavy eyebrows. "I wrote to you, Ecloge, with the information about his last day."

So that was how Ecloge and Alexandra knew so many details.

"We have the funeral pyre ready," said Phaon. "Would you like to see the preparations? They are outside, at the back of the villa."

No, I never want to see them. Never, never. But we trudged after the men, down a flight of stairs and out a door into a large cleared area. Hideously confronting us was a large pyre, its logs piled neatly, geometrically, a pyramid awaiting a torch. At the very top there was a level place for a litter to be placed.

"We have worked hard to procure this," said Phaon, a touch of pride in his voice.

Farther away was a rectangular hole with marble fragments lining its lip.

"What is this?" I asked, pointing to it.

"He directed us to dig his grave," said Epaphroditus.

I shuddered at the thing. Had he stood by and watched it take shape? O gods, how cruel.

I turned away and saw a hole in the back wall, recently dug. "And what is this?" I asked.

"We had to dig an entrance here so he could enter the cellar without being seen."

"He spent his last night in a cellar?"

"It was the safest place," said Sporus, speaking at long last.

"Please do not be distressed," said Phaon, when both Ecloge and Alexandra began weeping. He might as well have commanded the sun to stand still. We were overcome with the meanness of the surroundings, the humiliations heaped upon him—crawling through a broken wall in the basement of a freedman's villa to sleep alone in a dank cellar.

I had to keep my voice steady. "And where—where did the centurion find him?"

"Just here." He pointed to a place near the corner of the villa. There was a dark spot on the ground. Blood. "He heard the sound of the cavalry on the road just outside—we are close to it here—and quoted a line from the *Iliad*. Then it was time, if there was to be time."

Homer. Always Greece. I smiled, surprised that I could.

"May we go and prepare him now?" I asked. It had to be done. It could not wait.

"Yes. He is in the cellar. Not out of disrespect, you understand, but because it is cooler there."

Yes, that I understood.

They led us into the cellar down the regular steps. We descended into the chill, dim rooms, and walked through several before coming to one that had a table covered with a sheet. Tiny windows let in slivers of light, but it was necessary to light lamps in order to see.

"Could you leave us, please?" I asked, as we stood before the silent draped table.

"Yes," said Phaon. "You will see, there are casks of water, cloths, and towels here." He pointed to another table. They turned and left.

Now we were alone with him. Helplessly, we stood unmoving for several minutes. One of us had to draw back the cloth. None of us wanted to. At length I steeled myself to do it, and quietly approached the table. I took the cloth in both hands and pulled it away. I almost

recoiled when I saw him. Until that second I had not truly believed—
or rather, comprehended—that he was dead.

They had closed his eyes—a mercy—but not tended him otherwise.
The big gash on his neck had turned dark, but other than that he looked
lifelike. Death's changes had not yet advanced on him. He looked
younger, like the Lucius I had first known. I leaned over and kissed his
cold cheek. "Lucius is back," I told him. "I have my Lucius again."

Now to the grim task of uncovering him, washing him with care,
preparing him for the journey. It was an honor; it was a torture. At
length we clothed him in the white robes we had brought.

The men carried him outside on a litter. The day was cooling; the
sun threw slanting shadows. Before he was hoisted up onto the pyre, I
bent down and put the wreath on his head, smoothing out his hair—
always that unruly hair, now curling around the leaves. I kissed him
again, and whispered into his unhearing ear, "I saved you from a funeral pyre once, but this time I cannot, my love. But you said we would
never be apart in our souls again, and we are not." I pulled off the
bracelet and laid it on his chest. "I have come to you, as we promised.
I bring the bracelet back to you."

Alexandra came forward and put his prized cithara beside him on
the litter.

I had stepped back, but then I had to return to him. "Oh, my dearest, farewell," I said.

At a signal, the men lifted up the litter and positioned it at the top.
Then, using several torches, they set fire to it. As the flames rose, the
slaves came out of the house to watch.

I couldn't bear to see the flames devour him. I looked away, down
at the ground, but I could not blot out the sound of the wood snapping
and crackling, or the roar of the fire. Nor could I block the acrid stench
of smoke surrounding us.

Two days later, we made the mournful journey back into Rome,
carrying the ashes in an urn of plain pottery from my own work-
shop. It was stamped with my name and seal. Thus we would truly be

together forever. There was no hurry now; in fact it was advisable to delay to allow time for the sarcophagus and the altar with its balustrade to be in place.

As we rode slowly along, people lined each side of the road, the crowds becoming thicker as we got closer to Rome. Somehow they had learned of the ceremony at the Domitian mausoleum and stood in respect, watching us pass. The Via Salaria took us to the Pincian Hill, with its magnificent gardens on the high grounds. The family tomb was on the southwestern slope. As we approached, a crowd was waiting.

The tomb held the remains of members of the Domitian family, going back several generations. It was a large structure with niches and memorial plaques. I saw the names Gnaeus Domitius Ahenobarbus, his father, and Lucius Domitius Ahenobarbus, his grandfather the charioteer. Other plaques showed other names, going further back in time. Statues and marble vases were set at different levels.

We dismounted and walked slowly to the mausoleum's entrance, where a guard stood on duty. I carried the urn in both hands, holding it out in front of me, so it would be the first thing to enter the tomb. Before me, in the central area, was the red porphyry sarcophagus, gleaming and polished. They had managed to install it in time. The lid rested to one side; two uniformed attendants were waiting to help lower it into place. Above the sarcophagus was a new gleaming white marble altar surrounded by a balustrade of Thasian stone, as Ecloge had ordered.

Ecloge and Alexandra took their places beside me, in front of the sarcophagus. Its inside was dark; I could not see to the bottom. We were on our own to conduct whatever rites we wished.

I asked Ecloge to speak first. She addressed her words in a whisper to the urn. "You passed your entire life in joy, smiling, playing and happy, and delighted your soul with pleasures in the art of song. Now you rest among the dead while still youthful. This urn"—she reached out to touch it—"holds you in a narrow space and encloses your bones. May the earth rest lightly upon you."

Next Alexandra turned to touch the urn. "Evil spirits have cut your life short," she said, "like a storm from the south cuts a tender plant.

You were granted only half a life. But in that short half life you shone like the sun. May no one molest this, your resting place."

Silence fell. Now I must speak. I held the urn, trembling.

"You are Lucius again, returned to your family. May you join them in peace. May you find eternal joy. But know that I, who love you, have no joy forevermore, as you have hurried to where the Fates called you. This is all; more cannot happen. This was foreseen for us."

I stepped up to the dark box and lowered the urn into it. It was deep; my arms barely reached to the bottom. The urn made a dull noise as it touched its resting place. My fingers traced the top, caressing the smooth clay, before I withdrew my hands.

Moving back, I nodded to the workmen to proceed. They lifted the top and lowered it carefully into place, settling it so it sealed.

Carved into the lid was

LUCIUS DOMITIUS AHENOBARBUS
Age thirty years, five months, and twenty-five days

Nothing about his having been emperor. Just a name and his age. The powers that ruled now had forbidden anything else. But at least they had granted him a respectful burial.

Out into the bright sun, I saw the crowds, still waiting. They carried flowers, and one by one they came to the tomb and laid them on the sarcophagus.

Ecloge, Alexandra, and I climbed the hill and sought out one of the gardens there. The hill was known for its luxuriant gardens that afforded a fine view of Rome below us. I was drained, limp, but as I climbed, strength returned.

It was over. His life was over, ended here at this cold marble monument below us. I could see the stately Mausoleum of Augustus not far away, beside the Tiber. He had not wanted to be there; he was never really part of that family, for all he was the great-great-grandson of Augustus. Now he did not have to be; he had escaped at last.

"I think I will be buried where he died," said Ecloge suddenly. "Perhaps I shall use that grave already dug. Someone should, and take the sting from his having watched it being prepared."

"It is too early to be planning that," I said.

"I am many years older than he was. We can be gone tomorrow."

I was not so concerned with where I would eventually lie as I was with the long years stretching out before me without him. The emptiness would echo in my soul every day.

LXXV

LOCUSTA

Here I sit in my prison, still waiting for my fate to reveal itself. I am normally a patient person—my profession calls for it—but this exceeds even my gift for self-control, and I jump every time the door opens. I know many people connected to Nero have been executed, and that I may be joining them—soon. I have already been held here for months, after Galba took command in Rome.

His agents came to my academy, charging in, arresting my students, and hunting me down in my office. With no explanation of why they were arresting me, they hauled me off to Rome. But no explanation was needed: I was associated with the Neronian regime, and they were rounding up everyone they could find.

Before Galba arrived in Rome, which took a while, the news about Nero's fall had reached me out in the country. I mourned greatly for the young emperor, my friend. The reports of it were garbled. I was not sure if he had been able to avail himself of the poison I had given him or whether a grimmer end awaited him. Or perhaps there was no end at all, and he is in hiding. Some people believe that, and it is not impossible. The freedmen who were with him at an outlying villa have been enigmatic. Perhaps they lured him there to betray him to his enemies. Perhaps they were truly trying to help. We will never know. What we do know is that only a very few people ever claimed to see Nero dead, and the principal witness, Galba's henchman Icelus, had a vested interest in proclaiming him dead and hailing Galba as his successor.

It was Icelus who gave permission for Nero to have a proper funeral. But who is in the Domitian mausoleum? Could it be someone else, or could the tomb even be empty?

Nero was weary of being emperor. That I knew from my last conversation with him. It would be very like him to slip betimes away, to disappear into the east. Indeed his betrayer, Nymphidius, said he had fled to Egypt.

Ah, Nymphidius. I hope Nero *is* alive to know that his betrayer was slain by the Praetorians he had lied to in order to trick them into deserting Nero. Falling upon him, swords flashing, they cried that they were avenging Nero. Nymphidius was that lowest of the low, a double betrayer, for he tried to have the troops proclaim him emperor in place of Galba, claiming he was the son of Caligula. The self-purported son of Caligula now rests only the gods know where, but most likely in a ditch somewhere. Thus should perish all disloyal deceivers.

Nero's tomb (if indeed he is in it) has been continually decked with flowers by the common people. Galba has dismissed this by saying, "Nero will always be missed by the riffraff." Galba himself has already lost whatever support he had with the people who put him in power by refusing to pay the huge stipend promised to the Praetorians, saying, "I am accustomed to paying soldiers wages, not bribes."

He may not last long. But who will replace him? The family of Augustus is no more, snuffed out, gone. Someone must rule Rome, and that someone will have a family. But which family will prevail? I fear a civil war looming like the bloody ones that raged in the Republic.

Could Nero be alive? King Vologases of Parthia sent a special emissary to the Senate to ask them to honor Nero's memory. It is strong in the east, and revered. And there has been news of someone claiming to be Nero appearing in Greece, gathering followers, arming slaves. He is said to resemble Nero in looks and skill on the lyre and cithara, and many people in Greece have recently seen Nero and can verify whether he truly is the same man. He seems to have passed the test.

If so, will he return to Rome and oust Galba?

A sound at the door. It is opening, slowly. Perhaps Galba has decided he needs my services. Perhaps he will set me free. Perhaps it isn't Galba at all, but Nero returned.

I stand up, ready.

LXXVI

ACTE

The warm wind blowing over the grave has a heart of chill, a whisper that winter is nearer than it seems. So it is with me. Soon I will be sixty, and this will be my last journey here.

I lay late-summer flowers on the grave of Ecloge, who kept her vow to be buried in the grave prepared for Nero. On her marble gravestone is engraved CLAUDIAE ECLOGAE, PIISSIMAE—to Claudia Ecloge, most loyal. No higher virtue can be imagined than this.

Phaon is gone now, no one knows where; the villa is owned by someone else. He kindly allows Ecloge's grave to be tended and does nothing to discourage the stream of visitors who come to see where Nero took his last breath. Some still believe he is alive; of course I know better. But who can extinguish rumors that are determined to burn on and on, smoldering and smoking?

There have been at least three men eager to take advantage of the rumors—the so-called false Neros who impersonated him, relying on similar looks and musical skill. The first appeared in Greece only a few months after Galba's accession and gathered army deserters to his cause, as well as others who wished Nero back. He was cornered and captured on the island of Cythnus, off the coast of Greece.

The second one appeared ten years later, this time farther east. He claimed he had escaped the soldiers sent for him at Phaon's and had been in hiding ever since. He headed for Parthia, where he expected a warm welcome. The ruler did indeed welcome him and was ready to mount an effort to restore him to the throne, but his true identity as a Terentius Maximus was revealed, and he was executed.

The last one came ten years after that, some two years ago. He was embraced by the Parthians, who resisted Rome's demand to surrender him but were finally persuaded to. He, too, perished.

Nero, Nero . . . why do you keep returning in these teasing forms? Is your spirit still so restless?

I cast a look toward the corner where he had bled. All traces are gone now; the earth has long since drunk the blood, and plants have grown wild upon it. It has been twenty-three years since that day.

Now I must leave this sad spot and go to his grave.

I could seek the Pincian Hill without going through Rome itself, but as this may be my last visit, I want to see it one last time. So I choose the turn that takes me into the heart of the city, the city that has known six emperors since Nero. The year after he died unleashed wars between contenders for the throne. As there were no claimants from the original Julian family, anyone could entertain imperial dreams, and four did; that year is called the Year of Four Emperors. First there was Galba, who lasted only a few months, to be replaced by—yes!—Otho, who was replaced by Vitellius, who was replaced by Vespasian. Ten years later we got his son, Titus, as emperor, followed by the younger brother, Domitian, who reigns now.

As for Nero's companions and henchmen, their fates varied by emperor. Helios and Nymphidius were the first to go, executed in Galba's reign. Otho condemned Tigellinus, who had recovered from his illness only to die; he had to cut his own throat when he was given the command. Sporus committed suicide rather than become Vitellius's plaything. Epaphroditus lasted the longest but was executed by Domitian because he had failed to prevent Nero's suicide, an example an emperor could not condone.

The streets, as I enter them, are the usual noisy lanes, filled with people going about their business, as people do regardless of who wears the purple and lives in the palace.

The palace . . . the lower Golden House is no more. Vespasian destroyed it and replaced it with the looming structure I can see from across half the city: a gigantic amphitheater. I am approaching it now, with its sandy arches and shadowed niches; the roar from inside says there are gladiatorial games going on. Huge crowds mill around outside, so I will skirt the building.

Vespasian drained Nero's lake, filled it in, and put the amphitheater on top of it. He dedicated it as the Flavian Amphitheater. But irony reigns. Nero's colossus, still standing close by, has given the amphitheater the popular name *Colosseum*. So Nero still presides here.

Little else remains, though. Looking up at the Oppian Hill as I come closer, where the glorious pavilion used to be, Titus has constructed ugly baths. Some of the original pavilion remains, but its days are numbered. It was never finished and never will be.

In that it is like so much of Nero's legacy. His great enterprises and grand designs have been abrogated, aborted. The Liberation of Greece was rescinded by Vespasian. The Corinthian Canal was not completed. The Neronia were not continued. The only legacy he leaves behind is his music; his compositions are compiled in *The Master's Book* and are still performed. Art has indeed outlived stone and politics. That would please him.

It is better to go through the Campus Martius at this hour than the rest of the central city, so I will take that route. It is less crowded and has more open spaces. The public buildings here make Rome elegant and welcoming; visitors always remark on them. Today there are many strolling people, some eyeing the Pantheon, others the Augustus monuments farther up, the sundial and white marble Altar of Peace. Now in midday the shadow of the obelisk, serving as the gnomon for the sundial, is short. Nearby is the rotund Mausoleum of Augustus with its park, attracting sightseers and devotees.

Are you not glad to lie elsewhere? I asked Nero. The weight of that family pressed you down, and you would not want to rub shoulders with them there for eternity.

Lovely as this part of Rome is, it is not so lovely for condemned prisoners paraded in chains here in a mock Triumph, exposed to the jeers of the crowd before a public execution. Galba rounded up many from Nero's regime, including Helios and Locusta, and subjected them to this punishment.

I leave the city behind and am out in the open air, passing by gardens, smelling their dusty, late-summer scent. Ahead is the tomb of the Domitians. I see a small group of people at the entrance.

I approach them, curious as to who they are. They are of all ages; some seem to be foreigners, others Romans. There are even two legionaries.

"Why have you come?" I ask one of the families, a mother and two children.

"I have told the children about him," the woman says. "As this is a lovely day, I thought I would take them here."

"What have you told them?" *That he was insane, a tyrant, a monster?* That was the official story, peddled now by the Senate.

"That he was the most remarkable emperor we have had," she says. "He was not a warrior but an artist; he wanted to please the ordinary man, not the aristocrat; he raced chariots!" She laughs. "When shall we have such another?"

"Never, I fear," I say. Never, I know.

I climb the stairs into the sheltered interior. The sarcophagus is polished and clean; all around and on it are flowers, fresh ones. He is remembered.

I am here. This may be the last time. I am no longer young; I feel the changes in me, and the way back and forth from Velitrae grows longer. I have come from Ecloge's grave, which she shares with you. She was faithful unto death. So shall I be.

I run my hand over the smooth, cold stone of the sarcophagus. *I gave you back the bracelet. But I still have something you gave me long ago: the emerald eyepiece you used to see better at distance. I look at it and feel your vulnerability. You could see what lay close by but not what was far away.*

I touch the stone again, feeling the carved letters that spell his name.

A last farewell, my love, my friend. We shall not meet again until we see one another in the dim light of Hades. It will not be long. I can feel it. Wait for me.

AFTERWORD

This is the story of the last four years of the life of Nero Claudius Caesar Augustus Germanicus—whose five legal names are brimming with Roman history but who is now known to all merely as "Nero," joining that rare cadre of people for whom one name is enough and instantly recognizable.

In my prior novel *The Confessions of Young Nero*, I tell the story of how he grows to manhood and assumes the purple. But in many ways he did not come of age until the supreme test of the Great Fire of Rome. Rome was forever changed by it, and so was Nero. His relationships to the people in his life changed, his outlook on life changed, and his character changed. This volume begins with the Fire and ends twenty-three years after his death, giving us both the immediate repercussions of his life and reign and its somewhat longer aftermath.

During these four years, the second chapter of his life, come the events forever associated with him. At age thirty, after a succession of unique and unforgettable performances, he exited the stage of life.

But not completely. He is one of the few historical personages to have a busy posthumous existence. In the two decades following his death, there were at least three Nero impersonators who claimed to be the late emperor and gathered followers. Like Elvis, there were also numerous Nero "sightings" in various locations.

Today his name is a household word, when most of the other fifty-five Roman emperors have been forgotten. His image is unmistakable, as he dared to allow himself to be pictured as he really was on coins, double chin and all. It is not quite the sort of fame he had hoped for, but to have achieved it at all against such long odds is remarkable.

For the events of these four years of his life, we have the same main three ancient authorities: Tacitus, Suetonius, and Dio Cassius, with the crucial difference that Tacitus does not cover the last two years of his life, a lamentable gap. That makes it much harder to pinpoint the chronology of his sudden fall from power and to identify the details, which are murky. The other two, Dio Cassius and Suetonius, are much less interested in the context, which of course is what latter-day historians want to analyze.

All three have a well-known bias against Nero, writing at a later time and during the reign of a different dynasty, when it was important to belittle the accomplishments of the predecessor as much as possible. As a result, he has been entirely defined by his enemies, having had the bad luck that none of the countering accounts by people favorable to him have survived. Bits and pieces of additional information about Nero and his times are found in the writings of Pliny the Elder, Plutarch, Josephus, Dio Chrysostom of Prusa, Pausanias, Flavius Philostratus, St. Jerome, Martial, and others.

The modern historian Bernard Henderson says that with the reign of Vespasian (AD 69–79) "begins that systematic disparagement of Nero which consciously or unconsciously colors the whole of our extant records." Archaeologist Elisabetta Segala, author of the Superintendent of Archaeology of Rome's official guidebook to the Golden House, says, "The main sources for the history of Nero's principate— Tacitus (AD 54/55–120), Suetonius (AD 70–140), and Dio Cassius (AD 155–235)—all derive, directly or indirectly, from the political opposition and seem to be unanimously hostile to the emperor. Literary testimony and the Christian tradition, which soon identified Nero with the Antichrist, have all contributed to the formation of the totally negative image of the emperor which has come down to us."

Michael Grant, another modern historian, notes, "But much the most serious problem we have to confront still has to be mentioned. It consists of the long time that elapsed between Nero's death and the dates when these surviving accounts were written. Tacitus composed his *Annals* something like fifty years after Nero died, and Suetonius' *Life* [*of Nero*] was later still; while yet another hundred years had passed before Dio Cassius wrote. It is extraordinarily difficult to see what someone like Nero was really like when you are relying on authorities as late as that."

But help has finally arrived, as modern historians, trained to scientifically analyze material, such as coinage and manuscript texts, rather than take them at face value, have much more stringent standards of judgment. And recent archaeological findings, such as the discovery of that engineering marvel, Nero's rotating dining room, the *coenatio rotunda*, long thought to be just a legend, are altering our appreciation of, and opinion of, Nero and his reign in its setting. We can also judge him now in the context of performance art, in which he was a genius. In addition, our changing mind-set about subjects such as gender fluidity and identity and same-sex marriage make us see him in a new and more forgiving perspective. Such a simple shift in lighting can reveal new facets. The person I discovered was a truly visionary artist and far from the monster of cruelty his enemies had depicted. He didn't deserve the calumny his opponents heaped on him, and hopefully in our day people will finally come to view him as the complex person he was—certainly with faults but also with redeeming qualities.

It is always rewarding to return someone to his or her rightful place, and I hope that this volume helps to do that for Nero, or at least persuade people to stop and think about him a little differently.

In writing it, I had to make many choices of what to include, what to emphasize, and what to leave out, and I will explain them here for my readers. This volume covers many of the events that are integral to the legend of Nero. In the novel I follow the conviction of the historian Edward Champlin, who, in his book *Nero*, explains, "I have assumed that his actions were rational—that is, he was not crazy—and that much of what he did resonated far more with contemporary social attitudes than our hostile sources would have us believe." He mentions that "for most of Nero's actions, even the most notorious . . . we can find a purpose which may have nothing to do with the motives ascribed to him." In the novel, I have ascribed only motives to him that, to me, seem explanatory and likely.

With that in mind, let's review the main events of Nero's life covered in this novel.

First, the Great Fire of Rome has given rise to the saying, "Nero fiddled while Rome burned." Although Nero was not in Rome when it started, and he came rushing back and threw himself wholeheartedly into relief measures, a rumor started that he had stood and sung of the fall of Troy while watching the flames. He was known to have composed an epic on that subject and had performed it on stage, so it was a natural enough thought that the Fire was just too good a backdrop for him to pass up. There is no evidence that he did this, and the rumors have him performing in three different places.

After the Fire was over, the fact that he set aside large areas in the center of Rome for his new sprawling palace complex made people accuse him of starting the Fire to clear the area for his own purposes. In vain could he note that his own recently finished palace, the Domus Transitoria, had been lost in the Fire; in vain could he point out that the Fire had started in an area far from the new palace complex.

In truth, Rome was a firetrap and burned many times, always by accident. There is no reason to think this Fire was any different or set on purpose. And in spite of Nero's measures to make the city safer and avoid future fires, only sixteen years later, in AD 80, there was another big fire; although not as big as the one in AD 64, it still lasted three days.

Second, the first historical persecution of the Christians arose in the aftermath of the Great Fire of Rome. It is usually framed like this: Nero needed a scapegoat for the Fire, to shift the blame from himself, and he settled on the Christians. That is a simplistic version. The truth is that mysterious people were seen setting new fires and hindering the official firefighters during the height of the Fire. No one knew who they were; some even accused Nero of sending his agents out as arsonists.

Others suspected the Christians, who were seen at that time as criminals, antisocial nuisances, and a mysterious, un-Roman cult. Their waiting for the apocryphal "end time" made it credible that they were trying to hurry it along by destroying the world around them.

Nero probably genuinely believed that the Christians were involved, as did many others. The punishments meted out to them were in accord with Roman custom. Arsonists were burned. Criminals were crucified. Suetonius even lists the persecution of the Christians as one of the *good* things Nero did, illustrating the general contempt of them in Rome.

We do not know how widespread the persecution was. Contrary to common belief, people were not condemned for being Christians but for being arsonists. It is curious that this persecution is not attested to in the early Church writings. Did they not know about it? Or were the numbers small enough that at the time of the first records, the Church fathers were unfamiliar with it? That Peter and Paul were executed during this time is a legend. We do not know when they were actually executed or whether it was connected with this.

Afterward, to the Christians, since the letters of his name added up to 666 in Hebrew, he became the Beast of the Book of Revelation, and the belief of some people that he would return linked him to the Antichrist. As late as the twelfth century, his evil ghost was thought to inhabit crows nesting in a walnut tree near his tomb, so Pope Paschal II (1099–1118) ordered the tree cut down and a church built on the spot.

Third, Nero is accused of kicking his pregnant wife, Poppaea, to death. Dio Cassius says that he leapt upon her with his feet, either on purpose or accidentally. Suetonius says she was in ill health when he kicked her, angry that she scolded him for coming home late from the races. Tacitus says that he kicked her in anger but that some sources say he poisoned her, which Tacitus rebuts, saying, "this sounds malevolent rather than truthful, and I do not believe it—for Nero loved his wife and wanted children."

Modern historians tend to doubt any of this and think it is more likely she just died of a miscarriage, noting also that there is no record of Nero physically attacking anyone or being physically abusive to those around him.

The fourth shocking Nero legend, that he castrated an ex-slave who looked like Poppaea, married him, and called him her name, grows out of the death of Poppaea. As with all the other legends, it is much more complex than that. The freedman Sporus had an uncanny resemblance to Poppaea. Nero's grief over her death was almost pathological. He wore masks resembling her when he performed female parts on stage. But that, apparently, was not enough. In his grief for her, he attempted to re-create her, much as the James Stewart character does for the dead Madeleine in Alfred Hitchcock's *Vertigo*. It was a refusal to let go of someone in death, and as in the movie, one might even say it bordered on obsession. He did keep Sporus with him for the rest of his life, and Sporus was one of the few with him at his death. What Sporus thought of this we can never know. One assumes he was at least complaisant about it, for after Nero's death he committed suicide rather than go on with anyone else. It might also be noted that the "marriage" took place in Greece, where mythologizing and playacting was more routine, and people more tolerant, rather than in Rome, and seemed to be an act of theater.

The fifth big event in Nero's life, and his last spectacular, was his sixteen-month artistic and athletic tour of Greece, competing in all the major contests (Olympia, Delphi, Nemea, and Isthmia) as well as a host of minor ones. He competed in music (cithara), drama (classical tragedy), and sport (chariot racing). One might ask why in the world a Roman emperor would want to do this. One of his biographers, Michael Grant, says, "He was the first ruler in all recorded history, and indeed the only one of any real importance, to consider himself *primarily* as a singer and stage actor." It seems that from the very beginning he needed to create an identity for himself that had nothing to do with being a Julio-Claudian or emperor. Art became his refuge and, as pressures of his office increased, his escape. He needed to perform, and he needed to compete, and in Greece he would be competing at the highest level.

Unfortunately for him, it was impossible for him to have an impartial judgment on his talents, either in his own time or for posterity. People assume he must have been a poor singer or actor, and stories went around of his audience being held captive and feigning death to escape from the theater, women giving birth in the theater, and so on. They make amusing tales but are unlikely to be true. Being emperor did not mandate that he be untalented. It is more likely that he was quite good, or else he wouldn't have pursued those avenues. Still he could never know *how* good, because he could not get honest feedback. We do know that after his death his music compositions were preserved in *The Master's Book* and performed by others, which would indicate that they had merit, as there was no longer any need to flatter him.

We must address the *damnatio memoriae* issue. It is commonly stated that Nero underwent this official "damnation of memory," an erasure of his existence, as nearly as feasible. In truth this phrase is a modern one and not an official judgment enacted in ancient Rome; the term did not exist. It is true that when an emperor fell, his enemies did everything they could to blacken his name and desecrate his memorials, throwing over statues, chiseling his name out from monuments, and so on. This happened to Nero, although only a few months later, the statues reappeared in the Forum. This also happened to pagan statues vandalized by Christians. But these were spontaneous acts, not official ones.

In addition to addressing these widespread myths about Nero and setting the record straight, I also made some choices for my depiction of Nero and his world that were more personal.

As in the first book, I use feet and miles rather than kilometers, simply because the Romans did, although they vary slightly from our modern feet and miles. It seemed more in keeping with the time period. I also use modern place names, such as "Near Spain" rather than "Hispania Tarraconensis," which I feel the modern reader would more easily understand. I also try to avoid "Asia" because to the Romans it meant what we call Turkey. Likewise I avoided using "Africa" because the Romans meant it for the part of that continent bordering the Mediterranean, whereas we think of sub-Saharan Africa when we see that word.

For some very minor and entirely fictional characters, who exist only to present a letter or argue briefly in the Senate, then vanish from the narrative, I have used fictional names.

You will look in vain for the exact date of the eclipse in AD 64, for it is fictional.

In the novel I mention a bronze toy chariot that was given to Nero as a boy by the emperor Claudius. This chariot, the only replica model we have of an ancient Roman chariot, is in the British Museum and is often referred to as "Nero's chariot" although of course there is no proof it belonged to him.

The play *Octavia* is the only surviving historical play from ancient Rome. For a long time it was thought to have been written by Seneca, as it was found among his papers, and that played a part in its preservation. But it is now thought to belong to a later period—scholars are not agreed on exactly when—after the death of Nero, when it would have been safe to perform such a play, if indeed it was ever performed. Scholars are not sure of that, either. However, since it was important in the novel that Nero himself see what was being said about him, I left it with the old interpretation that Seneca had written it. We still don't know who wrote it or when.

The chronology of the Greek tour is very sketchy, as we are missing Tacitus, who was meticulous in compiling dates. Scholars have put together probable dates. We know Nero was in Corinth at the end of the tour because we have the date of his proclamation of the Liberation of Greece and that Helios arrived to bring him home shortly after that. It is interesting that the Corinthian Canal that was finally dug in the nineteenth century followed exactly the lines that Nero's engineers had excavated, and traces of the excavation were still there, along with an image of Hercules that was carved on the rock wall at one end of the canal by the workers.

A treasured survival from the Greek tour is a stela recording Nero's "Liberation of Greece" speech, which I quote in the novel. Oddly, it is the only speech of his that we possess, and it captures his language and histrionic flair. The carved inscription from grateful citizens was found in the Greek town of Akraiphia in Boeotia.

Likewise the chronology of the fall of Nero is murky. Much of the explanatory material of what went on is missing, with the result that it seems incomplete and puzzling to us. However, the description of the last day of Nero's life, in Suetonius, is a masterpiece of dramatic writing, almost Shakespearean. The tiny details—a barefoot, hasty midnight ride; brambles in his cloak; tepid water; mumbling to himself in the first, second, and third person in Greek and Latin; and finally his famous last words—"What an artist the world is losing!"—are incomparable in dramatic intensity.

I have chosen to omit mention of Statilia's former husbands prior to Vestinus—we are not sure how many there were or if Vestinus was her only one.

I chose to have Acte tell us of the aftermath of Nero's life, including the important information about the three false Neros and how he was regarded after some years had passed. Locusta as well provided a glimpse into the immediate aftermath. Unfortunately for her, her hopes of being freed were in vain, and she was executed, along with a number of other people from the Neronian regime, by Galba.

I have been blessed with many outstanding books and sources for my work. First, of course, are the three histories I mentioned earlier: Tacitus, *The Annals of Imperial Rome* (London: Penguin Classics, 1985); Suetonius, *The Twelve Caesars* (London: Penguin Books, 1986); and Dio Cassius, *Roman History, Books 61–70* (Cambridge, MA: Harvard University Press, 1925). For biographies, I found that the oldest (and still the longest one in English), Bernard W. Henderson's *Life and Principate of the Emperor Nero* (Philadelphia: Lippincott, 1903), was very good in providing many small personal details that helped make the book intimate. Michael Grant's *Nero: Emperor in Revolt* (New York: American Heritage Press, 1970) served as a basic go-to book for clear explanations and all pertinent facts. Miriam T. Griffin's *Nero: The End of a Dynasty* (New Haven, CT: Yale University Press, 1985) proved to be a treasure chest of information and analysis on him and the period. Stephen Dando-Collins's book *The Great Fire of Rome: The Fall of the Emperor Nero and His City* (Philadelphia: Da Capo Press, 2010) also has much more information than on just the fire, but it is excellent on that, and his *Nero's Killing Machine: The True Story of Rome's Remarkable Fourteenth Legion* (Hoboken, NJ: John Wiley & Sons, 2005) covers the war with Boudicca. Richard Holland's *Nero: The Man behind the Myth* (Stroud, UK:

Sutton, 2000) is good on the psychology of Nero, and Edward Champlin's *Nero* (Cambridge, MA: Belknap Press of Harvard University Press, 2003) is superlative in analyzing the person inside the myth and the method in his madness—if indeed it was madness. Last, from editors Emma Buckley and Martin T. Dinter, *A Companion to the Neronian Age* (Chichester, UK: Wiley-Blackwell, 2013) provides invaluable information on a variety of facets of Nero, military, mythological, artistic, and psychological.

Two excellent Seneca biographies, James Romm's *Dying Every Day: Seneca at the Court of Nero* (New York: Knopf, 2014) and Emily Wilson's *The Greatest Empire: A Life of Seneca* (New York: Oxford University Press, 2014), were very helpful. For Seneca's direct words, see *Seneca: Dialogues and Essays* (New York: Oxford University Press, 2008).

On some other topics, Patrick Faas's *Around the Roman Table: Food and Feasting in Ancient Rome* (New York: Palgrave Macmillan, 2003) is just what it says it is; Linda Farrar's *Ancient Roman Gardens* (Stroud, UK: Sutton, 1998) is a wonderful source for information on private and public gardens, and Roland Auguet's *Cruelty and Civilization: The Roman Games* (New York: Routledge, 1994) covers all aspects of the arena. T. G. Tucker's *Life in the Roman World of Nero and St. Paul* (New York: Macmillan, 1936), although written in 1910, has the most complete coverage, along with diagrams, of any book I've seen for details of daily living.

A newly published two-volume set edited by Andrea Carandini, *The Atlas of Ancient Rome* (Princeton, NJ: Princeton University Press, 2017) told me everything I ever wanted to know about sites in ancient Rome and revealed ones I hadn't even known existed.

For the material on the Greek Games, I relied on Panos Valavanis's massive *Games and Sanctuaries in Ancient Greece* (Los Angeles: J. Paul Getty Museum, 2004) and Stephen G. Miller's *Ancient Greek Athletics* (New Haven, CT: Yale University Press, 2004). Also helpful for the oracle at Delphi, visited by Nero during his time there, was William J. Broad's *The Oracle* (New York: Penguin, 2006). For the chariot racing scenes, Fik Meijer's *Chariot Racing in the Roman Empire* (Baltimore: Johns Hopkins University Press, 2010) was immensely informative.

A new book, Lauren Donovan Ginsberg's *Staging Memory, Staging Strife: Empire and Civil War in the* Octavia (Oxford, UK: Oxford University Press, 2017) examines the critically important history play that features Nero, shedding light on that mysterious drama and its context. Last, in dealing with the aftermath of Nero's reign and his legacy, I found Harriet I. Flower's *The Art of Forgetting: Disgrace and Oblivion in Roman Political Culture* (Chapel Hill: University of North Carolina Press, 2006) invaluable in clarifying that very confusing time.